CHILDLESS

CHILDLESS

A Novel

DR. JAMES DOBSON
AND KURT BRUNER

New York Boston Nashville

FaithWords
Hachette Book Group
237 Park Avenue
New York, NY 10017

faithwords.com

Printed in the United States of America

RRD-C

First Edition: October 2013
10 9 8 7 6 5 4 3 2 1

FaithWords is a division of Hachette Book Group, Inc.
The FaithWords name and logo are trademarks of Hachette Book Group, Inc.

The Hachette Speakers Bureau provides a wide range of authors for speaking events. To find out more, go to www.hachettespeakersbureau.com or call (866) 376-6591.

The publisher is not responsible for websites (or their content) that are not owned by the publisher.

Library of Congress Cataloging-in-Publication Data
Dobson, James C., 1936-
 Childless : a novel / Dr. James Dobson and Kurt Bruner. -- First edition.
     pages cm
 ISBN 978-1-4555-1315-4 (hardcover)—ISBN 978-1-4555-7605-0 (large print hardcover)—ISBN 978-1-4555-1314-7 (ebook)
 1. Christian fiction. I. Bruner, Kurt D. II. Title.
PS3604.O24C47 2013
813'.6--dc23
                              2012051320

In memory of the late Dr. Francis Schaeffer who warned us of the perilous future depicted in this book.

AUTHOR'S NOTE

When I was young my father gave me a poem presumably written in the sixteenth century by a woman named Ursula Southeil, better known as Mother Shipton. It contained a series of predictions about future events that have proven remarkably accurate. One of those predictions seemed to prophesy some of the present-day trends that inspired this book.

> *Then love shall die and marriage cease,*
> *And nations wane as babes decrease*

Nations wane when the old and feeble outnumber the young and productive. The best demographers tell us the growth in global population will soon end and then reverse due to an unprecedented drop in fertility taking place throughout the developed world. Places like Japan and Russia are already experiencing the economic turmoil caused by too few children trying to support a growing pool of aging citizens.

In *Fatherless* we explored one of the causes: men neglecting the honor and responsibilities of paternity. In *Childless* we'll ask what happens when sex is severed from the life-giving joys of maternity. Be forewarned, such questions require depicting ugly realities that come when we disregard the beauty and sanctity of the marriage bed.

As we said in Book One, a happy home is the highest expression of God's image on Earth. Marriage and parenthood echo heaven, something hell can't abide. This series is a fictional account of where the battle against human thriving is heading in the not-too-distant future. But it is also a celebration of God's design for families, which retains a resilient beauty and redemptive power the most ardent forces of hell cannot destroy.

James C. Dobson, PhD

CHILDLESS

September 1, 2043

Victor

The faint sound of doorbell chimes prompted Rebecca Santiago to click off the hair dryer. That's when she panicked. The oven timer! Her gown somewhere out of reach, she hastily grabbed Victor's gangly bathrobe while darting toward the kitchen in a futile effort to rescue her forgotten pumpkin scones.

Balancing the hot cookie sheet with her hand in an oven mitt, she opened the front door with the other hand. She rolled her eyes at the sound of an overnight delivery truck hastily speeding away from the driveway.

"You call that friendly service?" Rebecca shouted to the fleeing license plate before bending down to retrieve the thin package. It was small and flat like any of the countless legal documents that required her husband's attention. She tossed it aside before hurriedly disposing of the dozen smoldering lumps no longer suitable to serve with tea. As on every other Tuesday, the bridge club gals would arrive at eleven o'clock sharp. She had less than fifteen minutes to make her graying strands wavy and refurbish a face banished from makeup-free appearances decades ago.

The envelope sat ignored until four thirty that afternoon, when it caught Rebecca's eye. As she waved goodbye to Shelly, who, as usual, had overstayed her welcome by ninety minutes, she noticed it balanced conspicuously on the dining room table right next to a legal brief Victor had forsaken seven hours earlier.

"Gotta run," he had mumbled through a half-eaten piece of toast wedged between his teeth on his way out the door. "Lost track of time."

Rebecca sighed at the reminder of her husband's chief short-coming. She knew what few others could guess. The esteemed Victor Santiago, presiding judge in the Tenth Circuit Court of Appeals, was a man severely allergic to multitasking. Sipping coffee and reviewing legal opinions were two simultaneous activities that had squeezed checking the time out of his morning routine. She marveled that Victor managed to survive while away from her attentive hovering, let alone that he'd earned a notable reputation. But he had, thanks in large part to their thirty-two-year arrangement. The day Victor married Rebecca his formidable mind had entrusted all nonjudicial matters to his better half, and she had gladly assumed them.

Finding a pair of scissors, Rebecca slit the seal and let the contents fall onto the kitchen counter. A smaller envelope shaped like a greeting card displayed handwritten script.

To: Mrs. Rebecca Santiago
From: A Fan of the Judge

She smiled, anticipating another note expressing admiration for her husband's growing influence. She had a pleasant habit that had begun with her scrapbook of news clippings from Victor's years as prosecuting attorney. She loved saving mementos from key career milestones. Her favorite was the framed picture taken at the press conference announcing his appointment to the federal bench. Victor had protested when she placed it so prominently on display in the living room. But household décor fell within her jurisdiction. No matter how brilliantly worded his opinion on the matter, hers remained the deciding vote.

Rebecca hoped that no one, especially Victor, would ever suspect her least becoming custom: she routinely sorted through the office wastepaper basket to retrieve notes her husband might have discarded after dismissing thanks or a compliment from a client or colleague. Part of her role, she told herself, was to relish the accolades her husband considered irrelevant or undeserved.

Rebecca assumed this note came from yet another character witness offering evidence that her lifelong lover was also the most important legal mind on the planet. She slid the contents free and noticed a slight bulge from the folded letter inserted between the elegant panels of a card that must have been purchased from an upscale stationery store. She removed the page before reading the card's inscription.

Dear Rebecca:

I apologize for troubling you at home, and I regret any distress the enclosed may cause you. But I desperately need your assistance in what has become a most pressing, delicate matter. Thank you, in advance, for your cooperation.

Warmest regards,
A Manichean

She stared at the signature for several seconds, trying to place the name. Nothing came. Then she began unfolding the longer note to read the details of the mysterious request. Her mind raced ahead of her hands to offer possible scenarios, each seeming less plausible than the last.

A practical joke by her ornery brother? Keith hadn't even bothered fixing himself a sandwich since losing Kay. He wouldn't waste the little energy he had left concocting an elaborate gag. And even if he had, his hands shook too much for such graceful penmanship.

Perhaps some surprise Victor had arranged for her sixtieth? Of course her birthday remained weeks away, and Victor wasn't the type to plan such things. Then again, he could have received prods and help from his ever-thoughtful assistant Jennifer. Possible, but not likely.

Could it be a legitimate request to get involved with a case? Victor had presided over hundreds of decisions during his years on the bench. At his insistence, none had ever invaded the sanctuary of their home. On the one occasion he'd seemed tortured over a particularly challenging case she'd asked if he wanted to talk about it. But he had slammed the door on the possibility with a grateful kiss on her forehead.

Having dismissed all three alternatives Rebecca felt a rush of vague panic as she began reading the double-creased page.

Dear Victor:

Please forgive my sending this note to your wife Rebecca. Prior attempts to correspond through your assistant have proven unfruitful. I have yet to receive a single response to any of my previous letters regarding the wrongful death appeal involving NEXT Transition Services. As you know, many lives hang in the balance in this matter. That's why I was pleased the case fell to a man with the kind of wisdom and restraint you have demonstrated throughout your distinguished judicial career. But this case is far too important for any hint of ambiguity. That's why I must know where you stand before the scheduled ruling deadline of September 4th. Please consider Rebecca's future as you contemplate the following alternatives:

- *Option One: Assure me that you will indeed decide in favor of NEXT.*
- *Option Two: Bid your sweet wife farewell since you will die before issuing an opinion.*

Once again, I apologize for alarming Rebecca. But she deserves to know about the increasingly tense situation in which we find ourselves. I could not allow any of what might transpire to come as a surprise, and I trust that her intervention will motivate you to do what's right for everyone.

As always,
A Manichean
P.S. Kindly post your response at the following private forum address: ANON.CHAT.4398

Rebecca felt her legs weaken as she steadied herself with a dining room chair. She had always known that important work like Victor's came with certain risks. "So does driving a car or boarding a plane," her husband had always said reassuringly. He'd never bothered to mention possible assassination.

She took an overdue breath as her eyes returned to the only sentence on the page that mattered. *Bid your sweet wife farewell since you will die before issuing an opinion.*

The letter fell to the floor in union with Rebecca's sinking heart. She cradled her face in shaking hands, then closed her eyes to preview the scenes of a coming-soon nightmare.

Act One. She would plead with her husband. Beg him to cooperate.

Act Two. He would say no, stubbornly refusing to fear the same menacing threat that promised to keep her on edge for several fretful days and sleepless nights.

Act Three. A faceless stranger Rebecca might never detect would kill the man she could never live without.

PART ONE

Three Weeks Earlier

CHAPTER ONE

August 15, 2043

Tyler Cain drove through several blocks of boarded-up homes and vacant apartment buildings before reaching the familiar street. The neighborhood could have been any of a hundred half-abandoned sections of town. Denver had begun following in the footsteps of once-thriving cities like Detroit, Philadelphia, Chicago, and Boston. The national population had officially tilted downward only eighteen months earlier, but some regions had already transformed into empty havens of life free from the burden of kids.

Neighborhoods don't hide the signs of aging any better than the people who desert them. Decades earlier these homes had likely bustled with the sights and sounds of children heading off to school. They now served as rickety remnants of a bygone era. Few of the single-family dwellings appeared in use beyond the occasional crack dealer, palm reader, or senior citizen too poor or stubborn to leave an area the underfunded police no longer patrolled.

Tyler pulled his unwashed '28 Ford Mustang behind what he guessed to be an abandoned '22 Lexus. Two unrepaired flat rear tires suggested the vehicle had been pronounced dead after the prolonged torture of owner neglect. Tyler's car fit right in, providing the perfect camouflage for yet another mind-numbing stakeout.

With the flip of a tiny switch on the left rim of his sunglasses he looked toward the residence in question. He could have parked closer. But four hundred yards gave him a reason to use the vision-magnification feature that, he had convinced himself, would be well worth the extra expense. Tapping the lens twice, he zoomed in enough to confirm drawn draperies and a solitary car in the driveway.

Absolutely nothing was happening, as during most of his billable hours.

Tyler glanced at the clock while reaching for a slightly crumpled bag containing today's indulgence: two bacon cheeseburgers with extra pickles. Renee would not have approved, but he needed sustenance beyond the bird food she called a sensible diet. His girlfriend had always been a health nut. It was one of the things that had attracted him to her when they first met. Her fit forty-one-year-old figure remained the best part of an otherwise exasperating relationship. Daily jogs and calorie counting looked great on her, but they cramped his style. Besides, he was in better shape than most guys pushing fifty.

He looked in the visor mirror to inspect a face she had once called boyishly cute. No man wants to be either, so he had grown a slight goatee that now contained more gray than he had allowed his thinning hair to display.

Renee disapproved of facial hair almost as much as bacon burgers. "It itches me when we kiss," she had teased. "Itchy kissing can spoil the mood."

Fortunately she never followed through on the veiled threat.

So he continued ignoring her appeals to restore the aging baby face she had fallen in love with three years earlier.

While downing a final beefy bite with a sip of strawberry shake Tyler noticed a vehicle approaching from behind. He watched it grow in the driver's-side mirror as it slowed to a wary crawl. As the car crept past he recognized the woman's face from the photograph his client had provided. Her car continued rolling forward as she strained to find a legible address before pausing in front of the house Tyler had positioned himself to observe.

She remained seated inside for several minutes, apparently adding finishing touches to her makeup. When she finally opened the door Tyler tapped his lens for a closer look. Nearly attractive, she appeared old enough to be helping grown kids pack for college or spoiling her grandkids rather than getting dolled up in such a pleasantly inappropriate outfit.

Why do they care how they look? he wondered. The man waiting inside, Tyler assumed, would act out this week's sexual fantasy regardless. To guys with made-up names that change daily, the risk of getting caught was a bigger turn-on than high heels.

Tyler quickly grabbed his camera to snap five pictures of the woman, the first as she walked from the car and the fifth as she looked back from an opening front door to confirm secrecy. That's when he caught a glimpse of the man's face. He appeared a bit younger than the woman, his tentative eyes darting to and fro as if checking for a stalking lover who might catch him in the act. Five seconds later the door closed as the pair secured themselves within a renovated slum house far less attractive and sanitary than it had appeared in the online ad for this particular House of Delights.

So began Tyler's Monday-through-Friday afternoon routine of sitting outside this or some other den of iniquity to glean the scraps of a booming arranged hookups industry. It was all part of a predictable sequence for securing clients and earning a steadily mediocre income.

- Step One: Follow home whatever man or woman left one of the sordid establishments
- Step Two: Trace his or her address to identify a potential partner
- Step Three: Leave an anonymous note to plant a seed of suspicion and recommend a "trustworthy investigator" named Tyler Cain
- Step Four: Wait for the phone to ring

The process had kept Tyler so busy he no longer bothered asking his former supervising detective for legitimate investigation leads.

Business is great, he would boast when asked. *More work than I can handle paying me more than I deserve.*

In truth he felt like a crawdad bottom-feeding on the city's sludge to barely earn enough to match his former salary. He wondered how much longer he could muster the self-assured grin that masked the greatest regret of his life. Tyler should have never abandoned the force. He should have swallowed his pride when passed over for a promotion, rather than leave a job he loved.

Tyler swiped through the images he had captured to make sure the woman's face could be clearly identified and that the time marker didn't obstruct any important details. Satisfied, he smiled in anticipation of invoicing another heartbroken client. Receiving payment was the only part of the business Tyler still enjoyed. Years earlier he had imagined himself catching murderers and foiling international conspiracies like the handsome secret agents on television. But then he'd stumbled into a lucrative niche in the private detective business. A steady stream of insecure partners gladly paid his hourly rate to determine whether the loves of their lives were cheating.

Placing the camera aside, he settled in to await the woman's departure. He guessed it would be at least thirty minutes before he could snap the all-important exit photos, ample time to listen to a few weepy client recordings. They always phoned after receiving his invoice, because he included a personalized invitation to call if they needed a listening ear. Clingy lovers always trap and smother the next partner, so Tyler's business could thrive for many years on repeat business alone. In the early days he had scheduled face-to-face closure meetings, a touch of humanity that had earned him several word-of-mouth referrals. But he quickly ran out of time and patience for that routine. So he began offering to talk on a phone he rarely answered, resulting in a steady stream of extended messages. Ten minutes of listening to whiny, emotional bleating followed by quickly typing a message of condolence had proven nearly as productive with far less effort.

"Hi, Mr. Cain, this is Naomi Wilkerson." The voice broke, and there was a long, sniffling pause. Tyler rolled his eyes in recognition of a weakness he had come to despise in the people who paid him so well.

"I can't stop looking at the photographs you sent," she finally continued.

He recalled three sets of pictures taken over a span of six days.

"I showed them to Davey like you suggested. But when I asked him to explain he just ignored me and went back to sipping his beer and watching the game.

"I started kissing his hand and asked him if he still loved me, then I said I don't feel like he wants me the way he did when he first moved in. I tried to be strong because he gets mad when I cry. So I took a deep breath before asking him if he had slept with other women.

"He didn't get mad. He didn't react at all. He just turned slowly toward me and said, 'It's none of your business who I sleep with. And no, I don't want you like I did before.'

"I felt like a knife went into my heart. I ran to the bedroom and cried myself to sleep.

"Well, you can imagine my surprise when he woke me a few hours later to say he wanted to make love. I was so happy. When we finished he began to fall asleep. I cuddled in close and whispered in his ear that I will always love him, no matter what."

Same song, hundredth verse, Tyler thought, *a needy woman grasping for an apathetic man like a drunk caressing an empty bottle.* Tyler saw what Naomi refused to accept. Davey didn't love his partner the way she hoped for or deserved. He merely enjoyed their living arrangement and the on-demand sex afforded by a girl sleeping twelve inches away. But Naomi had invested too much of herself in the relationship to let him go. Better to keep a small part of Davey than lose all of herself.

"Anyway," the message continued, "I paid your invoice and I thank you for your hard work. I suppose it's possible that Davey made a mistake, possibly even slept with someone once. But I still think we have something special and I'm choosing to hope for the best. I don't know what I'd do without him. You're a very nice man, Mr. Cain. Your girlfriend is a lucky gal."

The comment reminded Tyler that he hadn't yet made dinner plans to celebrate his girlfriend's good fortune. She insisted they do something special every August seventeenth, the day they had met, in lieu of a nonexistent wedding anniversary.

Three years with one woman, he marveled.

Two more than I intended, he thought with a sigh.

This relationship, like his prior three, should have ended after a sensible nine or ten months, when infatuation wanes and daily habits annoy. Both happened with Renee after fifteen months, about the same time he found himself short on capital and scrambling for clients.

"I'll cosign," she had offered supportively when Tyler confessed his inadequate credit. Renee would have done anything for her man. Still would. So the relationship expanded from that of while-love-lasts lovers into that of until-the-loan-gets-paid business partners.

What made him most nervous was Renee's recent comment about her biological clock. As if afraid of a ticking bomb, the thought made him want to get away. Despite cutting corners and pinching pennies, however, he had only managed to pay down the outstanding balance on their joint loan by a few thousand dollars. It would be two more bottom-feeding years before he could retire the loan, before he'd feel right easing out of the relationship.

After tapping the DELETE MESSAGE icon Tyler typed and sent a brief note.

Hi Naomi:

I just got your message and wanted to wish you well. Thanks for sending payment. While I hope it won't be necessary, I am available if you or any of your friends find yourself in need of investigative services in future days.

Warm regards,
Tyler Cain, PI
P.S. Davey is lucky to have you.

Tyler felt a sudden urge to stretch his legs. He hesitated, concerned the distraction could cause him to miss the woman's exit. Checking the time, he noticed twenty minutes had passed. He had always called arranged hookups the illicit counterpart of drive-through fast food. Transaction and consumption occur

quickly. But he figured the two would spend time getting acquainted before going through the motions of awkward foreplay,
hesitant passion, and the rest. Perhaps another fifteen or twenty
minutes. Tyler decided to take a chance. He exited the car to
cool in the shade of a nearby tree.

That's when he received a call from Greg Smith, the one man
able to rescue Tyler from self-imposed exile.

CHAPTER TWO

"Smitty!" Tyler shouted with too much enthusiasm, leaning against the white bark of a full-leafed aspen. "How's my favorite former partner doing?"

"Fine, Cain. Just fine." Detective Smith had never been the most gregarious officer on the force, content to let his partner cover rituals like disingenuous backslapping for the both of them. He was even less inclined toward empty chatter now that he held the post of assistant chief.

"Great to hear from you," Tyler continued. "How's life at the top?"

He regretted the dig immediately. It wasn't Smitty's fault Tyler had been passed over. Greg Smith was a solid officer and a good man. He had earned every promotion, unlike the conniving Kory Sanders, who actually deserved snarky comments about maneuvering his way into a higher rank.

"To be honest, stressful," he replied. "But I won't bore you with my headaches."

Tyler paused for a fraction of a second. Would Smitty finally nibble on the line? Tyler had never actually asked his former partner to hire him back onto the force. But Smitty must have known.

"Can I do anything to help?" Tyler asked, trying to sound indifferently willing rather than desperately eager.

"Actually, you can."

Tyler jerked forward as if standing at attention. "Really?"

"That's why I called," Smitty continued. "The chief got an odd message from a staffer over at the Tenth Circuit this morning."

"Over on Stout Street?" A dumb question. The Federal Court of Appeals had been housed in the same building for more than a hundred years.

"I'm forwarding you the message."

Tyler instantly heard the ping of arrival in his ear.

"I know you have a full dance card, but could you squeeze in a quick call between cases? I think you're the right man for this one."

Tyler smiled. "What's the issue?"

"Can't say. The message is pretty cryptic, the kind we would ignore if it came from the average citizen. But this came from the courthouse to the chief's in-box."

"Say no more. 'When it comes from the top...'" Tyler began.

"'...we get to the bottom.'" Smitty finished the familiar mantra. "Probably just needs a courtesy call that will go nowhere. But I can't let this one fall through the cracks. You never know, it might generate some business."

Disappointed that Smitty hadn't called about an opening on the force or a juicy case like the ones they'd solved together in the glory days, Tyler resumed his leaning posture. "I'm on it. I'll call today."

"Thanks, Cain. I owe you one."

Tyler smiled at the notion of being owed anything by Smitty, the same man who'd sent one strong lead after another during Tyler's early, starving days as a private detective. What's more, his former partner treated Tyler with a respect that nearly made him feel legitimate by pretending not to know what kind of work kept Cain Investigations LLC above water. This call was yet another ploy to feed Tyler an assignment much more respectable than his usual fare. Captain Greg Smith was a very good man.

"Play message," he said.

"Greg, the chief asked me to forward you the attached for handling per the usual." Tyler couldn't place the voice. Perhaps the chief's office assistant? "Please close the loop with me and I'll let him know it's done. Thanks."

He continued listening until the forwarded portion began.

"Good morning. This is Jennifer McKay from Judge Santiago's office in the Tenth Circuit. We've encountered a sensitive situation and find ourselves in need of a private investigator that can be trusted with highly confidential information. I wonder if someone from your office could recommend a name or point us in the right direction. Thank you for any assistance you can offer. I will be available at this number all day."

Tyler felt a twinge of self-esteem while tapping his phone to pursue such a mysterious, potentially important case. It's not every day a federal judge calls the chief of police requesting a private detective recommendation.

"Jennifer McKay," a voice answered.

Her abruptness told Tyler he had reached a very busy person who skipped pleasantries to squeeze additional seconds into an overloaded schedule.

"Yes, Ms. McKay, my name is Tyler Cain. I'm following up on a request that came from the chief of police. I was told you were looking for a reliable private investigator."

"If such a thing exists." A sardonic laugh told Tyler she

ranked his profession only slightly above that of used car sales-man. "Do you have a recommendation for me?"

He allowed a momentary silence while considering the most advantageous posture in reply. "Actually, Assistant Chief Smith asked me to offer my services. I made no promises, but said I would give you a call. I'm very busy, but I owe him a favor."

"I'm so sorry," came the suddenly embarrassed answer. "I didn't mean to…" She paused to redirect. "I appreciate your call, Mr.…?"

"Cain. Tyler Cain," he said, glancing toward the house of ill repute to check for motion. Nothing.

"Listen, Ms. McKay, I stepped out of an important meeting to make this call. I can only give you a few minutes. Can you give me the gist of your situation quickly, or should I try you again in a day or two?"

A sense of apologetic urgency overtook the woman's voice. "Of course. I'm sorry. I'll make this brief."

He smiled at the results of his favorite tactic. He who cares least controls the conversation.

"Judge Santiago has received three letters that I consider threatening. We need someone to help us turn sparse details into meaningful clues so that we can decide next steps."

"Next steps?"

"Specifically, I need to decide whether to share the content of the letters with the judge."

"He hasn't seen them?"

"He won't let anything compromise his objectivity. I read all of his mail and screen out anything directly or indirectly touch-ing a case on his docket. He trusts me to handle them as I see fit until after he issues an opinion."

"And these letters touch an open case?"

"They do," she explained. "A pretty high-profile case."

The comment piqued Tyler's curiosity, but he continued feigning indifference. "Why not ask the police to look into it?"

"I'd like to avoid that if possible."

"Because?"

"It might force the judge to recuse himself from the case. If either lawyer learned of the threats they could claim his self-interest trumped their oral arguments."

"So you're certain the threats are credible?"

She hesitated. "Not certain. Quasi-worried. I've read a lot of messages sent to the judge over the years. Nothing like this before. It feels, I don't know, both quirky and diabolical. It's probably nothing. But it might be for real. I don't trust my gut on this one, so I'd like another set of eyes."

He appraised the voice. She seemed unaccustomed to qualms.

Tyler jumped when he noticed the front door of the house starting to open.

"Let me check my schedule and call you back," he said, scurrying toward the car. "I might be able to move an appointment to squeeze you in late this afternoon."

"That'd be perfect," Jennifer said gratefully.

Tyler ended the call while retrieving his camera. He pointed the lens in the general direction of the house to capture whatever images he could before the pair moved out of range. Luckily a few proved useful. The first revealed a smeared trace of lipstick on the man's earlobe that matched the color the woman had applied before entering the house. The other showed smeared streams of dark mascara on the woman's face, as if the fantasy she had anticipated had turned into a shameful nightmare.

The tearstains prompted a sudden burst of anger that caught Tyler by surprise. He reached for the source, remembering a frightened, shame-ridden victim from his last year on the force.

Raped by a lowlife who got his kicks defiling somebody's mom. It was Tyler who had placed the blanket over her slumped shoulders and brought a Dixie cup of room-temperature water for her to sip while waiting. It took thirty minutes to get a female officer to the station to console the woman toward a lucid statement. He spent the time gathering other evidence for the lab. He recalled a queasy repulsion at the lingering scent of the rapist's sweat and fluid on the back of the woman's torn skirt. It had proved useful in nailing the culprit.

Tyler watched the car pulling out of the driveway carrying a different kind of lowlife: one who had traumatized a woman *with* her consent. He wanted to follow the car to the man's home. He wanted to whip out the handcuffs he no longer carried and frighten the guy, possibly teach him a lesson about true manhood. But he restrained his temper and turned his car in the opposite direction. Tyler Cain was no longer a police officer authorized to right the wrongs of a world filled with ugly realities that, for now, helped him pay the bills.

CHAPTER THREE

Matthew Adams's steps felt lighter as he strolled toward the Campus Grinds coffee shop. He reread the words that lifted a weight his shoulders had been bearing the entire academic year.

Congratulations on maintaining a cumulative GPA of 2.30, more than adequate to release you from probationary status at the University of Colorado.

He had done it. The late nights memorizing study sheets and drafting essays had paid off. Matthew's dream could now shift from a remote possibility to a "more than adequate" pursuit. Sure, he still had three years of undergraduate to complete before applying for a master's and then a PhD program. But he was one important step closer to becoming a college professor, the aspiration his mom had died to make possible.

The money hadn't actually arrived yet. It remained in an interest-bearing account while the estate trustee resolved a few legal technicalities. But it would come, an assurance he had given the registrar's office when he learned it required tuition and other fees up front. The idea of making minimum payments on an academic loan did not trouble Matthew in the least. After all, his financial prospects looked every bit as promising as his burgeoning academic career.

Entering the coffee shop, Matthew accepted Sarah's bright greeting with a nod before slipping into the same chair he occupied whenever he arrived early for his scheduled shift. Placing his tablet on the table he began typing, eager to share the news with his favorite professor.

> *Dr. Vincent,*
> *Yahoo! See attached. I guess this makes me legit. Thanks for all the encouragement.*

Matthew looked up from the screen to think of others who might share in his excitement. None of his fellow students knew he had barely cleared the admittance hurdles, nor would they care. Most college freshmen still had pimples. Matthew had thinning hair. The few who knew his name weren't likely to admire his triumph. Thirty-five-year-old men should be teachers, not students. They should assign and grade papers, not barely escape academic probation.

Matthew pushed past a momentary sense of isolation to find Sarah's smile. He tried to curtail fantasizing about his wholesomely gorgeous shift manager now that she had a formal long-term partner. Sarah and the steroid-enhanced Ian had been living together for nearly a year, enough time to seriously dampen any hope that Matthew's unspoken admiration might blossom into something more. Still, he enjoyed any splash of her attention—the closest thing he felt to the feminine nurturing his mother could no longer give.

Mom would be excited, he thought. On a good day she would

have beamed with pride over the accomplishment, over a son she just knew would be a professor someday. On a bad day she would have been confused, would have asked what it meant only to misunderstand his explanation. Despite her hazy grasp, however, she would have placed her lean hand on his arm to offer a well-deserved squeeze.

But Janet Adams was no longer part of Matthew's life beyond warm recollections mixed with a diminishing regret. He told himself she had died a hero, that he hadn't forced his mother's decision. She had made a willing choice. His urgings had only bolstered her timidity and given her the reassurance needed to do what was best. For both of them. Why cling to a decaying body when the freedom of pure spirit could be achieved with a simple, painless procedure?

What a bodiless existence entailed seemed more mysterious now than it had eleven months earlier when Matthew had escorted his mother into an Aspen House transition room. That was part of the reason he looked forward to spending more time with a man who could shed light on the subject. As a freshman he hadn't been able to register for 200-level classes. As a sophomore, however, Matthew would sit under the formal instruction of Dr. Thomas Vincent. The recollection prompted a second brief message.

I plan to take METAPHYSICS 202 during fall semester. See you in class!

"Big news?"

He looked toward the voice to see Sarah clearing a nearby table. He relished both the view and the question.

"Actually, yes," came his mockingly smug reply. "You have the great honor of speaking to a world-renowned scholar."

"You got the 2.0?"

"Blew past it," he said. "Just got notice from the dean's office. She practically begged me to consider an associate professor position."

"Yeah, sure."

"But I said I want to finish my sophomore year before committing myself," he continued.

They shared a laugh as Sarah slapped him playfully with her towel.

"Seriously, Matt, that's great. Congratulations!"

He felt a single pat on his arm as she rushed back toward the counter. He wished she had added a slight squeeze.

"Thanks," he answered over his shoulder. "I'm pretty excited."

Celebration ended, Matthew glanced at the clock. Ten minutes until his shift began, enough time to let others in on the exciting news. But who? He considered his mom's former sitter. Donny would certainly act enthused. He might even genuinely admire his pal's accomplishment. But his occasional buddy had barely graduated from high school. Probably didn't even know the difference between a freshman and a faculty member. Donny hadn't read a book in forever. No. A moment like this required someone special, someone at or above his rising station rather than beneath it.

He thought for a moment longer. No one came to mind because, as he had told himself repeatedly, Matthew Adams lived in a relational Siberia.

"Maria Davidson," he whispered to himself, tapping the name on his screen. He had been sending her anonymous notes for months. Wasn't the occasion of his academic validation a perfect excuse to cross the line from secret admirer to high school classmate hoping to reconnect? Didn't people do such things? Sure they did, all the time. Would it be so wrong to send a message suggesting coffee or dinner? Of course it wouldn't.

He thought about the invitations he had received to attend their ten- and fifteen-year class reunions—where, he assumed, people went to learn whether the homecoming queen still turned heads and whether the geeky valedictorian had made millions. More to the point, people who never spoke to one another during high school had been known to hook up. Sixteen years can humble the most rigid caste systems, even those defending the popular elite from invasion by mortals like Matthew Adams. So while Maria Davidson declined Matthew's invitation to the senior prom in 2027, she might give him a chance in 2043.

Back then Maria had been the hottest girl at Littleton High School, while Matthew had little swagger and even less muscle mass. She had received nine invitations to the prom before Matthew's. He knew of at least five other guys who wanted to ask her but didn't have the confidence. He gave himself credit for at least taking that risk. He remembered that she wore a short, dark-blue, open-backed dress. Matthew went alone and spent the entire evening watching her from afar, seething whenever her date's groping hands touched her barely concealed body.

Sixteen years later he continued watching from afar, a pleasure that had become significantly easier nine months earlier when she'd accepted his anonymous request to join her "secret admirer" network. Every picture she posted told Matthew she remained amazing. Unlike those of the other former cheerleaders, her photos did not appear doctored. Even if they had been touched up here and there, you couldn't make here or there look that good unless you started with something great.

Mustering every ounce of his newly bolstered confidence, Matthew decided to do something he had imagined doing since the day he and Maria threw their graduation caps in the air. Alphabetical seating had put them only ten rows apart, the A's in row one and the D's in row eleven, but the distance between them couldn't have been greater. Today he lived within an easy drive, a gap he could quickly close by sending a note revealing his identity, asking her out, and, he let himself hope, receiving her "I'd love to" reply.

He opened her unique page and clicked the LET'S CHAT icon just below her smiling image.

Hello Maria:

It's me again. Thank you for your latest post. You get lovelier by the day!

I've never mentioned it in my prior messages, but I thought you would be interested to know that we have met. You and I attended Littleton High together. Class of '27. More than met, I asked you out. You probably won't remember me, but I certainly remember you. Who doesn't?

Anyway, I have recently experienced a bit of success…

He stopped typing. Was it unwise to suggest his success had been recent? Yes, women probably liked guys with a longer track record than two semesters of college. He deleted the last sentence to replace it with something better.

Anyway, I plan to be back in Littleton on business quite a bit in coming months and wondered whether you would be open to reconnecting. Perhaps we could meet for coffee or dinner? I promise I'm safe, although I'm not so sure how safe you are after reading your latest entry. But I'm willing to risk it.

I look forward to hearing back.

Matthew Adams

He sat back to review the draft. His message needed to strike the perfect balance between sincere admiration and playful flirting. Maria Davidson liked, and deserved, both. Pleased, he reached toward the SEND icon. But he paused for one last scan. Then he moved the cursor over the last two words and bounced thirteen taps on the DELETE key, clearing his real identity to replace it with his favorite pen name.

I look forward to hearing back.

A Manichean

CHAPTER FOUR

When his shift ended, Matthew logged into the registrar's system to confirm his fall schedule, something he had done at least a dozen times before. Like pinches to make sure he wasn't dreaming, Matthew enjoyed reminders of his good fortune. With only fifty openings in Dr. Vincent's class he had rushed to secure a spot two minutes after student access to the online registration system was opened. An hour later fifty other students, including three seniors, found themselves on a growing waiting list. He worried those seniors might do some last-minute jockeying to bump him out of his spot. That's why he went online to check his status often.

Matthew entered his student identification number followed by a password. An error message appeared. Assuming a typo he reentered the information. Another error message. This time he bothered to read it.

ACCESS DENIED DUE TO OVERDUE BALANCE.
CONTACT STUDENT FINANCIAL SERVICES TO SETTLE YOUR ACCOUNT.

Matthew cursed at the screen and the reminder of the university's student loan policy. It would carry an outstanding balance within a single academic year, but not into the next. He hadn't given the matter much thought back when he requested a loan, because he assumed the transition money would be freed up within a few short months. He'd fully intended to pay off the loan by winter break, then by the end of the spring semester, then by midsummer. With less than two weeks until fall classes began, however, he still hadn't received a dime.

Matthew quickly phoned the number on the screen.

"You have reached the Office of Student Financial Services at the University of Colorado." The recorded voice went on to offer Matthew more options than he could follow, none of which seemed promising. "If you wish to wait for the next available student assistance representative, please remain on the line. The current estimated wait is approximately ten minutes."

He swore again, then considered his options. Perhaps he should call back in the morning. No. Some senior might have snagged his slot in Dr. Vincent's class by then. He decided to wait, enduring the musical selection that sounded like a cross between a traditional Celtic folk song and a sleazy lounge-lizard ballad. Some music major must have landed a big break by convincing the university to use his laptop-produced album for hold music. Not a bad angle. What better way to reach a large captive audience?

Midway through the third near-identical song Matthew reached for something to occupy his numbing mind. He landed on a recollection that made his stomach tense. With all the excitement over planning his fall schedule, learning he had passed probation, and contacting Maria Davidson, he hadn't even considered the possibility he might not return to school. He had convinced himself that all would be well. But what if it wasn't?

Would he be stuck in a pointless job for another year, waiting for his money to clear? What if it never cleared? How would he endure the embarrassment? How could he continue to justify his mom's transition?

"Transitions are nothing more than suicide by a different name," Father Richard had said. He called it a mortal sin, Satan's attack on the very image of God. But Matthew refused to believe it. Matthew preferred the enlightened spirituality of Manichean philosophers to dogma he, like Dr. Vincent, had rejected. He reminded himself, yet again, that death brought freedom from the prison of the body. Spirit was pure and good. The body was bad. It decayed. So even if his mother's money remained beyond reach it would take nothing from the majesty of her choice.

As much as Matthew hated to think her heroic sacrifice might have been in vain, he refused to accept the possibility that it had been a sin.

"Thank you for holding, Mr. Adams. My name is Juanita. How may I help you?"

The interruption rescued Matthew from his quandary.

"Hi, Juanita," he began. "I just tried to sign in to confirm my fall schedule and got a notice that says—"

"I see that your account is past due," she interrupted. "Do you want to settle the balance today?"

"Actually, I was hoping to get a short extension."

"I'm afraid I'm not authorized to grant extensions into the new school year."

As he'd expected.

"I understand. I'm sure I'll have the money in hand shortly. But I'm concerned about losing my scheduled spots in several key classes. Is there any way to—"

"We don't reopen scheduled slots until ten days before the start of the semester."

Matthew felt a brief flood of relief followed by a rising panic. Classes were scheduled to begin on August twenty-seventh.

"So I only have a day?"

"Two days, actually," she offered generously.

"Two days, then. Will my schedule be locked until, let me see…August seventeenth?"

"That's correct."

"Thanks." He ended the call before she could recite her closing script and immediately dialed the number of the only man who could get him the necessary funds that quickly.

"Cedillo and Associates, how may I direct your call?"

It always impressed Matthew how professional Carol Cedillo seemed when answering her husband's office number. She sounded just like an efficient assistant sitting in the downtown law office Benjamin Cedillo didn't occupy and handling an appointment schedule he couldn't fill. You would never know Carol was standing in her kitchen, walking through the aisle of a grocery store, or in any of a hundred other locations speaking into a tiny microphone affixed to her earpiece.

"Hi Carol. It's Matthew Adams."

"Oh, hi, Matty."

Matthew grimaced, then smiled. He hated the nickname Carol Cedillo had given him while he was in diapers. A name he let only her get away with using.

"Is Ben around?"

"I think so. Hang on a second and I'll check. He might be watching television."

"Sorry to bother him this late in the day but it's kind of urgent."

"No worries," she said. "I'm sure he would love to talk to you."

Not likely, Matthew thought. It had been nearly six weeks since the two last spoke. The conversation had gone badly.

"There's nothing else I can do, Matt," Benjamin had insisted. "Aspen House says they refuse to take any action until the NEXT appeal is settled."

"Why can't you pressure Chuck Kohl?" Matthew had pushed. "He told me he would be happy to co-approve Mom's procedure."

"Which you didn't get in writing."

"Can't you say we had a verbal contract?"

"Sure, I can say it. But that would be next to impossible to prove. Your word against his."

That's when the conversation had turned ugly. Matthew questioned Benjamin's competence before suggesting he hoped to pocket the money himself.

"Watch yourself, young man," Ben had snapped back. "You know I won't get and wouldn't accept a penny of your mother's estate."

"Then you're holding things up out of spite. You're still upset over her decision."

"You're sure it was *her* decision?"

Matthew had resented the implication. "Of course it was her decision."

"Charles Kohl told me he isn't so sure about that."

"He's just covering himself. He signed off on the transition, for Pete's sake!"

"He signed off on her mental competence, not on whether he thought she felt coerced."

"I told you a hundred times, I didn't coerce her!"

"I know you believe that. But I can't prove it, nor could I get anyone at Aspen House to corroborate it."

Matthew didn't remember the rest of the conversation, only the cloud of anxious fury he'd felt when he left Ben's home office. During the six weeks that had passed since the encounter Matthew had tried to remain optimistic. He'd chosen to believe the man responsible for his mother's estate would find a loophole of some sort that would release enough money to pay off Matthew's freshman loan and fund his sophomore year.

He'd also tried to urge things along on two fronts. First he badgered the receptionist at Aspen House, a process he stopped after the third visit because Aspen House threatened him with a restraining order. His second effort was much more creative and far less sensible. He delivered several handwritten letters to the federal judge overseeing the NEXT appeal. It couldn't hurt to let the man who seemed to control his economic fate know the real-life ramifications of the court's decision.

"Hello, Matthew." Benjamin's voice lacked its customary warmth.

"Hi, Ben," Matthew said hesitantly. "How've you been?"

"Oh, you know, I've been out back rolling in the pile of money I'm earning from your mom's estate."

Matthew winced at the dig before swallowing his pride. "Look, Ben, I apologize for losing my temper, OK?"

He took Ben's silence as permission to continue.

"Listen, I only have about a week left before fall semester starts and they tell me I can't officially enroll until the balance from my freshman year is paid."

More silence.

"Anyway, I was hoping we could figure out a way to release some of Mom's money before—"

"Not gonna happen, Matt."

"Look, Ben, I said I'm sorry."

"Fine. I accept your apology. But this has nothing to do with what happened between us. Aspen House won't budge. End of story."

"So my money just sits in an account forever?"

"Not forever. Just until sometime in September."

"What happens in September?" Matthew asked.

"Opinions on the NEXT appeal will be issued."

"By Judge Santiago?"

Ben seemed surprised by Matthew's recall. "That's right. Judge Victor Santiago is the presiding judge. I forget the other two judges' names."

"Coates and Howatch," Matthew reminded him.

"Right again. I'm impressed."

Matthew decided not to tell Ben about the letters he had sent to Judge Santiago's office. "It's an important case to me."

"I bet it is," Ben said wryly. "Nothing gets people interested in the law like the risk of losing cold, hard cash."

"I'm not just interested because of the money," Matthew lied. "This case could determine the future of the whole transition industry."

"It could. Probably won't, though. I'm guessing they'll overturn the ruling against NEXT and everything will go back to normal."

"Including my inheritance?"

"If the Tenth Circuit Court decides in favor of NEXT I'm confident Aspen House will come around. Until then they're like every other transition clinic in the country, worried about an avalanche of wrongful death lawsuits."

Matthew found the whole legal mess confusing. How had a voluntary transition turned into a wrongful death case anyway? Why had a judge ruled against NEXT? Why had the court granted some dead debit's brother so much money? And what had made that case prompt so much debate in Congress over the president's Youth Initiative?

Whatever the reasons, the director of Aspen House had gotten nervous when Ben requested a digital copy of the neutral consent form after Matthew's mom transitioned. One day Chuck Kohl said he would send it. The next day Aspen House said he was no longer an employee. The request should have enabled Ben to tie up a last-minute detail for Matthew's inheritance. It had instead generated dozens of delay tactics and one large unpaid student loan.

"I can't keep waiting for some court's edict," Matthew said tensely. "The semester starts in a few weeks."

"I don't know what to tell you, Matt. Until that case gets resolved I simply can't release the money."

"And if it doesn't?" Matthew hated to ask. "What happens if they decide against NEXT?"

"You don't want to know."

"Yes, I do."

"If they uphold the decision against NEXT then all bets are off. The state of your mother's estate will most likely be decided by some judge using criteria on which I won't even try to speculate."

"Wait," Matthew said. "Are you saying I might not get the money at all?"

"It's a possibility. Remote. But possible."

Matthew suspected Ben took silent pleasure in the prospect, his voice betraying a hint of smug condemnation. The eighty-one-year-old lawyer had never liked transitions. He mocked the idea that snuffing yourself out just because you'd passed your prime was in any way noble or heroic. A devoutly nonreligious man, Ben never called transitions a sin as Father Richard had. He just resented them for making anyone over seventy-five feel guilty every time he enjoyed dinner at a nice restaurant or took a leisurely vacation. He intended to live as long and comfortably as possible, blissfully callous to the growing economic crisis facing the younger generation.

He seemed even more callous to Matthew's personal economic crisis.

"Selfish jerk," Matthew said after ending the call.

Three heads turned in his direction.

"Sorry. Not you," he said toward the trio. "I was talking to a stubborn old debit."

Each nodded in knowing solidarity. The young, after all, must stick together in a world increasingly plagued by aging parasites.

CHAPTER FIVE

It was late. Jennifer McKay had wanted it that way—to avoid… notice.

Tyler Cain stood between the massive white pillars of the Byron White United States Courthouse. He'd entered much taller buildings in downtown Denver, but none that evoked such grandeur. An echo of pride accompanied the clack of his heels as they ascended the massive marble stairs that led to the public entrance. Tyler had once been part of the justice system. He had a legitimate claim to the sense of satisfaction he should never have taken for granted or traded away for spite or easy money.

"Only a few minutes to closing time, sir," the security guard said as Tyler removed his belt and shoes before entering the body scanner.

"I'm meeting with—" He stopped himself. *Utmost confidentiality.* "I have a meeting on the third floor."

"You'll need to sign the register."

No paper trail.

"Could I just leave my wallet instead?"

"Mr. Cain?"

"Why, yes. How did you—"

"Go on through. Ms. McKay said she is expecting a confidential guest."

"Great. Thanks. Have a nice evening."

The guard nodded. "You too, sir."

After slipping into his shoes and fastening his buckle Tyler turned left down a marble hallway. He noticed a large portrait of an impressively dignified face. He didn't recognize the name of the person who had no doubt played an important role in the 150-year judicial history housed within these walls.

Tyler continued walking until he noticed a sign marked COURTROOM TWO. He stole a peek inside, letting his eyes adjust to the darkness enough to admire an impressively manicured trinity of judicial benches elevated loftily above a duo of wooden tables and chairs. This room, like four others located throughout the building, was a theater that hosted some of the best and brightest attorneys who had ever practiced law. Each of them received a mere fifteen minutes to make oral arguments that might sway the court. Tyler considered the human drama that took place whenever the trio of shadowy benches held a federal judge who must decide whether to uphold or overturn some lower court's ruling.

Moving past the clerk's office on the right he found a spiraling stairwell that led to the second-floor conference rooms. He took the time to peruse a hallway nearly as long as a football field, where he read dozens of forgotten names on portraits too far down the pecking order of historic significance to warrant main-floor exhibition. He then climbed the final flight of stairs to locate the office of Judge Victor Santiago.

He pushed through the large doors and was greeted by a series of polished walnut desks, their occupants now missing in action.

Even during his days on the force Tyler had never worked in such an opulent environment. He thought of his own "office" back home, a cluttered, secondhand desk that shared a corner of the extra bedroom with a box of old clothes destined for charity. He breathed in the rich aroma of importance he had never attained. Never wanted to attain. At least that's what he told himself now.

"Hello?" he called out, glancing at a clock on the wall. Ten minutes later than agreed, part of his plan to appear disinterested. Now he worried the strategy might have backfired. Perhaps Ms. McKay had thought Tyler unprofessional and given up on him.

"Mr. Cain?" a voice said from behind.

Tyler spun around to see a thirtysomething woman, her tightly bound hair and crisp clothing working hard to conceal an otherwise natural beauty. She appeared to be the kind of woman bent on achieving success through no-nonsense precision rather than good looks. Tyler made a mental note: *Driven, but…insecure.*

"Tyler Cain?" she asked.

He nodded. "Ms. McKay?"

"I'm so sorry to have kept you waiting." She ushered him past her vacated desk while retrieving a series of white business envelopes. Then she hurried through a nearby doorway. He followed her into the adjoining conference room. "Please, have a seat. Would you care for something to drink?"

Straight to business. Perhaps his plan hadn't backfired after all.

"No, thank you. I'm good."

She sat across from him, opened one of the envelopes, and slid the contents across the desk: one handwritten letter.

"This was the first letter Judge Santiago received."

He glanced to the bottom.

"A Manichean?"

"No idea. I can't find a record of the name in anything remotely associated with the NEXT case. Possibly an alias."

Tyler scanned the letter, trying hard not to seem terribly interested. He picked up the gist, however. Whoever this A Manichean was, he—or she, Tyler reminded himself, although the handwriting didn't exude femininity—seemed terribly concerned about the outcome of the NEXT Transition appeal, as though his or her own well-being hinged on the outcome. Tyler tossed the letter back onto the table. Jennifer slid him a second, then a third. In all three cases the writer asked the judge to correspond.

"I look forward to hearing from you soon," Tyler read aloud. "Please post your response at the following private forum address: ANON.CHAT.4398."

Tyler recognized the link format. ANON.CHAT sites were littered with titillating posts from illicit lovers trying to stay connected between trysts. The perfect forum to remain anonymous. The posting party controlled whether and how to reveal his or her identity. Very few ever did.

He rescanned the text of the final letter but found no explicit threat. All four of them could have been written by anyone interested in the case; possibly a snooping reporter or religious activist.

"It just sounds to me like a person worried the judge will make the wrong decision."

Jennifer visibly bristled at the remark. "And which decision would that be?" she said accusingly.

Defensive. Or maybe . . . protective.

Tyler shrugged. "You tell me what the wrong decision would be."

"Even if I knew Judge Santiago's opinion on the case," she said with brash self-importance, "I'm certainly not at liberty to tell you."

"Ms. McKay, I don't really care about where Judge Santiago lands on the specifics of"—he glanced back at the letter to jog his memory—"The specifics of the NEXT appeal. But you must suspect someone dangerous does care. Isn't that why you asked for the best private investigator available?"

"I'm sorry. You're right." Jennifer seemed to welcome Tyler's condescension. She seemed eager for someone to relieve her from an exhausting posture of strength. He sensed control moving to his side of the table.

"Listen, Mr. Cain. You've taken time out of your busy schedule to help, and here I am...well, I'm the one who asked you to come. It's just, usually we receive this kind of letter and forget about it. People send hastily written notes crafted in a moment of anger or frustration or even praise. End of story. But this feels different."

"You mentioned that on the phone."

"This case has serious implications for a lot of people no matter which way the judge decides."

"I thought appeals required three opinions. What about the other two judges?"

"I checked. No letters."

"What's your theory?"

"Both have published opinions in the past in transition-related cases. One leans for, the other against. I assume whoever wrote these letters knows enough about the judges to figure Judge Santiago's opinion will be the tiebreaker."

Tyler frowned at the unhelpful but likely theory. "Perhaps you can tell me who has the most to lose and gain from Santiago's decision."

"Well..." Jennifer hesitated. Tyler understood. He hadn't officially accepted the case. She couldn't risk saying much more. But he wouldn't commit to this case, no matter how great the opportunity, until they reached an agreement on compensation. *Keep playing it cool*, he told himself.

"Listen, Ms. McKay…"

"Jennifer."

"Fine. Jennifer. You don't know me from Adam. I get that. But if you want me to help you, you'll need to trust me."

"I understand. I'm sorry. It's just—"

"You don't like private investigators?"

"I don't have to like them, Tyler."

"Mr. Cain."

Her face reddened at the rebuff.

"Listen, Jennifer. I don't have to be here at all. You called asking for help, and I'm only here because I owe someone a favor. But we can end this now, if you prefer."

"No." She took a deep breath. "But please be advised that everything I tell you must remain confidential."

"Absolutely."

Jennifer gathered up the three letters, setting them in a neat pile before continuing. "Jeremy Santos, the plaintiff. He has the most to gain or lose. He received a very large award in punitive damages."

"For what?" Tyler preferred admitting ignorance in order to speed up the discovery process.

"He lost both his brother and his mother during a transition."

"A double transition?"

"No. It was his disabled brother's transition. The mother tried to stop the procedure and fell. Very sad."

"A transition and an accident. Then why the large settlement?"

"The boy scheduled the appointment while a minor."

"Oh. Let me guess. The mother hadn't approved?"

"That's right. The bottom line is that Jeremy Santos will lose a large sum of money if NEXT wins on appeal."

"What about NEXT?"

"They have even more to lose. And not just the settlement

money. Losing this appeal could force them to institute far more stringent approval requirements for all transitions."

"Is that so bad?"

"It could cut deeply into their business. The more hurdles volunteers face, the more likely they will change their mind. Even a twenty percent decline in transitions would mean nearly a billion-dollar hit per year."

"A billion? I had no idea," Tyler confessed.

"There is a lot of money at stake in this case. Especially when you consider the impact on President Lowman's Youth Initiative."

"Such as?"

"Fewer transitions mean higher senior-care costs and a drop in transition estate taxes," she explained. "Not a good time for either."

"So the White House may be worried about this case?"

"To be honest, Mr. Cain, you're the first person I've met who isn't concerned about this case." She seemed to enjoy the jab. "As you can see, the implications are enormous. Sooner or later this case will impact the household budget of anyone caring for an aging or disabled loved one."

Tyler raised his finger pausing the conversation to steal a moment. He retrieved his tablet and pretended to type a few notes while absorbing the scope of the case.

"I don't suspect NEXT incorporated itself. They're too big to risk open retaliation. But I suppose it could be some rogue individual within the company with something to lose. Maybe a person who slipped up on the Santos case who fears losing their job."

Tyler glanced at his empty page of notes before asking whether Jennifer could think of anyone else.

"Who knows? There are religious nuts all over the place who would love nothing more than to see NEXT take a serious fall."

"Religious nuts?"

"Sorry. I shouldn't call them that. But you know what I mean. There are people who would love to see the transition industry come to a screeching halt."

"Do you think that might include murder?"

"Murder?" Jennifer's gaze fell to the letters. "Do you think Judge Santiago's life is in danger?"

"I don't know what to think. I'm only exploring what you think, and what might be at stake."

Tyler found it difficult to continue feigning disinterest in a case infinitely more important than jilted lovers and forbidden sexcapades.

"When we spoke over the phone," he continued, "you seemed worried. Like a person fearful over something potentially… dangerous."

"I'm sure it isn't. At least…" Jennifer took another deep breath. "I don't know. The tone in the letters is—"

"—disconcerting?"

"Yes. As I said, in the past, the judge has received many letters on various cases. Some of them from wackos and religious diehards. He's maintained a strict policy of ignoring those letters. So it falls to me to decide what to do about them, if anything. Nothing's ever come of any of them in the past. But this one seems less nuts and more…calculating."

"I tend to agree with you," Tyler said. "But the motive behind these letters isn't clear. There's no way we can come up with concrete conclusions without further investigation. As you indicated, it's probably religiously motivated in some way, and perfectly harmless. But you never know."

Tyler felt himself leaning forward to again scan the mysterious content of the letters. He imagined himself tackling a case far more intriguing than anything he'd seen since leaving the force. For the first time in years he felt a hint of excitement over what tomorrow might bring. But he still couldn't appear eager. He flashed a purposeful glance to the clock on the wall above the door. Jennifer gathered the letters.

"So, do you think you can help?" she asked.

Tyler shrugged, then slipped a Cain Investigations, LLC business card from his jacket pocket. He jotted a number on the back and slid it across the table. "I'd be willing to do some preliminary investigation. My usual daily rate applies, of course."

A daily rate he had just doubled.

She took the card, glanced at it, then switched back into professional mode. "Fine. But once again I must insist that you keep this completely confidential. I don't want the police involved. No publicity at all. It could completely undermine perception of Judge Santiago's neutrality when rendering his opinion. I can't let anything happen that might force him to recuse himself from the case."

"I understand. Now, I do have one request. I'd like to take a copy of each of these letters."

"Of course. I've already made copies. You can take these. But please don't make any additional copies, electronic or otherwise. I wouldn't want anyone to get wind of their content until we know what...or who...we're dealing with."

———❧———

As Tyler made his way out, he paused again to admire the building's classic architecture and the inscriptions that made him wish he knew more judicial history. Then he noticed the massive bronze plaque displaying names of the former postmasters general. This building must have served as a major post office in early years.

Post office. A thought came to him. He pulled out the three letters and examined the postmarks. They seemed archaic in a day when nearly all communication took place through electronic tablets. Archaic, but in this case important. The postmark on all three letters indicated that they originated from southern Colorado. Which meant whoever sent the letters lived...here.

CHAPTER SIX

The ringtone blared through the car's speakers. Tyler checked the time on the dash, cringing. Renee was probably worried sick. Any deviation from the normal schedule required a call, a daily reality when you mixed private detective work with a somewhat paranoid girlfriend.

He ignored the melody as he eased his Mustang across the freeway and into the AutoDrive lane, north on Interstate 25. The vehicle accelerated quickly to cruising speed as he relinquished control. He had exactly seven minutes before his exit, just enough time to update his financial plan spreadsheet.

Tyler slid out his tablet and pulled up the calculator. He figured the Santiago case would entail a boatload of billable hours, every one of them moving him closer to his goal. The extra cash and a bit more scrimping should enable him to pay off the business loan in eighteen months—allowing him to escape the shackles of Renee's cosign. After...who knew how long? Three years plus another eighteen months? Practically married!

The phone rang again. No use putting off the inevitable. He sighed while tapping his earpiece.

"Hi, beautiful," he said in a pretty convincing tone.

"Don't 'Hi, beautiful' me," she chided. "You should have been here hours ago. Or at least called!"

"I'm sorry. It's just…well, I actually have some good news!"

"Are you almost home?"

She clearly had no interest in his good news. He felt a pail of chilly water soak his excitement over landing the Santiago case.

"Listen," he started, shifting into damage control mode. "I'm sorry about not calling, but when you hear why I think you'll—"

A slight sniffle on the other end of the line cut his words short. Something wasn't right.

"What's wrong?" Tyler asked, rising above his aggravation to sound genuinely concerned.

There was a pause, then, "It's nothing. We can talk about it when you get home. Just…can you pick up a few things at Bulrich's on the way? I'll forward you a list."

"Sure. I'll be home in fifteen." He was about to end the call, but decided to earn a few extra points. "Then we can talk."

"Fine."

Two minutes later his car signaled the Longmont exit ahead. He eased out of the AutoDrive lane, off Interstate 25, and onto the street that led to Bulrich's Organic Market. He pulled into the parking lot and then confirmed Renee's list had made it onto his tablet. He walked inside and moved straight to the liquor aisle to pick up an item she hadn't requested. Whatever the problem, he thought, a few glasses of wine could only help matters.

―⁓―

Tyler struggled to shove open the door to the house from the garage. Something was in the way. He managed to create enough of a gap to squeeze through, then stepped over the overstuffed box of used clothes sitting on the floor.

"Renee?" he called out, then placed the bag of locally grown veggies and bottle of wine on the kitchen counter.

Her voice hailed him from upstairs. "I'm in the guest room."

Guest room? They didn't have a guest room. Not really. There was a bed in there, sure. But it had been officially declared his "office" when he bought the rickety old desk Renee refused to allow anywhere downstairs. She called it a monstrosity. She wanted it out of sight, along with the mess typically strewn across its surface. So the desk and its owner were both relegated to the spare room.

A stack of clean blankets and two pillows sat like lumps in the hallway just outside the room. Not the old worn-out blankets, either. Tyler had grown accustomed to those from being banished to the extra bed, usually because Renee had caught him staring at another woman. These were the nice blankets, usually reserved for company.

He peeked inside. Renee's petite, fit form stood, motionless, dressed in a tight-fitting athletic top and spandex shorts, as though she were ready for an evening run. She was just standing there, staring.

"What are you doing?" he asked.

"Here," she said, startled into action. She pointed to the end of his desk nearest the wall. "Help me move this."

He obeyed, lifting the heavy end as they dragged it across the room. They set it down at an angle that would make it impossible for him to use, comfortably or otherwise.

"Is someone coming to visit?"

Renee turned her gaze toward Tyler's, then stepped forward, grabbing his arms and wrapping them around her waist in a hug. She caressed his stubbled jawline, then kissed him long and hard before pulling back and resting her head against his chest.

He drew her face to his and kissed her back. This wasn't about his being late and not calling. She was clearly upset about something. He slowly ran his fingers up her back to her long, dark hair. Then she pulled away.

"I can't," she said, a tear forming in her eye.

He kissed her nose, then her forehead. "Why not?"

"My dad called."

This time Tyler pulled away, seating himself on the edge of the desk. "What happened?"

Renee brushed away the tear, blinking several times before saying anything. Tyler felt momentarily awkward. He hated this kind of stuff. Renee's parents were always calling about something. Usually it was her mom complaining about Renee's dad and his crazy nonsense, or going on and on about their latest health woes. But rarely was it her dad who called.

"My mom fell. The ambulance came and, well, they're at the hospital now. They thought she might have broken her hip."

"Again?"

She nodded. "But I got through to my dad after I called you and apparently the doctors think she'll be OK. A bit bruised. She sprained her arm trying to catch herself."

Another tear.

"And you know my dad. He can't take care of himself worth anything if she's not there to cook and pick up after him."

Tyler tried to inject a bit of levity. "I don't think he'd remember to change his underwear if she didn't lay out his boxers for him."

"Exactly." She smiled, slightly. "So now I have to figure out what we're going to do."

"We?" It came out before Tyler could check himself.

"I was thinking they could come and stay with us. Just for a while."

"Here?" He glanced around the room, looking for any reason that wouldn't work. "They can't stay here. Imagine if your mom falls again while climbing the stairs? And this room…it isn't big enough for them! I can hardly squeeze around the bed! There's gotta be somewhere else. Somewhere better."

Renee perched herself on the edge of the bed. "I know, I know. But there is nowhere else. They certainly can't afford one of those rehabilitation centers right now. So I was thinking—and this is just for a week, two tops—that they could move in here and stay in our room."

Our room. That's what had come of living together three years. He missed the days when there was just *his* room. When any overnight guest was there for a short, no-strings-attached frolic. And now he was being asked to give up the master suite in exchange for this room. This very small room.

"It's downstairs," Renee stated over Tyler's silence. "No steps to manage. And there's a shower instead of a tub. It's perfect, really."

"But…it's *our* bedroom."

"I know. I'm sorry, Ty baby. But don't worry. We can celebrate our anniversary in here just as well as downstairs." She patted the mattress reassuringly.

He half-smiled, but that wasn't what he'd been thinking. In fact he'd forgotten, once again, about their upcoming anniversary. He'd been thinking that this wasn't what he had signed up for when Renee suggested moving in with him. At the time he'd naïvely thought it would make sex easy. No special dates or grand gestures required. Living together would mean that anytime he wanted it, all he had to do was roll over. And that's how things had been…at first.

But the longer they lived as domestic partners the more tension he felt over the increasingly intertwining and interdependent realities of their lives. Especially the business loan. And retiring that debt would require at least another eighteen months, a year and a half more of near-marriage.

He looked into the same eyes that had drawn him so deeply into the longest serious relationship he had ever endured. Her eyes were pleading while her lips formed an alluring pout. Truth was, he did care about Renee more than he wanted to admit. He couldn't throw her out in her time of need—especially over something like her mother falling.

Tyler reached out toward her. Their hands met, and he sighed. "You're right, of course," he heard himself say. Then he cursed silently.

Renee beamed. "You mean it?"

He shrugged.

She tugged him off the desk, kissing him again.

Tyler glanced around the still-disorganized room. "I guess we should finish getting this room in order."

"Later," Renee said. "I've got a surprise for you first."

He tried to like it. Or rather, he tried pretending to like it, but it was no use. Leeks and asparagus hardly made for a hearty dinner. Where was the meat? Where was the protein? This meal quite possibly ranked as the worst ever.

"So, you mentioned good news," Renee said over dessert: apple slices with honey and cinnamon.

"I did?"

"On the phone."

"Oh, right." He gladly set down his fork, shoving away his plate. "A new client."

Renee reached across the table with her fork and stabbed one of his apple pieces. "Another rich and jealous lover?"

He took a sip of wine, shaking his head. "No, no. Not like that. This one's different. Kind of a big deal, actually. Should be interesting. A bit of a mystery."

"Mystery sounds good."

"It is. Only...I don't know. My client doesn't want the police involved, and I'm a little uneasy."

"Police? Sounds serious."

"It is. I'll probably stop by to see what Smitty thinks...just in case."

His eyes landed on a frame on the mantel cycling through a series of pictures. He saw himself standing proudly alongside his old partner, both dressed to the hilt in their formal uniforms. Tyler hated that picture—a constant reminder of the life he'd traded away. But Renee loved it because, in her words, it made him look "hot," whatever that meant in reference to an almost-fifty-year-old guy. The rest of the photos held far less significance.

Standing with Renee at some ski lodge.

A solo shot of Renee making a cheesy smile, holding up a fish she'd caught during a tent camping trip they took together when they first met.

Then came Renee's family. Her father, his head mottled with age. Her mother, fragile and lean. Tyler had never really known his own father, and his mother had died before reaching such an advanced age. Ambushed at fifty-four by pancreatic cancer.

"So, when are they coming?" he asked, still staring at the picture frame.

"Hmm," Renee mumbled while finishing the last bite of apple off his plate. She swallowed hard. "Well, as soon as possible. Tomorrow would be good, but..."

She hesitated.

"But what?"

"Well. You know how much I hate the drive through the mountains alone and—"

"Renee," he said warily. "You do remember that I have work to do, right?"

"I know, I know. But...it will only take a few hours. Can't you come with me?"

Tyler felt anger in his throat as the afterglow of their earlier romp dwindled back to annoyance. Renee seemed eager to fit Tyler into the mold of her father, a man who had spent forty-some years of marriage doing anything his wife asked at the drop of a hat and sacrificing his dreams and desires for an existence Tyler would have found smothering. He told himself he had no intention of spending his life catering to the whims of a needy woman and, God forbid, potential kids.

He looked back toward Renee's relatively youthful face smiling beside his own from the picture frame. Would she end up as gaunt and decrepit as her mother? Would he end up like her father, sidelined by life with no real reputation to speak of or even hobbies to enjoy? Would he be stuck eating leeks and asparagus for the rest of his life?

"I...don't want to."

"Oh." Renee cast her gaze downward, then grabbed the dishes from the table and started toward the kitchen. "I understand. You're busy. I'm sorry to bring it up. I can manage. Somehow."

"Renee, don't be like that. I just got this case. It's important."

The dishes clattered into the sink. "No, really. I get it. Sometimes things are more important than...family."

"Renee!" he said, hoping to stand his ground. But it didn't matter. No further conversation would take place between the two of them for the rest of the night.

CHAPTER SEVEN

Julia Simmons watched her nephew jerk himself away from his mother's reach and then scan the mall parking lot for potential witnesses. No twelve-year-old boy likes to be surprised by a hug his friends might see. He huffed away as Maria Davidson wilted back toward the car, her dejected stroll in stark contrast to the hurried sprint she'd used to deliver Jared's forgotten backpack.

"Let me guess," Julia said as her sister slunk into the passenger seat. "He didn't say thank you."

Maria flashed an exaggerated pout. "I guess I'm off the cool list."

Julia laughed while putting the car into gear. "I don't think either of us is on Jared's cool list anymore."

Maria extended her arm as if to pause the car's forward movement. "Wait! What movie did he say they were seeing?"

"The one about micro-robots gone wild."

"That's right." Maria reached toward the dashboard to tap in the title *Micro-Predators II*. "Here it is. The movie ends at twelve thirty. Add an hour for them to get pizza afterwards—"

"—and that gives us until one thirty." Julia completed the

sentence. "We should go downtown. When was the last time we ate at Vesta?"

"Perfect!" Maria flashed a predatory grin. "Nothing like an upscale dipping grill to cheer up a mom banished from the domain of cool."

As they pulled out of the parking lot Julia considered the idea of her sister falling out of style. At thirty-five, Maria Davidson remained a remarkably attractive woman, her blond hair and effortless spunk creating a feminine charm other women couldn't help envying. She had never been shy about wearing the latest designer fashions. The outfit selected for today's sis lunch outing, for example, would turn every male head in the restaurant. While it was too risqué for Julia's taste or comfort, Maria enjoyed flaunting curves even her son's adolescent buddies found impossible to ignore. Regardless of Jared's attitude toward his mom, Maria Davidson would never be totally banished from the popular class.

"So, how's Troy?" Maria asked while checking her hair and makeup in the visor mirror.

"He's doing fine. A bit stressed lately. But fine."

"How was your night at the Omni?"

The question prompted a slight blush from Julia as she remembered celebrating six months with Troy.

"It was very nice." A smile lingered on her lips.

Maria's eyes shot in her sister's direction. "Julia Davidson," she said. "You naughty girl!"

"The name is Julia *Simmons*," she protested. "I'm his wife, remember? There's nothing naughty about it."

Both tried to suppress a sly grin.

"Well, I'm jealous. It's been a long time since I've been naughty."

Julia rolled her eyes. "You've got to be kidding. You just broke up with what's-his-name three or four months ago."

"Jonathan. And it's been six months."

"Right, Jonathan."

"Don't act like you forgot his name. He liked you first, remember?"

"And then he saw you and I became yesterday's news."

Maria looked out the window to avoid her sister's *I told you so* rebuke.

"I warned you about him," Julia said.

"You warn me about everyone I date."

Julia decided to retreat. "Anyway, Troy and I had a great time."

Maria softened. "Marriage looks good on you, Sis."

"Thanks. It feels good."

"I guess I was wrong about Troy."

"How's that?"

She hesitated. "You know. I said I thought you needed someone more...well—"

"More hip?"

Maria nodded uncomfortably. "You have to admit, he wasn't someone who would have shown up on my hot list. He was kind of, I don't know, peculiar."

Julia gently slapped her sister's arm. "He was not peculiar. He just got a bit tongue-tied around me. 'Smitten beyond words,' he used to say. I thought it was sweet."

"That's what I mean. He uses words like *smitten*. Who says things like that? I bet he still calls you *my lady*."

"Not anymore. I insisted he cut the noble-gentleman shtick."

"Good."

A brief silence passed between them.

"I remember what else you said," Julia reflected aloud. "You said I should find someone less religious."

Another nod. "I still think he needs to ease up a bit in that arena. You'll end up like Angie. Mark my words, the elegant Julia Davidson—"

"Simmons!"

"Sorry. The elegant Julia Simmons will become infamous for wearing frumpy sweat suits while pushing a double stroller through the neighborhood."

Julia winced at the reminder of a caricature her sister still couldn't shake. A caricature Julia herself had helped embed in the popular imagination throughout her award-winning career with RAP Media Syndicate.

"I seem to recall you also saying marital sex would put me to sleep." She turned toward Maria. "Trust me. You got that one wrong too."

They shared another sly smile.

"How are Kevin and Angie anyway?" Maria asked. "She looked so adorable at the wedding in her maternity bridesmaid's dress."

"I'll let you know next week. I'm flying out tomorrow afternoon with Troy to see them. Kevin has an important presentation he wants Troy to attend."

Maria lifted a single brow. "Really? You're going to DC?"

"Troy said he thinks it's time to release myself from self-imposed exile."

"Wow."

"I think I'm ready," Julia said.

"You don't sound convinced."

"I'm ready," she said. "I guess I'm just a bit apprehensive going back to the place where I nearly destroyed my best friend's marriage and ruined Kevin's political career."

"You didn't destroy or ruin anything," Maria objected. "You simply did your job."

It was the same thing Julia had told herself a hundred times before. She hadn't known her editor would play fast and loose with the *Breeders* story or that the pictures of Kevin with another woman had been staged. Still, she felt guilty about the wave of journalistic success the story had propelled.

"A job you quit, by the way," Maria continued. "You made it very clear you disapproved of what happened."

Julia accepted the reminder with a thin smile.

"Angie and Kevin are fine. You shouldn't worry."

"I know. I just wish—"

"Hush," Maria interrupted. "It'll be fine. You'll see."

Julia did her best to agree. "How's work?" she asked to change the subject.

"Oh, you know. Every other day we get another prediction of ruin."

"I thought things were turning around."

"Like I said, every *other* day."

"I'm sorry." Julia empathized with her sister's growing sense of insecurity. "Still looking for something better?"

"Who isn't?"

The question prompted Julia to make a mental note: *Finish the story on unemployment.* She had pitched a unique angle: a year-in-review feature that would connect the dots between twelve months of layoff and closure announcements and the dramatic spike in anxiety-induced depression. Nearly everyone who still had a job worried about losing it. When would the next shoe drop? Would there be another market crash? What if the government made another cut to the unemployment fund? Every news syndicate included a regular feature speculating about how the economy would change in the wake of what the *Wall Street Journal* now labeled *The Meltdown of 2042.* Every economist had a different viewpoint. None seemed to have a clue.

Julia had recently warmed to Troy's opinion. The crash had occurred after revised revenue projections confirmed the economy was chasing fertility rates over a steep cliff. The ratio of dependent seniors to younger workers was simply unsustainable. The pyramid had flipped, leaving too few productive young straining under the economic burden of an aging population. The past decade had brought a net decline in the number of households for the first time in the nation's history. Fewer households led to empty, unsellable homes. Lower property values led to lower consumer confidence, further reducing spending on goods and services. The resulting decline in corporate profits dried up most of the business capital necessary to invest in growth or innovation. Dominos fell in a predictable sequence. They would continue to fall.

Even shrinking the social safety net, while inevitable, hadn't helped. Some said the cuts might have deepened the crisis because business leaders had followed the government's lead. Nearly every sector of the economy took a hit, with the notable exception of the senior-care industry. That's why millions of former engineers, architects, manufacturers, sales managers, retailers, builders, and journalists found themselves giving baths and fixing diabetic meals for a living. The old still had access to the cash they hadn't spent raising kids.

Julia considered herself lucky. She had never had more work. One assignment after the next flowed to her independent writing business, most of them lucrative feature stories for a variety of online journals.

Maria was feeling the pinch more than her sister. But at least she had work. Only five employees at her salon remained full-time. A dozen others had had to leave without severance or accept a downgrade to part-time status.

"Dark zones," Julia whispered.

Maria strained to hear. "What's that?"

"Oh, something Troy mentioned the other day. He said we have so many dark zones in this economy that it makes the bright spots stand out more."

"Bright spots? Remind me."

"Kevin's proposal for stimulating the economy. Find pockets

of growth to copy their patterns. You know, bright needles in an otherwise dismal haystack."

"Oh yeah. I thought that proposal got killed."

"Not killed. Just ignored. Senator Franklin's austerity committee set it aside when the crisis hit. But Troy and Kevin seem to think there may be a window to resurrect the idea, especially since Franklin needs something positive to offset his slash-and-burn reputation. People won't support a presidential candidate whose chief accomplishment has been further pummeling a battered economy with one draconian cut after the next."

Maria appeared uninterested in matters so far removed from her own world.

"Anyway," Julia added quickly, "Troy suggested I should write stories on both."

"Both what?"

"Both dark zones and bright spots. You know, sections of the country in decline contrasted with those on the rise."

"Are any on the rise?"

"Troy says there are," Julia explained. "He thinks I should publish a series of features that would show how current policies touch everyday life. But I can't imagine who would pay me for the stories, and my plate is pretty full right now with the column and paid assignments like the series I owe Bing Media."

Julia shifted her concentration while easing the car onto the interstate, allowing Maria to steer the conversation to more pressing matters.

"I got an interesting message this week."

Julia recognized the lilt in her sister's voice. "Did you?"

"A guy. He seems interesting. Kind of mysterious."

"How'd you meet?"

"The usual."

"Not another one of your secret admirers! I thought you swore off—"

"I said I was taking a break, not that I'd sworn off exploring possibilities."

Julia stared straight ahead while motioning for Maria to spill the juicy details.

"He says we knew each other in high school."

"They all say that."

"Stop it."

"Sorry," Julia said sincerely. "I just worry about you, Sis. There are a lot of nutcases out there. And the sane ones could be driven nuts by the images you post. You need to be careful."

"I *will* be careful," Maria said glibly. "Besides, I haven't agreed to anything yet. But I am thinking about meeting him."

"When? Where?"

"Haven't decided yet."

"Promise me it will be during daytime and that you'll meet someplace besides your apartment or office. A public location in a different part of town."

"Of course."

"And bring a—"

"Can I please finish telling you about him before you knit my straitjacket?"

"Sorry," Julia said. "I'm listening."

"He said we knew each other in high school and that he asked me out."

"Who didn't?"

"Julia!" Maria shot daggers in her sister's direction.

"OK, I'll stop. But you do still hold the record for prom invitations at Littleton High."

Maria's glower morphed into a self-congratulatory smile. "Anyway, he has business in Littleton and wants to connect while in town."

"What kind of business?"

"Didn't say. But any man who has managed to keep a business going in these times must have his act together, right?"

Julia thought of her husband Troy. Difficult times had forced him out of Washington back to Denver to try salvaging his own business. He had been working day and night to keep things afloat.

"I guess he gets points for that," she said. "Would I have known him?"

"I think he signed the note with an online handle rather than his actual name. I checked the class annual. It wasn't in there. The closest I found were Mansfield and Manchester."

"Hip Manchester?" Julia asked with a laugh. "I remember him. What a goof!"

"I think that was our exit." Maria pointed to a passing Colfax Avenue sign.

"I'm taking Speer," Julia said. "It's a bit early for lunch so I thought we could stop by Troy's office to say hi. He could use the interruption. Do you mind?"

"Not at all. As long as you promise he won't call me Lady Maria. It makes me feel old."

"I told you. I outlawed the chivalrous lingo."

"Good."

They took the next exit onto Speer Boulevard, five minutes away from Troy's office, where Julia intended to grace her gallant gentleman with a much-needed kiss.

CHAPTER EIGHT

"Floor?" asked a thirtysomething gentleman, appreciating Maria's skirt and heels. His tailored suit and silk tie made the perfect package for a visible confidence.

"Ten, please," Julia replied.

"Me too," he said, tossing a wink toward the younger sister.

"Are you here to see Troy?" Julia asked.

"Yes, ma'am. Troy Simmons of TS Enterprises. You?"

"I'm Julia, Troy's wife." It felt good to say it when standing beside Maria. Her kid sister still turned heads like few other women. But Julia had managed something even less common, a committed relationship.

"Nice meeting you." A slight nod in Julia's direction finally acknowledged her presence. "Robert Wilkie."

"Hi, Robert. This is my sister."

Maria offered her hand to formalize the handoff from married to available woman. "Maria Davidson. A pleasure."

Julia marveled once again at the subtle movements and voice inflections that made her sister irresistible to the opposite sex.

In less time than it took an elevator to climb ten floors she had turned a complete stranger into a promising romantic prospect.

"What time is your meeting?" Julia asked as the doors slid apart.

The man glanced at his watch. "Eleven thirty. I'm a bit early."

Maria's eyes met Julia's. Both seemed to imagine the same scheme.

"Listen," Julia began. "I need to pop into my husband's office for a quick conversation. Do you mind keeping my sister company in the lobby for a few minutes? I won't be long."

Robert smiled at Maria, releasing Julia to approach a vacant assistant's desk in front of her husband's closed office door. She paused before entering at the sound of muffled conversation within. After a few moments she discerned a solitary, agitated voice.

"I understand you took a big hit last month, Marcos," Troy was saying. "Times are tough for all of us. But we moved forward in good faith assuming you would deliver your part of the funding."

Julia turned the handle to peer inside. She found Troy's eyes. He eagerly motioned her to enter but seemed a bit embarrassed by her sudden presence, as if she had stumbled upon a messy room in his otherwise tidy life.

He moved toward Julia to position himself for the expected embrace. Both waited impatiently while Troy listened to a voice apparently making more excuses or offering inadequate apologies.

"Listen, Marcos." He broke the silence. "All I need you to do is buy us both a few more days. I'm meeting Wilkie from Peak Capital for lunch in five minutes. I can't ask him to invest in a deal you plan to abandon or the conversation will end before we order appetizers. It'll be better for both of us if you hit the pause button until I can raise more cash. Two days."

Troy resumed listening while Julia reached for his left hand to pull it down from his forehead and place it around her waist. Then she removed the chewed-up pencil from his right hand to place it on the desk before forcing clenched fingers open onto her other hip. His frame seemed to welcome the soft distraction from beleaguered tension.

Julia didn't like or recognize the look in her husband's eyes. Troy's habitual confidence appeared shaken. Whatever deal he had made seemed very important. It also seemed to be unraveling.

"Fine," he said curtly. "I'll talk to you after three."

Troy took a deep breath after ending the call. Julia rose on tiptoe to offer her lips. He accepted them less enthusiastically than she had expected.

"Let's try that again," she ordered. "Only this time imagine I'm your wife rather than your sister."

He released a reluctant smile before accepting the invitation.

"Much better," she responded afterward. "Do you want to talk about it?"

She knew he did even as his head shook from side to side.

"No, thanks. I'm good. Especially now. This is a pleasant surprise."

She slid his hands upward until they cupped her face as if to frame a message she wanted him to hear.

"Troy Simmons," she began. "It's me, Julia, your wife. Talk to me."

He appeared reluctant, as if ashamed at her discovery of a chink in his masculine armor.

"A big deal?"

"One of the biggest," he explained. "I've called in every favor on this one. I've also met with most venture capitalists this side of the Rocky Mountains. They all like the concept but seem skittish. Everybody's nervous about another dip."

"I'm sure you'll make it work," she said reassuringly.

He fixed intently on her eyes while gently caressing her cheek with his thumb. "Don't worry your pretty head, my lady. Everything will be fine."

He gave her another quick peck on the lips that told her he didn't buy his own propaganda.

Julia let a momentary silence linger between them. Then she hesitantly asked a question he wouldn't like. "Have you talked to Kevin about it?"

She braced for impact. Troy took pride in his ability to navigate complex situations and in protecting his longtime partner. Kevin Tolbert had too much to worry about already, he insisted. That's why Troy had volunteered to move back to Denver in the first place. He missed the excitement of Washington DC and the influence of serving as Kevin's chief of staff. But somebody had to shore up what remained of their business holdings.

"No need," he lied. "Besides, I can update him in person tomorrow."

She decided to retreat.

"Are we still meeting at the Beltway Bistro?" He seemed eager to turn a corner. "I could use a good power-broker steak."

"Afraid not," she explained. "I got a message from Angie saying the baby is sick and asking if we mind coming to the house instead."

"Leah's sick?" he asked with concern.

"Not Leah...Ricky. Nothing serious, just a cough. Angie doesn't want to take any chances. I said we'd come over after we settle in at the hotel."

"How old is Ricky now?"

"Let's see. He was born about six weeks after our wedding." Julia began tapping fingers while running a mental tabulation. "Almost five months old."

Troy moved back toward the desk, his mind clearly someplace

else. Capitol Hill, Julia assumed. She knew that Troy loved his visits to Washington DC, where he breathed the air of an influence he'd held before the economic crisis forced him to re-assume the reins of TS Enterprises. The company he and Kevin had birthed and grown together had been hit hard during the prior twelve months. They had majority interests in seven distinct small businesses. Two had since gone under. A third was starting to sink. The money that had enabled Kevin to run for Congress and that allowed Troy to serve as his friend's loyal general was drying up. Now, rather than help steer the ship of state, Troy Simmons seemed to spend his days bailing water from leaky budgets.

"Earth to Troy," Julia teased.

"Sorry, babe," he replied. "Five months old. Wow."

She drew closer. "Are you sure you're OK? You seem worried."

"Just tired."

"Do you want to skip tonight's session? We fly out pretty early in the morning."

"Not a chance."

Troy definitely liked their Exploring Christianity class more than Julia. The weekly ritual took place in Reverend Ware's living room, where a half dozen lapsing pagans tried to understand the fine print before buying faith. Troy had insisted they attend together. Julia had reluctantly agreed, unsure whether she was ready to dive deeper into the religion she had recently come to admire from a safe distance. Christ appeared far less demanding from the sixteenth row on Sunday mornings than he did when she read his specific words. She wouldn't have minded skipping now and then, but Troy refused to miss a single session.

"I'm fine, babe, really." He reached for a blue blazer hanging on the arm of the desk chair. "I'm expecting a lunch appointment to arrive any—"

"Robert Wilkie," Julia interrupted. "He's in the lobby with Maria."

"You're kidding. He knows Maria?"

"No. Well, he does now. We met him in the elevator. He seemed smitten."

"Good." He chuckled. "I need every angle I can get with him. Maybe he'll make a deal if I offer to set him up with my sister-in-law."

"I think she's probably beating you to that punch right now."

They shared a laugh.

"Eating at Panzano?" Troy asked.

"Vesta."

"My next guess."

Troy retrieved his tablet from the desk and placed it in his jacket pocket. "Did you finish your column?"

"Nearly," Julia said, tightening her husband's tie. "It needs a few tweaks. I'll get it done after lunch. I might even have time to outline the Bing Media story they requested about—"

Julia cut herself off when a hint of tension returned to her husband's torso. While Troy had often said how proud he was of her journalistic resurgence, she feared it also spawned other feelings. Her rising notoriety highlighted his descent into obscurity. He had done the right thing by voluntarily leaving the circle of power to mind the shop. But such things could emasculate even the strongest male ego. Even though Troy hid it well, Julia felt his struggle.

"Oh, never mind about that. You have far more important things to think about right now. What do you say we go rescue your lunch partner from mine."

They left the office hand in hand. Julia noticed the still-vacant assistant's desk.

"Where's Maggie?"

"She left the third week of July."

"You haven't had an assistant for over a month?"

"Nope."

"No wonder you're feeling stressed. Any prospects?"

"I haven't really tried to find one," he admitted. "Can't afford the salary just now. I'm doing all right."

He placed his hand on her lower back to usher Julia away from another uncomfortable conversation. She refused to take the hint, pausing to glance at the adjoining office.

"Wait a minute," she said. "Wasn't that Steve Reynolds's office, your controller? Is he gone too?"

A sheepish nod. "Since late June."

"Then who's been managing the books?"

Troy bowed his head while raising his right hand like a schoolboy caught cheating in class.

"So you're doing Steve's job on top of everything else, and all without an assistant?"

"Look, Julia—"

"Why haven't you told me about this?" she interrupted. "No wonder you've been working such long hours and feeling so stressed!"

"I didn't want to burden you with—"

"Burden *me?* What about you?"

"I can handle it, babe. It's only temporary. You'll see."

She crossed her arms like a girl threatening to hold her breath.

"Please," he said. "I might be just one lunch meeting away from the solution. Let's talk about it later, OK?"

Julia forced herself to soften, unwilling to further upset Troy before an important meeting. "OK. But I want us to talk about it tonight."

"Deal."

As they rounded the corner Julia saw an all-too-familiar sight. Her sister sat cozily close to a man she had met minutes earlier, who was now enthralled with chatter about nothing in particular.

Julia smiled at the couple, then halted her advance and faced her husband to cut a different deal.

"No, I don't want to talk about it tonight," she whispered. "I want you to tell Kevin what's going on when we see the Tolberts tomorrow. You shouldn't have to carry this by yourself. I don't care how busy he is, Kevin is still your partner."

"Don't worry. I'll discuss everything with him tomorrow."

"Promise me," she insisted.

"I promise," he said in a hushed voice. "Now can we go? I really need the time with Robert if I'm going to make this deal work."

Satisfied, Julia squeezed her husband's hand. Then she turned toward the lobby to greet the potential investor with the most charming voice she could muster.

CHAPTER NINE

"We're gonna miss you," Sarah said while Matthew placed a chair on top of the table she had just finished cleaning.

"Thanks," he replied, forcing an upbeat grin. "Back at'cha."

The thud of the last wooden stool settling onto the flat surface created a disquieting sensation in Matthew. He had volunteered to stay and help Sarah close up shop, buying him a few extra minutes in a job he had never really liked but that had given him a place for nearly ten years.

Campus Grinds was where Matthew had voiced his frustration back when the University of Colorado rejected his first attempt to enroll, still one of the most disheartening moments of his life. His dream had died. Or so he'd thought at the time. His coworkers might not have cared all that much, but at least they offered a semblance of sympathy.

Watching Sarah clear the last bit of clutter from the counter prompted a twinge of grief. Matthew would miss her, his favorite of the many part-time employees who had come and gone over the years. He would miss waxing eloquent on a range of academic-sounding topics while she nodded with varying degrees of interest. The tiniest possible audience, she had given him a sense of validation the enrollment office seemed unwilling to bestow.

Sarah had been most thoughtful during his mother's worst years. A willing shoulder if he had been inclined to cry. But his mother's decline had fueled anger, not tears. So he never took her up on the offer.

"I'm not sure I ever told you how much I appreciated your kindness during my mother's illness." He paused to watch her reaction before saying more. She appeared momentarily puzzled, as if reaching to recall any sympathy she might have offered.

"Oh," she muddled, "don't mention it."

They both moved toward a small closet door in the corner behind the counter, where Sarah retrieved a broom and dustpan while Matthew grabbed a small garbage bucket he had filled and emptied hundreds of times before.

"How is she?" Sarah asked while maneuvering the broom into a corner.

"Who?" he asked.

"Your mom."

Matthew's brow furrowed. Then he remembered that he had never told Sarah about the transition. He'd told her about getting accepted as a full-time student. He'd sought and received her smiling approval when he said he could finally pursue his dream. But he hadn't mentioned his mother's death. Why would he? The money that would have freed him to quit his job still hadn't been released. Had that happened he might have told her about the inheritance. So, with the exception of a few shift-change requests to accommodate Tuesday and Friday classes, nothing was different about Matthew from what Sarah had observed over the prior four and a half years.

"My mom is…" he began, then stopped. "Actually, she's doing great. Never better."

He almost believed it after months of telling himself his mom was now free from the limitations of a decaying body.

"Glad to hear it." Sarah seemed eager to change subjects. "Remind me again why you're moving to Denver."

She knelt and positioned the dustpan in front of a freshly swept mound of dirt while handing Matthew the broom.

"Littleton, actually," he said.

"That's right. Littleton then."

He hadn't had time to invent an impressive reason for the change, so he told her the embarrassing truth. "I need to pay down my loan before I can fund another semester."

"I see," she replied, emptying the dustpan into the bucket. Then she stood and waited for the rest of a story he hadn't intended to tell.

"I grew up in Littleton. Lived there until about ten years ago when my mom retired."

"What brought you to Boulder?"

"Naïveté," he said, laughing. "I assumed living close would improve my chance of getting into the university. Mom agreed. Of course, she never went to college herself, so knew even less than I did about what it takes."

Matthew took two steps forward to accompany Sarah, who had inched her way toward the front of the shop for one last inspection of the floor.

"It took me seven years to get accepted, one of them driving to Front Range Community College to prove I have what it takes."

"Uh-huh," she said robotically.

He kept talking despite losing her attention. Closing duties completed, she appeared eager to lock up and head home.

"Anyway, there are more jobs in the Denver area. Besides, I

still have a few high school friends living in Littleton. I figure I'll hang there to save for ten or eleven months and then come back to school next fall."

Matthew was glad she didn't ask what job he had lined up. The only thing less impressive than cleaning coffee mugs was taking care of old people. But senior-care services paid a premium wage. Short of receiving the inheritance, he knew of no other way to get the kind of money necessary to enter his sophomore year.

They returned the cleaning supplies to the closet before Sarah retrieved her purse from behind the counter.

"Well," she began, "I guess this is goodbye for a while."

"For a while," he said with a tentative smile. "Thanks, again, for being a great shift boss. And for being a friend."

"You bet." She extended her free arm for a side embrace, less than he wanted but all he could expect.

"I'll miss you," Matthew heard himself say.

"Ditto," she said awkwardly. "So I'll see you in about a year?"

"For sure," he agreed. "In a year."

Matthew stood outside in the warm August air watching Sarah enter the locking code on the front door. They walked silently in the same direction, the space between them widening as each veered onto diverging paths.

He gradually slowed his pace until he found himself standing still on the university lawn while Sarah continued toward the parking lot. He waited for her to move out of visual range before turning back. Matthew needed to say one more goodbye before loading up the U-Haul and moving back to Littleton.

—∿∿—

Three hours earlier Professor Thomas Vincent had popped into the shop for his daily Brazilian coffee and invited

Matthew to stop by the office whenever his shift ended. He said he would be working late, code for an evening tryst with one of the female students eager to impress her teacher. Matthew smiled at the former priest fully recovered from a vow of chastity.

While approaching the philosophy building Matthew recalled the professor's instructions. He glanced up toward the outer window of the second floor. Drawing near he noticed light shining through opened blinds, his cue to climb the stairs.

"Hello, Matthew," Dr. Vincent said after opening the door. "Come on in."

The professor moved toward a dark wooden cabinet. "What are you drinking?"

Matthew shrugged. "Beer, I guess. Thanks."

Matthew walked toward a small sofa nestled between the professor's desk and bookshelf. Just before sitting he noticed the faint aroma of perfume only slightly more pungent than the lingering scent of Dr. Vincent's cologne. He moved to a different chair.

"Here you go." Dr. Vincent offered a cold bottle to his guest before raising his own. "To a successful freshman year."

Matthew mirrored his host with a nod before joining in a celebratory swig.

"And to your one year sabbatical before returning as a sophomore," Dr. Vincent said, repeating the ritual.

"'Sabbatical,'" Matthew mocked. "I like the sound of that. Although it's more like an exile."

"I'm sure everything will work out. You got this far. You'll find a way to keep going."

Matthew pressed his lips into a weak smile. "I guess."

Both men sat in silence for thirty seconds.

"So, tell me about the job. You said something about better pay but didn't mention what you'll be doing."

Matthew looked toward the bookshelf to avoid the professor's eyes. "I accepted an elder-care position."

"Really?"

"My first client lives in Littleton."

"East of Denver?"

"Right. A few blocks from my old high school."

"Friends?" Dr. Vincent asked.

"A few. There's a girl." Matthew left details of the relationship to his host's imagination rather than explain the pathetic reality.

"Anything serious?"

"Not yet." The truth. "But things seem to be progressing nicely." A stretch.

Another thirty seconds without words.

"Pretty lame, isn't it?" Matthew asked.

"What's that?"

"If you think about it, I'm right back where I started. No. Worse than where I started."

"How so?"

"Last year I couldn't go to school because I was broke and taking care of my mom. Now I'm in debt and will be taking care of a complete stranger."

"True. But you have a year of school under your belt."

"Right. And the loan to prove it," Matthew scoffed.

"Big accomplishments come through small moves, Mr. Adams."

The comment struck Matthew wrong. He felt anger rise as he recalled a year-old conversation with this same man. A conversation that had fueled a very *big* move.

"Do you consider it suicide if someone volunteers to transition?" Matthew had asked while wrestling with the most difficult quandary of his life.

"There's no such thing as a mortal sin," Dr. Vincent had assured him. "Just hard choices."

"Would you help your own mother transition, you know, if she asked you to?" Matthew had pressed further.

"Yes. I believe I would have helped her."

Matthew looked up from the bottle of beer toward his host. "I'm willing to make small moves. But I made a big move last year and I'm not sure it was the right thing to do."

"By helping your mom transition?"

More than help, he didn't confess.

"Listen to me, Matthew," Dr. Vincent insisted. "Your mother was in severe decline, am I right?"

A single nod.

"And she wanted to fund your dream?"

"She did," he acknowledged.

"Then you did the right thing by confirming her choice. There's no way either of you could have known the transition money would get held up in a legal mess."

"I guess you're right."

"Of course I'm right," Dr. Vincent decreed. "And it won't do either of you any good to second-guess the decision. Your mom's death wasn't a sin. Nor was it a waste. Even if the money never comes, the procedure put her out of her misery."

Matthew's stomach tensed. *Mom wasn't miserable, just forgetful.*

"What was the phrase you borrowed from that journalist?"

"Julia Davidson?"

"Davidson, right."

"'Free to thrive.'" Matthew recalled the title of a column that had eased his conscience. "She said something about using genetic prescreening to prevent defective babies. I thought it applied to people like my mom who deserve freedom from disease now."

"Your mother couldn't thrive while trapped in a decaying body."

Matthew pushed aside thoughts of his mother's smile and

touch to recall her failing memory, bathroom mishaps, and fits of anxiety. "I suppose not."

"There's no supposing about it," Dr. Vincent insisted. "You did the right thing, Matthew. I'm sure your mother would be proud of all you've accomplished this year."

He lifted his bottle for another toast. "To her heroic sacrifice."

They shared a drink.

"And to your hard work," he added.

"Thanks, Dr. Vincent," Matthew said. "I appreciate your encouragement."

"Just promise me you won't let this girlfriend in Littleton distract you from your goal. I expect to see you back here as soon as you resolve the transition money mess."

"I promise."

The host ushered his guest to the door, where both said their goodbyes before Matthew descended the stairs and began walking toward the parking lot. He felt much more at ease than he had when the day began, even allowing himself a hint of self-respect. A playful ping came from the device in his left pocket. Retrieving the source he tapped the tablet screen, where a brand-new image of Maria Davidson appeared. She had apparently posted it seconds earlier as another treat for her anonymous admirers. As usual, she looked amazing.

The moment prompted a satisfied smirk. In less than twenty-four hours Matthew would pack up his few possessions and move them to the home of an elderly client who lived a few short miles from the woman of his dreams. A woman Matthew hoped might become the kind of sweet distraction Dr. Vincent had warned him against.

CHAPTER TEN

Tyler waved his tablet over the police station parking meter until it acknowledged payment with a beep. Straining his left ear toward his shoulder he tried working out the kink in a neck that resented sleeping on the couch. After a series of comforting pops he stretched in the other direction. Renee had said he couldn't sleep in the master suite since she had cleaned the sheets for her parents. And joining her in the guest room would have required groveling, something he refused to do.

He approached the door in grumpy silence with a slight anxiety. He couldn't quite pinpoint what it was that troubled him about asking Smitty's advice. His old partner would keep the conversation completely confidential. But he still felt uneasy.

Tyler felt his pocket to confirm that he had remembered to bring the Santiago letters. Then he swallowed hard while crossing the threshold to reenter a former life.

A minute later Tyler found himself standing outside a window of bulletproof glass, behind which an unfriendly face eyed him skeptically. She said nothing while waiting for the day's first interruption to identify himself.

"Cain," he offered. "Tyler Cain. I'm here to see Smitty."

A disapproving scowl caused him to wonder what had happened to the perky brunette who used to occupy the receptionist station.

He nervously cleared his throat. "Or, I mean, Assistant Chief Smith."

A familiar voice called out from behind. "Cain?"

He spun around to see Kory Sanders, annoyingly happy to see him.

Tyler forced a smile in return, nodding. "Kory."

Kory slapped Tyler on the back, as if they had once been great friends.

They hadn't.

"What's happening?" asked the man who had weaseled his way into the post Tyler had deserved. "It's been a while. I haven't seen you since, oh, let me think, right after I became captain. Am I right?"

Kory smirked.

Pull out your gun and shoot me in the heart now, why don't you? Tyler thought.

"Uh. Yeah," he heard himself say.

"How's PI work treating you?"

"Great!" he lied. "Couldn't be better!" Which was almost true, given the new case.

Kory wore a doubtful smirk. "Riiiight."

Tyler suppressed an urge to slug his former nemesis.

"So, still with, oh, what was her name? Courtney?"

"Heck, no." Tyler snorted awkwardly. "Escaped that relationship years ago." Another forced laugh. "How about you? Anyone keeping you warm at night?"

"Off and on. You know how it is…I'm game if they're willing with no strings."

"I hear you," Tyler said. "My current live-in is a nice-enough gal. But it's about time I ended it."

The officer behind the glass glanced up, rolling her eyes.

"It's just getting, you know, complicated. She wants more from me than I—"

He stopped. Why in the world was he telling Kory Sanders about his relationship with Renee? Kory Sanders was a jerk. But Tyler found himself on the speeding train of a conversation heading nowhere good.

He lied again. "I think she wants a kid."

"Whoa, man," Kory said. "You gotta nip that one soon. That's why I have a strict policy: never live with a partner. Way too many expectations I'm not willing to meet."

Change the subject, Tyler thought. "I'm here to see Greg. Running an important case by him."

"Really?" Tyler could almost see the gears churning away in Kory's head. "Anything I can do to help?"

Tyler shook his head as he went for the dig. "Nah. Really needs someone…higher up."

Kory sniffed. "Gotcha. Well, you know where to find me if you change your mind." He rapped his knuckles twice on the counter before sliding two fingers across the entry scanner. The door buzzed open. "Don't be a stranger."

―⁓―

Tyler knocked assertively on the door with the sign that read GREGORY SMITH, ASSISTANT CHIEF OF POLICE.

"Smitty?"

His former partner glanced up from behind several stacks of

files and offered a wry smile. "Tyler Cain. To what do I owe the pleasure?"

Tyler set one foot over the threshold, waiting for an official invitation. "Got a few minutes?"

Smitty hesitated. Then he leaned back in his chair to wave him in. "You bet," he said, closing the folder in front of him. He tossed it onto one of the piles. "We've been in the computer age for nearly a century, and there's more paperwork now than ever!"

Smitty stood and moved to the front edge of his desk. Then he leaned back and crossed his arms. Tyler recognized the "keep it brief" stance, so he turned a chair around and leaned back to mirror his host's posture.

Their reunion felt awkwardly cordial, another reminder that Greg Smith was no longer Tyler's partner. The two had once trusted each other with their lives. They had been fairly close confidants who felt a bond forged patrolling neighborhoods, sipping doughnut-shop coffee, and enduring the boredom of more stakeouts than either cared to recall. But diverging streams of time's river had created an expanse Tyler could no longer pretend away.

He reached deep for something to restore their former amity. He found a useful memory: Smitty confiding in his partner during a rough spot in his relationship with Carol Anne. Were they still married?

"How's Carol Anne?" He felt his way lightly.

"Fine," Smitty said. "She's fine. We're fine, actually."

"Really? So you're not—"

"No." Smitty chuckled. "We're not apart. Actually, quite the opposite. We got some help, worked through our issues, and then, well…" He paused, reaching back to spin around a frame. "There's the result!"

A little girl who looked about two years old smiled cheesily at the camera, her hair decorated with ribbons and pigtails.

"Wow," Tyler said, not sure if Smitty considered fatherhood a coup or a curse. He'd never wanted children back in the day, one of many tense spots in the marriage. He had called kids conceived in the heat of passion "unplanned monkey wrenches thrown into the gears of life."

But the adoring grin Smitty flashed while displaying the photo suggested a change of heart.

"But I gather you're not here for a social visit," he said, spinning the frame back into place. "Is this about the case I sent your way?"

"Yes... and no."

Smitty frowned. "Well, which is it?"

"The judge's assistant insisted I keep the police out of this for now. Until I know more, at least. Officially speaking."

"But unofficially?"

"Unofficially, the whole thing makes me uneasy. There's a lot at stake, and I'm nervous the judge could be in danger."

"Which judge?"

"Can't say."

"Fine. So, unofficially, what's going on with this nameless judge?"

Tyler slid the letters from his pocket, holding them up but not quite offering them. "So far I've got three letters. Each mentions a big case on the nameless judge's docket. He or she also makes a request for direct communication, hoping to dialogue about the pending decision."

"He or she? No name?"

"Just a first initial and a last name."

Smitty lifted his eyebrows in a silent request for more.

"A Manichean," Tyler explained. "Might be a pen name. I found some information about an ancient religious sect called Manicheans, but nothing that seemed relevant to the case. Probably a coincidence."

"Has the judge responded to the sender?"

Tyler shook his head. "Not so far. I'm not even sure he's aware the letters exist."

"So what's the problem?"

"Each letter sounds more desperate than the last. Possibly more threatening. The first reads like a simple request to correspond anonymously. The second hints about unwelcome consequences of a wrong decision. The third expresses annoyance that the judge has ignored the sender's requests to dialogue."

Smitty stroked his clean-shaven chin in thought. "Any criminal record?"

"Nothing listed on my usual sources. Of course, they're always a bit out of date." Tyler hesitated before floating his first request. "Any chance I could run the name through the department database?"

"Done," Smitty said, uncrossing his arms, his standard end-of-meeting gesture.

Tyler didn't move, prompting Smitty to reluctantly resume an attentive stance.

"What else?" he asked.

"Scan the envelopes to see if forensics can find anything useful?"

"Also done."

"I've got a hunch about this one, Greg," Tyler began. "The same hunch I got on the Gilbert case."

As their eyes met, Tyler noticed Smitty's jaw begin to clench.

"Gilbert?" he asked.

Tyler nodded slowly as both minds regurgitated the details. The brutal murder of a young girl could have been prevented had the two disobeyed orders. The chief hadn't trusted Tyler's gut. He had wanted something concrete before approving an arrest. One anonymous lead wasn't enough to risk the embarrassment and backlash of hauling Travis Gilbert into custody. The respected businessman had donated generously to the mayor's campaign. But Tyler knew his low-life source had told the truth. Sure, it would have been risky acting on the word of a twenty-eight-year-old drug dealer. But it was even more risky, Smitty had argued, to sit back and do nothing while Gilbert committed murder to prevent a public scandal. The girl had gotten in over her head trying to blackmail Gilbert. They had met at a party. He enjoyed her for a while, then discarded her like a disposable toy. So she threatened to expose his "discreet habit" of using recreational drugs. But Gilbert figured it would save hassle and money to take her out of the picture. The girl's body disappeared until police uncovered her shallow grave behind a condemned suburban crack house six months after Tyler and Smitty were taken off the case.

"That's why I wanted to get another opinion," Tyler added. "You know, from the one person I trust on this kind of thing."

Smitty half-smiled, appreciatively. "Well, I think you're probably right."

Tyler frowned at the validation.

"Unofficially, I'd trust your instincts."

"But officially?"

"Officially, you already know what I'm going to say."

Tyler nodded, sighing. "No crime has been committed."

"We can't invest time or resources on someone who, from all appearances, simply wants to exchange words with a judge. Even hostile words." He waved his hand over the stacks of folders on his desk. "Look at this. I can't get on top of the pile as it is."

Tyler glanced down at the letters in his hand. He had anticipated Smitty's response, the same one he would have given had some private investigator shared the scenario back when he was a detective. The police can't get involved in a case based entirely on a hunch something *might* be wrong.

"I understand," Tyler responded.

"But I'll ask someone to run the name through our database for any additional leads."

"I appreciate that."

Smitty moved back around the desk to retake his seat. Recognizing the hint, Tyler slid the chair back into place before offering his hand across the desk.

"Thanks for the help, Smitty," he said. "And for the lead. You're a good man."

Smitty shook firmly, then retrieved a folder from the pile.

"Listen, Ty," Smitty said as Tyler moved toward the open door. "I miss working with you."

Tyler turned back toward his former partner to accept the badly needed sip of camaraderie. "Me too," he said.

"I gotta tell you, when you left the force, I thought you were crazy and…maybe even a little selfish."

"Ouch."

"No. Listen. I know there was bad blood between you and Kory, but it bothered me when you left. I won't lie, it hurt a little."

Both men blushed as honest sentiment invaded the conversation.

"But now I think it's exactly what needed to happen."

"What's that supposed to mean?" Tyler asked.

"It means losing my favorite partner forced me to reflect, you know, about what was happening at home."

A puzzled stare sat on Tyler's face.

"Carol Anne and I were a train wreck waiting to happen. And the truth is, all my venting to you wasn't helping matters. While I appreciated your encouragement it actually made things worse."

"Good to know," Tyler said self-deprecatingly.

"Oh, it wasn't your fault. It was mine. I heard what I wanted to hear. I mean, it's not like you had any experience with marriage. A married man has no business seeking advice from a carefree single buddy."

They shared a laugh. Tyler's less enthusiastic than Smitty's.

"I guess I wanted what you had."

Tyler nodded silently.

"But after you left I had to turn elsewhere. Long story short, Carol Anne and I got help. I learned to view love as a choice, not a feeling. That's when things improved."

Tyler shook his head, unsure of himself. "I'm not following you."

"I think someone up there used your departure for good even though it didn't make sense to either of us at the time."

"Someone up there?" Tyler asked callously. "You mean God?"

Smitty shrugged. "Perhaps."

A momentary silence lingered between them.

"Well, I'm glad my absence proved so helpful," Tyler ribbed as he turned back toward the door.

"Ever read the story of Esther?" Smitty asked.

"Esther who?"

"Just Esther. Look it up."

"OK. Because?"

"Because I think events can be orchestrated for purposes beyond our own intentions. The story of Esther describes a girl who had no clue that her crummy situation was being used to prevent an ancient holocaust."

"You don't say." Tyler tried to follow.

Smitty chuckled. "Just read the story. Bottom line, I disagreed with your decision to leave the force. I was ticked off. But that decision ended up salvaging my marriage." He reached for the picture frame. "And now I have this precious little girl."

"I see." Tyler finally connected the dots.

"Maybe something like that is happening for you. What if

God wants to use your gut to prevent something awful from happening to this judge?"

"A nice thought. But I seriously doubt God has anything to do with it."

"We'll see. Meantime, both officially and unofficially, I'm confident you'll figure it out. Come see me if things escalate to the point we can actually intervene."

"Gotcha." Tyler moved to the door. "Well, congratulations on your little girl there, I guess."

"Her name is Esther."

"Right." Tyler smiled. "Esther."

"It was good to see you, Ty. Don't be a stranger."

PART TWO

CHAPTER ELEVEN

Julia glanced toward her husband seated on the sofa across the room. He seemed more at ease than he had been in months. Spending time with Kevin had a calming influence on Troy, as did the escalating rivalry between the two older Tolbert children.

"It's my turn," six-year-old Tommy demanded, yanking his little sister's pajama hem.

"No!" Joy tightened her squeeze around Troy's torso to weather Tommy's assault.

Adult conversation paused yet again while Troy tried brokering a peace accord.

"I promised you each fifteen minutes," he said, checking the watch Tommy had been impatiently eyeing for eight minutes and forty-seven seconds. "Joy still has about seven minutes to go. Don't worry, buddy. I won't forget about you."

Tommy huffed, recrossing his arms to resume his leer at Joy's beaming face.

Two miniature tongues pierced through pressed lips toward one another.

"Tommy," Angie said sternly as the boy retrieved his tongue with lightning speed.

"She started it," he protested.

"You're the oldest," she replied before sealing his fate with a momentary glare.

Julia restrained a laugh at the childish dread only disapproving mommies can engender.

Angie looked back toward Julia. "How's he doing?"

"Good." Julia tried to believe it.

"Julia…" Angie flashed another motherly glare. "Really. How's he doing?"

"He misses Washington," she began. "No. He misses Kevin." They both looked back toward their husbands.

"And the kids," Julia added.

Angie offered a knowing nod. "They miss him too."

"The business has struggled, of course. But he doesn't talk to me about it. I get the feeling it makes him feel…I don't know…inadequate or something."

Angie's eyes smiled over her sip of tea.

"What?" Julia asked.

Angie tilted her head toward Kevin while cupping a hand to the edge of her mouth. "Sounds like someone else I know," she whispered. "When things get the worst he says the least."

Julia lowered her voice to match her friend's. "Why do they do that?"

Angie grinned widely before taking another drink. She looked like a woman eager to invite her friend into a secret society otherwise closed to newlywed brides.

"What?" Julia prodded again.

Angie looked back toward the men to confirm neither was listening.

"They *do* feel inadequate."

The revelation momentarily stunned Julia, then morphed into an elusive puzzle piece suddenly found.

"Why? I mean, both have accomplished so much at such a young age. Why should they feel inadequate?"

"Not should. Do. And I don't mean just Kevin and Troy. I'm talking about all men."

Julia thought of the men she'd dated before meeting Troy. Most carried themselves with a swagger that hid any hint of uncertainty. She remembered rebuking herself for craving their admiration and affection. *A successful and intelligent woman shouldn't need the attention of some egocentric man.* It's what she had written in her column and shouted at the mirror after countless disheartening dates. But watching her sister's romantic roller coasters and reading her readers' posts had convinced Julia that every woman struggled with a nagging insecurity just like her own. It had never occurred to her that the same might be true of men. Some men, perhaps. But Troy? And Kevin?

"Do you mean when things go wrong?" Julia asked.

"I mean almost always," Angie explained. "While brokering business deals and walking the halls of Congress my husband appears bold and self-assured."

Julia agreed. Kevin Tolbert came across as even more confident than Troy.

"And he is," Angie continued, "as long as he knows I respect him. But one look of disappointment or word of criticism from me and he becomes a different man. A smaller man."

"Smaller?"

"Less than he is when he senses my admiration."

Julia felt a familiar sense of indignation. "So we're supposed to stand on the sidelines wearing cheerleader outfits so they can win the big games. Is that it?"

Angie smiled disarmingly. "Something like that. But I hope

you wear something a bit racier than a cheerleader outfit now that you're married." She added a mischievous wink.

Julia suppressed a reluctant grin while marveling at her friend's unflappable confidence. Rather than take the bait Angie had redirected the potential quarrel like a seasoned mom distracting a child from a tantrum.

"You know what I mean," Julia snapped playfully.

"If there's anything I've learned about men during a decade of marriage it's that they desperately need their woman's admiration and respect. Why shouldn't they? I mean, God made two halves of a whole. Doesn't it make sense that men need us as much as we need them?"

"I guess I don't like thinking of it as a need," Julia admitted. "I love Troy. I want him. But *need* him?"

"That's right," Angie mocked. "I forgot. No man is an island. But a woman is different. She can go it alone."

Julia absorbed the rebuke. Probably even deserved it, she thought, after years of columns peddling an ideology that must have seemed shallow or silly to her newfound mentor. Angie would, of course, resent being called a mentor. The two had been high school friends reunited after a season of estrangement. Slowly drifting apart was the cowardly route Julia had chosen while falling in love with a world far removed from the kind of life Kevin and Angie Tolbert had built together. The kind of life, as Troy had hoped, she found it easy to admire.

But it remained difficult to choose.

"Point taken," Julia said, raising a hand of surrender.

Angie winked at her friend before lifting the mug back to her lips. "So," she began over the brim, "how's that discussion group with your pastor going?"

Julia sighed before glancing at a clock on the wall. "A new record," she said.

"Record for what?"

"For how soon you slipped into evangelist mode." She paused to calculate backward from her and Troy's arrival time. "Less than two hours."

In truth, Julia had hoped to avoid the subject. Yes, she had agreed to join Troy in the Exploring Christianity class. And yes, Pastor Alex had answered most of her toughest questions during the past few months. But Julia hated admitting to her hopeful friend that she hadn't yet decided to go as far as her husband. He had become an official follower of Jesus a few months earlier. Kevin had flown to Denver for the baptism, beaming with delight at his best friend's decision. Despite Angie's prayerful prods, however, Julia remained a straggler: open to the possibility, but hesitant. At times she felt an inexplicable yearning mixed with fear, as if nervously eager about her own likely plunge. But no decision as yet.

"I'm sorry." Julia regretted causing Angie's blush of unease. "I shouldn't have said that. The class is going well. Thanks for asking."

Angie smiled forgivingly. "You know I'm praying for you."

Julia nodded, then swallowed discomfiture at the idea of heavenly intervention. The thought of needing anyone, be it her husband, a dear friend, or even her Maker, stirred unwelcome but instinctual feelings. Might they explain her spiritual foot-dragging?

"I guess Pastor Alex is right," she confessed.

"About what?"

"He said the greatest barrier to becoming a Christian isn't any question or doubt."

"No?"

"No," Julia continued, "it's our pride."

Angie's brow lifted in surprised reaction to the admission. "Julia Simmons, proud?"

They shared a knowing laugh.

"Anyway," Angie said while gently touching her friend's arm. "They need us more than we realize."

Julia nodded to acknowledge Angie's return to the subject of husbands.

"I guarantee Troy needs you more than you think he does," Angie added.

"Then why doesn't he talk to me about what's going on?"

"Like what?" Angie asked.

"Like yesterday morning. I stopped by his office to say hi. He seemed happy to see me, but he also seemed nervous, like I had caught him in a secret."

"What kind of secret?"

"Like letting go of a few key staff members. And like failing to attract the kind of capital they need for a big deal he's trying to put together."

A look of concern invaded Angie's face. Julia regretted saying too much.

"I'm sure everything is fine," she added. "He plans to talk to Kevin about the situation tomorrow."

"He probably already has," Angie said. "Like I said before, when things are going the worst Kevin tells me the least."

Julia hesitated before deciding to say more. "Actually, he hasn't told Kevin yet. I insisted he do so."

Another look of apprehension from Angie.

"I think the business is struggling, Angie. Troy has been doing everything he knows to do without bothering Kevin with the details."

"Sam Gamgee," Angie mused aloud.

"Sorry?"

"From *The Lord of the Rings*," Angie added.

Julia recalled Troy's description of his relationship to Kevin. Sam Gamgee was the loyal companion of Frodo Baggins, bearer of the Ring. Kevin had been called to play a part Troy gladly supported, as Sam Gamgee eased the Ring-bearer's burden.

"That's right," Julia said. "Troy seems reluctant to saddle Kevin with bad news. He's trying to handle it himself."

Angie seemed reflective. "Did he say how bad it is?"

"You know how they are. Always putting the best spin on the situation."

Angie nodded silently.

"I didn't get a sense of imminent doom or anything like that. Just some tough decisions."

"Good." Angie seemed relieved. "I'm sure they'll sort it out together."

"I hope so," Julia said. "I think the whole mess has been wearing Troy down."

"Into a lesser man?"

Julia smiled at the reminder. "I suppose."

"Which means?" Angie directed.

"He needs a cheerleader?" Julia asked.

"I think you're catching on, girl!"

———

"My turn!" Tommy shouted from across the room. Protesting whimpers followed from three-year-old Joy. Both women watched in amusement as Kevin tried prying his daughter loose from Troy's lap.

"I'd better intervene," Angie said, moving toward the commotion.

Thirty seconds later Julia joined her husband on a tour of Tommy's bedroom, where he was eager to show "Uncle Troy" his collection of dead bugs and pricelessly worthless rocks. She then dismissed herself at Tommy's not-so-subtle insistence. He said it would be a violation of a soldier's honor to open his secret stash of battle supplies hidden in a box under the bed in the presence of "the fair maiden."

Troy knelt down before crossing his legs to mimic his mini comrade. Pausing at the bedroom door, Julia turned to enjoy one last look at her husband's face. The stress lines around his eyes so evident only hours earlier had vanished, like wrinkles on a crumpled shirt freshly ironed flat. Troy relished time with Kevin's kids. He would probably make a wonderful father.

The thought formed a knot in the pit of Julia's stomach.

CHAPTER TWELVE

It was nearly midnight when Julia and Troy stepped onto the hotel elevator. As the doors slid closed he pressed the top button, then took a step backward.

She noticed the illumined number. "Aren't we on floor seventeen?"

He nodded silently.

"Then why thirty-five?"

He turned and slipped his hands around her waist. "Twice as much time for mischief," he said, moving in for a kiss.

Julia put both hands against her husband's chest and gave a weak shove while punching the correct button. "Troy Simmons! I'm a respectable woman."

"You're also a beautiful woman," he said, drawing her body closer.

The kiss began about floor three and continued until briefly interrupted by a voice announcing their arrival.

She grabbed his hand and led him into the hallway, where they tiptoed quickly toward a door both yearned to enter and lock behind them.

Moments later, Julia sensed what little tension remained ebbing out of Troy's body as she removed his shirt. Then she heard a sound that halted their advance. Troy's sigh of pleasure and anticipation triggered the memory of another moment, another man. A wave of guilt slowed her throbbing pulse. It was not the first time Troy's touch had resurfaced old passions. She pulled back, then tried to resume. But a bewildered look told her he had noticed.

"Is something wrong?" Troy asked between winded breaths.

She pressed her lips to his, hoping the present reality could overpower the intruder from her past. No good. The taste of Troy's kiss only fueled the memory of the nameless encounter her body refused to forget. She pulled back again.

"I'm sorry." She sighed.

He placed his hand on hers, joining her on the edge of the bed. The two sat silently while Julia considered what to say.

"I forgot to bring protection." A lie. Claiming forgetfulness seemed better than admitting memories.

The comment clearly bothered him more than the interruption.

"Don't worry," Julia added. "I'm sure you can run down to the lobby to buy some. I'll shower and slip into—"

"I don't want to buy protection," he interrupted. "I just want to make love to my wife."

The comment startled Julia. "You know I'm not on the pill right now. And we don't like using—"

"I don't mean it like that."

"What then?" she asked, hugging a pillow to defend her body from the chilly air of an overhead vent.

Deep lines of stress reappeared on Troy's face. She knew he wanted to say something that he couldn't put into words.

Then it struck her. "You don't mean…"

She paused.

He nodded.

She swallowed back a sense of panic. "Troy. Be sensible."

"I'm tired of being sensible."

"We've only been married for six months," she reminded him. "We agreed we would consider kids after a few years."

"I know what we agreed. I was just hoping…"

He didn't need to finish. Julia recalled the look on her husband's face when Angie let him hold the new baby before dinner. He stared at little Ricky for at least five minutes, marveling at his fingers, earlobes, and toes. Then he volunteered to sit next to Leah to help her eat. Leah had held a special place in Troy's heart ever since Kevin told him about her genetic disorder. Tiny signs of fragile X syndrome had begun to appear, nearly indiscernible previews of her coming life filled with limitations and stares. They were nothing that would mark her as particularly unusual to the uninformed eye, but enough to cause Troy to hold her more tightly than he had the others.

Julia had said she was open to becoming a mom someday. She even had started to believe it. But she knew that Troy wanted to be a daddy now.

"Listen, babe," she said softly. "I think I'll be ready to talk about having kids soon, OK?"

"Why not talk about it now?"

"While in a romantic hotel room?" she asked playfully. "Not a good idea."

"Some people would call it the perfect time."

Julia felt her anxiety rise. Was Troy suggesting a blind conception? Did he honestly think she would consider such a risky option?

"Be serious." A nervous laugh.

He didn't respond.

"People don't do that anymore, Troy."

"Kevin and Angie do that," he retorted. "And they have four great kids."

Julia felt momentarily ashamed of her gut reaction, words that might have appeared in one of her columns a year or two earlier: *They have too many kids. Their irresponsibility brought an unproductive debit into the world.*

But Angie rejected the sensible approach to impregnation. She viewed kids as a gift to receive rather than a product to design. So she refused the common practice of screening out genetically defective embryos and letting a doctor implant the best and brightest. While Julia would no longer think of calling Angie a breeder, her friend fit the label.

"Listen, Troy, I want to give you children. I really do. But I can't imagine myself going that route. Making love is making love. We can do that here or anywhere you like. But making babies belongs in the clinic. I know you admire Kevin and Angie, but the thought of a blind conception scares me."

His shoulders slumped at another lost negotiation.

"I tell you what," she said with forced enthusiasm. "I'll make an appointment with the in vitro selection clinic as soon as we get home. We can start exploring options. OK?"

Troy seemed somewhat heartened by the suggestion as he moved slowly toward the minibar. He looked inside for a moment before retrieving a bottle of water.

"Do you want something?" he asked.

She removed the pillow from her body and spread her arms toward her husband. "Yes I do."

He looked away and opened his bottle to take a sip, suddenly immune to her advance.

"So, do you want to go to the lobby while I—"

"We have a big day tomorrow," he interrupted, passing two fingers across her cheek. "What do you say we get some sleep?"

Julia swallowed back the sting of rejection, trying to own the blame. "Are you sure?"

"I'm sure." He offered an affectionate smile.

She reached for the pillow to cover herself again.

CHAPTER THIRTEEN

Troy settled into the chair located immediately behind Kevin Tolbert's seat at the conference table. He felt at home, as if he had never left his role as intelligence officer and adviser to his friend. It was from this very location that he had fed Kevin talking points and supporting statistics on the day the congressman first introduced the concept of *bright spots* into the congressional vocabulary.

He leaned toward Julia, sitting nervously in the adjoining seat. "All's well," he said with a slight squeeze of her hand.

"So he doesn't mind?"

"Not at all. Kevin explained the situation. Anderson knows you no longer work with RAP Syndicate. You're attending as my wife rather than as journalist Julia Davidson."

"Julia Davidson Simmons," she corrected with a smile.

"Who were you talking to in the hall?" Troy asked.

Julia pointed toward an elegant fortysomething woman seated at the other end of the long conference table. "Trisha Sayers recognized me and made a fuss," she explained. "Wanted to catch up."

"Does she know you've gone over to the dark side?"

Julia laughed. "We only had a few seconds. The topic of marriage didn't come up."

Troy looked toward the clock on the wall: a few minutes before ten. If he knew anything about the host of this meeting, the discussion would start right on time. Brent Anderson, Senator Joshua Franklin's right-hand man, was a stickler for both punctuality and productivity. Troy had come to admire Anderson's efficiency back when he led the austerity coalition toward consensus. They debated and decided on a package of proposals in a matter of weeks, a monumental task that should have taken months. But they had been racing against time. Franklin knew that revised budget projections from the census would create panic in the markets. He wanted to strike quickly to position himself as a proactive leader in the midst of crisis. And while his timing did little to ease the economic collapse, it did propel him even higher in national polls.

Troy sensed that a similar urgency would likely characterize this discussion. Why else would Franklin have insisted that Anderson chair the meeting?

Kevin leaned back in his chair toward Troy, who leaped forward in response to a summoning motion.

"What's up?" Troy asked in a hushed voice.

"Look here." Kevin pointed to a page on the screen embedded in the conference table. "You were right."

Troy read quickly, trying to beat the countdown to meeting launch.

Comeback Coalition
August 2043 Agenda
ITEM A: NEXT Appeal Update (Anderson)
ITEM B: Youth Initiative Expansion Strategies (Florea)
ITEM C: Bright Spots Relaunch Proposal (Tolbert)

ITEM D: Projection Adjustments (Journeyman)
ITEM E: Press Relations Strategy (Sayers)
ITEM F: Broad Policy Framework (Anderson)

"Prime placement on the agenda," Kevin said with enthusiasm. "Who'd have thought?"

Troy cleared his throat in mock offense. "A certain former chief of staff would have thought," he jabbed. "I owe you a head-rub for questioning my instinct."

Kevin patted his head protectively as Troy retreated back to his chair.

"I nailed it," he whispered to Julia. "They're taking the bright spot approach much more seriously this round."

"They would have taken it seriously last year if I hadn't written the *Breeders* story," Julia said with regret.

"If you hadn't been assigned to that story you wouldn't be Mrs. Troy Simmons," Troy reminded her. "Besides, the timing is better now."

"How's that?"

"Everyone's nervous about how the NEXT appeal will land. They can't bank on growth in transitions to fund a recovery. A loss for NEXT could turn Kevin into Churchill."

"Winston Churchill? The chubby Brit?"

"The chubby Brit who everyone considered a nagging crackpot until his warnings became their reality."

"Got it. Kevin is the nagging crackpot warning them about trends they don't want to face."

"They'll have no choice but to face them when the transition industry takes a hit."

"*If* it takes a hit," Julia corrected.

"My gut tells me it already has. That's got to be the reason Franklin formed this coalition."

The sound of opening doors drew their eyes to the far end of the conference room, where Brent Anderson entered with an entourage of aides. He took the chair at the head of the table as the others settled into seven of the nine empty chairs that lined the walls.

The assembly complete, Troy looked at each face gathered, to identify potential allies and opponents. He recognized nearly every attendee. Several had served with Kevin on the austerity coalition in 2042. Others had participated in a long series of floor debates defending specific cuts that had been pieced together for a larger proposal. No one had liked the details he or she was defending. But they had no real choice. It was considered political suicide to oppose the only viable plan for preventing an economic free fall. In the end even liberals joined the fiscal conservatives, holding their noses while voting for what became commonly labeled the Franklin Austerity Plan. With his eye on the White House, Franklin now hoped to make another strategic move.

"Franklin's Comeback Plan," Troy whispered.

Julia eyed him inquisitively.

"That's what they'll call it," he continued. "They'll call whatever comes out of this dialogue Franklin's Comeback Plan. Ten to one says he'll use it as his calling card for the 2044 campaign. No politician wants to be known for cuts. He wants to offer a positive plan to rebuild the economy."

Troy hushed himself as Brent Anderson launched the meeting.

"I'd like to begin by thanking everyone for accepting Senator Franklin's invitation to participate on the comeback coalition," Anderson began. "As you no doubt read in the advance briefing I sent last Thursday, we've been asked to craft a viable strategy our party can rally around to restore this nation's economy back toward some semblance of health."

Troy typed and sent a note to Kevin's screen.

RESTORE HEALTH? MORE LIKE RAISE THE DEAD!

Kevin nodded slightly in inconspicuous agreement.

"The few of you who served on the austerity coalition last year," Troy heard Anderson continue, "will be familiar with the process I intend to use for this assignment that, I hope, will help us move quickly through what could otherwise become a daunting agenda. We must discuss very important and complicated matters in short order. Not an easy task. But it can be done if you will allow me to enforce a few simple rules of order."

Troy remembered the process well. Each agenda item would begin with a fifteen-minute fast-fire presentation followed by another fifteen for questions to clarify or enhance rather than debate. Anderson would have already leveraged his tough-minded tenacity to cull through the clutter of a million possible options to find the most promising ideas. He was the master of keeping committees focused on productive ends rather than wasting time on grandstanding or speculation about what might or even should be done. Under Anderson's direction this coalition would discuss only those items that met three simple criteria.

1. Was easy to explain in a sound bite.
2. Had solid data showing it would work.
3. Served Franklin's political agenda.

Kevin's backstage efforts to sell the idea of resurrecting the Bright Spots proposal must have convinced Anderson it satisfied all three.

"As the first item on the agenda suggests, we'll explore comeback options in anticipation of the decision scheduled to come out of the Tenth Circuit a few weeks from now. Senator Franklin has asked that we craft a proposal that can play well regardless of where things land on the NEXT appeal."

"Early indications?" asked Trisha Sayers, seated to Anderson's immediate right.

"Could go either way. Judge Coates leans for and Judge Howatch against. That makes Santiago the deciding vote. He has no track record of similar cases so we have no idea where he'll come down."

"Who appointed him?" came a question from the other side of the table.

"Obama."

"Must be an old bugger," someone said.

"Over thirty years on the bench," Anderson replied.

"Not good," added Sayers. "The older demographic leans against the Youth Initiative."

"By a two percent margin," Anderson responded. "A practically even split. Like I said, we have no idea where he'll land. That's why we need a plan that assumes either possibility. Remember, even if NEXT wins the appeal the case could go higher."

"The Supreme Court?" someone said. "They'll never accept the case."

Troy moved his head to get a better look at who had made the comment. Congresswoman Nicole Florea of Nevada.

"Why do you say that?" Kevin asked.

"It's a wrongful death case alleging inadequate approval measures." Her tone betrayed irritation at Kevin's question as well as his presence in the room. "Hardly worthy of our highest court's attention."

"I disagree." The comment came from a disheveled-looking gentleman leaning forward in his chair. "The NEXT case has major implications for the entire industry and the president's signature initiative. Every new hurdle people are required to jump creates a corresponding drop in transition volunteers. Hundreds of billions of dollars are at stake. I think the court will want a say on whether—"

"Rather than waste time in speculation," Anderson interrupted, "I'd like to ask each of you to read the executive briefing on the NEXT case after the meeting. It should arrive in your inboxes momentarily. Now, I'd like us to move on to the second item on the agenda. Nicole."

DID SHE BRING THE WITCH'S BROOM? Troy typed to Kevin, prompting a gently scolding slap from Julia.

"Stop it," she whispered. "Let him concentrate."

Troy leaned toward Julia to explain but decided he could defend his tactics after the meeting. Part of his role had always been to help Kevin keep things light. While his friend had an impressive mind, it was Congressman Tolbert's beguiling charm that usually won the day. An occasional quip deflected rising tensions and might help his performance during the Bright Spots portion of the agenda.

Nicole Florea had already thanked the committee for the opportunity to speak when Troy received a printed copy of her briefing delivered by a young man the congresswoman must have hired for front office décor. Printed pages meant it contained highly confidential information. The same young man would likely collect and shred the handouts after the presentation.

Florea burned five of her fifteen minutes reliving her glory days as leader of the Western States Conservative Coalition. She took credit for garnering the support necessary to help President Lowman pass the Youth Initiative over what she labeled the "sentimental qualms" of the religious wing of the party. Then she burned another five minutes trying to make the case that any serious attempt to drive an economic comeback required expanding the initiative to recruit a wider circle of volunteers.

Brent Anderson glanced at the clock. "Forgive me for interrupting, Nicole," he said impatiently. "But we have only allocated fifteen minutes. Did you want to explain the details of your proposal before we open up for questions?"

She appeared indignant at the idea that Anderson's rules of order might apply to her, apparently considering her autobiographical self-tribute and policy remix mere preliminaries before the meat of her presentation.

"Well, I did plan to walk us through details of the plan found on page three where I—"

"If I may," Anderson interjected, clearly eager to spare everyone another ten minutes of listening to the obvious. "I suggest you move us right to the bottom of page ten. I'm pretty sure most of us are familiar with the economic trend lines justifying your plan. It might be a better use of time to dive right into details of the proposal."

The redirect flustered the congresswoman more accustomed to giving speeches than to receiving direction. "Yes. Of course," she said, flipping pages of her own copy of the document.

Troy half listened to Nicole Florea's clumsy explanation while his eyes scanned ahead to her supposed solution. Kevin would be doing the same. Nothing new. She made yet another call to expand the president's Youth Initiative; to create greater incentives for potential transition volunteers. He had seen the language before. "Greater incentives" meant increased pressure. Make it easier to say yes so it would be harder to say no. America needed more of the elderly and disabled to get with the program. They were, after all, debits. They cost more than they produced. They spent personal wealth on themselves rather than releasing it to the younger, healthier generation. That's why so many had come to label them "selfish parasites" draining rather than fueling the economy by requiring time and attention from otherwise productive workers and entrepreneurs; those who contributed. Those who paid taxes.

Troy looked up from the page to cringe at the congresswoman's efforts to sell financial projections she clearly didn't understand. "So as you can see, a mere five percent volunteer rate among unproductive segments of the economy during the next three years will dramatically reduce the deficit while stimulating private sector growth."

Troy did the math. Depending upon where you drew the line between "productive" and "unproductive," 5 percent could mean between four and eight million new transitions on top of the roughly five million since the Youth Initiative began.

Kevin's daughter clearly fit within the "unproductive" classification. Little Leah would never live an independent life. She might always require care, placing her at the top of Nicole Florea's list of fitting volunteers for a simple procedure at one of the many conveniently located NEXT transition clinics.

Troy noticed a rising crimson hue on Kevin's neck.

So much for helping my friend keep things light, he thought.

CHAPTER FOURTEEN

"Any additional questions before we move to the next proposal?"

Brent Anderson appeared eager to get Nicole Florea back to her seat. Her presentation had run ten minutes longer than allocated.

"Good," he said before anyone could reply. "Congressman Tolbert."

Kevin finally had the floor.

"He still looks upset," Julia whispered to her husband.

A slight nod told her Troy agreed.

Kevin had managed to hold his tongue during the entire presentation. He had even resisted the urge to point out glaring mistakes in the projections. He must have needed the time to will himself calm. At least as calm as could be expected from a man listening to someone disparage his daughter's existence along with eight million other "unproductive" lives.

"Thank you, Mr. Anderson," he began after taking the kind of breath Troy recognized from their high school soccer days. His friend was determined to score. "Rather than review every detail in the briefing we just forwarded to your tablets I'll simply state the bottom line and invite questions."

Anderson chuckled at the jab against the long-winded Florea.

"You can review the charts on page six to see two trend lines that, on the surface, will seem counterintuitive," Kevin continued. "But I can assure you, the data is solid."

Two dozen hands began swiping their tablet screens to find the page.

"The first graph shows the economic trend lines we've all been reviewing with dismay these past few years with a deepening free fall over the past twelve months. Despite the brief flattening immediately after instituting the austerity measures approved in January, the month-to-month spiral shows no sign of slowing.

"The second chart, the one labeled 'Bright Spots,' shows a stark contrast. Most of the lines have been moving steadily in the other direction during the same period."

"Bright spots?" The question came from a voice Troy didn't recognize.

"That's what we call the communities showing sustained growth."

Anderson interrupted to suggest Kevin give a brief recap of the concept "for those who weren't part of the austerity coalition."

Troy smiled in admiration of a vintage Kevin Tolbert tactic. Keeping it short so they ask for more works better than droning on until they glance at their watches.

"If you insist," Kevin said. "We took the concept from a case I studied back in grad school. About fifty years ago a nonprofit group was given six months to solve child malnourishment in poor Vietnamese villages. A crazy deadline, since experts had identified a complex range of systemic problems intertwining to cause the epidemic. One guy cut through the complexity that had been paralyzing the experts. He asked what the mothers of the few healthy kids were doing differently from everyone else in the village. He figured if some kids thrive despite identical poverty, then there might be hope for the other kids. To make a long process short, they discovered a few simple habits among those families that made a huge difference."

"Give an example," Anderson said.

"Well, the mothers of the healthy kids divided daily rations into four small meals instead of two larger meals. They also snubbed cultural norms by feeding their kids foods widely considered low-class."

Anderson jumped in to add the punch line. "The relief agency called those families *bright spots* and used their success as a model for large-scale solutions."

Kevin stood silently as the eyes in the room shifted toward the front. Brent Anderson appeared embarrassed by his own outburst, which betrayed enthusiasm for Kevin's proposal.

"That's right," Kevin said with increased confidence. "And we did the same. We culled the data to find common characteristics among economic bright spots in this country. Every region has suffered the same downward pressures. But some seem to fare much better than others. We wanted to know what makes the difference and whether those differences can be encouraged elsewhere."

"And?" asked another voice. All eyes were back on Kevin.

"As the detail on page eight explains, these pockets of economic stability and growth match areas with the highest rates of fertility and the lowest percentage of transition volunteers."

"I thought we dealt with this nonsense last year," came an objection from the woman seated to Anderson's right.

"Please, Trisha," Anderson said, raising a hushing hand. "I'd like us to hold reactions and questions until Mr. Tolbert has finished explaining his proposal."

With a delegating gesture from their host Kevin picked up where he had left off.

"As these charts show, I propose that we find ways to incentivize growth. Look closely at the breakout on page seven labeled 'Dark Zones' and you'll see why expanding the Youth Initiative as Congresswoman Florea recommends would add to the long-term problem. Any short-term savings we might glean will only intensify the downward spiral. Ask any first-year MBA student worth his salt and he'll say a business can't just cut its way into prosperity. It must drive new innovation and reach new markets. The same is true on a national scale. Our nation can't transition...no, *kill* its way into health."

Nicole Florea shot to the edge of her seat, clearly aghast at Kevin's unnuanced word selection. But she said nothing. She just leered quietly while Kevin summarized his proposal three minutes ahead of schedule.

"In short," he said, "our economic woes stem from these dark zones. That's why we need more bright spots like those shown in the first graph. We need to make it easier for young people to marry and raise children and foster a society that welcomes the wisdom and support of our elderly rather than pressures them toward the grave. Take a long, hard look at the numbers, ladies and gentlemen. Our problem is not that we have too many old and disabled. Our problem is that we have too few young and healthy."

The room fell silent. Troy's eyes raced from one face to the next, trying to gauge reactions. He guessed a third might be modestly warm to Kevin's rationale. The rest looked like cougars frozen in position, awaiting Anderson's permission to pounce.

Which they did.

The next fifteen minutes brought a barrage of thrashing claws in Kevin's direction, each masked as appeals for more realistic, sensible strategies than the one presented by the young congressman from Colorado.

How would the Treasury Department absorb the massive hit if, as Kevin seemed to suggest, Congress made it harder for people to transition? The Youth Initiative had generated a trillion dollars in entitlement spending savings to date. The present budget assumed another two trillion over ten years. Where would those savings go if Grandma and Grandpa Citizen suddenly decided to stick around for another decade?

And even if committee members trusted the bright spots data, which few did, how could they advocate the notion of the federal government calling parenthood preferable to childlessness? That was a lead balloon that couldn't possibly pass Congress or be sold to the public. Dead on arrival.

But the cruelest swipe of all, the one that made all others seem tame, came from Trisha Sayers, when she asked a question so ugly it was hard to believe it had come from such a lovely mouth. The supermodel-turned-fashion-industry-tycoon might have retained her glamorous beauty despite the dog-eat-dog battles of business and politics, but she had apparently lost all tact.

"Excuse me?" Kevin asked across the table.

"I asked whether this isn't some sort of personal therapy," Trisha repeated, this time with less humor in her voice.

"Ms. Sayers," Brent Anderson said in an effort to intercept the confrontation. "There's no need to—"

"It's all right," Kevin said. "I'd like to answer the question if I may."

The tone of his friend's voice brought Troy back to ninth grade at Littleton High School. Kevin had confronted a kid named Eric who had been poking fun at an autistic eleventh grader named Edward. Eric had labeled him Ed the Sped.

Anderson paused momentarily. Then he nodded.

Kevin leaned down and swiped his tablet screen to find and

open a different file. He looked toward Troy, who shook his head slowly from side to side, hoping to dissuade his friend from saying something he might regret, then relaxed at Kevin's wink.

"I'm sending a photograph to your tablets now," Kevin began. "For those of you who don't know my family, I'd like to give you a bit of context for Ms. Sayers's question."

Trisha's mocking sneer softened to an embarrassed blush.

"This is my daughter Leah," he continued. "She'll turn two years old in a few months."

Several female attendees sighed in reaction to the child's toothy grin.

"Leah is what Ms. Sayers might call a debit."

"I never—" Trisha began.

"I know you wouldn't use the slang, Ms. Sayers. Nor would Congresswoman Florea. Nor would any of us in this room. But Leah has something called fragile X syndrome. I won't bother you with the details of her prognosis other than to say she will likely have severe intellectual disabilities her entire life. She may never be capable of living on the credit side of the ledger. So I guess that makes her a debit."

"Mr. Tolbert, there's no need to—"

"Please, Mr. Anderson, this will only take what remains of the time you've allotted my presentation."

A reluctant nod.

"I take it from Ms. Sayers's question that she thinks I have been advocating the bright spots idea out of some kind of guilt complex."

Trisha said nothing but gave a half nod of consent.

"You see, Ms. Sayers knows that my wife and I skipped the genetic screening process when we conceived Leah, just as we did with our three healthy kids. And despite her disability, we love and accept her as a gift. I suppose we should view her as defective. But we don't. And yes, we know we will be responsible for her the rest of our lives. We know that one or more of her siblings will accept responsibility for her after we're gone."

Kevin paused to take a sip from the glass of water sweating on the coaster in front of his place at the table. Three others followed suit in nervous solidarity with the successful congressman turned loving dad.

"I can assure you, Ms. Sayers, that I do not bring forward these ideas out of any sort of guilt. Nor do I advocate parenthood because I have more than the sensible one or two kids."

Several joined him in a self-deprecating laugh.

"And I don't show you Leah's picture to gain sympathy for my proposal. If the numbers make sense, vote with me. If they don't, move on."

Julia reached for and took Troy's hand as if anticipating Kevin's next words.

"I show you this picture to illustrate why I believe advocating bright spots will bring light to our darkening situation. With all due respect to Ms. Sayers and the honorable congresswoman from Nevada, those of you who have kids know what I mean when I say parenthood compels different choices than you would otherwise make."

Half of the room, including Brent Anderson, nodded in unison.

"Dads take extra shifts and second jobs. Moms cut coupons and launch home-based businesses. Grandparents buy birthday presents and watch grandkids, providing cheaper and better childcare while giving them something better to do than rot away in retirement villages.

"Take my family as a case in point. How much more do you think my wife and I save now that we have Leah?"

"Don't you mean spend?" asked Anderson.

"I mean save," Kevin explained. "We spend less on the things we would like to do for ourselves in order to invest in a long-term care fund for Leah. My colleague and I are in the process of buying another business I hope will create an income stream to cover my daughter's long-term needs."

Troy felt Julia look in his direction.

"Believe me. My love for Leah will motivate me to do everything I can to grow that business. And if the business grows, it will hire more workers. And if we hire more workers... well... you know the rest.

"Ladies and gentlemen, when we encourage bright spots we tap the most powerful natural resource on the planet. Families, not governments or businesses, motivate hard work and innovation, frugality and investment. They also provide the social safety net government can no longer afford."

"Trying to buy another business?" Troy heard Julia whisper. "Is that why you've been feeling so stressed?"

Troy raised a single finger to his lips as he strained to hear Kevin's final comment.

"But I've said enough. You can review the numbers for yourselves. All I ask you to do is open your minds to positive strategies that will spur growth rather than settling for defensive measures you think will diminish losses. Thank you for listening."

—⁓—

Brent Anderson appeared relieved as he received the handoff to regain control of the meeting. He also seemed pleased, as if he had secretly hoped Kevin would win the day.

Troy leaned forward as Kevin retook his seat. He pretended to pass a note as an excuse to offer his friend an affirming squeeze on the shoulder.

"You made us proud, Mr. Congressman," he whispered.

Kevin's nod seemed appreciative, if unconvinced.

The next agenda item burned about ten minutes in review-ing the impact of a slight decline in transition volunteers. The wrongful death decision against NEXT, Paul Journeyman ex-plained, had prompted extreme caution in the industry. Every transition provider in the country had suddenly started re-questing what no law required, co-approval by a neutral party. The seemingly commonsense safeguard added one more hur-dle for nervous volunteers to overcome. So the past year had seen fewer volunteers enroll than any year since the Youth Initiative began in 2036. As a result, higher-than-anticipated senior-care expenses would further drain public coffers while lower-than-projected inheritance capital would flow in the pri-vate sector.

"In short," Journeyman summarized, "the uncertainty created by the NEXT case has added tremendous downward pressure."

There were no questions beyond those swirling around Troy's head about faulty assumptions beneath the analysis. He decided he would review the data more closely later.

Trisha Sayers was given fifteen minutes to discuss how they might manage the media when Senator Franklin released the Comeback Coalition's proposals. She described the importance of timing, carefully worded spin, advance access to friends at RAP and Bing Syndicates, and about a dozen other steps she called "smart" and "proactive."

Troy rolled his eyes toward Julia.

"She's good," his wife whispered, to Troy's surprise. "Exactly the approach I would recommend to work the system in Franklin's favor."

An idea popped into Troy's head that he tucked away for later.

Anderson suggested a short break in an uncharacteristic show of mercy. Half the group hurried out to find a restroom. The other half, including Anderson, found isolated spots to make calls.

Kevin approached Troy and Julia. "Well?"

"You did great," Julia said with enthusiasm.

He smiled gratefully in her direction before looking Troy in the eyes. "Give me the body language numbers."

"I figure about a third are with you," Troy began. "But Anderson is one of them, so I'd call it about even."

"You think?" Kevin said with a trace of optimism.

"I'd bet your golden locks he's on the phone with Franklin right now for approval to railroad your proposal into the final plan."

"Not likely."

"Very likely," Troy argued. "Didn't you hear what Journeyman said about the decline in transitions?"

"I did. Good news from our perspective."

"It is. But it's also a mandate to find alternative solutions."

"A mandate from?" Kevin asked.

"A mandate from Franklin. Surely he's known about those numbers for weeks. He must have assembled this coalition because he anticipates trouble."

"What kind of trouble?" Julia asked.

"If NEXT wins the appeal you know Franklin will push full steam ahead on Nicole Florea's proposal."

Kevin gave a nod of annoyed agreement.

"But if NEXT loses…"

"He'll hold a press conference to pitch an alternative plan," Julia interjected.

"Exactly," Troy said to punctuate his wife's intuition.

"But two-thirds of this coalition want to throw me and my proposal out of the room," Kevin reminded him.

"Which is why I seriously doubt Anderson plans to call for a vote."

All three sets of eyes looked toward the front of the room. They saw Brent Anderson nodding into his phone in deferential agreement with, Troy presumed, a direct order from Senator Josh Franklin.

CHAPTER FIFTEEN

Irritation clawed up Tyler's spine at the man's voice calling from downstairs. Renee had roped Tyler into "keeping an eye" on her father while she took her mother to a follow-up appointment, "just for an hour or two." The moment she was out the door, he locked himself in his office—no, make that his new bedroom-slash-office-slash-closet space.

"Tyler?" Gerry called again.

Tyler squeezed out from between the desk and the wall and trotted down the steps, dismayed to find a stark-naked old man dripping water all over the floor.

"Geez, Gerry!" Tyler exclaimed, averting his gaze to his now-sopping carpet.

"I can't find any towels. Do you have any towels?"

"Did you try under the sink?"

Gerry pondered for a moment, then shook his head, splattering the walls like a wet dog.

Tyler nabbed a dishtowel from the kitchen and tossed it at his...well, what was he? Not father-in-law. No relation in any way whatsoever, and here Tyler was, being subjected to—this! "Use that in the meantime. And cover up, for Pete's sake," Tyler said.

Gerry smiled, then began drying off his hair.

"Listen, Gerry," Tyler said. "I've got a lot of work to do. So why don't you go put on some clothes and watch television or something."

A few minutes later Tyler was back at his desk, banging his head against the wall behind him in frustration before typing in his next search.

NEXT TRANSITION APPEAL.

A whole slew of search results popped up, although most were variations of the same. Antonio Santos's mother had died accidentally in a NEXT facility during Antonio's transition—trying to stop him, since he was, apparently, a minor at the time he volunteered. Jeremy Santos, Antonio's brother, filed a wrongful death suit and won. NEXT appealed, and now the case sat pending.

"With Santiago," Tyler murmured to himself.

He scrolled to the next article. Second verse same as the first. Then a third, and fourth. Nothing useful other than what he already knew—until he found Julia Davidson, RAP Syndicate. The name rang a bell. He poked at the title.

Jackpot! It appeared Ms. Davidson had already done a lot of legwork on this case, including an interview with Jeremy Santos, as well as the transition specialist involved. That could be interesting.

Name withheld on condition of anonymity.

Tyler swore under his breath. Still, a lot here, including connections to the government's Youth Initiative with potentially billions of dollars on the line. This case might actually be even larger than he had first believed. Jennifer McKay had already suggested Jeremy and NEXT as the most likely suspects to have written the letters. But there was a whole industry involved.

For now, however, the conspiracy theories would have to wait.

Back to Julia Davidson. He pulled up his Privacy Search account and found all her personal information, including direct contact accounts for both phone and messaging. For a few hundred bucks a year he had access to more private information than he could ever have accessed legally on the force. Everyone was afraid of the government butting into their lives where it didn't belong, but no one seemed to mind revealing anything and everything about themselves to the civilian population through cell phone records, social media, and the rest. Security scanners now knew and could report when someone walked into a store, what he bought, and in what size, all in the name of "targeted marketing" and "price reductions."

As for Julia, she was apparently married now with a different last name, and as luck would have it, living right here in the Denver area. He clicked the ESTABLISH CALL button and waited as the other end rang. With any luck he could meet with her today to learn everything she knew about the Santos case.

Less than thirty seconds later her auto response came back indicating she would be unavailable until after the weekend. No way to know whether she was actually gone or screening requests. He left a message indicating his desire to meet.

Julia Davidson would have to wait, which put Jeremy Santos on deck. Tyler looked up his info and placed the call.

"Hello?" the voice answered on the other end.

Within five minutes he had set up a meeting with Jeremy for that afternoon. Tyler glanced at the time, then grabbed his keys and headed downstairs, ready to escape the very moment Renee returned. She gave Tyler the evil eye in reaction to finding her father watching some old war movie in nothing but his under-wear.

—⁓—

Tyler hadn't expected to find Jeremy living in such a run-down apartment complex. Then he remembered. Winning an enor-mous case doesn't translate into cold, hard cash until after you survive the string of appeals. Jeremy's sofa was threadbare. The rest of the décor? Deteriorating bits and pieces showing neither a girlfriend's nor a mother's touch. The kid appeared broke, alone, and into who knew what kind of trouble.

Did desperate need motivate desperate measures? Tyler wondered as he fingered the threatening letters.

"Sorry about the mess," Jeremy said, indicating the piled-up dishes strewn around the room. "Haven't had much time to clean up lately."

"Working a lot?"

A nod. "Making a buck more than minimum wage." A shrug. "It pays the bills." A pause. "Barely."

Tyler smiled encouragingly, unsure if Jeremy's final statement was meant to inspire levity or compassion. "I read Ms. David-son's article about the NEXT case," he said. "And I know about the ongoing appeal. I'm confused about something, though."

"Shoot." Jeremy tossed the bangs from his eyes. He appeared unkempt, like someone wearily trying to find his way in life. Stuck in post-adolescence.

"I thought it was a wrongful death case."

"That's right."

"So, why haven't you at least received your"—Tyler hesi-tated, unsure of the correct wording—"inheritance?"

Jeremy laughed weakly, then gestured a wilted hand across the room. "You're lookin' at it."

"So, you got very little from your mother and brother's estate?"

Jeremy looked around with a sigh. "Less than little."

"I hope you don't mind me saying, but this appeal has to be pretty important to you, to your future. Financially speaking."

"You could say that. At the moment, I'm on a fast track to nowhere. I essentially work to live. Although I was able to pay for exactly two classes at Denver Community College. Passed both of them."

"Congratulations," Tyler said with a smile. "Any friends?"

"Nah. I burned through my few friends when I was still angry about what was happening to Antonio. Or more like what *wasn't* happening with me because of Antonio."

"Family?"

"I've got a dad. Somewhere. Maybe. Who knows? Other than that, I've got no one. Not even a girl." He laughed, uncomfortably.

Tyler pulled out the letters and spread them across the coffee table. "Have you seen any of these?"

Jeremy slid one close, glanced it over, then shook his head, his expression turning to one of concern. "No, I haven't. But...where did you get these? Are they for real?"

"Are you sure? Do you recognize the writing, maybe?"

He shook his head again, then locked his gaze on Tyler. "Wait a minute. You think I wrote these?"

Tyler shrugged, figuring there was little point in not being honest. "I don't know what to think. I'm still trying to investigate this whole mess. But the fact is, you're prime suspect number one. Let's face it, until this appeal is over, you're living in squalor. So I have to ask: did you write these letters?"

"No!" Jeremy shouted defensively. "Absolutely not!"

Tyler closely watched Jeremy's eyes, the poor man's lie detector. This was the moment of truth for a quick and easy investigation. *Bam, case closed.*

No such luck.

Jeremy returned Tyler's stare.

Both men realized the question of Jeremy's innocence had been resolved.

"Listen, kid," Tyler said, "as much as I'd like to discover who wrote these letters, I imagine you'll want to find out even more."

Jeremy settled back into his chair, nervously running his fingers through his hair. "It's got to be NEXT."

Tyler waited.

"They're trying to derail Judge Santiago's decision. They must think they're gonna lose the appeal. Oh man, this is intense."

Jeremy stood and walked toward the tiny kitchen. He came right back and sat. "What if these threats work? I can't keep going on like this. Hoping this whole thing will eventually end gets me through right now."

"I understand," Tyler said sympathetically. "It must be hard, having lost both your mother and your brother on the same day."

Was this going to turn into a counseling session? Years of holding weepy clients' hands had qualified Tyler more than he cared to admit. He'd consoled countless lovers through grief over cheaters. Was a death, or even two deaths, any different? Reassuring the boy might be as simple as inviting him to open up and talk about…his feelings.

"What was it like?"

Jeremy continued staring as if trying to decipher an algebra problem.

"Son," Tyler said more loudly.

"Sorry?"

"I asked what it was like. You know, losing them both so suddenly?"

Jeremy looked deeply into Tyler's eyes as if trying to gauge the stranger's heart. Then he stood again, this time walking toward the bedroom. He returned carrying a tablet. He placed it on the coffee table in front of Tyler's seat. "Watch this."

An icon labeled SANTOS BODIES awaited Tyler's initiating tap.

A video commenced playing. He realized immediately what it was. He had recorded countless others himself while investigating murder scenes. Someone had made a video record of the bodies in hopes of identifying clues to what had actually occurred on the day Jeremy's brother and mother died.

The first image was a small sign outside of what appeared to be a medical office complex. The large print read NEW DAY TRANSITION CENTER. Much smaller letters beneath said A SUBSIDIARY OF NEXT INC. just above an address, a contact code, and office hours.

A quick blink of the screen brought Tyler into a room containing about two dozen chairs and a few end tables with stacks of cheap tablets, the kind dentists and hospitals made available to occupy waiting patients.

"This is the reception area where Ms. Santos would have been sitting with Antonio before his procedure?" Tyler didn't recognize the voice. Female. Most likely a videographer contracted by the police department to document the scene.

A long silence followed as the woman awaited an answer to her question. The camera shifted, focusing on a slumping male form offering a silent nod in reply. Jeremy, twenty-four months earlier. He looked pale and shaken.

"Were you waiting with them?"

"No, ma'am," he said weakly.

Another blink and a new image. A narrow hallway with a series of doors bearing tiny signs indicating TRANSITION ROOM #1, TRANSITION ROOM #2, and so on. They stopped at room number four, where the woman invited Jeremy to step in front of the camera and open the door.

"Do you really need me to go back in?" he asked. "I already identified Mom's...I mean...I already identified the victim bodies. And I told the police officer everything I know. Can't you record without me in there?"

"I'm sorry, son," the woman said in a frail attempt to sound sympathetic. "But I don't have the authority to change the assignment. You'll be fine." She spoke like a woman who had grown callous to human loss, a hazard of her line of work. Get in, record the facts, and move on to the next case in your queue. Tyler remembered fighting the same tendency after being assigned to the homicide division.

"Can you call someone?"

"Not at this hour," the woman replied.

Tyler noticed a small time stamp in the bottom left corner of the shot:

[7:37 PM—AUGUST 17, 2041]

Less than five hours after Jeremy lost the two most important people in his life.

Tyler saw Jeremy's back obscure the scene. Then Jeremy opened the door inward, the camera following closely behind until he stepped out of the way.

The woman's voice assumed a more official diction, like that of a news anchor reporting live from the scene. "We've entered the room where Antonio Santos and his mother Sylvia Santos died within minutes of one another at approximately three o'clock mountain time."

The screen zoomed onto the body of the boy, starting with his face. All color had drained from the lips, cheeks, and ears. Tyler recognized the familiar, vacant stare of death.

"This is the cadaver of the late Antonio Santos, his body identified this afternoon by his biological brother"—the camera moved to Jeremy, his head bowed in awkward reverence—"Jeremy Santos."

The camera lingered for a moment, then returned to the corpse, this time offering a full-body review. A catheter remained unremoved, one end attached to a needle in the boy's arm and the other to an empty plastic pouch, the slight residue of yellow serum still clinging to the bottom of the bag.

That's when Tyler realized he had never actually been inside a transition room, or even a transition clinic. Like everyone else, he knew they existed. He even placed himself in the 68 percent of the population in favor of the president's Youth Initiative. Had probably parroted the common rationale about redeploying scarce resources rather than wasting them caring for debits. He imagined craggy, drooling seniors opting for a merciful release from dementia. An eighteen-year-old boy lying dead on a gurney didn't fit the picture of an industry he had always admired from the safe distance of opinion columns and political speeches.

Neither did the next image to appear on the tablet screen. A pool of drying blood escaping from its source, a woman's skull with matted hair splayed onto the floor and over her lifeless face. An assortment of male and female footprints had spread the dark redness throughout the room, evidence of a flurry of activity immediately following the fall.

"And this," the woman's voice explained, "is the body of Sylvia Santos, identified at three o'clock this afternoon by her biological son, Jeremy Santos."

Another shot of the wilted boy offering the faintest possible nod of confirmation.

"As you can see," the woman said, pointing the camera back toward the floor, "Ms. Santos died shortly after a fall that appears to have crushed the occipital bone on the bottom posterior of her skull. According to an attending nurse who checked for a pulse at three oh-seven, Ms. Santos died within seconds of the injury. That assumption will be confirmed by the coroner in due course."

The camera scanned the full length of the body. Other than signs of the nurse's efforts to confirm death, it appeared no one had touched the body. Few of the crime scenes Tyler had recorded while on the force had been so well preserved. No one had even bothered to reposition Jeremy's mother's legs after her death. They seemed postured to receive a husband, or birth a child. Tyler felt a rare blush at a sight less graceful than a mother would want to appear when identified by her grieving son.

He noticed a scalpel lying beside the woman's open palm. The alleged weapon the distraught mother grabbed at the last second to interrupt Antonio's procedure?

Having seen enough, Tyler tapped the screen to halt the video. "I'm sorry for your loss," he said inadequately.

Jeremy bristled. "I don't need your pity, you know. I'll be fine."

Tyler waited. Eventually Jeremy sighed.

"It was hard," he began. "Not just that day. All of it. You don't realize how incredibly dependent you become on someone depending on *you* until they don't need you anymore."

"Your mother?"

"Antonio."

"I see." Tyler glanced at the time, then sat back in his chair. The boy obviously needed to talk.

"Near the end, every minute of every day, everything revolved around Antonio. Of course, it hadn't always been that way. At first it was just little things. You know, like helping him get from one room to the next when he didn't have his crutches. No big deal.

"Of course, Mom worried about every little thing. I think that's because she could see, even early on, how things would eventually end. Me? I was too self-absorbed to realize that this was only going to get worse over time. And as it did, I'd lose more and more of myself."

"So, you felt bitter toward your brother?" Tyler asked.

"Yes and no. I wasn't bitter at *him*, really. I mean, how could I be? It wasn't like he chose his disease or could do anything to stop it. I mean, what teenaged brother really chooses needing his mommy or his only sibling to wipe his butt for him?"

Tyler thought of Renee's parents. He thought of Gerry dripping water all over his carpet. In some ways it didn't seem so different.

"But I guess I was bitter. What brother wants to do the wiping? It shouldn't have been just me and Mom. It should have been my dad, too. No. It shouldn't have been any of us. But I guess sometimes life deals you a crummy hand.

"Anyhow, eventually I had no life. Just helping take care of my brother. Even when I was at school, I felt guilty that I wasn't there for Antonio. I could barely concentrate. It was ironic, really. Me, the one who had every hope of becoming somebody, of making something of myself...I was the one who started failing. And Antonio, the one who could do less and less almost every day, never ever gave up trying. He was an inspiration, really."

Jeremy paused, choking back emotions. Tyler, however, was confused by his last statement. *An inspiration?* How could a helpless debit be an inspiration? Already, after just a few days, Renee's parents were wearing him down. Wearing both of them down. Renee was too exhausted for sex, and her parents were sucking away any and all free time. Even now Tyler felt the resentment festering.

He thought of Renee's face. Tired as she appeared, he had

never sensed resentment. It was as if she was immune. As if she took pride in caring for her parents.

Tyler saw an echo of the same baffling pride on Jeremy's face, now accompanying the salty puddles of moisture trying to escape the boy's eyelids.

"I'm sorry," Jeremy finally said. "It's just I never told him that. I never told him that he was an amazing brother. Maybe if I had, none of this would have happened."

"I'm sure he knew." Tyler was still trying to comprehend how one drew inspiration from suffering.

Jeremy seemed to read Tyler's mind. "I guess you couldn't understand. Antonio made the most of each day he had. Even when he could barely communicate, when he had to struggle for each and every syllable that came out of his mouth, he would always find a way to make everyone else feel better. He'd tell a joke, or type an encouraging word. Sometimes that's all he could do. One word."

Jeremy wiped the embarrassment from his cheeks with manly verve.

"And I had the audacity to feel sorry for myself," he said with a recovering snort. "I was such an idiot."

"But you have nothing to feel guilty about. I mean, you gave up your life to take care of your brother."

Jeremy shook his head. "No, Mr. Cain. Antonio is the one who gave up his life…for me. Or at least that's what he wanted to do."

"And would have done," Tyler surmised, "if NEXT had accepted the court's verdict."

Jeremy nodded silently while Tyler reached for his own tablet, knowing this investigation had only just begun.

CHAPTER SIXTEEN

"Holy...!" Donny groaned across the room, his voice stretched from an unexpectedly heavy load. "What on earth's in this one?"

Matthew glanced up from disassembling an upturned kitchen table. "Sorry, man. My books. All seven of the boxes in that corner are pretty heavy."

"Books? You have seven boxes of books? Ever hear of a digital reader? They've been around for something like a million years. Don't you think it's time to upgrade?"

"I have a digital reader, wise guy," Matthew said. "Those are collector copies. You know, print classics."

"Whatever," Donny said, rolling his straining eyeballs. "I'll send you the chiropractor bill."

They shared a forced laugh as Donny took his tenth jaunt through the front door toward the small U-Haul trailer latched to the back of Matthew's car.

"You sure that piece of junk is gonna make it all the way to Littleton pulling this load?" Donny teased upon returning.

"You let me worry about that," Matthew replied. "You just worry about trying to find a new guy-flick buddy."

"Already figured that one out," Donny said smugly. "We're gonna meet in the middle, Broomfield Virtual Cinema."

Matthew paused his wrench to glare in Donny's direction. "Broomfield isn't in the middle. That's about fifteen minutes from your place. I'd have to drive through Denver traffic. It would take me at least forty-five."

"I'm not the one moving. You should have to drive farther than me."

"I'm not the one who can't find another friend." Matthew realized it was the first time he had ever used the word to describe their relationship. "You're the pathetic hermit."

"Welcome to the club, buddy."

Matthew winced at the jab, knowing he had lost the banter. It was true that he had joined the club of live-in senior-care workers. He, like Donny, could easily sink in the social quicksand of a job that entailed watching television or scanning porn sites while providing what his employer described as "caring attention for that aging loved one who wishes to remain in the comfort and privacy of his or her own home." Matthew shook the image off by reminding himself the job was temporary. One year. Less if Judge Santiago decided the NEXT appeal as he should.

"Talk to your client yet?" Donny asked.

"In the morning," Matthew replied. "They sent me a keypad code so I could settle in my stuff tonight. They'll bring him over after breakfast."

"Name?"

"I forget." He felt slightly embarrassed by the admission. He remembered Donny's thoughtfulness while caring for Matthew's mother. Donny had always been careful to use her first name. He never called her Ms. Adams or ma'am. Always Janet.

"What's wrong with him?"

"Dunno. I think he's just old and ornery. The daughter said

they put him in a pretty nice senior home but that he keeps offending the residents and staff."

"A dirty old man?"

"Who knows? I guess I'll find out tomorrow."

—⁓—

Thirty minutes later they loaded the final piece of furniture into the trailer. Donny followed in his car as the two drove the hour to Matthew's new temporary residence. Turning east off Santa Fe Drive onto Church Avenue, Matthew saw the familiar campus of Arapahoe Community College, the one his favorite high school academic counselor had said Matthew should attend. A good idea in retrospect, since he could have completed his freshman and sophomore years with little hassle or expense. But the suggestion had offended him at the time. Way beneath his aspirations, even if fitting for his grade point average.

Turning left onto South Curtice Street he watched the campus shrink in the side-view mirror. Two hundred yards later a dashboard voice announced his arrival at the intended destination.

"What a dump!" Donny said as he folded his arms across his chest while leaning against the hood of his car.

It was. Brownish strands of thirsty grass had succumbed to invading weeds now claiming territorial rights. Faded mulch infested with stringy, naked vines filled flowerbeds that might have once displayed annual and perennial colors. Part of the gutter above the dented garage door hung loose. The exterior paint, a deep green that had been quite popular two decades earlier, offered glimpses of wood siding that should have been replaced back in the mid-twenties.

"Home sweet home," Matthew said with a sigh. "For now, anyway."

After tapping the keypad code Matthew eased the front door open like a man worried about waking a sleeping child. But the house was empty. His client had been away for months. The HOUSE FOR SALE sign leaned against the wall just beneath the entryway light switch, remnant of an abandoned plan A. According to the job notice, the old man was leaving a senior center to move back into his own home the following morning.

"What's that awful smell?" Donny muttered, holding his nose.

"Whew! Something must've died." Matthew opened both front windows to invite fresh air into the room. "The guy's daughter said she checked on the place every couple of weeks."

"Well she hasn't checked lately."

They spent the next ten minutes searching for the source of the foul odor. A small stream of dark blood on the kitchen floor led them to a jellifying rat hidden behind the refrigerator, an apparent victim of the small mousetrap still clinging to a rear claw.

"Must have tried dragging itself to shelter," Donny surmised. "Not a good omen for you, my man!"

Two hours later a dusk-lit breeze blew away much of the smell while the two men emptied the U-Haul trailer of the few belongings Matthew had decided to keep. The furniture, appliances, and decorations had met his mom's needs while she was alive. Now they entombed her memory. Matthew had decided to give most of them to charity.

"What do you say we order a pizza?" Donny said, looking up from a horizontal posture on the floor. "I'm starved and exhausted."

Matthew scanned the room to confirm the job had been accomplished. His new pillow sat on top of a floral bedspread that must have belonged to his client's daughter when she was a teenager. Beneath that was a mattress he feared would further stress his already aching back. But buying a new bed was out of the question, since he intended to save every penny possible to pay down his loan. Whether the inheritance money came or not, he had no intention of making live-in senior care a long-term career.

His books sat stacked along the wall that would have to double as a shelf. Most of his clothes hung on a dozen hangers in the closet or had been folded and placed in two open drawers. The rest of his belongings remained in a large box labeled "miscellaneous" on top of a dresser, where Donny had placed it compliantly.

"I guess I've gotten enough work out of you for one day," Matthew said with a grateful smile. "You've earned a meal."

Donny raised his head from the floor. "And a movie?"

"Can't," Matthew replied. "I need to shower and take care of a few things tonight and then get a good night's sleep. Gotta rest up. You know, first impressions and all."

"Do I ever," Donny said with a reluctant push against the floor. "And you might want to learn your client's name before he arrives in the morning."

"Good tip," said Matthew.

—⁓—

As Donny pulled away from the house, Matthew offered a single wave before clearing the empty pizza box and soda cans from the porch. They had decided to eat outside rather than defile the scent of pepperoni with the lingering stench of rat decay.

He showered away the grime of heavy lifting in the August heat, then moved into the front room to try enjoying his last evening alone by settling into what must have been the old man's favorite chair before the daughter moved him into an assisted living facility. Beside the chair was a small table on which sat a familiar icon. His mother had kept something similar beside her favorite chair. But her cross had been attached to rosary beads; this cross appeared on the cover of a book. Matthew flipped to the title page.

THE HOLY BIBLE
AUTHORIZED KING JAMES VERSION

He turned the book on its side and noticed dozens of dog-eared and worn pages in the last third. The Bible appeared quite old, possibly even from the glory days of early-twentieth-century publishing. Matthew recognized it as a leather-bound classic like one he had removed from the box Donny had complained most about carrying. Probably a collectible more valuable than the old man realized. Certainly too valuable to leave lying around in an empty house.

Matthew closed the Bible and placed it back on the table with gentle care, then tapped his tablet awake to find something that might distract him from a sinking feeling that had engulfed much of his day.

One message appeared. He glanced at the sender's name. It jolted him out of despondency.

Hi there!

OK. Your last message piqued my interest. I even went to the school annual to find your name. No A. Manichean listed. I assume you're using a handle. Here's the deal. We can meet on one condition. Send me your real name and a current picture, which is only fair since you seem to have been ogling my pictures for some time! (I'm glad you like them, by the way.) Then we can set a date. I get to pick the place. You get to pick up the check!

Your turn,
Maria Davidson

Matthew stood while rereading the note for a second opinion. After validating his good fortune he realized that he was standing. He sat back down to shoot back what he hoped would be a cleverly perfect reply. Before he could type a single word, however, he felt a slight panic. Did he even have a picture to send besides his license and student ID photos? He could shave and dress to take a shot with his tablet camera. But he felt like a goof when taking his own picture, and it always showed.

He quickly tapped his FAVORITES folder. He found several saved images of Maria and about a dozen other smiling beauties, but nothing of himself. He cursed. Then he remembered adding a headshot to his social network site about three years earlier. Two taps on the screen brought him to his home page. He smiled at the satisfactory image. But there was too much hair on his head. Maria would immediately peg him as insincere for posting such an outdated shot. He quickly replaced it with one of the stock cartoon images people used to conceal their own faces.

He considered sending a reply with no picture. But he didn't want to risk refusal, banishing him to the eternal torture of what might have been.

The seed of an idea rescued Matthew from total defeat. He set the tablet aside and walked to the bedroom to search through the unopened box filled with last-minute junk. Two minutes later he found what he'd hoped hadn't been discarded. Charles Kohl had taken a picture on the day of his mother's transition. He looked at his own face first. Not bad. Modest digital doctoring might even make him look ruggedly handsome. A relief!

Then he looked at the other face. He had never really examined it before. The photo had been hidden away in a drawer since the day it fell out of the envelope containing a thank-you note from Aspen House, which had included the picture as a memento of his mother's heroic choice. He saw it as a reminder of the burden he had borne and didn't care to recall.

Her eyes were more downcast than he remembered. Matthew had worked hard to make it a special day, to avoid any hint of what was really happening. He had told her they were visiting Aspen House so she could spend more time with the nice gentleman they had met earlier. A date, not an appointment. A chat, not a procedure. But the eyes staring at him through the photo now seemed to tell a truth he had refused to consider.

"I knew, Son. Sure, I went along. But I knew."

Matthew felt his hand start to tremble. He forced his gaze away from hers, then flipped the photo over. He walked to the living room, where he placed it on his tablet's scanner. Dragging the image into a photo-editing application, he isolated his own face. Moments later it looked like the kind of man he hoped Maria would want to meet, but enough like him to appear genuine.

He attached the picture to a note he decided to keep short but sweet.

Hi Maria:
   Here you go. I'll be in town this week. What do you say?

Matthew Adams

CHAPTER SEVENTEEN

The stream of unwelcome light inched its way across Matthew's eyelids but failed to rouse him, his aching lump clinging to the much needed haven of slumber. It was a different interruption that finally forced motion, the creaking swing of the door hinge followed by a gentle thump and high-pitched breathing. Someone had entered his room.

Matthew rolled over with great effort. He opened one eye, then the other. To his disorienting surprise he saw a ponytailed intruder sitting Indian-style beside his bed, looking up at his disheveled head with childlike wonder.

"Hello sir," she said, extending a hand and standing. "I'm Isabelle Gale. What's your name?" She looked no more than five or six years old. Her cheeks retained a pudgy cuteness left over from toddlerhood. But her mannered diction gave off an air of confident authority, like that of the de facto leader of her kindergarten reading circle.

Maneuvering his aching back and stiff legs, Matthew managed to achieve a sitting position on the edge of the bed.

"Matthew," he answered over the sandpaper sounds of a chin-scratch. "Matthew Adams." He cleared his throat of morning phlegm before accepting her offered hand. "Pleased to meet you, Miss Gale."

She giggled. Whether at the respectful title or Matthew's disheveled appearance was unclear.

Out of the corner of Matthew's eye he noticed movement near the foot of the bed. He turned to see a small forehead peering over the rumpled pile of blankets spilling off the edge onto the floor.

"And who's this?" he asked.

"That's Peter."

"Your little brother?"

"My older brother," Isabelle corrected.

"Really?" Matthew took a second look. Peter appeared timid. No, more than timid. Weak. And frightened.

"Hi there, Peter," he said to calm the boy's qualms. "Nice to meet you."

The boy froze, glaring at Matthew's extended hand as if it were an aimed rifle. Matthew pulled it back.

"He doesn't talk," Isabelle explained.

"How old is Peter?" Matthew didn't know whether to look at the boy or his proxy.

"Six and a half. Same as me. We're twins."

"You don't say."

"I was born two minutes after Peter. That's why Mommy calls him my big brother even though I'm taller by almost an inch."

"I see—" Matthew began before an adult voice interrupted the conversation.

"Isabelle!" Mom appeared flustered, and embarrassed. "I'm so, so sorry. I had no idea they were in here. I'm Marissa, Hugh Gale's daughter. I was distracted helping Dad with his oxygen tank. I apologize if they woke you."

"No worries," Matthew said to allay concern. "I'm Matthew Adams. We were just getting acquainted."

"You two come into the kitchen this instant," Marissa ordered as four little feet scurried obediently.

"Bye, Matthew," Isabelle said from the doorway.

"Mr. Adams," Marissa corrected, prompting another girlish giggle.

—⁓—

Five minutes later Matthew entered the kitchen to find Isabelle and Peter sitting at the counter. A scrumptious aroma told him they were eating some sort of toasted pastry. Both pairs of lips sipped from tiny straws protruding out of half-collapsed apple juice boxes. The table held several bags of groceries patiently awaiting their promotion to the pantry and refrigerator.

"Hi guys. Where's your mom?" Matthew asked.

"In there," Isabelle said after swallowing. She pointed toward the front room. "With Reverend Grandpa."

"Reverend Grandpa?"

"That's what we call him."

"Interesting," Matthew said, moving toward the doorway. He paused to take a deep breath before entering.

Father and daughter sat in silence. Marissa Gale was perched on the edge of the sofa with legs crossed at the ankle, her folded hands resting on her lap in polite impatience. She shot to her feet like a three-tour soldier noticing the arrival of her replacement. "Mr. Adams."

"Call me Matthew," he replied, stepping into the room.

"Matthew then. I don't believe you've met my father."

To Matthew's relief the man appeared modestly robust, his stout frame reclining comfortably in the chair Matthew had occupied twelve hours earlier. Hugh Gale looked more like a recently retired trucker than the death-courting skeleton Matthew had imagined. His forearms were particularly impressive, suggesting Hugh Gale had lifted weights in earlier life. It wasn't until Matthew repositioned himself in front of the man's seat that he noticed signs of disability: mechanical braces on his legs and a tiny oxygen tube protruding from his lower neck.

Matthew extended his hand. "Hello, Hugh. Pleased to meet you."

The man scowled. "Hugh?"

Matthew looked to the daughter to confirm he had heard the name correctly. Her eyes said he had, but that he had blundered nonetheless.

"Did I say you could call me Hugh?"

"Oh, I'm sorry," Matthew backpedaled. "Mr. Gale then."

Another scowl. "Mr. Gale?"

"My father prefers to be called *Reverend*." Marissa appeared embarrassed by the expectation.

"Reverend Grandpa!" the old man insisted.

Matthew searched the man's face. Was he testing Matthew's sense of humor or revealing an idiosyncrasy requiring careful navigation?

"Reverend Grandpa it is then," he decreed good-naturedly. "But only if you tell me where you got the title."

"I don't negotiate," Reverend Grandpa barked.

"Neither do I," Matthew said without blinking. Then held his breath.

The man slapped the armrest of his chair with a laugh. "Ha! I like this kid." A slight wheezing sound overtook his breathing before he continued. "Take no guff! That's always been my motto too."

Matthew and the daughter shared a sigh of relief.

"I got the title from little Pete."

"Peter," Marissa corrected. "How many times do I need to tell you, he wants to be called Peter?"

"You want to call him Peter. He prefers little Pete!"

Marissa shook her head. She seemed exasperated, as if she had lost this same argument on countless previous occasions.

"You mean the Peter sitting in the kitchen with Isabelle?" Matthew asked.

"One and the same. My favorite grandson!"

"Do you have other grandkids?"

"No sir," Reverend Grandpa said through a faint chuckle. "Just the twins."

"So he does talk?"

Marissa shot a surprised look at Matthew. "No, he doesn't speak. Hasn't said a word in the three years since his father died. But how did you know about that?"

"Isabelle told me. I'm sorry about your partner...or was it husband?"

"They weren't married," Reverend Grandpa said disapprovingly.

Marissa smiled dismissively at her father's quaint reaction.

"Thank you," she said to Matthew. "We were partners for three years. It was hard. I'm doing fine, but I worry about Peter since—"

"Little Pete will be just fine," Reverend Grandpa interrupted.

Matthew looked back toward his client. "So if he doesn't talk, when did he give you the title?"

The old man raised a hushing finger to his lips, then winked a smile at his new caregiver. Clearly the answer involved some secret grandpa/grandson pact.

"My father was a minister," Marissa explained.

"I'm still a minister!" came the gruff correction.

"A priest?" Matthew wondered aloud. He had never met a Father who was also a dad.

"Heaven forbid! Do you see me wearing a dog collar?" Reverend Grandpa touched the edge of his open-necked shirt. "I'm a Baptist preacher. I rely on this here book. I don't submit to some Roman pope!"

Matthew didn't know much about Baptist preachers, but it sounded as if Reverend Grandpa shared his own aversion to Catholic dogma. "Me neither," he said.

"That's good." The old man caressed the classic Bible Matthew had been admiring the prior evening. "We don't need a bunch of highbrow traditions or creeds. We have the word of God right here in black and white!"

Marissa rolled her eyes. "How about if we hit the pause button right there. I've heard this sermon before. You two can get acquainted later. I need to talk Matthew through instructions and then get Isabelle and Peter to school. I open today, so my shift starts in about an hour."

Reverend Grandpa raised a hand in surrender to his daughter's wishes while she moved toward the kitchen.

"I look forward to talking to you about religion, Reverend Grandpa," Matthew said as he started to trail Marissa. "I've been studying spirituality at college. We can compare notes."

"Anytime, my boy. Anytime."

—∿∿—

Matthew helped organize the groceries before joining Marissa at the kitchen table to run through her list of instructions. They quickly covered mundane matters like emergency and doctor phone numbers. Then she told him which foods not to prepare "no matter how much he shouts." He smiled at the daughter's attempts to change the diet of a man who must have spent all eighty-two of his years eating pretty much whatever he liked.

"Got it," Matthew said deferentially.

The most important instructions centered around managing and changing the oxygen tanks she called "vital to his daily survival."

"What happened?" Matthew asked. "I mean, your dad appears to be in pretty good shape. Why so much trouble breathing?"

"He had what should have been a mild heart attack a few years back. The old fool tried driving himself to the hospital. He got into an accident on the way. Ran off the road. No seat belt. His legs slammed into the dash pretty hard."

"I noticed the braces."

"They don't work as well as he had hoped. They help him stand, but he still needs the walker to get anywhere."

"No wheelchair?"

"I put it in the garage. Be warned. He hates it. Only lets us take it to places like the zoo or airport. You know, long-distance uses only. He says it makes him feel like an invalid."

"But he—"

Marissa raised her hand to interrupt. "I know, I know. But being an invalid and seeing yourself as one are two different things. You'll soon find out what I mean."

Matthew nodded, appreciating the heads-up.

"Anyway, the real damage of the accident was pulmonary. The extra strain on his heart from the internal bleeding and the time it took to move him caused some pretty serious damage. His ticker only pumps in first gear now. He needs more oxygen per red blood cell than his lungs can generate."

"Wow."

"That's why he needs someone around most of the time. A few minutes without oxygen and his system will start shutting down."

Matthew looked down at the list of instructions to confirm every detail.

Marissa placed her hand on Matthew's and said, "I want to thank you for accepting this job."

Looking into her eyes, Matthew tried to hide any of the discomfort he felt over the unexpected attention from a woman ten years his senior. Was her touch the affirming pat of a grateful daughter or the suggestive advance of a lonely woman?

"You bet," he said guardedly while trying to think of something to change the subject. "So the senior center didn't work out?"

She removed her hand. "A minor disaster!"

"Why? What happened?"

"In less than a month he had set a facility record for complaints from residents and staff."

"Anything I should know about?"

"You've already had a taste."

"The preacher stuff?"

"He figured God had placed him in the senior facility to rescue every lost soul from eternal damnation."

"I see."

"The straw that broke the camel's back happened last week. Dad decided to pull the fire alarm in the middle of afternoon naps as an illustration of Jesus's second coming."

Matthew flashed a quizzical look. "I don't follow."

"He thinks Jesus is going to blow a trumpet at any moment and come back to redeem his chosen people."

"Ah. So the fire alarm was—?"

"The closest thing he could find to a trumpet in order to wake unsuspecting heathens."

Matthew laughed at the image of Reverend Grandpa watching an unnerved crew of attendants frantically wheel groggy residents into the nursing home parking lot.

"I'll be sure to hide my trumpet."

Marissa joined Matthew's smile at an incident she seemed to

find amusing now that a solution to her father's care had been found. "You'll have your hands full, that's for sure," she said.

"We'll be fine," he said reassuringly. "Now you better get moving. I don't want to make you late for work."

Matthew finally closed the door to his bedroom ten hours later. Other than a few relatively harmless verbal jousts while he served meals to his client and helped him change into his bed-clothes, the two hadn't talked much. Reverend Grandpa seemed eager to enjoy his freedom from sterile smells and white walls with the simple pleasures of a good book and a long siesta. So, refusing to become the stereotype, Matthew kept himself busy with a list of self-assigned chores like watering dying grass and familiarizing himself with appliance dials.

As he crawled into bed he felt a surprising sense of usefulness. He'd almost forgotten what it was like to sink into a well-earned sleep after a particularly exhausting day caring for his mother. Despite resenting the work, he had always relished the satisfaction.

Just before turning out the light he remembered that it had been several days since he'd last checked his anonymous forum. He typed in a twelve-character pass-code to access what he hoped would be a thoughtful response from Judge Victor Santiago agreeing to dialogue on the NEXT appeal. But the forum listed no messages.

Then he heard the ping of a new message. He quickly tapped the bouncing icon.

Hi Matt:
I do remember you. And yes, I'd like to meet. How about 10 a.m. Monday at Enchanted Coffee near I-470?
Maria

Matthew stood, clasping his hands tightly together while pacing the tiny space between the bed and closet door. He moved back toward the tablet lying on top of the disheveled covers and reread the message. He spent the next thirty minutes suppressing an overwhelming urge to say a prayer of thanks.

CHAPTER EIGHTEEN

"Ooh. Let's pop in here," Angie blurted like a child startled by a candy store. "Their stuff is adorable!"

Julia glanced up at a sign that read TINY THREADS.

"Angie," she protested. "Kevin said to find something for you, not shop for the kids."

Too late. Her friend had already escaped into the treasury of infant and toddler apparel.

The time had been a gift from their husbands, a pleasant surprise since Julia had assumed she would spend the morning at the house with Angie watching the kids. Ricky still had a sniffle Leah seemed eager to mimic, which had killed their plans to dine at Tommy's favorite fast-food playland. A major disappointment since, he complained, McDonald's would soon renovate the space into a "stupid coffee lounge for grown-ups!" Made sense, Julia thought, in light of shifting demographics. But hard on a five-year-old losing his Neverland complete with burgers, shakes, and fries.

"You two go shopping," Kevin had suggested. "Buy yourself something nice. We can work here just as well as at my office."

Angie offered an obligatory refusal until Tommy cheered Uncle Troy's presence as a terrific consolation prize. That's when she gladly accepted.

Part of Julia liked the idea. Troy needed time with Kevin to discuss problems with the business. But he also loved hanging around the kids. Their exhausting demands seemed to charge rather than deplete her husband's batteries. Which worried another part of her.

She reluctantly followed Angie into the store, where she was confronted with the pleasing aroma of baby lotion innocence. Julia positioned herself next to a rack of pink newborn outfits and nervously fingered a pair of tiny booties half the size of the socks she had seen Angie drape over Ricky's pudgy toes. She felt out of place watching Angie scurry from one darling outfit to the next in a continued quest to coordinate Joy and Leah for their upcoming family photo.

Two hours earlier Angie had fled her home in eager anticipation of a morning away from the relentless demands of kids. "I really need the break," she had said. "I wanted to kiss Kevin when he suggested we go." No wonder the fifteen-minute drive to the outdoor mall had turned the car into a confession booth where Angie unloaded a series of hesitant complaints.

"This is the fifth week in a row one of the kids has been sick. I can't remember my last full night of sleep."

"Kevin tries. But he's been too busy to notice that I'm drowning."

"I hate those fund-raising dinners. I still haven't lost the last ten pounds of baby weight. I gave up trying to keep up with the trophy girlfriends."

"We got the results last week. Leah isn't progressing as well as we'd hoped. I cried myself to sleep Thursday night."

"Confidentially, there were days I hoped Kevin would lose his reelection bid."

"Some days I feel utterly alone."

Julia remembered her sister's warning. "You'll end up like Angie...wearing frumpy sweat suits while pushing a double stroller through the neighborhood."

Placing the booties on a nearby display rack, Julia watched Angie move toward the checkout counter. A bit of self-doubt notwithstanding, she was not frumpy in the least. Just a woman needing the kind of pampering a shopping-and-lunch outing might provide; perhaps splurging on a stylish new outfit would make her feel as beautiful as she remained. Yet there she was, cute as a button, standing in line to buy matching dresses for her little girls. How does a woman so eager for a break from Mommyville miss her children only hours after escape?

The sight made Julia aware of her growing unease.

"What do you think?" Angie asked, holding up the purchases.

Anxiety retreated in the glow of her friend's delight. "Perfect," she confirmed with a wink.

Julia heard Kevin's voice coming from Angie's phone.

"Hi, beautiful. Sure would like to talk to you." They were the identical words Troy's voice spoke when he called Julia.

"Is she OK?" Angie asked.

The look on Angie's face told Julia something had happened back at the house. The fingernail between her friend's teeth suggested the possibility of something serious.

"We can leave now if—" Angie paused in reaction to an apparent interruption from Kevin.

"Are you sure?" she asked, her face showing signs of uncertain compliance.

"Joy?" Julia asked when Angie ended the call.

"Leah," she replied with concern.

"Sniffles?"

"Diarrhea."

The word alone seemed to vanquish any baby lotion smell.

Julia frowned at the thought of yet another Mommyville reality she couldn't imagine herself handling.

"He said she's in the tub," Angie explained. "She likes taking a bath to get rid of the yucky feeling."

"Who doesn't?" Julia said tepidly. *Does it ever stop?* she wondered.

They spent the next thirty minutes finding distractions from thoughts of the mini-crisis their husbands might mishandle. They found three outfits Julia insisted Angie try, all of them flattering but none of them leading to a purchase.

They decided to enjoy the late-morning sunshine with a stroll toward the food court, where they saw a man proactively cooling lunchtime customers by opening a series of large umbrellas in the outside seating area.

"OK. Time to fess up, girl," Angie said abruptly, surprising Julia. "What's bothering you?"

"Bothering me?"

"Yes, you," she insisted. "I can tell there's something on your mind."

"I'm just worried about you," she lied. "I mean, the last thing you needed was another sick child."

"Comes with the job," Angie teased. "Besides, Kevin will muddle through."

Julia offered a thin smile.

"I upset you with what I said earlier, didn't I?" Angie continued. "I'm sorry. I didn't mean to dump on you like that. I just needed to tell someone what I'm feeling."

Julia slipped her arm into Angie's and bumped hips. "Don't worry about it. I understand."

She didn't want to say more. Angie's guess seemed an easier explanation than the truth. "But it's not what you said," she heard herself say.

"No? What then?"

Julia hesitated. *How to tell the mother of four kids that you resent your husband's push for a baby?*

"It's Troy," she began. "He wants more than I'm ready to give."

Angie stopped, her face seeming to flip through ugly possibilities that didn't fit what she knew of her husband's lifelong friend.

"Really? Like what?" she asked blankly. "He acts like he adores you."

"He does," Julia admitted with a tint of shame. "He's been wonderful to me. It's nothing like that."

"Then what's wrong?" Angie pulled them both toward a nearby bench. They sat.

Julia looked away from her friend's anxious eyes.

"Before we got married we discussed children," she began. "We agreed we would consider kids after a few years together."

She paused to watch a final umbrella rise in the distance.

"Troy wants kids now, doesn't he?" Angie said what Julia couldn't.

A single confirming nod.

"I'm not surprised. That scares you?"

Another hit, followed by a comforting stillness.

"I know how you feel."

Julia's head swung back toward Angie. "You do?"

"Of course I do." She took Julia's left hand in her own. "How do you think I felt when I found out I was pregnant with Ricky, that I was going to have a fourth child?"

For some reason Julia hadn't considered the question until that moment.

"One of my first thoughts was that you'd probably think I'd gone off the deep end!"

The comment prompted a nervous laugh. Then a prick of guilt.

"I'm so sorry," Julia said. "I must have made it more difficult for you."

"You and nearly everyone else on the planet. If I hadn't been thrown into a tailspin over the accusations against Kevin I would have been pretty upset about how you characterized people like me. Or should I say breeders like me."

The reminder of her feature's title made Julia blush. "Please forgive me. I know I hurt you and Kevin and I—"

"Stop it," Angie interrupted. "We've been over that ground a dozen times before. You're forgiven, OK? No more asking."

"I know, but—"

"Enough," Angie commanded.

Another single nod.

"I only mention the article because it put into words what I feel when people look at my life, my family."

"You have a beautiful family."

Angie smiled. "I think so. But it frightened me when I found out I was pregnant again. Did you know we had just received Leah's diagnosis a few weeks earlier?"

"It must have been scary."

"It was, for a few days. But then it became wonderful, just like my other three pregnancies."

"How?" Julia asked.

"How what?"

"How did it become wonderful? What changed your feelings?"

Angie seemed to wrestle within, as if reaching for words that didn't exist.

"When did you get past the fear?" Julia pressed further.

The question prompted a smile of realization. "I didn't."

"But you said—"

"I didn't say the fear disappeared. I said it became wonderful." She looked away, then back as if she had found a cue card on the horizon. "I guess the fear kind of lost itself in the wonder. Like leaning over the railing at Niagara Falls. Does that make sense?"

"I've never been."

"Go. It's a deafening force rushing over the edge and crashing on the rocks below. When you get close it looks and sounds like a million thunderous explosions per second. The second-most frightening, awe-inspiring experience you'll ever encounter."

"Second-most?"

Angie smiled silently while raising a single eyebrow.

Julia understood. "Oh, right."

"It's OK to be afraid, Julia."

She received Angie's squeeze with gratitude.

"Just don't let the fear keep you from the wonder."

"I think I get that part," Julia began. "But what about the rest?"

"What rest?"

"Today, for example. You couldn't even spend two hours away from the kids without a new worry to pull you back."

"I can't argue with that." Angie sighed.

"Do you ever resent the constant demands? Or giving up your career? I mean, be honest. What about your dreams? Your needs? Who looks after Angie?"

Angie started to say something, then held her tongue.

"What?" Julia asked. "Tell me."

"I'd rather not. Too holier-than-thou-sounding." She paused, seeming to gauge Julia's reaction before continuing. "You know, too religious."

Julia blushed at the nakedness of the comment. Then she joined Angie's lead by stepping over a line of candor. "Not too religious. Just religious. And I don't know about anyone else, but you've definitely lived holier than me."

They shared what seemed their first authentic laugh in years.

"Go ahead," Julia continued. "You were going to say?"

"I know I did a bit of whining earlier about the frustrations of motherhood. Forgive me for that. Being a mom often feels like one long string of sacrificial moments."

"Especially with so many. Does it ever stop?"

"Ask me in twenty years. Until then, I try to remember what Jesus said. 'If you want to find your life you must first lose it.'"

Julia nodded, remembering the sentiment from one of the Christianity classes she had attended with Troy. "I know that quote."

"He also said that unless a seed goes into the ground and dies, it can't give life."

"Meaning?"

"To me it means we find our true purpose and joy when we follow his example, when we give our lives away to others. It helps me view all of my little sacrifices for Kevin and the kids as my way of losing my life." She paused to lock eyes with Julia. "But I wouldn't trade the life I've found for anything in the world."

Kevin's voice interrupted the moment. "Hi, beautiful…"

"Speaking of the life I've found," Angie said before accepting the call. "I think it's time to rescue our men before they go over the Falls in a barrel!"

CHAPTER NINETEEN

The ancient world had conspired to create such architectural marvels as Rome's Coliseum, China's Great Wall, and India's Taj Mahal. Modern man had raised the stakes with the Panama Canal, Empire State Building, and Golden Gate Bridge. But none of them had outdone the genius on display in Tommy Tolbert's bedroom.

"This is it!" Troy announced as Tommy added a final Lego piece to a three-foot-high replica of the tallest building on the planet. "Ladies and gentlemen..."

He paused to make eye contact with both members of the audience. Kevin stood in the doorway with Joy at his knee. The official count might number three spectators, but little Ricky never actually lifted his head from Daddy's shoulder.

"...I proudly present the tenth wonder of the world, a three-hour construction effort that, according to the box, should only be attempted by individuals twice the age of our construction foreman. Please join me in congratulating an engineering genius, Mr. Tommy Tolbert!"

Joy clapped riotously while Kevin quietly raised his thumb in a show of fatherly pride. Tommy relished the moment, bowing deeply in self-congratulation while keeping the secret: Uncle Troy had helped him. A lot.

"What do you say we celebrate with sliced apples and peanut butter?" Kevin asked while confirming the baby's slumber. "I'll put Ricky in his bed and then we'll start the party."

Six minutes later the gang tapped milk cups in response to Daddy's congratulatory toast. Before he could sip, however, Troy leaned toward Leah's high chair for a second inspecting whiff.

"Keep her diaper fresh," Angie had coached Kevin on the phone. "Otherwise the diarrhea will cause a painful rash."

Troy was not going to let that happen. "I'll get this one."

The sound of the front door opening interrupted Kevin's grateful nod.

"Mommy!" Joy squealed in delight.

"Aunt Julia!" Tommy said, rushing from the table. "Come see what's in my room!"

Kevin and Troy insisted they could have handled the job. They even pretended offense at their wives' early return. But Angie had been right. The men hadn't found time to talk about any of the pressing matters each was eager to discuss.

"You two go for a walk," she commanded.

Four blocks later Troy halted their advancing footsteps. "Wait," he interrupted. "Are you saying what I think you're saying?"

Kevin flashed a triumphant grin. "Twenty percent."

"So a fifth of potential voters would support a Bright Spots platform?"

Kevin slapped his friend's back. "What's wrong, pal, didn't believe your own numbers?"

Troy's eyes followed a passing car while his mind tried to process the implications. Elections were won and lost on single-digit margins. Political fortunes were made and lost because of catering to voting blocs much, much smaller. His friend would likely become an important player in the minds of party leaders. They needed Kevin's influence to garner support among an important segment of the electorate.

Troy looked back toward Kevin. "What else did Anderson say?"

"He said Franklin thinks the Bright Spots proposal, properly positioned, could help his campaign."

"Properly positioned?" A yellow light. "What's that supposed to mean?"

Kevin resumed walking. "In a second. You said you wanted to hear the good news first."

"No I didn't," Troy said, trotting to catch up with Kevin. "I said I wanted the bad news but you overruled me, as usual."

"Oh yeah." Kevin laughed. "You need to understand the good news to help me think through how to react to the bad."

"React to what?"

"Brent Anderson ran his own version of our numbers. He said we were right about bright spot regions as the primary engines of population and economic growth. He said Franklin needs to attract votes and donors from these segments of the population if he's gonna win the election. Social conservatives still resent his support for the Youth Initiative."

"Yes, we do!"

A momentary silence while Kevin seconded Troy's motion with a nod.

Troy's yellow light shaded toward red. "Why do I get the feeling there's more? And that I won't like it?"

"Anderson said it would be political suicide to move quickly," Kevin explained. "Nicole Florea's crowd already fumes anytime Franklin even mentions the Bright Spots proposal. Imagine how they'll react if and when he makes it part of his platform."

"Let me guess," Troy groaned. "They want to take a 'balanced' approach."

Kevin halted his advance. "I can't believe it," he said, extending his arm toward Troy's chest. "That's exactly what he said."

"It's what they always say, Kevin!" Troy sounded angry. "But you can't make a balanced choice between east and west. If you're heading in the wrong direction you turn around. You don't stop and admire the view! Bright spots shine because they go against the flow of the majority. How on earth do you take a balanced approach to a one-hundred-and-eighty-degree turn?"

"I hear ya, buddy." Kevin took a deep breath as if trying to lower Troy's rising volume. Then he looked his friend in the eyes. "Listen, Troy. I don't agree with any of this. OK? I don't like it any more than you do. But I need to figure out how to play the hand I've been dealt."

Troy understood. "I'm sorry. Go on. I'm listening."

Kevin pulled his friend into the deep end by repeating what he had been hesitant to share. "Franklin says we need more transitions in light of the deepening economic free fall."

"More transitions? Has he even read...?"

"He's read our proposal, Troy," Kevin said sternly. "Anderson told me Franklin agrees with our long-term analysis. But he worries our approach could deepen the short-term crisis. That we need the cash infusion and savings generated by Youth Initiative policies."

"But—" Troy cut himself short. He couldn't argue. It would take a long time to reap the benefits of a pure Bright Spots agenda. Even in the unlikely event every family in the nation started having more kids immediately, the corresponding economic growth wouldn't outrun the soaring costs of an aging population for decades.

Resignation swept over Troy's face. "So what's the plan?"

Another deep breath released Kevin's reluctant explanation. "Franklin hopes to sell a big goal that he thinks will strike a positive, forward-looking tone."

"Why doesn't that make me feel better?" Troy mocked.

"He wants to increase fertility at twice the rate we increase transitions." Kevin held his tongue while Troy absorbed the news.

"Two births for every killing?"

Kevin remained silent a moment longer. "I said the rate of increase, not the raw number."

Troy did a mental calculation to correct his misunderstanding. "That's even worse!"

"I know. But the average voter will make the same mistake you just made. Speeches and sound bites will leave the impression he hopes to solve the long-term population crisis twice as fast as he wants to reduce the elderly population."

"An all-around swell guy!" Troy spat.

"I told you we wouldn't like it. But think for a second. What opportunities would such a policy present?"

Troy reluctantly obeyed, closing his eyes as if concentrating to calculate a restaurant tip.

"Well," he began, "in light of current trends, it would require some pretty aggressive incentives to motivate couples to have kids."

"My thoughts exactly," Kevin replied.

"But they'll probably also increase incentives for seniors to transition. Those trends have flattened. Most of the early adopters and sickly have already opted in, or rather out. Whatever you call it when they die. Anyway, the low-hanging fruit has already been plucked and destroyed. You know the snakes will want to expand into healthier, younger markets."

"I know," Kevin confessed. "But I don't think we can win that battle in this round. But we might be able to win on the other front."

Troy placed both palms on his head while filling his chest with air, his way of replacing hotheaded passion with a brainstorming cap.

"Besides," Kevin continued, "NEXT might lose their appeal. The Tenth District Court might give us a bigger victory than we could possibly hope to achieve in Washington."

"Let's hope," Troy said with a nod.

"Meanwhile, let's address the root of the problem." Kevin turned back toward the house, where they could pull out some scratch paper and pens to record whatever brilliance might transpire. "We can make a strong case that as fertility rates continue to drop the problem will get worse. I'll show pictures of Tommy, Joy, and Ricky, then your ugly mug. I'll say my kids will each have to work a second job just to cover their Uncle Troy's share of senior-care costs."

"Hey, don't toss me into the freeloader bucket yet. I still have time to have my own brood of kids."

The comment distracted Kevin's train of thought. "Really?"

Troy grinned awkwardly. "Well, a guy can hope."

"Have you and Julia been trying?"

Troy chose to divert. "I can't answer that. A gentleman always protects a lady's reputation." He flashed a thin smile.

It worked. Kevin returned to his point. "Anyway, I've been thinking. What if we started a privately funded research and capitalization organization?"

"Like a foundation?"

"Sort of. But more directive, like a venture capital operation.

A not-for-profit version of TS Enterprises. You know, do what we do well."

Troy winced. "To be honest, we're not doing it that well at the moment. In fact, we need to discuss a few pressing matters before I head back to Colorado."

"Fine," Kevin said dismissively to resume vision-casting. "We'll need an official-sounding name."

Troy thought about that for a moment. "How about something like the Center for Economic Health?"

"Perfect!" Kevin snapped. "The Center for Economic Health will exist to discover what's working in bright spot communities and provide seed funding for promising innovations that can help other regions foster bright spot habits."

"I like the sound of that," Troy added. "Although Nicole Florea will say we're subsidizing head-in-the-sand choices and creating a culture filled with environmentally irresponsible breeders."

"We'll worry about people like Nicole Florea later. First things first. Someone has to find, fund, and highlight what works so our nation doesn't advance the kind of failed strategies they tried in places like Russia and Japan. We can do better than just throwing money at single mothers to have another kid. We need married couples raising families."

Troy sensed a tinge of optimism in his friend's words. "Wait a minute," he said suspiciously. "You've already scripted this, haven't you?"

A sheepish grin.

"We aren't brainstorming from scratch, are we? You've given this some serious thought already."

"So?"

"Spill it!"

"Spill what?" Kevin asked defensively.

Troy threw his right arm around his friend's unsuspecting

neck and positioned his left hand for a torturous head-rub. "Don't make me do it, Kevin. You know I will."

"All right! All right!" Kevin pleaded while trying to rescue his face from an armpit moist with August heat. "Man alive, Troy!" Kevin used his shirt to wipe the stink from his face. "Ever hear of Speed Stick?"

"Spill it," Troy said calmly after releasing his victim.

"I think Franklin plans to give me a platform to present the Bright Spots policies."

"Anderson said that?"

"No. But I can read between the lines."

"Wow," Troy heard himself utter. "What kind of platform?"

"Who knows? But whatever it is, we'll need an organization that has my back. At this moment all we have is a bunch of spreadsheets showing bright spot communities have more kids and fewer transitions. We need more. We need to show how these communities make those trends easier and more likely. And most importantly, we need to find out what can be done to replicate those patterns in other regions."

The conversation reminded Troy of what he loved most about spending time with Kevin Tolbert. His friend's contagious enthusiasm had managed to find a silver lining despite very bad news. He smiled, reminiscing about times spent together finding turnaround potential in a failing business, selling investors on a plan neither fully knew could work, and garnering support for a congressional campaign both considered a long shot. He missed these moments feeding one another's creative juices and fanning the flame of a shared dream.

Despite the excitement of the present dream, however, Troy knew that it would be tough to turn it into reality while TS Enterprises remained short on cash.

Against every instinct within him, Troy forced himself to toss the wet blanket. "I gotta be honest, Kevin. I'm not sure we'll be able to bankroll this one. That's one of the things we need to discuss. I'm coming up short on investors for the Westar deal."

"What about Peak Capital? Didn't you meet with Wilkie?"

"He said he'll present it to the board."

"In other words, not a chance."

Troy's nod confirmed Kevin's conclusion. "All of our usual sources came up short. I don't know how we're gonna fund the Westar project, let alone pursue a whole new venture. Especially something as big as this."

They slowed their pace from blue-sky dreaming to rainy-day prudence.

"I'm sorry, Kevin."

As they eased toward the house, Troy felt a familiar squeeze on his shoulder. He tilted his eyes down toward his friend's earnest gaze.

"So, what do you say?" Kevin asked.

Troy knew what it meant. He had seen the same look of dogged determination on countless other occasions. *Damn the torpedoes, full speed ahead!* Kevin Tolbert would find a way to make the Center for Economic Health a reality. And when he did, the organization would need a leader, someone who could be trusted to implement Kevin's vision, someone who knew how to clarify and organize, but who also had the political instincts to smell the smoke of trouble long before it burst into flames of destruction. Someone who would rather die than disappoint or betray his best friend.

A few hours earlier a bewildered Tommy Tolbert had stood beside a mound of unassembled Legos. Now a second Tolbert genius needed Uncle Troy's help. A lot.

CHAPTER TWENTY

Julia's eyes landed on two passing images, as if a spotlight had selected each from the faceless herd of travelers rushing across her path. Troy had suggested she wait with the carry-on bags while he spoke to the airline boarding agent, the perfect occasion for a bit of people watching. Both scenes conspired to answer an unspoken question her day with Angie had posed.

The first spotlight framed a gentleman talking to no one, or rather someone out of sight, apparently using one of the new phone implants popular with techies. But he didn't look like a techie. He was strikingly handsome. A rugged shadow on his face suggested he had risen early, possibly for a power breakfast with a congressman or foreign ambassador. He wore a dark-gray suit, a deep-blue tie, and a casual grin that suggested an intimate chat rather than any kind of official conversation. *Of course*, she thought. *His office would be closed at this hour.*

Julia mentally filled in details. He was talking to a beautiful wife or partner back home in—what city? Phoenix. The man's smile was in reaction to a playful flirt from the woman he loved.

Both anticipated a passionate reunion after their long week apart.

Before she could complete the script, however, Julia noticed a different sort of smile as the man's eyes followed a passing woman clearly dressed to attract attention from the opposite sex. Not a quick, discreet glance. A long, hungry gaze that began the second he caught her approaching wink. It continued until she sashayed around a corner that took her beyond his line of vision. He stopped his advance, checked the time, then hastily wrapped up the phone conversation. He turned to follow the woman's path, presumably in pursuit of contact information for a possible rendezvous during his next trip.

Julia wondered if her husband had ever ogled other women while talking to her on the phone. She scowled at the man's back as the spotlight moved her eyes toward a second scene.

A heavyset woman, perhaps in her mid-forties. Too wide to be called glamorous, but pretty in the face. She shifted a purse from one shoulder to the other. That's when it became clear that she wasn't overweight, but pregnant. Julia guessed seven or eight months along. Seconds later the woman vanished from sight, slipping into the unisex restroom facilities after nearly colliding with a man rushing out the same door.

Julia again imagined the details. The woman appeared exhausted from a business trip that would have been much less taxing when she was young and skinny. Did she have a husband, like Troy, eager to become a dad? Or had she swallowed the same myth Julia had once advanced in her weekly columns? *Better to go it alone to defy outdated social constructs.*

She thought of Angie while sighing at her former folly. Of course things worked better when a man and woman partnered to raise kids. She thought of Kevin's Bright Spots presentation. Married couples with kids, for whatever reason, were much more likely to thrive than solo women. Even those bravely bearing kids without a partner ended up dependent upon someone, usually parents or the government. Or a sibling, like her own sister Maria who would have never made it without Julia's help during Jared's early years.

Julia scanned heads in a crowded line to find Troy standing at the counter. He appeared to be wearing down the defenses of an overworked agent. Then she looked back toward the restroom door. The pregnant woman exited, then checked her tablet for some urgent detail. Gate change information, Julia guessed. The woman shifted the weight of her purse from the side of a protruding belly.

Julia thought of what that belly meant for a woman midway between forty and fifty. Her child would get its driver's license when Mom turned sixty. If the baby was a girl who followed in her mother's footsteps she would have her own child in four decades, making the woman a grandmother at the age of eighty. Unless, of course, Grandma had already passed away or volunteered.

Julia felt her own tummy. Flat. Firm. Lifeless.

She noticed Troy walking in her direction. He winked at Julia, eyes so fixed on his bride that he failed to notice a passing miniskirt.

"I did it!" he announced triumphantly.

She smiled. "Did what?"

"I got us upgraded to first class."

"Nice."

"Only the best for my gal."

The achievement had augmented her husband's already excellent mood. The time spent with Kevin had lifted his spirits, as Julia had hoped.

She couldn't wait to cap off his day with the news now forming in her heart.

Thirty minutes later the flight attendant refilled Troy's glass while Julia pretended to read a novel. Despite a Pulitzer-winning journalism career, she found herself losing a battle to find the right words for such a big moment.

Are you ready to become a father? Not quite right. He'd always been ready.

I think it's time we moved toward parenthood. Way too prim. Besides, you didn't "move toward parenthood." You got pregnant.

Let's make a baby! Fun, but too abrupt.

"You OK?" Troy asked after sipping his soda. His voice betrayed concern.

She looked up casually from her tablet. "Fine," she said, reaching toward his torso and offering a slight squeeze. "Why do you ask?"

"You've been staring at the same page for about ten minutes."

She blushed. Time to fess up. "Yeah. I'm not all that interested in the story."

"And?" he pressed.

"And I've got a lot on my mind."

He shifted his weight to face her.

"I've been thinking about last night," she began. "I'm really sorry for shutting you down so quickly. You know, about having a baby."

"Me too," he said eagerly. "I shouldn't have pushed like that. Will you forgive me?"

She nodded silently, not sure whether she felt relief or disappointment.

"You're right," he continued. "We should wait a little longer."

"But I thought you wanted—"

"I did," he interrupted. "I do. But there's no need to rush. We have time."

He offered a supportive smile to seal a decision made on her behalf: another heroic gesture by the noble Troy Simmons.

Julia opened her mouth, but no words came.

"Which leads to the other thing I wanted to tell you." He looked like a boy eager to tell his mommy he had made a touchdown.

She felt a vague dismay, as if something important was rushing past them too quickly. She leaned forward to sort through feelings she had not known possible. Not for her, anyway. Her mind screamed words she had never spoken. Could never speak.

I want us to have a child.

Let's make love tonight, as soon as we get home.

No more caution.

Just spontaneous, abandoned love!

"Julia," his voice interrupted, "did you hear me?"

"Sorry," she returned. "Yes. You said Kevin needs something."

"He needs our help."

"Help with what?" she asked without interest.

"Things are moving fast with the Bright Spots proposal. It looks like Franklin wants to include it as a major emphasis during his campaign. Figures it will help him with a growing segment of the population."

She forced her full attention back into the conversation. "To raise money?" she asked.

"And votes. But yes, his campaign needs to raise money. I think he's struggling in dark zone regions where the austerity cuts hurt most. He needs bright spot support if he hopes to win."

She reached for her glass and sorted her thoughts while sipping cherry Fresca.

"Do you really think he'll back away from the Youth Initiative?"

"No, I don't. He'll speak out of both sides of his mouth, saying he wants to expand the economic potential of bright spots while continuing to glean the savings transitions generate."

"How does Kevin feel about that?"

"Same as me. He hates it." Troy borrowed Julia's tablet and began tapping the screen. "But we think it creates a window of opportunity."

"What are you looking for?" Julia asked.

"Here it is." He shifted the screen in her direction. "Kevin and I spent the afternoon outlining the framework for an organization he wants to launch called the Center for Economic Health." He gestured for her to read his draft document.

"You talked about a new project?" she said without noticing the words. "What about getting you some help with the business you already run?"

"If we don't help turn things around our business will sink along with the rest of the economy." He said it as if he was quoting Kevin. "Anyway, take a look."

She read the screen displaying a classic Troy Simmons template summarizing an organizational mission, strategy, and high-level budget.

"What does this mean?" She pointed to the fifth item listed under the Strategy section.

TELL THE STORIES (Julia via RAP Syndicate)

"It's one of the things I wanted to talk to you about," he replied. "The most powerful weapon in the battle for public opinion will be the media. And we don't have a prayer of getting a fair shake with any of the syndicates."

She knew what he would say next. Julia's journalistic star had been rising ever since the *Breeders* feature nearly destroyed Kevin Tolbert's reputation.

"You can't be serious," she protested. "You actually think RAP

Syndicate will let me advance the Bright Spots agenda? The current editorial board would kill any attempt to—"

"They would kill any attempt by the average journalist," he interrupted. "But there's a certain managing editor who might be open to a series of stories from a former columnist who resigned on his watch."

"Paul Daugherty?" she nearly shouted, then softened her voice to a vicious whisper. "Give me a break! I have no intention of asking Paul Daugherty for any favors. The man can't be trusted."

"No, he can't. But he owes you big. And he happens to work for the second-largest media empire in the nation."

"In case you've forgotten, I quit my job with RAP last fall. I haven't spoken to Paul in nearly a year. And I don't intend to talk to him for at least a few more decades!"

Troy held his tongue to let Julia's simmer cool.

"Listen, babe, you're one of the most widely read feature writers in journalism." Troy began stroking Julia's arm as if to caress away her tension. "Imagine the impact if RAP ran a series of features that put human faces on bright spot trends."

"But they won't. I know these people, Troy. They have editorial directives a hundred-eighty degrees opposite of Kevin's agenda."

"And the last feature you did for them hit very, very big," he reminded her. "I'm sure they'd love to snag a series with the famous Julia Davidson."

"Julia Simmons!"

"Not to them. They don't know or care that you're sleeping with the enemy."

He was right. Media syndicates didn't like it when a writer with a huge following suddenly started working for the competition. And since Julia remained an independent journalist, she could accept contracts from anyone.

"What would I say to Paul? 'Remember me? I'm the gal who

knows you stole my work on the *Breeders* feature to violate every rule of journalistic integrity. I don't trust you any farther than I could throw you. Wanna hire me back?'"

Troy smiled wryly. "Actually, yes."

She flashed a puzzled look.

"Think about it, babe," he continued. "Daugherty knows one word from you could end his career."

She didn't argue.

"And landing a series with you would be a feather in his cap."

It was true.

"But even Paul can't override the editorial board," she said. "The new owners of RAP Media are even less breeder-friendly than when I was on payroll, in part thanks to my feature."

"Which can serve our purpose. Imagine approaching Paul Daugherty with a series that explores the tension between economically disadvantaged neighborhoods and neighborhoods on the rise."

"Go on." She felt her creative juices begin to flow.

"The features could tell human interest stories highlighting the downward spiral of dark zone choices and the upward momentum of bright spots."

"I guess that could work," she confessed flatly.

"Not to mention leveraging your influence to sway public opinion on Kevin's proposal. All while maintaining the highest journalistic ideals."

"By implicitly blackmailing the editor?"

He laughed. "No. By presenting the reality of both sides. Communities with fewer kids and more transitions are in decline. That's a fact. Communities with higher fertility and lower transition rates are doing relatively well. A good journalist will put a face on both realities."

He leaned in to give her a peck on the forehead. "And you, Julia Simmons, are a very good journalist."

As Troy pulled back from the kiss Julia breathed the echo of his scent. Despite the two hours before they would arrive in Denver, the aroma made her feel at home.

"What do you say, babe?" he asked. "It *is* a key bullet on my strategy outline."

They shared a smile as Julia looked deeply into her husband's eyes. She thought of the man in the airport who pretended fidelity while chasing skirts. Troy would never do the same. She hoped it. She knew it.

She remembered another airport spotlight cast on a pregnant woman only five or ten years older than Julia. Had that woman's partner also agreed they had plenty of time, that they shouldn't rush into parenthood? Would accepting this assignment be the first of many postponements that might put Julia in the same boat a decade hence?

"You really think it would help?" she asked apprehensively.

"I do," Troy assured her. "And so does Kevin."

A fitting penance, she thought while pulling his hand toward hers to intertwine fingers. A tender squeeze gave the answer he wanted.

"Thanks, babe," he said, kissing her palm.

Julia reached for her glass and lifted it slowly to her lips. She didn't sip, distracted by the gentle, lingering presence of Troy's forearm on her abdomen. Flat. Firm. And lifeless.

CHAPTER TWENTY-ONE

Matthew spun the cap back onto a newly opened bottle of mouthwash while swishing the sting from cheek to cheek. He counted seconds toward the recommended sixty, but gave up at the halfway point. "Blah," he complained, spewing the clear liquid into the sink, wishing he had bought the mild, minty variety. But today was too important to take any chances. The stronger the better.

He ran a still-tingling tongue across his teeth while admiring the man staring back from the bathroom mirror.

Trimmed hair? *Check*.

Clean shave? *Check*.

Ironed shirt? *Check*.

Fresh cologne? *Check*.

Fresh breath? *Double check*!

Matthew wondered whether Maria Davidson was standing in front of her own bathroom mirror nervously anticipating their reunion. *Unlikely*, he guessed. She had probably suggested ten o'clock coffee because she could squeeze in a quick, cordial hello and be done with it. Maria had always been kind, even to the unpopular boys. Today's meeting was, for him, a shot at happiness. For her, he feared it was an act of charity.

He felt the abrupt jolt of three firm raps on the door.

"Matthew?" The slightly muffled voice sounded young and familiar. Isabelle?

"It's Mr. Adams!" came the faint sound of Marissa Gale correcting her daughter.

Matthew pulled the door open. He was greeted by two six-year-old faces, the first smiling boldly and the second dodging the scene.

"Hello there, Miss Gale," Matthew said.

She giggled while extending her hand for a proper greeting. "Hello, Mr. Adams. I told Peter you were probably in the bathroom."

"Hi, buddy," Matthew said to the pair of eyes peering around a protective corner. The boy then darted across the hall toward Reverend Grandpa's bedroom. The door quickly opened and closed to swallow his escape.

"My mother asked us to let you know we're here," Isabelle explained. "She said to say sorry for being late."

"Did she?"

"Yeah. It was Peter's fault."

"Isabelle," came another distant correction.

"OK. It was my fault too. We were playing Battleship and I only had one more ship to sink."

"I can understand that," Matthew said, glancing at the time. Thirteen past nine. "No worries. I wasn't going to leave for another few minutes anyway."

Isabelle surprised Matthew by grabbing his hand and leading him into the kitchen, where Marissa was unloading the dishwasher.

"You don't need to do that," Matthew protested. "I was going to—"

"Don't be silly," Marissa interrupted him. "From the looks of the place you've been keeping busy enough. This is your day off. Go and enjoy yourself. You deserve it."

She seemed overly grateful.

"You don't mind?" he asked, still feeling bad about requesting time off so soon after accepting the job.

"Are you kidding?" she said. "I half expected your message to say you wanted to quit. Wouldn't surprise me after two full days with Dad." She laughed nervously.

A brief silence.

"You won't, will you?" she asked timidly.

"Won't what?"

"Quit." She seemed a bit pale. "I mean, you'll give me a chance to find someone else if he gets to be too much to handle, right?"

He recognized the anxiety in Marissa's eyes. Matthew had felt it often the year his own mother crossed a fuzzy line from parent to dependent. He recalled a vague, persistent panic over a reality he hadn't been ready to accept.

She's getting worse, not better.

How much of my life will her illness put on hold? And what will it cost?

I'm not so sure I'm cut out for this.

Is anyone?

"Don't worry about it," Matthew reassured her. "Your dad's not so bad."

Marissa seemed relieved by the upbeat evaluation, honest or not.

"I think he might be a bit depressed, though," Matthew continued. "Stays in his room most of the time. I only see him when he rings the bell to let me know he needs help."

"Does he?" she asked.

"Ring the bell?"

"Yes. I mean, no. I mean, does he need very much help?"

"Only a few times a day. Otherwise I just bring his food and change his oxygen tank when it gets low. You know, like you showed me."

She nodded distantly.

"I mainly help him maneuver his legs when he wants to use the walker to get to the bathroom. He doesn't let me go in with him, so I assume he does fine on that front."

Marissa seemed reassured. "Good."

A brief pause.

"Good," she said again. "Well, I appreciate all you've done."

"Don't mention it," he said, feeling his empty pockets. "Oops. Forgot my tablet." He took a step toward the doorway. But he noticed Marissa positioning herself on the kitchen counter stool looking intent, as if she wanted to say more.

He waited. "Everything OK?" he asked.

She nibbled one side of her lower lip. "Fine. I'm fine."

"You sure?"

"It's nothing. I don't want to make you late."

The comment reminded him of the time. "OK," he said, starting toward the bedroom.

"It's just," she began, pausing his advance. "I worry. I wonder how long this is going to work. You know, a live-in arrangement."

The comment unsettled Matthew. He had just moved in. Just started this job.

"I know you don't mind him right now," she said. "But it's still the honeymoon period."

Matthew failed to connect any dots between the prior seventy-two hours and his images of a honeymoon.

"He always behaves at first. Even seems docile. He creates a false sense of security. Then, out of the blue, he goes in for the kill."

"The kill?" Matthew repeated nervously.

Marissa chuckled at Matthew's expression. "Sorry, bad choice of words. I mean he climbs onto his religious high horse. He'll start preaching at you soon. If he hasn't already."

Matthew shook his head. "Nothing yet. But I wouldn't sweat that. I'm kind of a spiritually oriented person myself. I've taken a few religion classes and plan to take more when I get back to school. Who knows, we might hit it off on that front."

"I doubt it." Marissa placed both hands, palms open, onto the counter. "But we can hope," she said in rebuke of her own pessimism.

Matthew sensed something else might be bothering Marissa. He waited a moment longer. Nothing came. "OK, then. I'll just go grab my tablet."

He moved swiftly down the hallway toward his open bedroom door, passing Isabelle en route. Her eyes were glued to some educational television program.

He searched the usual places, dresser top and side table. Nothing. Then he remembered. Reverend Grandpa had asked to borrow his screen to read the day's news.

While approaching the main bedroom Matthew heard a child's voice. *Peter?* He waited before knocking, pressing one ear against the closed door.

"And then the lady gave me this!" the boy said in a hushed tone, presumably raising some mysterious prize.

Isabelle was wrong. It seemed Peter could speak after all.

"My goodness!" came Reverend Grandpa's enthused voice. "Let me take a look at that."

Momentary silence.

"Looks like the genuine article," the old man continued. "Twenty dollars is a boatload of dough. What are you gonna do with it?"

"Hide it with the rest," Peter whispered. "I'm not telling

Mommy about it. She said we're running out of money. But she doesn't know about my secret supply."

Matthew heard subdued laughter, an intimate moment between conspiratorial masterminds. He pulled his ear away from the door and positioned his knuckles to knock, an intention halted when he heard Peter continue.

"I don't want you to go away, Reverend Grandpa. I want you to live at our house."

A brief gasp suggested the old man had been caught by surprise.

"Don't worry, Pete," Reverend Grandpa forced out after a hard swallow. "Your mommy and I discussed the money already. I'm gonna live right here, real close, for at least six months."

Six months? Is that what Marissa hadn't been able to say? The job ended in six months?

"Why not longer?" Peter was asking. "Why not always?"

"It's difficult to explain," the elder admitted. "But like I said, don't you worry about that right now. I need to stick around long enough to train my favorite apprentice, don't I?"

Another silence. Peter nodding?

"You still plan to take my place in the pulpit, don't you, buddy?"

Matthew chuckled at the thought of a boy who never spoke becoming a preacher. Or rather, a boy who spoke only to his grandfather.

Three gentle knocks on the door silenced the conversation within.

"What do you want?" came an unwelcoming bark.

Matthew hesitantly pushed the door open. "Excuse me Hugh…er…I mean, Reverend. Do you still have my tablet?"

"On the bed," came the terse reply, the old man's index finger pointing.

The smaller mastermind was crouched near the bedpost,

glowering with a look of disgust. Highly classified conversations should not be interrupted by such small concerns.

"Thanks," Matthew said apologetically, scooting out of the room.

He closed the door, then paused to listen. He smiled, anticipating more clandestine scheming. Then he remembered the time. Less than thirty minutes before his rendezvous with Maria Davidson. And nothing, not wild horses or the top-secret chatter of a mute child, could make him late.

CHAPTER TWENTY-TWO

She looked incredible.

Matthew had pulled into the parking lot a few minutes early, so he should have been the one sitting at a table watching for a semi-familiar face. But he instead parked his car twenty yards from the entry and slumped down in the seat to peer over the steering column until he spotted his, what? Date? Not really. Maria had only agreed to catch up with a guy from high school whom she would have described as an old acquaintance at best.

But she agreed to meet, he reassured himself. *And she actually came. So far, so good.*

He drank in one last look before approaching the entrance. She probably hadn't noticed his gaze, his face obscured by the words *Enchanted Coffee* stenciled on the glass. Maria only looked up from her tablet whenever the stir of the opening door prompted a brief glance. No extending neck. No hope-filled eyes. No pumping her ankle like a woman wondering if that special someone will arrive. Maria Davidson was, unlike Matthew, at ease.

Why wouldn't she be? The years had been very kind. Her face retained the frisky allure that had ensnared every fifteen-year-old boy during ninth grade. She wore a white sleeveless blouse and mid-length blue skirt that lay gently over her crossed legs. The tip of her foot peered out from the thin cotton edge as if offering his eyes the tiniest hint of those familiar, feminine limbs. Matthew had been admiring Maria's playfully provocative pictures for years, her online images searing themselves into his imagination. But now, moments away from their first real encounter since high school graduation, all he could think about was the trickle of nervous perspiration threatening to stain his new shirt.

Get out of the heat, you idiot, he chided himself. *Just go in and say hello.*

So he did.

"Maria?" he said, pretending only vague recognition.

After a slight hesitation she lifted an eyebrow of recognition, then stood to offer a cordial embrace. "Matt Adams," she said with a perky voice that matched the fragrance of her perfume. "How've you been?"

How to answer? *I'm flat broke. My mom's dead. And I quit college to take a job changing an old debit's oxygen. You?*

"Never better," he lied. "Let me take a look at you."

She turned to her side and lifted one leg while touching an index finger to her cheek like Betty Boop. He laughed at the same pose she'd used to flirt with boys back in high school. This was the first time the gesture had been intended for him.

"You look wonderful."

"You too," she said, reaching toward his neck.

He felt a flush of embarrassment as he realized she was fixing his right collar. "Thanks," he said sheepishly.

"Same old Matthew." She smiled while patting his shoulder like a puppy's head.

His heart sank. The last thing Matthew wanted was for Maria

to recall the awkward boy who'd had no business inviting her to the senior prom. He wanted her to see him as a new man. A successful man. Possibly even an attractive man.

"Can I get you something?" she asked, beating him to the punch.

"My treat," he insisted.

"OK, Mr. Big Spender!" she teased.

It took him a moment to react, wondering whether to make light or take offense. Her good-natured pat on his chest told him to play along.

"You know it," he chuckled. "Just got a bump in my allowance!"

She offered a polite but seemingly sincere laugh that boosted his confidence.

"I might even let you order a large," he said with a wink.

They spent the next few minutes dancing between questions about their ancient past and the sexually charged teasing they had started online. But much of it felt forced and out of place. That's when she eased the conversation toward Matthew's recent history.

"What sort of business are you in?"

He felt an immediate panic. He hadn't practiced how to answer questions about the supposed business that had brought him into town. He tried forcing his mind to offer options, but it refused to cooperate.

"You first," he said with relief. "Tell me what you do."

She appeared embarrassed by the question.

"I'm sorry," he added quickly. "I shouldn't make assumptions in this economy. So many people out of work."

"No, it's fine. I have a job, most days anyway."

He waited.

"Guess," Maria said with a gleam. "What do you think I do? No. Wait. What do you think I *should* do? That's more fun."

Matthew hesitated. Then he grinned. "Is this a game?"

A mischievous smile.

"OK," he began. "What should a woman with your charm and beauty do for a living?"

The mug paused in front of her lips as if she anticipated playful flirting or the perfect compliment.

He felt another panic. What did she hope to hear? Should he say something naughty, like lingerie model, or flattering, like teacher?

"A truck driver?" He chose funny.

Maria slapped his leg playfully.

"No?" he continued. "OK, give me another shot."

She lifted the mug back to her lips before lowering it again. "I style and color hair."

It fit. "Really?"

She nodded timidly.

"I bet you're really good at it," he said, refilling her sail with air.

"I am, actually," she confirmed. "But I'm looking for something better."

"Why?" he asked. "I mean, don't you like what you do?"

She seemed pleased by the question. "I do, actually. But unemployed people don't spend money on beauty. And those who do don't tip like they did before the crash."

Matthew understood. He had noticed a gradual shift in the appearance of middle-aged women, those who would have been salon regulars in better days.

A brief hush reminded Matthew that he still needed to answer Maria's question. He felt a bit less anxious knowing she had been self-conscious about her own career. Might he risk telling the truth?

"My turn," she said, filling the silence.

"OK," he said eagerly, realizing she intended to make the quiz multiple-choice. "What do you think I do?"

She uncrossed her legs and scooted to the edge of her chair. She began peering deeply into his face like a movie director deciding which angle to use for his close-up shot. Matthew waited as she pretended to gather clues from his blank stare.

"I've got it," she finally announced.

"Oh really," he said skeptically. "Just like that?"

"You're in the pharmaceutical industry."

He liked the option. He had managed so many of his mom's prescriptions that he could probably bluff without too much trouble.

"Close," he said. "But not quite."

She offered an irresistible but fleeting pout. "Don't tell me," she said, placing her index finger over his lips, her face contorted in concentration. "You drive a truck for a pharmaceutical company."

She laughed at her own effort to even the score, then pulled away from Matthew's finger as he tried to poke his revenge.

Another quiet moment as he thought about how much more impressive driving a truck would be than his real job.

"I don't want to bore you with the details"—a picture of Reverend Grandpa's wheelchair and oxygen tank invaded Matthew's mind—"but I work with medical equipment."

"Oh," she said with a hint of surprise.

He recalled the leg braces. "Mostly new mobility technologies."

He sensed intimidation in her rising brow.

"Sounds more impressive than it is, actually," he added. "But it pays the bills."

To his relief, she didn't ask any specific questions about his alleged field, allowing Matthew to imply and evade rather than outright lie. By the time he managed to change the subject Maria probably imagined him as a modestly successful businessman making a profit selling his wares to hospitals and senior-care facilities. Good enough, he thought.

Matthew noticed the sound of smooth jazz above the silence as they sipped their drinks.

"I guess Julia does pretty well," he said to keep the conversation alive. "I've read a few of her columns. My favorite is the one called *Free to Thrive.*"

She nodded evasively. Was she trying to recall the specific column or ignore her big sister's ubiquitous presence? It must be odd for a hairstylist, living in the shadow of her sister's journalism career. He quickly tried to think of another subject.

Maria did it for him. "This is my son Jared," she said, sliding a small tablet toward Matthew's side of the table.

"Wow," he said with genuine surprise. "I didn't know you had a kid."

She had never mentioned a child in any of her online posts. But then, why would she? Secret admirers want airbrushed girls, not diaper-changing moms.

Matthew recalled a column written by Maria's sister that seemed down on kids, so he'd assumed Maria felt the same. Apparently he'd assumed wrong.

"Looks like a great kid," he said. The look on Maria's face told Matthew this was the moment when other men had backed away. He shifted his eyes toward the boy's face. "How old?"

"Twelve, going on twenty," she said with a concise laugh.

He wondered about the rest of the story. The father? The circumstances? He decided not to pry.

"Would you like to meet him?"

"Really?" he erupted, realizing she had just said yes to a second date.

"Sure. If you want."

"I'd love to," he said in stunned delight. It had never occurred to Matthew that the Maria Davidson of his fantasy world might have real-world needs. Perhaps she longed for a man who admired her for being a mom. A man who might even like her kid.

She smiled broadly. "Great. When will you be back in town?"

He bobbled the question in his mind. Then he remembered. He had implied he was in town on business. She had no idea that he lived right up the road.

"Actually, I'll be here for a while…" He paused while reaching for more. "I have sort of a big deal in the works that needs a lot of my attention."

"Go big or go home," she said farcically, pretending a masculine voice.

"Excuse me?" he asked with confusion.

"Go big or go home," she repeated. "It's something one of my clients says all the time."

"What's it mean?" he asked.

"I guess it means don't waste time chasing little opportunities," she explained. "I thought of it when you said big deal."

The look in her eyes told Matthew that Maria found the idea of pursuing big deals rather than small matters attractive in a man. Attractive in Matthew. Or rather, in the Matthew he had let form in her mind.

—◊—

Twenty minutes later Matthew sat in his car unable to wipe an ecstatic grin from his face. His reunion with Maria Davidson had gone better than he could have hoped. And a second date was already on the calendar!

"Go big or go home," he repeated to himself, a new life slogan for a new Matthew Adams. Or at least a Matthew determined to become worthy of the kiss Maria had planted on his cheek before they parted.

He touched his fingers to the spot and savored the lingering hint of her perky scent.

"Go big or go home," he whispered while starting the engine. Peering into the rearview mirror he saw his own face frowning back at him.

Who are you kidding? it said accusingly. *You're not going big at all. In fact, you're dithering away time on a small opportunity. Changing oxygen tanks for Reverend Grandpa might earn enough extra to pay down part of your school loan, but it will never position you to seriously impress Maria or any other potential lover.*

Only his inheritance money would do that.

"I will go big!" Matthew shouted at his withering confidence while cutting off the engine. He opened the glove compartment to retrieve a pad of paper and a pen before walking back into the coffee shop. He sat down at the same table he and Maria had just left and began writing a letter.

Dear Judge Santiago:

Greetings once again. I apologize for sending yet another letter. But I have yet to receive any response to my earlier communications. Very important decisions have been placed on hold and I would appreciate input on your opinion in the case involving NEXT Transition Services. I realize you cannot correspond at length, but a simple, anonymous post would be greatly appreciated. I continue to await your response at the following forum address: ANON.CHAT.4398

I hope you will see fit to comply with my request.

Cordially,
A Manichean

Matthew reread the note. It lacked urgency.

Bigger!

He took a second sheet of paper to rewrite the note, this time with a revised ending.

I must insist that you comply with my request to avoid more drastic measures.

Respectfully,
A Manichean

CHAPTER TWENTY-THREE

Tyler plopped himself on a rotting park bench, tearing open the paper sack overflowing with fat and flavor: two bacon double cheeseburgers, extra mayo, large cheese fries, and a chocolate shake. Inhaling the lovely smell he realized he risked contaminating his clothes with an aroma that would sicken Renee. But he couldn't last another day without eating something that could make him smile.

A robin landed, curious enough to hop within a few feet before giving up and flying off. It was peaceful here. A great place to get things done. The rusting play structure had long been abandoned, the neighborhood possessed by those beyond childrearing years or those lacking any desire for the task. Vacant swings served as little more than a reminder of a quainter time when young mothers would bring their even younger children to play. Women who worked hard at pretending to enjoy themselves. At least, that's how Tyler had perceived it. He couldn't imagine his own mother actually enjoying places like this. Duty, that's what it was, not pleasure.

So why on earth Renee still hoped to have a kid escaped him. Worried him.

Tyler dug a floppy fry from the bag, shoved it into his mouth, then pulled out his tablet with his other, non-greasy hand. A small icon strobed subtly to indicate a new message. Julia Simmons. At first he couldn't place the name, then remembered—he had tried to contact the journalist who'd written the feature about Jeremy Santos. Tyler tapped to open the message full-screen.

Dear Mr. Cain:

I'm not sure if I'll be able to help you beyond what I wrote in the article. But I'd be happy to meet now that I'm back in town. Late Monday or early Tuesday, perhaps? Send me a few time options.

Regards,
Julia Davidson Simmons

He sent back a quick reply suggesting late afternoon.

The pounding of a man's running shoes approached. Tyler glanced up in time to see an elderly but fit jogger frown self-righteously at Tyler's half-eaten burger. The man passed by down the sidewalk.

"Yeah, well...which one of us is happier?" Tyler called out smugly...after the man was out of earshot, of course. Then he remembered, he was only here eating this sack of junk food to escape his live-in girlfriend and her parents. Not exactly the poster child for happiness.

Just then his tablet flashed and began to beep. He tapped his earpiece. "Tyler Cain," he slurred through a mouthful of burger.

"Mr. Cain?" the voice of Jennifer McKay said hesitantly.

Tyler forced a hard swallow and wiped his face. "Ms. McKay! I was just thinking about you."

"Why do I seriously doubt that?"

"Thinking about your case, I mean. I have a few leads, and so—"

"Mr. Cain. We have a problem. Can we meet?"

"Problem? What kind of a problem?"

"We received another letter. Hand-delivered to the security guard late yesterday, and...well. This one seems like an overt threat."

"Can you forward me a copy? I can take a look."

"No," Jennifer said firmly. "Once you go digital, you lose control. If this information gets in the wrong hands...well, we just can't chance it."

Tyler resented the thought of an unnecessary drive downtown. He could work the case just as easily from where he was with the tap of a SEND button. Jennifer McKay was being much too uptight about the whole thing.

He reminded himself that another meeting would translate into more billable hours.

"OK. Where should we meet?" He hoped it could be someplace far less...antiseptic...than before.

At least Tyler managed to finish his second burger, the fries, and the shake on his drive back to the Tenth District Federal Courthouse.

———

Jennifer's desk looked even more expansive now that Tyler's home desk sat nestled into a cramped corner. He slid his hand enviously across its surface, then noticed his own greasy fingerprint trail. He immediately wiped it away with his sleeve, an instinctive reaction against leaving Renee any potential "evidence."

"You mentioned having some leads," Jennifer said, turning

away from him to locate the most recent letter from the bottom filing cabinet drawer.

She stood upright, spun abruptly, and handed him the letter. He scanned it quickly. On the surface it wasn't much different from the others. Same signature. Same request for the judge to post an anonymous reply. But this one, unlike the three prior, had a greater sense of urgency. And the final line about "more drastic measures" caused concern.

Something has changed, thought Tyler. Whoever was writing these letters was becoming impatient to know the judge's decision. But who, he wondered, would benefit from a decision against NEXT besides Jeremy Santos?

"You're right," he said in Jennifer's direction. "This is a problem."

She sat down. "What do you think he means by drastic measures?"

"No idea. But it concerns me."

Tyler glanced around the office to find signs of adequate security. There was the check at the building entrance, of course. But after that, what would stop some crazy person like Mr. or Ms. Manichean from coming in here and creating a scene...or worse?

Jennifer apparently followed his gaze as it drifted to Santiago's office. "His office is locked at all times, even when we're working. Only he and I can get in during regular business hours."

"What about after?"

Jennifer frowned. "Mr. Cain, I can assure you Judge Santiago is in good hands here. There hasn't been a single violent incident in this building in over twenty-five years. I need you to focus on finding the person writing these letters. Let our security team handle things at the office."

"But I think—"

"We hired you to be a private detective," she said abruptly, "nothing more."

Tyler recalled Smitty's comment about being the right person for this job. He shoved the thought aside. "Ms. McKay, I need to be blunt. I get the distinct feeling you're more concerned with protecting yourself than protecting the judge."

"What?" The word erupted from Jennifer's lips, her gaze piercing. "Protecting myself? How dare you suggest that I..."

She paused to regain composure while lowering herself back into her seat, her manicured nails pressing firmly into the surface of the desk. "I would like an apology for that, Mr. Cain."

Tyler shrugged, trying to see how far she might go. "I just call it like I see it, is all."

"Really?" she answered, her eyes pinched into a condescending glare.

"Yes. Really. Listen, I don't get paid to be nice."

"You won't get paid at all if—"

"If what? You hired me to protect the judge."

"No. I hired you to look into these letters and find out who sent them."

Tyler decided to call her bluff. "Is there a difference?"

He let the question settle, then added another dig.

"You seem too afraid of losing your own job to look out for the judge's best interest."

She glared back, her arms crossed defensively. "The judge's best interest?" she began. "You have no idea what you're talking about, Mr. Cain. This is a federal appeals court, not a traffic court. Major issues are decided in this building. And Judge Santiago plays a very important part in that process."

"Why can't he let another judge handle this one?"

She rolled her eyes as if the question revealed inexcusable ignorance.

"This isn't like popping into a local magistrate's office and requesting a search warrant," Jennifer said derisively. "Let me educate you, Mr. Cain."

Tyler held his tongue. He knew next to nothing about federal appeals. But he was loath to let it show.

"There are three judges who render opinions in this court," she continued. "In this case, one of the three leans left, the other right. That leaves Judge Santiago as the only judge really open to the merits of both sides. So his is the opinion that truly matters. It also means there's no way on earth he'll ever allow anyone to influence his decision. He has asked me to shield him from that. So, yes, that is my job, if we're talking about jobs. And Judge Santiago is well aware of the risks. But he trusts me. And I admire his integrity, a rare quality in this day and age. Frankly, I'll do anything to make sure I don't let him down."

"Even if it gets him killed?"

A look of dread replaced the air of superiority on Jennifer's face. "Killed? Do you really think it could come to that?"

"I don't know what it could come to, Ms. McKay. But as a precaution—"

"Precaution is what we're paying you for," she snapped angrily, as if trying to balance her earlier show of fear. "Just find out who is sending these letters, and make sure they stop. Can you do that?"

He hesitated, looking toward the window to consider options. Part of him wanted to walk away from the whole mess. He was getting too old for lectures from self-important assistants, even ones as attractive as Jennifer McKay. But he also knew blowing this case was not an option. He might never get another lead from Smitty or anyone else on the force. Swallowing his pride in this instance might just get him back in the game. Besides, it was Santiago's business if he wanted to risk his life for some higher good.

He turned back toward Jennifer, who seemed to have softened.

"Listen," she said conciliatorily. "I wasn't going to tell you this so soon..."

"Tell me what?" he asked, upset that something had been withheld.

"That I'm authorized to pay beyond your daily rate on this case."

Tyler's head jerked toward her with a start.

"I can offer you a bonus of thirty thousand if you actually find the culprit."

Tyler tried to suppress a stunned reaction. A grin on Jennifer's face told him he'd failed. Thirty thousand dollars was more than enough to pay off the loan cosigned by Renee. With this one case he'd be able to return to bachelorhood a year and a half earlier than he had hoped.

Jennifer's smile grew. "Who's concerned more about his job now, Mr. Cain?"

He beamed in her direction, abandoning any pretense of indifference.

She stood and held out her hand. They shook.

Control had shifted unmistakably back into the hands of Jennifer McKay.

"Excellent," she said. "I look forward to a quick and tidy conclusion to this mess. I have the utmost confidence in you."

She's good, Tyler thought. *Very good*.

CHAPTER TWENTY-FOUR

"Mr. Cain?"

The woman extending her hand toward Tyler seemed assertive, like Jennifer McKay, but less forged. Comfortable in her own skin. Little wonder. Julia Davidson was a rare sight. Stunning but effortless beauty. Perfectly styled hair fell mid-length to merge feminine chic with a refined elegance. Her outfit was tasteful, implying rather than flaunting a lovely figure.

"Ms. Davidson," he said, accepting her greeting. Her left hand brushed a black strand from her face to return it to its proper place. That's when he noticed a ring. He remembered she had a new last name he couldn't recall.

"Call me Julia," she insisted.

He matched the offer. "Tyler. Thanks for meeting."

"Not a problem. I only hope I can help."

The hostess escorted them to a table situated next to a large window overlooking an outdoor parking lot. The same lot Renee frequented whenever she shopped at Bulrich's Organic Market.

"Would it be all right if we sat away from the window?" Tyler asked. He didn't need the agitation of defending an innocent lunch with a beautiful woman.

The hostess raised a surprised brow, then moved them to an inferior spot.

They made small talk while perusing menus. He learned about her recent marriage to Troy Simmons, who, it turned out, had spent time in Washington DC working with Congressman Kevin Tolbert. "I voted for Tolbert," Tyler boasted, claiming his share of credit for the newcomer's victory.

"I didn't," Julia said with a laugh. "But his wife and I have been friends since high school."

Tyler gave a curious glance.

"Don't ask," she said preemptively. "Let's just say that if you told me a few years ago I would end up married to a man like Troy Simmons, I would have said you were crazy."

"A hard marriage?" he heard himself ask. The same question he posed to potential clients. "Sorry," he added quickly. "None of my business."

She smiled at his embarrassment. "I guess every marriage is hard sometimes."

Tyler's phone vibrated, a welcome interruption. He glanced at the message.

FROM RENEE: CALL ME RIGHT AWAY

He begged Julia's pardon and tapped the RETURN CALL icon.

"Hi," he said with professional distance. "What's up?"

"'Hi'? 'What's up'?" Renee scolded. "Not 'Hi babe' or 'How are you?'"

"I'm in a meeting."

"Oh, sorry," she replied, a touch of warmth returning to her voice. "My tracker app says you're at Bear Rock Café. I'm just around the corner. I thought we might meet up for lunch. What time will you be done?"

"Can't do it," he said abruptly. *Why not?* "I'm, uh, booked up the rest of the day. I think I found an important lead in the new case."

"The case you won't tell me about?" she asked suspiciously.

He sensed hurt and paranoia overtaking the conversation. "I told you, I can't reveal—"

"I know what you told me," she interrupted. "Not much. That's what you told me. For all I know the case is a cover for a secret rendezvous with another woman."

Was she teasing or accusing? He looked at Julia nervously. Their lunch was completely innocent. It *was* about the case. He wasn't cheating on Renee. Granted, Julia was the kind of sharp, confident woman he found irresistibly attractive. And yes, he had wondered whether a marriage that was "hard sometimes" might mean she was open to advances. But he hadn't done anything wrong.

"Can we discuss this later?" he asked, aware of Julia's failed attempt to ignore the conversation.

"I'd rather not wait…" she said. Then the call ended.

"Renee?" he asked into the phone. No response. Had they lost a signal? Or had she hung up angry? Was she on her way over right now?

"Everything OK?" Julia asked as he returned the device to his pocket.

"Fine. Fine," he said while motioning toward the waitress, who took their orders and retrieved their menus. That's when Tyler got down to business.

"I read your story on the Santos case," he began. "I found it while doing research for a client."

"You mentioned that in your message. May I ask what type of client?"

He hesitated. But she needed the detail. "A federal official." He offered no title or name. But she was smart enough to connect the dots herself. "Confidentially, someone has been writing letters. It appears they're worried about the NEXT appeal decision. Now they're making threats."

"What kind of threats?"

"We can't be certain," he replied. "But I fear the worst."

"I see," she said with alarm. "How can I help?"

"I met with Jeremy Santos the other day," he began. "I figured him to be a prime suspect. You know, eager to get at the money tied up by the appeal."

Julia took a sip of water, her eyes offering a knowing smile. "And?"

"Dead end. That kid's no threat."

She nodded in agreement. "I felt bad for him. Very sad situation."

The sentiment offered a window into a tender side of the hard-hitting journalist. Tyler admired the sweet sympathy in her eyes.

The restaurant door opened. Tyler yanked his gaze away from Julia, expecting to see Renee charging in their direction. To his relief he saw an elderly couple shuffling toward the hostess desk.

"How's he doing?" Julia asked.

"The kid? Oh, he seems to be surviving. Just." He took a sip of water. "Anyway, I was hoping you could suggest other suspects. Did you come across anyone associated with the Santos story eager for NEXT to lose their appeal? Maybe a religious zealot trying to bring down a big transition provider? Or some other family with a wrongful death case waiting in the wings?"

Julia sat back to consider the question. She seemed to reach for details long forgotten. "Holly?" she asked herself. "No, not Holly. Hannah."

"Hannah who?"

"I'll need to find her last name. She's the transition specialist who was injured during the incident."

"I see," he said, jotting down the name while stealing another glance at the door. "Mad about the injury?"

"Not about the injury," Julia explained. "About the industry."

"But you said she works for NEXT."

"*Worked* for NEXT. She quit after the Santos deaths. A month later she contacted Jeremy and encouraged him to sue."

"Really?" Tyler said. "What's her piece of the pie?"

"None. At least that's what she told me."

"Then why tell Jeremy to sue?"

"She said she wanted to see more restrictions placed on the practice because it's easier to schedule a transition than to book a flight."

Tyler recalled the video images he had seen in Jeremy's apartment, including the lifeless stare of Antonio Santos's cold cadaver. He tried to imagine what it must have been like for Hannah or any other person to bear such sights as a routine part of the job.

"She called them sheep," Julia added.

"Called who sheep?"

"Transition volunteers. She said they aren't heroes but sheep going to the slaughter."

"How's that?"

"You should ask her yourself. I can find her contact information if you'd like."

Tyler knew he could just as easily find the information in the case file. But he preferred the opportunity for further correspondence. "That would be helpful. Thank you."

"I didn't get the impression Hannah was the type to do anything violent or rash," Julia added. "But she did mention struggling with depression. You never know."

"Right," Tyler responded.

The door opened again, this time with aggression. Tyler's head jerked. Another false alarm.

"You seem a bit jumpy. Is everything OK?"

"I'm good," he said apologetically, offering no explanation.

The food arrived. Tyler watched Julia as she bit into a potato chip. Not a baked veggie crisp as Renee would have forced him to order, but a greasy one with ruffles. He smiled in her direction. "You like potato chips?"

"Who doesn't?"

The perfect woman, he thought.

They both ate a few mouthfuls while Julia tried to recall other potential suspects. None came to mind.

"That's OK," Tyler said. "Give it more thought over the next few days. I'll start with Hannah. She sounds like a promising lead."

The phone vibrated again. Another call from Renee. The location tracker told him she was not in pursuit, but had driven home, probably in a huff. He ignored the call, then looked back toward his lovely lunch partner.

"So," he said, feeling more at ease. "What are you writing?" He had never really cared about journalism, but Julia seemed a good reason to start.

She swallowed down a bite of chicken salad sandwich. "I just got the green light from RAP for a series of features. Stories about dark zones and bright spots."

"The power grid?"

She laughed. "No. Economic regions. Dark zones follow general trends of financial decline. Bright spots show signs of growth. I plan to paint real-life portraits that embody the larger trends."

Tyler sensed an opportunity. "I don't traffic many light spots."

"Bright spots," she corrected with a charming grin.

"Right. Bright spots. But if dilapidated buildings and crack houses are any indication, I can probably introduce you to a few of my clients living in dark spots."

"Dark zones."

"Right."

"What kind of clients?" she asked.

He had made a misstep. Working with a federal official sounded impressive. Spying on cheating lovers sounded pathetic. Was pathetic.

"I can't reveal specifics for obvious reasons," he recovered, "but I serve a niche in the private investigation field that keeps me in touch with the lower classes."

Julia scrunched her nose at the slight.

"I mean, dark zone residents," he corrected himself.

"Well, I have a few bright spot families lined up already," she said. "They seem open to talking. But I'll have a harder time finding willing victims on the other end of the spectrum."

"Like?"

"Like people living in areas with higher concentrations of transitions."

Surprised, Tyler asked, "Don't you mean lower concentrations of transitions?"

"No, higher."

"But I always thought the point was to transition wealth to younger families."

"So they say." She paused. "Which reminds me. I'll also need households with few or no kids."

"Why's that?"

"Something about the combination of low fertility and high transitions correlates to economic decline."

"Hmm."

"Childless adults who've transitioned their parents would be the ideal interviews. Do you know any?"

Tyler tried reconciling the question with reality. Or, rather, with the reality he had always assumed.

"I know," Julia said to his bewildered stare. "It sounds counterintuitive. But the numbers don't lie. Trust me, my husband is an expert on this stuff."

Tyler frowned at the mention of a husband. Then he silently rebuked his imagination for entertaining possibilities.

"I can send you a list of dark zone streets and zip codes. Maybe you could look it over to see if you know anyone who'd be willing to chat. That would really help me out."

Her voice carried an appreciative detachment that made him feel like a guy hearing "We can still be friends."

"Sure thing," he agreed with a sigh. "I'll do what I can."

The phone vibrated: Renee calling, probably semi-distraught and eager to apologize for the earlier tiff. Tyler smiled at his girlfriend's predictable pattern.

"Excuse me," he said. "I need to take this call."

CHAPTER TWENTY-FIVE

Matthew sighed as he scraped half of Reverend Grandpa's lunch into the garbage can. It was something he had done a thousand times before while caring for his mom. He tried to recall when she'd begun leaving more food on her plate than she ate. Was it about the same time she'd started forgetting to take her medications? Or when the spark of determined strength in her eyes had surrendered to befuddled fear? Either way, he recognized diminished appetite as a sign of something wrong. Disease? Depression? No. Decay.

His client, like his mother, must be crying out for help. Why else would he specifically request a bean-and-cheese burrito for lunch and then shove it aside after a few pitiful bites? Why else would he keep himself cooped up in his bedroom like a man condemned to solitary confinement? During the five days Matthew had lived with Reverend Grandpa he had seen only one brief sign of passion: the covert scheming with his grandson. Even that, come to think of it, had sounded more like an effort to convince himself than an effort to cheer up Peter. Did Reverend Grandpa really intend to stick around for a long time?

Matthew finished the cleanup process and mentally checked off the third of five daily chores. Then he walked toward the laundry room, where a clump of damp towels awaited transfer from the washer to the dryer. He halted, trying to recall what the old man had told the boy. *Your mommy and I discussed the money already. I'm gonna live right here, real close, for at least six months.*

Of course!

Abandoning his to-do list, Matthew gave himself a much more important assignment.

———⁓———

"Free to thrive?" Reverend Grandpa said with a snigger. "Is that what they taught you up there in Boulder?"

Matthew couldn't quite read whether his client was intrigued or incensed.

The old man put both hands on his left leg brace, the first of three sequenced steps before standing. Matthew instinctively moved toward him, then remembered the rule: *Only assist when asked.* Afraid of another rebuke, Matthew reminded himself that his client was not, in Reverend Grandpa's words, "some helpless invalid!"

"Actually," Matthew answered, "the wording came from a column written by my girlfriend's sister." Mostly true. Maria Davidson might not yet qualify as his official girlfriend. But Julia was her sister.

"Oh, I see," Reverend Grandpa mocked. "So you got this entire cockamamy philosophy from a blogger?"

"Not the philosophy," Matthew corrected. "Just the *free to thrive* part."

The old man placed his right hand on the arm of his chair

while the other reached toward the top of his leg brace. Step two of three. Then he paused to look up, unimpressed, toward Matthew's face.

"Uh-huh," he said. "And the rest?"

Matthew wanted to mention the mountain of ancient sources, academic articles, and recent books he knew existed that would substantiate his philosophy. But in the moment only one touchstone of credibility came to mind.

"I've been studying under the chair of religious studies at the university. His name is Thomas Vincent." Matthew let the name linger in the air, waiting for his client to recognize the renowned scholar.

No raised eyebrow. No reaction at all.

"Dr. Thomas Vincent, PhD," Matthew added.

"Never heard of him."

Reverend Grandpa appeared distracted by the small icon affixed to the top of his leg brace. Despite repeated pressing, the hydraulic lift moaned without movement.

"Probably a low battery," Matthew said. "I better add recharging your brace to my daily routine."

"You do that," the man barked, reluctantly waving Matthew in his direction. "Don't just stand there like a worthless college boy. Help me up."

He bent down to receive Reverend Grandpa's weight.

Look who's calling me worthless, he thought while loaning the man his own limbs.

Five minutes and thirty-seven laborious steps later Reverend Grandpa settled into the front room recliner, inhaling rapidly through a suddenly stingy oxygen tube.

"You good?" Matthew asked.

A single nod.

Both men sat quietly until the deprived lungs were replenished.

"There." Reverend Grandpa sighed with some comfort. "So, what was it we were talking about?"

"Manichaeism," Matthew resumed. "Saint Augustine embraced it before he submitted to church dogma. I'm surprised you didn't study it in seminary."

A hint of vague familiarity appeared on the minister's face. "Fourth-century Augustine?"

"That's right," Matthew said eagerly. "You've heard of him?"

A laugh. "Of course I've heard of him. Bishop of Hippo. Wrote *Confessions*."

The title didn't ring a bell. "*Confessions?*"

"You know, his testimony."

"Testimony?"

"Good gravy, boy!" Reverend Grandpa exploded. "You haven't spent much time in church, have you?"

"Plenty. I went to parochial school."

The old man waved off the comment. "I'm not talking about catechism classes." His speech took on a melodic rhythm. "I'm talking about Bible-preaching, song-singing, amen-shoutin' church where people give a testimony of how God saved 'em from hell and damnation by his grace-givin' love!"

Matthew met the statement with a puzzled stare. Was he serious? Or was this another effort to pull the college boy's leg?

A smile on the minister's face told him it was both. "You'd need to be my age or older to remember what church was like back in the day."

"In what day?"

"Sunday!" he said as if delivering a punch line, laughing weakly. "At least, Sunday where I grew up."

Matthew watched his client's eyes enjoying a moment of reminiscence. They suggested deep bonds to a world quite different from the one Matthew inhabited. A universe far away, he assumed, from the one Reverend Grandpa's daughter had chosen.

"Did you raise Marissa in that kind of church?"

"I tried," he said dimly, placing his hand reverently on a book sitting beside him on the end table. It was the same vintage Bible Matthew had perused on the night he arrived at the house. "But times change, my boy. Times definitely change."

Matthew sensed the dismal cloud reclaiming Reverend Grandpa's disposition. He remembered his mission.

"So, Manicheans taught that the spiritual realm is good and the material world evil."

The comment seemed to pull Reverend Grandpa out of his descent. "And the incarnation?" he asked perceptively.

"A great question," Matthew said. "Church dogma says Jesus was God, a spirit, who became a man by taking on a material body."

"Amen!"

Matthew froze at the abrupt interruption.

"Sorry, old habit. It means I agree."

"OK. Well, anyway, some of his followers also created the myth of Jesus's bodily resurrection. The Manicheans, by contrast, understood that Jesus's resurrection was spiritual, not physical."

"They understood that, did they?"

"They did. And they saw Jesus as one who helped show us the way to God."

"Oh really. How?" Reverend Grandpa sounded as if he were humoring a child rather than engaging a foe.

"How what?"

"How'd he show us the way to God?"

"By transcending the prison of an evil, smelly, decaying body."

"So you think he died to escape stubbed toes and mosquito bites for some out-of-body existence?"

"Exactly."

"God didn't become flesh?"

"Didn't need to. Nor would it make sense. A perfect spirit wouldn't contaminate himself with an evil, material body."

"I see," the minister said. "And no bodily resurrection from the dead?"

"What for? The body decays. Only the spirit matters."

"Go on," Reverend Grandpa said, as if loosening a fishing line. "You say Augustine believed this?"

"He did. At least until he blindly accepted church dogma that condemned Manichean teachings as heresy."

"Those nasty church dogma guys!" Reverend Grandpa seemed to suppress a smile.

"Are you mocking me?"

"Not at all, my boy. I would never—" A bouncing torso interrupted the minister's explanation.

"You're laughing at me!"

The old man regained his composure with a snort. "I'm sorry, son. I'm just playing with you."

"But I'm serious!"

"I know you are." He suppressed another laugh. "If you only knew how many times I've heard some version of this same nonsense.

"*Jesus wasn't God, just an exceptional man.*

"*Jesus didn't rise bodily, he showed us the path to enlightenment.*

"Same song, two thousandth verse!"

"Have you ever asked yourself what it would mean if the Manicheans got it right and the Church got it wrong?" asked Matthew.

"They didn't get it right."

Matthew thought of Dr. Vincent. "Some very smart people think they did."

"I'm sure they do. But a lot of very smart people think and do some very dumb things."

"But if the Manicheans were right it would make a big difference, you know, in what you need to do six months from now."

Reverend Grandpa glowered at Matthew. "What do you mean, six months from now?"

Matthew swallowed hard at the realization he had said too much. "I didn't mean to hear."

"Hear what?"

"I overheard your conversation with Peter."

"Little Pete," he corrected. "What part of the conversation?"

"The part where you talked about money, and how you would be around for another six months."

The old man appeared confused. "And?"

"And, well, I assumed you were depressed because you plan to"—Matthew groped for the best word—"volunteer."

"Volunteer for what?"

"To transition. What else?"

The minister's face turned a furious shade of red. "So you brought up all this Manichean nonsense because you thought I was planning to commit suicide?"

"Not suicide. Transition."

"Same difference!" he barked. "Why in the world would I kill myself?"

"Well," Matthew scrambled, "you seemed a bit depressed. And then I heard you talking about money and a change in six months. I just assumed you wanted to help your daughter and grandkids."

The old man took a deep breath as if trying to submerge his rising ire.

"I do want to help Marissa and the kids," he began. "I've sat in that room thinking about little else. But, other than going back in time"—he slapped his leg brace and pinched his oxygen tube—"there aren't any good options."

Matthew sensed an intense self-doubt. No, self-condemnation. That would explain the depression.

"It was an accident," he said sympathetically.

"A stupid accident. And an avoidable accident if only I hadn't been too stubborn and cheap to add the accident anticipation package when I bought that car."

"Package?" Matthew wondered aloud. "I thought accident anticipation came standard on every vehicle."

"It does now. But not in the late twenties when I bought it."

"The twenties? Wow."

"Vintage, my boy. Vintage. Anyway, a measly thousand dollars then would have saved us a boatload of medical costs now. Plus I could've kept working for at least another decade. As it is, I'm probably gonna end up living with her and the kids."

"Is that so bad?"

"You tell me," Reverend Grandpa said. "Would you want the burden of me if you were my child? A child, incidentally, who's spent her whole life trying to get away from her religious nut of a father?"

Matthew held his tongue. He, too, had rejected a parent's religion. He knew what it was like to dread and then endure days on end managing doctor appointments, medication doses, overdue bills, and bathroom mishaps. The time and expenses of caring for a sick parent strangled dreams and killed options. They had reduced Matthew from budding professor to live-in caregiver.

"Six months is how much we have left on my reverse mortgage," he explained. "After that, no more income."

"What happens to the house?"

"The bank will own it. I can still live here until I die, but without the monthly check I can't afford utilities, upkeep..." He paused, glancing back toward Matthew. "Or help."

"I see."

"Either I'll move in with Marissa or she and the kids will

move in with me. We need to pool resources." A faint, humorless laugh. "Correction. We'll live off her paycheck."

Reverend Grandpa looked around the room as if scanning a gallery of better days. "Olivia and I bought this place when she was carrying Marissa. Seems like yesterday. Three hundred and sixty payments later it was all ours." He stopped, another reminiscent gaze sweeping over his eyes.

"How'd you lose her?" Matthew asked gingerly.

He cleared emotion from his throat. "Her ticker quit. Seventy-one years young."

"I'm sorry."

"Anyway, I've been living off the house's equity ever since the accident."

Matthew tried to imagine how it would feel, a proud father knowing he would soon be dependent on his little girl.

They sat silently, two men living in the wake of different misfortunes.

The elder finally spoke. "I should have listened to Olivia."

Matthew didn't follow.

"She wanted to give Marissa a sibling. Maybe two. I didn't think we could afford a houseful of kids on a preacher's salary."

"Sounds sensible to me," Matthew said reassuringly.

"Now I'd give anything if she had someone to share the burden. A brother maybe."

The minister put his hand on Matthew's shoulder like a wounded marine explaining how to disarm land mines. "Marry that girlfriend of yours, Matthew Adams." He moved his hand back to the side table, where his fingers gently caressed the book's leather binding. "And once you do, take some ancient advice."

"What's that?"

"Be fruitful and multiply."

Matthew smiled politely. "Forgive me," he said. "But you

could leave what little is left in your estate to Marissa, Isabelle, and Peter by doing the same thing millions of others in your situation have done. Volunteer."

"I can't do that," Reverend Grandpa insisted. "Never could."

Matthew heard a hint of hesitation and saw a touch of self-doubt in his client's eyes before they looked away. He decided to drop what was clearly an uncomfortable subject.

For now.

CHAPTER TWENTY-SIX

Tyler peered through the glass wall at three sleeping babies: two girls and a boy, judging from the colors of their caps. He knew he should think they were cute; but in all honesty, they looked a bit like misshapen aliens with oddly colored skin. Sights only their mothers could love.

Hannah Walker stood in the corner, hovering momentarily over a fourth baby, her stethoscope pressed against the child's chest. A boy, he noticed when she shifted her stance to perform some sort of test. The child suddenly let out a raspy, quavering scream of pain or irritation. Tyler sympathized with the little guy. One minute you're floating comfortably to the rhythmic echo of Mom's beating heart, the next you're being poked in the bottom by a colossal stranger with chilly hands. Next stop? Who knows? Spying for jealous lovers? Investigating obscure death threats?

"Welcome to the asylum, kid," he whispered through the glass. He sniffed his cup of lukewarm coffee before tossing it in a trash can next to the nursery entrance.

Hannah exited the hospital's newborn nursery, giving Tyler a quick smile.

"Sorry about that," she said, indicating down the hallway. "Where were we?"

"You enjoy your work?" It was more an observation than a question.

She smiled again, bigger this time. More genuine. Laugh lines formed to nearly obscure the slight scar along her lower jaw. "I really do."

"Quite a change from your previous line of work."

"Well, Mr. Cain, that's about the biggest understatement I've heard in all my life."

Tyler chuckled at himself. Hannah Walker had gone from helping push seniors out of this world to helping smuggle newborns in.

"It's OK, though," she went on. "I needed to find something positive if I was going to stay in the medical field. For over a year I kind of wallowed in self-pity after leaving New Day. This job came along, and it was serendipity." She paused. "I have this neighbor who believes in reincarnation. And sometimes I think that maybe, just maybe, these little ones are the souls of my former clients."

"You believe that?"

She pursed her lips with a slight shaking of the head. "No, not really. Wish I did, though. It would probably ease a bit of the guilt."

"Guilt for what?"

Hannah stopped their advance and turned partially toward Tyler. "One thousand, four hundred and twenty-three deaths," she said, her eyes still fixed down the hallway. "I stayed more than two years at New Day." The words dripped with disdain.

He said nothing. They resumed their stroll, rounding a corner under a sign that read BIRTH AND DELIVERY.

"Why did you? Stay, I mean."

She shrugged. "I don't know, honestly. At one time I thought I did."

A brief silence.

"At the time I think I had convinced myself I was helping heroes fulfill their destiny." A single laugh scoffed. "It took leaving to realize."

Tyler looked toward Hannah, waiting for the rest. Nothing came. "Realize what?" he asked.

"That I believed a lie. Wanted it to be true."

She met Tyler's eyes.

"No one likes to admit that about themselves, Mr. Cain. Especially when you're still living in the lie. So you go on, swallowing back sour bile while telling yourself you're part of some greater good."

She glanced upward, noticing the sign that summarized her new reality. She pointed toward it. "'Birth and Delivery,'" she read aloud. "Back then I sneered at breeders. Can you believe that? I actually made fun of the women who are helping me climb out of the pit."

"What pit is that?" he asked curiously.

"The one I helped dig. As of this morning it was eleven hundred and sixty-four graves deep. That little boy you saw me with in the nursery moved me one closer to the surface. Only eleven hundred and sixty-three to go."

"Sounds like a steep climb," Tyler said, from not knowing what to say.

"Believe me," she replied. "It's much easier climbing up than digging down. Like I said, I love my new job. Nine months now."

She paused, as if surprising herself with the comment.

"Nine months," she repeated. "Kind of ironic, isn't it?"

Tyler offered a weak smile of agreement before steering the conversation back.

"I see why you're *not* a fan of NEXT Transition Services."

She grimaced at the possibility. "Not in the least."

"You'd be pretty happy if they lost the appeal?"

"I wouldn't shed any tears if they lost. Other than possible tears of joy."

"Can you think of anyone else who would benefit if NEXT lost the appeal? Other than Jeremy Santos, that is?"

"Benefit?" Hannah Walker began, but an urgent ringtone erupted from the phone stuffed in her nursing scrubs pocket. She held a brief conversation on where to be for her next patient: a baby being born by C-section in just a few minutes. She ended the call, then glanced at Tyler, quite intently. "I'm sure there are plenty who would benefit, Mr. Cain. But why do you assume the person you are dealing with is *opposed* to NEXT? Does it say that explicitly in the letters?"

The question confused him. *Of course it does. Wait. Does it?* "Why do you ask?"

"Well, I'm sure there are many who want to see NEXT lose the appeal. But others would have far more to gain if they won."

Tyler had been so focused on Jeremy or some other lawsuit beneficiary he had barely considered the possibility. How stupid of him! *Losing my edge*, he thought with a sigh.

"The transition business is just that: a business. It's about making money, and a lot of it. Certain people will go to great lengths to make a buck. And when it comes to the old and afflicted, death pays handsomely."

"So you think it's NEXT?"

"Maybe. Or maybe someone with more to gain than NEXT."

"Like?"

Hannah shook her head as her phone beeped, then started down the hallway backward while finishing her thought. "I haven't a clue. That's for you to find out. But might I suggest you visit the clinic where I worked? See for yourself what goes on. You might find a lead or two. Goodbye, Mr. Cain."

And with that, she scurried off.

—∿—

New Day Transition Center seemed considerably smaller in person than it had in the video tour, at least from the outside. The brick exterior blended seamlessly into the surrounding establishments. It would be easy to miss unless you were looking. Probably on purpose. Despite the overall popularity of transition clinics, Tyler imagined there were still a few crazy zealots around eager to bomb the place if given half an opportunity. But here, nestled neatly between a pediatrician's office and that of a gynecologist specializing in reproductive screening, it felt rather harmless. Tyler laughed at the grouping.

It did seem odd, though. For a business set up to make lots of money, as Hannah Walker supposed, the interior seemed rather lackluster. Tyler wasn't even sure what he hoped to find here. He'd already seen the place, virtually, through the police recording. Maybe he needed to actually experience it for himself.

He glanced around the waiting room, where two elderly men sat with their fiftysomething children beside them. One was in a wheelchair, and the other had a canister of oxygen attached via clear plastic tubing to his nose. It was disturbingly quiet.

The receptionist smiled brightly. "Welcome to New Day, may I help you?"

Tyler was caught off guard, momentarily unsure of what to say. He glanced again at the man in the wheelchair. Probably the same age as Renee's father, or a few years beyond. A fleeting thought crossed his mind. What it would be like to see Gerry or

Katherine here, Renee holding his or her hand as they prepared to say their final goodbyes? She would never do it, of course. But the image gave him the needed reply.

"Yes," he said, bringing his gaze back to the young woman's. "It's my father-in-law, really. He's…well…"

"Oh, I understand. Hang on one moment." She stretched to check on the clients in the waiting room, as though fearing they had escaped, then handed Tyler a series of papers. "I'll have you meet with a counselor. In the meantime, you should read through this, making sure you, your partner, and his or her father understand everything fully."

Tyler continued playing the part as the receptionist leafed through the first several pages of legal mumbo jumbo. She stopped on the final page.

"This is the official application. The front is just basic personal information. You know. Name, date of birth, that kind of thing. On the back is a series of questions you—I mean your father-in-law—will need to answer after meeting with one of our counselors."

Tyler flipped the page to the back, scanning the list. On the surface they all seemed quite reasonable questions to ask oneself before deciding to die. But then Tyler realized how pointed some of them seemed. Like "Have you pre-identified allocation and distribution of your estate via a legal will?"

At the bottom, in barely legible fine print, was a revision number and date. It was recent, less than six months old. This was the eighth version of the form, in fact.

Ten minutes later Tyler sat on faux-wood-grained furniture across from a male counselor. A cheaply framed lithograph hung crookedly. The hint of fresh-breeze-scented air freshener wafted from a small plug-in behind the man. His nametag read LEO, probably short for Leonard.

Tyler had dutifully filled in the first page with Gerry's personal information, but held off on the questions targeting Gerry himself. Leo glanced at the form, then leaned forward, hands prayerfully folded.

"I know this must be a difficult time," he began.

Tyler nodded, then feigned an appreciative smile. "To be honest, I'm not even sure this is what he wants. But Renee…I mean, my wife, she's a bit overwhelmed right now."

"That's to be expected. No one should have to go through the process of having to see their parents slowly deteriorate to the point that they can't even take care of themselves. But we see it so often. And it doesn't have to be that way."

"But when's the right time?"

Leo leaned back too quickly, as if checking *Show compassion* off a mental list. It must have seemed Tyler didn't need convincing, just the proper motivation. "That's the tricky part," he said.

"Tricky?"

"Yes. See, transitions must be completely voluntary. We can't have overburdened children making decisions on behalf of their mother or father without absolute certainty that the parent understands and agrees to the process. That's the point of the second page. See there?"

"Yes."

"And so, assuming your wife is in agreement, the first step will be helping your father-in-law understand what kind of burden he has become to your wife. Sometimes that takes time and a little bit of patience."

"A little bit?"

Leo chuckled. "Or a lot. One of the volunteers sitting in our waiting room now had his first consultation nearly six months ago."

"Six months?" Tyler had spent less than ten days of hosting Gerry and Katherine in his house and already felt burned out.

"I know, but don't worry. Those are exceptional cases. If your father-in-law is already aware of his worsening condition, which is...?"

"Uh. Mild dementia."

"Oh, I'm so sorry," Leo said, briefly returning to a posture of pity, then continuing. "If your father-in-law can be made to see the toll his dementia is taking on your wife he'll be more open to volunteering. You can help that along some."

"Help it along?"

"Not that you want to push him into something he doesn't want to do."

"No," Tyler heard himself say.

"Like I said before, the decision must be completely voluntary. But sometimes the person less emotionally tied to the situation, such as yourself, can help them see the situation from a more clearheaded perspective. You know, help them focus on the benefits rather than just grieve the potential separation."

"Benefits?"

"Such as freeing resources for your wife, any grandchildren—"

"No kids."

"I see. Does she have a career, then? In a very real way, your father-in-law is probably holding her back."

Tyler's mind filled in other motivations. He and Renee hadn't had sex since the day her parents moved in. "I hadn't thought of it that way."

"Here," Leo said, handing the forms over to Tyler. "Take these. Discuss them with your wife. Look over the questions. And when you're convinced that your father-in-law is ready to answer them honestly, then you'll know the time is right."

Tyler folded the forms and slid them into his pocket before standing and offering his hand in thanks. Leo returned the gesture, escorting Tyler back toward the lobby. On the way Tyler caught a glimpse of the man in the wheelchair being moved through an open door. The sign overhead read TRANSI-TION ROOM #2.

In the waiting room Tyler noticed the man's daughter sitting quietly, dabbing a mascara-stained tear from each eye. She returned his glance. He sensed both relief and regret.

Hannah Walker had been right. He *was* surprised. Not because he had found any useful lead. He hadn't. He was surprised by the efficiency of the process. It had taken the NEXT staff less than thirty minutes to move him from a vaguely curious inquirer to a convinced salesman of their product. One or two sentences had emphasized that volunteering must be "completely voluntary." But they had seemed like legally required fine print, not sincere attempts to dissuade. Under other circumstances the encounter might have convinced Tyler to seriously explore a step he had never really put much thought into before.

Was Antonio Santos as easily convinced? he wondered.

Tyler forced the question out of his mind. Private detectives don't have the luxury of rabbit-trail thoughts. He got paid when he delivered. He put his Mustang in reverse, matching the direction of his case. The interviews with Julia Simmons and Hannah Walker had brought him no closer to finding the author of Judge Santiago's threatening letters. Nor to pocketing his thirty-thousand-dollar bonus.

CHAPTER TWENTY-SEVEN

Julia took a third glance at Tyler's text message to confirm the address.

> Austin Tozer said he would talk to you.
> Definite dark zone guy. His mom volunteered recently.
> Owes me a favor. Expecting you at 10 a.m. tomorrow.
> Address: 2210 Kingston Street in Aurora

She had the right place, unlikely as it appeared. What had she expected? A half-abandoned apartment building? A yard filled with knee-high weeds? A broken-down washing machine on the front porch? These were the images that came to mind whenever Troy mentioned dark zones. But Austin Tozer, whoever he was, lived in what appeared to be a modestly respectable neighborhood within jogging distance of the University of Colorado–Denver School of Medicine. Only peeling trim and graying roof shingles offered hints of the home's concealed age.

She felt a mild vibration from her tablet, a reminder that the scheduled time had arrived. Julia moved toward the recently painted front door, shaking her head in disbelief. Troy's scheme had actually worked. Paul Daugherty had jumped at the chance to present her concept to the editorial board, just as Troy had predicted. She frowned at the thought of Paul's likely pitch. *You'll never guess who I landed for the next weekend feature*! Julia hated the thought of Paul once again leveraging *her* work to increase *his* stature at RAP Media Syndicate. But it had to be done. Kevin needed this story. And many more.

When she reached the second of three porch steps Julia noticed a slight movement from the front window drapes. Had the man been watching her? For how long? Admiring eyes usually flatter a girl. But when hidden behind shadowy curtains they give her the creeps.

Before she could knock Julia noticed the door inching open. A partial face appeared from behind. Not a man. A woman? No. A girl. She looked Julia up and down as if eyeing an intruder before deciding whether to call the cops.

"Hi there," Julia said through the gap. "My name is Julia Sim—Julia Davidson. I'm here to see Mr. Tozer. Austin Tozer."

"Austin!" the girl shouted toward the back of the house. Then she disappeared, leaving Julia standing on the porch like a pizza delivery guy waiting for his tip.

A moment later the door fully opened. The man, like the house, caught Julia by surprise. She had, for some reason, expected a gruff, unshaven face and protruding beer belly. His thin torso and lean biceps lacked enough muscle tone to justify a tank top intended for less boyish forms. Patches of auburn whiskers splotched a face that could have used a shave but couldn't produce a beard. At first glance she assumed Austin was barely beyond adolescence. But his eyes and thinning hair said mid- to late thirties. Possibly older.

"Sorry," he said, motioning for Julia to enter. "Amanda never learned manners."

She stepped into the front room. "Your daughter?"

He laughed. "Nope. Childless by choice. She's my kid half sister. She lives with us."

They stood for a moment while Austin looked around the room, scratching his neck. He seemed nervous, as if he had expected someone different.

"Is this still a good time to chat?" she asked.

"Yes," he said quickly, glancing at the clock. "Perfect. Can I get you something? Water? Soda?"

Julia wasn't thirsty, but she accepted the offer anyway.

"Back in a flash," he said as if relieved by the opportunity to regroup. "Please, make yourself comfortable."

She moved to a chair situated across from the sofa, ideal for a face-to-face interview. When she sat, however, the cushion sank like a deflating balloon. Too many years had met too little padding. She scooted herself forward to find a patch of support while searching her tablet screen for a specific icon.

"May I record our conversation?" she asked as Austin reentered the room.

His face was hit with embarrassment. "I'm so sorry," he said, offering his hand to rescue Julia from the wrong chair. "I should have warned you about that." He quickly moved a pillow from the left side of the adjoining sofa. "Please. Sit here instead."

Finally settled, she repeated her question. "May I record our conversation?"

He nodded. "Do you plan to use my real name?"

"Would that be a problem?" she asked. "I prefer it when possible."

His eyes darted nervously at the other spot on the sofa, then back toward Julia. "Depends on what kinds of questions you ask," he said, taking the open seat. "I'll let you know when we're done."

Julia shifted her posture to face Austin, who was crossing and uncrossing his legs as if trying to assume the best position for an interview that suddenly felt like an awkward blind date.

Julia tapped the RECORD icon and placed the device on the space between them.

"Tyler Cain says the two of you are friends."

Austin appeared surprised by the comment.

"He said you owed him a favor." She smiled.

He didn't laugh. "More like I owe him money."

"Detective work?"

Austin chuckled. "That's what Tyler calls it. Did me more harm than good."

"I see," Julia said without curiosity.

"I hired him a few years ago when I thought Gwen was cheating on me. She still gets irate every time I get an outstanding invoice reminder."

"Gwen?"

"My partner. Been together nearly ten years." Austin pointed up and back to a picture hanging on the wall behind his head. "That's her there."

Julia stood to take a closer look. The woman in the photograph appeared older than Austin. Peering beyond the artificially blond hair and an outfit more suited for Austin's manners-deprived kid sister, she figured Gwen to be around forty. A self-conscious smile suggested a woman hoping to conceal teeth that had lost their former symmetry. There was a blotch on the right side of her neck just below the earlobe. A birthmark? Perhaps. But more likely a now-distorted tattoo applied to younger skin.

"She's lovely," Julia said generously.

"Thanks. I like her."

Julia smiled at the mystery of human attraction as she reclaimed her spot on the sofa. "How'd you connect?"

"The seventh tier of Virtuality."

"Virtuality?"

"A gaming universe. All my clan buddies made the switch to NuLIFE TREK. But I stuck with Virtuality. Call me old-school. Anyway, that's how we met. It's like we were meant to find each other. I'd probably still be living alone if Virtuality hadn't brought us together."

Julia smiled politely.

"Yep. Gwen and I hooked up online long before meeting face-to-face. Our avs were so hot together we just had to take it to level eight, if you know what I mean."

"Avs?"

"Avatars. You know, our other selves."

"Ah," Julia said with a nod, pretending to follow.

"Sorry she couldn't join us. The store called this morning offering a half-day shift."

"I understand," Julia said. "Take work when you can get it."

"You know it."

"How about you? Are you employed?"

Austin's sunken chest appeared to expand slightly. "I actually just started a new job last week."

"Congratulations."

Julia waited for details. None came.

"Nothing much, but a lot better than sitting around here all day waiting for Gwen to get home. You can only play so many solo levels before you need your av-mate to advance. Plus, we need the cash. Mom's estate was smaller than I expected. And the house still has a mortgage."

"Did the house belong to your mother?"

"Yep. Lived here with Amanda."

"Your sister?"

"Half sister."

"How old is Amanda?"

"Twelve. No. Eleven." He cursed. "I should probably keep better track of that now that I'm her legal guardian."

"So you and Gwen moved into your mother's house after her…passing?"

Austin shifted uncomfortably in his seat. "Before, actually."

A moment of silence.

"Go on," Julia prodded.

"Gwen and I moved in to help with Amanda after Mom got sick."

He lifted his eyes to meet Julia's. She held a sympathetic stare. He looked back toward the carpet.

"Well, not exactly sick. But she was pretty depressed."

"That's not true!"

Both looked toward the accusing feminine voice.

"Mom wasn't depressed. You were!"

Amanda stepped around a hallway corner that must have led to three bedrooms and a bath. Her appearance startled Julia even more than the outburst. She was darling, possessing a natural beauty diligently buried beneath the common trappings of a girl trying to look like a woman. Dark mascara hid a noticeable innocence that reminded Julia of her nephew Jared. Both kids inhabited that awkward age when children yearn to escape carefree-ness for the prison of forbidden knowledge. Her clingy top revealed the promise of breasts not yet blossomed. A short skirt flared suggestively, the latest design of fashion moguls hoping preteen girls would join their mothers as eye candy for hungry males.

"We were perfectly fine before you and Hen started mooching off Mom."

Austin frowned. "For the thousandth time, her name is Gwen. I hate it when you call her Hen!"

Julia resisted the urge to smile at Amanda's "henpecked" insinuation as the girl stormed out of the room. A door opened, then slammed.

Austin shook his head in a blend of anger and humiliation. "Like I said. She never learned manners." He breathed deeply. "Where was I?"

"You were telling me about your mother."

He looked as if his mind remained fixed on the accusation. He stood up and took a single step in Amanda's direction. Then he stopped.

"Right. My mother," he said, reclaiming his seat.

"She volunteered?" Julia already knew the answer thanks to Tyler's text.

"She *was* depressed," he insisted. Then he looked Julia in the eyes, as if realizing he had mischaracterized his mom's decision. "But that's not why she transitioned."

"She must have been fairly young," Julia suggested.

Austin reached for a tablet sitting on the table beside the sofa. He tapped the screen and handed it to Julia.

"That's her a few years back," he said as Julia studied the picture.

"I see where your sister gets her beauty."

"Half sister," Austin corrected.

Brother and half sister had clearly inherited different ends of the gene pool. Austin must have come from sperm lacking rugged good looks. The man who had partnered in Amanda's conception, by contrast, had merely jump-started a process that resulted in near-perfect transmission of feminine elegance from mother to daughter.

"Were they close?"

The question appeared to confuse Austin. "Was who close?"

"Amanda and her mother."

"Oh. I guess." He gave his answer another thought. "Actually, I'd say they oscillated between friends and enemies. Like a lot of mothers and daughters, I suppose."

Julia absorbed the comment. "It must have been tough to lose her mom at such a young age. Ten?"

"Yep. Wait." He cursed again, then started tapping fingers like a boy doing arithmetic. "Eleven. My mom volunteered a month after Amanda's eleventh birthday."

Julia tried to imagine the motivation for such a decision.

"In fact, Amanda's birthday played a role."

"How's that?"

"Gwen and I had been living here for about a year. That's when we noticed a growing sense of apathy in my mom. Some days it felt like despair."

"A year after you moved in?"

"Yes."

"Not before?"

"Before what?"

"Earlier you said you moved in to help with Amanda due to your mom's depression."

Austin's eyes shifted toward the wall. "That's right. We did," he said pensively. "Of course, that wasn't the only reason for the move."

Julia reminded herself that Austin's neighborhood officially qualified as "economically deprived."

"Was money a reason?"

"Both Gwen and I lost our jobs during the meltdown. Couldn't pay the rent. You know the rest."

Julia nodded.

"Anyway," he continued, "we thought it would be good for everyone if we pooled our resources."

"What kind of resources?"

A blank stare.

"You mentioned that your mother's estate was smaller than you thought."

"Actually, I didn't realize how small until later. Mom said her transition would provide more than enough to pay off the mortgage and establish a college nest egg for Amanda." He gave a single laugh. "Hardly."

Julia took a sip of soda. "What happened?"

"Bad math. She underestimated the transition service fees and inheritance tax rates. We barely got enough to pay off the mortgage."

"I thought you said you still had a mortgage."

"We do. The money would have been enough had I landed a steady job, which I didn't."

"So the money has been paying your monthly bills?"

He nodded.

"Even the portion intended for Amanda's college fund?"

Another, slower nod.

"Anyway," he continued, "shortly after Amanda's eleventh birthday Mom and Gwen did a bit of number crunching. Gwen's always been good with that sort of thing."

Julia looked up at the picture of Gwen, then at the elegant face smiling on Austin's tablet. "So your partner helped your mother decide to volunteer?"

"Yes and no. She helped her work through a decision tree I brought home from Aspen House."

"The NEXT clinic?"

"You know it?" Austin asked. "A really classy place."

"I've driven past it. Looks...nice."

"Anyway, it was clear we needed to do something drastic. I think Mom was the first one to say so."

He looked at the ceiling as if trying to recall his mother's precise words.

" 'We can't continue like this.' That's what she said. 'We need to make a major change.' "

"Why didn't you sell the house?" Julia asked.

"Impossible. She wouldn't even discuss it. A move would have been too unsettling for Amanda."

More than losing a mother? Julia thought.

"How did Amanda and your mom make it before you moved in?"

"Barely. That's how they made it," he said defensively. "Mom's paycheck covered their monthly expenses. No more. She wasn't saving anything for Amanda's future."

"What about after your move?"

He scowled. "We weren't moochers, if that's what you're suggesting!"

"I'm not suggesting anything," Julia said softly. "I'm just trying to understand what led your mother to volunteer."

"I had nothing to do with it," he insisted.

"Nothing to do with what?"

"With her decision. Gwen and Mom did all the talking. I kept myself out of it."

"I thought you said you brought a decision tree home from Aspen House."

He blushed. "I was just curious about how it all worked. You know, whether it might be a good option to consider."

"Was moving out one of those options?"

"I told you, Amanda—"

"I mean did it occur to you that it might help if you and Gwen moved out? If your mom and Amanda barely made it before you arrived, it must have been worse with three adults and a child living on one modest salary."

Austin began pinching uneasily at a patch of facial hair. His eyes appeared to be assessing what more, if anything, to say.

"Look, Ms. Davidson, I'm gonna shoot straight with you." He paused. "Mom drank."

"I see," Julia said sympathetically.

"She drank a lot. I found that out after we moved in."

Julia began assembling the pieces in her mind. A functional alcoholic stretched beyond what her frayed edges could handle. Drinking away the disappointments of a go-nowhere job, a do-nothing son, and a daughter increasingly at odds. A girl whose maturing features served as a daily reminder of her own waning beauty.

"Mom told Gwen she wanted to do something decent for her kids."

"Decent? As in leaving you the house?"

"Mainly the house. There were other assets. But the house mostly."

Austin looked as if more needed to be said. Julia waited.

"And we nearly lost it."

"Lost the house?"

A single nod. "Would have if Gwen hadn't got pregnant."

Julia looked up with a start. "Pregnant?"

"Twice in the past twelve months," he said with a curious enthusiasm.

"But I thought you said you and Gwen were childless by choice."

"We are," he replied matter-of-factly. "We sold them."

"Sold them!" Julia felt her right palm pressing against her abdomen.

"Two grand each. The embryotics market is booming."

A blank stare joined Julia's queasy feeling. She glanced at her tablet to make sure it was still recording what she was hearing. Then she willed herself back to a journalistic posture.

"Of course. Embryotics," she said, trying to connect the label.

Austin must have perceived her confusion. "You know. The

organic material used in everything from surgical attachment
tissue to those skin rejuvenation ointments used by rich old
ladies."

"Right," she heard herself say. "So you sold your girlfriend's
fetus?"

"Yep. Wish we'd discovered the market earlier. Prices have
been steadily rising for years."

"Who buys them?"

"Who doesn't? We responded to an ad that said elder cosmetic
innovations have overwhelmed traditional suppliers, or something like that. I don't recall the exact wording. All I know is that
they pay top dollar for a two-month fetus."

Julia swallowed hard as she recalled late-night commercials
for creams promising to "miraculously reverse your skin's aging
process" using "cutting-edge organic materials." The ads had
clearly targeted well-off women worried about age spots. Snake
oil priced high enough to seem legitimate.

The sound of an opening door forced Austin to his feet. He
appeared nervous, as if worried about how Gwen would react to
discovering an attractive woman sitting beside him on the sofa.

Austin relaxed, then scowled, when he realized it was just
Amanda.

Julia felt strangely warmed by the girl's arrival. "Hello," she
said enthusiastically.

Amanda smiled and offered a single wave. Then she
scrunched her nose at Austin.

"Where'd you go?" he demanded.

"Out." Nothing more.

"I'm glad you're back," Julia interjected, hoping to draw
the girl into the conversation. "I want to ask you a few questions as well."

Austin's head spun toward Julia with a look of incredulity.
"But—"

"I was just wrapping up my interview with your brother," Julia interrupted.

"Half brother," they corrected in unison.

"You don't mind if Amanda joins the conversation, do you, Austin?" Julia asked, eager for the girl to confirm or correct Austin's version of events.

He looked at Julia, then at Amanda, then back at Julia again. "Actually, I'd rather she didn't."

"Please, Amanda, will you join us?" Julia continued over Austin's protest.

"Sure," Amanda said proudly, moving toward the sofa.

"I said I'd rather she didn't," Austin repeated with conviction.

"What's the matter?" said Amanda. "Afraid I'll expose more of your bull?"

"Ms. Davidson, I must insist."

"I could really use her perspective for the story."

Austin stood in place for several awkward seconds, shifting his weight from side to side as if trying to decide a next move.

"Ok, I'll let you talk to her," he said. "But don't plan on using my real name," he said, as if threatening to take his ball and go home.

Julia considered the threat. "Actually, that might be best anyway. You know, more authentic knowing you had no reason to hide anything or embellish."

He continued standing for several silent seconds. "Tell you what," he finally said. "You two have a chat. I'm gonna go in the other room to...check in at work."

"Check in at work?" Amanda mocked. "What are you gonna check, whether you'll be on the grill or running the milkshake machine tomorrow?"

Austin's neck turned shades of both anger and humiliation on his way out of the room. He paused at the hallway to shoot Amanda a daggered glare before disappearing around the corner.

The girl flashed a triumphant grin before plopping herself Indian-style on the floor. Lines of obstinacy melted on her face as she offered Julia an admiring smile.

"You're really pretty," she said.

"Thanks. So are you."

The girl blushed. "Hen says I look like a tramp."

"A tramp?" Julia said, recalling the tart-like appearance of the woman in the photograph. "Well, you know better than that, don't you?"

Amanda appeared entranced by the graceful sophistication of Julia's clothes and the stylish cut of her dark, unbleached hair. She even seemed to admire the way Julia sat, which prompted a self-conscious glance at her own contorted posture. The girl repositioned herself on her knees while pulling a tiny skirt over her thighs with one hand and finger-combing her disheveled strands with the other.

"You look a lot like your mother," Julia said. "Your brother... I mean Austin showed me her picture."

Amanda smiled at the truth of it.

"She's dead. Killed herself last year."

"Yes, I heard that from Austin. Were you close to her?"

A shrug. "Sometimes."

"She went through a rough spell?"

Amanda looked toward the hallway, then back. "Yeah. Ever since the day Henpecked moved in with his Hen."

Julia let herself smile at the alias.

"Where'd you get that blouse?" Amanda asked, leaning in for a closer look. "Mmm. And that perfume? I like it."

"The blouse came from Standout."

"I love that store!" the girl said. "Mom let me order shoes from the clearance bin once."

"I don't remember where I got the perfume. It might have been a gift from my husband."

"You're married? For real?"

Julia laughed at the girl's astonishment. "For real. His name is Troy. He likes this perfume on me too."

Amanda giggled, prompting Julia to do the same.

"Can I see his picture?"

Julia complied by touching her tablet screen. "That's him."

"Oooh," Amanda sang. "You look good together. Where is this?"

"We were on our honeymoon in San Francisco."

"Your honeymoon? Nice." Amanda giggled again. "Kids?"

"No. Not yet."

"How come?"

"We've only been married for six months."

The girl appeared confused by the explanation, as if it had never occurred to her to associate marriage with having kids.

"So, Amanda, would you let me ask you a few questions for my story?"

"Your story?" she asked warily.

"I'm writing a feature about families that struggle financially. It's for RAP Syndicate."

The name didn't ring any bells for the girl.

"They own several online media channels."

"Do you ever write for *Gal Style*?"

"I don't. But RAP owns that one."

"Really? Cool."

Julia waited a moment while the girl considered.

"Why not?" Amanda said.

"Great!"

Julia again checked the tablet's recording status before diving in.

"Do you know why your mother volunteered?"

"Volunteered for what?"

"To transition."

"Oh. You mean why did she kill herself?"

Julia found the lack of nuance refreshing, and disturbing. "Yes. Why did she kill herself?"

"Austin." She said no more, as if her half sibling's name said it all.

"Why Austin?" Julia prodded.

"He moved Hen in with him. She took over the nest, if you know what I mean."

Julia nodded vaguely. Then she shook her head. "Actually, I don't know what you mean."

"Before Austin and Hen moved in Mom and I were doing fine."

"But Austin said he moved in to help when he realized your mom had been drinking."

"That's a pile of bull!"

"He said she wanted to…" *How to say it?* "To do something that might give you a better life."

"He's a liar!" she shouted toward the hallway before hushing herself. "She did it because Hen kept whining about her own crummy life. She convinced my mom to commit suicide so Austin could get the house."

"Didn't the house go to you?" Julia wondered aloud. "I mean. Wouldn't your mother have put the house in trust for your future?"

Julia knew what Amanda couldn't: that Austin would have hit obstacles trying to cosign for his mother's transition. More clinics were requiring confirmation from a neutral party, someone who would not receive any of the inheritance. At least not officially.

"Gwen!" Julia realized.

"What about her?"

Julia covered her mouth, suddenly aware she had spoken the name aloud. "Nothing. Sorry," she said.

"It doesn't matter now anyway," Amanda continued bitterly.

"Why's that?"

The girl searched her internal vocabulary list. "Moreclosure. Is that the word?"

"Do you mean *foreclosure*?"

"Foreclosure. That's it."

"The bank is foreclosing?"

"If that means we lose the house, yes. Although I guess Hen made enough fuss at the bank that we'll get to rent it back. We won't have to move out."

A few seconds of stillness passed between them.

"I wish *I* could move out," Amanda finally added. "I hate it here."

Julia looked into the girl's eyes. Resignation. And the acid of resentment.

"So you blame your brother for your mom's decision?"

"My half brother. Yes, I do."

"And Gwen?"

A nod. "Her too. But mostly Austin. He could have stopped it."

"Could he?"

"One word from him and Mom would have changed her mind. I know she was depressed. And yes, she drank. But who could blame her? Hen was making this place a living nightmare. I hate her!"

"Do you have anyone else? Relatives? Other siblings?"

"Nope. Just Austin and Hen."

A brief silence.

"I might take the school counselor's advice."

"What kind of advice?"

"She told me if things get bad enough I can request protection from the state."

The comment troubled Julia. "Protection? From what?"

A shrug. "Don't know. Misery? Depression? I just know she said kids without parents can go to live with the Foster family."

"I think you mean a foster home."

"That's it. A foster home. Believe me, I've thought about calling them more than once."

"For protection?"

"For a home. At least more of a home than this place."

"I see," Julia said softly.

"Anyway," Amanda sang while leaping to her feet. She took the seat beside Julia on the sofa and moved in close. "Got any more pictures from your honeymoon?"

Julia smiled at the girl's hand resting on her own. They spent the next few minutes swiping through photo album files, Amanda grilling Julia for details about Troy's business, her sister's wardrobe, her nephew's school, and the nickname of each child in the Tolbert clan.

Fifteen minutes later Julia said goodbye to a pouty Austin and accepted Amanda's invitation to walk her to the car. She sat in the driver's seat watching the eleven-year-old wave goodbye from the porch, then vanish behind the front door of her dark zone address.

As Julia pulled away from the curb she ran through scenes of a story now captured on her tablet's recorder.

An alcoholic single mother struggles to make ends meet.

An estranged son manipulates her into an early transition, then squanders away his sister's financial future.

An oddly matched couple sell their potential offspring for cash to a snake-oil salesman promising youthful vigor.

And a beautiful orphan girl awaits rescue, starving for attention and dreaming of the day she might escape the shadowy realm of 2210 Kingston Street to find a brighter life.

CHAPTER TWENTY-EIGHT

The refrigerator shelves held some hormone-free, antibiotic-free, pesticide-free, and, most importantly, flavor-free milk, fruits, and vegetables. Tyler clung to the door, hunched over, and rearranged a few items. Hope rose within him at the sight of a reusable plastic container. Leftovers. Some forgotten remnant of a meal he must have thought worth keeping. Then he remembered the mashed potatoes from four nights ago.

Renee never saved anything since, to her, only fresh foods deserved the honor of consumption. Tyler wasn't so picky. Anything that hadn't gone rancid or turned into a moldy science experiment should be given a sporting chance.

He pulled out the container and flicked off the lid excitedly before disappointment sank in. Add "Gerry's dentures" to the list of disqualified entrees. They sat balanced atop the pile of mashed potatoes like Noah's Ark on Mount Ararat, condensation flooding the valleys. They'd been missing for several days, forcing Gerry, Renee, Tyler—and the disembodied voice of Katherine calling out from the bedroom—to conduct a mad, unsuccessful hunt. Until now.

"Found your dad's teeth!" Tyler called out, tossing the container onto the counter and slamming the fridge closed. He was still hungry.

"What?" Renee said, arriving with a laundry basket on her hip.

Tyler pointed at the evidence. Renee leaned in close, barely glanced at it, then sniffed, wrinkling her nose at Tyler.

"Gross, huh?" he said.

"Yes," she said, pulling away with the back of her hand protecting her nose to prevent gagging. "But not that. You. When's the last time you changed? Your clothes stink."

Tyler sniffed at his underarm, shrugging. Cologne de Burrito Supreme from lunch.

"Give me your clothes."

"I'm kind of using them at the moment."

"I'm about to put a load in, so hand them over."

Tyler stripped off his shirt and pants and tossed them with a smile.

"You want these as well?" he asked, pulling at, then snapping the waistband of his boxers.

Renee rolled her eyes and stuffed his clothes into the basket before disappearing around the corner to head upstairs.

Drat! He glanced back at Gerry's teeth.

"Ty?" Renee called from the top of the steps. He rushed to the foot of the staircase and glanced up. "Take a shower, and then maybe we can meet up in the bedroom."

"Nice look." Gerry's voice smacked from the hallway, complete with grinning gums. His skimpy attire mirrored Tyler's.

Tyler looked down at himself, then back to Gerry, shaking his head. He suddenly worried Gerry had heard Renee's obvious come-hither call. "I thought you were in bed."

"Katherine can't sleep."

"Is her back hurting again?"

Gerry nodded. "Just came to get some water and Vicodin for her. Then I'll be out of your pants." He sniggered. "I mean out of your hair!"

"Very funny. I was just heading upstairs, so help yourself. Oh, and you might want to rescue your dentures from the potatoes."

———— ∿∿ ————

With one towel wrapped around his waist, Tyler dabbed moisture off his hair with another as he pushed open the bedroom door hoping to find Renee in next to nothing. Instead he found her on the bed, dressed in the same jeans and T-shirt she'd had on earlier. She was surrounded by several pieces of paper, tears on her reddened cheeks. She clutched one page tightly, her blank gaze moving up to meet his, saying nothing.

He blinked once, hard, then instinctively took a single step backward. What was this? A trick? Had she lured him up here just to yell at him? For what? He ran through a quick mental list of all the infractions he might have committed in the past couple of days, but came up empty. This couldn't be about the burrito, could it?

Renee said nothing as her glare shot piercing daggers. He wondered whether she intended to hold it all in, passive-aggressively, or let it rip. In the past, entire nights, days, even weeks could be ruined by one wrong word at a moment like this. So he stood in paralyzed silence. Then he imagined what could happen if he ignored her obvious distress. He chose the lesser risk.

"What's the matter?" he asked, forgoing any attempt to mind-read the problem and abandoning the fantasy he had indulged in while showering.

She waited, the tear on one cheek dripping to the page in her hand, drawing out the moment like a knife sliding slowly across taut skin. Finally she gathered herself enough to speak. "You want to kill my dad?"

Tyler squinted in confusion. Kill her dad? Why would he want to kill Gerry? Sure, he had flipped Tyler's life upside down, but any fleeting thoughts of murder were harmless catharsis. Nothing even remotely serious.

"Don't play dumb with me," she said, sitting up more bravely. "You want him dead. Probably both of them. Am I right? And you seriously thought I'd be OK with it? They're my parents, Ty! My flesh and blood!"

The final comment came out as a definitive jab. *They* were her flesh and blood, whereas he…wasn't. She had put Tyler in his place, and to his surprise, it stung. It was one thing for him to view Renee as expendable, but quite another for her to do the same to him. Out loud.

"Renee. I don't know what—"

"Don't deny it. I found the evidence in your pants pocket!"

For the first time Tyler examined the pages scattered about. They were the legal documents and partially filled-in application from New Day Transition Center.

"No, Renee, you don't understand!" He took a step forward to defend himself from what, he realized, might be the perfect way to end this relationship. Let her think it. Give her a reason to leave his house. His life.

No! he thought to his own surprise.

Renee held up the application, positioning it so Tyler could read it clearly. "What's not to understand?"

He wasn't sure what to say, how to explain it. She didn't know about the case with Judge Santiago. At least not specifically. He'd mentioned a new opportunity, that he was finally doing some real detective work with a real detective paycheck. But she didn't know how big it was, nor that it involved the transition industry. He wished now that he'd at least said that much. She would never believe he had just pretended to enroll her father to transition as part of a case.

"It doesn't mean anything," he heard himself saying. *Great! Now you sound like every one of your clients' cheating lovers.*

"Doesn't mean anything? You can't be serious. They're my parents!"

"No, listen. I'm working on this case. Remember, the one I told you about? There have been threats, and I need to make sure that…" He hesitated. What *was* the reason he'd gone to New Day? He really didn't know. A lead from a guilt-ridden former transition specialist that had gone nowhere?

"Make sure that what?" Renee pressed.

"You see, the entire transition industry hangs in the balance on this lawsuit appeal that—"

"I don't care about the transition industry."

"I know, but…a lot of people do and—" Suddenly Tyler wasn't sure he was talking to Renee. *A lot of people* included those who had nothing to do with the NEXT lawsuit or the Santiago case. He forced aside the hazy form of an emerging idea and brought himself back firmly to Renee. He stepped forward again, this time reaching to grab her hand. She jerked it away, but relented on his second attempt. "I needed to find out for myself what actually went on inside one of those clinics."

"I don't understand. Why my father?"

"It was the best I could come up with in the moment. I'm sorry. I never meant for you to even see these." He shoved aside the documents and climbed onto the bed, one knee at a time. "I just had to make it seem like, to them, I was serious."

Renee wiped a tear from her face, then sighed. "And were you?"

"Was I what?"

"Serious." Her gaze rose to his. "Because I know you hate every moment of them being here."

Tyler shook his head before looking away. She was right. He did hate it. The moments. But not them.

"I don't hate your parents," he finally said. "It's just...I interviewed this guy. His mother died, and his invalid brother transitioned. He had given up everything for his brother, including his own future. And after he was gone, Jeremy—the brother—he told me that even though he hated the situation he had been in, he missed his brother dearly. And that's how it is with your parents."

This time Renee was the one who appeared confused. "You missed my parents?"

"No. I mean, even though I don't like the situation we're in—and I'm just being honest—even though I don't like it, I know it's the right thing to do. Otherwise I never would have agreed to it to begin with."

"Do you mean that? Really?"

Tyler pursed his lips. Did he mean it? The words had just kind of fallen out of his mouth without much thought. Perhaps he'd become so accustomed to smoothing things over with Renee he was lying without even realizing it. But then again, maybe it really was how he felt. That taking in Renee's parents had been right. Katherine was practically bedridden. Gerry had managed to lose his own teeth in a container of mashed potatoes. They clearly could no longer manage by themselves. They needed Renee. He smiled. "Of course I mean it," he finally said to her, and to himself.

"Thank you." She took both his hands in hers, pressing his palms against her cool, wet cheeks. "But I need you to understand something. My parents are my priority right now. I mean, I love you. I want you. But they're my flesh and blood. If I'm ever forced to make a choice..."

She couldn't bring herself to say the rest.

He leaned forward and kissed her. "Don't worry. I get it."

She pulled back, smiling, then leaned her head against his chest before squeezing tightly. He returned the embrace, kissing the top of her hair tenderly. It felt nice, making up.

A voice came shouting from downstairs.

"Renee? Are you up there?"

Tyler tried to ignore Gerry's call, tried to distract Renee by kissing her neck just behind her ear. It didn't work.

"It's my dad."

"Ignore him. Five minutes."

"Renee? Your mother needs you. She needs to use the bathroom and I can't do it by myself."

Tyler tossed himself to the bed in defeat. "Fine. Go."

"I won't be long," Renee said with a wink. "I promise."

He knew better. Bathroom duty was a choreographed endeavor that took at least thirty minutes from start to finish. Tyler slipped under the covers, questioning his fleeting sense of love for Renee. Perhaps he'd confused his desire for passion with a willingness to continue this relationship indefinitely. He needed to regain control. This could be his life for a very long time if he didn't solve the Santiago case.

He drifted off to sleep, vaguely aware he was still hungry.

CHAPTER TWENTY-NINE

"Very nice," Dr. Vincent said as he watched Sarah walk away after delivering two steaming mugs to the table. "A friend of yours?"

"Sarah and I worked together," Matthew said, still enjoying the lingering scent of her *good to see you again* embrace. "We got pretty close."

Campus Grinds looked as it had every day of every year that Matthew had started and ended a shift. But it *felt* different sitting across from his mentor enjoying conversation instead of rushing to clear used napkins and empty mugs.

Both men took a first sip.

"How close?" Dr. Vincent asked with a wink.

Matthew's first instinct was to confirm the professor's suspicion with a bluff. But he had already exaggerated his progress with Maria, so decided to tell the truth. "Nothing like that. Just coworkers chatting to pass the time."

Dr. Vincent pulled out his phone, pointing and zooming toward the counter where Sarah was taking an order, and clicked a photo. Then he began voicing letters as he tapped "S. A. R. A. H." He paused, looking back at Matthew. "How do you spell her last name?"

Matthew recognized the professor's pattern. "She has a partner," he said protectively.

Dr. Vincent frowned like a wine connoisseur shaking an empty bottle. He hit the DELETE key.

"So, this girl in Denver," he said, getting them back to the conversation interrupted by the arriving drinks. "Any chance she'll keep you from returning to school next year?"

"Maria, from Littleton. And no, I don't see her keeping me from school. Although I do face other obstacles."

Dr. Vincent glanced at the time. "What do you say we spend twenty minutes overcoming your obstacles and leave the last ten for you to tell me about Maria?"

If only his financial problems could be solved so quickly.

"Actually, I wanted to discuss a different topic if that's OK with you."

The professor smiled. "You made the drive and bought the coffee so I suppose I should let you set the agenda. What's on your mind, Mr. Adams?"

"I'm working with a man who should transition," he said abruptly. "But he thinks it's wrong. And his daughter, who really needs him to volunteer, is scared to talk to him about it."

Dr. Vincent enjoyed a second drink while waiting for Matthew to say more.

"Well, not scared. More like perplexed. I think she likes the idea but vacillates between what she knows would be best and what she thinks would be wrong."

"So you've discussed this with both the father and the daughter?"

"I have. I raised it with my client after lunch a few days ago.

Then I spoke to his daughter yesterday. That's when I decided I needed your advice."

Dr. Vincent seemed pleased by Matthew's deferential regard. "I'm glad I was available. Tell me about the conversation with...what's the daughter's name?"

"Marissa. She's a bit older than me. Has two young kids."

"No partner?"

"Died a few years back. That's part of the reason the old man should transition. If he doesn't he'll need to move in with her and the kids."

The look on the professor's face told Matthew he didn't entirely see the problem.

"They don't get along," said Matthew.

Dr. Vincent continued to stare.

"And he's about to run out of money."

Finally an understanding nod. "I see. And his health?"

"Pretty bad. He can't walk. Breathes through a tube. Can't really be left alone."

"We decay," the professor said. They were the same words he had used when Matthew asked about his own ailing mother. And the words he used to explain Manichaeism to students and readers.

"Exactly!" Matthew said. "He's in decay and plans to make himself a burden to Marissa, Isabelle, and little Pete."

"The kids?"

"Yeah. Twins. About five or six years old."

"Hmm. Do they get along with their grandpa?"

The question carried weight, as if the professor thought affection might trump pragmatics.

Matthew recalled little Pete's secret conversation in his grandfather's room. "They get along," he replied. "But they've never had to live with Reverend Grandpa."

"Reverend Grandpa?" A chuckle.

"Don't ask," Matthew replied with a roll of his eyes. "He's sort of eccentric."

"I bet."

"He insists everyone call him Reverend. So the kids call him Reverend Grandpa." Matthew matched his mentor's smile as he thought of the comical man. "He used to be a preacher of some sort. Loves to read and quote from a vintage Bible he keeps in the front room."

The description flattened Dr. Vincent's grin into a disapproving sneer. "A literalist?"

Matthew didn't understand the question. "A what?"

"Does this Reverend Grandpa read the Bible as if it were literally true?"

"Seems to. Why?"

"What about the daughter?"

"What about her?"

"Does she share the old man's beliefs? You know, does she read the Bible literally?"

"I don't think she reads it at all. Like I said, she and her father don't get along."

"So she doesn't object to her dad volunteering for religious reasons?"

"I don't think so. She never mentioned any religious reasons. She just seemed afraid to talk to him about it."

"What did she say exactly?"

"Well," Matthew said, trying to recall. "I told her that I had asked Reverend Grandpa whether he had ever considered volunteering. She seemed both surprised and intrigued, especially when I explained your 'spirit good, body bad' concept."

"It's not entirely my concept," Dr. Vincent said with a reluctant hint of modesty. "Did Marissa seem open to transitions in theory?"

"I think so."

"So she didn't dismiss the process as immoral out of hand?"

"No."

"But she got nervous when you suggested a transition could help her specific situation?"

"Exactly! How'd you guess?"

"I've been teaching about enlightened spirituality for a long time now. The easy part is getting students to accept ideas in the abstract. It's much harder getting them to connect the dots to concrete realities like life and death. Humanity is hopelessly addicted to the embodied-personhood paradigm."

Matthew pretended to follow. "I guess," he said, returning to his dilemma. "One thing's for sure. Marissa Gale will never suggest a transition to Reverend Grandpa."

"But you did."

"Yes. I sensed he was depressed and assumed he had been considering volunteering. Boy, was I wrong!"

The two shared a laugh.

"Bit your head off, did he?"

A nod. "Yep. But I also sensed a tiny crack in the door, as if I had raised an option he would only consider under dire circumstances. That's why I mentioned it to Marissa. I even offered to help."

"Help? How?"

"I said I'd raise the topic with him again at the right moment. Possibly when he's feeling depressed or when he asks me to deposit his reverse mortgage check."

"Reverse mortgage?"

"He's been living on the house equity."

A nod of recall. "Right."

"Anyway, I said I could raise the subject at a time when he might be open to a different solution than burdening his daughter and grandkids. That's why I called your office. I was hoping you could help me come up with a few arguments that he might hear."

"I take it he doesn't like Manichean philosophy."

"Not at all. Dismissed my best points without a thought."

"I'm not surprised," the professor said. "Bible-thumpers aren't exactly known for their ability to think." He chuckled derisively.

"I guess. But he seems pretty smart. He's even read a book by Augustine."

"*City of God*?"

Matthew didn't recognize the title. "No. The book where Augustine described his religious conversion."

The former priest grimaced. "*Confessions*."

"So you know it?"

"All too well."

"Should I read it?"

"No."

The answer surprised Matthew. "No?"

The professor corrected himself. "I mean, yes, of course. But Augustine wrote *Confessions* after ditching Manichaeism for Christianity. His books won't help you convince an old literalist that it's OK to escape a decaying body."

"I see."

A brief silence.

"Let's get back to the daughter," the professor said. "Did she accept your offer to talk to the father about volunteering?"

"She didn't say yes. But she didn't say no either."

"Then you need to do it."

"Really?"

"Absolutely." Dr. Vincent appeared to have overcome any concerns about affectionate grandkids. "Does the family have money?"

"Not much. Like I said, he's burning through a reverse mortgage. Why do you ask?"

"I just wondered whether the daughter would be willing to pay down your school loan if you convince the old man to go through with it. You know, sort of like a finder's fee."

"Would that be, you know, ethical?"

Dr. Vincent rolled his eyes. "Why wouldn't it be? Anyone can donate to a university."

"I don't know. It feels sort of—"

"In fact," the professor interrupted, "I have a research project that's been on hold since the end of last semester when I lost my grant. If you can find me a donor I could easily create a full-scholarship intern position."

"Wait. You mean if Marissa donated to your research project you could get me back into school?"

"Not just Marissa. Anyone."

Matthew considered the possibilities.

"What about my mother's estate?"

The question seemed to confuse the professor. "I thought your mother's estate was held up until the NEXT appeal gets resolved."

"Yeah. But it's only held up because I'm the direct beneficiary. What if the money got donated to the university instead?"

Dr. Vincent smiled at the idea before showing a look of concern, as if trying to figure out how to avoid getting into trouble with the IRS. After a few seconds he appeared to imagine a loophole, or possibly a cheat. "We might just be able to make that work."

Ten minutes later Matthew sat alone at the same table staring at the bottom of an empty coffee mug. His breath quickened with excitement as he considered his next steps.

First, call estate trustee Benjamin Cedillo to relinquish his inheritance money to the University of Colorado.

Second, ask Maria Davidson on a date in order to celebrate his pending return to college.

CHAPTER THIRTY

Troy looked at Julia from his side of the sofa without saying a word. He had seemed distracted while reading the first draft of her story. It had made her nervous watching facial expressions and hearing sighs that she couldn't quite decipher. Was he impressed? Confused? Did he love it? Hate it? Perhaps the pause meant he was trying to think of what to say without hurting her journalist ego.

"Be honest. What do you think?"

Another, deeper sigh. One that she recognized.

Troy was agitated.

"Say something."

"They sold their babies on the black market?"

Julia felt relieved knowing she had appalled her first reader. That was the purpose of the feature, after all. To put a human face on dark zone trends. Although, in the case of Austin Tozer and the woman Amanda called Hen, *inhuman* might be the more fitting word.

Troy continued. "The guy convinced his fifty-eight-year-old mom to transition just so he could avoid getting a job?"

"I didn't say he said that, did I?" Julia asked, fearing she had misrepresented Austin's rationale.

Troy glanced down at the tablet to rescan a section of the article. "No. I guess I read that between the lines."

Good, thought Julia. The story had accomplished both of her goals. First, give the facts as presented. Second, show the truth as observed.

"And I didn't call what they did 'selling on the black market' since it's legal to sell a fetus. Right to privacy."

"But I specifically remember a provision in the Ethical Embryotics Act stating companies can only accept *donated* embryos from unsuccessful in vitro implantation."

"True," Julia said. "But that law only applies to companies supplying materials for medical uses. It never mentioned cosmetics, health supplements, or a dozen other product categories."

"Health supplements?"

"Embryotic-enhanced protein powder. Bodybuilders add it to shakes."

Troy's face took on a greenish hue. "We ingest human embryos?" he whispered as if asking forgiveness.

"*Soylent Green* come to life," Julia said.

"*Soylent Green?*"

"An old movie where human beings became part of the food supply due to overpopulation. Too many people for too little food."

Troy winced, then sighed. "Too *many* people? Oh for the days we worried about *that* problem."

"Austin Tozer and his partner fit the dark zones themes to a tee," Julia said. "They took two thousand dollars per potential kid to spend on video games and Pop-Tarts, clueless to how badly we will need those kids a few decades from now. How badly *they* might need them. I thought their story was poetically appropriate."

"Tragic poetry," Troy scoffed.

Julia waited for more.

"You did good, babe," Troy said as he kissed her forehead. "It captures the ugly side of dark zone trends. I can't imagine anyone reading this piece without questioning common assumptions behind the Youth Initiative."

"Thanks," Julia said. She sensed he wanted to say more. "And?" she asked.

He hesitated before speaking. "Well. I also can't imagine RAP Syndicate publishing this story as is."

"I have a deal with Paul. He promised to run what I deliver. No changes that I don't approve first."

"That's good," Troy replied. "But can we trust him?"

Julia knew what was behind the question. Paul Daugherty was the same editor who had radically altered Julia's *Breeders* feature a year earlier. He had merged Julia's work with a smear piece by Monica Garcia, a rising star at RAP thanks to great legs rather than winning prose.

"No, we can't trust him," she said. "But that's a risk we take."

He nodded in reluctant acceptance of the gamble. "Regardless," he said, "it's one of the most powerful things you've written. I'm proud of you." He gave her another kiss, this time on the lips. "And I'm grateful to you. I think this will help Kevin."

"Wait till you see my second story. Polar opposite of this one. My first bright spot family."

She began describing an interview she had done the prior afternoon: a couple married almost twenty years, with three kids, running a software support business they operated out of their home. The oldest son, seventeen years old, worked in the business part-time after school. The grandparents lived in the same house. Or rather in an apartment that adjoined the main structure and provided easy access so the younger kids could get

Grandpa's help with homework or assist Grandma chopping vegetables. Her favorite part of the story, she explained, was how the older and younger couples had pooled their resources after the crash, an ideal arrangement that enabled the younger pair to launch the business.

Midway through her description Julia realized Troy was nodding his head without really listening. She stopped talking, folded her arms with a huff, and waited the ten seconds it took for him to notice.

His distant stare finally saw her scolding face. "Sorry, babe," he said. "I'm listening."

"No. You're *trying* to listen. Not the same thing."

She was right.

"You might as well tell me what's on your mind," Julia insisted. "You'll find out what I was saying later when you read my second story."

He smiled sheepishly before he groaned. "I'm not sure you want to know."

Her mind jumped to Troy and Kevin's business. Another setback? Had the needed venture capital deal fallen through? "Now you *have* to tell me," she insisted.

"I spoke to Kevin about an hour ago. He said it seems like Senator Franklin may be up to something."

"Something bad?"

"Not necessarily bad. More like calculated. Franklin encouraged Kevin to approach a guy named Dimitri to help us fund getting the Center for Economic Health off the ground."

"Evan Dimitri?" she asked. "Isn't he the brains behind the Saratoga Foundation?"

"The brains and a big chunk of the cash," Troy said. "He's a major player behind Franklin's campaign. He even gave a large gift to Kevin's reelection PAC last year. That's why Franklin suggested Dimitri as a potential source of seed funding."

"Makes sense. So why the concern?"

"There's more. Kevin said Franklin is acting all chummy again, like he did before…"

Troy stopped.

"Say it. Before my *Breeders* story tarnished Kevin's reputation?"

A faint nod.

"Anyway, rumors are floating around that Franklin sees Kevin as a key ally to win the White House next year."

"I thought Franklin had been trying to distance himself from Kevin."

"He was. It appears that's changing."

"Isn't that a good thing?" Julia asked. "I mean, it can only help Kevin to gain access and influence, right?"

"Perhaps," Troy said warily. "But Franklin isn't known to do favors for other party leaders, even young up-and-comers like Kevin, unless he sees how it will advance his agenda or bolster his poll ratings. I can only think of one reason Franklin would start courting Kevin now."

Troy paused, giving Julia a moment to fill in the punch line.

"He wants Kevin's endorsement?"

Troy appeared confused by the suggestion. "No," he said. "Kevin's endorsement wouldn't mean much at this stage of the game. He's only a second-term congressman from a medium-size state."

"What then?" Julia asked impatiently.

"I think he might be considering Kevin for the ticket."

Julia gasped. "As in, *Tolbert for vice president* ticket?"

"Exactly. Think about it. The *Breeders* story tapped the disdain of a large swath of the population against people like Kevin Tolbert."

"Don't remind me," she said.

"But it also forced the party to face facts. They now acknowledge the existence of a sizable voting bloc that seems to be growing and that can afford to donate more than dark zone citizens."

"Franklin wants support from the breeders."

"Which Kevin's smiling face and family photo would embody better than anyone in the party. Traditional marriage. Four kids. All he needs is some platform to give voice to and garner support from a constituency no one else has tapped. A large influx of cash to establish the Center for Economic Health as a credible voice would position Kevin well."

"But you worry it would make Kevin beholden to Franklin."

"I'm not as worried about Franklin as I am about the guy funding Franklin's rise."

"Dimitri."

"Do you know what he did during the lunch meeting with Kevin? He flashed a two-million-dollar check in his face like a puppeteer dangling strings. The recipient line was blank. Then he placed the check in front of Kevin and handed him a pen. 'Fill in the name of your new organization,' he said."

"Two million dollars?"

"Twice what we had hoped to raise in seed funding."

"What did Kevin say?"

"He thanked Mr. Dimitri for the support, wrote 'Center for Economic Health' onto the check, and slid the pen back across the table."

"So you have two million to work with? That's terrific!" She noticed Troy's frown. "Isn't it?"

"It would be if not for what happened next. Dimitri slid the pen back toward Kevin and handed him another document. Kevin read it, then tore up the check."

Julia's eyes widened. "He tore up a two-million-dollar donation?"

"The document Dimitri wanted Kevin to sign would have

made us promise that the Center for Economic Health will only advocate policies that encourage increased fertility while leaving the second bright spot trend alone. 'I'm fine with you rallying support among voters who love kids,' Dimitri told him. 'That'll help us. But if you do anything to undermine the core of the Youth Initiative I'll drop you faster than a bowling ball!'"

"Meaning?"

"Meaning hands off the transition industry. No research showing it causes harm. No suggesting there have been abuses. No proposals that would curtail its growth."

"Did Kevin explain to him that transitions aren't bringing the promised growth?"

"He knows. He doesn't care."

"Why would a fiscal conservative like Dimitri support a practice that stagnates the economy?"

"Because he doesn't believe the evidence."

"But—"

"Correction," Kevin continued. "He doesn't *want to* believe the evidence because his company makes a fortune as the exclusive supplier of PotassiPass, the key chemical ingredient used in every NEXT transition."

No wonder Troy had been so distracted. So agitated.

"I'm sorry," was all she could think to say.

"Me too," he said, squeezing Julia's hand. "I've had a bad feeling about Evan Dimitri ever since…well…since the first time I saw his name."

"When was that?"

"A large donation check from out of the blue last year. No prior relationship. No connection whatsoever. Kevin met him for lunch alone and later with Franklin."

Troy paused as if watching wheels turn in his head. Then he turned back toward Julia. "It took guts for Kevin to tear up that check. But he may also have turned one of Franklin's most reliable friends into one of our wealthiest enemies."

"Let's hope not," Julia said as she reached for a silver lining. Nothing came. She instead placed her hand on Troy's tensed jaw. "Hey," she whispered sweetly. "Where's the man I married? The one who makes a living figuring out how to turn declining companies into thriving enterprises?"

She sensed his anxiety ease at her touch. She moved in closer, teasing his lips with her own.

"The man who discovered bright spots in an economy everyone else saw as a dark, mucky swamp?"

She wrapped both arms around Troy's neck while sliding from her side of the sofa onto his lap. She began nibbling his earlobe.

"The man who brightens my life every day and"—she tasted his upper neck—"the man with whom I plan to join the bright spots movement."

They kissed deeply for several seconds. Then Troy pulled his head back to look Julia in the eyes. "Wait. What did you just say?"

A sly grin followed by a fierce nod.

"So you want to? Now? Not in a few years?"

"Now," she said eagerly, recalling Angie's description of pregnancy and motherhood. It was like leaning over the railing at Niagara Falls, the fear overwhelmed by the wonder.

Her husband's fingers slid around her torso. Her body tingled with anticipation. Julia knew she was about to enjoy the first unprotected sex of her life.

And it surprised her to realize nothing had ever made her feel so safe.

CHAPTER THIRTY-ONE

Tyler sat in his car rereading the partially completed application he had taken from the New Day Transition Clinic. It stubbornly refused to give him even one additional clue. He took a first bite of his second doughnut before wiping the side of his mouth on a glaze-smeared napkin. He would have used the fresh napkin sitting on the passenger-side seat had it not held notes that, sadly, summarized his entire investigation.

The Facts

- 4 letters from "A Manichean"
- 3 polite. 4th seems a threat
- Jeremy = most to gain from NEXT loss
- Hannah hates them—possible suspect?
- New Day Clinic a bit pushy but legit

He needed more. He crammed the rest of doughnut number two into his mouth before attempting to speak a command.

"Please repeat," the device said in response.

Tyler swallowed without chewing and tried again. "Association search for A Manichean."

"Three thousand relevant results. Please specify to narrow."

"Within one hundred miles of Denver," he said while licking glaze from his thumb.

"Please repeat."

He sighed as he reached for the tablet. "I'll just type it in!"

"Thank you," the device said politely.

Two quick taps left a sugary smudge that reminded Tyler he still had four deliciously sticky fingers. He sucked the glaze from each while trying to clean the mess. Then he groaned at the streak left on the keyboard by the used napkin.

These notes are useless anyway, he thought while grabbing his case summary document. Seconds later the screen was legible again.

The phone rang in his ear.

"Tyler Cain," he answered.

"Good morning, Mr. Cain." He recognized the voice, but couldn't immediately place it. He glanced at the dash screen: JULIA DAVIDSON, JOURNALIST.

"Oh, hi, Ms. Davidson," he said with surprise.

"Simmons."

"Right. Ms. Simmons." *Probably calling to thank me*, he thought. "How'd it go with Austin?"

"Actually, quite well. I'm including his story in the series. Thanks for making the connection."

"Like I told you, Austin's definitely a dark zone kind of guy."

"The story won't use his real name, but you'll recognize him. It should run in the next few weeks."

The comment reminded Tyler to subscribe. "I look forward to reading it. Glad I could help."

"I'd like to return the favor," Julia began. "Something came up I think might prove helpful in your investigation."

"Really?" he said as if spotting a sliver of light through an overcast sky. "Let me hear it."

"During our chat you said the judge had received three letters, is that right?"

"Four, actually."

"Four letters then. And you said the person seemed urgent to know Santiago's opinion on the appeal?"

"That's right."

"Did the writer indicate whether he or she hoped the judge would decide for or against NEXT?"

Tyler glanced at the notes on his now-crumpled napkin and decided to play the odds. "Against."

"You're sure about that?"

He remembered Hannah Walker asking the same question. "Well, actually, the letters don't indicate one way or the other. But we've assumed—"

"Don't," Julia interrupted. "Don't assume the writer wants NEXT to lose the case. There are some very powerful people who need NEXT to win that appeal. Some of them might even go to extreme lengths in order to protect their interests."

"What kind of interests are you talking about?"

Tyler waited. Why the long silence? Was she trying to convince herself to say the rest? "Mrs. Simmons?"

"Please, call me Julia."

"OK, Julia. What kind of interests?"

She hesitated, then spoke. "It's probably totally unrelated to this case, but my husband learned of a conversation that took place in Washington that sheds light on the importance of the NEXT case."

"Go on," Tyler said.

Julia told him about the large check Kevin Tolbert had declined to accept from a man named Evan Dimitri.

"So this Dimitri guy has the exclusive supplier contract with NEXT?" Tyler chewed on the revelation for a moment. "And he threatened Congressman Tolbert?"

"Not exactly threatened. But he was clearly upset by Kevin's refusal."

He let the additional information settle. "I don't get it," he finally said. "I imagine those kinds of lunch conversations happen every day in Washington. Why did you think to mention this one? I don't see what it has to do with the Santiago case."

"Maybe nothing," she said. "But for whatever reason it made me think of you. I remembered you saying you thought those letters came from someone like Jeremy. Someone who has a lot to gain if NEXT loses its appeal."

"And you think I'm on the wrong track?"

"I do. I think you need to consider who has something to *lose* rather than something to gain. Evan Dimitri, among others, could lose a fortune in sales if anything undermines the transition industry."

"Like a wrongful death victory against NEXT."

"Exactly," she said.

Tyler's mind began racing as new possibilities breathed life into a dead-end investigation.

"Anyway," Julia was saying, "I wanted to mention it in case it could help you find the culprit."

"Thank you, Julia," he said. "It certainly can't hurt."

They ended the call. Tyler remembered his search and grabbed his tablet.

"Association search," he began. "Evan Dimitri and A Manichean."

"Please repeat."

He cursed, then began tapping the revised query onto the screen.

"No results," the tablet said disappointingly.

He deleted A MANICHEAN and hit SEARCH again. A string of results surfaced, most of them press releases about quarterly profits, emerging innovations, and recent acquisitions. Tyler tapped
the most promising. To his surprise it didn't bring him to a company site, but rather to the news posting page from a political
action group called the Saratoga Foundation.

Saratoga Foundation chairman Evan Dimitri recently announced the addition of fashion industry mogul Trisha Sayers to the board of directors. Ms. Sayers brings a wealth of
experience to the team derived from more than a decade
running one of the nation's largest retail chains and from
serving on a variety of presidential commissions including
the Youth Initiative coalition that helped the president craft
what became a sweeping plan to address the nation's steep
economic decline. Mr. Dimitri said he considers Ms. Sayers
an excellent addition to the board because she will bring…

A musical ping interrupted Tyler's reading. He looked at the
dash screen. A short text message.

FROM: JULIA DAVIDSON, JOURNALIST
Be careful, Mr. Cain. This case might end up carrying you into
the deep end of the pool.

CHAPTER THIRTY-TWO

"For Pete's sake!" Reverend Grandpa shouted from his perch. "Shut the door!"

Matthew should have knocked. He had been too eager to take one last peek at his freshly ironed collar and swish one last shot of mouthwash before leaving. He apologized at the mutually embarrassing intrusion and pulled the door closed as quickly as he had opened it. Then he heard the old man's voice mushroom from a slow, deep chuckle into a leg-brace-slapping roar of laughter.

"You should have seen the size of your eyeballs!" Reverend Grandpa said between guffaws, his voice slightly muffled by the bathroom door. "You looked like a little boy accidently skipping into the ladies' locker room!"

If only, Matthew thought. That would have been much less disturbing than the image now trapped behind his still-closed eyelids.

"Sorry, son," the old man said after one last snigger. "Thought you had left already. I shouldn't be long."

Matthew knew better. Besides, he had no desire to use the room now. "It's all right. I'm good. See you tonight."

"Have a good time, my boy."

Matthew walked back to the bedroom to grab a gift he had finished wrapping moments earlier. The box contained a framed picture of a photo he had clipped and saved from the Littleton High School annual; a little something he hoped Maria David-son would appreciate. Maybe even like.

"I'm off," he said, shooting Donny a wave.

"You're still here?" Donny said. "I thought you left."

"So did the Rev. I needed to wrap a little something." Matthew displayed the package.

Donny grinned and nodded.

"Thanks again for covering for me. I owe you one."

"No problem, man." Donny's eyes were fixed on a television screen mounted on the kitchen wall. "Sure you wouldn't rather hang out with us boys to watch the rest of the game?" He chuck-led at his own dumb question. Of course Matthew didn't want to watch baseball instead of go on his first official date with the most amazing woman on the planet. Still, he sweetened the deal by holding up a partially consumed bag of cheese puffs. "I brought your favorites."

"Tempting. But I'll pass."

Matthew started toward the back door, then looked back to-ward his in-a-pinch pal with a twinge of guilt. Should he have warned him about Reverend Grandpa's evangelistic fervor? Should he suggest steering clear of religious topics?

"Forget something?" Donny asked.

Matthew shook his head. "Good luck, buddy."

Donny shrugged, then looked back toward the game while tossing a single puff in the air to nearly catch it in his mouth.

As Matthew slipped out the door his phone rang from his front jeans pocket. He glanced at the screen and realized he needed to take the call, much as he hated any delays. "Hi, Ben," he answered. "Thanks for getting back to me."

"Hello, Matthew." Just as distant as the last time they'd spoken.

"How's Carol?" Small talk might help thaw the chill.

"How should she be?"

Matthew could tell Ben intended to make him work for every syllable of conversation.

"Give her my love."

"I will. Right after we get back from wasting another five hundred or a thousand dollars of your mom's estate on a romantic dinner and bottle of wine."

"Very funny. I never said you were—"

"What do you need, Matthew?" Ben asked as if speaking to a disruptive child raising his hand for yet another trip to the bathroom.

Matthew swallowed back contempt. Further antagonism in an already tense relationship wouldn't help matters.

"Did you get my message?"

"I did."

"Did it make sense?"

"It didn't."

Matthew inhaled deeply. "Well, I need to know whether I can redirect a portion of my mother's estate to the University of Colorado."

A brief silence told him wheels were turning in Ben's head.

"Ben? Did you hear me?"

"You can't do that," Ben said decisively.

"Why not?"

"I already told you, the money can't be released until—"

"It can't be released to *me*," Matthew interrupted. "But I'm asking if some of it can go to the university. You know, as a donation. I wouldn't get a penny."

Another spell of silence.

"Ben?"

"Why?"

Now Matthew went silent to consider options. Should he tell Ben the whole story? It might help if he knew Dr. Vincent had suggested the idea. Or would it be better to feed Ben information on a need-to-know basis?

"Matthew? What kind of scheme are you up to?"

"It's not a scheme," Matthew snapped as he placed the wrapped gift on the hood of his car to free a hand. He opened the door while admiring the package that symbolized his real goals. *Get back to school and become a professor. Do something with your life worthy of a woman like Maria Davidson.* "I just need to know if it can be done, OK?"

Matthew sensed the lawyer's subdued chafing. He didn't care.

"All right, Matty." Matthew hated when Ben used Aunt Carol's nickname for him. "I'll look into the possibility. Seems like a long shot, but I'll check it out."

Matthew had hoped to know before his date with Maria. A simple question, he assumed, with a quick yes-or-no answer. No such luck.

"When will you know?" Matthew pushed.

He heard Ben's familiar put-out sigh. "I'll see what I can do."

Each waited for the other to speak next.

"Thanks," Matthew relented. "I'll expect a call tomorrow."

He ended the call before Ben could respond.

Matthew knew Maria's eyes were trying to read his reaction. He had to say something, anything, now.

"Of course I don't mind."

He sensed her gaze sinking. Say more!

"In fact," he added quickly, "this is great!"

He hoped to sound convincing despite the shock. So much for a romantic dinner alone followed by, what had he expected, a trip back to her apartment? His first glance at her incredible outfit had said, *Yes*. Her son's sulking presence said, *Not a chance*.

Matthew recalled Maria's asking if he wanted to meet Jared on the day they'd had coffee. He had assumed she meant later, after the two of them spent time together. After they had hit it off. Not on their first real date, if that's what this was. Did she want the protection of a third wheel? Did the boy lack friends, someone to hang out with during his mom's date? Or maybe, he hoped, his presence meant Maria really liked Matthew, that she wanted him to see the full package sooner rather than later.

He realized he had been silent for a few seconds. "Put 'er there, buddy," Matthew said hastily, shoving his hand toward the boy.

Jared crossed his arms while turning to glower at his mother.

"Come on, man, don't leave me hangin'."

Which is exactly what the boy did.

Maria gave Matthew an embarrassed smile. "Sorry," she said.

Her eyes seemed like a plea for Matthew's help, triggering in him a curious sense of purpose. He tried to imagine the relationship between Maria and her twelve-year-old son, a boy who must be leery of the countless men hovering around his flower of a mom. Some of them, perhaps, had hurt her. Or him.

"Listen," he said, lowering his extended hand. No point in pretending with the boy. "I get it. You don't want to spend time becoming best friends with some old guy just because he likes your mom."

Maria seemed pleased by the comment.

Matthew looked at the restaurant hostess, who had already retrieved a pair of menus in anticipation of seating the "party of two" reserved under his name.

"And I'd be shocked if this young lady even has a table for three available."

The hostess looked toward the half-empty dining area, then back toward the trio. She followed Matthew's lead. "I'm afraid I only reserved a table for two, sir," she said with a complicit grin.

"So we have two choices," Matthew continued. "We can either call off the whole thing or"—he paused for dramatic impact—"we can jump in my car and head over to Conroy's to grab some burgers and shakes and then play a few rounds of Battalion Call."

The boy's brow lifted slightly at the mention of the vintage virtual warfare game. Then he forced his expression back to a frown, followed by a shrug.

"Sounds fun," Maria chirped. "What do you say, Jared?" She bumped him with a hip.

An hour later Matthew was sitting at a booth in front of empty burger wrappers and milkshake cups and a smattering of cold, neglected fries. He was listening to a grateful Maria confirm his suspicions. She did indeed have a rocky history with men.

"After that I promised Jared no more surprises. And I figured the best way to keep that promise was to bring him along."

"Makes sense to me," Matthew said as he glanced around the room to make sure the boy remained out of earshot. "He seems like a pretty good watchdog to keep away the wolves."

An embarrassed giggle. "Actually, too good. You're only my second date in the past six months."

Matthew dropped his jaw. "Not possible."

She blushed at the embarrassing secret and at the admiration in Matthew's eyes.

"How about you?" she asked. "I bet you've had a long line of women in your life."

He laughed awkwardly. "I wouldn't say a long line."

"What about Molly? I thought for sure she would pursue you after graduation."

The name didn't ring a bell at first. Then he remembered. "Jolly Molly Carson?" He blushed at the recollection. Maria had suggested Matthew ask Molly to the senior prom. It was the excuse she gave for rejecting his request. Said she couldn't go with a guy Molly crushed on. Molly Carson had a pretty face, but a heavy figure. Her quick wit made her good for a laugh. But not for a prom date.

"We never went out," Matthew said with a touch of offense. "I didn't even know she liked me."

"Who then?"

"Nobody you'd know," he said limply.

She seemed to sense her mistake. "Well, I'm glad."

His eyes met hers. "Glad? For what?"

"I'm glad you haven't been serious with many girls."

The comment surprised him, and pleased him. "Really? Why's that?"

Maria turned toward the gaming machines as if looking for Jared. "I don't know. I guess because it can include complications." She appeared reflective, as if wondering what life might have been had she made different choices. Then she turned back toward Matthew with what seemed a smile of sincere admiration. She slid her hand toward his. "You look good, Matthew. I'm glad you got in touch."

Feeling Maria's softness, he considered slipping to her side of the booth. But he stayed put. Maria Davidson had offered herself to many men over the years. Each, he assumed, had eagerly tasted a small piece of the delicious creature touching him now. But he wanted more than a fragment, more than a short-term fling. And getting what he wanted meant heeding the warnings of a wary watchdog named Jared.

His hand retreated tenderly to retrieve the gift he had placed on the bench beside him. "I brought you something."

A look of surprise. "What is it?"

"Open it and find out."

She did. A picture frame. She flipped it over to view the image.

"Do you remember this?"

Watching her eyes, he saw she clearly did not. No matter. "I've kept that picture framed in my room ever since high school."

She looked closer to examine the younger versions of them both. "Where did you get this picture?"

The question bothered him. She must have purchased their senior annual. Maria appeared in dozens of posed and spontaneous shots. But only one, this one, included Matthew Adams.

"It was in the annual," he explained. "That was us in the lunch room on February twelfth of our senior year."

"Right," she said guardedly. "I guess I missed this one."

A brief, awkward silence passed between them. What was she thinking?

"You know the exact date?" Maria asked.

"I sure do," he said proudly.

She shifted uncomfortably in her seat. Her soft allure seemed to harden, as if she were suddenly in the presence of a pesky stalker. It was the same look, he now remembered, she'd given him the day he asked her to go with him to the senior prom.

"That was great!" Jared shouted as he approached the booth. Both sets of eyes turned in the boy's direction, grateful for the interruption. Matthew forced a smile, still wondering what was on Maria's mind.

Jared slid into the open space beside his mom. The same space Matthew now thought he should have taken when he'd had the chance.

"Level eight!" the boy bragged in Matthew's direction. "I hit level eight that time!"

Matthew offered a thin smile of congratulation. "Whoa. You rock, dude!" he said like the dinosaur he felt himself becoming.

Had the picture reminded Maria that the mysterious Matthew Adams was not an overlooked gem from high school sweeping back into Littleton after building a successful business? He was the pimple-faced geek who had dared violate class system boundaries by crushing on the most desirable girl at Littleton High. A guy who, it turned out, had been obsessed with her since February twelfth of their senior year.

Maria pulled Jared close, a motherly embrace that seemed to double as a human shield protecting her from whatever danger Matthew suddenly posed.

"Geez, Mom!" the boy said while pulling away. He scanned the room for potential witnesses. Coast clear, he relaxed enough to notice the picture frame.

"Is that you?" he asked his mom, looking closer at the picture. She nodded. "Uh-huh."

He continued examining the image. "Who's the dorf?"

Maria's eyes met Matthew's. Both blushed at the embarrassing nature of the question. And at the truth of it.

"He wasn't a dorf." She gently slapped her son's arm. "He was a friend."

Not a *boy*friend. Not a long-lost love. Just a friend.

Maria quickly gathered the torn wrapping paper and bundled it around the frame before placing the gift beside her on the bench.

"Matthew brought it as a reminder of the good old days, didn't you, Matthew?"

He nodded as the boy exclaimed, "So you're the dorf?"

Another slap, this time less playful than the last.

Matthew smiled weakly until Maria broke the momentary

silence. "Why don't you two play another round together? You know, see if you can reach level nine."

Matthew started to object. Time to throw in the towel.

"I'm in!" Jared announced.

"I don't know," Matthew began before stopping himself at the thought that he might have been misreading Maria's body language. She wouldn't have suggested another round with Jared unless she wanted the two to continue bonding. Maybe the picture hadn't given her the creeps after all. Perhaps she was just reacting to an embarrassing reminder of her own age. Unlikely, he thought, but possible. Most women, even those as gorgeous as Maria Davidson, struggle with self-doubt.

"Come on," Jared prodded. "Just one more round."

"Why not?" Matthew said with a smile of renewed optimism.

"And then we should go," said Maria.

Jared frowned indignantly. "But you said I could order a dessert if I came along."

"Yeah, Mom," Matthew added. "We can't leave before I buy you two an ice-cream sundae."

She smiled at the label, and the offer. "All right," she relented. "We'll stay long enough for dessert."

"Great!" the duo said in unison, prompting another smile from the beautiful woman Matthew hoped was open to giving him another, less creepy, chance.

CHAPTER THIRTY-THREE

"I'm sorry, Mr. Cain," a pleasant female voice said through Tyler's earpiece. "Mr. Dimitri will be with you in a few minutes. He's wrapping up his other meeting now."

Tyler continued staring at his tablet screen. It displayed a still-vacant chair behind what looked like an empty news anchor desk. He'd seen countless nearly identical sets on television, with this or that pundit commenting on the latest White House decision, international incident, or celebrity hairstyle change.

"Like I said, I don't mind rescheduling if it would be more convenient." He half hoped the assistant would accept the offer, still a bit unnerved by his sudden inclusion in Evan Dimitri's "very busy schedule." Tyler's idea of a power lunch would be meeting Smitty for a sub sandwich. Dimitri, by contrast, routinely dined with senators and corporate titans. Tyler's greatest accomplishment had been putting a low-life murderer behind bars. Dimitri, from all appearances, had put presidential hopefuls in the White House.

"That won't be necessary, Mr. Cain. But thank you." The

woman spoke with more respect than Tyler deserved. He hadn't, after all, been entirely forthright when requesting the meeting.

It was true, he reminded himself, that he was investigating a case of suspected murder. Never mind no killing had yet occurred.

He actually had been a Denver detective...once upon a time.

And he did want input on the case from a well-respected businessman with unique expertise on the transition industry. And, he'd failed to mention, a strong motivation to intimidate Judge Santiago. Or kill him.

"Nice set," Tyler said to make small talk.

"Oh, yes, thank you," the woman's voice replied.

"I suppose Mr. Dimitri does a lot with the media?"

"Actually, not as much as you'd think. Necessary evil, if you know what I mean."

Tyler answered with a polite, unseen nod.

"He mostly uses it for board meetings, conference calls, and such. He prefers it over face-to-face meetings, which he considers an *unnecessary* evil. Except when it includes lunch." She laughed.

Tyler joined her chuckle. "I see."

A few more minutes of dead air.

"Sorry I'm late," Dimitri finally said while taking his seat, an obligatory comment that sounded more like an irritated bark. A ten-minute conference call with some detective named Tyler Cain was not, it seemed, on the top of his priority list.

Evan Dimitri appeared every bit as intimidating as his net worth. A solid frame matched a strong, determined jaw. His thick gray hair implied experienced maturity. And a four- or five-thousand-dollar suit fell awkwardly on a body more bruised rugby player than cultured CEO.

He barked again: "What do you want to know?"

Tyler had prepared himself for a few pointless pleasantries such as a comment about the weather or the latest major league rankings. But clearly Evan Dimitri disliked wasting time.

"Thank you for your time, Mr. Dimitri," Tyler began. "My name is—"

"Tyler Cain. I know. Denver police?"

"Yes," Tyler said instinctively. "I got the case from the assistant chief."

"Why didn't *he* call me?" A fair question from a powerful man.

"It's a somewhat unique situation requiring arm's-length handling. That's why it was assigned to me."

"Who are you?"

"A former officer now on special assignment."

"Former officer?" Dimitri glanced down, presumably at notes compiled by the executive assistant Tyler had convinced to schedule the meeting. "So you're not"—he paused to reread—"a homicide detective with the Denver police?"

"Retired to launch my own private investigation agency."

"Hmm," he said, clearly unimpressed. "So, what do you want to know?"

"I understand your company owns the patent on the Potassi-Pass serum."

A single nod.

"And that you have an exclusive supplier contract with NEXT Transition Services."

Dimitri huffed impatiently. "Do you plan to waste my time telling me what you already know or do you have a question?"

Tyler heard annoyed arrogance in Dimitri's voice, the same kind he had heard a thousand times during criminal interrogations. Apparently felons and power brokers felt a similar self-importance. Tyler knew how to respond. "Look, Mr. Dimitri," he said sternly, "I have no interest in wasting your time any more than my own. This will only take a few minutes."

Dimitri's smile suggested a respect for tough-skinned adversaries. "All right, Mr. Cain. I'll give you five."

Tyler realized he had acquired a measure of respect, but had lost half of his scheduled time.

"What do you know about the wrongful death decision appeal involving NEXT?"

"Same as anyone else. A greedy kid hopes to land a big payday from his mom's accidental death."

"Do you know the judges reviewing the appeal?"

A scowl. "Know them? Personally?"

Tyler hesitated. He had planned to feel his way through the conversation to find a less direct angle. But there was no time for tact.

"I mean have you corresponded with any of them?"

The question appeared to confuse Dimitri. "Corresponded? About what?"

"The case."

A caustic laugh. "Of course not."

Tyler watched Dimitri's eyes. He appeared to be telling the truth.

"Mr. Cain, I was told you wanted to discuss a murder case. Why are we talking about appeal court judges in a wrongful death lawsuit?"

Tyler wished he could hit pause and then rewind to restart the conversation on a less adversarial footing. He needed to gain Dimitri's confidence quickly. An idea came.

"I must ask you to keep what I'm about to share completely confidential," Tyler said, already regretting what he had decided to do.

"Of course."

"One of the federal judges issuing an opinion on the NEXT case has received letters that appear threatening."

Dimitri's eyebrows rose, but his face offered no indication of guilt. "Really?"

"Yes, sir." Tyler's tone changed, as if he were speaking to an ally helping with the case. "I was hoping you could help me think through who might be behind them."

For the first time since the conversation began Dimitri's eyes met Tyler's image on the screen. "Help you think it through?"

"That's right."

"So you can identify potential suspects?" He sounded, what, flattered?

"Exactly. I would really appreciate your opinion."

"Would you?" he asked flatly.

"Yes, I would," Tyler replied warily.

"Why me?"

"Excuse me?"

"Why me, Mr. Cain? You don't know me from Adam and I've certainly never heard of you. Yet out of the blue you decide to seek my advice solving a case involving NEXT."

Dimitri reached to accept a glass of something on the rocks from a feminine hand. He sipped, then smiled derisively. "What do you take me for, some kind of naïve fool?"

"No. Not at all. I just—"

"Who gave you my name?"

Tyler froze. *What to say?*

"Who told you to talk to me, Mr. Cain?"

"Two different sources suggested you could help me," he lied.

"Name them."

"I can't do that."

"Then this conversation is over. I don't have time for a goose chase prompted by anonymous leads. I'm a very busy man."

"Davidson." The name spilled from Tyler's lips before he could stop it.

Dimitri stared blankly. A good sign. Tyler sensed an opening window.

"Julia Davidson suggested I show someone like you the letters."

"Someone like me how?"

"Someone who understands both the business significance and the political significance of the NEXT appeal."

"I see," Dimitri said, appearing and sounding a bit more receptive. "Kim," he said into the air.

"Yes, Mr. Dimitri."

"Track down any communications or meetings I've had with a Julia…" He paused, shifting his eyes back toward Tyler.

"Davidson," he said, reluctantly filling in the blank.

"Julia Davidson."

"Yes, sir," the woman replied obediently.

Tyler knew Dimitri would connect the dots from journalist to husband to congressman. But he couldn't worry about that now. He had less than two minutes of Dimitri's attention left. The moment of truth had arrived. *Show him the letters and watch his eyes like you did with Jeremy Santos*, he coached himself.

A different voice protested within. "Once you go digital, you lose control," Jennifer McKay had warned. He pushed past the objection.

"Would you be willing to take a look?"

"At what?"

"At the letters."

Dimitri seemed intrigued. "What? Now?"

"Yes, sir. I can forward copies. All I need is a secure in-box and the assurance you'll destroy the files after our conversation."

Tyler waited as seconds chipped away at his remaining minutes.

"Any insight you can give would help. To be honest, we don't have many leads at the moment."

Dimitri smiled like a man accepting a stick of his favorite gum. "Kim will send you an in-box address, same one we use for confidential legal documents," he said, standing. "Send them while I take a leak."

The man disappeared from view while his voice trailed off. "Then you'll have another five minutes."

Glad for the restored time, Tyler quickly unfolded the letters to snap and save copies. Seconds later a link arrived on his screen. He hesitated, then hit SEND to complete the transfer.

He waited two minutes. Then he waited three more.

"Mr. Dimitri?" he said apprehensively.

No response.

He tried the woman. "Um, Kim? Is everything OK? The files should have arrived."

"They arrived, Mr. Cain," she responded matter-of-factly. "Mr. Dimitri is reading them now."

Tyler cursed within. He needed to watch Dimitri's pupils and decipher facial movements in reaction to the letters. How else would he be able to gauge guilt, surprise, confusion, or any other emotion?

"I don't see him. Where is he?"

"I'm right here," Dimitri said, resettling himself in the chair and lifting his eyes from the tablet in his hand. "I read the letters. Odd."

"Yes, they are," Tyler said. "Any other reactions?"

"Seems pretty straightforward to me," Dimitri offered.

"Really? How's that?"

"Judge Santiago needs to resign from the case. He's been compromised."

Tyler swallowed hard. *How much to say?*

"The judge hasn't been compromised because he hasn't actually seen the letters. I got them from an aide."

Dimitri waved his hand at the fact as if swatting an annoying insect. "No judge should issue an opinion on a case when some religious nut has made threats."

"Religious nut? Did you see something in the letters to suggest—"

"Isn't it obvious?" Dimitri interrupted. "Who else would want NEXT to lose the appeal? It's always the same people."

"The same people? Who?"

"Do you have any idea how many hostile letters come to my company every week, Mr. Cain? Ever since we landed the supplier contract with NEXT we've been targeted by every wacko on a mission to keep debits from ending their misery."

"Do you keep them?" Tyler asked, an idea forming.

"Keep what?"

"The wacko letters?"

"Beats me," Dimitri said. "Kim, do we keep the wacko letters?"

"I'm sure we have them on file somewhere, sir," she replied.

"Can I take a look?" Tyler asked. "You never know. I might find one with matching handwriting."

"Not likely."

"All the same, I'd like to try."

"Be my guest," Dimitri said curtly. "Kim…"

"On it, sir."

"Can I give you a bit of advice, Mr. Cain?" Dimitri continued.

"Please."

"I suggest you ignore these letters."

Was he offering advice or issuing a threat? "We can't just ignore them, Mr. Dimitri."

"Why not? You already said the judge is ignoring them."

"I didn't say he's ignoring them. I said he hadn't read them. He has a policy of delegating any messages related to an appeal to his aide until after issuing an opinion. So he won't even know these letters exist until September fourth."

"Why the fourth?"

"It's the day after the case will be decided and opinions released."

"I see," Dimitri said, his eyes shifting quickly toward a woman's hand appearing on the screen. He reached to receive a slip of paper. He read it aloud. "Julia Davidson is married to Troy Simmons, Congressman Tolbert's former chief of staff."

Needles of panic stung Tyler's neck and shoulders.

"So Congressman Tolbert gave you my name?"

"No, sir. I've never met the congressman."

"But you've met Troy Simmons?"

Tyler shook his head defensively.

Dimitri swore. Then he swore again. "What exactly are you trying to pull here, Mr. Cain?"

"I'm not trying to pull anything. I'm doing a job that—"

"You said your job was to investigate a possible threat, not to accuse honest citizens without a shred of evidence."

"I haven't accused you of anything."

"Oh no?" Dimitri's face flushed a furious red. "Why else would you have started this conversation by asking whether I had corresponded with the judge? And why didn't you tell me right up front that you were friends with Congressman Tolbert?"

"I told you, I've never met any congressman."

"Right. You've never met him," Dimitri scoffed. "I think you're lying, Mr. Cain. I think you know Tolbert and that you're trying to concoct a plausible story that will throw the trail off of a much more likely suspect."

Likely suspect? Tyler wondered.

"You got my name from the only congressman who has an ax to grind with the transition industry. The man who came crawling to me for reelection money last year but now thinks I'm too dirty to fund his Bright Spots crusade."

Tyler only vaguely recalled the term, something Julia had mentioned. No matter now. He racked his brain for a way to recover the moment. Nothing came but the realization his Hail Mary pass had been intercepted. Evan Dimitri now had the identity of a confidential source. Worse, he had digital copies of the documents Jennifer McKay had insisted Tyler protect.

"This conversation is over, Mr. Cain," Dimitri said after downing the last of his drink. "And you can assure Mr. Tolbert that I intend to speak to Josh Franklin about this little stunt."

Tyler reached deep to forge an intimidating tone. "I wouldn't do that if I were you. This is a highly sensitive investigation that—"

It was too late. The screen had already gone black, leaving Tyler wondering what, exactly, he had done. One thing was certain. He had stepped in something messy. And it smelled pretty bad.

CHAPTER THIRTY-FOUR

As far as Tyler could tell, Jennifer McKay's preoccupied gaze fell somewhere between the digital calendar of events hanging on the wall and whatever was beyond, as though she possessed X-ray vision. A desk phone handset was wedged firmly between her left shoulder and ear while she poked mindlessly at salad leftovers with a fork. The conversation seemed unimportant based on the brief utterances she made every few seconds.

"Hmm."

"Right."

"I see."

After nearly two minutes she was still completely unaware he was standing there. Finally Tyler rapped his knuckles hard on the desk surface to announce himself.

Startled, Jennifer simultaneously juggled the phone and spun around to locate the intruder. Seeing Tyler, she held up one finger, then ended the call with a curt "Let me call you back in a few minutes."

At this, Tyler plopped himself into one of two guest chairs.

"What are you doing here?" she said accusingly, nervously glancing around the otherwise empty office.

"We need to talk."

"Mr. Cain, I wish you had called first. Now's not a good time. Judge Santiago is in his chambers right this very moment. If he were to see you here—"

"Tell him I'm your long-lost cousin, then."

"I don't have any long-lost cousins."

Tyler hoped to gain the upper hand to head off a repeat of their last encounter. He leaned forward with an air of importance. "Does it matter?"

Taking a long deep breath, Jennifer finally relaxed enough to lean back in her chair. "I'm assuming this is about the letters."

Showing up unannounced had served his purpose. Tyler glanced around the office. Aside from the guard at the building's entrance, he hadn't been approached by anyone asking why he was there, nor had anything stopped him from walking right into this office without Judge Santiago's personal assistant even noticing. What would prevent someone from breaking through into Judge Santiago's chambers? Above the doorway a metal conduit led up through the ceiling. Probably wiring for an alarm system of some kind, but too little too late to stop a potential killer with a grudge.

As he'd hoped, she followed his gaze around the room.

"You're completely unprepared, Ms. McKay."

"Excuse me?"

"What if I had been a gunman?"

"There are metal detectors. No guns allowed."

He nodded toward a decorative lamp sitting on the edge of her desk. "Blunt-force trauma to the head is just as deadly."

Jennifer instinctively raised her hand to the back of her head protectively, combing her fingers through her hair in a vain attempt to seem unfazed. "Are you trying to scare me, Mr. Cain? Because as I already told you, safety is not a concern here. Unless you have information to suggest we *should* be concerned..."

This time it was Tyler who eased back into his chair. Mission accomplished. Jennifer McKay was on the defensive. He had the upper hand. A little fear was a powerful way to hook a listening ear.

"I *might* have information," he said, dangling a proverbial carrot.

Jennifer glanced toward Santiago's chambers again, then back to Tyler, her demeanor sharpening. "You *might*? Is that short for 'I don't have a single lead'?"

She was onto him already.

"No," Tyler lied, hoping to recover. "It's code for 'I have a potential lead, but I need something to help smoke out the author to know for sure.' Something from you."

"From me?"

"I need you to reply to the letters."

She shot up immediately. "I already told you I can't—"

"You can't do that. Yes, I know. But the stakes on this case might be higher than either of us originally imagined. Much higher."

Which was true. Maybe.

"Really?" Jennifer said doubtfully, then turned and slid open one of her desk drawers, pulling out a photograph. She laid it out on the desk and shoved it over for Tyler to see.

It was a picture of a little girl in pink pajamas holding tightly to a rag doll. It reminded him, vaguely, of the photo Smitty had shown of his daughter, with her larger-than-life innocent smile. But aside from that slight resemblance, the photo seemed unremarkable.

"Is she...yours?" Tyler asked.

Jennifer shook her head. "Gosh, no! I'm far too busy to have a partner, let alone a family! No, this little girl represents the outcome of an eight-year battle her parents had in the court system, fighting for the right to adopt the frozen embryo of the mother's brain-dead sister. An auto accident prevented implantation, and there was no legal precedent in allowing such an adoption without a parent's written consent. In fact, the sister had left instructions to donate any unused embryos to science. But here she is, almost twelve years after the legal battle began. She's four."

Tyler glanced at the little girl one more time, then slid the photo back. "She's cute. But I don't see how this matters to this case."

Jennifer sighed. "It matters because you still seem to underestimate the importance of Judge Santiago's work."

"What are you talking about? I've never said his work wasn't important."

"Not directly. But I need you to understand. This little girl—Hope is her name—she's a reminder. She's alive today because of an opinion Judge Santiago issued several years back."

"And?"

Jennifer frowned as if Tyler had missed her obvious point. "The stakes in Judge Santiago's cases are always higher than we know, Mr. Cain. Not just in this case."

"Fine. But hear me out, please."

"I'm listening," she said grudgingly.

"There just aren't enough useful clues in the letters themselves. And if I try to approach the suspect directly, there could be dangerous ramifications."

"Such as?"

"Such as ... retaliation."

"Retaliation against whom? Santiago?"

"Perhaps."

She shook her head, clearly frustrated. "There you go with

the suppositions again. Perhaps. Might. Possibly. I need more than that."

For a moment Tyler considered mentioning his conversation with Evan Dimitri. But he stopped himself. He just couldn't be certain. Yes, Mr. Dimitri had something to lose—a lot to lose, actually—but Tyler had been unable to watch his eyes, leaving him no choice but to believe Dimitri when he said he knew nothing about the letters. Besides, he couldn't tell her about the conference call without mentioning that he had violated her insistence that no one see the letters. Worse than see them, Tyler had scanned and sent digital copies!

"I can't give you more. Not yet. But what if you contacted the author on *behalf* of Judge Santiago? It doesn't have to be the judge himself. He doesn't even have to know about it. You can do it. I just need you to establish actual communication. I'll coach you on what to say."

Tyler stopped talking when he realized Jennifer was not even pretending to consider his suggestion.

Just then the door to Judge Santiago's chambers opened, and out came an impeccably dressed man with thinning gray hair. He closed the door behind himself and double-checked to see it was locked by rattling the handle. When he spun around, he looked surprised.

"Oh!" he exclaimed, then took a step forward. "I didn't realize we had any further appointments today, Jennifer."

Tyler rose respectfully. "It's an honor to meet you in person, sir."

Santiago smiled, then said, "Well, I'd say the honor is mine, but I have no idea who you are!"

"Oh, right. I'm..." Tyler searched frantically for an appropriate ruse.

"—the caterer," Jennifer finished for him, "for your wife's surprise birthday party."

"Ah, yes! Then it is an honor to meet you," Santiago said more enthusiastically. He accepted Tyler's outstretched hand and shook it vigorously before frowning. "Although I must admit you don't fit the part."

Tyler tried to release his grip, unsuccessfully. "Excuse me?"

"Caterer. You don't fit the part. Handshake's all wrong. Clothing choice. If I had to guess, I'd say you worked as some sort of public servant. A fireman, perhaps?"

Tyler smiled at the suggestion.

"Or maybe a security guard," the judge added.

Tyler furrowed his brow then went with the judge's first guess by playing the part of caterer. "It takes a lot of strength in the hands to properly prepare hors d'oeuvres!"

Both men laughed politely.

"Oh, don't worry about that," Santiago reassured him. "The trick will be pulling it off without anyone other than myself and Ms. McKay here knowing. My wife always has a way of finding out about any surprise. I think she has my office bugged or something!"

Tyler smiled. "I see."

Then Santiago pulled his coconspirator in close, glancing at Jennifer before whispering in his ear. "I don't care what she says...you just make sure to serve something men like us can really sink our teeth into. I'm tired of all those delicate finger foods with names I can't even pronounce. Got it?"

Tyler liked the judge already. He quickly pulled back and winked.

Santiago freed Tyler's hand. "Well, I must be off. My beautiful wife Rebecca awaits my return!"

And with that he turned and rushed out the door.

"Caterer?" Tyler said to Jennifer as he sat back down. "Well, he seems like a nice guy. Good judge of character."

"Yes, Mr. Cain. Exactly. He pegged you in three seconds flat."
After several moments of silent tension she added, "Are you finished, then? Because as I told you I can't risk compromising his
role."

He pursed his lips in frustration, then blurted out, "Doesn't a
death threat compromise his role?"

"Please. A request for dialogue is not a death threat, Mr. Cain.
You aren't hearing me on this. It doesn't matter if Judge Santiago
merely knows about the letters, if he actually reads the letters, or
if he opens dialogue with the person who wrote the letters. Even
if I were to dialogue with the author on his behalf, there would
be the appearance of impropriety. The appearance. That's all it
takes for someone to declare Santiago unfit to render an opinion."

"Well, then, it might be time we convinced the judge to resign
from the case. For his own protection."

"Protection from what?"

Tyler ran his hand over the back of his head, staring up at
the ceiling, tired of this game. What else could he say? He had
vast experience in these matters. She should just trust his expert
opinion.

Then he remembered the forensic report; a small detail that
might mean nothing. But he needed something, anything, that
would imply progress.

"I think the author of these letters is on the move," he finally
said, taking a completely different tack.

"On the move?"

"It appears the first three letters were sent from outside the
area. In the vicinity of Boulder, actually. While the most recent
letter was probably sent locally."

It was no more than a possibility. The envelopes showed mi-
croscopic traces of DNA from staff members who work at a
Boulder postal processing facility. But that only meant the let-

ters had *been* there, not that they had necessarily been sent from there. Still, it seemed a plausible theory.

"And?" Jennifer McKay continued staring, waiting impatiently for some juicy revelation.

"And I think it's an indication of the author's obsession with this case. His next move might be to confront Judge Santiago in person."

"I'm sorry, Mr. Cain," she said. "But Judge Santiago pays me to make hard calls. I simply can't tell the judge about these letters until you have some shred of evidence that tells me he is in real danger. I need more than hunches and assumptions."

"But I just told you..."

"People move all the time," she interrupted. "They also drop letters off at different post boxes. Boulder and Denver are not that far apart. What you have is circumstantial at best."

"It's just...a gut instinct I have. And when my gut tells me something, I find it's best not to ignore it!"

"Then don't ignore it. Find out who sent these letters, like I hired you to do in the first place."

Tyler felt a rising sense of desperation. He was going nowhere fast with this conversation. He feared Jennifer's stubbornness might be Santiago's undoing. Not to mention his own. He decided to appeal to her one last time. *Less confrontational*, he told himself.

"Just think it over," he began. "Message me if you change your mind. Ultimately, it's your decision."

"Yes. It is," she agreed. "And I don't need to think about it since I'm certain I won't change my mind."

The words of Julia Simmons crossed Tyler's thoughts. *Be careful, Mr. Cain. This case might end up carrying you into the deep end of the pool.* And it had. Deeper than he'd imagined.

This case had begun as a much-needed distraction from his usual pathetic clients. Then it escalated into a high-stakes gamble. Now he feared he had bet too many chips. Perhaps it was time to fold.

While the car carried him toward home in the AutoDrive lane Tyler made a decision.

"I'm done with this case," he told the windshield, resolutely. "I'll bill for time served. Then I'll resign."

The car responded by saying, "AutoDrive disengaging. Switching to manual mode."

"My thoughts exactly," he said. He took the steering wheel, the small measure of control it afforded a welcome change of pace from the unruly mess he had made during the past twenty-four hours.

CHAPTER THIRTY-FIVE

Julia noticed three brochures lying on the table beside an unoccupied waiting-room chair. She selected the middle one, titled *Genetic Screening: The Loving Choice*. She took a seat and began reading. The opening paragraph seemed familiar. It could easily have been paraphrased from one of the many columns on the subject she had published during her years working for RAP Syndicate.

For as long as women have had babies they've been asked the same question.

"Do you want a boy or a girl?"

And they've given the same answer.

"We just want a healthy child."

But there was little they could do besides taking prenatal vitamins or avoiding drugs, alcohol, and cigarettes.

Thankfully, today's parents can take steps to dramatically increase the likelihood of delivering a healthy bundle of joy. And when it comes to the child's sex the choice is literally yours!

This office is a proud member of HEALTH ASSURANCE, an alliance of caring gynecologists who serve the needs of women opting for genetic screening and physicians partnering with families to radically reduce lifelong medical expenses by accepting only prescreened pediatric patients.

Julia recalled praising the insurance companies and physicians who had created the Health Assurance network. It made sense to give parents who had opted for genetic prescreening lower rates, since their offspring showed dramatically fewer incidences of disability and disease. Within a few years nearly half of all new mothers paid lower premiums and deductibles than their "blind conception" counterparts. Doctors would only accept new patients who had been prescreened, an easy way to cut costs for everyone. Before long it became difficult to find a pediatrician unless you had prescreened. Only a handful of older doctors on their way to retirement were willing to treat the higher-cost kids. Even they began demanding cash payments up front, since, they discovered, healthcare authorities questioned every treatment before delaying or denying payment. So in less than a decade, Julia recalled, financial prudence had pushed nearly every woman away from blind conception toward what the brochure called *the loving choice*.   .

What better way to show your child love than to give her or him all of the advantages that come with prescreening?

Julia noticed her hand cradling her tummy. Had the passion she'd enjoyed with Troy made today's visit more than research for another dark zone story? She had felt a bit queasy before breakfast. Did morning sickness occur within twenty-four hours? If so, would a urine sample even detect pregnancy this early?

She shook off the questions, reminding herself she had always felt slightly nauseated when preparing to deceive.

The first lie had occurred when she went online to make an eight a.m. appointment for Troy and a ten a.m. appointment for herself. Julia tried to imagine the look that must have been on her husband's face when a nurse handed him the sample container a few hours earlier. He must have turned bright red. The thought prompted a quiet snigger.

The second lie had taken place a few minutes earlier when Julia checked in for her own appointment. "My name is Julia Simmons," she had said. "I'm here for my preconception consultation."

The process was pretty straightforward. The male partner submitted a sample so the lab could test the viability of his sperm. The potential mother then received an examination to determine whether she was a good candidate for implantation. What exactly that entailed Julia didn't know; probably checking to confirm the woman wasn't already pregnant, her ovaries still produced healthy eggs, and her uterus could maintain a pregnancy. Assuming all was well, the woman would be scheduled for some sort of ovarian stimulation to harvest as many eggs as possible for fertilization. The more embryos produced, the brochure explained, the more options from which to choose the best possible offspring.

"Julia Davidson?"

The voice didn't sound familiar. Nor had Julia given her maiden name. She looked toward an open door where a cute, thirtyish woman stood as if inviting her to enter. Julia stuffed the brochure in her purse to finish reading later.

"I'm Julia," she said with an inquisitive smile. "Have we met?"

"No. But I'm a big fan of your column."

Of course.

"Oh, um, thanks," Julia muttered while glancing around the room. Two of the five women seated in the waiting room were flashing warm grins in her direction. So much for undercover research.

She walked toward the woman and glanced at her name tag. "Hello, Lynette. Very pleased to meet you."

A lie. She hadn't wanted to meet anyone while trying to stay under the radar. No matter, she reassured herself, as long as she avoided hinting at the real reason for her visit.

As soon as the door closed behind them Lynette became as giddy as a teenage girl suddenly face-to-face with her favorite pop star. She caught Julia by surprise with a hug. "I can't tell you what an honor it is to have you visit our office," Lynette was saying over Julia's shoulder.

"Oh my," Julia said with a gentle pat on Lynette's back. Rather than taking the hint to separate, however, the woman tightened her squeeze. Julia finally pulled herself away.

"Sorry," Lynette said with a wink. "My partner tells me I get a bit over-enthusiastic."

Julia smiled weakly. "No worries."

They stood for a few more seconds until Lynette finally remembered her role. "This way," she said, extending her arm toward a scale.

Julia went through the motions as if planning for an in vitro selection pregnancy with her husband Troy.

"I must confess," Lynette said while taking Julia's pulse, "I was shocked when I recognized your face. Julia Davidson is the last woman I would have expected to go with Troy Simmons."

She knows Troy?

"I met him this morning. He seemed..." she paused as if trying to find a different word.

"Uptight?"

"Well, yes." Lynette appeared embarrassed. "But very handsome," she added as a consolation.

Julia felt suddenly protective. "We've been married for six months."

"I understand," Lynette said with consequence.

"Understand what?"

"The six-month bug. Pretty common here."

Lynette seemed to notice Julia's puzzled expression.

"We get quite a few couples in here trying to seal the partnership."

"Seal? What do you mean?"

"You know, making a kid together. Nothing bonds two people like a mini-us."

"Right," Julia said.

"I could tell right away Troy was different than most of the guys we see."

"How's that?"

"He didn't accept the stimulant aids for starters."

"Stimulant aids?"

"A gentle term for porn. He said he would be fine without it. Seemed a bit embarrassed by the offer."

Julia smiled at the description of her noble gentleman. Memories of their recent love-fest would have been more than adequate to aid Troy's contribution to the ruse.

"When I realized who you were I assumed there must have been some mistake. Julia Davidson married?"

"I guess wonders never cease," Julia offered.

"You can say that again." Lynette was shaking her head while jotting down the last of Julia's stats. She handed her a cup. "I'll need a urine sample, then we'll draw some blood."

Julia nodded.

"I almost got married once," Lynette said as Julia was turning the doorknob.

"Is that right?"

"Yep."

"Why almost?" Julia asked.

Lynette flashed a wide grin. "I guess I discovered your columns in the nick of time!"

The woman was shaking her head as if amazed by the irony as Julia slipped into the hallway toward the designated bathroom.

After capturing a urine sample Julia stood in front of the mirror. The same mirror, she assumed, Troy had looked into two hours earlier. She wondered how she would feel if this had been a real appointment rather than an act. It felt unseemly standing in the same spot where her husband had donated half of the required ingredients; as if they were two workers on an assembly line rather than participants in an intimate, one-flesh union.

"So this is how babies are made," she said to the woman in the mirror.

Two quick raps on the door followed by a muffled voice. "Ms. Davidson? Is everything OK?" Apparently she had fallen behind the usual assembly time line.

Julia took a deep breath in anticipation of the next scene of her performance. Then she opened the door. "Everything's fine. Please, call me Julia."

Lynette smiled at the invitation. "OK, Julia. Let's go to the consultation room to discuss next steps and options."

Julia's phone, the one she was supposed to have turned off in the waiting room, rang. Lynette looked at her with playful condemnation. She apologized while retrieving the device from the bottom of her purse and then glancing at the screen.

Tyler Cain.

She started to tap the IGNORE icon but hesitated while trying to recall what might have prompted the call. Did he have another dark zone contact she might interview? Another question about the Santiago case?

"Do you need to take that?" Lynette asked thoughtfully.

"Do you mind?" she asked while tapping the ACCEPT icon.

"Second door on the left," Lynette whispered while pointing down the hall. "I'll join you there in a minute."

Julia nodded at Lynette while turning her attention to the voice on the phone. "This is Julia."

"Hi, Ms. Simmons," Tyler began. "Can you talk?"

Julia began walking in the direction of the consultation room. "For a second. What's up?"

"I just wanted to bring you up to speed on the Santiago situation."

Situation?

"I've decided to end the investigation."

"Really? Did you find out who—"

"No I didn't," he said as if mad at the question. "But the judge isn't taking my advice; or rather the judge's aide. Either way, I don't like to waste people's money. If they won't listen to me, I can't help them."

Julia waited for more. Tyler remained quiet. Was that it? If so, why call Julia about the decision? If he had more, why not just say it?

"And?" she prodded.

"And, um…" A hesitation. "And I just wanted to say thanks for your help."

Julia sensed the call was about more than wrapping up the loose end of thanking a source. What wasn't Tyler saying?

"Are you sure there isn't more?"

"Like what?" he said too quickly. And too defensively.

"I don't know." She recalled their last conversation. "Did you identify any other potential leads?"

"Like Evan Dimitri?"

"Well, not him specifically. But yeah, people who might want to protect NEXT rather than harm it?"

Another long silence. Julia sensed Tyler struggling with an internal tug-of-war. Why? What had he really called to tell her?

"Mr. Cain? Is there something else you want to—"

"Like I said," he interrupted. "I wanted to thank you for your help and let you know I'm off the case."

"OK. Thanks for the update," she said in puzzled deference.

"And I appreciate your keeping our conversations strictly confidential."

"Of course."

"Good luck on your dark zone story. I'll let you know if I think of other leads on that front."

"Please do," she said before realizing the call had ended.

After a few seconds Julia noticed she was standing in the doctor's consultation room, the place where she would learn about next steps and options. Julia walked toward one of two seats positioned before a modestly cluttered desk. Her eyes landed on a small grouping of photographs on the wall that depicted what appeared to be a ski trip with friends; an older couple, possibly Lynette's parents; and Lynette sitting with two other women toasting the photographer with glasses filled with a dark wine: a celebration of some sort, possibly her graduation from medical school?

Then she noticed the diploma. UNIVERSITY OF COLORADO was stenciled boldly across the top, followed by smaller text she couldn't read, presumably the same congratulatory script used on countless other certificates ending with "has conferred upon" before the graduate's name; in this case, LYNETTE ROSE WRIGHT. Then more small text followed by DOCTOR OF MEDICINE.

As if on cue, the graduate entered the room. Julia felt old as she watched Lynette remove her doctor's smock. Stylish and pretty, Lynette reminded Julia of Maria a few years back. She appeared to be in her late twenties, thirty tops. More like the unattached, childless girlfriend with whom you would go shopping than an MD to whom you would go for pregnancy advice.

"All set?" Lynette asked.

"Yes, thank you. Nothing urgent."

"Good." Lynette sat beside Julia rather than occupying the seat behind the desk. Then she tapped her tablet screen and held it between them for shared viewing: a checklist of steps followed by a series of questions.

"We've completed most of the pre-consultation items."

Julia glanced at the list. Only a few boxes remained unchecked.

"I need to review the lab results to confirm what I've seen today," Lynette explained, "but on the whole I'd say you shouldn't have any problems." She looked to Julia with a congratulatory smile.

Julia felt herself tear up in response to the gesture. The reaction embarrassed her. "I'm sorry," she said while reaching for a tissue.

"Don't be," Lynette replied while touching her famous client's forearm. "This is very good news for a woman of your age."

A woman of my age?

"Half of the women I see past age thirty-five aren't good candidates."

"Half?"

"More maybe," Lynette explained.

"So only half of the women my age can have a child?"

"Half of the women your age who make appointments with my office. The rest don't want a child."

"Of course," said Julia.

"Of those who do, less than half are good candidates for in vitro implantation. There are a dozen reasons."

"Are there other options? You know, for the women you can't help?"

Lynette appeared to be recalling clients who had hit the snooze button on their biological clock once too often. "Not really," she finally said despondently. "But you look good. I think we'll be able to harvest a good selection of eggs. So, barring any surprises, I expect you'll be choosing a child within a few short months."

The comment reminded Julia of her agenda. "Tell me how that works. You know, the actual screening process?"

"My lab does most of the work," Lynette replied. "In the typical case we fertilize between five and eight eggs. About half of those will meet specs."

"Meet specs?"

"Sorry. Standard specifications. We analyze the genome sequence of each zygote to screen out any with likely defects or chronic diseases. The process has become remarkably precise. A recent batch detected propensities for both bipolar and attention deficit hyperactive disorders." She said it like a proud mom bragging on the accomplishments of her genius kid. "Anyway, we eliminate those zygotes before presenting you with the good options."

Julia suppressed an urge to grab her tablet to capture notes. Today she was a patient exploring motherhood, not a reporter conducting research.

"Assuming you have both possibilities you'll select the child's sex, unless of course you want it to be a surprise. Then we get to pick."

"How often does that happen?"

"Not very. Most people know what they want. Usually a boy, come to think of it. But I like to make a big deal about it when we do. I call the office staff together and we hold hands in a circle."

"To pray?" Julia guessed.

"To flip the ceremonial coin. Heads a girl. Tails a boy. At last count we had a pretty even mix of the two. I guess random chance would improve the odds for us gals."

Lynette laughed at her own quip while Julia wondered which sex she and Troy might select. Then she felt her suddenly queasy tummy. Had random chance already beaten them to the punch?

The doctor looked back at the list. "I should get the results from your husband's sample later today. After that we'll get you scheduled for your first infusion of a fertility stimulant and, if all goes well, invite a few of your eggs to the dance."

Julia forced a thin smile.

"Any questions?"

"Just one," Julia said after a slight hesitation. How to say it? "You mentioned eliminating some of the zygotes. Can I ask what happens to them?"

Lynette gently slapped her own cheek as if suddenly recalling a skipped step. "Oh yes," she said. "I almost forgot." She drew Julia's attention to the tablet and pointed beneath the action items toward a column of unasked questions.

"We need you to provide direction on how you want us to handle the embryotic material."

The comment reminded Julia of the conversation with Austin Tozer that had prompted her decision to make the appointment. He had gotten two thousand dollars per embryo. Would she receive a similar offer?

Lynette began reading a script from the tablet. "In order to respect the ethical sensibilities of our clients we request input on the preferred method of disposal for any excess embryotic materials resulting from your treatments."

Julia braced herself for the first of three questions.

"Are you undergoing this process with the intent of carrying and delivering a full-term baby?"

Julia tried to imagine another reason to schedule an in vitro selection consultation. "Yes I am," she answered. "But may I ask what it would mean if I said no?"

"We'd assume you plan to donate."

"Donate? To what?" Julia wasn't sure she wanted an answer.

"To the embryotics supply."

"Is that like the blood supply?" Julia blushed at her own ignorance.

"Sort of," Lynette explained. "But more like an organ donation to a specific beneficiary. Usually a family member asks relatives for donations when they schedule any kind of surgery that might require tissue repair or mild regeneration of internal organs. Embryos from close relatives make the best donors since the body can better assimilate organic material with a similar genome sequence."

Julia nodded, a look of vague comprehension triggering Lynette's second question.

"Would you like the attending physician to decide the best means of disposal for any unused zygotes?"

Julia considered how to reply. "What does that mean?"

"It means you give us permission to choose the best course of action depending upon a variety of factors."

Julia knew a dodge when she heard one: lots of words with no real answer. "What factors?"

Lynette seemed suddenly hesitant to say more, perhaps remembering that she was talking to a journalist. "Oh, you know, the usual. Which field of study would benefit most from access to the material? Things like that."

"For money?"

"Excuse me?" the doctor sounded offended.

Pull back, girl, Julia told herself. She had begun sounding like an antagonistic reporter rather than a curious client.

"I mean," she said in the least threatening voice she could muster, "are there any financial incentives for selecting one disposal strategy over another?"

"Incentives for whom?" Lynette asked indignantly.

Julia decided to change course quickly. "For me."

The doctor's tension seemed to dissipate. "Oh, that," she said with a relieved smile. Lynette looked back to the tablet to read the final question.

"Do you wish to dispose of excess embryotic materials in any of the following manners?" She looked toward Julia before reading off a menu of fifteen or twenty official-sounding organizations requesting targeted donations. Each needed a specific variable. Male or female. Caucasian, Asian, African-American, or mixed-race. One requested embryos that would have red hair. But none of them offered money.

"I'm curious," Julia said after Lynette completed the list, "whether there are any organizations willing to—" She stopped herself.

"Yes, there are," Lynette volunteered. Then she tapped a small icon located at the very bottom of the screen before handing it to Julia.

The tablet displayed a long list of businesses. Julia quickly scanned to identify names associated with health supplements and cosmetics. None appeared clearly marked.

"I'm not allowed to recommend any specific companies," Lynette was saying, "but I can tell you that some offer more compensation than others."

Julia felt a wave of shame. Not for her lies. For her discovery.

Dear God, she thought. Or perhaps prayed. *What have we become?*

"Would you like a copy of the file to review with your partner?"

"Husband," Julia said.

"Right, sorry. Would you?"

"Please," Julia said while handing the tablet back. She thanked the doctor for the information as she stood to leave the room.

"You can stop by the front desk to make a next appointment," Lynette said warmly. "I look forward to seeing you again."

Julia nodded while extending her hand. Lynette ignored the offer, opting instead for another demonstrative hug.

It took Julia a split second to return the gesture. It was more physical intimacy, she mused, than Lynette's clients experienced while conceiving a child.

The thought reminded Julia that nothing had been said about her urine sample. Wouldn't they know immediately if she was pregnant?

"So, I guess I'm not expecting?" she asked as if checking a minor detail. "I assume we couldn't proceed if I were."

The question seemed to startle Lynette. "Oh," she said while reaching for her tablet, apparently to check Julia's pregnancy test results. "Yes, we would recommend a different approach in that case. Could you be?"

Julia nodded guiltily, knowing Lynette probably frowned upon spontaneous, unprotected marital sex. "A small chance," she confessed.

The doctor tapped and swiped the screen until she found the tidbit of data needed to answer Julia's question. "Let's see here."

Julia held her breath.

"Congratulations!" she said after one final swipe. "You're clear."

"Oh," Julia replied with a weak smile. "I see. That's good. A relief," she lied. "Thanks for checking."

"You bet. See you soon."

"Yes. See you soon."

Julia walked past the receptionist's desk, then through the lobby and out the door. A door she hoped she would never have to enter again.

CHAPTER THIRTY-SIX

Julia lowered the music and dimmed the dining room lights. The table looked exquisite beneath two lustrous flames dancing to the smooth sounds of romantic jazz. She smiled in anticipation of inviting her husband to do the same as soon as he arrived home from the office.

She had considered sending Troy a text message suggesting they meet at his favorite restaurant. She would have spent the last part of the meal rubbing her foot against his leg while they took turns feeding one another spoonfuls of his favorite dessert.

But she changed her mind. A candlelit dinner at home would be better: less time between suggestion and action. Rather than whisper during dessert she would *be* the dessert.

Julia went to her closet and flipped through the possibilities. Which was Troy's favorite? Short teddy or lingering gown? How could she know when he seemed equally pleased by all of them? She finally chose. White. The perfect color for a night that she hoped would move their union from two people in love to one flesh in partnership.

Since the day Julia met Troy Simmons she'd known he wanted to be a father. It was in the lobby of Apostles' Church in Washington DC. She had accepted Angie's invitation to attend a service while in town. She should have known Angie would use the occasion for matchmaking. Troy clearly loved the Tolbert kids, especially when they called him "Uncle Twoy." But he also seemed to love the dream of little feet running into his arms and hearing his own child shouting, "Daddy!"

Julia never would have imagined herself going on a date with a man like Troy, let alone accepting his hand in marriage. Marriage itself, she had believed, was an archaic institution. What a difference a year can make! Here she was now, planning an intimate evening with a man she'd never intended to marry, hoping to conceive a child she never wanted to have. Or so she had thought. Apparently our deepest desires eventually trump our most persuasive objections.

A sudden noise startled Julia. Troy arriving home early? No, a timer alerting her that the crescent rolls were ready to remove from the oven.

While placing the last roll into a basket on the table, Julia checked the clock. Troy should be another twenty minutes, plenty of time for her to shower and slip into his surprise. The phone rang. She glanced at the television screen to read the caller's identity. Not Troy calling to say he would be late. Just Dr. Wright's office, probably calling to give her the detailed results of fertility tests she assumed were fine. She decided to ignore the call, instead rushing into the master bathroom for her most important preparations.

Fifteen minutes later Julia found herself moving from one spot to another, trying to decide which location best fit the occasion. She imagined Troy's face when he walked through the door to delicious smells, dim lights, and an alluring bride lounging on the sofa or waiting invitingly at the table.

Only one unfinished detail remained. She reached for her tablet to restart the programmed sequence of Troy's favorite jazz artists. She noticed a bouncing icon reminding her of the ignored call, now a waiting message with an attachment. She tapped it to pass the remaining moments, expecting Lynette's assistant to say she had forwarded the formal test results and ask when Julia wanted to begin the in vitro process. She instead heard the doctor's voice.

"Hi, Julia. I've attached results of the full range of tests we ran today. As expected, you look healthy."

Julia smiled at the surprising feeling of relief.

"But I wanted to explain the results on page six of the attached summary so you will understand your options," Lynette continued. "Don't worry. I've helped plenty of couples in the same situation. Call my office when you can and we'll set up a consultation. OK? We'll talk then."

Options for what? Julia wondered. *I thought she said I looked healthy.*

Even though Troy could walk through the door at any second, Julia had to know what was on page six. She tapped the attachment icon to open the document. She tried her best to decipher the medical jargon, including two "possible causes" with labels that meant nothing to her; *epididymitis* and something called *Young syndrome*. She looked at the top of the page for any clues that might inform what she was reading. That's when she realized this was a summary of Troy's sperm sample. But what did it mean? Was it something bad? Lynette mentioned she had helped other couples in the same situation. What situation?

She moved toward the door to peek outside. No sign of Troy's car. She went back to her tablet and quickly entered the unfamiliar words into a medical terminology search engine. All five of the top results carried the same disturbing label.

Causes of male infertility.

She began scanning the first article. Apparently epididymitis was some sort of blockage preventing sperm from releasing to its fruitful destiny. But that included a list of symptoms Troy had never experienced such as fever and pain. The only other potential culprit, *Young syndrome*, was described as having "no known effective treatment or cure."

Did this mean she and Troy couldn't conceive naturally? Could they conceive at all?

Julia heard the familiar sound of the opening garage door announcing Troy's arrival. She quickly swiped out of the screen and tossed her tablet beneath a throw pillow. She had never decided whether to stay on the sofa or move to the dining room. She chose the latter, buying a few extra seconds to absorb the news and decide whether and how to tell her husband.

The thought of telling Troy prompted unwelcome grief. "Not now!" she said aloud, grabbing one of the perfectly placed napkins to dab her moistening eyes.

The last thing she wanted was for Troy to see her in tears. This was supposed to be a romantic evening of thrilling intimacy, not a cry-fest over possible bad news.

But she knew in her soul that it was more than *possible* bad news. Why would the doctor call unless the results suggested her husband could never be a daddy?

Another wave of sorrow invaded, this one too strong for Julia to swallow back. She heard the doorknob turning. What to do? She darted from the dining room back into the master bedroom. Better for Troy to enjoy the surprise and anticipation of a candlelit room than wonder what had triggered his wife's uncontrollable tears.

She rushed to the bathroom and closed the door before splashing cold water onto her puffing cheeks. She would let Troy assume she was still getting ready to greet him with an alluring smile. A smile she commanded her disobedient face to produce.

Julia reached deep to summon the strong, controlling woman she had been before falling in love with Troy. The girl who had maintained a cool demeanor during a year of nightmarish dreams. The journalist who had confronted Washington power brokers with prudent diplomacy. The woman who could use the same iron will to finish what she had started a few hours earlier. She had planned a night of bliss with her husband. So a night of bliss is what she intended to give.

"Hi, babe," she heard Troy saying from the dining room. "What's all this?"

She took a deep, restorative breath before replying. "A little surprise. I'll be out in a minute."

She used the time to reapply a bit of makeup. Troy would never guess she had been crying, even if his eyes managed to peel themselves away from her gown. Then she opened the bedroom door to find her husband nibbling on a crescent roll at the dining table, his shoulders slumped as if he was contemplating his own brand of dispiriting news.

She moved toward Troy, glad the music covered the sound of her approach. She slid her arms around his chest to offer an embrace both needed.

She whispered into his ear, "Welcome home, Mr. Simmons."

Her touch and voice prompted a smile. He pulled her hand to his lips and gently kissed her soft skin. Julia sensed he was trying to push past exhausted discouragement to receive her wonderful but poorly timed gift.

"This looks terrific," he said while rubbing her arm.

She moved to the chair beside him. His eyes turned to saucers. She blushed, then giggled.

"You look terrific!" He gasped to recover his stolen breath.

They kissed. Then they kissed again.

"I hope you're hungry," Julia said.

His eyes sank as if the comment reminded him of a lost appetite. Then he looked back at the candlelit arrangement. At the enormous effort his wife had gone to for him. "Starved," he said with forced enthusiasm.

She placed a single finger on his chin to move his eyes back in her direction. "Troy Simmons. Tell me what's wrong."

His eyes sank again. "Is it that obvious?"

"I'm afraid so. But thank you."

"For what?"

"For trying to enjoy my surprise."

He leaned toward her for another kiss, which she refused to accept.

"No food or dessert until you tell me what's wrong."

"There's dessert?"

She stood and then turned to give him a full view of her sheer outfit. "Yes, there is." Both smiled as she sat again. "Now, what happened?"

Troy released a lengthy sigh. "I got a call from Brent Anderson today."

"Franklin's right-hand man?"

"He called to warn me. No, to scold me."

"For what?"

"That's just it. I have no idea what he was talking about. He accused me of seriously undermining Kevin's opportunity for broader influence in the Franklin coalition. I asked what I had done, but he accused me of playing dumb as if I knew what I'd done. Then he told me to back off with Dimitri."

"Evan Dimitri?"

"I suppose. But I haven't had any contact at all with Evan Dimitri."

A prickly thought entered Julia's mind. She pushed it aside and said, "That's odd."

"Very odd. I can only assume he's upset about the refused donation check. But that was Kevin. I was a thousand miles away minding the shop."

"Maybe he thinks you put Kevin up to it."

"Unlikely. I'm nothing to Dimitri and Anderson: an invisible gofer who runs reports and accepts assignments."

"You're a lot more than that!" Julia protested. "Kevin relies on you for, well, for everything."

He touched her cheek in appreciative acceptance of the reassurance. "I know that."

"And Kevin knows it!"

He smiled at her resolve. "And Kevin knows it. But I can't imagine why Anderson would call me."

"Maybe he called Kevin too."

"He didn't. I checked."

"What did Kevin say?"

"Not much." Troy's shoulders slumped again. "Just that he would follow up with Anderson."

A prickly thought Julia couldn't dismiss. Had Tyler Cain contacted Evan Dimitri in response to her call?

"What if someone else used your name?" she asked.

"Used my name for what?"

"To gain access to Dimitri."

"Who would do that? And why?"

Julia dismissed the possibility again. "Never mind," she said. "I'm just thinking out loud."

A brief silence as both tried to imagine what would suddenly turn Anderson against Troy. Against Kevin.

"It must be the donation thing," Troy finally said. "Nothing else makes sense. Kevin refused Dimitri's check, meaning he rejected the attached strings. That must have upset Franklin."

"I guess," Julia agreed. "Which means you did nothing wrong."

He looked up as if relieved by the verdict.

"It also means there's no reason I shouldn't reheat our dinner." Julia stood and reached for the serving dish.

Troy's hand caressed the thin fabric that barely concealed her thigh. "And dessert?"

"The dessert is still warm," she said, sitting on Troy's lap. Her lips moved toward his ear, the breath of each whispered word seeming to deepen his desire. "Would you rather skip dinner?"

She sensed the tension releasing from both husband and wife with each escalating touch.

Thirty minutes later Troy was sitting at the table, a new man.

"I made it to the clinic today," he said casually while spreading a slab of butter onto a freshly heated roll.

Julia's body stiffened. "Did you?"

"Talk about awkward. I had to go into a bathroom and..." He stopped short, then fast-forwarded. "I had to hand my sample to an office aide who looked young enough to be my daughter. Embarrassing."

"Thanks for doing that," Julia said. "It will help my next story."

"How about you?" he asked.

"What?"

"Weren't you supposed to go today as well?"

"Oh, that." A slight hesitation. "I had a consultation appointment. Learned quite a bit." *Keep it short. Don't elaborate. Change the subject.*

"And?" he said, preempting her strategy.

"And I found out there are a bunch of businesses that buy unused embryos, just like Austin Tozer said. They try to get you to donate as the preferred disposal method for what they call excess embryotic material. But I asked one question about financial incentives and the doctor showed me several options for selling instead."

Troy huffed angrily in her direction. "Are you serious?"

Julia nodded.

"No wonder I got a bad feeling the second I walked into the place," he continued. "Their process gave me the willies. A father should be more than a nameless, faceless cog in the wheel. They handed me a dirty magazine and said, 'Have at it'!"

"Troy!" Julia blushed while slapping his shoulder playfully.

"Well, it's true," he said. "And dehumanizing."

She had to agree. "Having a child should be beautiful, not mechanical."

As she placed another roll on his plate Troy put his hand lovingly on her waist. "You're beautiful," he said. "Thank you, Julia."

She smiled, knowing he meant more than the roll.

"That's how babies are supposed to be made." He winked while placing his hand on her abdomen. "And you never know."

A wave of guilt. *Should I tell him?* she wondered. *No. Not now. Why spoil a beautiful moment? Tell him in the morning.*

Troy buried his head in Julia's bosom. "You're a gift," he said. "I love you."

She placed her hands on his head and began caressing his hair. "I love you too," she said, swallowing back a returning sorrow, an emotion that she would try to hide but that she knew would keep her awake late into the night. "I love you too."

CHAPTER THIRTY-SEVEN

"Hello, Mr. Matthew," little Pete said, extending his hand forcefully.

Reverend Grandpa beamed as he smiled at Matthew, who accepted the gesture with delighted shock.

"Hello, Mr. Peter," Matthew said, shaking the boy's hand. "Great to see you again."

It must have been the longest conversation Peter Gale had had with anyone besides Reverend Grandpa since his father's death. For sure the only words Matthew had actually seen coming out of the kid's mouth. And the happiest he'd ever seen the old man appear.

Little Pete looked toward his grandpa like a private waiting for the sergeant to say, "Dismissed." A congratulatory wink released the boy to flee the room in embarrassed gratification.

"I'm impressed," Matthew said.

"I told you he's a smart kid," the old man bragged.

Matthew didn't recall being told any such thing. He nodded in agreement anyway.

The reverend continued. "All he needed was a little time. Next stop, the pulpit."

"The what?"

"The pulpit. You know, a preacher's podium."

"You call it a pulpit? Why?"

Reverend Grandpa rolled his eyes and waved a hand to bat away Matthew's ignorance. "Never mind."

"So you want Peter to be a preacher when he grows up?"

"Not really."

The answer surprised Matthew. "But I thought—"

"Little Pete is the one who wants to be a preacher like his granddad. I figured I could use his goal to help him start talking again."

Matthew remembered overhearing his client's earlier conversation with Peter. "He's been secretly talking to you for a while, hasn't he?"

Reverend Grandpa nodded. "Welcome to a very exclusive club, my boy."

"I'm honored."

"You should be," he said matter-of-factly. "It took an hour of coaching to get him to say those three words to you today."

Matthew smiled at the accomplishment. He tried to imagine how the death of a father might traumatize a little boy. What kind of pain had forced the child into such a self-imposed cone of silence? Having never known his own father, Matthew couldn't relate to the loss. But he had occasionally sensed himself grieving the absence.

Reverend Grandpa inhaled deeply as if accepting well-deserved congratulations. Then he inhaled again, unnaturally. The third attempt alarmed Matthew, prompting him to bend down and check the gauge on the old man's oxygen tank. The usually green light was bright red. He had seen yellow before, but never red. Wasn't there supposed to be an audible tone when the tank fell below the minimum safe level? No matter now; Matthew had to move fast.

The old man continued gasping for air as if suffering a heart attack while running a marathon in the summer heat. Matthew hurried toward the closet to retrieve a replacement tank. He panicked at the sight of one already depleted container, then darted out of the room toward the kitchen pantry, where they kept an emergency backup tank.

By the time he returned Peter and Isabelle were on either side of their grandpa, each holding a hand while frantically patting the old man's back in a useless effort to help.

Thirteen seconds later Matthew turned a knob to release the life-sustaining gas into Reverend Grandpa's lungs. A few replenishing breaths later the old man appeared to calm. The children, however, remained visibly shaken.

"What the—" Matthew stopped short, remembering the presence of children. "What on earth happened? I never heard the caution tone. This tank shouldn't have dropped into the red zone that fast!"

"My fault," Reverend Grandpa confessed after relishing a few more oxygen-rich breaths. "I hit the silence button to stop the racket while coaching Pete. We were so close to a breakthrough I didn't want the interruption."

"Dropping dead would have been a whole lot more of an interruption than asking me to change tanks!" Matthew scolded.

"Drop dead?" Isabelle shouted. "You mean he could have died?"

Matthew hesitated as post-panic anger arrived. "Yes, he could have died. Stupid old man!"

Peter jerked his head toward the mouth that had dared utter such an offense.

"He's not stupid!" the boy said. "You are!" Peter ran out of the room.

Isabelle's jaw dropped. "Grandpa," she said while her eyes fixed on the spot where she'd last seen Peter. "Peter said a whole sentence. Out loud!"

"Actually, two sentences," the old man said with a chuckle that quickly escalated into a roar of amused relief.

Isabelle ran after her brother.

"You've been honored again, my boy!" Reverend Grandpa said between guffaws.

"Great," Matthew replied, still irritated by the old man's carelessness.

He spent the next fifteen minutes rounding up every oxygen tank in the house. Four empty containers went into a box next to the front door to be put in Marissa's car as soon as she returned from her errands to get the kids. He found one additional full tank in a corner of the garage and placed it in his client's closet where it belonged for easy retrieval during the next stupidity-induced incident.

An hour later Marissa drove away with the box and the kids. Isabelle remained true to her pledge not to mention the little scare to Mom who, Grandpa had insisted, would make a big fuss over nothing. Matthew had calmed himself enough to speak to the old man, determined to say things he needed to hear whether he liked them or not.

"Did you see the look on Peter's and Isabelle's faces today?" Matthew began. "You nearly scared them to death when you were wheezing for air."

"It was a silly mistake. I'm still alive, and the kids are fine."

"What if I hadn't been nearby? What if you had died?"

The question seemed to anger the old man. And bother him.

"It wasn't my time to go yet."

"Thanks to me," Matthew said.

"Thanks to God," the old man countered. "You were just his instrument. If he wanted me home, I'd be there."

Matthew didn't follow. "What are you talking about? You are home."

Another look of exasperation. "I mean my home beyond the clouds."

A continued blank stare.

"Heaven!"

"Oh," Matthew said, finally understanding. The comment prompted an idea. "Speaking of heaven, I need to talk to you about something."

The reverend motioned Matthew in his direction. "Well, if we're going to chat about something important, let's do it in the living room. Help me up, will you, son?"

Matthew loaned the old man his arm as he stood to position himself in front of his walker. Then Reverend Grandpa firmly squeezed Matthew's shoulder as if acknowledging a debt of gratitude.

"Thanks, my boy," he said with what sounded like sincere affection.

A few minutes later the two sat side by side in the living room, Reverend Grandpa in his favorite chair and Matthew on the sofa. No eye contact, just as Matthew preferred for this particular conversation.

"I think God wants me to tell you something."

The old man seemed pleasantly surprised by the comment. "He does, does he?"

"Yes."

"Which God?"

Matthew turned toward the question. "What?"

"Which God told you to say something to me? The one I believe in or the one you believe in?"

Matthew didn't know how to respond, prompting the old man's playful sigh.

"Look, son, my God speaks through the Bible, not through

a college boy." The sting of offense quickly dissipated as Reverend Grandpa added, "Even a college boy I've grown fond of."

"I still need to say something to you. Promise me you'll listen and at least consider what I've got to say. I think I've earned that."

A deferential nod. "OK. Take the pulpit."

Matthew tried to remember the reference.

"I'm all ears," the old man added.

Matthew swallowed hard before diving into his hastily planned speech. "I think Marissa wants you to volunteer."

He paused to let the words sink in.

"And I think that you want what's best for her and the kids, so I think you need to consider the option."

There, he'd said it.

"Marissa told you that?" Reverend Grandpa asked with injury in his voice.

"No. She didn't say she wants you to transition. But I can tell."

"How?"

"By the look in her eyes when I suggested it. I can tell she feels the same way I felt when facing a similar situation with my mom."

"You lost your mom?"

"Long before she died." Matthew sensed the old man looking at him as he kept his own eyes fixed on the wall.

"What happened?" Reverend Grandpa asked gently.

"We decay."

"Excuse me?"

Matthew looked at his client. "It's something my religious studies professor told me. It was certainly true of my mom. She had been deteriorating for years before she finally volunteered."

"She killed herself?"

Matthew turned back toward the wall. "No. She didn't kill

herself. She sacrificed herself. For me." He felt the admission moisten his eyes. He swallowed back the growing lump in his throat. "She wanted me to go to college in order to become a teacher. But her medical expenses were burning through our savings." He looked at his client. "Just like you're burning through yours."

Reverend Grandpa looked away. He was either ashamed of himself or angry at Matthew. Probably both.

"So she decided to escape."

"Escape?"

"Escape the decay. Transcend the limitations of physical existence to follow in Jesus's footsteps."

"Jesus's footsteps?"

"That's what I wanted to tell you. I think God wants you to know you've misunderstood. You see Jesus as someone who rose from the dead like a death-conquering hero. But he was actually showing us the path to our true destiny."

"Which is?"

"Which is to transcend the limitations of a decaying body by becoming a death-embracing mystic. To escape the body."

Matthew noticed Reverend Grandpa reaching at an awkward angle as he twisted his torso while shoving a hand deep into his pocket.

"What are you doing?" Matthew asked. "Do you need some help?"

"No need for help. I'll have it in just a...ah...here it is."

The old man held up a small pocketknife. Matthew wondered why on earth he had been carrying a tool used by campers and hunters. Perhaps a keepsake preserving bygone memories?

"I had planned to wrap this as a gift for little Pete," Reverend Grandpa began, "to celebrate today's big accomplishment."

What did a celebration gift have to do with Matthew's speech? Was the old man even listening?

"But I think you need it more." Reverend Grandpa pulled open what appeared to be a dangerously sharp tip. He flipped the knife around to hold it by the blade. "Here you go."

Matthew accepted the gift with a confused gaze. "Thanks, I guess. But why do you think I need this more than Peter?"

"So you can slit your own throat."

"What?" Matthew asked, covering his Adam's apple protectively with his other hand. "Slit my throat?"

"Or should I say, set yourself free?" A scathing laugh.

Matthew handed the knife back, rejecting the ridiculous notion.

"What's the matter, my boy? Don't believe your own philosophy? Or is it just something you believe when it applies to old debits like me?"

Matthew stood to leave the room. "I was trying to be serious," he said with disgust. "My mom's death isn't something to joke about."

"No, it isn't," Reverend Grandpa agreed. "Nor is it something to compare to Jesus's sacrifice on a cross!"

Matthew sensed his client's rising indignation.

"Death-embracing mystic? Nonsense! You have no clue what you're talking about, boy. Jesus Christ was not showing us the way to some harebrained enlightenment. He was giving his life as a payment for sin. My sin. Your sin. Even your mom's sin."

"What's that supposed to mean?"

"Your mom committed suicide, Matthew. No matter how much you try to dress it up as a heroic act, it was taking the most precious gift God gives us. Not to mention adding another coffin to the bonfire of human dignity."

The words made Matthew too furious to speak. How dare the old man call his mom's transition a sin! Even if it had been wrong, she hadn't done it. Matthew had. He was the one who had convinced her frail mind to volunteer. He was the one who had put the sword of guilt into her back as she walked the plank of "heroic sacrifice." He was the one who had chosen to heed the advice of Dr. Vincent rather than the warnings of Father Richard.

It wasn't a sin! Matthew tried to believe. *It was the right decision.*

"You're the one who has no idea what you're talking about!" Matthew finally retorted. "My mother was a good woman. She did what you're too selfish and cowardly to do. She's better off today because of it. And so am I!"

Matthew stormed out of the room, ignoring Reverend Grandpa's effort to coax him back.

"Sit down, my boy…" The bedroom door slammed to shield Matthew from noisy words he had no interest in hearing.

He spent the next few minutes trying to quell an irrational desire to grab the old man's knife and silence him for good. He instead grabbed his tablet from the top of the dresser and searched the PICTURES folder to find a portrait of his mother. He found one taken in her better days, when she still retained an echo of girlish beauty, a reminder of what she had been before dementia started stealing her away.

"I'm sorry, Mom," he heard himself whisper. "I thought it was for the best. But now I can't even get to the college money you left me."

He closed his eyes. Then he cursed.

When he opened his eyes he noticed a bouncing icon at the bottom of his digital screen. An unopened message from Maria Davidson! His mood lifted immediately as he tapped.

Hi Matt:

  It was great catching up after so many years. I'm afraid I'm entering a pretty busy season of life, so it probably isn't a good idea to try getting together again before you head back to your mysterious life. But I had a wonderful time and appreciated you taking an interest in Jared. Thanks for reconnecting. Be happy and be good.

Maria

Matthew read the letter twice before the meaning finally sank in. Maria Davidson had just said goodbye. Or rather, good riddance!

He cursed again as he let the tablet fall to the floor.

I won't let this happen, he thought. Then he frantically searched his dresser drawers to locate some stationery and a pen.

CHAPTER THIRTY-EIGHT

Sitting at her dining room table, Rebecca Santiago tried to push past her fear. Her weakness. She picked the letter up from the floor and read it one last time.

Dear Victor:

Please forgive my sending this note to your wife Rebecca. Prior attempts to correspond through your assistant have proven unfruitful. I have yet to receive a single response to any of my previous letters regarding the wrongful death appeal involving NEXT Transition Services. As you know, many lives hang in the balance in this matter. That's why I was pleased the case fell to a man with the kind of wisdom and restraint you have demonstrated throughout your distinguished judicial career. But this case is far too important for any hint of ambiguity. That's why I must know where you stand before the scheduled ruling deadline of September 4th. Please consider Rebecca's future as you contemplate the following alternatives:

- *Option One:* Assure me that you will indeed decide in favor of NEXT.
- *Option Two:* Bid your sweet wife farewell since you will die before issuing an opinion.

Once again, I apologize for alarming Rebecca. But she deserves to know about the increasingly tense situation in which we find ourselves. I could not allow any of what might transpire to come as a surprise, and I trust that her intervention will motivate you to do what's right for everyone.

As always,
A Manichean
P.S. Kindly post your response at the following private forum address: ANON.CHAT.4398

Rebecca walked into the kitchen, where a small stack of dirty teacups and saucers reminded her that she had been plunged into a different universe from the one she had inhabited only a few minutes before. Hadn't she just waved goodbye to Shelly, the last straggler from a chatty afternoon with friends? Hadn't she intended to complain to Victor about the tragedy of burned pumpkin scones? It was part of their daily ritual over dinner to share the high points and low points of their day. She suddenly had a new, dreadful low to report. And it couldn't wait until dinner.

She found the phone and pressed the image of Victor smiling back at her. She heard his recorded voice begin the custom greeting made for her ears only.

"Hi, Rebecca. There's two things I want to do at this moment. First, answer your call. Second, tell you how much I love you. Unfortunately, I'm probably in session at the moment. So I'll have to settle for saying that I love you. I'll call back as soon as I can."

She smiled. Then she panicked. What if he could *never* talk to her again? What if the crazy killer had been impatient and decided not to wait until September fourth after all?

She quickly tapped another image. A live voice answered. *Thank God*!

"Jennifer?" It was all she could say, her fear and sorrow surfacing at the relief.

"Rebecca?" Jennifer responded to the sound of crying. "What's wrong? What happened?"

Jennifer McKay had been like a daughter to the Santiagos. There was no one Rebecca would rather have called, short of Victor himself.

"Rebecca? Are you hurt?" Jennifer was asking through the phone with urgent concern.

She finally regained a semblance of composure. "I'm all right, Jennifer." Then she swallowed back another ocean of moisture and took a deep breath. "But I'm afraid for Victor. We need to do something to protect him!"

She had never said anything like it before. Victor had always been the sentry in their relationship. It was his job to worry about his frail bride. Rebecca knew herself to be weaker than she wished. She relied on Victor's strength. But in this moment she would settle for Jennifer's.

"A letter arrived today," she continued. "Somebody wants to kill my Victor!"

No response.

"Did you hear me, Jennifer? I said—"

"Did the letter specifically mention killing?"

"Yes, of course. Why would I make something like that up?"

"Is the letter signed?" Jennifer asked.

Why doesn't she seem alarmed?

"I'm afraid, Jennifer. I'm so afraid."

"Listen to me, Rebecca. I need to know if there is a signature."

Rebecca walked back to the dining room to find the letter and search for a name. "Someone named Manichean," she replied. "Why, what's going on?"

Before Jennifer could respond Rebecca saw a line in the letter she hadn't noticed before.

Prior attempts to correspond through your assistant have proven unfruitful.

"You've received other letters, haven't you?"

"Yes, we have. But don't worry. We have a detective investigating the situation."

A detective? Situation? Rebecca felt her fear becoming anger. "What situation? And why didn't you tell me about this? Why didn't Victor tell me?"

A long, torturous silence. Jennifer finally answered. "Rebecca, Victor doesn't know about the letters."

She couldn't believe her ears. Why would Jennifer keep such an important secret from her boss? From Rebecca's husband? "What do you mean?"

Jennifer explained everything: Victor's policy of ignoring any correspondence related to an open case, her role of deciding how to handle each situation, and why in this instance she had chosen to hire a private investigator rather than go to the police.

Rebecca looked back at the signature. *A Manichean.* "Do you have any idea of his identity?"

A two-second delay. "We have a few leads."

Rebecca sensed the truth. They had no idea. "I want to talk to Victor immediately," she insisted.

"I understand," Jennifer said. "But, please, can you read me the letter? Word for word."

She did, her voice breaking again when she reached the ultimatum.

"He's going to kill my Victor!" she said, the panic recoloring her voice. "We have to tell him now!"

A momentary hush meant Jennifer must have been assessing her dilemma. If she did as Rebecca suggested she would be violating Victor's policy. A policy Rebecca both admired and suddenly hated.

"Listen, Rebecca," Jennifer began. "The judge will be in session for at least another ninety minutes. Security is on high alert due to the earlier letters, so nothing can happen to him here."

"Nothing can happen to him? Come on, Jennifer. *Anything* could happen!"

"Please, Rebecca. I promise we'll protect him. But I need to come over and see that letter right away. I'll call the detective and we'll meet you there. Then we'll decide. One hour, that's all I ask."

Rebecca considered the request. What would Victor want her to do? She knew the answer immediately.

"OK," she said reluctantly. "One hour."

The call ended. Rebecca felt light-headed. She sat back down at the dinner table where her living nightmare had begun. Then she refolded the note, slid it back into the envelope, and wrapped her arms around a delicate frame now home to the consuming demon of terror.

PART THREE

CHAPTER THIRTY-NINE

Jennifer McKay was sitting on the living room sofa beside a distraught woman who was downing the last swig of a drink that was not, Tyler presumed, her first. Although he had never seen her before, Tyler knew the woman immediately: the judge's wife, understandably shaken.

He glanced toward the dining room table, then groaned at the sight of Assistant Chief Greg Smith. Tyler had hoped to arrive in time to read the letter first and then debrief his former partner rather than the other way around. Jennifer had said she'd phoned the police before calling Tyler. He had raced through downtown Denver in slow motion behind rush-hour traffic hoping to beat Smitty to the house. No such luck.

Tyler heard the clack of a dead bolt latching behind him as an officer closed the front door. The sound prompted a glance from Smitty, who looked up from the letter to offer a summoning wave.

"Tyler," he said in a hushed voice.

"Smitty," Tyler replied with a nod. "What've we got?"

It was the same question he'd asked a hundred times before, back when he and Smitty had investigated everything from petty burglary to serial homicide. But this time it felt impertinent. They were no longer partners. Tyler wasn't on the force. Nor was he an effective private investigator—he had failed to prevent whatever threat Smitty was reading.

He quickly corrected himself. "I mean, what have *you* got?"

Smitty handed Tyler the page. "Take a look for yourself."

He did. Then he glanced in Jennifer's direction. She was rubbing Rebecca Santiago's forearm to offer comfort. Their eyes met. His shot an *I told you so* rebuke. Hers stubbornly refused any *I should have listened* regret.

"I was afraid of this," he said while following Smitty around the corner to speak in private. Tyler wanted his former partner to believe the letter hadn't been a surprise. And in a way it hadn't. Tyler's gut had told him the situation could escalate. He had told Jennifer she should write back to smoke out the culprit. That she should alert the judge so that he could resign from the case to protect his life. "Maybe now Ms. McKay will take my advice," Tyler continued.

"What advice is that?"

"Tell the judge about the letters."

"You mean he doesn't know?"

"No sir. He has a strict policy against paying attention to any correspondence related to an active case."

Smitty sighed. "Of course."

Tyler waited a moment to let Smitty appreciate his dilemma. "I have a few potential suspects," he lied. "But I need the judge to write back so we can spring the trap."

Smitty looked at Tyler questioningly but said nothing. Then he glanced back into the living room.

"Ms. McKay, may I speak to you for a moment?" he asked. "That is, if Mrs. Santiago doesn't mind."

The woman shook her head deferentially while reaching for the bottle of brandy sitting strategically beside her now-empty glass. "Go ahead, Jennifer. I'll be fine."

Jennifer appeared grateful for the promotion from comforter to collaborator. She clearly disliked the thought of Tyler and Smitty discussing next steps without her input.

She joined them in the dining room, where Tyler still hoped to control the situation. He spoke first. "Smitty and I were just discussing the need to show this letter to the judge—"

"No!" she interrupted. "This is a very important case and he's only a few days away from issuing an opinion. The judge would be very upset if we—"

"Come on!" Tyler said, too loudly. He hushed himself before continuing. "You can't be serious. The man's wife is sitting in the next room so alarmed she's drowning her fears in booze. I think it's about time you woke up to what's happening here, Ms. McKay."

"I know exactly what's happening here, Mr. Cain! And I know exactly what Judge Santiago would want."

"You're just too stubborn to admit I was right!" Tyler added before Smitty raised a hand to silence the whispered spat.

"Ms. McKay is right," he began.

Tyler's head jerked in Smitty's direction, then back toward Jennifer, who appeared equally startled.

"What?" Tyler said.

"I don't think we need to show Judge Santiago this letter."

Jennifer grinned in triumph as Tyler weighed his response. How to save face? More importantly, how to protect the judge? Then it struck him.

"We don't have a choice," he said. "His wife will tell him the second she sees him."

"No, she won't," Jennifer said with surprising confidence. "I explained the situation. She knows the judge better than anyone. She knows he would want us to wait until after he issues an opinion."

Tyler peered back around the corner toward the shaken woman. "Look at her, for Pete's sake! Even if she managed to keep her mouth shut, which seems highly unlikely, the judge will know by looking at her that something's up." He turned toward Smitty. "Imagine the fallout if it gets out that the police knew about this threat and didn't try to stop it."

"I didn't say we wouldn't try to stop it," Smitty said. "I said I don't think the judge needs to see the letters. We can inform him of a threatening situation without specific details. If we do our job properly, there's no reason we can't let the man do his."

If we do our job properly. A dig at Tyler's failed investigation?

"We'll tell the judge that we have evidence he may be the target of an assassination attempt," Smitty continued. "Then we'll tell him it's related to a court case without saying which or what decision the suspect demands. The judge can make his own decision on whether he wants more detail or not."

"He won't," Jennifer insisted as Tyler seethed.

"We'll see," Smitty replied. "But for now, tell me everything either of you knows so that we can determine the best course of action."

Jennifer reminded Smitty that she had called the chief of police to request a recommendation for a private investigator. She sounded like a disappointed customer complaining to the store manager.

Then Tyler shared what little he had learned from the earlier letters. He decided to leave out the part where he called Evan Dimitri. No need to further sully his reputation by describing the blunder. A mistake that had gotten him nowhere and, he told himself, was probably irrelevant to the case.

Smitty sighed reflectively after listening to Tyler's debrief.

"So," he began, "our only real clues are the postal facilities in which the letters were processed and an odd pseudonym."

"A Manichean," Tyler inserted in an attempt to prove useful.

"Right," Smitty said without interest as he considered options. "Here's what we're going to do. Ms. McKay, I want you to inform the judge of a threat."

"Of course," she said, obviously pleased by Smitty's wise tactic.

"Tyler, I want you to further analyze this new letter."

Smitty handed the note to his former partner, who accepted it eagerly and with relief. "You got it, boss," he said, grateful to still be on the team.

"I'll assign an officer to guard the judge's house and another to his chamber until he either resigns from the case or issues an opinion."

"Only two officers?" Jennifer asked, like a still-disgruntled customer.

"It's two more than I can afford, Ms. McKay," Smitty explained.

She huffed. "We have security guards at the courthouse already. Would it be possible to assign both officers to the house? I'm sure it would make Mrs. Santiago feel much more secure."

A single nod. "Done."

Tyler joined Smitty in offering reassurance to Mrs. Santiago before heading to his car. He closed himself in and breathed deeply the sun-warmed air. As the engine engaged, the date and time appeared on the dashboard. September 1, 2043. Only three days until Judge Santiago was scheduled to issue an opinion on the wrongful death appeal initiated by NEXT Transition Services.

He had less than seventy-two hours to find the culprit. And, he hoped, to prove himself worthwhile to his former partner.

CHAPTER FORTY

The bartender reached for the empty glass. "Another round?"

The question interrupted Tyler's concentration. "What's that?"

"I asked if you need a refill."

"Oh, yeah, thanks. Diet cola."

The man smirked at an order more suited to a fast-food joint than his establishment. "You sure you don't want something stiffer? You look like you could use it."

"Not tonight." Tyler pointed to his open tablet. "Still on duty."

The man went away for a moment and returned with a fresh glass of ice. He slid it forward along with an unopened can of soda. "Enjoy."

Tyler nodded, then resumed his digital doodling, jotting down each new clue found in the latest letter.

WANTS NEXT INC. TO WIN THEIR APPEAL
CLEAR DEATH THREAT
DIFFERENT HANDWRITING?

Tyler deleted the last line when he realized the differences were too slight to suggest another author. It was probably the same hand more nervous due to rising stakes. He continued reviewing the list.

SENT BY COURIER VS. POST

The first three letters had been sent from the Boulder area. The fourth from Denver. This one had no origination postal code or any other mark suggesting a location. It had come on a delivery truck Rebecca Santiago hadn't been able to describe.

VERY RESPECTFUL TONE

As in the earlier letters.

WRITER KNOWS WIFE'S FIRST NAME

Easy enough to find with a simple online search of news clippings.

In short, nothing useful.

Tyler took a sip of his soda to cool a rising anger at Smitty's decision. At this very moment Jennifer McKay was informing the judge of a vague threat rather than insisting that he correspond with the writer or resign from the case.

He scanned the letter again, resting his eyes on the postscript.

P.S. Kindly post your response at the following private forum address: ANON.CHAT.4398

Why not send a short note promising to decide in favor of NEXT? It would neutralize the threat and, perhaps, provide a few additional clues. The judge could ignore the promise and decide the case as he saw fit. By then they might even have caught the culprit.

But Tyler knew the suggestion would fall on deaf ears. Judge Santiago would rather risk his life than undermine his integrity, a fact Tyler found both exasperating and laudable. He wondered what, if anything, he himself would risk his own life to protect. Certainly not his integrity. That was already in the toilet.

Tyler glanced again at the signature line.

A MANICHEAN

It must mean something. But what?

He quickly typed the name into a search field for what must have been the tenth time since taking the case. The same useless list of results appeared.

That's when it struck him. Maybe the words weren't a pseudonym at all. Maybe they were a description. Not a first initial and last name, but a title, like A CANADIAN or A DENVER BRONCOS FAN.

He looked at the list of links again to spot any group or organization that might accept members. Perhaps a religious order, or a club, or an online chat association with dues. Nothing fit.

He narrowed the search criteria to anything near Boulder. Twenty results: two of the top five included the name Dr. Thomas Vincent, chairman of the Religious Studies department at the University of Colorado.

"Bingo!" Tyler said aloud.

"Nope," the bartender responded while wiping the counter. "But we host a poker match every Monday night."

Tyler chuckled at the misunderstanding, then tapped the first link. Apparently this Dr. Vincent fellow taught a course on ancient religious controversies in the very city from which the first letters had been sent.

He tapped the second link and learned Dr. Vincent had also written a book about Manichaeism. The author's biography said he was a leading authority on a wide range of philosophies that had been largely rejected by the early Christian church.

Tyler launched another search, this time typing the name Thomas Vincent in conjunction with Boulder, Colorado. A long list of results surfaced: video highlights from prior lectures, free downloads from an upcoming book about something called Gnosticism, and a whole string of spicy photos posted by college-age girls to his personal attention. Tyler pulled up several of the pictures before ordering himself to focus on the task at hand.

He dialed the number listed on the university's website. A recorded female voice answered, accompanied by a pleasant musical selection. He glanced at the time. Past office hours.

He tapped Smitty's image to ask for help. Within ten minutes he had Dr. Vincent's private number compliments of a citizen-watch database law enforcement agencies could access with a proper warrant. A warrant Jennifer McKay had gladly procured from the judge.

He dialed the number. A voice answered. "Thomas Vincent."

Tyler found himself at a loss for words. What to say? He couldn't mention the letters. After all, the professor was a possible suspect.

"Hello," Tyler began hesitantly. "Forgive me for the intrusion, but is this the same Dr. Vincent who wrote the famous book on a religious movement known as Manichaeism?"

A brief laugh from the other end of the line. "I'd hardly call it famous. Academic works don't sell many downloads. But yes, I'm the author. To whom do I have the pleasure of speaking?"

A nice-sounding man. Very respectful. Just like the letters.

"Tyler Cain. I'm doing research on a project and was encouraged to call you for help. I'm told you're the most respected voice in your field."

A bit of flattery couldn't hurt, especially when talking to an academic who seemed more distinguished than famous.

"Well, I'm happy to do what I can," Dr. Vincent said. "Who recommended me?"

Tyler felt a slight panic. What to say? "I'm embarrassed to say it, but I forgot the person's name. We met on a plane and struck up a conversation."

"A student of mine?"

"I think so."

"Hmm. A young woman?"

Tyler thought for a second. Play the odds. Other than in the movies, killers tend to be male. "A man."

"Really?"

"Is that surprising?" Tyler asked.

"I don't give this number out to many of my male students."

Tyler glanced back at the spicy pictures. *What a life*! he mused.

"Well, no matter," the professor continued. "How can I help?"

"I was hoping you could point me in the right direction on something."

"I'll do what I can."

Should he risk mentioning the signatures? Without eye contact Tyler would have no way of sensing the professor's reaction. What if Dr. Vincent had written the letters? Or delivered them? Would this call ruin any hope of cornering the culprit? Maybe. But Tyler was running out of time and options. He decided to chance it.

"Do you know anyone who would call himself a Manichean?"

"A Manichean?"

"Yes, sir."

"Well, yes. Of course."

"Really? Who?"

"Well, the most notable would be Augustine."

Tyler quickly grabbed his tablet. "Could you spell that name?"

The professor laughed at the request. "Certainly you're familiar with Saint Augustine."

"Saint?"

"Fourth century. Bishop of Hippo." Dr. Vincent's voice sounded suspicious; he had been tipped off by Tyler's appalling ignorance.

"Truth is," Tyler began, "I don't know much about ancient religions or philosophy or anything of the sort."

A brief silence. "What's this about? Who gave you this number?"

"The police."

"The police?" Dr. Vincent said with alarm. "Why would the police give you my private number? Come to think of it, why do they even *have* my private number?"

Tyler couldn't see the professor's eyes, but his voice carried no hint of guilty avoidance. Tyler decided to come clean by telling Dr. Vincent about the letters.

"I see," the professor responded after listening in silence.

"Do you have any idea who would be eager for NEXT to win its appeal and describe himself as a Manichean?"

Dr. Vincent thought for a moment before mumbling something beneath his breath. Possibly a name.

"What's that?" Tyler asked.

"I had a student this past year who seemed particularly interested in Manichean philosophy. As it happens, he also has a transition inheritance tied up with his late mother's estate. I think he might have mentioned something about the NEXT lawsuit, but I couldn't say for sure."

"What's the student's name?"

The professor hesitated. "I can't imagine this young man doing anything so stupid. He wants to be a teacher. And he's worked very hard."

"You'd be surprised what people will do when they get desperate," Tyler said. "I just want to ask the guy a few questions. Can you please tell me his name?"

Another pause. "His name is Matthew. Matthew Adams."

"Thank you, Dr. Vincent. Does Matthew Adams live in student housing on campus?"

"He's no longer a student. He plans to return to school next year if he can—" The professor stopped short.

"If he can what?" Tyler pushed, sensing the professor knew more than he wanted to reveal. "If he can get the money?"

"Yes."

Double bingo!

"Which will happen if the transition inheritance is released?"

"I suppose," Dr. Vincent agreed grudgingly.

"Do you have any idea where we might find Mr. Adams now?" Tyler asked. "Please, Dr. Vincent, this could be a matter of life and death."

The professor explained that Matthew had left Boulder to take an elder-care job in the Denver area.

"And when did you last speak to Mr. Adams?"

"Last week. He came to me for advice on dealing with his client."

"Did he mention an address? Give you a phone number? Anything like that?"

"I'm afraid not," Dr. Vincent replied, as if relieved by his own ignorance. "Like I said. Somewhere in the Denver area."

Tyler thanked the professor and left the door open for a follow-up inquiry before ending the call.

He had a name.

He had a general location.

And he still had two days.

Tyler smiled in self-congratulation as he reached for the soda can to refill his glass. Then he paused, motioning toward the bartender, who was refilling a collection of empty nut bowls.

"I think I'll have that stiff drink now," he said. "I'm suddenly in the mood to celebrate."

CHAPTER FORTY-ONE

It felt good to receive Maria's long embrace, the sorrow Julia had managed to conceal from Troy for the past thirty-six hours finally erupting into her sister's nurturing arms. It had only taken three gently spoken words.

"I'm sorry, Sis."

Despite her embarrassment, Julia thanked Maria for listening, for caring, and for promising not to say anything to Troy.

The two now sat on a large rock in silence, holding hands as they had when they were little girls during a thunderstorm. A streak of early-morning sunlight peered over the nearby mountains, brightening the stony trail they intended to hike.

Maria spoke first. "Are they certain? No chance at all?"

"Not much. The doctor mentioned a surgical option. But that rarely helps." Julia paused to swallow back another flood of tears. Then she continued. "She said most couples in our situation use a sperm bank."

"Would Troy be open to that?"

"He wants a child badly." Julia wiped her nose with a tissue she had retrieved from her jogging suit pocket. "But he wants *our* child. How would he feel about a baby that was half me and half some other guy? Could he love that child like he would his own flesh and blood?" She shrugged. "I don't know. And I'm afraid to ask."

Maria placed her hand on Julia's shoulder. "What are you afraid of?"

"Afraid he'll say yes. You know Troy. He'll do whatever he thinks would make me happy. But would it make *him* happy? I'm afraid I'd never really know how he felt about a child that his wife had with a complete stranger."

"Julia!" Maria said sternly. "You make it sound like you're contemplating a one-night stand. It's not like that. Couples use sperm donors all the time."

Julia laughed self-consciously. "I know, I know," she said with a sigh. "I'm probably being silly. Of course it's not wrong. But it still doesn't feel quite right. At least not for Troy. Or for me."

Maria nodded quietly, waiting a few seconds, then stood up. "Do you still want to go?"

Julia nodded, glad to move beyond self-pity. She loved nothing more than a brisk walk along Bear Creek Lake to help clear her head and regain perspective.

Neither said anything for thirty or forty paces. Then Maria asked, "Have you thought about adoption?"

The question raised a different cloud over Julia's demeanor. Not personal grief, but the memory of a disturbing discovery. While researching dark zone trends Julia had learned there was a five-year waiting list for adoptable infants. Five years!

"There aren't any babies available," she said without explanation.

"You can't be serious. There must be some babies in need of a good home."

"Very few. It seems harvesting pays better than delivery."

The comment appeared to startle Maria. She stopped walking and turned toward her sister. "What did you say?"

"Fetus harvesting. It's become a fairly large industry supporting the embryotic supply chain."

"The what?"

"You know: surgical repair material, cosmetics, health supplements. That sort of thing."

It took a moment for Maria to connect the dots. "Wait. You mean that's what they mean when they say 'embryotics'?"

Julia nodded. "You can sell a two-month-old fetus for a few thousand dollars. So, unless you want to raise a child, what's the motivation for women to invest nine months getting fat, visiting doctors, and buying prenatal vitamins? It's illegal to sell a live baby due to human trafficking laws. But embryos can be sold without hassle or questions."

Maria appeared every bit as troubled as Julia had been when confronted with the naked facts. But the process had never been a secret. It had just remained hidden in plain sight thanks to naïve indifference, or perhaps willful ignorance. In the back of Julia's and Maria's minds they must have known that someone, somewhere had been harvesting embryos. Like everyone else, they had chosen not to ask where the raw materials fueling the public's enhanced appearance and extended years came from. The look on Maria's face reminded Julia of her own earlier epiphany. They were like two children stumbling upon a suspicious dog kennel beside their daddy's butcher shop.

Eager to move beyond the depressing and dark, Julia raised a lighter subject as they continued their walk. "So, tell me about your date. How was the reunion with the high school mystery suitor?"

Maria smiled, then frowned. "Well, despite your worst fears he didn't turn out to be a mass murderer hoping to rape and strangle me."

Julia laughed at the reminder of her overprotective warnings. "That's good news. So, what's his name?"

"Matthew."

"And?"

"And we met for coffee."

"A public place. Very good. You listened to me. Did you meet during daylight hours like I—"

Maria slapped her sister's arm.

"Ouch! What was that for?"

"Love pat," Maria said playfully. "Yes, Julia, we met in the daytime. Now will you quit with the hovercraft questions?"

"Sorry. Tell me about him."

"I didn't remember him at first. But he sure knew me. He could tell you what I was wearing the day we sat together in the cafeteria, what I said when I refused his invitation to the prom, and how many pictures I've posted online in the past year."

"Sounds creepy to me."

"It wasn't like that. At least not at first. I thought it was kind of sweet. Flattering."

"Maria," Julia said severely. "That's how it always starts with you. They look. They like. They flatter. They enjoy. And then they leave."

"Not this time. I ended it before reaching the 'enjoy' phase."

Julia was genuinely surprised. "Really? Just like that? What happened?"

"He didn't pass the Jared test."

"The what?"

"Jared made me promise I would introduce him to any guy I liked enough for a potentially serious relationship. So he came with me on my second date with Matthew. It didn't go well."

"What happened?"

"Nothing really. Jared just got bad vibes. He wants me to marry someone like your Troy. This guy didn't come close."

"Was he mean?"

"No. Quite nice actually."

"Then what?"

Maria appeared to be searching for the right word. "Needy. No, weak. That's the word. He didn't seem like the kind of guy who would put me before himself. At least that's how Jared read him."

"I see. Disappointed?"

"A bit. He was cute. And it was my first real date in six months. But I'm learning not to trust my own first impressions."

They walked another quarter mile before either spoke again.

"I'm proud of you, Sis," Julia finally said. "I bet it made Jared feel good knowing you respected his opinion enough to end the relationship."

"It did." A sigh. "I'm OK with the decision. There was something odd about Matthew anyway. It kind of gnawed at me but I couldn't put my finger on it. At least not until after Jared gave him the thumbs-down. Then I remembered feeling something was off-kilter when he first contacted me. He used a really weird online handle."

"A lot of guys do that when using online connection services."

"I know. But most use something fun like 'Lover Boy' or 'Dream Man.' Matt used something pretty strange. I can't remember it exactly. *A Manichu* or *A Mannequin.* Something like that."

Julia stopped in her tracks.

Maria took several steps before noticing, then turned back. "What?"

"Was it *A Manichean?*"

"That's it!" Maria said with surprise. "How on earth did you know?"

Six minutes later both sisters were sitting in Julia's car.

"That's the same name I got from a Dr. Vincent I called last night," Tyler Cain's voice was saying through the stereo speakers. "He's a professor on ancient religions in Boulder who said Matthew Adams recently moved from Boulder to Denver to take an elder-care job. Triple bingo!"

"An elder-care job?" Maria said. "He told me he was in town on business."

"Did he mention an address?" Tyler asked.

"No. I assumed he was staying in a hotel."

Tyler cursed. "Well, I already tried the address change information service. They list the Boulder address he left but nothing on this end."

"No mail-forwarding mailing address?" Julia asked.

"One of those rental box places. I had planned to try tracking it down this morning."

"But there must be a hundred of those places in the Denver area."

"Three hundred and twenty-seven, actually. Smitty said the police have no record of credit card use since Matthew moved from Boulder. He seems to have gone underground. No address. Cash purchases. So I have to start with what I've got."

"Who's Smitty?" Maria asked.

"My former partner with the Denver police."

"Did you check for an active bank account?" Julia suggested. "Surely that would have his new address."

"I couldn't get any information over the phone. My call routed to somebody named 'Jeremy' in one of those foreign call centers in North Korea or Vietnam. You know how they talk. Anyway, I plan to stop by the major bank branches when they open this morning, right after I get a compulsory cooperation document from Smitty."

"Wait a minute," Julia said while looking at her sister. "Maria was in touch with Matthew last week."

"A few days ago, actually. But I told you. I sent him a Dear John message. It's over between us."

"I bet you said goodbye in a way that would keep the door open in case you ever changed your mind."

"Julia!" Maria reacted with offense.

"I'm right, aren't I?"

A nod.

"I thought so."

"That's perfect!" Tyler interjected. "Maria, I need you to send Matthew Adams another message."

"Saying what?" she asked. "Matt's not likely to respond if I tell him the police want to talk to him."

"No," Tyler agreed. "But I bet he'd respond if you told him you would like to see him again."

"That you'd *love* to see him again," Julia corrected as she shoved her tablet in front of Maria.

She reluctantly accepted the device. "I'm not so sure about this. What if he—"

"Please, Maria, just type whatever Mr. Cain suggests."

She did, carefully following Tyler's wording to request a rendezvous later that afternoon.

Just before Maria hit SEND, Julia placed her hand on her sister's arm, then suggested one last action. She reached for the tablet and pointed. "Wink."

"Excuse me?"

"I said wink at the camera. We're attaching a snapshot."

Maria glowered at her sister. Then dutifully obeyed.

CHAPTER FORTY-TWO

Nothing was going to keep Matthew from getting to Bear Creek Lake by six. Not even Reverend Grandpa's ill-timed attempt at making amends. Feeling bad for what he had said about Matthew's mother, the old man suggested the two might grab a burger together. "My treat!" he had said with a sheepish grin.

But even if Matthew had wanted to accept some lame apology, he wouldn't have gone. Maria Davidson had made that impossible by retracting her rejection note. Why else would she suggest a picnic dinner and say she would love to see him again? Reverend Grandpa could fend for himself for a few hours, even if it meant Matthew abandoning his post. Or losing his job.

He triple-checked the destination to confirm the precise location suggested in Maria's mischievous note.

I'll be waiting near the trailhead wearing white shorts and a bright yellow sleeveless blouse. (Easy to spot from a distance and enjoy up close!)
Go to coordinates 39.653182,-105.148349.

I'll wait exactly ten minutes. If you don't arrive I'll figure you aren't coming.

But I really, really hope you do!

He looked urgently at the dashboard clock for the eighth time in as many minutes. Assuming a hundred-yard walk from the parking area he should make it with time to spare. He took a deep breath while turning left onto Kumpfmiller Drive. One turn later he saw Maria in the distance. She was, as promised, easy on the eyes. Her blond hair was pulled back, revealing a lovely neck that matched lightly tanned limbs. She looked even better than he had imagined, her upper legs partially concealed behind a small picnic basket dangling from her coupled hands. She appeared to brighten when she spotted Matthew's approaching smile.

As he slammed the car door, Matthew waved in Maria's direction. She lifted the basket slightly as if offering evidence of her intentions, then turned onto the trail and began walking into the trees. He laughed to himself, still stunned by his sudden good fortune, before starting toward her. Then he stopped and turned back toward the car to grab the love note he had planned to send. Now he could watch her read it and, he hoped, relish her reaction.

"Maria," he called into the trees. "Wait up. I've got something for you."

No answer.

He trotted to the trailhead, where he found a path beneath the shade of unwieldy tree branches.

"Maria," he repeated, half hoping she would continue the game of hide-and-seek.

But this time she called back. "I'm over here by the lake."

He turned left toward the voice.

"Just beyond the clump of trees."

Matthew's mind raced through the possibilities. Would he find her lounging on a blanket beside two freshly poured glasses of wine? Or perhaps in a bikini with her bare toes caressing the water's edge? Or, dare he hope, taking a plunge wearing nothing but an invitation for him to join?

"Mr. Adams?"

The male voice startled Matthew. He looked left toward an approaching stranger who somehow knew his name.

"Have we met?" Matthew asked while instinctively extending a cautious hand.

The man matched the offer with a firm shake. "My name's Tyler Cain. I've been trying to track you down."

Track me down? Matthew thought while scanning the shore for signs of Maria. He noticed a trace of yellow and white moving quickly on the other side of a tree-lined path.

"Ms. Davidson won't be able to join us," Tyler explained.

"Us?" Matthew said with confusion. "What are you talking about? Maria and I arranged to meet here for...a...picnic. Who are you?"

"I'm a private investigator working with the Denver police. I've been investigating threats made against Judge Victor Santiago."

Matthew cursed, once in alarm and again at Maria's apparent betrayal. But how could she have known about the letters? Had he accidentally mentioned them during their first date? No, he hadn't.

"Threats? Against a judge?"

"That's right."

"What does that have to do with Maria? Or me?"

The detective reached into a backpack he had placed onto the path. Did he have a gun? Bounty hunter handcuffs? No. He pulled out a small stack of handwritten notes Matthew recognized immediately.

"What are those?"

"I was hoping you could help me figure that out," Tyler said while offering the papers. "Like I said, I've been investigating a case involving the judge. But I need your help piecing together some of the clues."

"*My* help?" Matthew felt himself start to panic. "Why me?"

"Two different people suggested I talk to you."

"Who?" he demanded.

"Dr. Thomas Vincent from UC–Boulder, for one. He's an expert on this word here." Tyler pointed to the signature line at the bottom of the first note. "I'm not entirely sure how the professor pronounced it."

"Manichean," Matthew read without thinking. He quickly feigned ignorance. "Is that how you say it?"

"Sounds about right," Tyler confirmed.

Matthew looked up. What to say? "Who else suggested talking to me?"

"Maria's sister, Julia Davidson. She's been helping me on the case and said you had signed notes to Maria using this same word."

Of course! Sisters always share intimate love-life details. Maria must have shown Julia his messages. Matthew hated to imagine what Maria must think of him now.

But he had an even more troubling concern. What did the police believe? And what did this private investigator know?

"Listen, Mr. Cain—"

"Call me Tyler, please."

"Tyler then. You've gotta believe me. I never meant any harm. I just wanted to communicate with the judge. I thought maybe—"

"No, Mr. Adams," Tyler pounced. "You didn't think. A thinking person doesn't send death threats to a sitting judge. A thinking person doesn't sign those threats with the same screwball name he uses to woo women."

"Death threats? I never sent any death threats."

Matthew quickly unfolded and reread the first note he had sent to the judge. Then he read two more. "I just asked the judge to correspond with me about the case. To consider the real-life impacts on people like me if he—"

Tyler took the stationery pages back from Matthew. Then he retrieved another from his pack. This one photocopied since, Matthew assumed, the original was sitting in a protective plastic bag at police headquarters. "This letter arrived yesterday, Mr. Adams," Tyler said. He began reading aloud. "Bid your sweet wife farewell since you will die before issuing an opinion." He stopped and looked into Matthew's eyes. "Sounds a heck of a lot like a death threat to me."

Matthew appeared startled as he quickly yanked the page from Tyler's hand. He felt the color draining from his face as he read.

"I've never seen this letter before in my life," he said in a voice that sounded every bit as guilty as the detective had assumed him to be.

"Yeah. And I'm the Easter bunny," Tyler mocked.

"I'd never kill—" The image of his mom's slumping corpse interrupted Matthew's defense. "I'd never *murder* anyone! You've got to believe me."

CHAPTER FORTY-THREE

Tyler glanced at the page, then back at the ball of anxiety standing before him. "Save it for the police, Mr. Adams," he said. "My job is to follow the evidence trail wherever it leads and then hand everything over to the authorities. I'm just glad I tracked you down before you did something *really* stupid."

"Wait!" Matthew grabbed Tyler's wrist as if trying to keep him from leaving. "Listen to me. I didn't write this letter. I admit I wrote those." He pointed at Tyler's pack. "But not this one. Look here, even the writing looks different."

It did. A little.

"Please, Mr. Cain, I just wanted to get the judge to seriously consider the impact of his decision. I admit it was stupid. But I never intended to hurt the man. I swear I'm no assassin."

Tyler reached into his pack to find and retrieve the letter Jennifer McKay had shown him only a few days earlier. He scanned the page until he found the damning line.

"Even if you hadn't written this last letter," he said, "you still threatened the judge."

"No I didn't!" Matthew protested.

"Then how am I supposed to interpret this line, 'comply with my request to avoid more drastic measures'?"

A look of surrender came over Matthew's face, as if he had forgotten about the earlier threat.

"I shouldn't have said it like that," he confessed.

"But you did say it like that."

"I know," Matthew said. "I was trying to go big."

Tyler didn't follow.

"Forget it." Matthew's head was hanging in defeat. "It doesn't matter now anyway."

Tyler noticed moisture forming in Matthew's eyes. Liquid fear. As much as he wanted to believe the clear, indisputable evidence, something inside told him the guy was harmless. Dumb. Rash. Perhaps even conniving. Matthew Adams certainly fit the part of an uptight coward who would send anonymous, threatening letters. But he looked nothing like the sort who could walk into a federal courthouse and shoot to kill. With so many actual murderers walking free thanks to high-paid defense attorneys, and knowing what happens to weak men thrown in with hardened predators, Tyler would have hated to see Matthew spend a decade in a federal penitentiary.

"Do you have a lawyer?" Tyler asked.

Matthew wiped his face, then looked up self-consciously. "Not really. Just my uncle Ben. He handles my mom's estate. We don't get along."

"You'll need a good defense lawyer," Tyler said while rummaging through his backpack. He pulled out a pad and pen, then jotted down a name and number. "Call this guy," he said.

Matthew read the scribbling. "A friend of yours?"

"More like an enemy," Tyler replied. "But he's good at his job. Got several guys off I tried to put behind bars. You'll need someone like him. Expensive. But effective."

"I can't afford expensive." He looked Tyler in the eyes. "I guess I'm sunk."

Tyler shrugged. "Maybe not. They'll go easier on you if you come clean. You never know. You might even get a good plea bargain."

"What's that?"

"They'll charge you with plotting to assassinate a federal judge. A conviction would carry a long minimum sentence. If you admit to something less, perhaps violation of federal postal regulations, the judge could be much more lenient."

"I see," Matthew said into the air.

Tyler suddenly realized he had no script for the next scene of this drama. He had been 100 percent focused on finding and confronting Judge Santiago's potential assassin. It hadn't occurred to him what to do if the threat proved innocuous. Should he offer to drive Matthew to the station and hand him off to Smitty for questioning? Or should he show compassion? Let him go home to wrap up details of a life that was certain to change for the worse?

He decided to pull out his phone and point it at Matthew's face. Matthew frowned in reaction.

"I need to know where you'll be and how to reach you," Tyler said. "I'll send the information with this picture to a friend on the force. They'll want to talk to you. Tell them what you've admitted to me and you'll be OK."

Matthew gave the information. "Do you really think they might go easy on me?"

"I do."

But he didn't. Courts weren't likely to show much mercy to a guy who had threatened to murder a sitting judge. They might go light on someone who had threatened a congressman or senator. Possibly even the president. But a fellow judge? Not a chance.

"Go home, Mr. Adams," Tyler said. "Call a lawyer and wait for the police."

He had probably made the wrong decision. Smitty would have told Tyler to bring in the suspect personally. Immediately. "Don't let him out of your sight!" he'd have ordered. But Tyler wanted to give Matthew time and space to think through a plausible excuse for his folly. Which is exactly what Tyler knew it had been, a series of idiotic decisions by a desperate fool. Still, to be safe, Tyler shadowed Matthew's car from a discreet distance. He followed him to the house, then parked several hundred yards away to observe. The same routine he had used in countless stakeouts for jealous clients. As an added precaution he also placed a tiny observation camera on the rear porch. He could watch both through his car's windshield and tablet's screen.

Several hours of inaction gave Tyler time to think. Part of him rested comfortably in the knowledge that he had found the culprit, solved the case. But another part of him felt uneasy, as if one or two pieces of the puzzle didn't fit. The look on Matthew's face, for one, when Tyler showed him the final letter. He appeared genuinely surprised, as if he had no recollection of writing it. And the handwriting. There were differences, no matter how slight. Was it possible Matthew hadn't sent the final note after all?

No. Not possible. Who else would have sent it? Matthew must have intentionally altered the script. That's why he had been so eager to draw attention to the differences.

Tyler tapped an image on the dash menu. Three rings later he heard Smitty's voice message accept the call.

"Hi Smitty, it's Tyler. Great news. I found the guy who wrote the letters to Judge Santiago." Hearing the words prompted a swell of self-congratulation. He had solved the case. He had saved the judge from possible assassination. A job well done. "He's no real threat. I'm sending you the suspect's picture and the information on where you can have him picked up for questioning. I would keep the security detail at the judge's home for a few days to play it safe, but I think we can rest easy on this one."

He ended the call. No need to mention any doubts. Smitty would trust Tyler's assessment that it had been a one-man operation. The same man who had driven home in the still-parked car and entered the still-closed front door Tyler had grown tired of watching.

His stomach rumbled as Tyler eased away from the curb. He frowned, then smiled at the thought of rewarding his investigative genius with a double cheeseburger and a chocolate shake. A few minutes later he pulled up to the drive-through window of the only burger joint still open. He ordered value meal number six. Then he imagined Renee's disapproving gaze.

Renee!

In all the excitement over finding and confronting Matthew Adams he had forgotten to call her to say he wouldn't make it home in time for dinner. He quickly tapped her image on the dash.

"Tyler Cain, I'm very upset with you!" A recording made for his specific number for this specific occasion. "I don't ask for much. Just a bit of courtesy. I made a very special meal tonight. I also bought a new nightgown. But you won't be enjoying either. There's a pillow and blanket in the den. I hope you get a major crick in your neck!"

The message ended abruptly. He imagined her slamming a vintage phone receiver onto the cradle in a huff.

Banished to the sofa! So much for celebrating success with his gal, his first meaningful accomplishment since, well, since too long ago to remember.

"Did you want to add a hot cherry pie to that order?" the drive-through voice asked, short-circuiting Tyler's pity party.

He looked at the clock. Much too late for a deep-fried indulgence sure to trigger middle-of-the-night heartburn.

Renee would definitely not approve.

"Sure!" he answered defiantly. "And top it with vanilla ice cream."

CHAPTER FORTY-FOUR

Julia snuggled in close to caress her husband's chest while enjoying the gentle movement of his fingertips up and down her bare shoulder. Exactly what she needed after a long, eventful day. She had connected the dots between her sister's mysterious suitor and Tyler Cain's elusive suspect, helped orchestrate a seductive bait and switch where Maria was the bait, and then tried to calm her kid sister's nerves while driving away from the scene. Maria had finally gone home with Jared after a very late dinner that included giving Troy a play-by-play description of the whole fiasco.

"Are you sure she'll be OK?" Troy asked while staring up at the ceiling. "This Matthew guy won't come after her, will he?"

"She'll be fine," Julia said. "Tyler told me he decided to follow the car home to keep an eye on the house until the police arrive. But he wasn't concerned. He said the guy was no real danger to anyone but himself."

"Good."

A moment of tender silence passed.

"Kevin called this afternoon."

"He did?" Julia said while sitting up to wrap herself in the disheveled sheet. The day's adventure had dominated all conversation to the point that she had neglected to ask about Troy's day.

"He told me to tell you he liked your first feature and that he's eager to see the second."

"Does he think they might help?"

"Can't hurt."

She waited for more. Nothing came. "Has he heard any more from Franklin?" she asked.

"He has. It seems the whole Dimitri thing blew over. Anderson said they managed to convince him I wasn't behind whatever made him so mad."

Julia remembered Brent Anderson's earlier threat, "Back off with Dimitri."

"If they don't think it was you or Kevin, who do they think *was* behind it?"

"No clue. Doesn't matter. They've moved on to the next potential scandal and we're back on their 'useful' list."

Julia sighed. "Doesn't it bother you?"

"Doesn't what bother me?"

"The whole game. You know. They consider Kevin an asset one day and a liability the next. They call you a brilliant player on Monday but try to distance themselves from you on Friday. It's not fair. It's not right."

Troy leaned on his side to mirror Julia's posture. "No, it's not right. But it is what it is. Neither Kevin nor I expected politics to smell pretty. Cleaning up a mess sometimes means working around garbage. But it's part of the price you pay when trying to do something significant."

"I'd call it a pretty big price."

One shoulder gave a half shrug. "Maybe. But someone needs to be a voice for the weak and vulnerable. Might as well be us."

"I guess. I just wish…" She stopped when she noticed Troy fiddling with the edge of the silk sheet she had turned into a toga. He lifted the edge, pretending to steal an indiscreet peek. Julia slapped his hand playfully. Then she smiled. "Again?"

"Aren't you ovulating?" he asked with a wink. "How 'bout doubling our odds?"

Julia's smile melted as the grief her sister's adventure had interrupted mounted another invasion.

"What do ya say?" Troy began moving his lips toward hers.

Julia's head slid slightly back before she could overrule the motion. Hoping he hadn't noticed, she willed her arms around his torso to hold him tightly. But it was no good. She knew that he sensed something was wrong. She sat up again, revealing a single tear disobediently falling onto her cheek.

His finger touched the moist insurgent. "Hey there now. What's this about?"

The sweet, clueless tone of Troy's voice opened another breach in the dam. A second tear fell, then two more. She knew that if she spoke a river of sorrow would drown her explanation in a flood of misunderstood emotion.

Julia wanted to tell her husband how much she loved him, that she wished with all her heart a second round of intimacy could double their chances. But she knew what she couldn't say. That their union would never conceive the blessing of a child. Never give Troy what he wanted more than anything in the world.

"Oh, it's nothing," she finally managed. She kissed him gratefully, then inhaled a breath of composure. "I'm just tired. Do you mind waiting until morning?"

He appeared to believe her. "Of course," he answered while grabbing a tissue to wipe final remnants of wetness from her face. "Let's wait until morning."

Troy kissed her forehead before rolling onto his side of the mattress.

Julia slipped into the bathroom to wash her face and find an oversized T-shirt to wear. That's when she noticed a woman she barely recognized staring back at her from the mirror. Was this the same woman who had once celebrated the drop in global fertility? The girl who had disregarded marriage as an outdated institution and motherhood as the valley of the inept? The journalist who'd fed a mountain of myths to nine million approving readers? "The fewer carbon footprints polluting the planet the better!" she'd once scoffed. Now she would give anything to conceive, deliver, and nurture one into a son or daughter of her own. Troy would have wanted a boy. Or would he have? He loved hanging out with Tommy. But he seemed smitten with Joy and Leah. He might want a girl after all.

Julia let her imagination carry her into an alternate future. She envisioned dressing her toddler in frilly dresses. She saw herself shopping for a new outfit with a preteen daughter eager to look pretty when Daddy took her to the symphony or father-daughter dance. She pictured a cute, precocious girl as she had been herself during adolescence. Sort of like Amanda, Austin Tozer's half sister. She and Julia had seemed to hit it off the way she might have with her own child.

Another tear began to form at the thought of what a wonderful daddy Troy would have made. Unlike her own father, Troy would never have abandoned his family. He would have modeled loving strength and heroic sacrifice. He would have shown their little girl what a man could be. What a man should be.

But that day would never come. Troy couldn't produce a child of his own. And the prospect of finding a baby to adopt was, at best, remote.

Julia wiped away the tear while turning off the bathroom light. She walked back to the bed and slid gently under the covers. Then she leaned in close to Troy's ear. "Good night, darling," she whispered.

His undecipherable grunt told her he was asleep. She smiled, patting his back while settling onto the billowy comfort of her pillow.

That's when it struck her. Amanda! She sat up with a start.

If Troy could be such a wonderful adoptive uncle to the Tolbert kids, why couldn't he be a wonderful adoptive father to a girl with no parents of her own, a girl who hated living with her self-centered half brother and embryo-selling wife?

"Troy," Julia said, shaking her husband awake.

"What? What?" he said in dazed confusion while his hands felt around the bed as if swatting bugs.

Julia clicked on the lamp, causing Troy's eyelids to scrunch tightly together at the sudden, blinding brightness. She bolstered her courage by lifting his hand to her lips for a reinforcing kiss.

"Troy, honey, we need to talk."

CHAPTER FORTY-FIVE

A sudden surge of fear forced Rebecca Santiago awake. When had she dozed off? She looked at the bedroom television screen. Credits were rolling from the movie she had hoped would help keep her awake until her husband got home. She looked at the clock. Half past midnight! Three hours earlier Victor had promised he should be home soon.

She felt herself breathing faster. It was the start of a panic attack like the one she had endured during the blizzard of 2037 when Victor decided to drive home instead of stay at the office as she'd asked him to. "The roads are too slick," she had said. "You'll slide into a ditch and freeze to death." It took him more than an hour, but he made it home safe and sound. Her panic was for naught then. She tried to believe it was equally pointless now.

She got out of bed, clicked off the television, and found her gown before moving to the window to open the blinds. The police car was still parked out front. She squinted for a better look. It appeared the officer's head was leaning against the glass in sound sleep. Not much comfort.

Rebecca opened the bedroom door and moved into the kitchen, where she hoped to find Victor sitting in front of a bowl of cereal enjoying a late-night snack after a longer-than-expected day in his chambers. But the room was dark. She rushed to the back door to check for Victor's car in the garage. Empty!

She told herself to stay calm, that he was probably in his office sipping a cup of cold coffee while tweeking a written opinion on that big case. He had said it needed to be finished by morning. It wouldn't be the first time he had burned the midnight oil to hit a deadline.

But he had never done so while a death threat hung over his head!

She tapped her husband's image on the phone, then heard his recorded voice.

"Hi, Rebecca. There's two things I want to do at this moment. First, answer your call. Second…"

"No!" she shouted at the phone.

She dialed again. The same result.

The phone fell to the floor as Rebecca raced toward the front door. Seconds later she was sitting in the passenger side of the police car pleading with an officer whose name she couldn't recall to drive to the courthouse as fast as possible.

Rebecca felt both overwrought and foolish standing outside the courthouse. She hadn't thought to grab the latest entry code. Victor always left it for her in an envelope sitting in his sock drawer. She rarely used it, relying on Jennifer or a guard to open the door whenever she came to meet Victor for lunch or surprise him with a fresh-baked afternoon snack. Of course, neither his assistant nor security was in the building at such a late hour.

And since her telephone lay on the floor back home she couldn't call Jennifer for help. It took nearly fifteen minutes for the officer to track down someone who could help him gain access to the judge's private chambers. The delay was agony for Rebecca, who spent every second imagining one awful scenario after another. The patient young officer tried comforting her by suggesting it would be even more difficult for a potential assassin to reach the judge than it had proven for them. That didn't make her feel any better.

As soon as they reached the third-floor office wing Rebecca noticed the outer door was slightly ajar. Would Jennifer have left without locking the door behind her? No, not when Victor remained inside working. She was almost as protective of Victor as Rebecca. Something was wrong.

"Please, ma'am, let me go in first," the officer insisted.

Rebecca ignored the suggestion, rushing through the door, past Jennifer's desk, and into Victor's now-dark office.

The light came on in reaction to the motion. She looked toward the chair where she had imagined finding Victor slumped over his desk in a pool of blood. It was empty. She rushed past a row of bookshelves to peer into his conference room, where she had imagined her husband dangling by the neck from a noose suspended from the ceiling. But the room was empty.

Rebecca heard the sound of the officer's footsteps finally catching up with her frantic search.

"He's not here!" she shouted while grasping both of the officer's arms. "Where could he be? Dear God, where is my Victor?"

The officer gave her a blank gaze. "Perhaps he left before we arrived. He might be at the house looking for you right now."

But she knew better. She knew they would find Victor's car parked in his private space. And she knew something dreadful had happened to her husband.

"No. He must be here somewhere," she insisted while running back out the front office door. "Victor!" she shouted to her left, then to her right. "Where are you, sweetheart?"

She heard the officer's voice utter a muffled obscenity, drawing her back into Victor's chambers.

She entered the office again. No sign of anyone. A moment of dread passed before she saw the open door of Victor's private bathroom.

The officer stepped toward her without a word.

"What?" Rebecca asked urgently.

"Ms. Santiago, please, stay right where you are."

"Why? What is it?"

He lowered his head like a rookie trying to recall the official protocol for nightmares.

"The judge."

"You found him?" she asked, rushing past his protective blockade.

"Please, ma'am…"

It was too late. She saw what the officer had cursed. Victor, lying on the floor with eyes wide open as if staring at her from the realm of the dead. No blood or hangman's rope. Just her husband's empty form.

She fell onto his lifeless body, then tried lifting him to her breast. His corpse spurned the effort like a steadfast bag of sand. It was the first show of affection he hadn't returned in three decades. And the last, Rebecca suddenly realized, that she would ever attempt.

CHAPTER FORTY-SIX

As soon as Tyler entered the detective wing of headquarters he came face-to-face with the last person he wanted to see.

"Cain," Kory Sanders said with a solemn nod that carried a hint of derision. Tyler's old rival clutched a mug of java while leaning against the wall beside a pretty young detective Tyler didn't recognize. She added her own nod, then gave the once-over to the fumbling private investigator who had failed to prevent Judge Santiago's assassination.

"Sanders," Tyler responded flatly. "Seen Smitty this morning?"

Sanders tilted his head toward a hallway without a word before resuming whispered speculations about how badly Cain had botched the job or how dumb it had been for Smitty to assign such a big case to a washed-up former detective.

"Thanks," Tyler said, lowering his eyes. If only they knew the whole embarrassing truth. He had actually found the suspect, had confronted him and followed him home. But rather than have Matthew Adams arrested Tyler pitied the guy and handed him the name of a defense attorney. Maybe the chief had been right in promoting Sanders instead of Tyler after all. Had Sanders ever made such a fatal miscalculation? Had anyone?

Tyler walked toward the conference room where he knew Smitty would be waiting.

As he approached the row of glass-walled offices Tyler spotted Jennifer McKay, who had already arrived. Of course she had. She must have been up much of the night trying to console a grief-stricken Rebecca Santiago. She looked even more exhausted than Tyler despite his aching back and stiff neck, compliments of the sofa. His only consolation was that Renee had felt bad after he told her about Smitty's call.

"Oh no!" she had said. "When did it happen?"

"Last night," Tyler explained while hurriedly zipping his pants and buttoning his shirt. "The judge's wife and a cop found the body around one o'clock this morning."

"That's seven hours ago. Why didn't they call sooner?" she asked.

Tyler was still asking himself the same question. Shouldn't Smitty have had someone phone him immediately? No one knew more about the suspect. But then, Tyler reminded himself, he was no longer part of the force. Gathering evidence after an assassination was the domain of public officials, not private investigators who ranked one step above anonymous tipsters. Besides, obtaining an arrest warrant in the middle of the night and tracking down Matthew Adams would have been Smitty's all-consuming priority.

As he approached the closed door Tyler noticed a third person in the room with Smitty and Jennifer, probably the officer who had been with Mrs. Santiago when they found the judge's body. He looked even more spent than Jennifer.

Smitty waved Tyler in eagerly, as if he had been impatiently waiting to take an important next step in the process.

"Sorry it took so long to get here," Tyler said. Of course he had come faster than anyone should have expected, his crumpled shirt and morning breath offering sufficient evidence of a mad rush. "I just got the call twenty minutes ago."

"Close the door," Smitty ordered.

Tyler obeyed. "Any trail yet?"

Smitty seemed confused by the question. "Trail?"

"On Matthew Adams's location."

Smitty looked at the other two, who must have already known what Tyler didn't. "Didn't they tell you on the phone?"

Tell him what? All Tyler knew was that Judge Santiago had been killed and that Smitty had wanted him in the conference room as soon as possible. He had assumed Smitty wanted help tracking down the fugitive. Not because Tyler was the best man for the job, but because he had been the last person to see Matthew Adams before letting him roam free for a midnight murder.

"We found Mr. Adams right where your message said he would be. He was at the home of an elderly gentleman named Hugh Gale. Of course, he claims to know nothing about the killing."

"You questioned him already?" Tyler asked in stunned surprise. "Wait. You found him sitting at the house?"

"Yep. Not too bright, I gather. I mean, who commits murder and then returns to the same address he just gave to a guy investigating death threat letters?"

Tyler felt the rebuke. "Look, Smitty, I'm really sorry about—"

Smitty raised his hand to silence Tyler. "Not now."

"I parked outside his house for several hours after—"

"I said not now."

Tyler's gut tightened at the realization he had let Smitty down. But his apology would need to wait. "So what was Matthew doing when you picked him up?"

DR. JAMES DOBSON & KURT BRUNER

"He told my guys he had been sitting in the front room reading most of the night."

"Reading? Reading what?"

"An old Bible," Smitty said. "Claims he was trying to find something to calm his nerves after meeting with you."

"He told you we met?"

"He did. Said you suggested he wait at the house and expect our arrival. He seemed pretty calm until the officer said he was under arrest for the murder of Judge Victor Santiago. That's when the guy went into a meltdown, claimed he knew nothing about any murder and that he never intended to hurt anyone. You know the litany."

Tyler said nothing. Something didn't fit. Why would a killer wait for the police to arrive, knowing a mountain of evidence existed to pinpoint him as the murderer? He had seen the letters. He had even confessed to writing most of them.

"Did you get much out of him?" Tyler asked.

"Not since he made his one phone call."

"Defense lawyer?"

"Yep. Clammed up after that. I'm getting ready to go in and try again. I need more. All we have is circumstantial evidence right now. I'm hoping he'll slip up and say something we can use in court. I need you to listen for anything that might feed the right line of questioning."

"Certainly."

"I'm especially interested in these," Smitty said, handing Tyler two clear plastic bags. "We found them stuffed in a trash container just outside the judge's chambers."

Tyler examined the first bag. It contained a needle and a catheter about two feet long. The second held one of those clear bags hospitals use to hold IV fluids. It was empty except for small traces of a yellow liquid. The label read "PotassiPass."

"I know this chemical," Tyler said, remembering the brand

name from the summary he had read of the Santos wrongful death case. "It's the chemical NEXT Transition Services uses with clients."

Smitty and Jennifer eyed one another as if the comment had confirmed their hunch.

"Who could get that for him?" Smitty asked.

"Who couldn't?" the other officer said. "All you would need to do is find a transition clinic employee willing to swipe a bag for you."

"Or take one out of a clinic yourself," Smitty suggested.

Tyler didn't follow.

"The suspect's mother transitioned about a year back," Smitty explained. "I bet he stole some of the serum then."

Plausible, Tyler had to agree. But something still didn't seem right. Why would Matthew have stolen transition chemicals months before he even knew Judge Santiago would be assigned the case?

He followed Smitty to the next room. Jennifer and the other officer joined him as they took their seats behind a two-way mirror. On the other side sat a clearly shaken Matthew Adams, who was fidgeting with a pencil. Tyler remembered the routine. Hand the uncooperative suspect a pencil and paper as you leave the interrogation room and suggest he write down a confession "for his own good" so the judge might go easy on him. The page appeared blank.

As Smitty walked out of the room Jennifer turned toward Tyler. "I owe you an apology," she whispered.

He turned toward her dark form. "For what? I'm the one who blew this case."

"I should have listened to you." Tyler sensed tears of regret in her voice. "If I had warned the judge he would still be alive."

"And you'd have lost your job," Tyler said generously. "You did what he ordered you to do."

She sighed. "Still." A pause. "I'm sorry."

"Me too," Tyler said faintly while reaching to pat her slumping shoulders. "Me too."

They saw Smitty closing the door behind him as he entered the brightness beyond the glass.

"There's a sick irony in all of this," Jennifer whispered in Tyler's direction while awaiting Smitty's first question. "The same drug used to transition Antonio Santos ended up killing the man who was about to decide in favor of the plaintiff."

"What?" Tyler said. "He was going to come down in favor of NEXT? I thought he was leaning the other way."

"So did most people," Jennifer replied. "But I proofed his draft opinion. He was going to say NEXT did nothing wrong. The boy was an adult when he transitioned regardless of what day he applied. The law doesn't require parental approval after eighteen."

"So NEXT is off the hook?"

"Would have been. Now the appeal will get assigned to a new trio of judges. Could be months before that happens."

Tyler looked through the glass at the nervous suspect. A few more days and Judge Santiago would have freed up Matthew's urgently needed inheritance money. His mother's estate would have been released thanks to NEXT's successful appeal.

Then Tyler thought of Jeremy Santos, who wanted the court to confirm the malevolence of a system that had caused his brother's and mother's deaths. NEXT should pay for what it had done to the two people Jeremy loved more than anyone on earth. Ever since watching the gruesome footage taken at the clinic on the fateful day of their deaths, Tyler had unconsciously hoped the same.

"Do you have anything else to tell me?" Smitty was asking.

Matthew sat silent while biting the end of his pencil.

Smitty took the sheet of paper from in front of the suspect. Blank. "Nothing to write?"

"I told you already," Matthew said in exhausted desperation. "I didn't kill anyone."

"Well, someone did," Smitty said. "Someone who, like you, goes by the pseudonym Manichean. Someone who, like you, wants to see NEXT win its appeal. And someone who, like you, had access to these." Smitty tossed the plastic bags onto the table in front of Matthew. "Do you want to tell me where you got them?"

Matthew bent closer to examine the bags. He seemed to recognize the contents but appeared alarmed by their presence.

A sudden knock on the interrogation room door drew Smitty's attention. "Sir," a male voice called into the room, "I have the autopsy report."

Smitty moved away from the table. Matthew seemed relieved by the momentary interruption, as if he needed time to figure out what was going on or how to spin his story.

Then Smitty reentered the room, reading what must have been a summary of key details from the autopsy. At the same moment the door to the observation room opened to receive a man holding what appeared to be an identical page.

"What's he reading?" Jennifer asked in the man's direction.

"Here," he replied, handing the report to Jennifer. "Read for yourself."

Tyler leaned toward Jennifer and squinted to make out the words.

CAUSE OF DEATH: Heart attack triggered by potassium chloride poisoning
  TIME OF DEATH: 6:35 p.m.

Tyler jumped up from his chair with a start. All three pairs of eyes darted in his direction, then turned toward the sound of

Smitty's voice. "Where were you between six and eight o'clock last evening?" he was asking.

"We have the wrong man!" Tyler shouted toward the glass.

"What?" Jennifer said in unison with both officers.

"I said we have the wrong man."

"Why do you say that?"

"Because I was questioning Matthew Adams near Bear Creek Lake at the time of the assassination!"

CHAPTER FORTY-SEVEN

Evan Dimitri approached the same black limousine that had carried him to his corporate jet earlier in the day. A man wearing a cap stood beside the open door extending a much-needed glass of brandy that he accepted without a word before slipping inside. Then the driver trotted to the front of the vehicle and awaited instructions.

"Home," Dimitri grunted.

It had been a long day meeting with a board of directors he neither needed nor liked. More of the same claptrap, fretting about matters he had completely in hand. Yes, profits had dipped slightly as a result of the NEXT appeal. Yes, the pending Tenth District ruling could sink all hope of hitting revenue targets. And yes, he did agree it would be wise to develop a short-term contingency plan while considering diversification options.

Dimitri hated the thought of how much time he had wasted addressing the board's concerns. They needed to trust him. He knew exactly what had to be done. In fact, he had already set solutions in motion.

He glanced at the time. Might there be news so soon? Or had the police done a better job than usual of avoiding leaks? He tapped an icon embedded in his armrest to wake a flat screen positioned over the bar. Then he kicked off his shoes while taking a sip of his favorite post-nonsense drink. A query box appeared.

"Find any news about the NEXT appeal or Judge Victor Santiago," he said. Almost instantaneously the two most recent stories appeared.

4:34 PM Breaking News

- FEDERAL JUDGE FOUND DEAD IN DENVER CHAMBERS

6:21 PM Breaking News

- PERSON OF INTEREST QUESTIONED IN SUS-PECTED JUDICIAL ASSASSINATION

He watched the first clip. It revealed that one of the judges hearing the NEXT wrongful death case had died suddenly of an apparent heart attack. The same judge many political and corporate titans feared would tip the scales against the transition industry. Dimitri knew that Judge Santiago's death, while tragic for the family, could be a boon to company stock when markets opened the following day. He smiled at the realization that profits, for now, remained safe from the unpredictable actions of a crusading judge.

The second clip revealed that someone "close to the case" said police had questioned an unnamed man with some connection to what they now feared might have been an assassination. No mention of any accomplices or a conspiracy. A probable lone killer.

Dimitri gave an approving nod in response to the sparse details before tapping an icon that prompted the voice of his ever-available assistant Kim.

"Yes, sir."

"Get me Dean Myerson."

Moments later another voice came on the line. "You saw the news?"

"I did. Any surprises?"

A long silence. "Actually, yes. The suspect walked after questioning. I didn't see that coming."

Dimitri cursed. "He walked? Did they charge him?"

"Murder. But something happened during the interrogation that made them drop it down to suspected mail fraud. The Manichi guy's lawyer demanded they release him to his oversight."

"It's pronounced *Manichean*," Dimitri said, feeling a shade of concern. "What about our letter?"

"As far as I can tell they still think the guy wrote it."

A look of reassurance came over Dimitri's face. "Good. That's perfect." He took another sip of brandy.

"I guess," Dean replied.

"Keep me posted if anything changes."

"Will do, sir."

Dimitri ended the call before summoning Kim back onto the line.

"I'm here, sir," she said.

"I need you to draft a message to the board of directors. Tell them we've received word that a decision in the NEXT case will be delayed until they can assign a new team of judges. We can expect business as usual for the rest of the fiscal year."

"Got it."

"Send me a draft to proof later tonight."

"As you wish," she said before being cut off.

His short-term problem had been resolved, buying him time to finalize a longer-term growth strategy he had been considering for months. He felt a sudden surge of creative energy demanding he flesh out the concept further.

"Driver?"

"Sir?"

"I've changed my mind. Take me to the office."

CHAPTER FORTY-EIGHT

Renee slid a covered plate in front of Tyler. He had offered to serve, but she had insisted he join her parents at the table and seemed excited about whatever gourmet bird food she had been preparing. He was trapped. But he didn't mind. Not really. He had never found her more attractive.

Perhaps it was because Renee had spent every waking moment of the past few days trying to lift him out of the dumps. She had apologized at least a dozen times for banishing him to the sofa on the night before the terrible day. And then there was the refrigerator surprise. He found an unopened Hostess snack sitting on the shelf right next to a gallon of soy milk. Never mind that he hated soy milk. It was the thought that counted.

But that wasn't the reason. Something else had made Renee more appealing.

Tyler reached for the mystery plate to peek under the makeshift lid before feeling a slap at his hand.

"Not yet," Renee said playfully. "Wait until I serve everyone."

He grinned sheepishly toward Gerry and Katherine. Neither paid him any attention. Gerry was enamored with the spoon that doubled as a mirror he was using to peer up his left nostril. Katherine sipped her glass of water, staring in blissful contentment as usual.

Tyler continued watching Renee in search of what had changed. She had the same perky face, cute hairstyle, and slight figure. A guilt-induced cupcake notwithstanding, she maintained the same obsession with all things healthy and tasteless. And her nonstop hovering while trying to cheer him up, while appreciated, had started to make him feel claustrophobic. He almost wanted to go back to work. Almost, but not quite. He couldn't bear to take on another jealous-lover case. Not after coming so close to doing something important again.

Tyler noticed Renee sitting down to join them at the table. Then she smiled in his direction.

"Smells delicious," he said. "What is it?"

"You'll find out in a minute."

Despite low expectations Tyler prepared himself to react with delight. He'd love to find a pile of garlic-and-bacon mashed potatoes next to a pecan-crusted chicken breast. But he knew it was more likely he'd discover steamed cauliflower with a tofu garnish. Either way, Renee deserved an enthusiastic response.

He looked across the table at Gerry and Katherine. Then he looked back at their daughter, now placing a napkin on her lap.

"Ready?" she asked like a giddily excited girl.

"I'm ready," Tyler replied in the most energetic voice he could muster as Gerry finally placed the spoon back on the table.

"Then take a look."

It was worse than Tyler had imagined. Some sort of green slimy base possibly made of boiled spinach beneath what appeared to be a baked slab of…what? Certainly not any kind of meat he had ever eaten.

"Baked eggplant!" Renee announced proudly. "I've been trying to find a good recipe forever. This one said it tastes just like fried chicken but with less than half the calories and much, much less fat."

"Mmm," Tyler said in anticipation of a meal he was sure to hate. "Sounds wonderful."

He took a big bite. The texture felt more like warmed squash than crispy chicken. He chewed, slowly at first. He considered saying something but realized a second and third mouthful would mean more to Renee than the most perfectly worded compliment.

"Do you like it?" her eyes asked.

Tyler recalled a comment from Smitty. "Love is a choice, not a feeling."

"I love it!" he willed himself to say.

Renee leaped from her seat to hug Tyler's neck. Startled at first, he moved his arms around her waist and invited her to sit on his lap.

"Tyler Cain!" she pretended to protest. "Not in front of the children."

Renee's parents smiled at the comment. That's when it struck him.

Gerry and Katherine!

"I need you to understand something," Renee had said a few days before. "My parents are my priority right now. I mean, I love you. I want you. But they're my flesh and blood."

With a single gutsy declaration Renee had transformed herself from a weak, clingy lover into something else. Something better. She had made a choice to do what was right by her folks even if it meant losing the man she loved. Losing him! And rather than pushing Tyler away, the resolve had drawn him toward her like nails to a magnet. He knew that Renee loved him. But he also realized that she didn't *need* him. The subtle change made her someone he wanted to pursue rather than flee; someone strong enough to expect him to do what was right, and to become his best. A woman who deserved better than she had received. Better, perhaps, than he could possibly ever give.

For the first time in a while Tyler felt lucky to have her in his life. Possibly because he realized he had almost driven her out of it.

Tyler had taken the Santiago case hoping for a high-paying gig that would inch him closer to freedom from what he saw as Renee's needy, demanding presence. Had he successfully prevented the assassination he would have received a handsome bonus. He could have paid off their joint loan. Today might have been the day he sent Renee packing and returned to the carefree existence he thought he wanted. Instead, he was starting to realize, it was the day he would invite Renee to add meaning to his miserable excuse for a life. But when? How? Certainly not while sitting across from her nostril-ogling dad.

Tyler did his best to remain enthusiastic while enduring the rest of his meal. As soon as he finished, Renee scooped a second serving onto his plate. He wanted to say, "No more, thank you. I'm stuffed!" But her beautiful eyes won the moment. He took another bite.

"Oh," she said. "I nearly forgot to tell you, Smitty called today while you were napping."

He had been "napping" much of the past two days.

"He asked if you could drop by tomorrow afternoon."

Not a chance, Tyler thought. The last place he wanted to be right now was the police station. He didn't need another reminder of his ineptitude or another sniggering glare from the likes of Kory Sanders.

"I said you'd be there around two o'clock."

"You said what?"

"Come on, babe. It'll do you good. You need to get out."

He swallowed back a protest. Renee was probably right. Nothing good would come of another day moping around the house. Besides, Smitty had been kind. He had refused to let Tyler own the blame for Judge Santiago's death. "You were right about Matthew Adams," Smitty had insisted. "The guy was no assassin."

So who was? There were countless possibilities. Unlikely as it seemed, the letters from Matthew Adams were an uncanny coincidence. He'd happened to write a series of benign letters at the same time someone else was planning an assassination. Someone, perhaps, with more to gain than Matthew. Or more to lose.

"I don't know," Tyler objected weakly. "I'm not sure I'm ready to—"

"You're ready," Renee interrupted. "And you're good at what you do."

He looked away, wishing he could agree. Then he felt Renee's hand on his jaw forcing his gaze in her direction.

"Do you hear me?" she said. "You're a very good detective. That's what Smitty thinks, anyway."

It took five seconds for the comment to sink in. "What?"

"He told me you followed the evidence where it led and that every detective on his team would have reached the exact same conclusions you did."

"He said that?"

"He did. I bet he wants to talk to you about a job."

"Unlikely." Tyler knew better. The force was still over budget. Smitty needed to cut rather than add positions.

"Or maybe he has another case for you to solve."

The possibility sounded good to Tyler. He certainly had no appetite for another House of Delights stakeout.

"OK," he relented. "I'll go."

Renee grinned with satisfaction while taking another bite.

Tyler couldn't help smiling back.

Gerry chose that moment to enter the conversation. "Dog-gone it," he said. "When do you plan to stop pussyfooting around and make an honest woman out of my daughter?"

"Daddy!" Renee shouted with a blush while Katherine looked up in apparent delight.

"Well," Gerry continued, "it's obvious neither one of you is going anywhere. Why not make it official?"

Tyler said nothing at first. A few days earlier he would have assumed Renee had orchestrated the moment. But the look on her face said she was equally surprised, equally embarrassed.

What none of the others could know was that Smitty had raised the same point two days before. "You should marry Re-nee," he had said after asking about their relationship. "She deserves to be happy. So do you."

Smitty had come to see marriage as a gift rather than a burden; a source of happiness rather than stress. He'd even invited Tyler to meet with a pastor from his church. "Premarital counseling would help you get off on the right foot," he had suggested.

Renee looked at Tyler. She appeared unsettled. "I'm sorry," she whispered toward his ear. "Daddy shouldn't have said that."

"You're right," Tyler whispered back. "He shouldn't have said it."

Then Tyler stood up from the table.

"Come on, Tyler, don't be upset," Gerry began. But Tyler raised his hand to silence the old man.

"No," he said insistently. "I have every right to be upset. And I am. I'm very upset."

Renee looked distraught, as if her father had ruined their otherwise perfect evening.

"I'm upset at myself for letting you beat me to the punch," Tyler continued. Then he bent down on one knee in front of Renee, who seemed uncertain how to respond. Was she protecting herself from thinking what was happening was actually happening? "Renee," Tyler said after kissing her hand, "I have a question to ask you that's long overdue."

Tears of uncertain joy began forming in her eyes.

"Will you marry me?" he asked.

A flood of emotion released as Renee nodded breathlessly.

Tyler accepted her kiss while Gerry and Katherine reached for one another's hand.

"Oh, wait!" Tyler said suddenly as if realizing he had made a big mistake. "I take it back."

"What?" Gerry said. "Take it back?"

"I need twenty-four hours."

"What for?" Katherine asked timidly.

"I need a ring to do this properly," he said to Renee's obvious relief. Then he stood. "Can I ask you again tomorrow?"

"Yes. Yes. Yes," she shouted through tears with an even more vigorous nod.

Tyler returned to his seat, proud of his own courageous act. Reckless? Perhaps. But he knew it felt right. Knew it *was* right.

Renee accepted a hug from her mother while Tyler stabbed his fork into another bite of food. He raised it mindlessly to his mouth and began chewing. The flavor, he suddenly realized, was starting to grow on him.

CHAPTER FORTY-NINE

Matthew rubbed the patch of irritated skin that had formed beneath the metal bracelet he had been forced to wear around his ankle. The tracking device was gone. But the itchy reminder of his virtual incarceration made him boil with a fury he couldn't have suppressed even if he'd wanted to. And he didn't want to. He had every right to be angry, every reason to hate. But hate whom? Everyone!

He hated Maria Davidson. He would have given anything to make her happy. But she'd lied to him. Betrayed him. Pretended he had a chance with her. It was all a lie!

He hated Tyler Cain. The detective had said he believed Matthew. So why hadn't he let him off the hook? Why suggest the police arrest him for sending a few harmless letters?

He hated the police. They knew full well Matthew hadn't murdered the judge. Why force him to wear a digital dog leash until they got to the bottom of the case? They had already asked him every possible question. He had no more answers to give: no idea who might have written the final letter, why the person had used Matthew's pen name, or how the person had mimicked his earlier letters to near-perfection.

He hated whoever had written those letters.

And Matthew hated his professor. The detective had said Thomas Vincent had helped them connect the dots to Matthew's interest in Manichean philosophy. Dr. Vincent was no priest, and certainly no saint. But he still should have kept their conversations confidential.

Matthew had even decided to hate Judge Santiago. Why hadn't he issued a favorable opinion on the NEXT appeal? If he had done so sooner all would have been well. The judge would still have been alive and Matthew would have been able to access the money in his mother's estate. Money that rightfully belonged to him!

The sound of Reverend Grandpa's stupid bell rang again in Matthew's ears. He had been ignoring the sound for five minutes. Let the old man get his own dinner for once! Or go hungry. Maybe then he'd think twice before poking fun at matters he was too muddleheaded to grasp.

"Such a tragedy," Reverend Grandpa had said while watching the news about Judge Santiago's demise.

Matthew had looked in the old man's direction, at first holding his tongue. But that didn't last. He was in no mood for passivity. He needed to win at something. Why not demolish the Bible-thumping fool in a head-to-head debate? "It's not a tragedy. Death is freedom, the spirit's escape from a decaying body."

His anger boiled again at the recollection of words his former mentor had taught. But the words were still true, even if the man teaching them wasn't.

"Nonsense!" Reverend Grandpa retorted. "The body is every bit as sacred as the spirit. Human beings aren't ghosts. We're embodied spirits."

"You should have thought of that before you drove your car

into a ditch," Matthew said. "Now look at you. A worthless body that's nothing but a burden…on you and everyone else. The real tragedy is you taking up space and using up money that could help Marissa, Isabelle, and Peter."

Matthew could tell the old man felt the sting of rebuke. He wanted him to. Matthew hated Reverend Grandpa.

The bell continued ringing. Matthew finally got up with a huff and walked into the room where he had left the old man fifteen minutes before.

"What?"

"I don't think this is going to work out any longer."

"What are you talking about?"

The old man shifted uncomfortably in his chair. "I think we need to end your contract."

The old man was firing him? It figured. Why not add CANNED to Matthew's growing list of the week's calamities, right after DUMPED, FRAMED, and ARRESTED?

He wouldn't give Reverend Grandpa the satisfaction.

"Fine. I quit!" Matthew shouted while turning toward his room.

"I didn't mean right this second," the old man said with alarm. "I meant we should pick an end date and—"

"I don't care what you meant," Matthew said, walking back toward his client. "I'm telling you that I quit. Today. Right now! Consider this your ten-minute warning. Find some other bump-on-a-log babysitter."

Matthew went to his room to pack a bag of his most important items. He would return for the rest of his things once he got settled in, where? Who knew? Someplace. Anyplace that wasn't here.

Screw the police! He was innocent. They had no right to know where he went.

Screw Maria and Professor Vincent! They no longer deserved his admiration.

And screw Reverend Grandpa! He could find someone else to fix meals and change oxygen tanks.

Matthew heard a loud thud coming from the other room. His first impulse was to rush toward the sound. He instead spent several more minutes throwing socks and T-shirts into an open travel case and stuffing his toothbrush and shaver into the side pocket. He checked the bag. Then he checked it again. It appeared he had everything needed to make a dramatic, immediate exit.

As he moved back down the hallway Matthew heard panicked wheezing. He let the bag fall to the floor, then rounded the corner. That's when he saw Reverend Grandpa on the floor reaching desperately in Matthew's direction. His hand held the detached portion of an air tube that must have been damaged when the old man tried lunging toward a walker sitting three or four feet beyond.

No sound of escaping air came from the oxygen tank. The time Matthew had been packing would have been more than enough for it to empty itself.

The old man pointed frantically down the hall. Matthew remembered the extra tank stored in the bedroom closet. But he hesitated, giving himself two seconds for an uncommon sense of clarity.

Why prolong the inevitable? The old man should end his misery.

The family needed his dwindling resources.

Every reasonable person would call Reverend Grandpa a debit, someone who should volunteer for the greater good.

For Marissa's good.

Who needed a clinic or transition form? The old man's death, no matter how achieved, would bring the same result.

A reduced burden on society.

And a spirit free to thrive.

Matthew looked back toward a man afraid to do what was right. He needed Matthew's help. Matthew's courage.

He thought of the questions that would be asked. Why hadn't Matthew been around to prevent the accident? Simple. The old man had fired him. He'd left at the client's insistence.

He wondered how Marissa would react to the discovery. Would she suspect him of neglect? Worse? Perhaps. But she would be too relieved, too grateful, to contradict Matthew's explanation.

Then he thought of the kids. What if the boy or Isabelle found the body rather than Marissa? Would little Pete ever speak another word? He forced the question out of his mind. A greater good often comes at a price. Peter would be fine. In time.

Matthew retrieved his bag and walked quickly toward the door. He did his best to ignore the sounds of tortured suffocation. A transition would have been so much easier. Swift. Painless. Dignified. But the old man had made his choice.

Then Matthew made his exit.

As the door closed behind him Matthew stood on the front porch. In the sudden stillness he inhaled deeply, the fresh evening air offering a measure of calm to his rapidly beating heart. He instinctively turned back, his fingers wrapping themselves around the handle. He paused. This was a defining moment of belief. Walking away was right. It was compassionate. If by some small chance he was wrong, Reverend Grandpa's God could intervene. He was a God, the old man had said, who had cared enough about physical bodies to assume one. A God of miracles who could prevent his demise, or even raise him from the dead.

He released the handle, his heart racing even faster. He recalled a similar moment from a year before when he had lent his mother courage she didn't possess. When he had watched her take her final breath. He felt the rage of resentment rising within. Her transition, while setting her free, had brought him none of the promised results.

No college fund.

No Maria Davidson.

No real hope of a teaching career.

If the Supreme Being cared about his creation, loved his children, why hadn't he done anything for Matthew's mom? Or for Matthew? Or for the old man suffocating on the floor within?

He took a step off the porch and looked into the evening sky. Then he added one more name to his growing list.

Matthew Adams hated God.

CHAPTER FIFTY

"Pleased to meet you, Beth," Troy said after standing to greet the woman who was apologizing for running behind schedule. Julia smiled warmly from her chair while joining thirty seconds of polite but meaningless small talk about the traffic and warm temperatures.

Austin Tozer and his partner, the woman Amanda had called Hen, appeared to resent Beth's presence, rolling their eyes impatiently in reaction to the ritual of social etiquette. A cold glance suggested this wasn't the first time the couple had met the child welfare agent.

Troy returned to his wife's side at a kitchen table that retained a sticky residue. Julia imagined the couple hastily clearing away dishes in reaction to the doorbell. It would have been much better to meet in Troy's office. More professional and more like home turf. But she had eagerly accepted the demand they meet at Austin's home. Julia was just glad the couple had agreed to get together, no matter how reluctantly.

As Beth Morris settled into her chair, Austin made a preemptive strike. "I don't want to lose Amanda."

It was what Julia had feared after three calls in the prior two days. During the first conversation Austin had loved the thought of getting rid of Amanda so that he and Gwen could live a normal life, whatever that meant. By the second call his posture had softened considerably from that of a fed-up guardian stuck watching a she-brat to that of a sentimental brother inseparably linked to his precious little sister. He had suggested postponing the conversation but backed down when Beth Morris sent a message insisting they proceed as scheduled.

"We've grown very close," Austin continued. He shot a glance toward his partner as if hoping she would mouth his next lines. "I love Amanda, and so does Gwen." Austin took Gwen's hand clumsily as if realizing he had omitted the scripted gesture. "She's like our daughter. She needs us." He seemed to cringe as Gwen's fingers squeezed firmly. "And we need her," he added.

Julia couldn't believe her ears and didn't believe Austin's words. She glanced at Beth, who was jotting notes onto a tablet. Then she looked at Troy, who winked reassuringly in her direction.

Troy had been remarkably receptive to what Julia now feared had been an impulsive idea. She should have given him more time to grieve the disheartening news of their infertility. And that's exactly how she described it. Not *his* infertility. *Their* infertility.

"I can't get pregnant," was all she had said. It wasn't a lie. But the whole truth, she feared, would destroy her husband. Right or wrong, she couldn't allow that. So they held each other and cried themselves to sleep. Julia waited until morning to mention fostering. She waited until lunch to say anything about Amanda Tozer, a name Troy didn't recall from her dark zones story.

"I changed her name in the feature," Julia reminded him. "She needs a real family. She needs a daddy."

Now, two days later, they found themselves sitting across the table from two conniving opportunists. Austin and Gwen must have done some research on Troy's and Julia's past successes before crafting a scheme to make money off of Amanda's departure.

"I understand how you must feel," Troy said in response to Austin's prepared speech.

Julia wanted to call Austin's bluff. But she held her tongue, trusting her husband's instincts.

Troy continued, "It must be difficult to contemplate losing your sister so soon after saying goodbye to your mother."

It clearly hadn't occurred to Austin to connect the two losses. "Yes. Yes it is."

"Very difficult," Gwen added while wiping an invisible tear from her cheek. "She's a wonderful girl."

Beth Morris looked up from her pad. "Where is the wonderful girl?" she asked. "I thought she was supposed to join us. I'd like to get her perspective since she's old enough to speak into this decision."

"She's still at school," Austin said uncomfortably.

Beth glanced at the time. "The school day ended an hour ago."

"She rarely comes straight home," he said. "Besides, I don't think it would be wise to include her just yet. I mean, we are discussing sending her away from her home."

"Are we?" Beth asked abruptly. "I thought you said you had changed your mind."

Austin sent a panicked look to Gwen. "Well, that's not exactly what I meant."

Beth looked back at her notes. "You said, and I quote, 'I don't want to lose Amanda.'"

"That is what you said," Troy added.

"What he meant to say," Gwen interjected, "is that losing Amanda will be more difficult than we realized at first."

Julia fumed quietly at the lie. They wouldn't miss her in the least!

"So you are open to the idea?" Beth asked.

"Well, yes," Austin replied. "But we were sort of hoping to reach an agreement of some kind."

Gwen's eyes became daggers pointed toward her partner's loose tongue.

"An agreement of some kind?" Beth asked. "Could you be a bit more specific?"

"You know," Austin said hesitantly, clearly in unscripted territory.

"No, Mr. Tozer, I don't know. Please enlighten me."

"My mother's transition instructions placed Amanda's share of the money in trust. We receive interest on that investment to cover the cost of raising her. When she's old enough we are supposed to use the principal as a college fund."

"How much will she receive?"

"Um, well, it's not *quite* that simple," Austin stammered. "Our expenses have been much higher than anticipated and my employment history has been less lucrative than we had hoped. So—"

"So you borrowed against Amanda's share of the money," Julia finally said, no longer able to restrain herself.

Beth's head shot in Austin's direction. "Is that true, Mr. Tozer?"

Austin squirmed uneasily.

"Do you have any idea what it costs to raise a girl like Amanda?" Gwen interjected in her partner's defense. Then her eyes zeroed in on Julia. "I realize our bills would be pocket change to some people. But they keep us pretty stressed."

Julia started to react, but Troy stepped in.

"I'm sure it's been very expensive," he said. "But those expenses will only rise the longer Amanda stays with you. Won't you let us help?"

Austin's eyes brightened as if Troy had finally caught his skillfully concealed hints. "Help? Help how?"

"What was the total value of Amanda's share of the inheritance?"

"Fifty thousand dollars," Gwen said without delay, a number far higher than the meager sum Austin had implied during his interview with Julia.

Troy appeared momentarily surprised by the sum, then continued setting the trap. "As you know, Mr. Tozer, my wife is writing a feature story about people in dire economic circumstances thanks to the financial meltdown."

Austin nodded.

"I read the portion about you, although your name isn't used. I told her I thought the story would be much more powerful if it included a photograph of you and Gwen."

"Really?" Austin's partner said. "You think so?"

"I do. And, of course, it would be best to use your real name."

"Of course," Gwen agreed.

Troy looked back at Austin. "Mr. Tozer, what if I paid you a lump sum for permission to use your real name and photograph in that story?"

It took Julia a moment to follow Troy's lead, wondering where on earth he planned to get that kind of cash. Then she understood.

"That'd be perfect," she added enthusiastically. "The syndicate always prefers real names and photos when possible."

"I suppose we could do that," Austin answered warily. "How much?"

"Mr. Simmons," Beth said in an effort to take control of a conversation clearly moving out of bounds, "I don't think it prudent to continue this—"

"Please, Ms. Morris, just one thing more," he interrupted. "Julia, tell him what you found."

Julia reached into her shoulder bag to retrieve a tablet.

"What?" Austin asked. "What did you find?"

"I believe you know a private investigator named Tyler Cain. Is that right?"

Austin squirmed in his chair while receiving a threatening glower from Gwen who, Julia recalled, had been furious after Austin hired Tyler to spy on her.

"Well, he provided me with some information he thought might prove useful to my story."

"What sort of information?" Gwen asked.

"Apparently you subscribe to several rather graphic pornography services."

Austin blushed in Beth's direction. Julia looked at Gwen. She appeared unfazed by the revelation.

"And?" he asked defiantly.

"And your preference options include early adolescent girls."

Austin swallowed nervously while Beth looked disapprovingly in his direction.

"And that you've selected hair color and body styles remarkably similar to Amanda's."

"Let me see that," Beth ordered while reaching toward Julia's tablet.

"Now wait just a minute," Austin said while getting up from the table. "My entertainment options are nobody's business but my own!" He glanced sheepishly in Gwen's direction. "It's perfectly legal material."

"It may be legal, Mr. Tozer," Beth said sternly. "But these preference options raise very serious questions about your suitability as a guardian for a child who matches your parameters."

Austin cursed. He grabbed a bunched-up napkin from the

kitchen counter and threw it furiously toward the wall. It fell limply onto the floor.

"Take her then," he finally said. "Who needs her anyway?"

A moment passed before Beth Morris broke the silence. "Mr. Tozer, are you saying you will not protest the Simmons's request to pursue foster adoption of Amanda?"

He looked toward Gwen. Her eyes threatened. He no longer cared.

"Yes. That's what I'm saying."

His shoulders sank in defeat as he began leaving the room.

"Mr. Tozer. Can I ask one last question?" Julia asked.

He nodded, his face still looking toward the door.

"Where can we find Amanda?"

CHAPTER FIFTY-ONE

The car pulled close to a dying playground blemished by over-grown weeds and discolored monkey bars. Julia recognized Amanda fifty yards in the distance. She was sitting alone on a rusting swing that rocked to and fro without intent, a girl lost in solitary thought.

"Do you want me to go with you?" Troy asked.

"Give us a minute alone first. It might be better that way."

He nodded in agreement before kissing Julia on the cheek.

"Are you sure this is a good idea?" she asked. "I mean, we haven't even been married a year. Are we ready to become instant parents of an adolescent girl we barely know?"

"Correction," he said with a smile. "You barely know her. I've never met her."

She sighed at the truth of it.

"I can't explain it," he added. "But I have a strong feeling this is right for us. As if…" He hesitated.

"As if God is leading us?" she asked, giving him permission to take the conversation places she had too often resisted going.

A nod. "Yeah. Something like that."

"I'm sorry, Troy."

"Sorry for what?"

"I don't know. For dragging my feet about motherhood. And for making you feel…"

Words failed her. But the gentle touch of Troy's masculine fingers against the softness of her cheek told her he understood.

"Go on." He nudged her toward the car door. "We'll be fine."

Julia made it as far as the monkey bars when Amanda noticed her approaching form. Ten more steps and she suddenly realized who it was.

"Ms. Davidson!" Amanda said enthusiastically. "Is that you? Remember me? Amanda Tozer?"

Julia laughed. "Of course I remember you, Amanda. I came to see you."

The girl looked confused. "Me? Not Austin?"

"I already spoke to your brother. He told me you might be here."

"My half brother," she insisted. "He sent me a message saying to hang out here until he calls. Said I couldn't come home right away. Not that I wanted to anyway. He was meeting with you?"

"He was," Julia answered, reaching toward Amanda's disheveled head of hair.

"I know. Bad hair day again," she said. "I wish I had straight hair like you. It's so pretty. You're so pretty."

Julia moved toward the swing beside Amanda's. "Mind if I join you?"

"Really?"

"I'd like to chat. Then I'd like to introduce you to someone."

She looked toward the vehicle in the distance. "Your husband?"

"Yes. Troy."

"Really? Cool!"

Julia started pumping her legs back and forth. "I think I remember how to do this."

"Easy as pie!" Amanda said, pumping her legs to demonstrate for a novice.

They swung in delightful silence for a few moments while Julia tried to put herself in Amanda's shoes. A near-stranger was about to ask if she wanted to leave the home of her deceased mother, the only home the girl had ever known. How to approach the subject?

"Amanda," Julia began, "I met with your brother because I want to ask you something."

"Me? Really? What?"

Both swings eased themselves toward stillness. Julia turned toward the girl to meet her eyes.

"Do you remember when you said you wanted to call the Foster family?" Julia laughed at the recollection.

Amanda nodded. "Sure do."

"Well, I made some phone calls to get information on how you could move in with a foster family."

A series of rapid-fire questions shot in Julia's direction. "Really? You did? For me? Wow! What'd you find out?"

"If the right family comes along, and if your brother—"

"My half brother!"

"Right, sorry. If Austin doesn't oppose the arrangement, the process can move fairly quickly."

"How quickly?"

"Depends on how fast the family can complete applications, get a home study done, attend training, that sort of thing."

Amanda sat listening intently to every word.

Julia swallowed hard. "So, I was wondering—"

She didn't finish the question. Amanda's arms flew around Julia's neck. "Yes, yes, yes!" she shouted as they tilted off balance, sending both bodies to a worn patch of gravel below.

Tears flooded Julia's eyes as the girl planted her cheeks with six or seven kisses.

"I get to live with you?" she shouted between pecks. "And with your husband? Like a real family?"

Julia sat up with some effort. Then she patted the ground beside her to offer Amanda an adjoining spot.

"Everything's already in progress," she finally said. "So if you'll have us, we'd be honored to have you."

"You'll be my foster family?"

"For a while," Julia answered. "Until we qualify for full adoption."

That's when emotion filled Amanda's eyes. "You mean it?" she managed to say after a long silence.

Julia nodded decisively. "I mean it."

They sat on the gravel for several minutes while Julia explained the why, what, how, and when of a process she didn't fully grasp herself. "I'm not quite sure of all the details," she said. "But we'll figure them out as we go. Right now, there's a man over there who can't wait to meet you."

They stood. Then Amanda intertwined her fingers with Julia's as they began to walk.

Troy opened the car door in the distance. Then he stood beside the vehicle, the look on his face reminding Julia of the day he'd asked her on their first date. But he seemed less anxious, more resolute, as if about to accept an adventure neither he nor Julia could begin to comprehend.

Their eyes met. He winked as if never more proud of his friend, his lover, and his partner in the task of becoming a bright spot in Amanda's darkening world.

ABOUT THE AUTHORS

Dr. James Dobson is the Founder and President of Family Talk, a nonprofit organization that produces his radio program, "Family Talk with Dr. James Dobson." He is the author of more than thirty books dedicated to the preservation of the family. He has been active in governmental affairs and has advised three U.S. presidents on family matters. Dr. Dobson is married to Shirley and they have two grown children, Danae and Ryan, and two grandchildren. The Dobsons reside in Colorado Springs, CO.

Kurt Bruner serves as Pastor of Spiritual Formation at Lake Pointe Church and on the adjunct faculty of Dallas Theological Seminary. A graduate of Talbot Seminary and former Vice President with Focus on the Family, Kurt led the teams creating films, magazines, books, and radio drama. As President of HomePointe Inc., he helps local church leaders create an ongoing culture of intentional families. Kurt is the best-selling author of more than a dozen books. Kurt and his wife, Olivia, have four children and live in Rockwall, Texas.

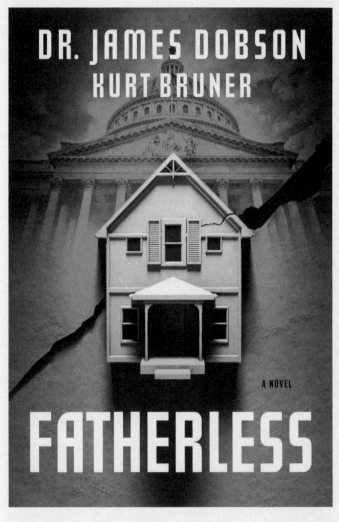

A NOVEL

FATHERLESS

Start at the Beginning

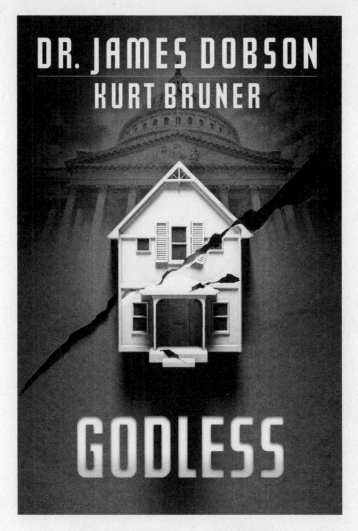

Summer 2014

DR. JAMES DOBSON

harrylangdon.com

Dr. Dobson wasn't ready to retire when he left Focus on the Family in February 2010. He knew that God had given him a mission and a message many years ago, and that God had not yet lifted that assignment from him.

Dr. Dobson felt God directing him to start a new ministry, which he did in March 2010, to continue the important work of strengthening families, speaking into the culture, and spreading the gospel of Jesus Christ. He called the new organization *Dr. James Dobson's Family Talk*.

In July of 2012, Dr. Dobson filmed a new series titled **"Building a Family Legacy"** that combines new and relevant sessions with some of the classic presentations from his original film series recorded in 1978 and seen by over 80 million people worldwide. This timeless family resource will be available in 2013.

DR.JAMES
DOBSON'S
familytalk™

The voice you trust
for the family you love

Be a Bright Spot

Explore the demographic and sociological trends portrayed in this book and celebrate the resilient beauty of God's design for marriage and parenthood. Kurt's blog invites readers to help turn the tide by becoming a bright spot. Go to **KurtBruner.com**

Kurt leads a network of innovative local churches creating a culture of intentional families. Subscribe to the free executive briefing and learn how your church can join the movement at **DriveFaithHome.com**

TRICKS

TRICKS

AN 87TH PRECINCT NOVEL BY

ED McBAIN

ARBOR HOUSE

New York

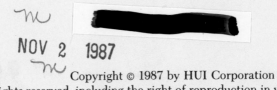
Copyright © 1987 by HUI Corporation
All rights reserved, including the right of reproduction in whole or in part in
any form. Published in the United States of America by Arbor House
Publishing Company and in Canada by Fitzhenry & Whiteside Ltd.

Manufactured in the United States of America

10   9   8   7   6   5   4   3   2   1

Library of Congress Cataloging in Publication Data

McBain, Ed, 1926–
Tricks: an 87th Precinct novel.

I. Title.
PS3515.U585T7   1987   813'.54   87-11350
ISBN 0-87795-927-7

This is for
Russell Wm. Hultgren

The city in these pages is imaginary.
The people, the places are all fictitious.
Only the police routine is based on established
investigatory technique.

1

The pair of them came down the street streaming blood.

No one paid any attention to them.

This was the city.

The taller of the two wore a blood-stained blue bathrobe. Blood appeared to be oozing from a half-dozen crosshatched wounds on his face. His hands were covered with blood. The striped pajama bottoms that showed beneath the hem of the robe were spattered with blood that seemed to have dripped from an open wound in his belly, where a dagger was plunged to the hilt.

The shorter person, a girl—although it was difficult to tell from the contorted mask of her face—wore only a paisley-patterned nightgown and high-heeled, pink pom-pommed bedroom slippers. Her garments screamed blood to the unusually mild October night. An ice pick was stuck into her chest, the handle smeared with blood. Blood was matted in her long stringy hair, bright red blood stained her naked legs, and her ankles, and the backs of her hands, and her narrow chest where it showed above the top of the yoke-necked nightgown.

She couldn't have been older than twelve.

The boy with her was perhaps the same age.

They were both carrying shopping bags that seemed stained with blood as fresh as that of their wounds. There could have been something recently severed from a human body inside each of those bags. A hand perhaps. Or a head. Or perhaps the bags had become blood-soaked only from proximity to their own bodies.

They came running up the street as though propelled by the urgency of their wounds.

"Let's try here," the boy said.

Several teeth appeared to be missing from his mouth. The black gaps were visible when he spoke. A thin line of red painted a trail from his lower lip to his chin. The flesh around his right eye was discolored red and black and blue and purple. He looked as if someone had beaten him severely before plunging the dagger into his belly.

"This one?" the girl asked.

They stopped before a street-level door.

They knocked frantically on the door.

It opened.

"Trick or treat!" they shouted in unison.

It was 4:10 P.M. on Halloween night.

The four-to-midnight shift at the 87th Precinct was only ten minutes old.

"Halloween ain't what it used to be," Andy Parker said.

He was sitting behind his desk in the squadroom, his feet up on the desk, his chair tilted dangerously, as if burdened by the weight of the shoulder holster slung over its back. He was wearing rumpled trousers, an unpressed sports jacket, unshined black shoes, dingy white socks, and a wash-and-wear shirt with food stains on it. He had got his haircut at a barber's college on the

Stem. There was a three-day-old beard stubble on his face. He was talking to Hawes and Brown, but they were not listening to him. That didn't stop Parker.

"What it is, Devil's Night steals from it," he said, and nodded in agreement with his observation.

At their own desks, the other detectives kept typing.

"Years ago," Parker said, *"tonight* was when the kids raised hell. Nowadays, you got church dances, you got socials at the Y, you got all kinds of shit to keep the kids out of trouble. So the kids figure Okay, they want us to be good on Halloween, so we'll pick another night to behave like little bastards. So they invented Devil's Night, which was last night, when we got all the windows busted and the eggs thrown."

Across the room, the typewriters kept clacking.

"You guys writing books or what?" Parker asked.

No one answered him.

"I'm gonna write a book one of these days," Parker said. "Lots of cops write books, they make a fortune. I had plenty experience, I could prolly write a terrific book."

Hawes looked up for a moment, and then scratched at his back. He was sunburned and peeling. He had returned only Monday morning from a week's vacation in Bermuda, but his skin was still the color of his hair. Big red-headed man with a white streak in the hair over the left temple, where he'd once been slashed. He had not yet told Annie Rawles that he'd spent some very pleasant hours with a girl he'd met down there on the pink sands.

"This guy Wamburger in L.A., he used to be a cop," Parker said, "I think with Hollywood Division. He writes these big bestsellers, don't he? This other guy, Kornitch, he writes them, too, he used to be a cop in New York. Ain't nobody who didn't used to be a cop can write books sound real about cops. One of these days, I'm gonna write a big fuckin' best-seller, I'll go live on a yacht in the south of France. Get these naked broads diving off the boat while I sit there doing nothing."

3

"Like now," Brown said.

"Yeah, bullshit, I already finished my work," Parker said. "This shift's been too fuckin' quiet. Whose idea was it to put on extra men, anyway?"

"The lieutenant's."

"So what's the use of seven guys when nothin's happening? Who's on, anyway? And where the fuck are they?"

"Cruising," Hawes said. "Out there looking for trouble."

He was thinking he himself would be looking for trouble if he told Annie what had happened in Bermuda, even though his arrangement with her was a loose one. Separate apartments, occasional conjugal visits, like they gave prisoners down in Mexico. Anyway, he'd *asked* Annie to come with him to Bermuda, hadn't he? Annie said her vacation wasn't till February. He asked her to change her vacation. She said she had to be in court all that week. She also said she hated Bermuda. He went down alone. Met this girl who practiced law in Atlanta. She'd taught him some legal tricks.

"It's so quiet, you could hear a pin drop," Parker said. "I coulda been home sleeping."

"Instead of sleeping here," Brown said, and went to the water cooler. He was a hefty, muscular black man, standing some six-feet four-inches tall and weighing two hundred and twenty pounds. There was a glowering look on his face as he pulled a paper cup from the holder and then stabbed at the faucet button. He always looked glowering, even when he was smiling. Brown could get an armed robber to drop his piece just by glowering at him.

"Who's sleeping?" Parker said. "I'm resting, is all. I already finished my work."

"Then why don't you start writing your book?" Hawes said.

"You could write all about how Halloween ain't what it used to be," Brown said, crumpling the paper cup and going back to his desk.

"It ain't," Parker agreed.

4

"You could write about it's so quiet on Halloween, your hero has nothing to do," Hawes said.

"That's the truth," Parker said. "This phone ain't rung once since I come in."

He looked at the phone.

It did not ring.

"I'll bet that bothers you a lot," Brown said. "The phone not ringing."

"Nothing to do," Hawes said.

"No ax murders out there," Brown said.

"I had an ax murder once," Parker said, "I could maybe write about that."

"It's been done," Hawes said.

"Be a big fuckin' best-seller."

"I don't think it was."

" 'Cause maybe a cop didn't write it. You got to be a cop to write best-sellers about cops."

"You got to be an ax murderer to write best-sellers about ax murders," Brown said.

"Sure," Parker said, and looked at the phone again.

"You got nothing to do," Hawes said, "whyn't you go down the hall and shave?"

"I'm working on my Miami Vice look," Parker said.

"You look like a bum," Brown said.

"I *am* a bum," Parker said.

"You got to be a bum to write best-sellers about bums," Brown said.

"Tell that to Kennedy," Hawes said.

"Teddy? I didn't know he wrote books," Parker said. "What does he write about? Senators?"

"Go shave," Hawes said.

"Or go write a book about a barber," Brown suggested.

"I ain't a barber," Parker said.

He looked at the phone again.

"You ever see it this quiet?" he asked.

"I never even *heard* it this quiet," Brown said.

"Me, neither," Parker said. "It's like a paid vacation."

"Like always," Brown said.

"I once had a lady choked to death on a dildo," Parker said. "Maybe I could write about that. I had a lot of cases I could write about."

"Maybe you could write about the case you're working now," Brown said.

"I ain't working nothing right now."

"No kidding?"

"I finished all my work. Everything wrapped up till the phone rings."

"Maybe the phone's out of order," Hawes said.

"You think so?" Parker said, but he made no move to lift the receiver and listen for a dial tone.

"Or maybe none of the bad guys are doing anything out there," Brown said.

"Maybe all the bad guys went south for the winter," Hawes said, and thought again about Bermuda, and wondered if he should come clean with Annie.

"Fat chance," Parker said. "This weather? I never seen an October like this in my entire life. I once had a case, this guy strangled his wife with the telephone cord. I'll bet I could write about that."

"I'll bet you could."

"Hit her with the phone first, knocked her cold. Then strangled her with the cord."

"You could call it *Long Distance*," Brown said.

"No, he was standing close to her when he done it."

"Then how about *Local Call*?"

"What's wrong with *Sorry, Wrong Number*?" Parker asked.

"Nothing," Hawes said. "That's a terrific title."

"Or I could write about this guy got drowned in the bathtub. His wife drowned him in the bathtub. That was a good case."

6

"You could call it *Glub*," Brown said.

"*Glub* ain't a best-selling title," Parker said. "Also, she cut off his cock. The water was all red with his blood."

"Why'd she do that?" Brown asked, truly interested now.

"He was fuckin' around with some other broad," Parker said. "You shoulda seen the guy, he was a tiny little runt. His wife came in while he was taking a bath, she shoved him under the water, good-bye, Charlie. Then she cuts off his cock with his own straight razor, throws it out the window."

"The razor?"

"No, the cock. Hit an old lady walking by in the street. Hit her right on top of the head, knocked this plastic flower off her hat. She bends down to pick up the flower, she sees the cock laying on the sidewalk. Right away she wonders who she can sue. She picks it up, runs to her lawyer with it. Goes running down the street with this cock in her fist, in this city nobody even blinked."

"Carella and I once worked a case," Hawes said, "where this guy cut off another guy's hands."

"Why'd he do that?"

"Same reason. Love."

"That's *love*?"

"Love or money," Hawes said, and shrugged. "The only two reasons there are."

"Plus your lunatics," Brown said.

"Well, that's a whole 'nother ball game," Parker said. "Your lunatics. I once had a lunatic, he killed four priests before we caught up with him. We ast him why he was killing priests. He told us his father was a priest. How could that be, his father a priest?"

"Maybe his mother was a nun," Brown said.

"No, his mother was a registered nurse. Fifty years old, but gorgeous. Peaches Muldoon, her name was. Her square handle, I mean it, she was from Tennessee. Told me her son was nuts for sure, and she was glad I nailed him. Peaches Muldoon. A redhead. A real racehorse."

7

"Who'd *she* say the father was?"

"Her brother," Parker said.

"Nice case," Hawes said.

"Yeah. Maybe I oughta write about that one."

"You're not a priest."

"Sometimes I *feel* like a priest," Parker said. "You know the last time I got laid? Don't ask."

"Maybe you oughta go look up Peaches," Brown suggested.

"She's prolly dead by now," Parker said, giving the idea serious consideration. "This was maybe ten years ago, this case."

"She'd be sixty by now," Hawes said.

"If she ain't dead, yeah. But sixty ain't old, you know. I laid a lot of sixty-year-old broads. They have lots of experience, they know what they're doing."

He looked at the phone again.

"Maybe I *will* go shave," he said.

The two women knew each other well.

Annie Rawles was a Detective/First working out of the Rape Squad.

Eileen Burke was a Detective/Second who worked out of Special Forces.

They were in Annie's office discussing murder.

The clock on the wall read 4:30 P.M.

"Why'd they drag *you* in?" Eileen asked.

"My experience with decoys," Annie said. "I guess Homicide's getting desperate."

"Who caught the squeals?"

"Guy named Alvarez at the Seven-Two."

"In Calm's Point?"

"Yes."

"All three?"

"All three."

"Same area of the precinct?"

8

"The Canal Zone, down by the docks. You'd think you were in Houston."

"I've never been to Houston."

"Don't go."

Eileen smiled.

She was five-feet nine-inches tall, with long legs, good breasts, flaring hips, flaming red hair, and green eyes. There was no longer a scar on her left cheek. Plastic surgery had taken care of that. But Annie wondered if there were still internal scars.

"You don't have to take this one," she said. "I know it's short notice."

"Well, tell me some more," Eileen said.

"Or it can wait till *next* Friday. Shit, Homicide only called me an hour ago. Told me Alvarez wasn't making any headway, maybe the spic needed a helping hand. Homicide's words, not mine."

"Good old Homicide," Eileen said, and shook her head knowingly.

She wondered if Annie had doubts about her handling this one. She hadn't handled a really difficult one since the accident. Calling it an "accident" made it easier to think about. An accident was something that could happen to anyone. Something that needn't necessarily happen again. An accident wasn't a rapist slashing open your left cheek and then taking you by force.

Annie was watching her.

Eyes the color of loam behind glasses that gave her a scholarly look, black hair cut in a wedge, firm cupcake breasts on a slender body. About the same age as Eileen, a bit shorter. As hard and as brilliant as a diamond. Annie used to work out of Robbery, where she'd blown away two guys holding up a midtown bank. Blew them out of the air. If she hadn't been frightened by two seasoned hoods facing a max of twenty, would she have any sympathy for a decoy cop running scared?

9

Well, I've been on the job, Eileen thought, I'm *not* running scared.

But she was.

"When was the first one?" she asked.

"The tenth. A Friday night, full moon. Alvarez thought maybe a loonie. Then the second one turned up a week later, the seventeenth. And another one last Friday night."

"Always Friday night, huh?"

"So far."

"So tonight's Friday, so Homicide wants a decoy."

"So does Alvarez. I spoke to him right after I got the call. He sounds smart as hell, but so far he hasn't got a place to hang his hat."

"What's his thinking on it?"

"You don't know the Zone, huh?"

"No."

"Then you missed what I was saying about Houston."

"I guess so."

"There's an area bordering the Ship Canal down there, it's infested with hookers and dope. Sleaziest dives I've ever seen in my life. The docks on the Calm's Point Canal run a close second."

"Are they hookers then? The victims?"

"Yes. Hookers."

"All three?"

"One of them only sixteen years old."

Eileen nodded.

"What'd he use?" she asked.

Annie hesitated.

"A knife," she said.

And suddenly it all played back again in Eileen's head. . . .

Her hand going for the Browning .380 automatic tucked into her boot, Don't force me to cut you, *the pistol coming free of its holster, moving into firing position—and he slashed her face. Sudden fire blazed a trail across her cheek. She dropped the gun at*

10

once. Good girl, *he said. And slashed her pantyhose and the pant-ies underneath. . . .*

And . . .

And thrust the cold flat side of the knife against her . . . against her . . .

"*Want me to cut you here, too?*"

She shook her head.

No, please, *she thought.*

And mumbled the words incoherently, No, please, *and said them aloud at last,* "No, please. Please. Don't . . . cut me again. Please."

"*Want me to fuck you instead?*"

"*Don't cut me again.*"

Annie was watching her intently.

"Slit their throats with a knife," she said.

Eileen was covered with cold sweat.

"So . . . I . . . I guess they want me to play hooker, is that it?" she said.

"That's it."

"New girl in town, huh?"

"You've got it."

"Cruising? Or have they set up . . . ?"

"They're planting you in a place called Larry's Bar. On Fair-view and East Fourth."

Eileen nodded.

"Tonight, huh?"

"Starting around eight."

"That's early, isn't it?"

"They want to give him enough rope."

"Where do I check in?"

"The Seven-Two. You can change there."

"Into what? The hookers today look like college girls."

"Not the ones working the Canal Zone."

Eileen nodded again.

11

"Has Alvarez picked my backups?"

"One. A big beefy guy named . . ."

"I want at least two," Eileen said.

"I'm your other one," Annie said.

Eileen looked at her.

"If you want me."

Eileen said nothing.

"I'm not afraid of using the piece," Annie said.

"I know you're not."

"But if you'd feel better with another man . . ."

"Nothing's going to make me feel better," Eileen said. "I'm scared shitless. You could back me with the Russian army, and I'd still be scared."

"Then don't do it," Annie said.

"Then when do I stop being scared?" Eileen asked.

The room went silent.

"Homicide asked me to get the best decoy I knew," Annie said softly. "I picked you."

"Thanks a lot," Eileen said.

But she smiled.

"You *are*, you know."

"I *was*."

"*Are*," Annie said.

"Sweet talker," Eileen said.

And smiled again.

"So . . . it's up to you," Annie said, and looked up at the clock. "But you've got to let me know right away. They want everything in place by eight tonight."

"Who's this big beefy guy?"

"His name's Shanahan. Irish as Paddy's underwear, six-feet tall, weighs at least two hundred pounds. I wouldn't want to meet him in a dark alley, believe me."

"I *would*," Eileen said. "I'd like an hour with him before I hit the street. Can he be in the squadroom by seven?"

"You'll do it then?"

"Only 'cause you're the other backup," Eileen said, and smiled again.

But she was trembling inside.

"This guy who killed them," she said. "Do they have any idea what he looks like?"

"Alvarez says he's got some statements that seem to jibe. But who knows what he'll look like tonight? If he comes in at all."

"Terrific," Eileen said.

"One thing for sure, though."

"Yeah?"

"He's passing himself off as a trick."

The saw ripped through wood, ripped through flesh and bone along the middle of the wooden box and the middle of the woman. Blood gushed from the track the saw made, following the sharp teeth. The saw itself was bloody when at last he withdrew it from box and woman. He looked up at the wall clock. 5:05 P.M. He nodded in grim satisfaction.

And lifted the lids on both sides of the box.

And the woman stepped out in one piece, grinning, and held her arms over her head, and the audience began to applaud and cheer.

"Thank you, thank you very much," the man said, bowing.

The audience was composed mostly of boys and girls between the ages of thirteen and eighteen because the performance was being held at the high school on North Eleventh. The principal of the school, Mr. Ellington, beamed contentedly. Hiring the magician had been his idea. A way to keep these restless teenagers happy and occupied for an hour or so before they hit the streets. He would make a little speech after the performance was over, which should be any minute now. He would tell them all to go home and have a good dinner and then put on their costumes and go out for a safe and sane Halloween in the secure knowledge that among the rights granted in a democracy was freedom of assembly—like the assembly they'd had this evening—and also

13

freedom of assembly in the streets, but *not* the freedom to perform malicious mischief, definitely not. That would be his pitch. The kids, grateful for an hour's entertainment, would—he hoped—follow his directives. No one from Herman Raucher High would become involved in vandalism tonight. Nossir.

He watched now as the magician's assistant rolled the wooden box off the stage. She was a good-looking blonde, in her late twenties Ellington guessed, wearing a sequined costume that exposed to good advantage her long, long legs and her exuberant breasts. Ellington noticed that most of the boys in the auditorium could not take their eyes off the assistant's long legs and the popping tops of her creamy white breasts. He himself was having a little difficulty doing that. She was back on stage now, wheeling a tall box. A vertical one this time. The magician—whose name was Sebastian the Great—was wearing tails and a top hat. Ellington looked up at the clock. This was probably the closing number of the act. He hoped so because he wanted to make his little speech and get the kids the hell out of here. He had promised Estelle he would stop by on the way home from school. Estelle was the lady he stopped by to see every Wednesday and Friday afternoon, when his wife thought he had meetings with the staff. Estelle's legs weren't as long, nor were her breasts as opulent as those on the magician's assistant, but then again Estelle was forty-seven years old.

"Thank you, kids," Sebastian the Great said, "thank you. Now I know you're all anxious to get out there in the streets for a safe and sane Halloween, and so I won't keep you much longer. Ah, thank you, Marie," he said to his assistant.

Her name's Marie, Ellington thought, and wondered what her last name was, and wondered if she was listed in the phone book.

"You see here a little box—well, not so little because I'm a pretty tall fellow—which I'm going to step into in just a moment . . . thank you, Marie, you can go now, you've been very helpful, let's have a nice round of applause for Marie, kids."

14

Marie held her hands up over her head, legs widespread, big smile on her mouth, and the kids applauded and yelled, especially the boys, and then she did a cute little sexy turn and went strutting off the stage in her high heels.

"That's the last you'll see of Marie tonight," Sebastian said.

Shit, Ellington thought.

"And in just a few minutes, you'll see the last of me, too. What I'm going to do, kids, I'm going to step inside this box . . ."

He opened the door on the face of the box.

"And I'm going to ask you all to count to ten . . . out loud . . . one, two, three, four, and so on—you all know how to count to ten, don't you?"

Laughter from the kids.

"And I'm going to ask your principal, Mr. Ellington, to come up here—Mr. Ellington, would you come up here now, please?—and when you reach the number ten, he's going to open the door of this box, and Sebastian the Great will be gone, kids, I will have disappeared, vanished, poof! So . . . ah, good, Mr. Ellington, if you'll just stand here beside the box, thank you. That's very good." He took off his top hat. Stepping partially into the box, he said, "I'm going to say good-bye to you now . . ."

Applause and cheering from the kids.

"Thank you, thank you," he said, "and I want to remind you again to please have a safe and sane Halloween out there. Now the minute I close this door, I want you to start counting out loud. And when you reach ten, Mr. Ellington will open the door and I'll be gone but not forgotten. Mr. Ellington? Are you ready?"

"Ready," Ellington said, feeling like an asshole.

"Good-bye, kids," Sebastian said, and closed the door behind him.

"One!" the kids began chanting. "Two! Three! Four! Five! Six! Seven! Eight! Nine! Ten!"

Ellington opened the door on the box.

Sebastian the Great had indeed vanished.

15

The kids began applauding.

Ellington went to the front of the stage, and held up his hands for silence.

He would have to remind the kids not to try sawing anybody in half, because that had been only a trick.

The station wagon pulled up to the curb in front of the liquor store on Culver and Ninth. The big woman behind the wheel was a curly-haired blonde in her late forties, wearing a blue dress with a tiny white floral print, a cardigan sweater over it. A kid was sitting beside her on the front seat. Three more kids were in the back of the car. The kids looked perhaps eleven or twelve years old, no older than that.

They threw open the doors and got out of the car.

"Have fun, kids," the blonde behind the wheel said.

The kids were all dressed like robbers.

Little black leather jackets, and little blue jeans, and little white sneakers, and little billed caps on their little heads, and little black masks over their eyes. They were all carrying shopping bags decorated with little orange pumpkins. They were all holding little toy pistols in their little hands. They went across the sidewalk in a chattering little excited group, and one of them opened the door to the liquor store. The clock on the wall behind the counter read 5:15 P.M. The owner of the store looked up the moment the bell over the door sounded.

"Trick or treat!" the little kids squealed in unison.

"Come on, kids, get out of here," the owner said impatiently. "This is a place of business."

And one of the little kids shot him in the head.

Parker had shaved and was back in the squadroom, rummaging through the file cabinets containing folders for all the cases the detectives had successfully closed. In police work, there was no such thing as a solution. You never *solved* a case, you closed it out. Or it remained *open*, which meant the perpetrator was already in Buenos Aires or Nome, Alaska, and you'd *never* catch him. The Open File was the graveyard of police detection.

"I feel like a new man," Parker said. In fact, he looked like the same old Parker, except that he had shaved. "Muldoon," he said, "Muldoon, where are you, Muldoon?"

"You really gonna call a sixty-year-old lady?" Brown asked.

"Peaches Muldoon, correct," Parker said. "If she was well-preserved at fifty, she's prolly still got it all in the right places. Where the fuck's the file?"

"Look under Aging Nurses," Hawes said.

"Look under Decrepit Broads," Brown said.

"Yeah, bullshit, wait'll you see her picture," Parker said.

The clock on the squadroom wall read 5:30 P.M.

"Muldoon, here we go," Parker said, and yanked a thick file from the drawer.

The telephone rang.

"Who's catching?" Parker asked.

"I thought you were," Brown said.

"Me? No, no. You're up, Artie."

Brown sighed and picked up the phone.

"Eighty-Seventh Squad," he said, "Brown."

"Artie, this is Dave downstairs."

Sergeant Murchison, at the muster desk.

"Yeah, Dave."

"Adam Four just responded to a 10-20 on Culver and Ninth. Liquor store called Adams Wine & Spirits."

"Yeah?"

"They got a homicide there."

"Okay," Brown said.

"You got some people out, don't you?"

"Yes."

"Who? Can you take a look for me?"

Brown reached across the desk for the duty chart.

"Kling and Carella are riding together," he said. "Meyer and Genero are out solo."

"Any idea which sectors?"

"No."

"Okay, I'll try to raise them."

"Keep in touch."

"Will do."

Brown hung up.

"What?" Hawes asked.

"Homicide on Culver. There goes the neighborhood."

The telephone rang again.

"Take a look at this picture," Parker said, coming over to Brown's desk. "You ever see a body like this one?"

"Eighty-Seventh Squad, Hawes."

"Look at those tits," Parker said.

"Hello, who am I talking to, please?" a woman's voice asked.

"Detective Hawes."

"Legs that won't quit," Parker said.

"My husband's gone," the woman said.

"Yes, ma'am," Hawes said, "let me give you the number for . . ."

"My name is . . ."

"It'll be best if you call Missing Persons, ma'am," Hawes said. "They're specially equipped to deal with . . ."

"He disappeared here in *this* precinct," the woman said.

"Still . . ."

"Does that look like a fifty-year-old broad?" Parker asked.

The telephone rang again. Brown picked up.

"Eighty-Seventh Squad, Brown," he said.

"Artie? This is Genero."

"Yeah?"

"Artie, you won't believe this."

"What won't I believe?" Brown asked. He looked up at Parker, covered the mouthpiece, and whispered, "Genero."

Parker rolled his eyes.

"It happened again," Genero said.

18

"My name is Marie Sebastiani," the woman on Hawes's phone said. "My husband is Sebastian the Great."

Hawes immediately thought he was talking to a bedbug.

"Ma'am," he said, "if your husband's really gone . . ."

"I'm at this restaurant, you know?" Genero said. "On Culver and Sixth?"

"Yeah?" Brown said.

"Where they had the holdup last night? I stopped by to talk to the owners?"

"Yeah?"

"My husband is a magician," Marie said. "He calls himself Sebastian the Great. He's disappeared."

Good magician, Hawes thought.

"And I go out back to look in the garbage cans?" Genero said. "See maybe somebody dropped a gun in there or something?"

"Yeah?" Brown said.

"I mean he's *really* disappeared," Marie said. "Vanished. I went out back of the high school where he was loading the car, and the car was gone, and so was Frank. And all his tricks were dumped in the driveway like . . ."

"Frank, ma'am?"

"My husband. Frank Sebastiani. Sebastian the Great."

"It happened again, Artie," Genero said. "I almost puked."

"What happened again?"

"Maybe he just went home, ma'am," Hawes said.

"No, we live in the next state, he wouldn't have left without me. And his stuff was all over the driveway. I mean, expensive *tricks.*"

"So what are you saying, ma'am?"

"I'm saying somebody must've stolen the car and God knows what he did to Frank."

"Artie?" Genero said. "Are you with me?"

"I'm with you," Brown said, and sighed.

"It was in one of the garbage cans, Artie."

19

"What was in one of the garbage cans?"

"Which high school is that, ma'am?" Hawes asked.

"Herman Raucher High. On North Eleventh."

"Are you there now?"

"Yes. I'm calling from a pay phone."

"You stay right there," Hawes said, "I'll get somebody to you."

"I'll be waiting out back," Marie said, and hung up.

"Artie, you better come over here," Genero said. "The Burgundy on Culver and Sixth."

"What is it you found in . . . ?"

But Genero had already hung up.

Brown slipped into his shoulder holster.

Hawes clipped his holster to his belt.

Parker picked up the telephone receiver.

"Peaches Muldoon, here I come," he said.

5:40 P.M. on Halloween night, the streets dark for almost an hour now, the city off daylight savings time since the twenty-sixth of the month. All the little monsters and goblins and devils and bats out in force, carrying their shopping bags full of candy from door to door, yelling "Trick or Treat!" and praying no one would give them a treat with a double-edged razor blade in it.

Brown looked at his watch.

Along about now, his wife, Caroline, would be taking Connie around. His eight-year-old daughter had previewed her costume for him last night. She'd looked like the most angelic witch he'd ever seen in his life. All next week, there'd be sweets to eat. The only people who profited from Halloween were the candymakers and the dentists. Brown was in the wrong profession.

He had chosen to walk to the Burgundy Restaurant on Culver and Sixth. It wasn't too far from the station house, and a cop—if Genero could be considered one—was already on the scene.

The night was balmy.

God, what an October this had been.

Leaves still on the trees in the park, dazzling yellows and reds and oranges and browns, daytime skies a piercing blue, nighttime skies pitch-black and sprinkled with stars. In a city where itchy citizens took off their overcoats far too early each spring, it now seemed proper and fitting that there was no need to put them on again quite yet. He walked swiftly toward Culver, turning to glance at E.T. hurrying by with Frankenstein's monster on one side and Dracula on the other. Smiling, he turned the corner onto Culver and began walking toward Sixth.

Genero was waiting on the sidewalk outside the restaurant. He looked pale.

"What is it?" Brown asked.

"Come on back," Genero said. "I didn't touch it."

"Touch what?" Brown asked. But Genero was already walking up the alleyway on the right-hand side of the restaurant.

Garbage cans flanked either side of the restaurant's back door, illuminated by an overhead flood light.

"That one," Genero said.

Brown lifted the lid on the can Genero was pointing to.

The bloody upper torso of a human body was stuffed into the can, on top of a green plastic garbage bag.

The torso had been severed at the waist from the rest of the body.

The torso had no arms.

And no head.

"Why does this always happen to me?" Genero asked God.

2

"I once found a hand in an airlines bag," Genero said.

"No shit?" Monoghan asked without interest.

Monoghan was a Homicide cop. He usually worked in tandem with his partner Monroe, but there had been two homicides in the Eight-Seven tonight, a few blocks apart from each other, and Monoghan was here behind the restaurant on Culver and Sixth, and Monroe was over at the liquor store on Culver and Ninth. It was a shame; Monoghan without Monroe was like a bagel without lox.

"Cut off at the wrist," Genero said. "I almost puked."

"Yeah, a person could puke, all right," Monoghan said.

He was looking down into the garbage can where the bloody torso still rested on the green plastic bag.

"Nothing but a piece of fresh meat here," he said to Brown. Brown had a pained look in his eyes. He merely nodded.

"M.E. on the way?" Monoghan asked.

"Called him ten minutes ago."

"You won't need an ambulance for this one," Monoghan said. "All you'll need is a shopping bag."

He laughed at his own little witticism.

He sorely missed Monroe.

"Looks like a man, don't it?" he said. "I mean, no knockers, all that hair on the chest."

"This hand I found," Genero said, "it was a man's, too. A great big hand. I nearly puked."

There were several uniformed cops in the alley now, and a couple of technicians sniffing around the back door of the restaurant, and a plainclothes lady cop from Photo taking her Polaroids. Crime Scene signs already up, even though this *wasn't* a crime scene in the strictest sense of the word, in that the crime had almost certainly taken place elsewhere. All they had here was the detritus of a crime, a piece of fresh meat—as Monoghan had called it—lying in a garbage can, the partial remains of what had once been a human being. That and whatever clues may have been left by the person who'd transported the torso to this particular spot.

"It's amazing the number of dismembered stiffs you get in this city," Monoghan said.

"Oh, boy, you're telling *me*?" Genero said.

Monoghan was wearing a black homburg, a black suit, a white shirt, and a black tie. His hands were in his jacket pockets, only the thumbs showing. He looked like a sad, neat undertaker. Genero was trying to look like a hip big-city detective disguised as a college boy. He was wearing blue slacks and a reindeer-patterned sweater over a sports shirt open at the throat. Brown penny loafers. No hat. Curly black hair, brown eyes. He resembled a somewhat stupid poodle.

Monoghan looked at him.

"You the one found this thing here?" he asked.

"Well, yes," Genero said, wondering if he should have admitted this.

23

"Any other parts in these other garbage cans?"

"I didn't look," Genero said, thinking one part had been plenty.

"Want to look now?"

"Don't get prints on any of those garbage-can lids," one of the techs warned.

Genero tented a handkerchief over his hand and began lifting lids.

There were no other parts.

"So all we got here is this chest here," Monoghan said.

"Hello, boys," the M.E. said, coming up the alley. "What've we got here?"

"Just this chest here," Monoghan said, indicating the torso.

The M.E. peeked into the garbage can.

"Very nice," he said, and put down his satchel. "Did you want me to pronounce it dead, or what?"

"You could give us a postmortem interval, that'd be helpful," Monoghan said.

"Autopsy'll give you that," the M.E. said.

"Looks of this one," Monoghan said, "somebody already *done* the autopsy. What'd he use, can you tell?"

"Who?" the M.E. said.

"Whoever cut him up in pieces."

"He wasn't a brilliant brain surgeon, I can tell you that," the M.E. said, looking at the torn and jagged flesh where the head, arms, and lower torso had been.

"So what was it? A cleaver? A hacksaw?"

"I'm not a magician," the M.E. said.

"Any marks, scars, tattoos?" Brown asked quietly.

"None that I can see. Let me roll it over."

Genero noticed that the M.E. kept referring to it as "it."

The M.E. rolled it over.

"None here, either," he said.

"Nothing but a piece of fresh meat," Monoghan said.

❖ ❖ ❖

Hawes was wearing only a lightweight sports jacket over a shirt open at the throat, no tie, no hat. A mild breeze riffled his red hair; October this year was like springtime in the Rockies. Marie Sebastiani seemed uncomfortable talking to a cop. Most honest citizens did; it was the thieves of the world who felt perfectly at home with law-enforcement officers.

Fidgeting nervously, she told him how she'd changed out of her costume and into the clothes she was now wearing—a tweed jacket and skirt, a lavender blouse and high-heeled pumps— while her husband, Sebastian the Great, a.k.a. Frank Sebastiani, had gone out behind the high school to load the car with all the *little* tricks he used in the act. And then *she'd* gone out back to where she was supposed to meet him, and the car was gone, and he was gone, and his tricks were scattered all over the driveway.

"By *little* tricks . . ." Hawes said.

"Oh, you know, the rings, and the scarves, and the balls, and the bird cage . . . well, all this stuff all over the place here. Jimmy comes with the van to pick up the boxes and the bigger stuff."

"Jimmy?"

"Frank's apprentice. He's a jack of all trades, drives the van to wherever we're performing, helps us load and unload, paints the boxes when they need it, makes sure all the spring catches are working properly . . . like that."

"He dropped you both off today, did he?"

"Oh, yes."

"And helped you unload and all?"

"Same as always."

"And stayed for the performance?"

"No, I don't know where he went during the performance. Probably out for a bite to eat. He knew we'd be done here around five, five-thirty."

"So where is he now? Jimmy?"

"Well, I don't know. What time do you have?"

Hawes looked at his watch.

"Five after six," he said.

25

"Gee, I don't know *where* he is," Marie said. "He's usually very punctual."

"What time *did* you get done here?" Hawes asked.

"Like I said, around five-fifteen or so."

"And you changed your clothes . . ."

"Yes. Well, so did Frank."

"What does he wear on stage?"

"Black tie and tails. And a top hat."

"And he changed into?"

"Is this important?"

"Very," Hawes said.

"Then let me get it absolutely correct," Marie said. "He put on a pair of blue slacks, and a blue sports shirt, no pattern on it, just the solid blue, and blue socks, and black shoes, and a . . . what do you call it? Houndstooth, is that the weave? A sort of jagged little black and blue weave. A houndstooth sports jacket. No tie."

Hawes was writing now.

"How old is your husband?" he asked.

"Thirty-four."

"How tall is he?"

"Five-eleven."

"Weight?"

"One-seventy."

"Color of his hair?"

"Black."

"Eyes?"

"Blue."

"Does he wear glasses?"

"No."

"Is he white?"

"Well, of *course*," Marie said.

"Any identifying marks, scars or tattoos?"

"Yes, he has an appendectomy scar. And also a meniscectomy scar."

"What's that?" Hawes asked.

"He had a skiing accident. Tore the cartilage in his left knee. They removed the cartilage—what they call the meniscus. There's a scar there. On his left knee."

"How do you spell that?" Hawes asked. "Meniscectomy?"

"I don't know," Marie said.

"On the phone, you told me you live in the next state . . ."

"Yes, I do."

"Where?"

"Collinsworth."

"The address?"

"604 Eden Lane."

"Apartment number?"

"It's a private house."

"Telephone number, area code first?"

"Well, I'll give you Frank's card," she said, and dug into her shoulder bag and came up with a sheaf of cards. She took one from the stack and handed it to Hawes. He scanned it quickly, wrote both the home and office phone numbers onto his pad, and then tucked the card into the pad's flap.

"Did you try calling home?" he asked.

"No. Why would I do that?"

"Are you sure he didn't go home without you? Maybe he figured this Jimmy would pick you up."

"No, we were planning on eating dinner here in the city."

"So he wouldn't have gone home without you."

"He never has."

"This Jimmy . . . what's his last name?"

"Brayne."

"Brain? Like in somebody's head?"

"Yes, but with a Y."

"B-R-A-Y-N?"

"With an E on the end."

"B-R-A-Y-N-E?"

"Yes."

"James Brayne."

27

"Yes."

"And his address?"

"He lives with us."

"Same house?"

"A little apartment over the garage."

"And *his* phone number?"

"Oh, gee," she said, "I'm not sure I remember it."

"Well, try to remember," Hawes said, "because I think we ought to call back home, see if either of them maybe went back there."

"They wouldn't do that," Marie said.

"Maybe they got their signals crossed," Hawes said. "Maybe Jimmy thought your husband was going to take the stuff in the car . . ."

"No, the big stuff won't fit in the car. That's why we have the van."

"Or maybe your husband thought you were getting a ride back with Jimmy . . ."

"I'm sure he didn't."

"What kind of a car was your husband driving?"

"A 1984 Citation. A two-door coupe."

"Color?"

"Blue."

"License-plate number?"

"DL 74-3681."

"And the van?"

"A '79 Ford Econoline."

"Color?"

"Tan, sort of."

"Would you know the license-plate number on that one?"

"RL 68-7210."

"In whose name are the vehicles registered?"

"My husband's."

"Both registered across the river?"

"Yes."

"Let's find a phone, okay?" Hawes said.

"There's one inside," she said, "but calling them won't do any good."

"How do you know?"

"Because Frank wouldn't have dumped his tricks all over the driveway this way. These tricks cost money."

"Let's try calling them, anyway."

"It won't do any good," Marie said. "I'm telling you."

He dialed Sebastiani's home and office numbers, and got no answer at either. Marie at last remembered the number in the room over the garage, and he dialed that one, too. Nothing.

"Well," he said, "let me get to work on this. I'll call you as soon as . . ."

"How am I going to get home?" Marie asked.

They always asked how they were going to get home.

"There are trains running out to Collinsworth, aren't there?"

"Yes, but . . ."

"I'll drop you off at the station."

"What about all those tricks outside in the driveway?"

"Maybe we can get the school custodian to lock them up someplace. Till your husband shows up."

"What makes you think he'll show up?"

"Well, I'm sure he's okay. Just some crossed signals, that's all."

"I'm not sure I want to go home tonight," Marie said.

"Well, ma'am . . ."

"I think I may want to . . . could I come to the police station with you? Could I wait there till you hear anything about Frank?"

"That's entirely up to you, ma'am. But it may take a while before we . . ."

"And can you lend me some money?" she asked.

He looked at her.

"For dinner?"

He kept looking at her.

"I'll pay you back as soon as . . . as soon as we find Frank. I'm

29

sorry, but I've only got a few dollars on me. Frank was the one they paid, he's the one who's got all the money."

"How *much* money, ma'am?"

"Well, just enough for a hamburger or something."

"I meant how much money does your husband have on him?"

"Oh. Well, we got a hundred for the job. And he probably had a little something in his wallet, I don't know how much."

Which lets out robbery, Hawes thought. Although in this city, there were people who'd slit your throat for a nickel. He suddenly wondered how much money he himself was carrying. This was the first time in his entire life that a victim had asked him for a loan.

"I'm sort of hungry myself," he said. "Let's find the custodian and then go get something to eat."

Monroe looked bereft without Monoghan.

The clock on the liquor-store wall read 6:10 P.M.

He was standing behind the cash register, where the owner of the store had been shot dead a bit more than an hour earlier. The body was already gone. There was only blood and a chalked outline on the floor behind the counter. The cash register was empty.

"There was four of them," the man talking to Meyer said.

Meyer had been cruising the area when Sergeant Murchison raised him on the radio. He had got here maybe ten minutes after it was all over, and had immediately radioed back with a confirmed D.O.A. Murchison had informed Homicide, so here was Monroe, all alone, and looking as if he'd lost his twin brother. He was wearing a black homburg, a black suit, a white shirt, and a black tie. His hands were in his jacket pockets, only the thumbs showing. He looked like a sad, neat undertaker. Meyer wondered where Monoghan was. Wherever he was, Meyer figured he'd be dressed exactly like Monroe. Even if he was home sick in bed, he'd be dressed like Monroe.

Meyer himself was wearing brown slacks, a brown cotton turtleneck, and a tan sports jacket. He thought he looked very dapper tonight. With his bald head and his burly build, he figured he looked like Kojak, except more handsome. He was sorry Kojak was off the air now. He'd always felt Kojak gave bald cops a good name.

"Little kids," the man said.

This was the third time he'd told Meyer that four little kids had held up the liquor store and shot the owner.

"What do you mean, little kids?" Monroe asked from behind the cash register.

"Eleven, twelve years old," the man said.

His name was Henry Kirby, and he lived in a building up the street. He was perhaps sixty, sixty-five years old, a thin, graying man wearing a short-sleeved sports shirt and wrinkled polyester slacks. He'd told first Meyer and then Monroe that he was coming to the store to buy a bottle of wine when he saw these little kids running out with shopping bags and guns. Monroe still couldn't believe it.

"You mean *children*?" he said.

"Little kids, yeah," Kirby said.

"Grade-schoolers?"

"Yeah, little kids."

"Pre-pubescent twerps?" Monroe said.

He was doing okay without Monoghan. Without Monoghan, he was being Monoghan and Monroe all by himself.

"Yeah, little kids," Kirby said.

"What were they wearing?" Meyer said.

"Leather jackets, blue jeans, sneakers and masks."

"What kind of masks?" Monroe asked. "Like these monster masks? These rubber things you pull over your head?"

"No, just these little black masks over their eyes. Like robbers wear. They were robbers, these kids."

"And you say there were four of them?"

"Four, right."

"Ran out of the store with shopping bags and guns?"

31

"Shopping bags and guns, right."

"What kind of guns?" Monroe asked.

"Little guns."

"Like twenty-twos?"

"I'm not so good at guns. These were little guns."

"Like Berettas?"

"I'm not so good at guns."

"Like little Brownings?"

"I'm not so good at guns. They were little guns."

"Did you hear any shots as you approached the store?" Meyer asked.

"No, I didn't. I didn't know Ralph was dead till I walked inside."

"Ralph?" Monroe said.

"Ralph Adams. It's his store. Adams Wine & Spirits. He's been here in this same spot for twenty years."

"Not no more," Monroe said tactfully.

"So where'd these kids go when they came out of the store?" Meyer asked.

He was thinking this sounded like Fagin's little gang. The Artful Dodger, all that crowd. A cop he knew in England had written recently to say his kids would be celebrating—if that was the word for it—Halloween over there this year. Lots of American executives living in England, their kids had introduced the holiday to the British. Just what they need, Meyer thought. Maybe next year, twelve-year-old British kids'd start holding up liquor stores.

"They ran to this car parked at the curb," Kirby said.

"A vehicle?" Monroe said.

"Yeah, a car."

"An automobile?"

"A car, yeah."

"What kind of car?"

"I'm not so good at cars."

"Was it a big car or a little car?"

32

"A regular car."

"Like a Chevy or a Plymouth?"

"I'm not so good at cars."

"Like an Olds or a Buick?"

"A regular car, is all."

"They all got in this car?" Meyer asked.

"One in the front seat, three in the back."

"Who was driving?"

"A woman."

"How old a woman?"

"Hard to say."

"What'd she look like?"

"She was a blonde."

"What was she wearing?"

"I really couldn't see. It was dark in the car. I could see she was a blonde, but that's about all."

"How about when the kids opened the doors?" Monroe asked. "Didn't the lights go on?"

"Yeah, but I didn't notice what she was wearing. I figured this was maybe a car pool, you know?"

"What do you mean?"

"Well, the kids were all about the same age, so they couldn't all be *her* kids, you know what I mean? So I figured she was just driving maybe her own kid and some of his friends around. For Halloween, you know?"

"You mean the kid's mother was a wheelman, huh?"

"Well . . ."

"For a stickup, huh? A wheelman for four eleven-year-olds."

"Or twelve," Kirby said. "Eleven or twelve."

"These kids," Meyer said, "Were all of them boys?"

"They were *dressed* like boys, but I really couldn't say. They all went by so fast. Just came running out of the store and into the car."

"Then what?" Monroe asked.

"The car pulled away."

"Did you see the license plate?"

"I'm not so good at license plates," Kirby said.

"Was it you who called the police?" Meyer asked.

"Yes, sir. I called 911 the minute I saw Ralph laying dead there behind the counter."

"Did you use this phone here?" Monroe asked, indicating the phone alongside the register.

"No, sir. I went outside and used the pay phone on the corner."

"Okay, we've got your name and address," Monroe said, "we'll get in touch if we need you."

"Is there a reward?" Kirby asked.

"For what?"

"I thought there might be a reward."

"We're not so good at rewards," Monroe said. "Thanks a lot, we'll be in touch."

Kirby nodded glumly and walked out of the store.

"Halloween ain't what it used to be," Monroe said.

"You just got yourself another backup," Kling said.

"No," Eileen said.

"What do you mean no? You're going into one of the worst sections in the city . . ."

"Without you," she said.

". . . looking for a guy who's already killed . . ."

"Without *you*, Bert."

"Why?"

They were in an Italian restaurant near the Calm's Point Bridge. It was twenty minutes past six; Eileen had to be at the Seven-Two in forty minutes. She figured five minutes over the bridge, another five to the precinct, plenty of time to eat without hurrying. She probably shouldn't be eating, anyway. In the past, she'd found that going out hungry gave her a fighter's edge. Plenty of time to eat *after* you caught the guy. Have two martinis after you caught him, down a sirloin and a platter of fries. After you caught him. If you caught him. Sometimes you didn't catch him. Sometimes he caught you.

She was carrying her hooker threads and her hardware in a tote bag sitting on the floor to the left of her chair. Kling was sitting opposite her, hands clasped on the tabletop, leaning somewhat forward now, blond hair falling onto his forehead, intent look in his eyes, wanting to know why she didn't need a tagalong boyfriend tonight.

"Why do you think?" she asked.

The chef had overcooked the spaghetti. They'd specified *al dente* but this was the kind of dive where the help thought Al Dente was some guy with Mafia connections.

"I think you're crazy is what I think."

"Thanks."

"Damn it, if I can throw some extra weight your way . . ."

"I don't want you throwing anything my way. I've got a guy who's twice your size and a woman who can shoot her way out of a revolution. That's all I need. Plus myself."

"Eileen, I won't get in your way. I'll just . . ."

"No."

"I'll just be there if you need me."

"You really don't understand, do you?"

"No, I don't."

"You're not just another cop, Bert."

"I know that."

"You're my . . ."

She debated saying "boyfriend" but that sounded like a teenager's steady. She debated saying "lover" but that sounded like a dowager's kept stud. She debated saying "roommate" but that sounded like you lived with either another woman or a eunuch. Anyway, they weren't actually living together, not in the same apartment. She settled for what had once been a psychologist's term, but which had now entered the jargon as a euphemism for the guy or girl with whom you shared an unmarried state.

"You're my S.O.," she said.

35

"Your what?"

"Significant Other."

"I should hope so," Kling said. "Which is why I want to . . ."

"Listen, are you dense?" she asked. "I'm a cop going out on a job. What the hell's the matter with you?"

"Eileen, I . . ."

"Yes, *what*? Don't you think I can cut it?"

She had chosen an unfortunate word.

Cut.

She saw the look on his face.

"That's just what I mean," she said.

"What are you talking about?"

"I'm not going to get cut again," she said, "don't worry about it."

He looked at her.

"This time I shoot to kill," she said.

He took a deep breath.

"This spaghetti tastes like a sponge," she said.

"What time are you due there?"

"Seven."

He looked up at the clock.

"Where are they planting you?"

"A bar called Larry's. On Fairview and East Fourth."

"This guy Shanahan, is he any good?"

"I hope so," she said, and shoved her plate aside. "Could we get some coffee, do you think? And how come you're chalking off Annie?"

"I'm not . . ."

"I'd trade a hundred Shanahans for Annie."

"Calm down, Eileen."

"I'm calm," she said icily. "I just don't like your fucking attitude. You want to hand wrestle me? Prove you can go out there tonight and do the job better than I can?"

"Nobody said . . ."

"I can do the job," she said.

36

He looked into her eyes.

"I can do it," she said.

He didn't want to leave the parts where they'd be found too easily, and yet at the same time he didn't want to hide them so well that they wouldn't be discovered for weeks. This was tricky business here. Putting the pieces of the jigsaw in different places, making sure he wasn't spotted while he was distributing the evidence of bloody murder.

He'd dropped the first one behind a restaurant on Culver, near Sixth, figuring they'd be putting out more garbage when they closed tonight, hoping they'd discover the upper torso then and immediately call the police. He didn't want to scatter the various parts in locations too distant from each other because he wanted this to remain a strictly local matter, one neighborhood, one precinct, *this* precinct. At the same time, he couldn't risk someone finding any one of the parts so quickly that there'd be police crawling all over the neighborhood and making his job more difficult.

He wanted them to put it all together in the next little while.

Two, three days at the most, depending on how long it took them to find the parts and make identification.

By then, he'd be far, far away.

He cruised the streets now, driving slowly, looking for prospects.

The other parts of the body—the head, the hands, the arms, the lower torso—were lying on a tarpaulin in the trunk.

More damn kids in the streets tonight.

Right now, only the little ones were out. In an hour or so, you'd get your teenyboppers looking for trouble, and later tonight you'd get your older teenagers, the ones *really* hoping to do damage. Kick over a garbage can, find a guy's arm in it. How does that grab you, boys?

He smiled.

Police cars up ahead, outside a liquor store.

Bald guy coming out to the curb, studying the sidewalk and then the street.

Trouble.

But not *his* trouble.

He cruised on by.

Headed up to the Stem, made a right turn, scanning the storefronts. Kids swarming all over the avenue, trick or treat, trick or treat. Chinese restaurant there on the right. All-night supermarket on the corner. Perfect if there was a side alley. One-way side street, he'd have to drive past, make a right at the next corner, and then another right onto Culver, come at it from there. Stopped for the red light at the next corner, didn't want some eager patrolman pulling him over for a bullshit violation. Made the right turn. Another light on Culver. Waited for that one to change. Turned onto Culver, drove up one block, made another right onto the one-way street. Drove up it slowly. Good! An alley between the corner supermarket and the apartment house alongside it. He drove on by, went through the whole approach a second time. Guy in an apron standing at the mouth of the alley, lighting a cigarette. Drove by again. And again. And again and again until the alley and the sidewalk were clear. He made a left turn into the alley. Cut the ignition, yanked out the keys. Came around the car. Unlocked the trunk. Yanked out one of the arms. Eased the trunk shut. Walked swiftly to the nearest garbage can. Lifted the lid. Dropped the arm in it. Left the lid slightly askew on top of the can. Got back in the car again, started it, and backed slowly out of the alley and into the street.

Two down, he thought.

3

The police stations in this city all looked alike. Even the newer ones began looking like the older ones after a while. A pair of green globes flanking the entrance steps, a patrolman standing on duty outside in case anybody decided to go in with a bomb. White numerals lettered onto each of the globes: 72. Only the numbers changed. Everything else was the same. Eileen could have been across the river and uptown in the Eight-Seven.

Scarred wooden entrance doors, glass-paneled in the upper halves. Just inside the doors was the muster room. High desk on the right, looked like a judge's bench, waist-high brass railing some two feet in front of it, running the length of it. Sergeant sitting behind it. On the wall behind him, photographs of the mayor and the police commissioner and a poster printed with the Miranda-Escobedo warnings in English and in Spanish. Big American flag on the wall opposite the desk. Wanted posters on the bulletin board under it. She flashed her shield at the sergeant, who merely nodded, and then she headed for the iron-runged steps at the far end of the room.

Rack with charging walkie-talkies on the wall there, each unit stenciled PROPERTY OF 72ND PRECINCT. Staircase leading down to the holding cells in the basement, and up to the Detective Division on the second floor, hand-lettered sign indicating the way. She climbed the steps, apple green walls on either side of her, paint flaking and hand-smudged. She was wearing sensible, low-heeled walking shoes, a cardigan sweater over a white cotton blouse and a brown woolen skirt. The hooker gear was still in the tote bag, together with her hardware.

Down the corridor past the Interrogation Room, and the Clerical Office, and the men's and women's toilets, and the locker rooms, through a wide doorway, and then to the slatted wooden rail divider with green metal filing cabinets backed up against it on the inside. Stopped at the gate in the railing. Flashed the potsy again at the guy sitting behind the closest desk.

"Eileen Burke," she said. "I'm looking for Shanahan."

"You found him," Shanahan said, and got to his feet and came around the desk, hand extended. He was not as big as Annie had described him, five-eleven or so, maybe a hundred and seventy pounds, a hundred and eighty. Eileen wished he were bigger. Black hair and blue eyes, toothy grin, what Eileen's father used to call a black Irishman. "Mike," he said, and took her hand in a firm grip. "Glad to have you with us. Come on in, you want some coffee?"

"Sounds good," she said, and followed him through the gate in the railing and over to his desk. "Light with one sugar."

"Coming right up," he said, and went to where a Silex pot of water was sitting on a hot plate. "We only got instant," he said, "and that powdered creamer stuff, but the sugar's real."

"Good enough," she said.

He spooned instant coffee and creamer into a cup, poured hot water over it, spooned sugar into it with the same white plastic

40

spoon, stirred it, and then carried the cup back to his desk. She was still standing.

"Sit down, sit down," he said. "I'll buzz Lou, tell him you're here."

He looked up at the clock.

Ten minutes to seven.

"I thought you and Annie might be coming over together," he said, and picked up the phone receiver. "Good lady, Annie, I used to work with her in Robbery." He stabbed at a button on the base of the phone, waited, and then said, "Lou? Eileen Burke's here, you want to come on back?" He listened. "No, not yet." He looked at the clock again. "Uh-huh," he said. "Okay, fine." He put the receiver back on the cradle. "He'll be right here," he said to Eileen. "He's down the hall in Clerical, thought you might want to look over the reports on the case. We been working it together, Lou and me, not that we're getting such hot results. Which is why Homicide's on our backs, huh?"

She registered this last silently. She did not want a backup harboring a grudge over Homicide's interference. Some cops treated a tough case as if it were a sick child. Nurse it along, take its temperature every ten minutes, change the sheets, serve the hot chicken soup. Anybody else went near it, watch out. She hoped that wasn't the situation here. She wished the Seven-Two had *asked* for assistance, instead of having it dumped on them.

"How's the coffee?" Shanahan asked.

She hadn't touched it. She lifted the cup now. Squadroom coffee cups all looked alike. Dirty. In some squadrooms, the detectives had their initials painted on the cups, so they could tell one dirty cup from another. She sipped at the coffee. The imprint of her lipstick appeared on the cup's rim. It would probably still be there a month from now.

"Okay?" he said.

"Yes, fine," she said.

"Ah, here's Lou," he said, looking past her shoulder toward the railing. She turned in the chair just in time to see a slight, olive-complexioned man coming through the gate. Small mustache under his nose. Thick manila file folder in his right hand. Five-nine, she estimated. Moved like a bullfighter, narrow shoulders and waist, delicate hands. But you could never tell. Hal Willis at the Eight-Seven was only five-eight and he could throw any cheap thief on his ass in three seconds flat.

"Burke?" he said. "Nice to see you." No trace of an accent. Second- or third-generation American, she guessed. He extended his hand. Light, quick grip, almost instant release. No smile on his face. "Lou Alvarez," he said. "Glad to have you with us, we can use the help."

Party manners? Or a genuine welcome? She wished she knew. It would be her ass on the line out there tonight.

"I've got the file here," he said, "you might want to take a look at it while we're waiting for Rawles." He looked up at the clock. Still only five minutes to seven, but he nodded sourly. Was this an indication that he thought all women were habitually late? Eileen took the manila folder from him.

"You can skip over the pictures," he said.

"Why?"

Alvarez shrugged.

"Suit yourself," he said.

She was looking at the photographs when Annie walked in.

"Hi," Annie said, and glanced up at the clock.

Seven sharp.

"Hello, Mike," she said, "how's The Chameleon these days?"

"Comme-çi, comme-ça," Shanahan said, and shook her hand.

"We used to call him The Chameleon," she explained to Eileen, and then said, "Annie Rawles," and offered her hand to Alvarez.

"Lou Alvarez."

He took her hand. He seemed uncomfortable shaking hands with women. Eileen was suddenly glad it would be Shanahan out there with her tonight.

"Why The Chameleon?" she asked.

"Man of a thousand faces," Annie said, and looked at the photograph in Eileen's hand. "Nice," she said, and grimaced.

"Never mind the pictures," Alvarez said, "the pictures can't talk. We got statements in there from a couple of girls working the Zone, they give us a pretty good idea who we're looking for. Homicide's been pressuring us on this from minute one. That's 'cause the mayor made a big deal in the papers about cleaning up the Zone. So Homicide dumps it on us. You help us close this one out," he said to Eileen, "I'll personally give you a medal. Cast it in bronze all by myself."

"I was hoping for gold," Eileen said.

"You'd better take a look at those other pictures," Shanahan said.

"She don't have to look at them," Alvarez said.

"Which ones?" Eileen asked.

"You trying to spook her?"

"I'm trying to prepare her."

"She don't have to look at the pictures," Alvarez said.

But Eileen had already found them.

The earlier photographs had shown slashed faces, slit throats. These showed rampant mutilation below.

"Used the knife top and bottom," Shanahan said.

"Uh-huh," Eileen said.

"Slashed the first girl in a doorway two blocks from the bar."

"Uh-huh."

"Second one in an alleyway on East Ninth. Last one on Canalside."

"Uh-huh."

"What I'm saying is watch your step," Shanahan warned. "This ain't your garden variety weirdo jumpin' old ladies in the park. This is a fuckin' animal, and he means business. You get in the slightest bit of trouble, you holler. I'll be there in zero flat."

"I'm not afraid to holler," Eileen said.

"Good. We ain't trying to prove nothing here, we only want to catch this guy."

"I'm the one who catches him," Alvarez said, "I'll cut off his balls."

Eileen looked at him.

"What'd these other girls tell you?" Annie asked.

She did not want Eileen to keep studying those pictures. Once around the park was once too often. She took them from her hand, glanced at them only cursorily, and put them back into the folder. Eileen looked up at her questioningly. But Alvarez was already talking.

"You familiar with the Canal Zone, you know most of the girls work on the street," he said. "A car pulls up, the girl leans in the window, they agree on a price, and she does the job while the trick drives them around the block. It's Have Mouth, Will Travel, is what it is. But there's a bar near the docks where you get a slightly better-class hooker. We're talking comparative here. None of these girls are racehorses."

"What about this bar?" Annie said.

"It's called Larry's, on Fairview and East Fourth. The girls working the cars go in there every now and then, shoot up in the toilet, fix their faces, whatever. But there's also some girls a little younger and a little prettier who hang out there looking for tricks. Again, we're talking comparative. The girls on the meat rack outside get only five bucks for a handjob and ten for a blow-job. The ones working the bar get double that."

"The point is," Shanahan said, "the three girls he ripped were working the bar."

"So that's where you're planting me," Eileen said.

"Be safer all around," Alvarez said.

"I'm not looking for safe," she said, bristling.

"No, and you're not a real hooker, either," Alvarez said, bristling himself. "You stand out there on the street, you keep turning down tricks, the other girls'll make you for fuzz in a minute.

You'll be standing out there all alone before the night's ten minutes old."

"Okay," she said.

"I want this guy," he said.

"So do I."

"Not the way I want him. I got a daughter the age of that little girl in there," he said, wagging his finger at the folder.

"Okay," Eileen said again.

"You work the bar," Alvarez said, "you get a chance to call your own shots. You played hooker before?"

"Yes."

"Okay, so I don't have to tell you how to do your job."

"That's right, you don't."

"But there are some mean bastards down there in the Zone, and not all of them are looking to carve you up. You better step easy all around. This ain't Silk Stocking work."

"None of it is," Eileen said.

They both glared at each other.

"What'd they say about him?" Annie asked, jumping in.

"What?" Alvarez said.

Still angry. Figuring Homicide had sent him an amateur. Figuring she'd be spotted right off as a plant. Fuck you and your daughter both, Eileen thought. I know my job. And it's still *my* ass out there.

"These girls you talked to," Annie said. "What'd they say?"

"What?"

"About the guy, she means," Shanahan said. "This ain't gospel, Annie, this is maybe just hookers running scared, which they got every right to be. But on the nights of the murders, they remember a guy sitting at the bar. Drinking with the victims. The three he ripped. Same guy on three different Friday nights. Big blond guy, six-two, six-three, maybe two hundred pounds, dressed different each time, but blending in with everybody else in the joint."

45

"Meaning?"

"Meaning Friday-night sleaze. No uptown dude looking for kicks."

"Do you get any of those?" Eileen asked.

"Now and then," Shanahan said. "They don't last long in the Zone. Hookers ain't the only predators there. But this guy looked like one of the seamen off the ships. Which don't necessarily mean he *was*, of course."

"Anything else we should know about him?"

"Yeah, he had them in stitches."

"What do you mean?"

"Kept telling them jokes."

Eileen looked at him.

"Yeah, I know what you're thinking," Shanahan said. "A stand-up comic with a knife."

"Anything else?"

"He wears eyeglasses," Alvarez said.

"One of the girls thinks he has a tattoo on his right hand. Near the thumb. She's the only one who mentioned it."

"What kind of tattoo?"

"She couldn't remember."

"How many girls did you talk to?"

"Four *dozen* altogether," Alvarez said, "but only two of them gave us a handle."

"What time was this?" Annie asked. "When they saw him at the bar with the victims?"

"Varied. As early as nine, as late as two in the morning."

"Gonna be a long night," Annie said, and sighed.

Shanahan looked up at the clock.

"We better work out our strategy," he said. "So we can move when he does. Once he gets Eileen outside . . ."

He let the sentence trail.

The clock ticked into the silence of the squadroom.

"Do they know you down there in the Zone?" Eileen asked.

Shanahan looked at her.

"Do they?"

"Yes, but . . ."

"Then what the hell . . . ?"

"I'll be . . ."

"What good's a backup who . . .?"

"You won't recognize me, don't worry."

"No? What does the bartender say when you walk in? Hello, Detective Shanahan?"

"Six-to-five right this minute, you won't know me when I walk in," Shanahan said.

"Don't take the bet," Annie said.

"Will I know you if I have to holler?"

"You'll know me then. Because I'll be there."

"You're on," Eileen said. "But if I make you, I go straight home. I walk out of there and go straight home. Understood?"

"I'd do the same. But you won't know me."

"I hope not. I hope I lose the bet."

"You will," Annie promised.

"I didn't like your shooting him," the blonde at the wheel of the station wagon said. "That wasn't at all necessary, Alice."

Alice said nothing.

"You fire the guns in the air to scare them, to let them know you mean business, that's all. If that man you shot is dead, the rest of the night could be ruined for us."

Alice still said nothing.

"The beauty part of this," the blonde said, "is they never expect lightning to strike twice in the same night. Are you listening, kiddies?"

None of the kids said a word.

The digital dashboard clock read 7:04.

"They figure you do a stickup, you go home and lay low for a while. That's the beauty part. We play our cards right tonight, we go home with forty grand easy. I mean, a Friday night? Your liquor stores'll be open, some of them, till midnight, people stocking up for the weekend. Plenty of gold in the registers, kids, there for the taking. No more shooting people, have you got that?"

The kids said nothing.

The eyes behind the masks darted, covering both sides of the avenue. The slits in the masks made all the eyes look Oriental, even the blue ones.

"Especially you, Alice. Do you hear me?"

Alice nodded stiffly.

"There she is," the blonde said, "number two," and began easing the station wagon in toward the curb.

The liquor store was brightly lighted.

The lettering on the plate-glass window read FAMOUS BRANDS WINE & WHISKEY.

"Have fun, kids," the blonde said.

The kids piled out of the car.

"Trick or treat, trick or treat!" they squealed at an old woman coming out of the liquor store.

The old woman giggled.

"How *cute!*" she said to no one.

Inside the store, the kids weren't so cute.

The owner had his back to them, reaching up for a half-gallon of Johnny Walker Red.

Alice shot him at once.

The thirty-year-old account executive standing in front of the counter screamed.

She shot him, too.

The kids cleaned out the cash register in less than twelve seconds. One of them took a fifth of Canadian Club from the shelves. Then they ran out of the store again, giggling and yelling, "Trick or treat, trick or treat!"

"Hello, Peaches?" the man on the telephone said.

"Yes?"

"I've been trying to reach you all day. My secretary left your number, but she didn't say which agency you're with."

"Agency?"

"Yes. This is Phil Hendricks at Camera Works. We're shooting some stuff next week, and my secretary thought you might be right for the job. How old are you, Peaches?"

"Forty-nine," she said without hesitation. Lying a little. Well, lying by eleven years, but who was counting?

"That's perfect," he said, "this is stuff for the Sears catalogue, a half-dozen mature women modeling housedresses. If you'll give me the name of your agency, I'll call them in the morning."

"I don't have an agency," Peaches said.

"You don't? Well, that's strange. I mean . . . well, how long have you been modeling?"

"I'm not a model," Peaches said.

"You're not? Then how'd my secretary . . . ?"

There was a long, puzzled silence on the line.

"This *is* Peaches Muldoon, isn't it?" he said.

"Yes," she said, "but I've never . . ."

"349-4040?"

"That's the number. But your secretary must've . . ."

"Well, here's your name and number right here in her handwriting," he said. "But you say you're not a model?"

"No, I'm an RN."

"A what?"

"A registered nurse."

"Then how'd she . . . ?"

Another puzzled silence.

"Have you ever *thought* of modeling?" he asked.

"Well . . . not seriously."

"Because maybe you mentioned to someone that you were looking for modeling work, and this got to my secretary somehow. That's the only thing I can figure."

"What's your secretary's name?"

"Linda. Linda Greeley."

"No, I don't know anyone by that name."

"*Did* you mention to someone that you might be interested in modeling?"

"Well . . . you know . . . people are always telling me I should try modeling, but you know how people talk. I never take them seriously. I mean, I'm not a kid anymore, you know."

"Well, forty-nine isn't exactly *ancient,*" he said, and laughed.

"Well, I suppose not. But people try to flatter you, you know. I'm not really beautiful enough to do modeling. There's a certain type, you know. For modeling."

"What type *are* you, Peaches?" he asked.

"Well, I don't know how to answer that."

"Well, how tall are you, for example?"

"Five-nine," she said.

"How much do you weigh?"

"I could lose a little weight right now," she said, "believe me."

"Well, there isn't a woman on earth who doesn't think she could stand to lose a few pounds. How much *do* you weigh, Peaches?"

"A hundred and twenty," she said. Lying a little. Well, lying by ten pounds. Well, twenty pounds, actually.

"That's not what I'd call *obese,*" he said. "Five-nine, a hundred-twenty."

"Well, let's say I'm . . . well . . . zoftig, I guess."

"Are you Jewish, Peaches?"

"What?"

"That's a Jewish expression, zoftig," he said. "But Muldoon isn't Jewish, is it?"

"No, no. I'm Irish."

"Red hair, I'll bet."

"How'd you guess?" she asked, and laughed.

"And isn't that a faint Southern accent I detect?"

"I'm from Tennessee originally. I didn't think it still showed."

"Oh, just a trace. Which is why zoftig sounded so strange on your lips," he said. "Well, I'm sorry you're not a model, Peaches, truly. We're paying a hundred and twenty-five a hour, and we're shooting something like two dozen pages, so this could've come to a bit of change. Do you work full time as a nurse?"

"No. I do mostly residential work."

"Then you might be free to . . . ."

He hesitated.

"But if you're not experienced . . ."

He hesitated again.

"I just don't know," he said. "What we're looking for, you see, is a group of women who are mature and who could be accepted as everyday housewives. We're not shooting any glamor stuff here, no sexy lingerie, nothing like that. In fact . . . well, I don't really know. But your inexperience might be a plus. When you say you're a zoftig type, you don't mean . . . well, you don't look *too* glamorous, do you?"

"I wouldn't say I look glamorous no. I'm forty-nine, you know."

"Well, Sophia Loren's what? In her fifties, isn't she? And she certainly looks glamorous. What I'm saying is we're not looking for any Sophia Lorens here. Can you imagine Sophia Loren in a housedress?" he said, and laughed again. "Let me just write down your dimensions, okay? I'll discuss this with the ad agency in the morning, who knows? You said five-nine . . ."

"Yes."

"A hundred and twenty pounds."

"Yes."

"What are your other dimensions, Peaches? Bust size first."

"Thirty-six C."

"Good, we don't want anyone who looks *too*, well . . . you get some of these so-called *mature* models, they're big-busted, but very flabby. You're not flabby, are you?"

"Oh, no."

"And your waist size, Peaches?"

"Twenty-six."

"And your hips?"

"Thirty-six."

"That sounds very good," he said. "Are your breasts firm?" he asked.

"What?"

"Your breasts. Forgive me, but I know the ad agency'll want to know. They've had so many of these so-called mature models who come in with breasts hanging to their knees, they're getting a little gun-shy. Are your breasts good and firm?"

Peaches hesitated.

"What did you say your name was?" she asked.

"Phil Hendricks. At Camera Works. We're a professional photography firm, down here on Hall Avenue."

"Could I have your number there, please?"

"Sure. It's 847-3300."

"And this is for the Sears catalogue?"

"Yes, we begin shooting Monday morning. We've already signed two women, both of them in their late forties, good firm bodies, one of them used to model lingerie in fact. Do me a favor, will you, Peaches?"

"What's that?" she said.

"Is there a mirror in the room there?"

"Yes?"

"Does the phone reach over there? To where the mirror is?"

"Well, it's right there on the wall."

"Stand up, Peaches, and take a look at yourself in that mirror."

"Why should I do that?"

"Because I want an objective opinion. What are you wearing right now, Peaches?"

"A blouse and a skirt."

"Are you wearing shoes?"

"Yes?"

"High-heeled shoes?"

"Yes?"

"And a bra? Are you wearing a bra, Peaches?"

"Listen, this conversation is making me a little nervous," she said.

"I want your objective opinion, Peaches."

"About what?"

"About whether your breasts are good and firm. Can you see yourself in the mirror, Peaches?"

"Listen, this is really making me *very* nervous," she said.

"Take off your blouse, Peaches. Look at yourself in your bra, and tell me . . ."

She hung up.

Her heart was pounding.

A trick, she thought. He tricked me! How could I have been so dumb? Kept *talking* to him! Kept *believing* his pitch! Gave him all the answers he . . .

How'd he know my first name?

I'm listed as P. Muldoon, how'd he . . . ?

The answering machine. Hi, this is Peaches, I can't come to the phone just now. Of course. Said he'd been trying to reach me all day. Hi, this is Peaches, I can't come to the phone just now. Got the Muldoon and the number from the phone book, got my first name from the answering . . .

Oh, God, my *address* is in the book, too!

Suppose he *comes* here?

Oh dear God . . .

The telephone rang again.

Don't answer it, she thought.

It kept ringing.

Don't answer it.

Ringing, ringing.

But Sandra's supposed to call about the party.

Ringing, ringing, ringing.

If it's him again, I'll just hang up.

She reached out for the phone. Her hand was trembling. She lifted the receiver.

"Hello?" she said.

"Peaches?"

Was it him again? The voice didn't sound quite like his.

"Yes?" she said.

"Hi, this is Detective Andy Parker. I don't know if you remember me or not, I'm the one who locked up your crazy . . ."

"Boy, am I glad to hear from *you!*" she said.

"How about that?" Parker said, putting up the phone. "Remembered me right off the bat, told me to hurry on over!"

"You're unforgettable," Brown said. He was at his desk, typing a report on the torso they'd found behind the Burgundy Restaurant. Genero was looking over his shoulder, trying to learn how to spell dismembered.

The squadroom was alive with clattering typewriters.

Meyer sat in his dapper tan sports jacket typing a report on the kids who'd held up the liquor store and killed the owner.

Kling was at his own desk, typing a follow-up report on a burglary he'd caught three days ago. He was thinking about Eileen. He was thinking that right about now Eileen was in Calm's Point, getting ready to hit the Zone. He was thinking he might just wander over there later tonight. He looked up at the clock. Seven-fifteen. Maybe when he got off at midnight. See what was happening over there. She didn't have to know he was there looking around. A third backup never hurt anybody.

"So," Parker said, "if nobody needs me here, I think I'll mosey on over."

"Nobody needs you, right," Meyer said. "We got two homicides here, nobody needs you."

"Tell me the truth, Meyer," Parker said. "You think those two homicides are gonna be closed out tonight? In all your experience, have you ever closed out a homicide the same day you caught it? Have you?"

"I'm trying to think," Meyer said.

"In all my experience, that never happened," Parker said. "Unless you walk in and there's the perp with a smoking gun in

54

his hand. Otherwise, it takes weeks. Months sometimes. Sometimes *years.*"

"Sometimes *centuries*," Brown said.

"So what's your point?" Meyer said.

"My point is . . . *here's* my point," he said, opening his arms wide to the railing as Carella came through the gate. "Steve," he said, "I'm very glad to see you."

"You are?" Carella said.

He was a tall slender man with the build and stance of an athlete, brown hair, brown eyes slanting slightly downward to give his face a somewhat Oriental look. Tonight he was wearing a plaid sports shirt under a blue windbreaker, light cotton corduroy trousers, brown loafers. He went directly to his desk and looked in the basket there for any telephone messages.

"How's it out there?" Brown asked.

"Quiet," Carella said. "You got back okay, huh?" he asked Kling.

"I caught a taxi."

Carella turned to Parker. "Why are you so happy to see me?" he asked.

" 'Cause my colleague, Detective Meyer Meyer there, sitting at his desk there in his new jacket and his bald head, is eager to crack a homicide he caught, and he needs a good partner."

"That lets me out," Carella said. "What kind of homicide, Meyer?"

"Some kids held up a liquor store and shot the owner."

"Teenagers?"

"Eleven-year-olds."

"No kidding?"

"You gotta get yourself some lollipops," Brown said, "bait a trap with them."

"So is everybody all paired up nice now?" Parker asked. "You got Genero . . ."

"Thanks very much," Brown said.

"Meyer's got Steve . . ."

"I only stopped by for some coffee," Carella said.

"And I got Peaches Muldoon."

"Who's that?"

"A gorgeous registered nurse who's dying to see me."

"Sixty years old," Brown said.

"That's an old *lady!*" Genero said, shocked.

"Tell him."

"You ever date a nurse?" Parker said.

"Me?" Genero said.

"You, you. You ever date a nurse?"

"No. And I never dated a sixty-year-old lady, either."

"Tell him," Brown said.

"There is nothing like a nurse," Parker said. "It's a fact that in the book business if you put the word nurse in a title, you sell a million more copies."

"Who told you that?"

"It's a fact. A publisher told me that. In this office where they stole all his typewriters, this was maybe a year ago. A nurse in the title sells a million more copies."

"I'm gonna write a book called *The Naked and the Nurse,*" Brown said.

"How about *Gone with the Nurse?*" Meyer said.

"Or *Nurse-22?*" Carella said.

"Kid around, go ahead," Parker said. "You see me tomorrow morning, I'll be a wreck."

"I think you'd better stick around," Brown said. "Cotton's all alone out there."

"Bert can go hold his hand, soon as he finishes writing his book there."

"What book?" Kling asked, looking up from his typewriter.

"Me," Parker said, "I'm gonna go do a follow-up on a homicide investigation."

"Ten years old," Brown said.

"I thought you said eleven," Carella said, puzzled.

56

"The homicide. Ten years ago. He arrested a nut was killing priests. The nurse is his mother."

"The *kids* are eleven years old," Meyer said. "The ones who did the liquor store guy. Or twelve."

"That's what I thought," Carella said. He still looked puzzled.

"Any further objections?" Parker asked.

They all looked at him sourly.

"In that case, gentlemen, I bid you a fond adoo."

"You gonna leave a number where we can reach you?" Brown asked.

"No," Parker said.

The phone rang as he went through the gate and out into the corridor.

Watching him go, Brown shook his head and then picked up the phone receiver.

"Eighty-Seventh Squad, Brown."

"Artie, this is Dave downstairs," Murchison said. "You're handling that body in the garbage can, ain't you?"

"*Piece* of a body," Brown said.

"Well, we just got another piece," Murchison said.

4

Hawes had to keep telling himself this was strictly business.

Bermuda had been one thing, Bermuda was a thousand miles away, and besides he'd asked Annie to go along with him. This was another thing. This was the big bad city, and Annie lived here and besides he had a date with her tomorrow night, and furthermore Marie Sebastiani was married.

As of the moment, anyway.

The possibility existed that her husband had run off on his own to get away from her, though why anyone would want to abandon a beautiful, leggy blonde was beyond Hawes. If that's what had happened, though—Sebastian the Great tossing his junk all over the driveway and then taking off in the Citation—then maybe he was gone forever, in which case Marie wasn't as married as she thought she was. Hawes had handled cases where a guy went out for a loaf of bread and never was heard from since. Probably living on some South Sea island painting naked natives.

One case he had, the guy told his wife he was going down for a *TV Guide*. This was at eight o'clock. The wife sat through the eleven o'clock news, and then the Johnny Carson show, and then the late movie, and still no hubby with the *TV Guide*. Guy turned up in California six years later, living with two girls in Santa Monica. So maybe Sebastian the Great had pulled the biggest trick of his career, disappearing on his wife. Who knew?

On the other hand, maybe the lady's concern was well-founded. Maybe somebody had come across Frank Sebastiani while he was loading his goodies in the car, and maybe he'd zonked the magician and thrown his stuff out of the car and took off with the car and the magician both. Dump the magician later on, dead or alive, and sell the car to a chop shop. Easy pickings on a relatively quiet Halloween night. It was possible.

Either way, this was strictly business.

Hawes wished, however, that Marie wouldn't keep touching him quite so often.

The lady was very definitely a toucher, and although Hawes didn't necessarily buy the psychological premise that insisted casual body contact was an absolute prerequisite to outright seduction, he had to admit that her frequent touching of his arm or his shoulder or his hand was a bit unsettling. True enough, the touching was only to emphasize a conversational point—as when she told him again how grateful she was that he was taking her to dinner—or to indicate this or that possible restaurant along the Stem. He had parked the car on North Fifth, and they were walking westward now, heading downtown, looking for a place to eat. At seven thirty-five on a Friday night there were still a lot of restaurants open, but Marie had told him she felt like pizza and so he chose a little place just south of the avenue, on Fourth. Red-checkered tablecloths, candles in Chianti bottles, people waiting in line for tables. Hawes rarely pulled rank, but now he casually mentioned to the hostess that he was a detective working out of the Eight-Seven and he hadn't had anything to eat since he came on at four o'clock.

"This way, officer," the hostess said at once, and led them to a table near the window.

As soon as the hostess was gone, Marie said, "Does that happen all the time?"

"Does what happen?"

"The royal treatment."

"Sometimes," Hawes said. "You sure you only want pizza? There's plenty other stuff on the menu."

"No, that's what I really feel like. Cheese and anchovies."

"Would you like a drink?" he asked. "I'm on duty, but . . ."

"Do you really honor that?"

"Oh, sure."

"I'll just have beer with the pizza."

Hawes signaled to the waiter, and then ordered a large pizza with cheese and anchovies.

"Anything to drink?" the waiter asked.

"A draft for the lady, a Coke for me."

"Miller's or Michelob?"

"Miller's," Marie said.

The waiter went off again.

"This is really very nice of you," Marie said, and reached across the table to touch his hand briefly. A whisper touch. There, and then gone.

"As soon as we get back to the squadroom," Hawes said, "I'll call Auto again, see if they turned up anything on either of the vehicles."

He had made a call to Auto Theft from the custodian's office at the high school, reporting both the Citation and the Econoline, but he knew what the chances were of finding either vehicle tonight. He didn't want to tell her that.

"That would be a start," she said. "If they found the cars."

"Oh, sure."

A pained look crossed her face.

"I'm sure he's okay," Hawes said.

"I hope so."

"I'm sure."

He wasn't at all sure.

"I just keep thinking something terrible has happened to him. I keep thinking whoever stole the car . . ."

"Well, you don't know that for a fact," Hawes said.

"What do you mean?"

"Well, that the car was stolen."

"It's gone, isn't it?"

"Yes, but . . ."

He didn't want to tell her that maybe her husband had driven off on his own, heading for the wild blue yonder. Let the lady enjoy her pizza and her beer. If her husband had in fact abandoned her, she'd learn it soon enough. If he was lying dead in an alley someplace, she'd learn that even sooner.

He didn't bring up Jimmy Brayne again until after they'd been served.

She was digging into the pizza as if she hadn't eaten for a week. She ate the way that woman in the *Tom Jones* movie ate. Licked her lips, rolled her eyes, thrust pizza into her mouth as if she were making love to it. Come on, he thought. Strictly business here.

"He's normally reliable, is that right?" he said.

"Who?"

"Jimmy Brayne."

"Oh, yes. Completely."

"How long has he been working for you?"

"Three months."

"Started this July?"

"Yes. We did the act at a big Republican picnic on the Fourth. That was the first time Jimmy helped us."

"Carrying the stuff over in the van . . ."

"Yes."

"Picking it up later."

"Yes."

"Did he know where he was supposed to pick you up tonight?"

61

"Oh, sure. He dropped the stuff off at the school, of course he knew."

"Helped you unload it?"

"Yes."

"When was that? What time?"

"We got there about three-fifteen."

"Drove into the city together?"

"Frank and I were following the van."

"And Jimmy left the school at what time?"

"As soon as everything was on stage."

"Which was when?"

"Three-thirty, a quarter to four?"

"And he knew he was supposed to come back at five-thirty?"

"Yes."

"Is it possible he went someplace with your husband?"

"Like where?"

"For a drink or something? While you were changing?"

"Then why was all the stuff on the sidewalk?"

"It's just that . . . well, *both* of them disappearing . . ."

"Excuse me," the waiter said. "Officer?"

Hawes looked up.

"Officer, I hate to bother you," the waiter said.

"Yes?"

"Officer, there's somebody's arm in one of the garbage cans out back."

It was ten minutes to eight on the face of the clock on the locker-room wall.

They could have been teenagers swapping stories about their boyfriends.

Nothing in their conversation indicated they were going out hunting for a killer.

"Maybe I should've gone down later," Annie said. "The trial ended on Wednesday, I could've gone down then." She stepped into her short skirt, pulled it over her blouse and pantyhose, zipped up the side, fastened the button at the waist. "Trouble is, I wasn't sure I *wanted* to go."

"But he asked you, didn't he?" Eileen said.

"Sure, but . . . I don't know. I got the feeling he was just going through the motions. I'll tell you the truth, I think he wanted to go down there alone."

"What makes you think so?" Eileen asked.

She was wearing a low-cut blouse, and a wraparound skirt as short as Annie's, fastened on the right-hand side with a three-inch-long ornamental safety pin. The pin would be a last-ditch weapon if she needed it. If she needed it, she would poke out his eyes with it.

She was sitting on the bench in front of the lockers, pulling on high-heeled boots with floppy tops. A holster was strapped to her ankle inside the right boot. The pistol in the holster was a .25-caliber Astra Firecat automatic, with a two-and-a-half-inch barrel. It weighed a bit less than twelve ounces. Six-shot magazine, plus one in the firing chamber. She would pump all seven slugs into his face if she had to. There was a six-shot, .44-caliber Smith & Wesson hammerless revolver in her handbag. Plus a switchblade knife. Rambo, she thought. But it won't happen to me again. She was wearing two pairs of panties under her pantyhose. Her psychological weapons.

"I just . . . I don't know," Annie said. "I think Cotton's trying to end it, I just don't know."

She reached into the locker for her handbag, took out her cosmetics kit.

Eileen was standing now, looking down into the boots.

"Can you see this gun?" she asked.

Annie came over to her, lipstick in her hand. She looked down into the floppy top of the boot on Eileen's right foot.

"You might want to lower the holster," she said. "I'm getting a glimpse of metal."

63

Eileen sat again, rolled down the boot top, unstrapped the holster, lowered it, strapped it tight again.

"Maybe you should've gone down there, had it out with him," she said.

"Well, that would've ended it for sure. A man doesn't want a showdown on his vacation."

"But if he *wants* to end it . . ."

"I'm not sure of that."

"Well, what makes you think he *might* want to?"

"We haven't made love in the past two weeks."

"Bert and I haven't made love since the rape," Eileen said flatly, and stood up and looked down into the boots again.

"I'm . . . sorry," Annie said.

"Maybe that'll change tonight," Eileen said.

And Annie suddenly knew she was planning murder.

The old lady's name was Adelaide Davis, and she had seen the kids going into the liquor store on Culver and Twelfth. She was now standing outside on the sidewalk with Carella and Meyer. Inside the store, two ambulance attendants were hoisting the body of the owner onto a stretcher. Monroe was watching the operation, his hands in his jacket pockets. A tech from the Mobile Lab unit was dusting the register for fingerprints. The M.E. was kneeling over the second body. One of the attendants said, "Up," and they both lifted the stretcher and then stepped gingerly around the M.E. and the other body.

A crowd had gathered on the sidewalk. This was still only eight o'clock on a balmy Friday night, a lot of people were still in the streets. The ambulance attendants went past Mrs. Davis and the two detectives. Mrs. Davis watched them as they slid the stretcher into the ambulance. She watched them as they carried another stretcher back into the store. Patrolmen were shooing back the crowd now, making sure everyone stayed behind the barriers. Mrs. Davis felt privileged. Mrs. Davis felt like a star. She

64

could see some of her neighbors in the crowd, and she knew they envied her.

"I can't believe this," she said. "They looked so cute."

"How many were there, ma'am?" Carella asked.

Mrs. Davis liked Carella. She thought he was very handsome. The other detective was bald, she had never favored bald men. Wait'll she told her daughter in Florida that she'd witnessed a murder—*two* murders—and had talked to detectives like on television.

"Oh, just a handful of them," she said.

"How many would you say?" Meyer asked.

"Well, they went by very fast," she said. "But I'd say there were only four or five of them. They all jumped out of the station wagon and ran into the store."

"It was a station wagon, huh? The vehicle?"

"Oh, yes. For certain."

"Would you know the year and make?"

"I'm sorry, no. A blue station wagon."

"And these kids ran out of it with guns in their hands, huh?"

"No, I didn't see any guns. Just the shopping bags."

"No guns," Carella said.

"Not until they got inside the store. The guns were in the shopping bags."

"So when they got inside the store, these little boys pulled the guns and . . ."

"No, they were little girls."

Meyer looked at Carella.

"Girls?" he said.

"Yessir. Four or five little girls. All of them wearing these long dresses down to their ankles and little blonde wigs. They looked like little princesses."

"Princesses," Carella said.

"Yes," Mrs. Davis said. "They had on these masks that covered their entire faces, with sort of Chinese eyes on them—slanted,

65

you know—well, maybe Japanese, I guess. Well, like *your* eyes," she said to Carella. "Slanted, you know?"

"Yes, ma'am."

"And rosy cheeks painted on the masks, and bright red lips, and I think little beauty spots near the mouth. They were absolutely beautiful. Like little Chinese princesses. Or Japanese. Except that they were blonde."

"So they had on these Chinese-looking masks . . ."

"Or Japanese . . ."

"Right," Meyer said, "and they were wearing blonde wigs . . ."

"Yes, curly blonde wigs. Like Little Orphan Annie, except she's a redhead."

"Curly blonde wigs, and long dresses."

"Yes, like gowns. They looked like darling little princesses."

"What kind of shoes, ma'am?" Carella asked.

"Oh. I don't know. I didn't notice their shoes."

"They weren't wearing *sneakers,* were they?"

"Well, I really couldn't see. The gowns were very long."

The ambulance attendants were coming out with the second body now. The M.E. was still inside, talking to Monroe. Mrs. Davis looked down at the body as it went past. Before tonight, she had never seen a dead body except in a funeral home. Tonight, she'd just seen two of them close up.

"So they ran into the store," Carella said.

"Yes, yelling 'Trick or treat.' "

"Uh-huh," Carella said. "And pulled the guns . . ."

"Yes. And shot Mr. Agnello and the man who was in the store with him."

"Shot them right off?" Meyer said.

"Yes."

"Didn't say it was a stickup or anything, just started shooting."

"Yes. Mr. Agnello and the man with him."

"What happened next, ma'am? In the store. Did you keep watching?"

"Oh, yes. I was scared to death, but I kept watching."

"Did you see them clean out the cash register?"

"Yes. And one of them took a bottle of whiskey from the shelf."

"Then what?"

"They came running out. I was standing over there, to the left, over there, I'm not sure they saw me. I guess maybe they would've shot me, too, if they'd seen me."

"You were lucky," Carella said.

"Yes, I think I was."

"What'd they do then?" Meyer asked.

"They got back in the station wagon, and the woman drove them off."

"There was a woman driving the car?"

"Yes, a blonde woman."

"How old, would you know?"

"I really couldn't say. A sort of heavyset woman, she might've been in her forties."

"By heavyset . . ."

"Well, sort of stout."

"What was she wearing, would you remember?"

"I'm sorry."

Monroe was coming out of the liquor store.

"This the witness here?" he asked.

"A very good witness," Carella said.

"Well, thank you, young man," Mrs. Davis said, and smiled at him. She was suddenly glad she hadn't told him she'd wet her pants when she saw those little girls shooting Mr. Agnello.

"So what've we got here?" Monroe said. "An epidemic of kindergarten kids holding up liquor stores?"

"Looks that way," Carella said. "Where's your partner?"

"Who the hell knows where he is?" Monroe said. "Excuse me, lady."

"Oh, that's perfectly all right," she said. This was just like cable television, with the cursing and all. She couldn't wait to phone her daughter and tell her about it.

"Same kids, or what?" Monroe asked.

67

"What?" Mrs. Davis said.

"Excuse me, lady," Monroe said, "I was talking to this officer here."

"Little girls this time," Meyer said. "But it sounds like the same bunch. Same blonde driving the car."

"Nice lady, that blonde," Monroe said. "Driving kids to stickups. What kind of car, did you find out?" He turned to Carella. "What it is, the fart at the other store couldn't . . . excuse me, lady."

"Oh, that's perfectly all right," she said.

"A blue station wagon," Meyer said.

"You happen to know what year and make, lady?"

"I'm sorry, I don't."

"Yeah," Monroe said. "So all we got is the same big blonde driving four kids in a blue station wagon."

"That's about it," Meyer said.

"There wasn't homicides involved here, I'd turn this over to Robbery in a minute. You better give them a buzz, anyway."

"I already did," Meyer said. "After the first one."

One of the techs ambled out of the store.

"Got some bullets here," he said. "Who wants them?"

"What do they look like?" Monroe asked.

The technician showed him the palm of his hand. A white cloth was draped over it, and four spent bullets rested on it.

"Twenty-twos maybe," he said, and shrugged.

Mrs. Davis leaned over to look at the technician's palm.

"So, okay, lady," Monroe said, "you got any further business here?"

"Cool it," Carella said.

Monroe looked at him.

"I'll have one of our cars drop you home, Mrs. Davis," Carella said.

"A taxi service, they run up here," Monroe said to the air.

"Cool it," Carella said again, more softly this time, but somehow the words carried greater menace.

Monroe looked at him again and then turned to Meyer.

"Bag them bullets and get them over to Ballistics," he said. "Call Robbery and tell them we got another one."

"Sounds like good advice," Meyer said.

Monroe missed the sarcasm. He glared again at Carella, and then walked to where his car was parked at the curb.

Wait'll I tell my daughter! Mrs. Davis thought. A ride in a police car!

The patrolmen riding Charlie Four were approaching the corner of Rachel and Jakes, just cruising by, making another routine run of the sector when the man riding shotgun spotted it.

"Slow down, Freddie," he said.

"What do you see, Joe?"

"The van there. Near the corner."

"What about it?"

Joe Guardi opened his notebook. "Didn't we get a BOLO on a Ford Econoline?" He snapped on the roof light, scanned the notebook. "Yeah, here it is," he said. In his own handwriting, he saw the words "BOLO tan '79 Ford Econoline, RL 68-7210. Blue '84 Citation, DL 74-3681." The word BOLO stood for Be On the Lookout.

"Yeah," he said again. "Let's check it out."

The two men got out of the car. They flashed their torches over the van. License plate from the next state, RL 68-7210.

They tried the door closest to the curb.

Unlocked.

Freddie slid it all the way open.

Joe came around to the passenger side of the van. He slid the door open there, leaned in, and thumbed open the glove compartment.

"Anything?" Freddie asked.

"Looks like a registration here."

He took the registration out of a clear-plastic packet containing an owner's manual and a duplicate insurance slip.

69

The van was registered to a Frank Sebastiani whose address was 604 Eden Lane in Collinsworth, over the river.

The movie had let out at seven o'clock, and they had stopped for a drink on the Stem later. They had begun arguing in the bar, in soft, strained voices, almost whispers, but everyone around them knew they were having a fight because of the way they leaned so tensely over the small table between them. At first, the fight was only about the movie they'd seen. She insisted it had been based on a novel called *Streets of Gold*, by somebody or other, and he insisted the movie'd had nothing whatever to do with that particular novel, the movie was an original. "Then how come they're allowed to use the same title?" she asked, and he said, "They can do that 'cause you can't copyright a title. They can make the shittiest movie in the world if they want to, and they can call it *From Here to Eternity* or *The Good Earth* or even *Streets of Gold*, like they did tonight, and nobody in the world can do a damn thing about it." She glared at him for a moment, and then said, "What the hell do you know about copyright?" and he said, "A hell of a lot more than you know about *anything*," and by now they were really screaming at each other in whispers, and leaning tensely over the table, eyes blazing, mouths drawn.

They were still arguing on the way home.

But by now the argument had graduated to something more vital than an unimportant little novel called *Streets of Gold* or a shitty little movie that hadn't been based upon it.

They were arguing about sex, which is what they almost always argued about. In fact, maybe that's what they'd really been arguing about back there in the bar.

It was almost eight-thirty but the streets were already beginning to fill with teenagers on the prowl. Not all of them were looking for trouble. Many of them were merely seeking to let off adolescent energy. The ones out for fun and games were wearing costumes that weren't quite as elaborate as those the toddlers and later the teenyboppers had worn. Some of the teenage girls, using the excuse of Halloween to dress as daringly as they wished, walked the streets looking like hookers or Mata Haris or go-go dancers or sexy witches in black with slits up their skirts to their thighs. Some of the teenage boys were dressed like combat marines or space invaders or soldiers of fortune, most of them wearing bandoliers and carrying huge plastic machine guns or huge plastic death-ray guns. But these weren't the ones looking for trouble. The ones looking for trouble weren't dressed up for Halloween. They wore only their usual clothing, with perhaps a little blackening on their faces, the better to melt into the night. These were the ones looking to smash and to burn. These were the ones who had caused Lieutenant Byrnes to double-team his detectives tonight. Well, *almost* double-team them. Seven men on instead of the usual four.

The arguing couple came up the street toward the building where they lived, passing a group of teenage girls dressed like John Held flappers, sequined dresses with wide sashes, long cigarette holders, beaded bands around their foreheads, giggling and acting stoned, which perhaps they were. The couple paid no attention to them. They were too busy arguing.

"What it is," he said, "is there's never any spontaneity to it."

"Spontaneity, sure," she said. "What you mean by spontaneity is jumping on me when I come out of the shower . . ."

"There's nothing wrong with . . ."

"When I'm all clean."

"When do you *want* to make love?" he asked. "When you're all dirty?"

"I sure as hell don't want to get all *sweaty* again after I've just taken a shower."

"Then how about *before* you take your shower?"

"I don't like to make love when I feel all sweaty."

"So you don't like to do it when you're sweaty and you don't like to do it when you're *not* sweaty. When *do* you . . . ?"

"You're twisting what I'm saying."

"No, I'm not. The point I'm trying to make . . ."

71

"The point is you're a sex maniac. I'm trying to cook, you come up behind me and shove that humongous thing at me . . ."

"I don't see anything wrong with spontaneous . . ."

"Not while I'm cooking!"

"Then how about when you're *not* cooking? How about when I get home, and we're having a martini, how about . . . ?"

"You know I like to relax before dinner."

"Well, what the hell is making love? *I* find making love relaxing, I have to tell you. If *you* think making love is some kind of goddamn strenuous *obstacle* course . . ."

"I can't enjoy my cocktail if you're pawing me while I'm trying to re . . ."

"I don't consider *fondling* you *pawing* you."

"You don't know how to be gentle. All you want to do is jump on me like a goddamn *rapist!*"

"I do not consider passion *rape!*"

"That's because you don't know the difference between making love and . . ."

"Okay, what's this all about? Tell me what it's all about, okay? Do you want to quit making love *entirely*? You don't want to do it *before* your shower, you don't want to do it *after* your shower, you don't want to do it while we're *drinking* or while you're *cooking* or while we're watching television, or when we wake up in the morning, when the hell *do* you want to do it, Elise?"

"When I feel like doing it. And stop shouting!"

"I'm not *shouting*, Elise! When do you want to do it? Do you *ever* want to do it, Elise?"

"Yes!" she shouted.

"When?"

"Right now, Roger, okay? Right here, okay? Let's do it right here on the sidewalk, okay?"

"Fine by me!"

"You'd do it, too, wouldn't you?"

"Yes! Right here! *Anywhere!*"

"Well, I wouldn't! You'd have done it at the goddamn *movies* if I'd let you."

"I'd have done it in the bar, too, if you hadn't started *arguing* about that dumb movie!"

"You'd do it in church!" she said. "You're a maniac, is what you are."

"That's right, I'm a maniac! You're driving me crazy is why I'm a maniac!"

They were entering their building now. He lowered his voice.

"Let's do it in the elevator, okay?" he said. "You want to do it in the elevator?"

"No, Roger, I don't want to do it in the goddamn elevator."

"Then let's take the elevator up to the roof, we'll do it on the roof."

"I don't want to do it on the goddamn roof, either."

He stabbed angrily at the elevator button.

"Where *do* you want to do it, Elise? *When* do you want to do it, Elise?"

"Later."

"When later?"

"When Johnny Carson goes off."

"If *we* were on television," he said, "and Johnny Carson was watching *us*," he said, "and he had a big hard-on . . ."

"We happen to *live* here, Roger."

". . . do you think Johnny Carson would wait till *we* were off to do it? Or would Johnny Carson . . . ?"

"I don't care what Johnny Carson would do or wouldn't do. I don't even *like* Johnny Carson."

"Then why do you want to wait till he's off?"

The elevator doors opened.

At first they thought it was a stuffed dummy. The lower half of a scarecrow or something. Blue pants, blue socks, black shoes, black belt through the trouser loops. A Halloween prank. Some kids had tossed half a stuffed dummy into the elevator.

73

And then they realized that a jagged, bloody edge of torn flesh showed just above the dummy's waist, and they realized that they were looking at the lower torso of a human being and Elise screamed and they both ran out of the lobby and out of the building and up to the pay phone on the corner, where Roger breathlessly dialed 911.

The cruising cops in Boy Two responded within three minutes.

One of the cops got on the walkie-talkie to the Eight-Seven.

The other cop, although he should have known better, went through the stiff's trousers and found a wallet in the right hip pocket.

Inside the wallet, which he also shouldn't have touched, he found a driver's license with a name and an address on it.

"Well, here's who he is, anyway," he said to his partner.

5

"What this is," Parker said, "you had an obscene phone call, is what this is."

"That's what I figured it was," Peaches said.

She still looked pretty good. Maybe like a woman in her early fifties. Good legs—well, the legs never changed—breasts still firm, hair as red as he remembered it, maybe with a little help from Clairol. Wearing a simple skirt and blouse, high-heeled shoes. Legs tucked up under her on the couch. He was glad he'd shaved.

"They're not all of them what you think they're gonna be," Parker said. "I mean, they don't get on the phone and start talking dirty right away—well, some of them do—but a lot of them have a whole bagful of tricks, you don't realize what's happening till they already got you doing things."

"That's *just* what happened," Peaches said. "I didn't realize what was going on. I mean, he gave me his *name* and . . ."

"Phil Hendricks, right?" Parker said. "Camera Works."

"Right. And his address and his phone number . . ."

"Did you try calling that number he gave you?"

"Of *course* not!"

"Well, I'll give it a try if you like, but I'm sure all that was phony. I had a case once, this guy would call numbers at random, hoping to get a baby-sitter. He'd finally get a sitter on the phone, tell her he was doing research on child abuse, smooth-talked these fifteen-, sixteen-year-old girls into slapping around the babies they were sitting."

"What do you mean?"

"He'd tell them how important it was in their line of work to guard against their own tendencies, everybody has such tendencies—this is him talking—and child abuse is an insidious thing. And he'd have them interested and listening, and he'd say, 'I know you yourself must have been tempted on many an occasion to slap the little kid you're sitting, especially when he's acting up,' and the fifteen-year-old sitter goes, 'Oh, boy, you said it,' and he goes, 'For example, haven't you been tempted at least once tonight to smack him around?' and she goes, 'Well . . .' and he goes, 'Come on, tell me the truth, I'm a trained child psychologist,' and before you know it, he's got her convinced that the best way to *curb* these tendencies is to *release* them, you know, in a therapeutic manner, slap the kid gently, why don't you go get the kid now? And she runs to get the kid and he tells her to give the kid a gentle slap, and before you know it he's got her beating the daylights out of the kid while he's listening and getting his kicks. That was this one case I had, I may write a book about it one day."

"That's fascinating," Peaches said.

"Another case I had, this guy would look in the paper for ads where people were selling furniture. He was looking for somebody selling a kid's bedroom set, you know? Getting rid of the kiddy furniture, replacing it with more mature stuff. He knew he'd get either a youngish mother or a teenage girl on the phone—it's usually the girls who want their furniture changed when they get into their teens. And he'd start talking to them about the furniture, either the mother if she was home, or the teenage girl if the mother was out, and while he was talking to them, because it would be a long conversation, you know, what kind of bed is it, and how's the mattress, and how many drawers in the dresser, like that, while he was on the phone he'd be . . . well . . ."

"He'd be masturbating," Peaches said.

"Well, yes."

"Do you think the man who called me tonight was masturbating while he talked to me?"

"That's difficult to say. From what you told me, he either *was* already, or was leading up to it. He was trying to get you to talk about your body, you see. Which is still very nice, by the way."

"Well, thank you," Peaches said, and smiled.

"Sounds to me like that's what would've set him off. Getting you to strip in front of the mirror there. You'd be surprised how many women go along with something like that. He hooks them into thinking they've got a shot at modeling—there isn't a woman alive who wouldn't like to be a model—and then he gets them looking at themselves while he does his number."

"That's when I began to realize," Peaches said.

"Sure."

"When he told me to take off my blouse."

"Sure. But lots of women don't realize even then. You'd be surprised. They just go along with it, thinking it's legit, never guessing what's happening on the other end."

"I'm afraid he might come here," Peaches said.

"Well, these guys don't usually do that," Parker said. "They're not your rapists or your stranglers, usually. Don't quote me on that, you got all *kinds* of nuts out there. But usually your telephone callers aren't your violent ones."

"Usually," Peaches said.

"Yes," Parker said.

77

"Because he has my address, you see."

"Um," Parker said.

"And my name is on the mailbox downstairs. With the apartment number."

"I know. I saw it when I rang the bell. But that says P. Muldoon."

"Sure, but that's what's in the phone book, too. P. Muldoon."

"Well, I doubt he'll be coming around here. He may not even call again. What I'd do, though, if I was you, I'd change that message on your answering machine. Lots of single girls, they do these fancy messages, music going in the background, they try to sound sexy, it makes the caller think he's got some kind of swinger here. Better to just put a businesslike message on the machine. Something like, 'You've reached 123-4567,' and then, 'Please leave a message when you hear the beep.' Strictly business. You don't have to explain that you can't come to the phone because everybody *knows* they caught the machine. And of course you shouldn't say, 'I'm out just now,' or anything like that, because that's an invitation to burglars."

"Yes, I know."

"The point is most people today are familiar with answering machines, they *know* they're supposed to leave a message when they hear the beep, so you don't have to give them a whole list of instructions, and you don't have to sound cute, either. Your friends hear that cute little message a coupla hundred times, they want to shoot you. An obscene caller hears that cute little message, he figures he's got a live one, and he'll keep calling back till he can get you talking."

"I see," Peaches said.

"Yeah," Parker. "Do you have any male friends who can record a message for you?"

"Well . . ."

"Because that's usually the best thing. That way any nut who's running his finger down the book for listings with only a first initial, he comes across P. Muldoon, he gets a man's voice on the an-

78

swering machine, he figures he got a Peter Muldoon or a Paul Muldoon, but not a Peaches Muldoon. He won't call back. So that's a good way to go unless you're afraid it'll scare off any men who may be calling you legitimately. That's up to you."

"I see," Peaches said.

"Yeah," Parker said. "Now with this guy who called you tonight, he already knows there's a Peaches Muldoon living here, and he already got you going pretty far with his little routine, so he may call you back. What we'll do if he keeps calling you, we'll put a trap on the line . . ."

"A trap?"

"Yeah, so we can trace the call even if he hangs up. You've got to let me know if he calls again."

"Oh, I *will*," Peaches said.

"So that's about it," Parker said. "Though maybe he won't call again."

"Or come here."

"Well, like I said, I don't think he'll do that. But you know how to reach me if he does."

"I really appreciate this," Peaches said.

"Well, come on, I'm just doing my job."

"Are you on duty right now?" she asked.

"Not exactly," he said.

"Wanna come to party?" she said.

Marie Sebastiani was showing them another card trick.

"What we have is three cards here," she said. "The ace of spades, the ace of clubs, and the ace of diamonds." She fanned the cards out, the ace of diamonds under the ace of spades on the left and the ace of clubs on the right. "Now I'm going to put these three aces face down in different parts of the deck," she said, and started slipping them into the deck.

Five detectives were watching her.

Carella was on the phone to Ballistics, telling them he wanted a fast comeback on the bullets the techs had recovered at Famous

Brands Wine & Liquors. The guy at Ballistics was giving him a hard time. He told Carella this was almost a quarter to nine already, and he went off at midnight. The lab would be closed till eight tomorrow morning. He was telling Carella the report could wait till then. Carella was telling him he wanted it right away. Meanwhile, he was watching Marie's card trick at the same time.

The other four detectives were either standing around Carella's desk, or else sitting on parts of it. His desk resembled a convention center. Brown was standing just to the left of Carella, his arms folded across his chest. He knew this was going to be another good trick. She had done four card tricks since Hawes came back to the squadroom with her. This was after Hawes had called Brown from a little pizza joint on North Fourth to say one of the people there had found an arm in a garbage can out back. Brown had rushed on over with Genero. Now they had three pieces. Or rather the Medical Examiner had them. The upper torso and a pair of arms. Brown was hoping the M.E. would be able to tell him whether or not the parts belonged to each other. If the parts didn't match, then they were dealing with maybe three separate corpses. Like the three cards Marie Sebastiani now slipped face down into various places in the deck.

"The ace of spades," she said. "The ace of diamonds." Sliding it into the deck. "And the ace of clubs."

Genero was watching the cards carefully. He felt certain he'd be able to catch the secret here, though he hadn't been able to on the last four tricks. He wondered if they were breaking some kind of regulation, having a deck of cards here in the squadroom. He was hoping the M.E. would call to say they were dealing with a single corpse here. Somehow, the idea of a single chopped-up corpse was more appealing than three separate chopped-up corpses.

Meyer was standing beside him, watching Marie's hands. She had long slender fingers. The fingers slipped the cards into the deck as smoothly as a drug dealer running a knife into a competitor. Meyer was wondering why those little kids had changed their clothes before pulling the second stickup. He was also wondering whether there'd be a third stickup. Were they finished for the night? Nitey-nite, kiddies, beddy-bye time. Or were they just starting?

Hawes was standing closest to Marie. He could smell her perfume. He was hoping her husband had abandoned her and run off to Hawaii. He was hoping her husband would call her from Honolulu to say he had left her. This would leave a cold, empty space in Marie's bed. Her proximity now was stupefyingly intoxicating. Hawes guessed it was her perfume. He had not yet told her that the blues had located the van. No word on the Citation yet. Maybe hubby and his apprentice had flown off to Hawaii together. Maybe hubby was gay. Hawes glanced at Marie's pert little behind as she leaned over the desk to pick up the deck of cards. He was sorely tempted to put his hand on her behind.

"Who'd like to shuffle?" she asked.

"Me," Genero said. He was sure the secret of all her tricks had something to do with shuffling.

Marie handed the deck to him.

Meyer watched her hands.

Genero shuffled the cards and then handed the deck back to her.

"Okay, Detective Brown," she said. "Pick one of those three cards. Either the ace of clubs, the ace of diamonds, or the ace of spades."

"Clubs," Brown said.

She riffled through the deck, the cards face up, searching for it. When she found the ace of clubs, she pulled it out, and tossed it onto the desk. "Detective Meyer?" she said. "How about you?"

"The ace of spades," he said.

"I don't get it," Genero said.

Marie was looking through the deck again.

"Where's the trick?" Genero said. "If you're looking at the cards, of *course* you're going to find them."

"Right you are," she said. "Here's the ace of spades."

81

She tossed it onto the desk.

"Which card do *you* want?" she asked Genero.

"There's only one card left."

"And which one is that?"

"The ace of diamonds."

"Okay," she said, and handed him the deck. "Find it for me."
Genero started looking through the deck.

"Have you found it yet?" she asked.

"Just hold on a minute, okay?" he said.

He went through the entire deck. No ace of diamonds. He
went through it a second time. Still no ace of diamonds.

"Have you got it?" she asked.

"It isn't here," he said.

"Are you sure? Take another look."

He went through the deck a third time. Still no ace of diamonds.

"But I saw you put it back in the deck," he said, baffled.

"Yes, you did," she said. "So where is it?"

"I give up, where is it?"

"Right here," she said, grinning, and reached into her blouse,
and pulled the ace of diamonds out of her bra.

"How'd you do that?" Hawes asked.

"Maybe I'll tell you sometime," Marie said, and winked at
him.

The telephone rang. Carella was sitting closest to it. He picked
up.

"Eighty-Seventh Squad, Carella," he said.

"Steve, this is Dave downstairs. Let me talk to either Brown or
Genero, okay? Preferably Brown."

"Hold on a sec," Carella said, and extended the receiver to
Brown. "Murchison," he said.

Brown took the receiver.

"Yeah, Dave?"

"I just got a call from Boy Two," Murchison said. "It looks like we maybe got an ID on that body been turning up in bits and pieces. A couple found the lower half in their building, in the elevator. *If* it's the same body. Wallet in the guy's hip pocket, driver's license in it. You better run on over there, I'll notify Homicide."

"What's the address?" Brown asked, and listened. "Got it," he said, writing. "And the couple's name?" He listened again. "Okay. And the name on the license? Okay," he said, "we're rolling." He put the receiver back on the cradle. "Let's go, Genero," he said, "the pieces are coming together. We just got ourselves the lower half. Name tag on it, this time."

"This trick is called The Mystic Prediction," Marie said, and began shuffling the cards.

"What do you mean, name tag?" Genero asked.

"The dead man's carrying a wallet," Brown said.

"How?"

"What do you mean *how*? In his *pocket* is how."

"I'm going to ask any one of you to write down a three-figure number for me," Marie said.

"You mean he's wearing pants?" Genero said.

"Unless there's a pocket sewn on his ass," Brown said.

"You mean there's *pants* on the lower half of the body?"

"Whyn't we run on over and see for ourselves, okay?"

"Who wants to write down three numbers for me?" Marie asked. "Any three numbers?"

"And his name's in the wallet?" Genero said.

"On his driver's license," Brown said. "Let's go."

Both men started for the railing. Kling was coming back from the men's room down the hall. He opened the gate and made a low bow, sweeping his arm across his body, ushering them through.

"So what's his name?" Genero asked.

"Frank Sebastiani," Brown said.

And Marie fainted into Kling's arms.

* * *

Annie Rawles was already in place when Eileen pulled up out-side Larry's. The clock behind the bar, a big ornate thing rimmed with orange neon, read five minutes to nine. Through the plate-glass window, Annie could see the white Cadillac edging into the curb. The bartender could see it, too. They both watched with casual interest as the driver cut the engine, Annie nursing a beer, the bartender polishing glasses. The man behind the wheel of the car was big and black and wearing pimp threads.

They both watched as Eileen got out of the car on the curb side, long legs flashing and signaling, little hidden pistol tucked into one of those soft sexy boots, high-stepping her way toward the entrance door now.

Mr. Pimp leaned across the seat, rolled down the window on the curb side.

Yelled something to Eileen.

Eileen sashayed back, bent over to look in the window.

Short skirt tight across her ass, flashing, advertising.

Started shaking her head, waving her arms around.

"She's givin' him sass," the bartender said.

Southern accent you could cut with a butter knife. Maybe this wasn't so far from Houston after all.

"An' he don't like it none," the bartender said.

Mr. Pimp came storming out of the car on the driver's side, walked around the car, stood yelling at her on the sidewalk.

Eileen kept shaking her head, hands on her hips.

"Won't stop sassin' him, will she?" the bartender said.

And suddenly Mr. Pimp slapped her.

"Whomp her good," the bartender said, nodding encourage-ment.

Eileen staggered back from the blow, her green eyes blazing. She bunched her fists and went at him as if she'd kill him, but he shoved her away, turned her toward the bar, shoved her again, toward the door of the bar this time, and then strutted back to the Caddy, lord of all he surveyed. Eileen was nursing her cheek. She glared at the Caddy as it pulled away from the curb.

Act One had begun.

Four pieces had become one piece.

Maybe.

They showed her the bundle of clothing first.

Black shoes, blue socks. Blue trousers. Black belt. White Jockey undershorts. Blood stains on the waistband of the trousers and the shorts.

"I . . . I think those are Frank's clothes," Marie said.

Some coins in one of the pants pockets. A quarter, two dimes, and a penny.

No keys. Neither house keys nor car keys.

A handkerchief in another pocket.

And a wallet.

Black leather.

"Is this your husband's wallet?" Brown asked.

"Yes."

Her voice very soft. As if what they were showing her demanded reverence.

In the wallet, a driver's license issued to Frank Sebastiani of 604 Eden Lane, Collinsworth. No credit cards. Voters Registration card, same name, same address. A hundred and twenty dollars in twenties, fives, and singles. Tucked into one of the little pockets was a green slip of paper with the words MARIE'S SIZES hand-lettered onto it, and beneath that:

> Hat: 22
> Dress: 8
> Bra: 36B
> Belt: 26
> Panties: 5
> Ring: 5

Gloves:	6½
Stockings:	9½ (Medium)
Shoes:	6½B

"Is this your husband's handwriting?" Brown asked.

"Yes," Marie said. Same soft reverential voice.

They led her inside.

The morgue stank.

She reeled back from the stench of human gasses and flesh.

They walked her past a stainless-steel table upon which the charred remains of a burn-victim's body lay trapped in a pugilistic pose, as though still trying to fight off the flames that had consumed it.

The four pieces of the dismembered corpse were on another stainless-steel table. They were casually assembled, not quite joining. Lying there on the table like an incomplete jigsaw puzzle.

She looked down at the pieces.

"There's no question they're the same body," Carl Blaney said.

Lavender-eyed, white-smocked. Standing under the fluorescent lights, seeming neither to notice nor to be bothered by the intolerable stink in the place.

"As for identification . . ."

He shrugged.

"As you see, we don't have the hands or the head yet."

He addressed this to the policemen in the room. Ignoring the woman for the time being. Afraid she might puke on his polished tile floor. Or in one of the stainless-steel basins containing internal organs. Three cops now. Hawes, Brown, and Genero. Two cases about to become one. Maybe.

The lower half of the torso was naked now.

She kept looking down at it.

"Would you know his blood type?" Blaney asked.

"Yes," Marie said. "B."

"Well, that's what we've got here."

Hawes knew about the appendectomy and meniscectomy scars because she'd mentioned them while describing her husband. He said nothing now. First rule of identification, you didn't prompt the witness. Let them come to it on their own. He waited.

"Recognize anything?" Brown asked.

She nodded.

"What do you recognize, ma'am?"

"The scars," she said.

"Would you know what kind of scars those are?" Blaney asked.

"The one on the belly is an appendectomy scar."

Blaney nodded.

"The one on the left knee is from when he had the cartilage removed."

"That's what those scars are," Blaney said to the detectives.

"Anything else, ma'am?" Brown asked.

"His penis," she said.

Neither Blaney nor any of the detectives blinked. This wasn't the Meese Commission standing around the pieces of a corpse, this was a group of professionals trying to make positive identification.

"What about it?" Blaney asked.

"There should be a small . . . well, a beauty spot, I guess you'd call it," Marie said. "On the underside. On the foreskin."

Blaney lifted the corpse's limp penis in one rubber-gloved hand. He turned it slightly.

"This?" he asked, and indicated a birthmark the size of a pinhead on the foreskin, an inch or so below the glans.

"Yes," Marie said softly.

Blaney let the penis drop.

The detectives were trying to figure out whether or not all of this added up to a positive ID. No face to look at. No hands to examine for fingerprints. Just the blood type, the scars on belly and leg, and the identifying birthmark—what Marie had called a beauty spot—on the penis.

"I'll work up a dental chart sometime tomorrow," Blaney said.

"Would you know who his dentist was?" Hawes asked Marie.

"Dentist?" she said.

"For comparison later," Hawes said. "When we get the chart."

She looked at him blankly.

"Comparison?" she said.

"Our chart against the dentist's. If it's your husband, the charts'll match.'"

"Oh," she said. "Oh. Well . . . the last time he went to a dentist was in Florida. Miami Beach. He had this terrible toothache. He hasn't been to a dentist since we moved north."

"When was that?" Brown asked.

"Five years ago."

"Then the most recent dental chart . . ."

"I don't even know if there *is* a chart," Marie said. "He just went to somebody the hotel recommended. We had a steady gig at the Regal Palms. I mean, we never had a *family* dentist, if that's what you mean."

"Yeah, well," Brown said.

He was thinking Dead End on the teeth.

He turned to Blaney.

"So what do you think?" he said.

"How tall was your husband?" Blaney asked Marie.

"I've got all that here," Hawes said, and took out his notebook. He opened it to the page he'd written on earlier, and began reading aloud. "Five-eleven, one-seventy, hair black, eyes blue, appendectomy scar, meniscectomy scar."

"If we put a head in place there," Blaney said, "we'd have a body some hundred and eighty centimeters long. That's just about five-eleven. And I'd estimate the weight, given the separate sections here, at about what you've got there, a hundred-seventy, a hundred-seventy-five, in there. The hair on the arms, chest, legs, and pubic area is black—which doesn't necessarily mean the *head* hair would match it exactly, but at least it rules out a blonde or a redhead, or anyone in the brown groupings.

This hair is very definitely *black*. The eyes—well, we haven't got a head, have we?"

"So have we got a positive ID or what?" Brown asked.

"I'd say we're looking at the remains of a healthy white male in his late twenties or early thirties," Blaney said. "How old was your husband, madam?"

"Thirty-four," she said.

"Yes," Blaney said, and nodded. "And, of course, identification of the birthmark on the penis would seem to me a conclusive factor."

"Is this your husband, ma'am?" Brown asked.

"That is my husband," Marie said, and turned her head into Hawes' shoulder and began weeping gently against his chest.

The hotel was far from the precinct, downtown on a side street off Detavoner Avenue. He'd deliberately chosen a fleabag distant from the scene of the crime. *Scenes* of the crime, to be more accurate. Five separate scenes if you counted the head and the hands. Five scenes in a little playlet entitled "The Magical and Somewhat Sudden Disappearance of Sebastian the Great."

Good riddance, he thought.

"Yes, sir?" the desk clerk said. "May I help you?"

"I have a reservation," he said.

"The name, please?"

"Hardeen," he said. "Theo Hardeen."

Wonderful magician, long dead. Houdini's brother. Appropriate name to be using. Hardeen had been famous for his escape from a galvanized iron can filled with water and secured by massive locks. Failure Means a Drowning Death! his posters had proclaimed. The risks of failure here were even greater.

"How do you spell that, sir?" the clerk asked.

"H-A-R-D-E-E-N."

"Yes, sir, I have it right here," the clerk said, yanking a card. "Hardeen, Theo. That's just for the one night, is that correct, Mr. Hardeen?"

"Just the one night, yes."

"How will you be paying, Mr. Hardeen?"

"Cash," he said. "In advance."

The clerk figured this was a shack-up. One-night stand, guy checking in alone, his bimbo—or else a hooker from the Yellow Pages—would be along later. Never explain, never complain, he thought. Thank you, Henry Ford. But charge him for a double.

"That'll be eighty-five dollars, plus tax," he said, and watched as the wallet came out, and then a hundred-dollar bill, and the wallet disappeared again in a wink. Like he figured, a shack-up. Guy didn't want to show even a glimpse of his driver's license or credit cards, the Hardeen was undoubtedly a phony name. Theo Hardeen? The names some of them picked. Who cared? Take the money and run, he thought. Thank you, Woody Allen.

He calculated the tax, made change for the C-note, and slid the money across the desk top. Wallet out again in a flash, money disappearing, wallet disappearing, too.

"Did you have any luggage, sir?" he asked.

"Just the one valise."

"I'll have someone show you to your room, sir," he said, and banged a bell on the desk. "Front!" he shouted. "Checkout time is twelve noon, sir. Have a nice night."

"Thank you."

A bellhop in a faded red uniform showed him to the third-floor room. Flicked on the lights in the bathroom. Taught him how to operate the window air-conditioning unit. Turned on the television set for him. Waited for the tip. Got his fifty cents, looked at it on the palm of his hand, shrugged, and left the room. What the hell had he expected for carrying that one bag? Rundown joint like this—well, that's why he'd picked it. No questions asked. In, out, thank you very much.

He looked at the television screen, and then at his watch.

A quarter past nine.

Forty-five minutes before the ten o'clock news came on.

He wondered if they'd found the four pieces yet. Or either of

90

the cars. He'd left the Citation in the parking lot of an A & P four blocks north of the river, shortly after he'd deep-sixed the head and the hands.

Something dumb was on television. Well, *everything* on television was dumb these days. He'd have to wait till ten o'clock to see what was happening, if anything.

He took off his shoes, lay full length on the bed, his eyes closed, and relaxed for the first time today.

By tomorrow night at this time, he'd be in San Francisco.

6

Eileen came out of the ladies' room and walked toward the far-
thest end of the bar, where a television set was mounted on the
wall. Quick heel-clicking hooker glide, lots of ass and ankle in it.
She didn't even glance at Annie, sitting with her legs crossed at
the cash-register end of the bar. Two or three men sitting at
tables around the place turned to look at her. She gave them a
quick once-over, no smile, no come-on, and took a stool next to
a guy watching the television screen. She was still fuming.
In the mirror behind the bar, she could still see the flaming
imprint of his hand on her left cheek. The bartender ambled
over.

"Name it," he said.

"Rum-Coke," she said. "Easy on the rum."

"Comin'," he said, and reached for a bottle of cheap rum on
the shelf behind him. He put ice in a glass, short-jiggered some

rum over it, filled the glass with Coke from a hose. "Three bucks even," he said, "a bargain. You be runnin' a tab?"

"I'll pay as I go," she said, and reached into her shoulder bag. The .44 was sitting under a silk scarf, butt up. She took out her wallet, paid for the drink. The bartender lingered.

"I'm Larry," he said. "This's my place."

Eileen nodded, and then took a sip of the drink.

"You're new," Larry said.

"So?" she said.

"So I get a piece," he said.

"You get shit," Eileen said.

"I can't have hookers hangin' around in here 'cept I get a piece."

"Talk to Torpedo," she said.

"I don't know nobody named Torpedo."

"You don't, huh? Well, ask around. I got a feeling you won't like talking to him."

"Who's Torpedo? The black dude was slapping you around?"

"Torpedo Holmes. Ask around. Meanwhile, fuck off."

"You see the lady sittin' there at the end of the bar?" Larry said.

Eileen looked over at Annie.

"I see her."

"She's new, too. We had a nice little talk minute she come in. I'm gettin' twenty percent of her action, just for lettin' her plant her ass on that stool."

"She ain't got Torpedo," Eileen said. "You want to get off my fuckin' back, or you want me to make a phone call?"

"Go make your phone call," Larry said.

"Mister," Eileen said, "you're askin' for more shit than you're worth."

She swung off the stool, long legs reaching for the floor, picked up her bag, shouldered it, and swiveled toward the phone booth. Watching her, Annie thought God, she's good.

In the phone booth, Eileen dialed the hot-line number at the Seven-Two.

Alvarez picked up.

"Tell Robinson to get back here," she said. "The bartender's hassling me."

"You got him," Alvarez said, and hung up.

Detective/Second Grade Alvin Robinson worked out of the Seven-Three, near the park and the County Court House. The team at the Seven-Two was certain he wouldn't be made for a cop here in the Canal Zone, and were using him tonight only to establish Eileen's credentials as a bona fide hooker. He wouldn't be part of the backup team, though Eileen might have wished otherwise. She was still annoyed that he'd hit her that hard—even though she knew he'd been going for realism—but in the Caddy on the way over he'd sounded like a tough, dependable cop who knew his business.

He walked into the bar not ten minutes after she placed her call. Eyes challenging, sweeping the room under the wide brim of his hat, everyone in the joint looking away. He did a cool pimp shuffle over to where Eileen was sitting, and put his hand on her shoulder.

"That him?" he asked, and cocked his head to where Larry was filling a jar with tomato juice. Eileen merely nodded. "You," Robinson said, and pointed his finger. "Come here."

Larry took his time ambling over.

"You givin' my fox trouble?" Robinson said.

"You got a phone in that pussy wagon of yours?" Larry said, toughing it out though he'd never seen a meaner-looking black man in his life. Everybody in the bar was looking at them now. The guys at the tables, the one who'd been watching television a minute earlier.

"I ast you a question," Robinson said.

"I read her the rules, pal," Larry said. "The same rules . . ."

"Don't pal *me*, pal," Robinson said. "I ain't your fuckin' pal, and I don't live by no rules. If you never heard of Torpedo Holmes, then you got some quick learnin' to do. Nobody cuts my action, man. Nobody. Less he's lookin' for some *other* kinda cut I'd be mighty obliged to supply. You got that?"

"I'm tellin' you . . ."

"No, you ain't *tellin'* me nothin', mister. You *list'nin'* is what you doin'." He reached into his wallet, took a frayed piece of glossy paper from it, unfolded it, and smoothed it flat on the bar. "This's from *L.A. Magazine*," he said. "You recognize that picture there?"

Larry looked down at a color photograph of a big black man wearing a red silk lounge robe and grinning cockily at the camera. The room in the background was opulent. The caption under the picture read: *Thomas "Torpedo" Holmes at Home.*

Robinson thought the resemblance was a good one. But even if it hadn't been, he firmly believed that most white men—especially a redneck like this one—thought all niggers looked alike. Thomas "Torpedo" Holmes was now doing ten years at Soledad. The article didn't mention the bust and conviction, because it had been written three years earlier, when Holmes was riding too high for his own good. You don't shit on cops in print, not even in L.A.

"I'm assumin' you don't know how to read," Robinson said, "so I'll fill you in fast." He snatched the article off the bartop before it got too much scrutiny, folded it, put it back into his wallet again. Eileen sat looking bored. "Now what that article says, man, is that not even L.A.'s finest could lay a finger on me, is what that article says. An' the same applies right here in *this* city, ain't no kinda law can touch me, ain't no kinda shitty bartender . . ."

"I *own* this place!" Larry said.

"You list'nin' to me, man, or you runnin' off at the mouth? I'm tellin' you I don't cut my action with nobody, not the law, not nobody else runnin' girls, and most of all not *you.*"

"This ain't L.A.," Larry said.

"Well, no shee-it?" Robinson said.

"I mean, I got rules here, man."

"You want me to shove your rules up your ass, man? Together with that jar of tomato juice? Man, don't tempt me. This little girl here, she's gonna sit here long as she likes, you dig, man? An' if I'm happy with the service she gets, then maybe I'll drop some other little girls off every now an' then, give this fuckin' dump some class." His wallet came out again. He threw a fifty-dollar bill on the counter. "This is for whatever she wants to drink. When that's used up, I'll be back with more. You better pray I don't come back with somethin' has a sharp end. You take my meanin', man?"

Larry picked up the bill and tucked it into his shirt pocket. He figured he'd won a moral victory. "What's all this strong-arm shit?" he asked, smiling, playing to the crowd now, showing them he hadn't backed down. "We're two gentlemen here, can't we talk without threatening each other?"

"Was you threatenin' me?" Robinson said. "I didn't hear nobody threatenin' me."

"What I meant . . ."

"We finished here, man? You gonna treat Linda nice from now on?"

"All I said to the lady . . ."

"What you said don't mean shit to me. I don't want no more phone calls from her."

"I don't mind a nice-looking girl in the place," Larry said.

"Good. An' I don't mind her bein' here," Robinson said, and grinned a big watermelon-eating grin. He put his hand on Eileen's shoulder again. "Now, honey," he said, "go easy on the sauce. 'Cause Daddy got some nice candy for you when the night's done."

"See you, Torp," she said, and offered her cheek for his kiss.

Robinson gave Larry a brief, meaningful nod, and then did his cool pimp shuffle over to the door and out to the white Cadillac at the curb.

From the other end of the bar, Annie said, "I wish *I* had a man like that."

The third liquor-store holdup took place while Alvin Robinson was doing his little dog-and-pony act for the owner of Larry's Bar, but the blues didn't respond till nine-thirty, and Carella and Meyer didn't arrive at the scene till nine thirty-five, by which time Robinson was already driving back toward the Seventy-Third Precinct.

This time, nobody had been killed—but not for lack of trying. Martha Frey, the forty-year-old woman who owned and operated the store on Culver and Twentieth, told them that four of them—wearing clown suits, and pointed pom-pommed clown hats, and white clown masks with bulbous red noses and wide grinning red mouths—had started shooting the minute they walked in. She'd grabbed for her heart and fallen down behind the counter in what she hoped was a very good imitation of someone who'd been mortally wounded. It had occurred to her, while they were cleaning out the cash register, that one of them might decide to put a "coop dee gracie," as she called it, in her head while she was lying there playing possum. None of them had. She considered it a miracle that she was still alive, four little guns opening up that way, all of them at the same time. She wondered if maybe they'd hit her after all. Was it possible she was now in shock and didn't know she'd been hit? Did the detectives see any blood on her?

Meyer assured her that she was still in one piece.

"I can't believe they missed me," she said, and made the sign of the cross. "God must have been watching over me."

Either that, or they were nervous this time around, Carella thought. Three times in the space of four hours, even your seasoned pro could spook. No less a handful of grade-schoolers.

97

"Did you see who was driving the car?" Carella asked.

"No," Martha said. "I was tallying the register for the night. I usually close at nine on Fridays, but this is Halloween, there's lots of parties going on, people run short of booze, they make a last-minute run to the store. This was maybe twenty after when they came in."

The Mobile Lab van was pulling up outside the store.

"Techs'll be here a while," Carella said. "They'll want to see if there's anything on that register."

"There ain't anything *in* it, that's for sure," Martha said mournfully.

"Did they say anything to you?" Meyer asked. "When they came in?"

"Just 'Trick or Treat!' Then they started shooting."

"Didn't say, 'This is a stickup,' anything like that?"

"Nothing."

"Hello, boys," one of the techs said. "Kiddy time again?"

"School let out again?" the other tech said.

"How about when they were cleaning out the register?" Meyer asked, ignoring them.

"One of them said, 'Hold it open, Alice.' I guess he meant the shopping bag."

"Alice?" Carella said. "A girl?"

"A woman, yes," Martha said.

Carella thought this was carrying feminism a bit too far.

"Well, this little girl . . ." he started to say, but Martha broke in at once.

"A *woman*," she said. "Not a little girl. These weren't *children*, Detective Carella, they were *midgets*."

He looked at her.

"I used to work the high-wire with Ringling," she said. "Broke my hip in a fall, quit for good. But I still know midgets when I see them. These were *midgets*."

"What'd I tell you, Baz?" one of the techs said. "I shoulda taken your bet."

"Midgets," the other tech said. "I'll be a son of a bitch."

Me, too, Carella thought.

But now they knew what they were looking for.

And now they had a pattern.

Peaches and Parker were the only ones not in costume.

"What are you supposed to be?" a man dressed like a cowboy asked.

"I'm a cop," Parker said.

"I'm a victim," Peaches said.

"I'll be damned," the cowboy said.

Parker showed his shield to everyone he met.

"Looks like the real McCoy," a pirate said.

Peaches lifted her skirt and showed a silent-movie director a black-and-blue mark on her thigh.

"I'm a victim," she said.

She had got the black-and-blue mark banging against a table on her way to the bathroom one night.

The silent-movie director, who was wearing jodhpurs and carrying a megaphone, said, "That's some leg, honey. You wanna be in pictures?"

The girl with him was dressed as Theda Bara. "That's an anagram for Arab Death," she said.

Parker looked into the front of her clingy, satin, low-cut dress, and said, "You're under arrest," and showed her his shield.

In the kitchen, Dracula and Superman and Scarlett O'Hara and Cleopatra were snorting cocaine.

Parker didn't show them his shield. Instead, he snorted a few lines with them.

Peaches said, "You're kinda fun for a cop."

This was the first time in a good many years that anyone had told Parker he was kind of fun, for a cop or anything else. He hugged her close.

She went, "Oooooo."

A white man in blackface, dressed as Eddie Murphy dressed as the Detroit detective in *Beverly Hills Cop* said, "I'm a cop," and showed Parker a fake shield.

"I'll go along quietly," Parker said, and hugged Peaches again.

"Way I figure it," Kling said, "we go over there soon as we're relieved. Maybe get to the Zone around midnight, a little after."

"Uh-huh," Hawes said, and looked up at the wall clock.

Ten minutes to ten. Less than two hours before the relieving shift began filtering in.

"They don't even need to know we're there," Kling said. "We take one of the sedans, just cruise the streets."

They were sitting at his desk, talking in whispers. Across the room, Brown was getting a description of Jimmy Brayne. He was right now ready to bet the farm that Sebastian the Great's apprentice was the one who'd done him in and chopped him up in pieces.

"This guy's extremely dangerous," Kling said. "Juked three people already."

"And you think they may need help, huh?" Hawes said. "Annie and Eileen?"

"More the merrier," Kling said.

"White or black?" Brown asked.

"White," Marie said.

"His age?"

"Thirty-two."

"Height?"

"About six feet."

"Annie never even mentioned she was going out on this," Hawes said. "I talked to her must've been . . ."

"She didn't get the call from Homicide till late this afternoon. That's the thing of it, Cotton. They pulled this whole damn thing out of a Cracker Jack box."

"Weight?" Brown said.

"About a hundred and eighty? Something like that."

"Color of hair?"

100

"Black."

"Eyes?"

"Brown."

"I mean, would *you* go out there with only two backups?" Kling said. "Where the guy's armed with a knife, and already boxed three people?"

"Those don't sound like bad odds," Hawes said. "Three to one? All three of them loaded. Against only a knife."

"*Only*, huh? My point is, if Annie and this Shanahan guy stay too close to her," Kling said, "he won't make his move. So they have to keep their distance. But if he breaks out, who's covering the backfield?"

"Any identifying scars, marks, or tattoos?" Brown asked.

"Not that I know of."

"Any regional accent or dialect?"

"He's from Massachusetts. He sounds a little like the Kennedys."

"What was he wearing when you left the house today?"

"Let me think."

She was sitting on a bench under the squadroom bulletin board, her hands folded on her lap. Her face was still tear-stained. Brown had one foot up on the bench, a clipboard resting on his knee. He waited.

"Blue jeans," she said. "And a woolen sweater, no shirt. A V-necked sweater. Sort of rust-colored. And sneakers. And . . . white socks, I think. Oh, yes. He wears a sort of medallion around his neck. A silver medallion, I think he won it in a swim meet. A high school swim meet."

"Wears it all the time?"

"I've never seen him without it."

"Have you discussed this with Eileen?" Hawes asked.

"Yeah, I mentioned it at dinner," Kling said.

"Told her you want to go over there?"

"Yeah."

"To the Zone?"

"Yeah."

"What'd she say?"

"She told me she could handle it."

"But you don't think she can, huh?"

"I think she can handle it better with a few more people on the job. They shoulda known that themselves, Homicide. And also the Seven-Two. Putting two women on the street against . . ."

"Plus Shanahan."

"Well, I don't know this Shanahan, do you?"

"No, but . . ."

"For all I know . . ."

"But you can't automatically figure he's a hairbag."

"I don't know what he is. I *do* know he's not gonna care as much about Eileen as *I* care about her."

"Maybe that's the problem," Hawes said.

"Does he wear a wristwatch?" Brown asked.

"Yes," Marie said.

"Would you know what kind?"

"One of those digital things. Black with a black band. A Seiko, I think. I'm not sure."

"Any other jewelry?"

"A ring. He wears it on his right pinky. A little gold ring with a red stone. I don't think it's a ruby, but it looks like one."

"Is he right-handed or left-handed?"

"I don't know."

"What do you mean?" Kling said.

"I mean, why don't you leave it to them?" Hawes said.

Kling looked at him.

"They're experienced cops, all of them. If Homicide or the Seven-Two hasn't put an army out there, it's maybe 'cause they think they'll spook him."

"I don't see how two more guys is gonna make an *army*," Kling said.

"These guys can smell traps," Hawes said, "they're like animals in the jungle. Anyway, they'll be carrying walkie-talkies, won't they? Annie, Shanahan? Maybe even Eileen. There'll be rmp's cruising the Zone, they're not gonna be alone out there. Any one of 'em calls in a 10-13 . . ."

"I don't want her getting cut again," Kling said.

"You think *she* wants to get cut again?" Hawes said.

"Tell me what happened before you left the house today," Brown said. "Was he behaving differently in any way?"

"Same as always," Marie said.

"Did he get along okay with your husband?"

"Yes. Well, he wants to be a magician, you see. He studies all the tricks the famous magicians did—Dai Vernon, Blackstone, Audley Walsh, Tommy Windsor, Houdini, Ballantine—all of them. He keeps up with all the new people, too, tries to dope out their tricks. And my husband is . . ."

Her face almost broke.

"My husband . . . was . . . very patient with him. Always willing to explain a sleight, or a pocket trick, or a stage illusion . . . helping him with his patter . . . taking the time to . . . to . . . show him and . . . and guide him. I don't know how he could've done something like this. I'll tell you the truth, Detective Brown, I'm willing to give you anything you need to find Jimmy, but I can't believe he did this."

"Well, *we* don't know that for sure, either," Brown said.

"That's just what I mean," Marie said. "I just pray to God something hasn't happened to *him*, too. I just hope somebody hasn't . . . hasn't killed them *both*."

"How do *you* get along with him?" Brown asked.

"Jimmy? I think of him as a brother."

"No friction, huh? I mean, the three of you living in the same house?"

"None whatever."

"So what does that mean?" Kling asked. "You won't go with me?"

"I don't think *you* should go, either," Hawes said.

"Well, I'm going."

"She knows her job," Hawes said flatly. "And so does Annie."

"She *didn't* know her job when that son of a bitch . . ."

Kling caught himself. He took a deep breath.

"Take it easy," Hawes said.

"I'm going out there tonight," Kling said. "With you or without you."

"Take it easy," Hawes said again.

Brown walked over.

"Here's the way I figure it," he said to Hawes. "You caught the Missing P, I caught the pieces. Turns out it's the same case. I figure maybe Genero ought to go back to cruising, find all that trouble in the streets the loot's worried about. You and me can team up on this one, how does that sound to you?"

"Sounds good," Hawes said.

"I'll go tell Genero," Brown said, and walked off.

"You okay?" Hawes asked Kling.

"I'm fine," Kling said.

But he walked off, too.

The precinct map was spread out on the long table in the Interrogation Room. Meyer and Carella were hunched over the map. They had already asked Sergeant Murchison to run a check on any circuses or carnivals that happened to be in town. They did not think there'd be any at this time of year. In the meantime, they were trying to figure out where the midgets would hit next.

"Midgets," Meyer said, shaking his head. "You ever bust a midget?"

"Never," Carella said. "I busted a dwarf once. He was a very good burglar. Used to crawl into vents."

"What's the difference?" Meyer asked.

"A midget is a person of unusually small size, but he's physically well-proportioned."

"So? Dopey and Doc were well-proportioned, too."

"That's the movies," Carella said. "In real life, a dwarf has abnormal body proportions."

"Can you name all the Seven Dwarfs?" Meyer asked.

"I can't even name Snow White," Carella said.

"Go on, give it a try."

"Anyone can name the Seven Dwarfs," Carella said.

"Go ahead, name them."

"Dopey, Doc . . ."

"I gave you those two free."

"Grumpy, Sleepy, Sneezy . . . how many is that?"

"Five."

"Bashful."

"Yeah?"

"And . . ."

"Yeah?"

"Who's the seventh one?" Carella said.

"Nobody can name all seven of them," Meyer said.

"So tell me who he is."

"Think about it," Meyer said, smiling.

Carella hunched over the precinct map. Now the goddamn seventh dwarf would bother him all night long.

"First hit was here," he said, indicating the location on the map. "Culver and Ninth. Second one here. Still on Culver, three blocks east. Next one was Culver and Twentieth."

"They're working their way uptown on Culver."

"First one at . . . have you got that timetable?"

Meyer opened his notebook. "Five-fifteen," he said. "Second one at a little after seven. Third one about forty minutes ago."

"So what's the interval?"

"Five-fifteen, seven-oh-five, nine-twenty. Figure two hours, more or less."

"Time to change their costumes . . ."

"Or maybe we're dealing with *three* gangs here, did that occur to you?"

"There aren't that many midgets in the world," Carella said.

"You figured out the seventh dwarf yet?"

"No." He looked at the map again. "So the next one should be

105

further uptown on Culver, and they should hit around eleven, eleven-thirty."

"*If* there's a next one."

"And unless they speed up the timetable."

"Yeah," Meyer said, and shook his head again. "Midgets. I always thought midgets were law-abiding citizens."

"Just be happy they aren't giants," Carella said.

"You got it," Meyer said.

"Huh?" Carella said.

"Happy. That's the seventh dwarf."

"Oh. Yeah."

"So what do you want to do?"

"First let's check Dave, see if he came up with any circuses or carnivals."

"That's a long shot," Meyer said.

"Then let's call Ballistics again, see if they got anything on the bullets."

"We'll maybe get a caliber and make," Meyer said, "but I don't see how that's gonna help us."

"And then I guess we better head uptown," Carella said, "case Culver, see which stores are possibles for the next hit."

"You figuring on a plant?"

"Unless there's a dozen of them."

"Well, it's getting late, there won't be many open."

Carella folded the map.

"So," he said. "Murchison first."

She was still sitting on the bench, weeping softly, when Hawes approached her.

"Mrs. Sebastiani?" he said.

Marie looked up. Face tear-streaked, blue eyes rimmed with red now.

"I'm sorry to bother you," he said.

"No, that's all right," she said.

"I wanted to tell you . . . we found the van, but we still haven't located the Citation. You said Brayne drove the van into the city today . . ."

"Yes."

"So maybe the techs'll be able to lift his prints from the wheel. He hasn't got a criminal record, has he?"

"Not that I know of."

"Well, we'll run him through the computer, see what we come up with. Meanwhile, if the techs lift anything, and if we find the Citation, then maybe we'll know if he's the one who drove it away from the school. By comparing prints from the two wheels, do you see?"

"Yes. But . . . well, we *all* drove both cars a lot. I mean, you'll probably find my prints and Frank's together with Jimmy's. If you find any prints."

"Uh-huh, yes, that's a possibility. But we'll see, okay? Meanwhile, Detective Brown has already put out a bulletin on Brayne, and we'll be watching all railroad stations, bus terminals, airports, in case he . . ."

"*You'll* be watching?"

"Well, not Brown and me personally. I mean the police. The bulletin's gone out already, as I said, so maybe we'll get some results there. If he's trying to get out of the city."

"Yes," Marie said, and nodded.

"Brown and I are gonna run back to the high school, see if anybody there saw what happened in that driveway."

"Well . . . will anyone *be* there? I mean, won't the teachers. . .?"

"And the kids, yes, they'll be gone, that'll have to wait till morning. But the custodian'll be there, and maybe *he* saw something."

"Will it be the same custodian who was there this afternoon?"

"I don't know, but we're going to check it out, anyway."

"Yes, I see."

"Meanwhile, I wanted to know what *you* plan to do. Do you have any relatives or friends here in the city?"

"No."

"Then will you be going back home? I know you're short of cash . . ."

"Yes, but there was money in Frank's wallet."

"Well, the lab'll be running tests on the wallet and everything in it, so I can't let you have that. But if you want me to lend you train fare, or bus fare . . . what I'm asking is whether or not you plan on going home, Mrs. Sebastiani. Because, honestly, there's nothing more you can do here."

"I . . . I don't know what I want to do," she said, and began crying again, burying her face in an already sodden handkerchief.

Hawes watched her, awkward in the presence of her tears.

"I'm not sure I want to go home," she said, her voice muffled by the handkerchief. "With Frank gone . . ."

The sentence trailed.

She kept sobbing into the handkerchief.

"You have to go home sometime," Hawes said gently.

"I know, I know," she said, and blew her nose, and sniffed, and wiped at her eyes with the back of her hand. "There are calls I'll have to make . . . Frank's mother in Atlanta, and his sister . . . and I guess . . . I suppose I'll have to make funeral arrangements . . . oh God, how are they going to . . . what will they . . .?"

Hawes was thinking the same thing. The body was in four separate pieces. The body didn't have hands or a head.

"That'll have to wait till autopsy, anyway," he said. "I'll let you know when . . ."

"I thought they'd already done that."

"Well, that was a prelim. We asked for a preliminary report, you see. But the M.E.'ll want to do a more thorough examination."

"Why?" she asked. "I've already identified him."

"Yes, but we're dealing with a murder here, Mrs. Sebastiani, and we need to know . . . well, for example, your husband may have been *poisoned* before the body was . . . well . . ."

He cut himself short.

He was talking too much.

This was a goddamn grieving widow here.

"There are lots of things the M.E. can tell us," he concluded lamely.

Marie nodded.

"So . . . *will* you be going home?" he asked.

"I suppose."

Hawes opened his wallet, pulled out two twenties and a ten.

"This should get you there," he said, handing the money to her.

"That's too much," she said.

"Well, tide you over. I'll give you a ring later tonight, make sure you got home okay. And I'll be in touch as we go along. Sometimes these things take a little while, but we'll be work . . ."

"Yes," she said. "Let me know."

"I'll have one of the cars drop you off," he said. "Will you be going home by train or . . . ?"

"Train, yes."

She seemed numb.

"So . . . uh . . . whenever you're ready, I'll buzz the sergeant and he'll pull one of the cars off the street. I'd drive you myself, but Brown and I want to get over to the school."

Marie nodded.

And then she looked up and said—perhaps only to herself— "How am I going to live without him?"

7

Genero was annoyed.

He was the one who'd found the first piece of the body, and now all *four* pieces were out of his hands. So to speak. He blamed it on seniority. Both Brown and Hawes had been detectives longer than he had, and so they'd immediately taken charge of a juicy homicide. So here he was, back on the street again, cruising like a goddamn patrolman. He was more than annoyed. He was enormously pissed.

The streets at a quarter past ten were still teeming with people ... well, sure, who expected this kind of weather at the end of October? Guys in shirt sleeves, girls in summer dresses, everybody strolling up the avenue like it was summertime in Paris, not that he'd ever been there. Lady there on the corner with a French poodle, letting the dog poop right on the sidewalk, even though it was against the law. He wondered if he should arrest

110

her. He considered it beneath his dignity, a Detective/Third having to arrest a lady whose dog was illegally pooping. He let the dog poop, drove on by.

Made a cursory tour of the sector.

Who else was out here?

Kling?

Came onto Culver, began heading east.

Past the first liquor store got robbed tonight, then the second one . . .

What had they been talking about back there in the squad-room? Meyer and Carella. Midgets? Was it possible? Midgets holding up liquor stores? Those little Munchkins from *The Wizard of Oz* holding up *liquor* stores, for Christ's sake? He didn't know what kind of a world this was getting to be. He thanked God every night before he went to sleep that he had been chosen to enforce law and order in the kind of world this was getting to be. Even if sometimes he had a good ripe murder yanked out of his hands. The only way to get ahead in the Department was to crack a good homicide every now and then. Not that it had done Carella much good, all the homicides he'd cracked. Been a detective for how many years now? Still only Second Grade. Well, sometimes people got passed over. The meek shall inherit the earth, he thought. Still, he wished he'd had an honest crack at that homicide tonight. He was the one found the first piece, wasn't he?

Onto Mason Avenue, the hookers out in force, well, Halloween, lots of guys coming uptown to look for the Great Pumpkin. Went home with the Great Herpes and maybe the Great AIDS. He wouldn't screw a Mason Avenue hooker if you gave him a million dollars. Well, maybe he would. For a million, maybe. That one on the corner looked very clean, in fact. But you could never tell. Anyway, she was Puerto Rican, and his mother had warned him against fooling around with any girls who weren't Italian. He wondered if Italian girls ever got herpes. He was positive they never got AIDS.

111

Swinging north again, up one of the side streets, then onto the Stem, all gaudy and bright, he really loved this part of the . . .

"Boy One, Boy One . . ."

The walkie-talkie lying on the seat beside him. Dispatcher trying to raise . . .

"Boy One."

Answering.

"10-21 at one-one-four-one Oliver, near Sixth. Apartment four-two. 10-21 at one-one-four-one Oliver, near Sixth. See the lady."

"What was that apartment again?"

"Four-two."

"Rolling."

A burglary past, couple of blocks down and to the south. No need for a detective on the scene. If it had been a 10-30, an armed robbery in progress, or even a 10-34, an assault in progress, he'd have responded along with the blues. He guessed. Sometimes it was better not to stick your nose into too many things. A 10-13—an assist officer—sure. Man called in for help, you got to the scene fast, *wherever* you were.

Ran uptown on the Stem for a couple of blocks, made a right turn at random, heading south toward the park. He'd swing onto Grover there, parallel the park for a while, then run north to the river, come back down Silvermine, take a run around the Oval, then back south on . . .

Up ahead.

Four teenagers.

Running into the building on the corner.

Just a glimpse of them.

Blue jeans and denim jackets.

Something in their hands.

Trouble?

Shit, he thought.

He eased the car over. No parking spaces on the street, he

double-parked in front of the building and picked up the walkie-talkie.

"Eight-Seven," he said, "D.D. Four."

Calling home, identifying himself. One of the six unmarked sedans used by the Detective Division.

"Go ahead, Four."

"Genero," he said. "10-51, four in number, at twelve-seventeen North Eleventh."

"Stay in touch, Genero."

He'd identified the four teenagers as a roving band, a noncrime incident, and he hoped that was what it turned out to be. Getting out of the car, he pulled back the flap of his jacket and was clipping the walkie-talkie to his belt when a loud whooshing sound erupted from inside the building. He almost dropped the walkie-talkie. He looked up sharply. Flames! In the lobby there! And running out of the building, the four teenagers, one of them still carrying in his right hand what looked like a Molotov cocktail. Instinctively, Genero yelled, "Stop! Police!" and yanked his service revolver from its holster.

The kids hesitated for only a moment.

"Police!" he shouted again.

The one with the firebomb held a Zippo lighter to the wick and hurled the bottle at Genero.

The bottle crashed at his feet. Flames sprang up from the sidewalk. He threw both hands up to protect his face, and then immediately stepped back and brought his right hand down again, pistol level, firing into the wall of fire, through the wall of fire, two quick shots in succession.

Somebody screamed.

And suddenly they were on him. They jumped through the flames like circus performers, three of them hitting him almost simultaneously, knocking him to the pavement. He rolled away from the fire, tried to roll away from their kicks. He brought the gun hand up again, fired again, three shots gone now, heard someone grunt. Don't waste any, he thought, and one of them kicked him in the head. He went blank for an instant. His finger tightened reflexively on the trigger. The gun exploded wild, close to his own ear. He blinked his eyes. He was going. He fought unconsciousness. Someone kicked him in the shoulder, and the sharp pain rocketed into his brain and brought him back. Four shots gone, he thought. Make the next ones count. He rolled away again. He blinked them into focus. Only two of them on their feet now. The third one flat on his back near the entrance to the building. Fourth one lying on the sidewalk dangerously close to the fire. He'd hammered two of them, but there were still two to go, and only two shots left in the gun.

His heart was pounding.

But he took his time.

Waited till the lead kicker was almost on him, and then shot for his chest.

Second one right behind him, almost knocked off his feet when his buddy blew back into him. Genero fired again. Took the second one in the left shoulder, sent him spinning around and staggering back toward the wall of the building.

Genero could hardly breathe.

He got to his feet, fanned the empty gun at them.

Nobody seemed to be going anywhere.

He backed off a pace, pulled cartridges from his belt, loaded them into the cylinder, counting . . . four, five, six and ready again.

"Move and you're dead," he whispered, and yanked the walkie-talkie from his belt.

Detective/Third Grade Richard Genero had come of age on the eve of All Hallows' Day.

The school custodian who answered the night bell was the same one who'd locked Sebastian the Great's tricks in a storeroom earlier this afternoon. Peering through the grilled upper glass panel of the door at the back of the building, he recognized Hawes at once, unlocked the door, and let him in.

" 'Evening, Mr. Buono," Hawes said.

"Hey, how you doing?" Buono said.

He was a man in his late sixties, thinning gray hair, thin gray mustache over his upper lip. Pale blue eyes, somewhat bulbous nose. He was wearing coveralls. A flashlight was in one of the pockets. He clipped his ring of keys to a loop on the pocket.

"This is my partner, Detective Brown," Hawes said.

"Nice to meetcha," Buono said. "You come back for the stuff?"

"Well, no," Hawes said. "Few questions we'd like to ask you."

Buono immediately figured they knew he was stealing supplies from the classroom closets.

"Hey, sure," he said, and tried to look innocent. He locked the door behind them, and said, "Come on over the office, we can talk there. My friend and me were playing checkers."

They walked down a yellow-tiled, locker-lined corridor. They passed a wall clock that read twenty minutes past ten. They made a left turn. More students' lockers on either wall. A bulletin board. A poster reading:

COME CHEER THE TIGERS!
Saturday, Nov. 1, 2:00 P.M.
RAUCHER FIELD

To the right of that, another poster announcing:

SEBASTIAN THE GREAT!
HALLOWEEN MAGIC!
Auditorium. 4:00 P.M.

Beneath the lettering was a black-and-white photograph of a good-looking young man wearing a top hat and bow tie, grinning into the camera.

115

"Okay to take that poster?" Brown asked.

"Which one?" Buono said.

"The magician."

"Sure," Buono said, and shrugged.

Brown began pulling out the tacks.

"Come in handy, we find the head," he said to Hawes, and then folded the poster and put it in his inside jacket pocket.

Buono led them further down the hall, opened a door at the end of it. A sparsely furnished room. An upright locker, green in contrast to the reds, yellows, and oranges of the lockers in the halls. Long oak table, probably requisitioned from one of the administration offices. Four straight-backed chairs around it, checker board on one end of it. Coffee pot on a hot plate on one wall of the room, clock over it. Framed picture of Ronald Reagan on the wall opposite.

"This here's my friend, Sal Pasquali," Buono said.

Pasquali was in his late sixties, early seventies, wearing brown trousers, brown shoes and socks, a pale yellow sports shirt, and a brown sweater buttoned up the front. He looked like a candy-store owner.

"These people here are detectives," Buono said, and looked at Pasquali, hoping he would understand what the look meant: Watch your onions about the chalk, and the paste, and the pencils, and the erasers, and the reams of paper.

Pasquali nodded sagely, like a Mafia don.

"Pleased to meetcha," he said.

"So," Buono said, "sit down. You want some coffee?"

"Thanks, no," Hawes said.

The detectives pulled out chairs and sat.

Buono could see Brown's gun in a shoulder holster under his jacket.

"We were just playing checkers here," Pasquali said.

"Who's winning?" Brown asked.

"Well, we don't play for money or nothing," Pasquali said.

Which meant that they did.

116

Brown suddenly wondered what these two old farts were hiding.

"I wanted to ask whether you saw anything that happened outside there this afternoon," Hawes said.

"Why?" Buono said at once. "Is something missing?"

"No, no. Missing? What do you mean?"

"Well, what do *you* mean?" Buono said, and glanced at Pasquali.

"I meant when the cars were being loaded."

"Oh."

"When Mr. Sebastiani was out there loading his tricks in the Citation."

"I didn't see him doing that," Buono said.

"You weren't out there after he finished the act, huh?"

"No. I didn't come on till four o'clock."

"Well, he'd have been out there around five-thirty."

"No, I didn't see him."

"Then you have no idea who might've dumped that stuff out of his car . . ."

"No idea at all."

"And driven off with it."

"No. Five-thirty, I was prolly down the north end of the building, starting with the classrooms there. I usually start cleaning the classrooms down the north end, it's like a routine, you know. Tradition."

"That's near the driveway, isn't it? The north end?"

"Yeah, the back of the building. But I didn't see anything out there. I mean, I *mighta* seen something if I was looking—there's windows in the classrooms, you know. But I wasn't looking for nothing. I was busy cleaning up the classrooms."

"You say you came on at four . . ."

"That's right. Four to midnight."

"Like us," Brown said, and smiled.

"Yeah?" Buono said. "Is that your shift? Whattya know? You hear this, Sal? They got shifts like us."

117

"What a coincidence," Pasquali said.

Brown still wondered what they were hiding.

"So you came on at four . . ." Hawes said.

"Yeah. Four to midnight. There's a man relieves me at midnight." He looked at the clock on the wall. "Be here in a few hours, well, less. But he's like just a watchman, you know."

"If you came on at four . . ."

"Yeah." A nod.

"Then you weren't here when the Sebastianis arrived, were you? They would've got here about a quarter after three. You weren't here then, is that right?"

"No. Sal was here."

Pasquali nodded.

"Sal works from eight to four," Buono said. "He's the *day* custodian."

"Shifts," Pasquali said. "Like you."

"He can't stay away from the place," Buono said. "Comes back to play checkers with me every night."

"I'm a widower," Pasquali explained, and shrugged.

"Did you see the cars when they arrived?" Brown asked him. "Tan Ford Econoline, blue Citation?"

"I seen one of them out there," Pasquali said. "But not when it came in."

"Which one did you see?"

"Little blue car."

"When was this? When you saw it?"

"Around . . . three-thirty, was it?"

"You asking me?" Buono said. "I wasn't here three-thirty."

"Three-thirty, it musta been," Pasquali said. "I remember I was heading out front, where the school buses come in. I usually go out there, talk to the drivers."

"They'd have been setting up the stage by then," Hawes said.

Brown nodded.

"And the van was already gone."

Brown nodded again.

118

"Did you see any people out there?" Hawes asked Pasquali. "Carrying things in? Unloading the cars?"

"All I saw was the one car."

"Blonde woman in her late twenties? Two men in their early thirties?"

"No," Pasquali said, and shook his head.

"Were the doors open?"

"What doors?"

"On the car."

"They looked closed to me."

"Anything lying in the driveway there?"

"Nothing I could see. What do you mean? Like what?"

"Tricks," Hawes said.

"Tricks?" Pasquali said, and looked at Buono.

"They done a magic show this afternoon," Buono said. "For the kids."

"Oh. No, I didn't see no tricks out there."

"You didn't happen to wander by that driveway later on, did you? Around five-thirty? When they were loading the . . ."

"Five-thirty I was home eating my dinner. I made a nice TV dinner for myself."

Hawes looked at Brown.

"Anything?" he asked.

Brown shook his head.

"Well, thanks a lot," Hawes said, and shoved back his chair.

"I'll let you out the building," Buono said.

The detectives followed him out of the office.

As soon as they were gone, Pasquali took out his handkerchief and mopped his brow.

At twenty minutes past ten, Larry's Bar was buzzing with activity.

Not a table empty. Not a stool unoccupied at the bar.

Eileen was sitting at one of the tables now, talking to a blonde hooker named Sheryl who was wearing a red skirt slit up one

119

side, and a white silk blouse unbuttoned three buttons down. There was nothing under the blouse. Sheryl sat with her legs spread, her high heels hooked on the chair's top rung. Eileen could see track marks on her naked white thighs. She was telling Eileen how she'd come to this city from Baltimore, Maryland. Eileen was scanning the room, trying to figure out which one of these guys in here was her backup. Two waitresses, who could have passed for hookers themselves—short black skirts, high heels, overflowing white peasant blouses—were busily scooting back and forth between the tables and the bar, avoiding grabs at their asses.

"Got off the bus," the girl said, "first thing happens to me is this kindly old man asks can he help me with my valise. Had to be forty years old, am I right, a nice old man being friendly. Asks me have I got a place to stay, offers to get me a taxi to the Y, says 'I'll bet you're starving,' which I was, takes me to a hamburger joint, stuffs me with burgers and fries, tells me a nice young girl like me—I was only seventeen—had to be careful in the big, bad city, lots of people out there waiting to victimize me."

"Same old bullshit," Eileen said.

She figured there were only two men who could be Shanahan. Guy sitting there at one of the tables, talking up a hooker with frizzied brown hair, he had a hook nose that could've been a phony, black hair and blue eyes like Shanahan's, about his height and weight, wearing horn-rimmed eyeglasses. He could've been Shanahan.

"Well, sure, you know the story already," the girl said. "Mr. Nice turns out to be Big Daddy, takes me to his apartment, introduces me to two other girls living there, nice girls like me, he says, has me smoking pot that same night and shooting horse before the week is out. Turned me out two days later with a businessman from Ohio. Guy ast me to blow him, I didn't know what the fuck he meant. Man, that seems like ages ago."

"How old are you now?" Eileen asked.

"Twenty-two," Sheryl said. "I'm not with Lou no more . . .

that was his name, Lou . . . I got me a new man, takes good care of me. Who you with?"

"Torpedo Holmes," Eileen said.

"Is he black, or what?"

"Black."

"Yeah, mine, too. Lou was white. I think the white ones are meaner, I really do. Lou used to beat the shit out of me. That first time, after the guy from Ohio, you know, where I didn't know what to do, Lou beat me so I couldn't walk. Had a dozen of his buddies come up the next morning, one after the other, twelve of them, teach the little hayseed from Baltimore how to suck a cock. Broke in my ass, too. That was when I *really* got turned out, believe me. The guy from Ohio was child's play. In fact, everything after that night with Lou's buddies was child's play."

"Yeah, they can be rotten when they want to," Eileen said.

Guy sitting there talking to Annie was the other possibility, though she doubted Shanahan would've made such obvious contact. Brown eyes, but those could be contacts if he was playing this real fancy. Wearing a plaid jacket that made him look wider than Shanahan. Sitting on a stool, so Eileen couldn't tell how tall he was. But he was a possibility.

"This guy I got now . . . you know Ham Coleman?"

"I don't think so."

"Hamilton? Hamilton Coleman?"

"Yeah, maybe."

"Black as his name. Coal, you know. Coleman. Hung like a stallion, likes to parade around the pad with only a towel around him, dares the girls to snatch it off. Quick as a bullfighter. You snatch off the towel, he gives you a little treat. My poison is still hoss—well, you know, that's what Lou hooked me on. But some of the girls—there's six of us with him—they dig the nose candy, and he gets them whatever they need, good stuff too, I think he has Colombian connections. It's like a game he plays with the towel, snatch it off, suck his big dick, he lays the dope on you. I mean, it's just a game, 'cause he keeps us supplied very nice, any-

121

way. It's kind of cute, though, the way he struts around in that towel. He's really okay. Ham Coleman. You ever think of moving, you might want to come over. We don't have any redheads. That your real hair?"

"Yeah," Eileen said.

" 'Cause mine is straight from a bottle," Sheryl said, and laughed.

She still had a little-girl's laugh. Twenty-two years old, hooked on heroin, in the life since she was seventeen. Thought Ham Coleman with his towel was "kind of cute."

"What I'm really hoping for . . . well, this is just a *dream*, I know," she said, and rolled her eyes, "but I keep asking Ham about it all the time, who knows, it might really come true one day. I keep asking him to set us up like real call girls, you know, hundred-buck tricks, maybe two hundred, never mind dropping us here in the Zone where we're like common *whores*, you know what I mean? I mean, you and me, we're just common whores, ain't we? When you get right down to it?"

"Uh-huh. And what does he say?"

"Oh, he says we ain't got the class yet to be racehorses. I tell him class, shit. A blowjob's a blowjob. He says we still got a lot to learn, all six of us. He says maybe in time he'll set up a class operation like what I got in mind. So I tell him *when*? When we're all scaley-legged hookers, thirty, forty years old? Excuse me, I guess maybe you're in your thirties, I didn't mean no offense, Linda."

"Don't worry about it," Eileen said.

"Well, we all have our dreams, don't we?" Sheryl said, and sighed. "My dream when I first came to this city was I'd become an actress, you know? I was in a lot of plays in high school, in Baltimore, I figured I could make it big as an actress here. Well, that was just a dream. Like being a hundred-dollar call girl is probably just a dream, too. Still, you got to have dreams, am I right? Otherwise . . ."

"You girls gonna sit here talking to each other all night?"

The man standing by the table had padded up so quietly that he startled both of them. Blond guy, Eileen figured him at five-eleven, around a hundred and seventy pounds, just like Shanahan. Wearing dark glasses, she couldn't see the color of his eyes. The blond hair could be a wig. Moved a bit like Shanahan, too, maybe he *was* Shanahan. If so, he'd just won the bet. One thing he wasn't was the killer. Not unless he'd lost three, four inches, thirty pounds, a pair of eyeglasses, and a tattoo near his right thumb.

He pulled out a chair.

"Martin Reilly," he said, and sat. "What's a nice Irish lad doing in a joint like this, right?"

Voice heavier than Shanahan's. Calm's Point accent. Turtle Bay section, most likely. Lots of Irish families still there.

"Hi, Morton," Sheryl said.

"Martin," he corrected at once.

"Ooops, sorry," Sheryl said. "I'm Sheryl, I know just how you feel. When people call me Shirley, it really burns my ass."

"You know what really burns my ass?" Reilly said.

"Sure. People calling you Morton."

"No," Reilly said. "A little fire about this high."

He held out his hand, palm down, to indicate a fire only high enough to burn a man's ass.

"That one has hair on it," Eileen said, looking bored.

"Like the palm of my hand," Reilly said, and grinned. "All those months at sea, ladies, a man marries his hand."

Still grinning. Rows of even white glistening teeth, the better to eat you with, my dear. If Shanahan had capped teeth like that, he'd be starring on *Hill Street Blues*.

"You just get in?" Sheryl asked.

"Docked tonight."

"From where?"

"Lebanon."

"Ain't there no girls there in Lebanon?" Sheryl said, and rolled her eyes.

123

"Not like you two," he said.

"Oooo, my," she said, and leaned over the table so he could look into the front of her blouse. "So what are you looking for?" she asked, getting straight to the point. "A handjob's fifteen," she said, quoting high, "a blowjob's twenty-five, and Miss Puss is forty."

"How about your friend here? What's your name, honey?" he asked, and put his hand on Eileen's thigh.

"Linda," she said.

She let his hand stay on her thigh.

"That means beautiful in Spanish."

"So they tell me."

"How much for both of you? Do I get a better price for both of you?"

"You're getting a bargain as it is," Sheryl said.

"Tell you what," Reilly said, and slipped his hand up under Eileen's skirt. "I'll give you . . ."

"Mister," Eileen said, and caught his hand at the wrist. "You ain't given us *nothing* yet, so don't grope the goods, okay?"

"I'm sampling it."

"You get what you see, you don't need samples. This ain't a grocery store honors coupons."

Reilly laughed. He folded his hands on the table top.

"Okay, let's talk numbers," he said.

"We're listening," Sheryl said, and glanced at Eileen.

"Fifty for the both of you," Reilly said. "Around the world."

"You talking fifty for *each* of us?" Sheryl said.

"I said *both* of you. Twenty-five each."

"No way," Sheryl said at once.

"Okay, make it *thirty* each. And you throw in a little entertainment."

"What kinda entertainment?" Sheryl asked.

"I wanna see you go down on the redhead here."

Sheryl looked at Eileen appraisingly.

"I hardly know her," she said.

124

"So? You'll get to know her."

Sheryl thought it over.

"Make it fifty apiece, we'll give you a good show," she said.

"That's too much," he said.

"Then fuck off," Sheryl said. "You're wasting our time here."

"I'll tell you what," Reilly said. "I'll make it forty apiece, how's that?"

"What are you?" Sheryl said. "A Lebanese rug merchant?"

Reilly laughed again.

"Forty-five," he said. "For each of you. And a ten-dollar bonus for whoever brings me off first."

"Count me out," Eileen said.

"What's the matter?" Reilly asked, looking offended. "That's a fair and honest deal."

"It really is, you know," Sheryl said.

"Sheryl can show you a good time all by herself," Eileen said, doing a fast tap dance. "I don't work doubles."

"Then what the fuck were we talking about here?" Reilly asked.

"You were doing all the talking," Eileen said. "I was only listening."

Reilly dismissed her at once.

"You got any other girlfriends in here?" he asked Sheryl.

"How about the frizzied brunette over there?" she said.

Reilly looked over to where the brunette was still in conversation with one of the other Shanahan possibilities.

"That's Gloria," Sheryl said. "I worked with her before."

"Is she a muff-diver?" Reilly said. "Or is she like your friend here?"

"She *loves* pussy," Sheryl said, lying. "You want me to talk to her?"

"Yeah, go talk to her."

"That's forty-five apiece," Sheryl said, cementing the deal, "and a ten-buck bonus." She was figuring they'd do a little show, then take turns blowing him, and share the extra ten for fifty each. Which wouldn't be bad for an hour's work. Maybe less than an hour if he'd been at sea as long as he'd said. "A hundred in all, right?"

"A hundred is what I said, ain't it?"

"It's just I have to tell Gloria," Sheryl said, and got up, long leg and thigh flashing in the slit skirt. "Don't go away, honey," she said, and walked over to the other table.

"You're in the wrong business," Reilly said to Eileen.

Maybe I am, Eileen thought.

There were four liquor stores on Culver Avenue between the last one hit on Twentieth, and the eastern edge of the precinct territory on Thirty-Fifth. After that, it was the neighboring precinct's problem, and welcome to it. They drove up Culver to the last store, and then doubled back to the one on Twenty-Third. The digital dashboard clock read 10:32 P.M.

The store was empty except for a man behind the counter who was slitting open a carton of Jack Daniels sour mash. He looked up when the bell over the door sounded, saw a burly bald-headed guy and another big guy with him, and immediately placed his hand on the stock of the shotgun under the counter.

"What'll it be, gents?" he asked.

Hand still on the shotgun stock, finger inside the trigger guard now.

Meyer flashed the potsy.

"Police," he said.

The hand under the counter relaxed.

"Detective Meyer," he said. "Detective Carella. Eighty-Seventh Squad."

"What's the problem?" the man said.

He was in his early fifties, not quite as bald as Meyer, but getting there. Brown eyes, slight build, wearing a gray cotton work jacket with the words ALAN'S WHISKIES stitched in red on the breast pocket.

"Who are we talking to, sir?" Meyer asked.

126

"I'm Alan Zuckerman."

"Is this your store, sir?"

"It is."

"Mr. Zuckerman," Carella said, "there've been three liquor-store holdups on Culver Avenue tonight. Starting on Ninth and working uptown. If there's a pattern—and there may not be—your store's next in line."

"I'm closing in half an hour," Zuckerman said, and turned to look at the clock on the wall behind the counter.

"They may come in before then," Meyer said.

"You don't know me, huh?" Zuckerman said.

"Should I know you?" Meyer said.

"Alan Zuckerman. I was in all the papers last year this time." He looked at Carella. "*You* don't know me, either, do you?"

"I'm sorry, sir, I don't."

"Some cops," Zuckerman said.

Meyer glanced at Carella.

"This very precinct, they don't know me."

"Why should we know you, sir?" Carella asked.

"Because last October I shot two people came in the store to rob me," Zuckerman said.

"Oh," Carella said.

"With *this*!" Zuckerman said, and yanked the shotgun from under the counter.

Both detectives backed away.

"*Bang!*" Zuckerman said, and Meyer flinched. "One of them falls on the floor screaming! *Bang,* the other barrel! And the second one goes down!"

"I seem to recall that now," Meyer said. "Mr. Zuckerman, you can put up the shotgun now, okay?"

"Made all the papers," Zuckerman said, the gun still in his hands, his finger inside the trigger guard. "Shotgun Zuckerman, they called me, the papers. They had the story on television, too. Nobody tried no tricks here since, I can tell you that. It's been a year already, a little more than a year."

127

"Well, these people tonight," Meyer said, "Mr. Zuckerman, could you please put up the gun?"

Zuckerman slid the gun under the counter again.

"Thank you," Meyer said. "These people tonight, there are four of them. All of them armed. So your shotgun there, if all four of them start shooting . . ."

"Shotgun Zuckerman can take care of them, don't worry."

"What we were thinking," Carella said, "is maybe we could lend you a hand."

"Sort of ride shotgun to your shotgun," Meyer said, nodding.

"Backups, sort of," Carella said.

"Only in case you need us."

"Otherwise we'll butt out."

Zuckerman looked at them.

"Listen," he said at last, "you want to waste your time, that's fine by me."

He yanked the phone from the receiver the moment it rang.

"Hello?" he said.

"Hi," Marie said.

"Where are you?"

"Metro West. I'm catching the ten forty-five home."

"How'd it go?"

"Tough night," she said. "Any trouble on your end?"

"Nope. They made identification, huh? I saw it on television."

"I was the one who made it. Where'd you leave the Citation?"

"Behind an A & P near the river."

" 'Cause I don't think they found it yet."

"Who's on the case?"

"A salt-and-pepper team. Brown and Hawes. Big redhead, big black guy. In case they come snooping."

"Why would they?"

"I'm saying in case. They're both dummies, but you oughta be warned. They got a bulletin out . . . they asked me for descriptions. They're gonna be watching all the airports. What flight are you on?"

"TWA's one twenty-nine. Leaves at twelve-oh-five tomorrow afternoon."

"What time do you get to Frisco?"

"Four forty-seven."

"I'll try you at the hotel around six-thirty. You'll be registered as Jack Gwynne, am I right?"

"All the dead ones," he said, and laughed. "Like Sebastian the Great."

"Give me the number of the Hong Kong flight again?"

"United eight-oh-five. Leaves Frisco at one-fifteen Sunday, gets there around eight the next morning."

"When will you call me?"

"Soon as I'm settled."

"You think that passport'll work?"

"It cost us four hundred bucks, it *better* work. Why? You running scared?"

"Nerves of steel," she said. "You shoulda seen me with the cops."

"No problem with the ID, was there?"

"None."

"You did mention the cock?"

"Oh, sure."

"Little birthmark and all?"

"Come on, we went over this a hundred times."

"*You* went over it a hundred times."

"And hated every minute of it."

"Sure."

"You *know* that, damn it."

"Sure."

"You going to start on me again?"

"I'm sorry."

"You oughta be. All we've been through."

"I said I was sorry."

"Okay."

There was a long silence on the line.

"So whattya gonna do till noon tomorrow?"

"Thought I'd go down for a drink, then come back and get some sleep."

"Be careful."

"Oh yeah."

"They know what you look like."

"Don't worry."

Another silence.

"Maybe you oughta call me later tonight, okay?"

"Sure."

"Be careful," she said again, and hung up.

8

"Torpedoman ain't gonna like this," Larry said.

"Who asked you?" Eileen said.

"For a working girl, all you done so far is sit and drink."

"Guess it just ain't my lucky night," Eileen said.

"Whattya talkin' about? I already seen you turn down a dozen guys."

"I'm particular."

"Then you shouldn't be in this dump," Larry said. "Particular ain't for the Canal Zone."

Eileen knew he was only pointing out the obvious: the name of the game was money, and a hooker working a bar wasn't a girl at the Spring Cotillion. You didn't tell a prospective John your card was filled, even if he looked like Godzilla. Larry was already suspicious, and that was dangerous. Get a few more guys giving her the fish eye, and she could easily blow the *real* reason she was here.

Sheryl and the frizzied brunette were still out with the blond sailor, but Eileen was ready to bet her shield they'd be back in business the moment they returned. There was no way any enterprising girl could avoid making a buck in here. The bar was in incessant motion, a whorehouse with a liquor license and a transient crowd. Any man who came in alone walked out not five minutes later with a girl on his arm. According to Shanahan, the girls—even some of them on the Canalside meat rack—used either a hot-bed hotel up the street or any one of fifty, sixty rooms for rent in the Zone. They usually paid five bucks for the room, got a kickback from the owner and also a share of the three bucks the John paid for soap and towels. That way, a twenty-dollar trick could net a girl the same twenty when all was said and done. Plus whatever tip a generous John might decide to lay on her for superior performance.

She glanced down the length of the bar to where Annie was sitting in earnest conversation with a little Hispanic guy wearing jeans, boots, and a black leather jacket studded with chrome. Looked like Annie was having the same problem. The only difference was that she could step outside every now and then, make it look like she was drumming up trade on the street. Eileen was glued to the bar. The bar was where the killer had picked up his three previous victims. She tried to catch Annie's eye. They had figured out beforehand that if they wanted to talk they'd do it in the ladies' room, not here in public. Eileen wanted to dope out a scam that would cool Larry's heat.

"Torpedoman's gonna whip your ass," he said.

"You wanna make a little side bet?" Eileen said. "You wanna bet I go home with six bills before the night's over?"

Annie finally looked over at her.

Eye contact.

Brief nod of her head.

Eileen got off the stool and started for the ladies' room. The Hispanic guy sitting next to Annie got off his stool at the same time. Good, Eileen thought, she's ditching him. But the Hispanic guy walked straight toward her, meeting her halfway down the bar.

"Hey, where you goin', Mama?" he said. Loud voice for a little twerp, Spanish accent you could cut with a machete. Little brown eyes, mustache under his nose, looked like an undernourished biker in his leather jacket.

"Got to visit my grandma," Eileen said.

"You gran'ma can wait," he said.

Behind him, down the bar, Annie was watching them.

Another brief nod.

All right already, Eileen thought. As soon as I *shake* this guy.

The guy wasn't about to be shaken. He gripped Eileen's elbow in his right hand, began steering her toward the stool she'd abandoned—"Come on, Mama, we ha' biss'niss to talk abou'" —same loud voice, you could hear him clear across the river, fingers tight on her elbow, plunked her down on the stool—"My name iss Arturo, I been watchin' you, Mama"—and signaled to Larry.

"You want me to wet my pants?" Eileen asked.

"No, no, I sornly don' wann you to do that," he said.

Larry ambled over.

"See wha' my frien' here iss drinkin'," Arturo said.

She couldn't make a fuss about the ladies' room now, not with Larry standing right here and already believing she was turning down tricks left and right. Spot Annie trailing her in there, they'd *both* be out of business.

"Larry knows what I'm drinking," she said.

"Rum-Coke for the lady," Larry said, "it's still prom night. How about you, amigo?"

"Scotch on dee rahss," Arturo said. "Twiss."

Larry started pouring.

"So how much you get, Mama?" Arturo asked.

"What are you looking for?"

"This swee' li'l ting here," he said, and put his forefinger on her lips.

133

"That'll cost you twenty," she said.

Going price, in case Larry was listening. Which of course he was.

"You got someplace we can go, Mama?"

"Plenty of rooms for rent around here."

Everything kosher so far. But Larry was still here.

"How much do I pay for dee room?" Arturo asked.

"Five."

Larry raised his eyebrows. He knew the girls usually paid for the room themselves but he figured Linda here was hustling the little spic. Maybe she *would* go home with six bills tonight, who the hell knew?

"Muy bien, muchacha," Arturo said.

"Rum-Coke, scotch-rocks with a twist," Larry said, sliding the drinks closer to them. "Six bucks, a bargain."

Arturo put a ten-dollar bill on the counter. Larry started for the cash register at the far end. As soon as he was out of earshot, Arturo whispered, in perfect English, "I'm on the job, play along."

Eileen's eyes opened wide.

At the far end of the bar, Annie gave another brief nod. Larry rang open the register, put the ten in the drawer, took four bills out of it, slammed the drawer shut again, and then started back toward where they were sitting, sipping at their drinks now. Arturo had his hand on Eileen's knee, and he was peering down the front of her blouse. She was saying, " 'Cause like, you know, I'm a working girl, Artie, so I'd like to get started, if that's okay with you."

"Hey, no sweat, Mama," he said. "We can tay dee booze wid us."

"Not in *my* good glasses," Larry said, and immediately began transferring the drinks to plastic cups.

Eileen was already off the stool. She turned to Larry and said, "Glad you didn't take that bet?"

Larry shrugged.

He watched them as they picked up the cups and walked away from the bar. He was thinking he wouldn't mind a piece of that himself. As they started out the door, they almost collided with a man coming in at the same time.

"Oh, I beg your pardon," he said, and stepped aside to let them through.

Larry was sure he'd seen the guy before. He was at least six-feet two-inches tall, with wide shoulders and a broad chest, thick wrists, big hands. He was wearing jeans, sneakers, a little tan cap, and a yellow turtleneck sweater that matched the color of his hair. He looked like a heavyweight fighter in training.

"You're not *leaving*, are you?" he asked Eileen.

She breezed right past him, ignoring him.

But her heart was suddenly pounding.

Annie sat at the bar wearing a short tight black skirt, purple tube top cradling her cupcake breasts, high-heeled black patent leather shoes, face heavily pancaked, blood-red lipstick on her mouth, eyes lined in black, lids tinted to match the blouse, looking more like a hooker than any of the real ones in the place.

She thought Terrific. Here he is.

All we need is this little trick of fate.

Eileen walking out while he walks in.

Eileen loaded to the gunnels, me wearing only a .38 in my handbag, terrific.

Eileen the decoy, me the backup, and in he walks.

Terrific.

If it's him.

He sure as hell looked like the blond guy Alvarez and Shanahan had described. No eyeglasses, but the same height and weight, the same bulk.

Standing just inside the doorway now, looking over the place, cool, confident in his size, ready to take on any guy in the place, mop up the floor with him, this cat had nothing to worry about, oh no, handsome as the devil, oh so cool, scanning the room, checking out the girls, then walking up toward the bar, passing the cash register where she sat . . .

"Hi," she said. "Wanna join me?"

"Danny Ortiz," Arturo said on the street outside. "Detective/Second, Undercover Narcotics. I got a call from Lou . . ."

Lou, Eileen thought. Not Lou the friendly white man who'd turned out Sheryl, if that was her real name. In novels, everybody had different names so you could tell them apart. In real life, Lou could be a pimp and a detective at the same time. Lou Alvarez of the Seven-Two.

". . . said I ought to check out Larry's Bar, see his decoy needed some help. Described you and Rawles, sat with her, talked her up, she told me the Johns were hitting on you like locusts. Am I screwing anything up?"

Lou Alvarez, calling his buddy Danny Ortiz in Narcotics, asking him to run on over here, hit on the decoy, take her out of the joint to preserve her credibility.

"You saved my life," Eileen said.

Bit of an exaggeration, but at least he'd saved her cover.

"So you wanna neck or anything?" Ortiz said. "Pass the time?"

"That's the best offer I've had all night," she said. "But I gotta get back in there."

Ortiz looked at her.

"Our man just walked in," she said.

His size was intimidating. He filled the stool, filled the bar, seemed to fill the entire room. Sitting next to him, Annie was scared. If this was the guy . . .

"So what's your name?" she asked.

"What's yours?"

"Jenny," she said.

"I'll bet."

Deep voice rumbling up out of his barrel chest.

"Well," she said, "my straight handle is Antoinette Le Fevrier, but who'll believe that on a hooker?"

"Oh, is that what you are?" he asked.

Voice almost toneless. Bored attitude. Looking in the mirror, checking out the other girls in the place even as he talked to her.

"No, I'm a famous brain surgeon," Annie said, and smiled.

He did not smile back. Turned to look at her. Eyes the color of steel. A chill ran up her spine. Where the hell was Shanahan?

"You still didn't tell me your name," she said.

"Howie," he said.

Sounded square enough to be true.

"Howie what?"

"Howie's enough," he said, and folded his hands on the table-top. No tattoo on either one of them. Was he, or wasn't he? "So what you do is make love to strangers, huh?" he said. "For money."

She didn't want this guy to ask her outside. Not with only the .38 in her bag and Shanahan nowhere in sight.

"That's my job. You interested?"

"You're not my type," he said.

"Oh? And what's your type?" she asked. Keep him talking. Keep him interested till Eileen walked back in. And if Eileen *didn't* walk in soon, then talk him into taking *her* outside to make his move. If Shanahan was anywhere around, he'd be tracking both of them.

"I like them younger," he said. "And fresher."

"Well, what you see is what you get," she said.

"You seem too far gone."

"Uh-huh," she said, "practically ancient." One of the dead girls had been sixteen. The others were in their twenties. Keep him here, she thought. Don't let him wander off to any of the younger girls in here, or they'll drift away together and he'll score another one tonight.

"I mean, what can I tell you?" she said. "I'm not a teenager, but I'm pretty good for an old lady."

He turned to look at her again.

No smile.

Christ, he was chilling.

"Really?" he said.

"Really."

Come-on look in her eyes. She licked her lips. But she had only the .38 in her bag. No backup artillery. And Shanahan God knew where. Ortiz heading back home soon as he cleared Eileen, wham, bam, thank you, ma'am, or so it would appear to Larry.

"Ten for a handjob," she said, "how about it? Twenty for a blowjob, thirty if you want the pearly gates."

"My, my," he said. "You really are a seasoned pro, aren't you?"

"Exactly what I am," she said. "How about it?"

"No, you're too far gone," he said.

Eyes on the mirror again. The blonde who'd been talking with Eileen earlier was back now, together with her frizzied brunette friend. Both of them young and looking for more action. His eyes checked them out. Stick with me, pal, she thought. Here's where the action is.

"Are you a cop?" he asked without even looking at her.

Mind-reader, she thought.

"Sure," she said. "Are you a cop, too?"

"I used to be," he said.

Oh, shit, she thought. A renegade. Or a malcontent.

"I can always tell a cop," he said.

"You wanna see my badge?" she said.

Deliberately using the word badge. A cop called it a shield.

"Are you with Vice?" he asked.

"Oh, man, *am* I," she said. "Clear down to my tonsils."

"I used to be with Vice," he said.

"So *I'm* the one who caught myself a cop, huh?" she said, and smiled. "Well, Howie, that makes no difference to me at all, the past is the past, all water under the bridge. What do you say we take a little stroll up the street, I'll show you a real good ..."

"Get lost," he said.

"Let's get lost together, Howie," she said, and put her hand on his thigh.

"You understand English?" he said.

"French, too," she said. "Come on, Howie, give a working girl a ..."

"Get *lost* !" he said.

A command this time.

Eyes blazing, big hands clenched on the bartop.

"Sure," she said. "Relax."

She got off the stool.

"Relax, okay?" she said, and walked down to the other end of the bar.

Inexplicably, her palms were wet.

Guy sitting next to him at the bar was running a tab, twenty-dollar bill tucked under the little bowl of salted peanuts. Big flashy Texan sporting a diamond pinky ring, a shirt as loud as he himself was, and a black string tie held with one of those turquoise-and-silver Indian clasps. He was drinking martinis, and talking about soybeans. Said soybeans were the nation's future. No cholesterol in soybeans.

"So what do *you* do?" he asked.

"I'm in insurance."

Which wasn't too far from the truth. Soon as Marie made the insurance claim ...

"Lots of money in insurance," the Texan said.

"For sure."

At double indemnity, the policy came to two hundred grand. More money than he could make in eight years' time.

"By the way, my name's Abner Phipps," the Texan said, and extended a meaty hand.

He took the hand. "Theo Hardeen," he said.

"Nice to meet you, Theo. You gonna be in town long?"

"Leaving tomorrow.

"I'm stuck here all through next week," Phipps said. "I hate this city, I truly do. There're people who say it's a nice place to visit, but I can't even see it for that. Worth your life just walkin' the streets here. You see that thing on television tonight?"

"What thing is that?"

The black bartender was listening silently, standing some six feet away from them, polishing glasses. The clock on the wall read ten to eleven. Shows'd be breaking soon, he wanted to be ready for the crowd.

"Somebody chopping up a body, leaving pieces of it all over town," Phipps said, and shook his head. "Bad enough you *kill* somebody, you got to chop him up in pieces afterward? Why you suppose he did that, Theo?"

"Well, I'll tell you, Abner, there're all kinds of nuts in this world."

"I mean, there're two rivers in this city, Theo. Why didn't he just throw the whole damn *body* in one of them?"

That's where the head is, he thought. And the hands.

"Still," Phipps said, "if you got a body to get rid of, I guess it's easier to dump in sections. I mean, somebody sees you hauling a corpse around, that might raise suspicion, even in *this* city. An arm, a head, whatever, you can just drop in a garbage can or down the sewer, nobody'll pay any attention to you, am I right, Theo?"

"I guess maybe that's why he did it."

"Well, who can figure the criminal mind?" Phipps said.

"Not me, that's for sure. I have a hard enough time selling insurance."

"Oh, I'll bet," Phipps said. "You know why? Nobody likes to think he's gonna kick off one day. You sit there tellin' him how his wife's gonna be sittin' pretty once he's dead, he don't want to hear that. He wants to think he's gonna live forever. I don't care *how* responsible a man he is, it makes him uncomfortable talkin' about death benefits."

"You hit it right on the head, Abner. I talk myself blue in the face, and half the time they're not even listening. Explain, explain, explain, they don't know what the hell I'm talking about."

"People just don't listen anymore," Phipps said.

"Or they don't listen carefully enough. They hear only what they want to hear."

"That's for sure, Theo."

"I'll give you an example," he said, and then immediately thought Come on, he's too easy. On the other hand, it might teach him a valuable lesson. Chatting up a stranger in a bar, no real sense of how many con artists were loose and on the prowl in this city. Teach him something he could take back home to Horse's Neck, Texas.

He reached into his pocket, took out a dime and a nickel.

"What have I got here?" he asked.

"Fifteen cents," Phipps said.

"Okay, open your hand."

Phipps opened his hand.

"Now I'm putting this dime and this nickel on the palm of your hand."

"Yep, I see that, Theo."

"And I'm not touching them anymore, they're in your hand now, am I right?"

"Right there on the palm of my hand, Theo."

"Now close your hand on them."

Phipps closed his hand. The bartender was watching now.

"You've got that fifteen cents in your fist now, am I right?"

"Still there," Phipps said.

"A dime and a nickel."

"A dime and a nickel, right."

"And I haven't touched them since you closed your hand on them, right?"

"You haven't touched them, right."

"Okay, I'll bet you when you open your hand, one of them won't be a dime."

"Come on, Theo, you're lookin' to lose money."

"Man's lookin' to lose money for sure," the bartender said.

"I'll bet you the twenty dollars under that peanut bowl, okay?"

"You got a bet," Phipps said.

"Okay, open your hand."

Phipps opened his hand. Fifteen cents still on his palm. Same dime, same nickel. The bartender shook his head.

"You lose," Phipps said.

"No, I win. What I said . . ."

"The bet was that one of these coins wouldn't be a dime no more."

"No, you weren't listening. The bet was that one of them wouldn't be a dime."

"That's just what . . ."

"And one of them isn't. One of them's a nickel."

He slid the twenty-dollar bill from under the peanut bowl, and tucked it into his jacket pocket. "You can keep the fifteen cents," he said, and smiled and walked out of the bar.

The bartender said, "That's a good trick to know, man."

Phipps was still looking at the fifteen cents on the palm of his hand.

Genero was a celebrity.

And he was learning that a celebrity is expected to answer a lot of questions. Especially if he shot four teenagers. There were two people waiting to ask questions now. One was a roving investigative reporter from Channel 6. The other was a Duty Captain named Vince Annunziato, who was filling in for the Eight-Seven's Captain Frick. The reporter was interested only in a sensational news story. Annunziato was interested only in protecting the Department. He stood by silently and gravely while the reporter set up the interview; one sure way to get the media dumping on cops was to act like you had something to hide.

"This is Mick Stapleton," the reporter said, "at the scene of a shooting on North Eleventh Street, here in Isola. I'm talking to Detective/Third Grade Richard Genero, who not forty-five minutes ago shot four teenagers who allegedly started a fire in the apartment building behind me."

Annunziato caught the "allegedly." Protecting his ass in case this thing blew up to something like the Goetz shootings in New York. Guy with a hand-held camera aimed at Stapleton, another guy working some kind of sound equipment, third guy handling lights, you'd think they were shooting a Spielberg movie instead of a two-minute television spot. Crowds behind the police barriers. Ambulances already here and gone, carting away the four teenagers. Annunziato was happy they weren't black.

"Detective Genero, can you tell us what happened here?" Stapleton asked.

Genero blinked into the lights, looked at the red light on the front of the camera.

"I was making a routine tour of the sector," he said. "This is Halloween night and the lieutenant put on extra men to handle any problems that might arise in the precinct."

So far, so good, Annunziato thought. Care and caution on the part of the commanding officer, concern for the citizenry.

"So you were driving past the building here . . ."

"Yes, and I saw the perpetrators running into the premises with objects in their hands."

"What kind of objects?" Stapleton asked.

Careful, Annunziato thought.

"What turned out to be firebombs," Genero said.

"But you didn't know that at the time, did you?"

"All I knew was a roving band running into a building."

"And this seemed suspicious to you?"

"Yes, sir."

"Suspicious enough for you to draw your gun and . . . ?"

"I did not unholster my revolver until fire broke out in the premises."

Good, Annunziato thought. Felony in progress, reason to yank the piece.

"But when you first saw these youngsters, you didn't know they were carrying firebombs, did you?"

"I found out when the fires went off inside there, and they came running out."

"What did you do then?"

"I drew my service revolver, announced that I was a policeman and warned them to stop."

"And did they stop?"

"No, sir, they threw one of the firebombs at me."

"Is that when you shot at them?"

"Yes, sir. When they ignored my warnings and came at me."

Good, Annunziato thought. Proper procedure all the way down the line. Firearm used as a defensive weapon, not a tool of apprehension.

"When you say they came at you . . ."

"They attacked me. Knocked me over and kicked me."

"Were they armed?"

Careful, Annunziato thought.

"I did not see any weapons except the firebombs. But they had just committed a felony, and they were attacking me."

"So you shot them."

"As a last resort."

Perfect, Annunziato thought.

"Thank you, Detective Genero. For Channel Six News, this is Mick Stapleton on Eleventh Street."

With the edge of his hand, Stapleton made a throat-slitting gesture to his cameraman, and a brief "Thanks, that was swell" to Genero, and then walked quickly to where the mobile van was waiting at the curb.

Annunziato came over to where Genero was standing, looking surprised that it was over so fast.

"Captain Annunziato," he said. "I've got the duty."

"Yes, sir," Genero said.

"You handled that okay," Annunziato said.

"Thank you, sir."

"Handled *yourself* okay with them four punks, too."

"Thank you, sir."

"But you better call home now, tell 'em we're taking you off the street."

"Sir?"

"Few questions we'll have to ask you downtown. Make sure we get all the facts before the bleeding hearts come out of the woodwork."

"Yes, sir," Genero said.

He was thinking the goddamn shift would be relieved at a quarter to twelve, but he'd be downtown answering questions all night.

Train speeding through the night now, leaving behind the mills and factories just over the river, coming into rolling green land where you could see the lights of houses twinkling like it was Christmas instead of Halloween.

By Christmas they'd be sitting fat and pretty in India someplace.

Person could live on ten cents a day in India—well, that was an exaggeration. But you could rent yourself a luxurious villa, staff it with all the servants you needed, live like royalty on just the interest the two hundred thousand would bring. New names, new lives for both of them. Never mind trying to live on the peanuts Frank had earned each year.

She sighed heavily.

She'd have to call his mother as soon as she got home, and then his sister, and then she guessed some of his friends in the business.

145

Had to get in touch with that detective again, find out when she could claim the body, arrange for some kind of funeral, have to keep the casket closed, of course, she wondered how soon that would be. Today was Friday, she didn't know whether they did autopsies on the weekend, probably wouldn't get around to it till Monday morning. Maybe she could have the body by Tuesday, but she'd better call an undertaker first thing in the morning, make sure they could handle it. Figure a day in the funeral home—well, two days, she guessed—bury him on Thursday morning. She'd have to find a cemetery that had available plots, whatever you called them, maybe the undertaker would know about that. Had to have a stone cut, too, HERE LIES FRANK SEBASTIANI, REST IN PEACE—but that could wait, there was no hurry about a stone.

She'd call the insurance company on Friday morning.

Tell them her husband had been murdered.

Make her claim.

She didn't expect any problems. Sensational case like this one? Already on television and in one of the early morning papers she'd bought at the terminal. MAGICIAN MURDERED, the headline read. Bigger headline than he'd ever had in his life. Had to get himself killed to get it.

Two hundred thousand dollars, she thought.

Invest it at ten percent, that'd bring them twenty thousand a year, more than enough to live on like a king and queen. A maharajah and maharanee was more like it. Go to the beach every day, have someone doing the cleaning and the cooking, have a man polishing the car and doing the marketing, buy herself a dozen saris, learn how to wrap them, maybe get herself a little diamond for her nose. Even at eight percent, the money would bring in sixteen thousand a year. More than enough.

And all they'd had to do for it was kill him.

The train rumbled through the night, lulling her to sleep.

✿   ✿   ✿

He approached Eileen almost the moment she sat down at one of the tables.

"Hi," he said. "Remember me?"

No eyeglasses, no tattoo, but otherwise their man down to his socks. The eyeglasses he'd worn on his earlier outings could have been windowpane. The tattoo could have been a decal. Her heart was beating wildly. She didn't realize until this moment just how frightened she really was. You're a *cop*, she told herself. *Am* I? she wondered.

"I'm sorry," she said, "have we met?"

"Mind if I sit down?"

"Please do."

The prim and proper hooker.

But crossed her legs anyway, to show him thigh clear to Cincinnati.

"I'm Linda," she said. "Are you looking for a good time?"

"That depends," he said.

"On what?"

"On what you consider a good time."

"That's entirely up to you."

"I noticed you when I was coming in," he said. "You were leaving with a little Puerto Rican."

"You're very observant," she said.

"You're a beautiful woman, how could I miss you?"

"What's your name?" she asked.

"Howie."

"Howie what?"

"Howie gonna keep 'em down on the farm."

He had them in stitches. Shanahan's words. Kept telling them jokes. A stand-up comic with a knife.

"So what're you interested in, Howie?"

"Let's talk," he said.

"Candy store's open," she said. "You want to know how much the goodies cost?"

147

"Not right now."

"Just say when, Howie."

He folded his hands on the tabletop. Looked into her eyes.

"How long have you been hooking, Linda?"

"First time tonight," she said. "In fact, I'm a virgin."

Not a smile. Not even the *hint* of a smile. Some stand-up comic. Just sat there looking into her eyes, big hands folded on the table.

"How old are you?"

"You should never ask a woman her age, Howie."

"Early thirties, in there?"

"Who knows?" she said, and rolled her eyes.

"What's your real name?"

"What's yours?"

"I told you. Howie."

"But you didn't tell me Howie what."

"Howie Cantrell," he said.

"Eileen Burke," she said.

The name would mean nothing to him. If he was their man, he'd learn soon enough who Eileen Burke was. If he was looking for action, her name wouldn't mean beans to him.

"Why are you using Linda?" he asked.

"I hate the name Eileen," she said. Which wasn't true. She'd always thought the name Eileen was perfect for the person she was. "Linda sounds more glamorous."

"You're glamorous enough," he said, "you don't need a phony name. May I call you Eileen?"

"You can call me Lassie if you like."

Still no smile. Totally devoid of a sense of humor. So where was the comedian? Flat, steel-gray eyes reflecting nothing. But were they the eyes of a triple murderer?

"So where're you from, Howie?"

"I'll ask the questions," he said.

"Now you sound like a cop."

"I used to be one."

148

Bullshit, she thought.

"Oh?" she said. "Where?"

"Philadelphia," he said. "Do you see that girl sitting at the bar?"

"Which one?" Eileen asked.

"In the black skirt. With the short dark hair."

He was indicating Annie.

"What about her?"

"I think she's a cop," he said.

Eileen burst out laughing.

"Jenny?" she said. "You've got to be kidding."

"You know her?"

"She's been hooking since she was thirteen. Jenny a cop? Wait'll I tell her!"

"I already told her."

"Mister, let me tell *you* something about hookers and cops, okay?"

"I know all about hookers and cops."

"Right, you're a cop yourself."

"*Used* to be one," he said. "I can always tell a cop."

"Have it your way," she said. "Jenny's a cop, you're a cop, I'm a cop, when you're in love the whole world's a cop."

"You don't believe I used to be a cop, do you?"

"Howie, I'll believe anything you tell me. You tell me you used to be a Presbyterian minister, I'll believe you. An astronaut, a spy, a . . ."

"I was with the Vice Squad in Philly."

"So what happened? Didn't you like the work?"

"It was good work."

"So how come you ain't doing it no more?"

"They fired me."

"Why?"

"Who knows?" he said, and shrugged.

"Can't stay away from the job, though, huh?"

"What does that mean?"

149

"Well, here you are, Howie."

"Just thought I'd drop by."

"You been here before?"

First leading question she'd asked him.

"Couple of times."

"Guess you like it, huh?"

"It's okay."

"Come on, Howie, tell me the truth." Teasing him now. "You really dig the girls here, don't you?"

"They're okay. Some of them."

"Which ones?"

"Some of them. Lots of these girls, you know, they're in this against their will, you know."

"Oh, sure."

"I mean, they were forced into it, you know."

"You sure you were a Vice cop, Howie?"

"Yes."

"I mean, you sound almost *human*."

"Well, it's true, you know. A lot of these girls would get out of it if they knew how."

"Tell me the secret. How do I get out of it, Howie?"

"There are ways."

A big, wiry, gray-haired guy walked over from the bar. Had to be in his mid-fifties, grizzled look, sailor's swagger. Wearing jeans and white sneakers, blue T-shirt, gold crucifix hanging on a chain outside the shirt, metal-buttoned denim jacket open over it. Right arm in a plaster cast and a sling. Shaggy gray eyebrows, knife scar angling downward through the right brow and partially closing the right eye. Brown eyes. Thick nose broken more than once. Blue watch cap tilted onto the back of his head. Shock of gray hair hanging on his forehead. He pulled out a chair, sat, and said, "Buzz off, Preacher."

Howie looked at him.

"Buzz off, I wanna talk to the lady."

"Hey mister," Eileen said, "we're . . ."

"You hear me, Preacher? Move!"

Howie shoved back his chair. He glared angrily at the guy with the broken arm, and then walked across the bar and out into the street. Annie was already up and after him.

"Thanks a lot," Eileen said. "You just cost me . . ."

"Shanahan," he said.

She looked at him.

"Put your hand on my knee, talk nice."

The midgets came in at a minute before eleven.

Shotgun Zuckerman was ready to close the store.

They came in yelling "Trick or treat!"

Alice opened fire at once.

("It was us taking all the risk," she said at the Q & A later. "Never mind what Quentin told us. If anybody pegged us for little people, we were finished. It was better to kill them. Easier, too.")

Zuckerman didn't even have a chance to reach for the shotgun. He went down dead in the first volley.

Meyer and Carella broke out of the stockroom the moment they heard the bell over the door sound. By the time they came through the curtain shielding the front of the store from the back, Zuckerman was already dead.

In the station wagon outside, the blonde began honking the horn.

"Police!" Meyer shouted, and Alice opened up with a second volley.

This wasn't a cops-and-robbers movie, this was real life.

Neither of the detectives got off a shot.

Meyer went down with a bullet through his arm and another through his shoulder.

Carella went down with a bullet in his chest.

No tricks. Real blood. Real pain.

Three of the midgets ran out of the store without even glancing at the cash register. The only reason Alice ran out after them, without first killing the two cops on the floor, was that she thought there might be more cops in the place.

This came out during the Q & A at ten minutes past two on the morning of All Hallows' Day.

9

The more Parker presented himself as a *fake* cop, the more he began feeling like a *real* cop. Everybody at the party kept telling him he could pass for a detective anywhere in the city. Everybody told him his shield and his gun, a .38 Smith & Wesson Detective Special, looked very authentic. One of the women—a sassy brunette dressed as a Las Vegas cigarette girl, in a flared black skirt and a flimsy top, high-heeled black shoes, and seamed silk stockings—wanted to hold the gun but he told her cops didn't allow straights to handle dangerous weapons. He had deliberately used police jargon for "honest citizens." In this city, a straight was anyone victimized by a thief. In some cities, victims were called "civilians." In any city, a thief was anyone who wasn't a cop, a straight, or a civilian. To the cops in this city, most thieves were "cheap" thieves.

A homosexual wearing a blonde wig, a long purple gown, and amethyst earrings to match, objected to the use of the word

153

sale of arms to Iran had provided unauthorized funds for Nicaraguan rebels.

This was straying into intellectual territory beyond Parker's scope.

He laughed, anyway.

Pornography was something he dealt with on a daily basis, and he believed straights ought to keep their noses out of it, period. Complicated and illegal arms deals were something else, and he never wondered about them except as they might effect his line of work. When you dealt with cheap thieves day and night, you already knew that they weren't only in the streets but also in the highest reaches of government. He didn't say this to anyone here at the party because he was having too good a time, and he didn't want to get too serious about cause and effect. He didn't even think of it consciously as cause and effect. But he knew, for example, that when a star athlete was exposed as a coke addict, the kids playing pickup ball in the school yard thought, "Hey, I gotta try me some of that shit." He also knew that when somebody high up in government broke the law, then your punk dealing grams of crack in the street could justify his actions by saying, "See? *Everybody* breaks the law." Cause and effect. It only made Parker's job harder. Which was maybe why he didn't work too hard at the job anymore. Although tonight, *playing* at the job, he felt as if he was working harder at it than he had in years.

It was really very peculiar.

He told everybody that one day he was going to write a book about his experiences.

"Ah-ha!" somebody said, "you're a *writer!*"

"No, no, I'm a cop," he protested.

"So how come you want to be a writer?" someone else said.

" 'Cause I ain't got the guts to be a burglar," Parker said, and everyone laughed again.

He'd never realized he was so witty.

At a little after eleven, Peaches suggested that they move on to another party.

155

Which is how Parker got to meet the wheelman and one of the midgets on the liquor-store holdups.

There were a lot of things bothering Brown about the Sebastiani case.

The three most important things were the head and the hands. He kept wondering why they hadn't turned up yet. He kept wondering where Jimmy Brayne had dropped them.

He also wondered where Brayne was right now.

The blues from the Two-Three, armed with the BOLO that had gone out all over the city, had located the blue Citation in the parking lot of an A & P not far from the River Dix. The techs had crawled over the car like ants, lifting latent prints, collecting stain samples, vacuuming for hairs and fibers. Anything they'd got had already been bagged and sent to the lab for comparison with whatever had been recovered from the Econoline van. Brown had no illusions about the lab getting back to them before sometime Monday. Meanwhile, both cars had been dumped—which left Brayne without wheels. His last location had been in the Twenty-Third, where he'd dropped the Citation, way over on the south side of the city. Was he now holed up somewhere in that precinct? Had he cabbed east, west, or north to a hotel someplace else? Or was he already on an airplane, bus, or train heading for parts unknown?

All of this bothered Brown.

He also wondered why Brayne had killed his mentor and employer.

"You think they're making it?" he asked Hawes.

"Who?"

"Brayne and the woman."

"Marie?"

The possibility had never occurred to Hawes. She had seemed so honestly grieved by her husband's disappearance and death. But now that Brown had mentioned it—

"I mean, what I'm looking for is some motive here," Brown said.

"The guy could've just gone beserk, you know. Threw those tricks all over the driveway, ran off in the Citation . . ."

"Yeah, I'm curious about that, too," Brown said. "Let's try to dope out a timetable, okay? They come into the city together, Brayne in the van, Marie and her husband in the Citation . . ."

"Got to the school around a quarter past three."

"Unloaded the car and the van . . ."

"Right."

"And then Brayne went off God knows where, said he'd be back at five, five-thirty to pick up the big stuff."

"Uh-huh."

"Okay, they finish the act around five-fifteen. Sebastiani changes into his street clothes, goes out back to load the car while Marie's getting out of her costume. She comes out later, finds the stuff all over the driveway and the Citation gone."

"Right."

"So we got to figure Brayne dumped the van on Rachel Street sometime between three-thirty and five-fifteen, grabbed a taxi back to the school, and cold-cocked Sebastiani while he was loading the car."

"That's what it looks like," Hawes said.

"Then he chops up the body—where'd he do that, Cotton? Blood stains in the Citation's trunk, you know, but nowhere else in the car."

"Coulda done it anywhere in the city. Found himself a deserted street, an abandoned building . . ."

"Yeah, you could do that in this city. So he chops up the corpse, loads the pieces in the trunk, and starts dropping them all around town. When he gets rid of the last one, he leaves the car behind that A & P and takes off."

"Yeah."

"So where's the motive?"

"I don't know."

"She's an attractive woman," Brown said.

Hawes had noticed that.

"If she was playing house with Brayne in that apartment over the garage . . ."

"Well, you've got no reason to believe that, Artie."

"I'm snowballing it, Cotton. Let's say they had a thing going. Brayne and the woman."

"Okay."

"And let's say hubby tipped to it."

"You're thinking movies or television."

"I'm thinking real-life, too. Hubby tells Brayne to lay off, Brayne's still hungry for her. He chops up hubby, and him and the woman ride off into the sunset."

"Except Brayne's the only one who rode off," Hawes said. "The woman's . . ."

"You think she's home yet?" Brown asked, and looked up at the clock.

Ten minutes past eleven.

"Half hour or so to Collinsworth," Hawes said. "She was catching the ten forty-five."

"Whyn't we take a ride out there?" Brown said.

"What for?"

"Toss that apartment over the garage, see we can't find something."

"Like what?"

"Like maybe where Brayne's heading. Or better yet, something that links him to the woman."

"We'll need a warrant to toss that garage."

"We haven't even got jurisdiction across the river," Brown said. "Let's play it by ear, okay? If the lady's clean, she won't ask for a warrant."

"You want to call her first?"

"What for?" Brown said. "I love surprises."

✿ ✿ ✿

Kling waved so long to them as they headed out of the squad-room. He looked up at the clock. The graveyard shift should be here in half an hour or so—O'Brien, Delgado, Fujiwara and Willis. Fill them in on what had gone down on the four-to-mid-night, grab one of the sedans, and head for Calm's Point. Make himself invisible in the Zone, just another John looking for a little Friday-night sport. But keep an eye out for Eileen.

He thought she was dead wrong about this one.

His being there in the Zone could only help an undercover sit-uation that had been hastily planned and recklessly under-manned.

This time, *he* was the one who was dead wrong.

They sat at the table talking in whispers, just another hooker and a potential trick. Negotiating the deal, Larry figured. Never seen the guy with the broken arm in here before, wondered who'd be on top in the sack, might get a little clumsy with that arm in a sling. Wondered about that and nothing else. The place was still busy, there was booze to be poured.

"Howie Cantrell is his real name," Shanahan whispered. "Used to be with Vice in Philly, that's all straight goods. Went off his rocker six years ago, first started beating up hookers in the street, then began preaching salvation to them. The Philly P.D. didn't so much mind the beatings. Worse things than beatings go down in Vice. But they didn't like the idea of a plainclothes min-ister on the force. They sent him up for psychiatric, and the shrinks decided he was under considerable stress as a result of his proximity to the ladies of the night. Retired him with full pen-sion, he drifted first to Boston, then here, started his missionary work all over again in the Zone. Everybody calls him the Preacher. He looks for the young ones, spouts Jesus to them, tries to talk them out of the life. Takes one of them to bed every now and then, for old times' sake. But he's harmless. Hasn't raised a hand to anybody since Philly let him go."

"I thought he was our man," Eileen said.

"We did, too, at first. Dragged him in right after the first murder, questioned him up and down, but he was clean as a whistle. Talked to him again after the second one, and again after the third. Alibis a mile long. We shoulda warned you about him. Be easy to make the mistake you made. How's it going otherwise?"

"I almost lost my virginity, but Alvarez bailed me out."

"Who'd he send?"

"Guy named Ortiz. Narcotics."

"Good man. Looks eighteen, don't he? He's almost thirty."

"You coulda told me I'd have help."

"We're just full of tricks," Shanahan said, and smiled.

"You gonna plant yourself in here?" Eileen asked.

"Nope. I'll be outside. Watching, waiting."

"Who grizzled up your hair?" she asked.

"The Chameleon," he said, and grinned.

"I hope you can *see* through that eye."

"I can see just fine."

"And I hope our man doesn't want to arm wrestle," she said, glancing at the cast.

Across the room, Annie was coming back into the bar. She walked to where Larry was standing, put four dollars on the bartop and said, "Your end, pal."

"Why, thank you, honey," he said, "much obliged," and tucked the bills into his shirt pocket, figuring the four represented twenty percent of whatever she'd got for her last trick. I *do* love an honest hooker, he thought, and immediately wondered if she'd short-changed him.

Annie wandered over to where Eileen and Shanahan were sitting.

"Your blond friend went home," she said. "Caught a bus on the corner."

"That's okay," Eileen said, "I'm still waiting for Mr. Right."

Annie nodded, and then walked over to a table on the other

side of the room. She wasn't alone for more than a minute when a big black guy sat down next to her.

"She needs help," Eileen whispered.

"Bring her outside," Shanahan said, and then rose immediately and said in a voice loud enough for everyone in the bar to hear, "I'll see you around the corner, honey."

Eileen went over to Annie and the black man.

"I got a one-armed bandit waiting in a car around the corner," she said. "He's looking for a hands-on trio, me driving, him in the middle, both of us dancing his meat around the block. You interested in a dime for ten minutes' work?"

"Dimes add up," Annie said, and immediately got to her feet.

"Hurry on back, hear?" the black man said.

"I did not appreciate all the shooting," Quentin Forbes said, looking petulant. He was still wearing the dress, pantyhose, and low-heeled walking shoes he'd worn while driving the station wagon, but the long blonde wig was hooked over the arm of a ladder-backed wooden chair. "There was no need for such violence, Alice. I warned you repeatedly . . ."

"It was only insurance," she said, and shrugged.

"The costumes were all the insurance we . . ."

"The costumes were bullshit," Alice said.

She was a beautiful little blonde woman in her late thirties, blue eyes and a Cupid's-bow mouth, perfect legs and breasts, four-feet two-inches tall and weighing a curvaceous seventy-one pounds. In the circus, she was billed as Tiny Alice. This went over big with homosexual men. She had changed out of the clown costume they'd worn on the last two holdups, and was now wearing a dark green dress and high-heeled pumps. To Forbes, she looked wildly sexual.

"Did you want the cops to think three *separate* gangs of kids were holding up those stores?" she asked.

"I wanted to confuse the cops, was all," Forbes said. "If you want to know what *I* think, Alice, I think your shooting spree was what brought them down on us, is what I think."

"We should have finished them off," she said. "If you hadn't started honking the horn . . ."

"I honked the horn to warn you. The moment I saw them coming from the back room . . ."

"We should have finished them off," she said again, and took a tube of lipstick from her handbag and went to the mirror on the wall.

"The point of the costumes," Forbes insisted, "was to . . ."

"The point was you wanted to put on a dress," Alice said. "I think you enjoy being in drag."

"I do indeed," Forbes said. "First time I've been in a woman's pants in more than a month."

"Braggart," Corky said.

She was slightly taller than Alice, a bad failing for a midget, but she was prettier in a delicate, small-boned, almost Oriental way. She, too, had changed into street clothes, a black skirt and a white silk blouse, a pink cardigan sweater, high-heeled patent leather pumps. She looked like a tiny, young Debbie Reynolds.

The two men who'd been in on the holdups were sitting at the table, still wearing their clown suits, counting the money.

"That's five thousand here," one of them said.

High Munchkin voice, wearing glasses, brown eyes intent behind them. His name was Willie. In the circus, he was billed as Wee Willie Winkie. Next month, he'd be down in Venice, Florida, rehearsing for the season. Tonight he was helping to stack and count the money from four stickups—well, *three* actually, since they hadn't got anything but cops on the last one. The stickups had been Forbes' idea, but Corky was the one who talked Willie into going along, said it'd be a good way to pick up some quick off-season change. Corky was his wife, and Alice was her best friend. This made Willie nervous. Alice was the only one who'd shot anyone tonight. The others had all fired their pistols well over the heads of the store owners, the way Forbes had told them to.

"What we should do," Willie said to the other man at the table, "we should both of us count each stack."

His hands were sweating. He was still very nervous about this whole thing. He was sure the police would come breaking in here any minute. All because of Alice. He had never heard of a midget doing time in prison. Or getting the electric chair. He did not want to be the first one in history.

"Can I trust you little crooks to give me a true count?" Forbes asked.

"You can help count it, you want to," the other man at the table said.

He was older than the other midgets, shorter and more delicate than even the women. His name was Oliver. In the circus, he was billed as Oliver Twist. He never understood why. He had red hair and blue eyes, and he was single, which was just the way he wanted it. Oliver was a great ladies' man. Full-sized women loved to pick him up and carry him to bed. Full-sized women considered him too darling for words, and they were never threatened by his tiny erect pecker. Full-sized women were always amazed that they could swallow him to the hilt without gagging. In some ways, being a midget had its benefits.

"Here's another five," Willie said, and slid the stack to Oliver, who began riffling the bills like a casino dealer.

"My rough estimate," Forbes said, "is we took in something like forty thousand."

"I think that's high," Alice said.

Standing at the mirror, putting on her lipstick. Lips puckered to accept the bright red paint, pretty as a little doll. Forbes had tried making her last year when they were playing the Garden in New York. She'd turned him down cold, said he would break her in half, although he knew she was sleeping with half the Flying Dutchmen. Corky watched her intently, as if hoping to pick up some makeup tricks.

"Twelve, thirteen thousand each store," Forbes said, "that's what I figure. Thirty-five, forty thousand dollars."

"There wasn't any thirteen in that store with the lady owner," Oliver said.

He was the one who'd cleaned out the register after Alice shot that lady in the third store. They weren't supposed to talk in the stores, but he'd yelled, "Hold it *open,* Alice!," because Alice's hands were trembling, and the bag was shaking as if there was a snake in it trying to get out.

"Mark my words, forty," Forbes said.

"Here's another five," Willie said.

"Fifteen already," Forbes said. "Mark my words."

Turned out, when all was said and done, that there was only thirty-two thousand.

"What'd I tell you?" Alice said.

"Somebody must be skimming," Forbes said, and winked at her.

"What does that come to?" Corky asked. "Five into thirty-two?"

"Something like sixty grand apiece," Oliver said.

"You *wish,*" Alice said.

"Six, I mean."

Willie was already doing the long division on a scrap of paper. "Six-four," he said.

"Which ain't bad for a night's work," Forbes said.

"We should've finished those cops," Alice said idly, blotting her lipstick with a piece of Kleenex. Willie shivered. He looked at his wife. Corky was staring at Alice's mouth, a look of idolatrous adoration on her face. Willie shivered again.

"What I'm gonna do right now," Forbes said, "is get out of this dress, and put on my own clothes, and then I'm gonna go partying. Alice? You wanna come along?"

She looked him up and down as if seeing him for the first time. Then she shrugged and said, "Sure. Why not?"

164

* * *

She called her mother-in-law the moment she was in the house.

The place felt empty without him.

"Mom," she said. "This is Marie."

Crackling on the line to Atlanta.

"Honey," her mother-in-law said, "this is a *terrible* connection, can you get the operator to ring it again?"

Terrific, she thought. I'm calling to tell her Frank is dead, and she can't hear me.

"I'll try again," she said, and hung up, and then dialed the operator and asked her to place the call. Her mother-in-law picked up on the second ring.

"How's that?" Marie asked her.

"Oh, much better. I was just about to call *you*, this must be psychic." Susan Sebastiani believed in psychic phenomena. Whenever she held a seance in her house, she claimed to converse with Frank's father, who'd been dead and gone for twenty years. Frank's father had been a magician, like his son. "What it is," she said, "I had this terrible premonition that something was wrong. I said to myself, 'Susan, you'd better call the kids.' Are you okay? Is everything all right?"

"Well . . . no," Marie said.

"What's the matter?" Susan said.

"Mom . . ."

How to tell her?

"Mom . . . this is very bad news."

"What is it?"

"Mom . . . Frank . . ."

"Oh, my God, something's happened to him," Susan said at once. "I knew it."

Silence on the line.

"Marie?"

"Yes, Mom."

"What happened? Tell me."

165

"Mom . . . he's . . . Mom, he's dead."

"What? Oh, my God, my God, oh, dear God," she said, and began weeping.

Marie waited.

"Mom?"

"Yes, I'm here."

"I'm sorry, Mom. I wish I wasn't the one who had to tell you."

"Where are you?"

"Home."

"I'll come up as soon as I can. I'll call the airlines, find out when there's . . . what happened? Was it an automobile accident?"

"No, Mom. He was murdered."

"What?"

"Someone . . ."

"What? *Who?* What are you talking about? Murdered?"

"We don't know yet, Mom. Someone . . ."

She couldn't bring herself to tell his mother that someone had chopped up his body. That could wait.

"Someone killed him," she said. "After a show we did this afternoon. At a high school up here."

"Who?"

"We don't know yet. The police think it might have been Jimmy."

"Jimmy? Jimmy Brayne? Who Frank was teaching?"

"Yes, Mom."

"I can't believe it. Jimmy?"

"That's what they think."

"Well, where is he? Have they questioned him?"

"They're still looking for him, Mom."

"Oh, God, this is terrible," Susan said, and began weeping again. "Why would he do such a thing? Frank treated him like a brother."

"We both did," Marie said.

"Have you called Dolores yet?"

166

"No, you're the first one I . . ."

"She'll have a heart attack," Susan said. "You'd better let me tell her."

"I can't ask you to do that, Mom."

"She's my daughter, I'll do it," Susan said.

Still weeping.

"I'll tell her to come there right away, you'll need help."

"Thank you, Mom."

"What is it from her house? An hour?"

"Tops."

"I'll tell her to get right there. Are you okay?"

"No, Mom," she said, and her voice broke. "I feel terrible."

"I know, I know, sweetie, but be brave. I'll come up as soon as I can. Meanwhile, Dolores will be there. Oh, my God, so many people I'll have to call, relatives, friends . . . when is the funeral going to be? They'll want to know."

"Well . . . they'll be doing an autopsy first."

"What do you mean? Chopping him up?"

Silence on the line.

"You didn't give them permission to do that, did you?"

Opportunity right there to tell her he was *already* chopped up. She let the opportunity pass.

"They have to do an autopsy in a murder case," she said.

"Why?"

"I don't know why, it's the law."

"Some law," Susan said.

Both women fell silent.

Susan sighed heavily.

"All right," she said, "let me call Dolores, let me get to work. She'll be there in a little while, will you be okay till then?"

"I'll be fine."

Another silence.

"I know how much you loved him," Susan said.

"I did, Mom."

"I know, I know."

167

Another sigh.

"All right, honey, I'll talk to you later. I'll try to get a plane to-night if I can. You're not alone, Marie. Dolores will be right there, and I'll be up as soon as I can."

"Thank you, Mom."

"All right now," Susan said, "I have to go now. Call me if you need me."

"Yes, Mom."

"Good night now, honey."

"Good night, Mom."

There was a small click on the line. Marie put the receiver back on the cradle. She looked up at the clock on the kitchen wall. Only forty minutes left to what had been the longest day of her life.

The clock ticked noisily into the stillness of the empty house.

The clock on the hospital wall read twenty-five minutes past eleven.

Lieutenant Peter Byrnes had not yet called the wives. He would have to call the wives. Speak to Teddy and Sarah, tell them what had happened. He was standing in the corridor with Deputy Police Commissioner Howard Brill, who'd come uptown when he'd heard that two detectives had been shot in a liquor-store stakeout. Brill was a black man in his early fifties; Byrnes had known him when they were both walking beats in River-head. About the same size as Byrnes, same compact head and in-telligent eyes; the men could have been cast from the identical bullet mold, except that one was black and the other was white. Brill was upset; Byrnes could understand why.

"The media's gonna have a ball," Brill said. "Did you see this?"

He showed Byrnes the front page of one of the morning tab-loids. The headline looked as if it had been written for a sensa-tional rag that sold at the local supermarket. But instead of

MARTIAN IMPREGNATES CAMEL or HITLER REINCAR-
NATED AS IOWA HOUSEWIFE, this one read:

MIDGETS 2—COPS 0
POLICE CAUGHT SHORT

"Very funny," Byrnes said. "I got one cop in intensive care,
and another one in surgery, and they're making jokes."

"How are they?" Brill asked.

"Meyer's okay. Carella . . ." He shook his head. "The bullet's
still inside him. They're digging for it now."

"What caliber?"

"Twenty-two. That's according to the slugs we recovered in
the store. Meyer took two hits, but the bullets passed through."

"He was lucky," Brill said. "They're worse than a goddamn
forty-five, those low-caliber guns. Hit a man where there's real
meat, the bullet hasn't got the force to exit. Ricochets around inside there like it's bouncing off furniture."

"Yeah," Byrnes said, and nodded bleakly.

"Lot of shooting tonight," Brill said. "You'd think it was the
Fourth of July, 'stead of Halloween. Your man clean on that
other one?"

"I hope so," Byrnes said.

"Four teenagers, Pete, the media *loves* kids getting shot.
What's the report on their condition?"

"I haven't checked it. I ran over here the minute . . ."

"Sure, I understand."

Byrnes guessed he should have checked on those kids before
he'd come over here—not that he really cared *how* they were,
except as their condition reflected on his squad. On his block, if
you were looking for trouble with a cop, you should be happy
you found it. But if Genero had pulled his gun without prudent
care and reasonable cause, and if one of those punks died, or
worse yet ended up a vegetable . . .

"How smart is he?" Brill asked.

"Not very."

" 'Cause they'll be coming at him, you know."

"I realize that."

"Where is he now?"

"Still downtown. I think. I really don't know, Howie. I'm sorry, but when I heard about Meyer and Carella . . ."

"Sure, I understand," Brill said again.

He was wondering which of the incidents would cause the Department the biggest headache. A dumb cop shooting four kids, or two dumb cops getting shot by midgets.

"Midgets," he said aloud.

"Yeah," Byrnes said.

Tricky, he thought.

I know that.

Coming back to the same bar a fourth time.

But that's part of the fun.

Look the same, act the same, makes it more exciting that way. Big blond guy is who they're looking for, so Heeeeeere's *Johnny,* folks! No description in the newspapers yet, but that's the cops playing it tricky, too.

Tricks all around, he thought.

Suits me fine.

By now they're thinking psycho.

Some guy who once had a traumatic experience with a hooker. Hates all hookers, is systematically eliminating them. They ought to boot up their computer, check with Kansas City. In Kansas City, it was only two of them. Well, when you're just starting, you start small, right? In Chicago, it was three. Good night, folks! Do my little song and dance in each city, listen to the newspaper and television applause, take my bow, and shuffle off to Buffalo. Slit their throats, carve up their pussies, the cops *have* to be thinking psycho. I'll do four of them here, he thought, and then move on. Two, three, four, a nice gradual escalation.

Let the cops think psycho.

A psycho acts compulsively, hears voices inside his head, thinks someone's commanding him to do what he's doing. Me, I never hear voices except when I'm listening to my Sony Walkman. Comedians. Walk along with the earphones on, listen to their jokes. Woody Allen, Bob Newhart, Bill Cosby, Henny Youngman . . .

Take my wife. Please.

For our anniversary, my wife said she wanted to go someplace she'd never been. I said, How about the kitchen?

My wife wanted a mink coat, and I wanted a new car. We compromised. I bought her a mink coat and we keep it in the garage.

Walk along, listen to the comics, laugh out loud, people probably think I'm nuts. Who cares? There isn't anyone *commanding* me to kill these girls—

Ooops, excuse me, I beg your parmigiana. Mustn't get the feminists on my back, they'd be worse to deal with than cops. Next city, maybe I'll do five. Get five of them and then move on. Two, three, four, five, nice arithmetical progression. Keep moving, keep having fun, just the way Mother wanted it. What's the sense of life if you can't enjoy it? Live a little, laugh a little, that's the thing. These women—got it right that time, Ms. Steinem—are *fun* to do.

Try to dope *that* one out, officers.

Keep on looking for a psycho, go ahead.

When all you're dealing with is somebody as sane as Sunday.

Larry's Bar.

Welcome home, he thought, and opened the door.

"What'll it be?" Larry asked him.

"This guy comes into a bar, has a little monkey on his shoulder."

"Huh?" Larry said.

"This is a joke," he said. "The bartender asks him 'What'll it

171

be?' The guys says, 'Scotch on the rocks,' and the monkey says, 'Same for me.' The bartender looks at both of them and says, 'What are you, a ventriloquist?' The monkey says, 'Were my lips moving?'"

"That's a joke, huh?" Larry said.

"Gin and tonic," he said, and shrugged.

"How about your monkey?"

"My monkey's driving," he said.

Larry blinked.

"That's another joke."

"Oh," Larry said, and looked at him. "You been in here before?"

"Nope. First time."

" 'Cause you look familiar."

"People tell me I look like Robert Redford."

"Now *that's* a joke," Larry said, and put the drink in front of him. "Gin and tonic, three bucks, a bargain."

He paid for the drink, sat sipping it, eyes on the mirror.

"Nice crop tonight, huh?" Larry said.

"Maybe."

"What are you looking for? We had a Chinese girl in here ten minutes ago. You dig Orientals?"

"This samurai comes home from the wars," he said.

"Is this another joke?"

"His servant meets him at the gate, tells him his wife's been making it with a black man. The samurai runs upstairs, breaks down the bedroom door, yanks out his sword, yells, 'Whassa this I hear, you make it with a brack man?' His wife says, 'Where you hear such honkie jive?'"

"I don't get it," Larry said.

"I guess you had to be there."

"Where?"

"Forget it."

"We got some nice black girls in here tonight, if that's what you're lookin' for."

172

Larry was thinking about his twenty-percent commission. Drum up a little trade here.

"This old man goes into a whorehouse . . ."

"This ain't a whorehouse," Larry said defensively.

"This is another joke. Old guy, ninety-five years old. He tells the madam he's looking for a blowjob. The guy's so frail he can hardly stand up. The madam says, 'Come on, mister, you've had it.' He says, 'I have? How much do I owe you?' "

"Now *that's* funny," Larry said.

"I know a hundred jokes about old people."

"*That* funny, it wasn't."

"This old guy is sitting on a park bench, crying his heart out. Another guy sits next to him, says . . ."

"Hi."

He turned.

A good-looking blonde girl was sitting on the stool next to his.

"My name's Sheryl," she said. "Wanna party?"

10

The minute he saw her, he knew she was going to be more fun than any of the others. Something in her eyes. Something in her smile. Something in the way she plumped her cute little bottom down on the bar stool, and crossed her legs, and propped one elbow on the bar, and her chin on her hand, and looked him mischievously in the eye—a fun girl, he could tell that at once.

"Well, well, well, hello, Sheryl," he said.

"Well, well, well, hello to you," she said.

"Barkeep," he said, "see what the lady'll have."

"Barkeep, I love that," Sheryl said.

A fun girl. He knew it.

"So what'll it be?" he asked.

"What are *you* drinking?"

"Gin and tonic."

"I'll have the same," she said.

"A gin and tonic for the lady," he said to Larry, and then immediately, "This guy walks into a bar . . ."

"You already told this one," Larry said.

"This is another one. Guy walks into a bar, says, 'See that cat over there?' Everybody looks at the cat. Big tomcat with an enormous tail. The guys says, 'I'll bet any man in the house my penis is longer than that cat's tail.' Everybody wants to bet him. Hundred-dollar bills come out all over the place. The guy says to the bartender . . ."

"Gin and tonic," Larry said, "three bucks, a bargain."

"You should learn not to interrupt a story," he said.

"Tell 'im," Sheryl said.

"The guy says to the bartender, 'Okay, measure us.' So the bartender takes out a tape measure, goes over to the cat, measures the cat's tail, and says, 'Fourteen inches.' They guy nods and says, 'Okay, now measure my penis.' The bartender measures the penis. 'Eight inches,' he says. 'You lose.' The guy looks at him. 'Excuse me,' he says, 'but exactly *how* did you measure that cat's tail?' The bartender says, 'I put one end of the tape against his asshole and the other end . . .' and the guy says, 'Would you mind showing me the same consideration?' "

Sheryl burst out laughing.

Larry said, "I don't get it. You owe me three bucks."

He paid for the drink. Sheryl was still laughing.

A fun girl.

"What's your name?" she asked.

"Robert Redford," he said, which wasn't too far from the truth in that his first name really was Robert.

"I believe you," she said, and winked at Larry. "What do people call you? Rob? Bob? Bobby?"

"Bobby," he said, which was absolutely the truth.

"And how does *your* tail measure up against that cat's, Bobby?"

"Want to find out?" he said.

"Oooo, yes," Sheryl said, and rolled her eyes.

"Think that might be fun, huh?" he said.

"I think it'd be *loads* of fun," she said. "I'll tell you what I get, Bobby. A handjob's . . ."

"Not yet," he said.

"Well, you see, Bobby, I'm a working girl. So whereas there's nothing I'd enjoy more than sitting here all night with you . . ."

He put a twenty-dollar bill on the bartop.

"Let's say we're running a tab," he said.

"You mean you and me? Or you and Larry?"

"You and me. The twenty's yours. It buys twenty minutes, a dollar a minute. We'll talk about renewing the option when the meter runs out. How's that sound, Sheryl?"

"No problem," she said, and scooped up the bill.

"Four bucks of that is mine," Larry said, and held out his hand. Sheryl made a face, but she gave him the twenty, and watched him as he walked down to the cash register to make change.

"So where you from, Bobby?" she asked.

"Most recently? Chicago. Before that, Kansas City."

Playing it recklessly. Those were the two cities exactly. But that's what made this so exciting. Playing the game for the ultimate risk.

Larry was back with her change. "Here's your sixteen," he said, handing her three fives and a single.

"You take out a fourteen-inch whanger in here," she said, "Larry'll want twenty percent of it."

"I never yet seen nobody with a fourteen-incher," Larry said.

"You been looking?" she asked, and winked at Bobby and put the bills into her handbag. "What Larry does, he checks out the men's room for fourteen-inchers."

"This soldier is in the men's room taking a shower," Bobby said. "All the other guys in his company . . ."

"Is this another one?" Larry said.

"I thought I told you not to interrupt my stories," Bobby said. "Stories like yours . . ."

"Be quiet," he said.

176

He spoke the words very softly.

Larry looked at him.

"Do you understand?" he said. "When I'm telling a story, be quiet."

Larry looked into his eyes.

Then he shrugged and walked to the other end of the bar.

"Serves him right," Sheryl said. "Let me hear the story, Bobby."

"This soldier is taking a shower. All the other guys in his company are crowded around the stall, looking in at him, craning for a look at him. That's because the guy has a penis that's only an inch long. Finally, the guy can't take it anymore. He turns to them and yells, 'What's the matter? You never seen anybody with a hard-on before?' "

Sheryl burst out laughing again.

From the other end of the bar, Larry grimaced sourly, and said, "Very funny."

"So which one are you, Bobby?" Sheryl asked. "The fourteen-incher or the inch-long wonder?"

"I thought we weren't going to hurry," he said.

"Listen, it's your money," Sheryl said. "Take all the time you need."

"I mean, I thought we were having fun here," he said.

"We are," she said.

"I mean, isn't this fun?"

"I love your stories, Bobby," she said.

"You're a fun girl," he said. "I can tell that."

"That's what I've been told, Bobby."

"I mean, I'll bet you like to do new and exciting things, don't you?"

"Oh, sure," she said. "I even did it with a police dog once."

"That's not what I meant. I meant *new* things. Exciting things."

"Well, to me that was new. Six guys watching while I did it with a police dog? That was new."

177

"It may have been new, but I'll bet it wasn't exciting," Bobby said.

"Well, I have to admit, when the dog went down on me that was sort of exciting. He had like this very raspy tongue, you know? Like sandpaper. I guess you could say that was sort of exciting. I mean, once you got past the idea of him being a *dog*, which was disgusting, of course."

"Sheryl," he said, "I think you're terrific, I really do. We're going to have a lot of fun together, you'll see."

"Oh, I'm sure."

"We're going to do some new and very exciting things."

"I can hardly wait," she said.

"Lots of laughs," he said.

"I already find you very funny," she said.

"This midget goes into a men's room," he said. "And there's a guy standing there at one of the . . ."

This second party was even better than the first one had been.

Parker was having the time of his life.

At the first party, he'd got drunk enough to believe he was really a writer passing himself off as a cop who only wanted to be a writer. At this party, he didn't tell anyone he was a cop because no one was in costume here, it wasn't that kind of a party. But even without the masquerade, he was having a marvelous time. Maybe because there were all sorts of interesting people here, most of them women. Or maybe because these interesting women all found *him* interesting.

This was very amazing to him.

He thought he was just being his usual shitty self.

It turned out that the woman whose apartment they were in was celebrating her sixty-third birthday tonight, which was why there was a party in the first place, never mind Halloween. Her name was Sandra, and she was the one Peaches had been expecting a call from earlier tonight, which was the only reason she'd answered the phone after that heavy-breathing creep got off the line. Sandra was her next-to-best friend; her best friend was the woman who'd thrown the costume party. Still, Peaches liked Sandra a lot, especially because she never expected a present on her birthday. She was a bit surprised, therefore, and somewhat annoyed, when Parker flatly and rudely expressed the opinion that no one over the age of sixty should be asked to blow out all the candles on a birthday cake in a single breath. And she was even more surprised when Sandra burst out laughing and said, "Oh, baby, how true! Who the hell needs such a humiliating stress test?"

Everyone laughed. Even Peaches.

Sandra then blew out all the candles in a single breath, and pinched Parker on the behind and asked him if he'd like the candles on *his* cake blown. "Out," she added.

Everyone laughed. Except Peaches.

A little later on, encouraged by the attention a lot of these very interesting women were paying to ideas he'd never even known he'd had, Parker ventured a bit closer to home and suggested to a lady trial lawyer that *anyone* committing a murder was at least a little bit crazy and that therefore the "legal insanity" defense was meaningless. The lady lawyer said, "That's very interesting, Andy. I had a case last week where ..."

It was astonishing.

Parker said to a woman wearing horn-rimmed eyeglasses and no bra that he found pornographic movies more honest than any of the nighttime soaps on television, and the woman turned out to be a film critic who encouraged him to expand upon the idea.

Parker told a woman writer—a *real* writer—that he never spent more than five pages with any book if he wasn't hooked by then, and the woman expounded upon the importance of a book's opening and closing paragraphs, to which Parker said, "Sure, it's like foreplay and afterplay," and the woman writer put her hand on his arm and laughed robustly, which Peaches did not find at all amusing.

Peaches, in fact, was becoming more and more irritated by the fact that Sandra had invited her to a party where the women outnumbered the men by an approximate two-to-one and where Parker was suddenly the center of all this female attention. She had liked it better when they were a couple pretending to be a cop and a victim. They were *sharing* something then. Now Parker seemed to be stepping out on his own, the small-time flamenco dancer who'd been offered a movie contract provided he ditched his fat lady partner. This miffed Peaches because for Christ's sake she was the one who'd introduced him to show biz in the first place!

When the female midget walked in at twenty-five minutes to twelve, Peaches immediately checked out the man with her. Burly guy going a bit bald, but with a pleasant craggy face, and a seemingly gentle manner. Five-ten or -eleven, she guessed, merry blue eyes, nice speaking voice now that she heard him wishing Sandra a happy birthday. Sandra took their coats and wandered off, muttering something about mingling. Peaches moved in fast before the other sharks smelled blood on the water. She introduced herself to the man and the midget—

"Hi, I'm Peaches Muldoon."

"Quentin Forbes. Alice . . ."

—and then took the man's arm before he could finish the midget's name, and said, "Come on, I'll get you a drink," and sailed off with him, leaving the midget standing there by the door looking forlornly and shyly into the room.

Parker had never seen a more beautiful woman in his life.

He went over to her at once.

"Small world," he said.

And to his enormous surprise—the night was full of surprises—she burst out laughing, and said, "I feel like a fire hydrant waiting for an engine company. Where's the bar?"

Hal Willis came into the squadroom at twenty minutes to midnight. The teams usually relieved at a quarter to the hour, and so he was early—which was a surprise. Nowadays, ever since

180

he'd taken up with Marilyn Hollis, he was invariably late. And rumpled-looking. He was rumpled-looking tonight, too, giving the impression of a man who'd leaped out of bed and into his trousers not five minutes earlier.

"Getting a bit brisk out there," he said.

He was wearing a short car coat over slacks and a sports jacket, no tie, the top button of his shirt unbuttoned. At five-feet eight-inches tall, he was the shortest man on the squad—even shorter than Fujiwara, who was of Japanese descent—but Willis knew judo and karate, and he'd fooled many a cheap thief who'd fig-ured him for a pushover. He took off the coat and hung it on the coatrack, glanced idly at the bulletin board, and then looked at the duty chart to see who'd be sharing the shift with him. He moved like a man underwater nowadays. Kling attributed his eternal weariness to Marilyn Hollis. Eileen said Marilyn Hollis was poison. Maybe she was right. Kling looked up at the clock.

"Let me fill you in," he said.

He told Willis about the four teenagers Genero had shot.

"Genero?" Willis said, amazed.

He told Willis about the four midgets who'd held up a series of liquor stores.

"Midgets?" Willis said, amazed.

He told Willis that Carella and Meyer had taken three bullets between them and were both at Buenavista Hospital.

"You going over there?" Willis asked.

"Maybe later. I have to run out to Calm's Point."

He looked up at the clock again.

"Brown and Hawes caught a homicide," he said, "all the pa-perwork is on Brown's desk. There's a picture of the victim, too, a magician. They found him in four separate pieces."

"Four pieces?" Willis said, amazed.

"There's a number you can reach them at in Collinsworth, case anything breaks. They got an all-points out on a guy named Jimmy Brayne."

"Good evening, gentlemen," O'Brien said from the slatted rail

181

divider, and then pushed his way through the gate into the squadroom. "Winter's on the way." He was indeed dressed for winter, wearing a heavy overcoat and a muffler, which he took off now and carried to the coatrack. Willis wasn't happy to be partnered with O'Brien. O'Brien was a hard-luck cop. You went on a call with O'Brien, somebody was bound to get shot. This wasn't O'Brien's fault. Some cops simply attracted the lunatics with guns. On Christmas Day, not too long ago—well, not too long ago by *precinct* time, where sometimes an hour seemed an eternity—O'Brien and Meyer had stopped to check out a man changing a flat tire on a moving van. A moving van? Working on Christmas Day? The man turned out to be a burglar named Michael Addison, who'd just cleaned out half a dozen houses in Smoke Rise. Addison shot Meyer twice in the leg. Brown later dubbed the burglar Addison and Steal. This was pretty funny, but the bullets in Meyer's leg weren't. Willis—and everyone else on the squad—was convinced Meyer had got himself shot only because he'd been partnered with O'Brien. Still, he'd been shot again tonight, hadn't he? And he'd been working with Carella. Maybe in this line of work, there were bullets waiting out there with your name on them. In any event, Willis wished O'Brien was home in bed, instead of here in the squadroom with him.

"Steve and Meyer took a couple, did you hear?" he said.

"What are you talking about?"

"Some midgets shot them," Kling said.

"Come on, midgets," O'Brien said.

Kling looked up at the clock again.

"I'll be checking out a car," he said to no one.

"You want a cup of coffee?" O'Brien asked Willis.

It was only fifteen minutes before the beginning of All Hallows' Day.

In the Roman Catholic and Anglican churches, the first day of November is a feast day upon which the church glorifies God for all his saints, known or unknown. The word "hallow" derives

182

from the Middle English *halowen,* further derived from the Old English *hālgian,* and it means "to make or set apart as holy; to sanctify; to consecrate." All Hallows' Day and Hallowmass are now archaic names for this feast; today—except in novels—it is called All Saints' Day. But it has always been celebrated on the first day of November, which in Celtic times was coincidentally the first day of winter, a time of pagan witches and ghosts, mummery and masquerade. Wholly Christian in origin, however, are the vigil and fasting that occur on the day before.

On the eve of All Hallows' Day, a Christian and a Jew kept vigil in a corridor of the Ernest Atlas Pavilion on the fourth floor of Buenavista Hospital.

The Christian was Teddy Carella.

The Jew was Sarah Meyer.

The clock on the corridor wall read 11:47 P.M.

Sarah Meyer had brown hair and blue eyes and lips her husband had always considered sensual.

Teddy Carella had black hair and brown eyes, and lips that could not speak, for she had been born deaf and mute.

Sarah had not seen the inside of a synagogue for more years than she cared to count.

Teddy scarcely knew the whereabouts of her neighborhood church.

But both women were silently praying, and they were both praying for the same man.

Sarah knew that her husband was out of danger.

It was Steve Carella who was still in surgery.

On impulse, she took Teddy's hand and squeezed it.

Neither of the women said a word to the other.

Neither of the women said a word to the other.

They spotted him the moment they came back into the bar. Annie knew he was their man. So did Eileen. They headed immediately for the ladies' room.

A black hooker wearing a blonde wig was standing at the sink, looking into the mirror over it, touching up her lipstick. She was a woman in her early forties, Eileen guessed, wearing a black dress and a short, fake fur jacket, going a bit thick in the middle and around the ankles. Eileen was certain she had just come in off the meat rack on the street outside.

"Getting chilly out there, ain't it?" the woman said.

"Yeah," Annie said.

"I'd park in here a while, but Larry gets twenty percent."

"I know."

"My man take a fit I give away twenty percent of the store."

There was a knife scar across the bridge of her nose.

She must have been pretty once, Eileen thought.

"One last pee," she said, and went into one of the stalls.

Annie lighted a cigarette. They chatted idly about how cold it was. The black hooker chimed in from behind the closed door of the stall, reporting on the really cold weather in Buffalo, New York, where she used to work years ago. They waited for her to flush the toilet. They waited while she washed her hands at the sink.

"Have a nice night," she said, and was gone.

"He's our man, isn't he?" Eileen said at once.

"Looks like him."

"Hitting on the wrong hooker."

"You'd better move in," Annie said.

"Sheryl won't like it."

"She'll like a slab even less."

"Will Shanahan know he's here?" Eileen asked.

"He'll know, don't worry."

Eileen nodded.

"You ready for this?" Annie asked.

"I'm ready."

"You sure?"

"I'm sure."

Annie searched her face.

"Because if you . . ."

"I'm ready," Eileen said.

Annie kept searching her face. Then she said, "Let's go then," and tossed her cigarette into one of the toilet bowls.

The cigarette expired with a short tired hiss.

He was telling another joke when Eileen took the stool on his right.

Blond. Six-two, six-three. Two hundred and ten easy. Eyeglasses. A tattoo near his right thumb, a blue heart lined in red, nothing in it.

". . . so he says to the old man, 'What's the matter? Why are you crying?' The old man just keeps sitting there on the park bench, crying his eyes out. Finally he says, 'A year ago, I married this beautiful twenty-six-year-old girl. I've never been happier in my life. Before breakfast each morning, she wakes me up and blows me, and then she serves me bacon and eggs and toasted English muffins and piping hot coffee, and I go back to bed and rest till lunchtime. Then she blows me again before lunch, and she serves me a hot, delicious lunch, and I go back to bed again and rest till dinnertime. And she blows me again before dinner and serves me another terrific meal, and I fall asleep until morning when she wakes me up again with another blowjob. She's the most wonderful woman I've ever met in my life.' The guy looks at him. 'Then why are you crying?' he asks. And the old man says, 'I forgot where I *live!*'"

Sheryl burst out laughing.

Eileen was thinking about the dead hookers he'd had in stitches.

"This guy's marvelous," Sheryl said, still laughing, leaning over to talk across him. "Linda, say hello to Bobby, he's marvelous."

"Hello, Bobby," Eileen said.

Terrific name for a slasher, she thought.

"Well, well, well, hello, Linda," he said, turning to her.

"Me and Bobby's running a tab," Sheryl said. "Which by the way, time's almost up."

"That right?" Eileen said.

"Just having a little fun here," Bobby said.

"The real fun comes later, honey," Sheryl said. "This is just the warm-up."

"I hear redheads are a lot of fun," Bobby said. "Is that true?"

"I haven't had any complaints," Eileen said.

She was wondering how she could get rid of Sheryl. If they were running a bar tab . . .

"But they burn in the sun," Bobby said.

"Yeah, I have to watch that."

"Just don't go out except at night, that's all," Sheryl said. "Listen, Bobby, I hate to be pushy, but your time's running out. You said twenty bucks for twenty minutes, remember?"

"Uh-huh."

"So take a look at the clock. You got about a minute left."

"I see that."

"So what do you say? We're having fun here, am I right?"

"Lots of fun."

"So how about another twenty, take us into Saturday?"

"Sounds like a good idea," he said, but he made no move for his wallet. Sheryl figured she was losing him.

"Matter of fact," she said, "whyn't you put Linda on the tab, too?"

"Thanks, no, I've been drinking too much tonight," Eileen said.

"This ain't a booze tab," Sheryl said. "This is accounts receivable. What do you say, Bobby? Lay a couple of twenties on the bar there, you buy both of us till a quarter past. Double your pleasure, double your fun. And later on, you still interested, we do a triad."

"What's a triad?" he asked.

"I read it in a book. It's like a two-on-one. A triad."

"I'm not sure I could handle two of you," he said.

But Eileen could see the sudden spark of ambition in his eyes. Blue to match the blue in the tattooed heart near his thumb. Seriously considering the possibility now. Take them *both* outside, slash them both, maybe go for a third one later on, do the hat trick tonight.

She didn't want a civilian getting in the way.

She had to get rid of Sheryl.

"I don't work doubles," she said.

A risk.

"How come?" Bobby asked.

"Why should I share this?" she said, and put her left hand on his thigh. He thought she was going for the meat. She was frisking him for the knife. Found it, too. Outlined in his right-hand pants pocket, felt like a six-incher at least. Maybe eight.

A shiver ran up her spine.

Sheryl was getting nervous. Her eyes flicked up to the clock again. The twenty minutes were gone, and she didn't see another twenty bucks coming out of his wallet. She was afraid she'd already lost him. So she tried again, appealing not to *him* now, but to the redheaded hooker sitting on his right, a sorority sister, so to speak, someone who knew how tough it was to earn a buck in a dog-eat-dog world.

"Change your mind, Linda," she said.

There was something almost plaintive in her voice.

"Come on, okay? It'll be fun."

"I think Linda might be more fun alone," Bobby said.

Eileen's hand was still on his thigh. Off the knife now, like finding the knife was an accident. Fingers spread toward his crotch.

Sheryl looked up at the clock again.

"Tell you what," she said. "I'll make it only ten bucks for the next twenty minutes, how's that? We'll sit here, I'll let you tell me some more of your jokes, be a lot of fun, what do you say?"

A last desperate try.

"I say it's up to Linda here. What do you say, Linda?"

"I told you. I don't do doubles."

Flat out. Get rid of her.

"You heard her," he said.

"Hey, come on, what kinda . . . ?"

"So long, Sheryl," he said.

She got off the stool at once.

"You're some cunt, you know that?" she said to Eileen, and turned away angrily and walked toward a table where three men were sitting drinking beer. "Who wants me?" she said angrily, and pulled out a chair and sat.

"I hate it when the fun goes out of it," Bobby said.

"We'll have lots of fun, don't worry," Eileen whispered, and tightened her hand on his thigh. "You want to get out of here this minute? I get ten bucks for a handjob . . ."

"No, no, let's talk a while, okay?" He reached into his right hip pocket, pulled out his wallet. Big killer, she thought, keeps his wallet in the sucker pocket. "Same deal as with Sheryl, okay? A buck a minute, here's a twenty"—reaching into the wallet, pulling out a bill, looking up at the clock—"we'll see how it goes, okay?"

"What is this?" Eileen asked. "An audition?"

"Well, I'd like to get to know you a little before I . . ."

He cut himself short.

"Before you what?" she said.

"You know," he said, and smiled, and lowered his voice. "Do it to you."

"What would you like to do to me, Bobby?"

"New and exciting things," he said.

She looked into his eyes.

Another shiver ran up her back.

"You cold?" he asked.

"A little. The weather's changing all of a sudden."

"Here," he said. "Take my jacket."

188

He shrugged out of the jacket. Tweed. He was wearing a blue flannel shirt under it, open at the throat. Blue to match his eyes and the tattooed heart near his thumb. He draped the jacket over her shoulders. There was the smell of death on the jacket, as palpable as the odor of smoke hanging on the air. She shivered again.

"So what do you say?" he asked her. "A buck a minute, does that sound all right?"

"Sure," she said.

"Well, good," he said, and handed her the twenty-dollar bill.

"Thanks," she said, and looked up at the clock. "This buys you till twenty past," she said, and tucked the bill into her bra. She didn't want to open her bag. She didn't want to risk him spotting the .44 in her bag, under the silk scarf. She was going to blow his brains out with that gun.

"Nothing for our friendly barkeep?" he asked.

"Huh?"

"I thought he got twenty percent."

"Oh. No, we have an arrangement."

"Well, good. I'd hate to think you were cheating him. You don't cheat people, do you, Linda?"

"I try to give good value," she said.

"Good. 'Cause you promised me a lot of fun, didn't you?"

"Show you a real good time," she said, and nodded.

Across the room, Annie was in conversation with the frizzied brunette who'd earlier partnered with Sheryl. The place was beginning to thin out a bit. There'd be a new shift coming in, Eileen guessed, the morning people, the denizens of the empty hours. He'd paid for twenty minutes of her time, but he'd dumped Sheryl without a backward glance, and she couldn't risk losing him to any of the other girls here. Twenty minutes unless he laid another bill on the bar. Twenty minutes to get him outside on the street, where he'd moved on the other three women. Show him a real good time, all right. Punish him for what he'd done.

Make him pay for the three women he'd killed. Make him pay, too, for what a man named Arthur Haines had done to her face . . . and her body . . . and her spirit.

"So where are all the jokes?" she asked.

"Jokes?"

"Sheryl said you're full of jokes."

"No, Sheryl didn't say that."

"I thought she said . . ."

"I'm sure she didn't."

A mistake? No. Back off a bit, anyway.

"She said she'd settle for ten bucks, sit here with you, let you tell her some more jokes . . ."

"Oh. Yeah."

"So let me hear one."

"I'd rather talk about you right now."

"Sure," Eileen said.

" 'Cause I find that fun, you know. Learning about other people, finding out what makes them tick."

"You sound like a shrink," she said.

"Well, my father's a shrink."

"Really?"

"Yeah. Practices in L.A. Lots of customers out there. You know what L.A. stands for?"

"What?"

"Lunatic Asylum."

"I've never been there, so I wouldn't . . ."

"Take my word for it. Every variety of nut in the—do you know the one about the guy who goes into a nut shop?"

"No."

"He stutters badly, he says to the clerk, 'I'd l-l-like to b-b-buy a p-p-pound of n-n-nuts.' The clerk says, 'Yes, sir, we have some very nice Brazil nuts at three dollars a pound.' The guy says, 'N-n-no, that's t-t-too high.' So the clerk says, 'I've also got some nice almonds at two dollars a pound.' The guy says, 'N-n-no, that's t-t-too high, t-t-too.' So the clerk says, 'I've got some peanuts at a dollar a pound,' and the guys says, 'F-f-fine.' The clerk weighs out the peanuts, puts them in a bag, and the guy pays for them. The guy says, 'Th-thank you, and I also w-w-want to th-thank you for n-n-not m-m-mentioning m-m-my im-p-p-pedi-ment.' The clerk says, 'That's quite all right, sir, and I want to thank you for not mentioning my deformity.' The guy says, 'Wh-what d-d-deformity?' The clerk says, 'Well, I have a very large nose.' The guy says, 'Oh, is that your n-n-nose? Your n-n-nuts are so high, I th-thought it was your p-p-pecker.'"

Eileen burst out laughing.

The laughter was genuine.

For the briefest tick of time she forgot that she was sitting here at the bar with a man she felt reasonably certain had killed three women and would do his best to kill her as well if she gave him the slightest opportunity.

The laughter surprised her.

She had not laughed this heartily in a long time. She had not laughed since the night Arthur Haines slashed her cheek and forced himself upon her.

She could not stop laughing.

She wondered all at once if the laughter was merely a release of nervous tension.

But she kept laughing.

Tears were rolling down her cheeks.

She reached into her bag for a tissue, felt under the silk scarf, touched the butt of the .44, and suddenly the laughter stopped.

Dabbing at her eyes, she said, "That was very funny."

"I'm going to enjoy you," he said, smiling, looking into her eyes. "You're going to be a good one."

11

Alice was telling him that a lot of men got turned on by midgets, did he realize that?

Parker realized it. She was a perfect little doll, blonde hair and blue eyes, beautifully formed breasts and well-shaped legs. She was wearing a green dress that hugged the womanly curves of her body, legs crossed, one foot jiggling in a high-heeled green slipper.

He said, "I read a lot of these men's magazines, you know . . ."

"Uh-huh," she said, nodding encouragement. Drink in her right hand, cigarette in her left.

"And there's all sorts of letters from men who get turned on by all sorts of women."

"Uh-huh."

"Like, for example, there are many men who are sexually attracted to women with back problems."

"Back problems?" Alice said.

"Yes. Women who wear braces."

"I see," she said.

"And there are men who enjoy one-armed women."

"Uh-huh."

"Or even double amputees."

"Uh-huh."

"Or women who are color blind."

"Color blind, right."

"But I've never seen any letters from men who find *midgets* sexually attractive. I wonder why. I mean, I find *you* very attractive, Alice."

"Well, thank you," she said. "But that's what I was saying. A *lot* of men get turned on by midgets."

"I can understand that."

"It's what's called the Snow White Syndrome."

"Is that what it's called?"

"Yes, because she was living with those seven dwarfs, you know."

"That's right, I never thought of that. I mean, if you look at it that way, it could be a dirty story, couldn't it?"

"Well, sure. Not that dwarfs are midgets."

"No, no. They *aren't*?"

"No. Midgets are perfectly proportioned little people."

"You certainly are perfectly proportioned, Alice."

"Well, thank you. But my point is, with so many men being attracted to female midgets . . ."

"Uh-huh."

"You think you'd see midgets in ads and all."

"I never thought of it that way."

"I mean, wouldn't you like to see me modeling lingerie, for example?"

"Oh, I would."

"But instead, if you're a midget, you have to join a circus."

"I never thought of it that way," he said again.

"Have you ever seen a midget working as a clerk in a department store?"

"Never," he said.

"Do you know why?"

"Because you can't see over the counter?"

"Well, that's one reason, of course. But the main reason is there's a lingering prejudice against little people."

"I'll bet there is."

"Short has become a dirty word," Alice said. "Have you ever seen a short movie star?"

"Well, Al Pacino is short."

"On my block, Al Pacino is a *giant,*" she said, and giggled.

Parker loved the way she giggled.

"Have you ever seen a movie where there are midgets making *love?*" she asked.

"Never."

"We *do* make love, you know."

"Oh, I'll bet."

"Have you ever seen a midget fireman? Or a midget cop?"

He had not yet told her he was a cop. He wondered if he should tell her he was a cop.

"Well, they changed the requirements, you know," he said.

"What requirements?"

"The height requirements. It used to be five-eight."

"So what is it now?"

"You can be any height. I know cops you can fit them in your vest pocket."

"You mean a midget can become a cop?"

"Well, I don't know about *midgets*. But I guess . . ."

"Because I can shoot a gun as good as anybody else, you know. I used to do an Annie Oakley act in the circus. Little Annie Oakley, they called me. That was before I got to be Tiny Alice."

"You *are* tiny," he said. "That's one of the things I find very sexually attractive about you."

"Well, thank you. But what I'm asking, if I applied to the po-

lice department ... to become a woman cop, you know ...
would they accept me? Or would they think *short*? Do you see
what I mean?"

"I don't think of you as short," Parker said.

"Oh, I'm short, all right."

"I think of you as delicate."

"Well, thank you. There's this man Hans, he's one of the Flying Dutchmen, an aerial act, you know?"

"Uh-huh."

"He wrote me this very hot love letter, I memorized it. What
made me think of it was your use of the word delicate."

"Well, you are delicate."

"Thank you. Would you like to hear the letter?"

"Well ... sure," Parker said, and glanced over his shoulder to
see where Peaches was. She was nowhere in sight. "Go ahead,"
he said.

"He said he wanted to disrobe me."

"Take off your clothes, you mean."

"Yes. He said he wanted to discard my dainty delicate under
things ... that's what made me think of it, delicate."

"Yes, I see."

"And pat my pubescent peaks ... this is him talking now, in
the letter."

"Yes."

"And probe my pithy pussy, and manipulate my miniature
mons veneris and Lilliputian labiae ..."

"Uh-huh."

"And caress my compact clitoris and crisp pauciloquent pubic
patch. That was the letter."

"From one of the Flying Dutchmen, huh?"

"Yes."

"He speaks good English."

"Oh, yes."

"That isn't the guy you're with tonight, is it? The guy you
came in with?"

"No, no. That's Quentin."

"He's not one of the Flying Dutchmen, huh?"

"No, he's a clown."

"Oh."

"A very good one, too."

"So how long have you been in town? I didn't even know the circus was here, I'll tell you the truth."

"Well, we're not here. We won't be here till the spring sometime. We go down to Florida next month to start rehearsing the new season."

"Oh, so you're just visiting then, is that it?"

"Yeah, sort of."

"You're not married or anything, are you?"

"No, no. No, no, no, no, no."

Shaking her head like a little doll.

"How long will you be in town?"

"Oh, I don't know. Why?"

"I thought we might get together," Parker said, and shrugged.

"How about the big redhead you're with?"

"Peaches? She's just a friend."

"Uh-huh."

"Really. I hardly know her. Alice, I've got to tell you, I've never met a woman as delicate and as attractive as you are, I mean it. I'd really like to get together with you."

"Well, why don't you give me a call?"

"I'd like that," he said, and took his pad from his pocket.

"That's *some* notebook," she said. "It's bigger than I am."

"Well, you know," he said, and wondered again if he should tell her he was a cop. Lots of women, you told them you were a cop, it turned them off. They figured all cops were on the take, all cops were crooks. Just because every now and then you accepted a little gift from somebody. "So where can I reach you?" he said.

"We're staying at Quentin's apartment. The four of us."

"Who's the four of us? Not the Flying Dutchmen, I hope."

"No, no, they went back to Germany, they'll be joining us in Florida."

"So who's the four of you?"

"Willie and Corky . . . they're married . . . and Oliver and me. And of course Quentin, whose apartment it is. Quentin Forbes."

"What's the address?" Parker asked.

"Four-oh-three Thompson Street."

"Downtown in the Quarter," he said, nodding. "The Twelfth."

"Huh?"

He wondered if he should explain to her that in this city you didn't call the Twelfth the "One-Two." Any precinct from the First to the Twentieth was called by its full and proper designation. After that, it became the Two-One, the Three-Four, the Eight-Seven, and so on. But that would have meant telling her he was a cop, and he didn't want to chance losing her.

"What's the phone number there?" he asked.

"Three-four-eight . . ."

"*Excuse* me."

Voice as cold as the second day of February, hands on her hips, green eyes blazing.

"I'd like to go home now," Peaches said. "Did you plan on accompanying me? Or are you going to play house all night?"

"Uh . . . sure," Parker said, and got to his feet. "Nice meeting you," he said to Alice.

"It's in the book," Alice said, and smiled up sweetly at Peaches.

Peaches tried to think of a scathing midget remark, but nothing came to mind.

She turned and started for the door.

"I'll call you," Parker whispered, and ran out after her.

The house was a white clapboard building with a white picket fence around it. A matching white clapboard garage stood some twenty feet from the main structure. Both buildings were on a street with only three other houses on it, not too far from the turnpike. It was two minutes past midnight when they reached the house. The first day of November. The beginning of the Celtic winter. As if in accordance, the weather had turned very cold. As they pulled into the driveway, Brown remarked that all they needed was snow, the turnpike would be backed up all the way to Siberia.

There were no lights burning on the ground floor of the house. Two lighted windows showed on the second story. The men were inappropriately dressed for the sudden cold. Their breaths plumed from their mouths as they walked to the front door. Hawes rang the doorbell.

"Probably getting ready for bed," he said.

"You wish," Brown said.

They waited.

"Give it another shot," Brown said.

Hawes hit the bell button again.

Lights snapped on downstairs.

"Who is it?"

Marie's voice, just inside the door. A trifle alarmed. Well, sure, midnight already.

"It's Detective Hawes," he said.

"Oh."

"Sorry to bother you so late."

"No, that's all . . . just a minute, please."

She fumbled with the lock, and then opened the door. She *had* been getting ready for bed. She was wearing a long blue robe. Laced ruff of a nightgown showing in the V-necked opening. No slippers.

"Have you found him?" she asked at once.

Referring to Jimmy Brayne, of course.

"No, ma'am, not yet," Brown said. "Okay for us to come in?"

"Yes, please," she said, "excuse me," and stepped back to let them in.

Small entryway, a sense of near-shabbiness. Worn carpeting, scarred and rickety piece of furniture under a flaking mirror.

"I thought . . . when you told me who you were . . . I thought you'd found Jimmy," she said.

"Not yet, Mrs. Sebastiani," Hawes said. "In fact, the reason we came out here . . ."

"Come in," she said, "we don't have to stand here in the hall."

She backed off several paces, reached beyond the door jamb for a light switch. A floor lamp came on in the living room. Musty drapes, a faded rug, a thrift-shop sofa and two upholstered armchairs, an old upright piano on the far wall. Same sense of down-at-the-heels existence.

"Would you like some coffee or anything?" she asked.

"I could use a cup," Brown said.

"I'll put some up," she said, and walked back through the hall and through a doorway into the kitchen.

The detectives looked around the living room.

Framed photographs on the piano, Sebastian the Great doing his act hither and yon. Soiled antimacassars on the upholstered pieces. Brown ran his finger over the surface of an end table. Dust. Hawes poked his forefinger into the soil of a potted plant. Dry. The continuing sense of a house too run down to care about—or a house in neglect because it would soon be abandoned.

She was back.

"Take a few minutes to boil," she said.

"Who plays piano?" Hawes asked.

"Frank did. A little."

She'd grown used to the past tense.

"Mrs. Sebastiani," Brown said, "we were wondering if we could take a look at Brayne's room."

"Jimmy's room?" she said. She seemed a bit flustered by their presence, but that could have been normal, two cops showing on her doorstep at midnight.

199

"See if there's anything up there might give us a lead," Brown said, watching her.

"I'll have to find a spare key someplace," she said. "Jimmy had his own key, he came and went as he pleased."

She stood stock still in the entrance door to the living room, a thoughtful look on her face. Hawes wondered what she was thinking, face all screwed up like that. Was she wondering whether it was safe to show them that room? Or was she merely trying to remember where the spare key was?

"I'm trying to think where Frank might have put it," she said.

A grandfather clock on the far side of the room began tolling the hour, eight minutes late.

One . . . two . . .

They listened to the heavy bonging.

Nine . . . ten . . . eleven . . . twelve.

"Midnight already," she said, and sighed.

"Your clock's slow," Brown said.

"Let me check the drawer in the kitchen," she said. "Frank used to put a lot of junk in that drawer."

Past tense again.

They followed her into the kitchen. Dirty dishes, pots, and pans stacked in the sink. The door of the refrigerator smudged with handprints. Telephone on the wall near it. Small enamel-topped table, two chairs. Worn linoleum. Only a shade on the single window over the sink. On the stove, the kettle began whistling.

"Help yourselves," she said. "There's cups there, and a jar of instant."

She went to a drawer in the counter, opened it. Hawes spooned instant coffee into each of the cups, poured hot water into them. She was busy at the drawer now, searching for the spare key. "There should be some milk in the fridge," she said. "And there's sugar on the counter there." Hawes opened the refrigerator. Not much in it. Carton of low-fat milk, slab of margarine or butter, several containers of yogurt. He closed the door.

"You want some of this?" he asked Brown, extending the carton to him.

Brown shook his head. He was watching Marie going through the drawer full of junk.

"Sugar?" Hawes asked, pouring milk into his own cup.

Brown shook his head again.

"This may be it, I really don't know," Marie said.

She turned from the drawer, handed Brown a brass key that looked like a house key.

The telephone rang.

She was visibly startled by its sound.

Brown picked up his coffee cup, began sipping at it.

The telephone kept ringing.

She went to the wall near the refrigerator, lifted the receiver from its hook.

"Hello?" she said.

The two detectives watched her.

"Oh, hello, Dolores," she said at once. "No, not yet, I'm down in the kitchen," she said, and listened. "There are two detectives with me," she said. "No, that's all right, Dolores." She listened again. "They want to look at the garage room." Listening again. "I don't know yet," she said. "Well, they . . . they have to do an autopsy first." More listening. "Yes, I'll let you know. Thanks for calling, Dolores."

She put the receiver back on its hook.

"My sister-in-law," she said.

"Taking it hard, I'll bet," Hawes said.

"They were very close."

"Let's check out that room," Brown said to Hawes.

"I'll come over with you," Marie said.

"No need," Brown said, "it's getting cold outside."

She looked at him. She seemed about to say something more. Then she merely nodded.

"Better get a light from the car," Hawes said.

Marie watched them as they went out the door and made their way in the dark to where they'd parked their car. Car door opening, interior light snapping on. Door closing again. A moment later, a flashlight came on. She watched them as they walked up the driveway to the garage, pool of light ahead of them. They began climbing the steps at the side of the building. Flashlight beam on the door now. Unlocking the door. Should she have given them the key? Opening the door. The black cop reached into the room. A moment of fumbling for the wall switch, and then the light snapped on, and they both went inside and closed the door behind them.

The bullet had entered Carella's chest on the right side of the body, piercing the pectoralis major muscle, deflecting off the rib cage and missing the lung, passing through the soft tissue at the back of the chest, and then twisting again to lodge in one of the articulated bones in the spinal column.

The X rays showed the bullet dangerously close to the spinal cord itself.

In fact, if it had come to rest a micrometer further to the left, it would have traumatized the cord and caused paralysis.

The surgical procedure was a tricky one in that the danger of necrosis of the cord was still present, either through mechanical trauma or a compromise of the arterial supply of blood to the cord. Carella had bled a lot, and there was the further attendant danger of his going into heart failure or shock.

The team of surgeons—a thoracic surgeon, a neurosurgeon, his assistant, and two residents—had decided on a posterolateral approach, going in through the back rather than entering the chest cavity, where there might be a greater chance of infection and the possibility of injury to one of the lungs. The neurosurgeon was the man who made the incisions. The thoracic surgeon was standing by in the event they had to open the chest after all. There were also two scrub nurses, a circulating nurse, and an anesthesiologist in the room. With the exception of the circulating nurse and the anesthesiologist, everyone was fully gowned and gloved. Alongside the operating table, machines monitored Carella's pulse and blood pressure. A Swan-Ganz catheter was in place, monitoring the pressure in the pulmonary artery. Oscilloscopes flashed green. Beeps punctuated the sterile silence of the room.

The bullet was firmly seated in the spinal column.

Very close to the spinal cord and the radicular arteries.

It was like operating inside a matchbox.

The River Dix had begun silting over during the heavy September rains, and the city had awarded the dredging contract to a private company that started work on the fifteenth of October. Because there was heavy traffic on the river during the daylight hours, the men working the barges started as soon as it was dark and continued on through until just before dawn. Generator-powered lights set up on the barges illuminated the bucketsful of river slime scooped up from the bottom. Before tonight, the men doing the dredging had been grateful for the unusually mild weather. Tonight, it was no fun standing out here in the cold, watching the bucket drop into the black water and come up again dripping all kinds of shit.

People threw everything in this river.

Good thing Billy Joe McAllister didn't live in this city; he'd have maybe thrown a dead baby in the river.

The bucket came up again.

Barney Hanks watched it swinging in wide over the water, and signaled with his hand, directing it in over the center of the disposal barge. Pete Masters, sitting in the cab of the diesel-powered dredge on the other barge, worked his clutches and levers, tilting the bucket to drop another yard and a half, two yards of silt and shit. Hanks jerked his thumb up, signaling to Masters that the bucket was empty and it was okay to cast the dragline out over the river again. In the cab, Masters yanked some more levers and the bucket swung out over the side of the barge.

Something metallic was glistening on the surface of the muck in the disposal barge.

Hanks signaled to Masters to cut the engine.

"What is it?" Masters shouted.

"We got ourselves a treasure chest," Hanks yelled.

Masters cut his engine, climbed down from the cab, and walked across the deck toward the other barge.

"Time for a coffee break, anyway," he said. "What do you mean a treasure chest?"

"Throw me that grappling hook," Hanks said.

Masters threw the hook and line to him.

Hanks tossed the hook at what appeared to be one of those aluminum cases you carried roller skates in, except that it was bigger all around. The case was half-submerged in slime, it took Hanks five tosses to snag the handle. He pulled in the line, freed the hook, and put the case down on the deck.

Masters watched him from the other barge.

Hanks tried the catches on the case.

"No lock on it," he said, and opened the lid.

He was looking at a head and a pair of hands.

Kling arrived in the Canal Zone at thirteen minutes past midnight.

He parked the car on Canalside and Solomon, locked it, and began walking up toward Fairview. Eileen had told him they'd be planting her in a joint called Larry's Bar, on Fairview and East Fourth. This side of the river, the city got all turned around. What could have been North Fourth in home territory was East Fourth here, go figure it. Like two different countries, the opposite sides of the river. They even spoke English funny over here.

Larry's Bar.

Where the killer had picked up his three previous victims.

Kling planned on casing it from the outside, just to make sure she was still in there. Then he'd fade out, cover the place from a safe vantage point on the street. Didn't want Eileen to know he was on the scene. First off, she'd throw a fit, and next she might spook, blow her own cover. All he wanted was to be around in case she needed him.

He had put on an old pea jacket he kept in his locker for unexpected changes of weather like the one tonight. He was hatless and he wasn't wearing gloves. If he needed to pull the piece, he didn't want gloves getting in the way. Navy-blue pea jacket, blue jeans—too lightweight, really, for the sudden chill—blue socks and black loafers. And a .38 Detective Special in a holster at his waist. Left hand side. Two middle buttons of the jacket unbuttoned for an easy reach-in and cross-body draw.

He came up Canalside.

The Beef Trust was out in force, despite the cold.

Girls huddled under the lamp posts as though the overhead lights afforded some warmth, most of them wearing only short skirts and sweaters or blouses, scant protection against the cold. A lucky few were wearing coats provided by mobile pimps with an eye on the weather.

"Hey, sailor, lookin' for a party?"

Black girl breaking away from the knot under the corner lamp post, swiveling over to him. Couldn't be older than eighteen, nineteen, hands in the pockets of a short jacket, high-heeled ankle-strapped shoes, short skirt blowing in the fresh wind that came off the canal.

"Almos' do it for free, you so good-lookin'," she said, grinning widely. "Thass a joke, honey, but the price is right, trust me."

"Not right now," Kling said.

"Well, *when*, baby? I stann out here much longer, my pussy turn to ice. Be no good to neither one of us."

"Maybe later," Kling said.

"You promise? Slide your hand up under here, take a feel of heaven."

"I'm busy right now," Kling said.

"Too busy for *this*?" she said, and took his hand and guided it onto her thigh. "Mmmmm-*mmmmm*," she said, "sweet chocolate pussy, yours for the takin'."

"Later," he said, and freed his hand and began walking off.

"You come on back later, man, hear?" she shouted after him. "Ask for Crystal."

He walked into the darkness. On the dock, he could hear rats rustling along the pilings. Another lamp post, another huddle of hookers.

"Hey, Blondie, lookin' for some fun?"

White girl in her twenties. Wearing a long khaki coat and high heels. Opened the coat to him as he went past.

"Interested?" she said.

Nothing under the coat but garter belt and long black stockings. Quick glimpse of rounded belly and pink-tipped breasts.

"Faggot!" she yelled after him, and twirled the coat closed as gracefully as a dancer. The girls with her laughed. Fun on the docks.

Made a right turn onto Fairview, began walking up toward Fourth. Pools of light on the sidewalk ahead. Larry's Bar. Two plate-glass windows, beer displays in them, entrance door set between them. He went to the closest window, cupped his hands on either side of his face, peered through the glass. Not too crowded just now. Annie. Sitting at a table with a black man and a frizzied brunette. Good, at least one backup was close by. There at the bar. Eileen. With a big blond guy wearing glasses.

Okay, Kling thought.

I'm here.

Don't worry.

From where Shanahan sat slumped behind the wheel of the two-door Chevy across the street, he saw only a big blond guy looking through the plate-glass window of the bar. Six feet tall, he guessed, give or take an inch, broad shoulders and narrow waist, wearing a seaman's pea jacket and blue jeans.

Shanahan was suddenly alert.

Guy was still looking through the window, hands cupped to his face, motionless except for the dancing of his blond hair on the wind.

Shanahan kept watching.

The guy turned from the window.

No eyeglasses.

Might not be him.

On the other hand . . .

Shanahan got out of the car. It was clumsy moving with the right arm in a cast, but he'd rather be made for a cripple than a cop. Guy walking up the street now. How come he wasn't going in the bar? Change of M.O.? Shanahan fussed with the lock of the car door, watching him sidelong.

Minute the guy was four car lengths away, Shanahan took off after him.

The bar was baited with Eileen, but there were plenty of other girls out here on the street. And if this guy was suddenly changing his pattern, Shanahan didn't want *any* of them dying.

Eileen didn't like the tricks her mind was beginning to play.

She was beginning to like him.

She was beginning to think he couldn't possibly be a murderer.

Like the stories you read in the newspapers after the kid next door shot and killed his mother, his father, and his two sisters. Nice kid like that? all the neighbors said. Can't believe it. Always had a kind word for everyone. Saw him mowing the lawn and helping old ladies across the street. This kid a killer? Impossible.

Or maybe she didn't *want* him to be a murderer because that would mean eventual confrontation. She knew that if this was the guy, she'd have to end up face to face with him on the street outside. And the knife would come out of his pocket. And . . .

It was easier to believe he couldn't possibly be the killer.

You're tricking yourself, she thought.

And yet . . .

There really were a lot of likable things about him.

Not just his sense of humor. Some of his jokes were terrible, in fact. He told them almost compulsively, whenever anything in the conversation triggered what appeared to be a vast computer-bank memory of stories. You mentioned the tattoo near his thumb, for example—the killer had a tattoo near his thumb, she reminded herself—and he immediately told the one about the two girls discussing the guy with the tattooed penis, and one of them insisted only the word Swan was tattooed on it, whereas the other girl insisted the word was Saskatchewan, and it turned out they were both right, which took Eileen a moment to get. Or you mentioned the sudden change in the weather, and he immediately reeled off Henry Morgan's famous weather forecast, "Muggy today, Toogy tomorrow," and then segued neatly into the joke about the panhandler shivering outside in the cold and another panhandler comes over to him and says, "Can you lend me a dime for a cup of coffee?" and the first guy says, "Are you kidding? I'm standing here bare-assed, I'm shivering and starving to death, how come you're asking *me* for a dime?" and the second guy says, "Okay, make it a nickel," which wasn't very funny, but which he told with such dramatic flair that Eileen could actually visualize the two panhandlers standing on a windy corner of the city.

Outside, the city beckoned.

The night beckoned.

The knife beckoned.

But inside, sitting here at the bar with the television set going, and the sound of voices everywhere around them, the world seemed safe and cozy and warm, and she found herself listening intently to everything he said. Not only the jokes. The jokes were a given. If you wanted to learn about him, you had to listen to his jokes. The jokes were some sort of defense system, she realized, his way of keeping himself at arm's distance from anyone. But scattered in among the incessant jokes, there were glimpses of a shy and somewhat vulnerable person longing to make contact—until another joke was triggered.

He had used up his first twenty dollars five minutes ago, and was now working on the second twenty, which he said should take them through to twelve-forty.

"After that, we'll see," he said. "Maybe we'll talk some more, or maybe we'll go outside, depends how we feel, right? We'll play this by ear, Linda, I'm really enjoying this, aren't you?"

"Yes," she said, and guessed she meant it.

But he's the killer, she reminded herself.

Or maybe not.

She hoped he wasn't.

"If you add up these twenties," he said, "a dollar a minute, you'll be getting a third of what my dad gets in L.A., he gets a hundred and fifty bucks for a fifty-minute hour, which ain't bad, huh? For listening to people tell you they have bedbugs crawling all over them? Don't brush them on me, right? Well, I guess you know that one, I guess I've already told that one."

He hadn't told that one. But suddenly, as he apologized for what he'd mistakenly thought was repetition, she felt oddly close to him. Like a married woman listening to the same jokes her husband had told time and again, and yet enjoying them each time as if he were telling them for the first time. She knew the "Don't-brush-them-on-me" joke. Yet she wished he would tell it, anyway.

And wondered if she was stalling for time.

Wondered if she was putting off that eventual moment when the knife came out of the pocket.

"My father was very strict," he said. "If you have any choice, don't get raised by a psychiatrist. How's your father? Is he tough on you?"

"I never really knew him," she said.

Her father. A cop. On the beat, they used to call him Pops Burke. Shot to death when she was still a little girl.

In the next instant, she almost told him that her *uncle* and not her father was the one who'd had the most telling influence on her life. Uncle Matt. Also a cop. Whose favorite toast was, "Here's to golden days and purple nights." An expression he'd heard repeated again and again on a radio show. Recently, Eileen had heard Hal Willis's new girlfriend using the same expression. Small world. Even smaller world when your favorite uncle is sitting off-duty in his favorite bar making his favorite toast and a guy walks in with a sawed-off shotgun. Uncle Matt drew his service revolver and the guy shot him dead. She almost told Bobby she'd become a cop because of her Uncle Matt. She almost forgot in that instant that she herself was a cop working undercover to trap a killer. The word "entrapment" flashed into her mind. Suppose he isn't the killer? she wondered. Suppose I blow him away and it turns out—

And realized again that her mind was playing tricks.

"I grew up in a world of don't do this, don't do that," Bobby said. "You'd think a shrink would've known better, well, I guess it was a case of the shoemaker's children. Talk about repression. It was my mother who finally helped me to break out. I make it sound like a prison, don't I? Well, it was. Do you know the one about the lady walking along the beach in Miami?"

She shook her head.

She realized she was already smiling.

"Well, she sees this guy lying on the sand, and she goes up to him and she says, 'Excuse me, I don't mean to intrude, but you're very white.' The guy looks up at her and says, 'So?' The lady says, 'I mean, most people they come down to Miami, they lie in the sun, they get a nice tan. But you're very white.' The guy says, 'So?' The lady says, 'So how come you're so white?' The guy says, 'This is prison pallor, I just got out of prison yesterday.' The lady shakes her head and says, 'How long were you in prison?' The guys says, 'Thirty years.' The lady says, 'My, my, what did you do, they put you in prison for thirty years?' The guy says, 'I killed

210

my wife with a hatchet and chopped her up in little pieces.' The woman looks at him and says, 'Mmmm, so you're single?' "

Eileen burst out laughing.

And then realized that the joke was about murder.

And then wondered if a murderer would tell a joke about murder.

"Anyway, it was my mother who broke me out of prison," Bobby said, "and she had to die to do it."

"What do you mean?"

"Left me a lot of money. Do you know what she said in her will? She said, 'This is for Robert's freedom to risk enjoying life.' Her exact words. She always called me Robert. 'Robert's freedom to risk enjoying life.' Which is just what I've been doing for the past year. Kissed my father off, told him to shove it, told him I'd be happy if I never saw him again, and then left L.A. forever."

She wondered if there were any warrants out on him in L.A.

But why would there be any warrants?

"Went to Kansas City, had a good time there . . . got the tattoo there, in fact, what the hell, I'd always wanted a tattoo. Then on to Chicago, lived it up there, too, plenty of money to take risks, Linda. I owe that to my mother." He nodded thoughtfully, and then said, "He's the one who killed her, you know."

She looked at him.

"Oh, not literally. I mean he didn't stick a knife in her or anything. But he was having an affair with our housekeeper, and she found out about it, and it broke her heart, she was never the same again. They said it was cancer, but stress can induce serious illness, you know, and I'm sure that's what caused it, his fooling around with Elga. The money my mother eventually left me was the money she'd got in the divorce settlement, which I think was poetic justice, don't you? I mean, him raising me so strictly— while he's fooling around with that Nazi hooker, mind you—and my mother giving me *his* money so I could lead a richer life, so I could risk enjoying life. I think that was the key word, don't you?

In the will? Risk. I think she wanted me to take risks with the money, which is what I've been doing."

"How?" Eileen asked.

"Oh, not by investing in hog bellies or anything," he said, and smiled. "By living well. Living well is the best revenge, isn't it? Who said that? I know *somebody* said that."

"Not *me!*" Eileen said, and backed away in mock denial.

"Don't brush them on me, right?" he said, and they both laughed.

He looked at the clock.

"Five minutes left," he said. "Maybe we'll go outside then. Would you like to go outside then? When the five minutes are up?"

"Whatever you want," she said.

"Maybe that's what we'll do," he said. "Have a little fun. Do something new and exciting, huh? Risks," he said, and smiled again.

He had a very pleasant smile.

Transformed his entire face. Made him look like a shy little boy. Blue eyes soft, almost misty, behind the eyeglasses. Shy little kid sitting in the back row, afraid to raise his hand and ask questions.

"In a way, you know," he said, "it *has* been a sort of revenge. What I've been doing with the money. Traveling, having a good time, taking my risks. And getting even with him, in a way, for Elga. Our housekeeper, you know? The woman he tricked my mother with. Deceiving her all those years. A shrink, can you imagine? Holier than thou, and he's laying the goddamn housekeeper. I mean, my mother was the one who put him through medical school. She was a schoolteacher, you know, worked all those years to put him through school, do you know how long a psychiatrist has to go to school? It's very difficult to believe that women can be so callous toward other women. I find that very difficult to believe, Linda. I mean, Elga behaving like a common hooker . . . excuse me, I don't mean any offense. Excuse me, really," he said, and patted her hand. "But, you know, you hear all this talk about sisterhood, you'd think she might have had some sense of concern for my mother, I mean the woman was married to him for forty *years*!" He grinned suddenly. "Do you know the one about this man who comes to his wife, they've been married forty years, he says to her, 'Ida, I want to do it like dogs.' She says, 'That's disgusting, Sam, doing it like dogs.' He says, 'Ida, if you won't do it like dogs, I want a divorce.' She says, 'Okay, Sam, we'll do it like dogs. But not on our block.'"

Eileen nodded.

"Didn't like that one, huh?"

"Mezz' a mezza," she said, and see-sawed her hand on the air.

"I promise we won't do it like dogs, okay?" he said, smiling. "How would you like to do it, Linda?"

"You're the boss," she said.

"Have you ever seen a snuff movie?" he asked.

"Never," she said.

Here it comes, she thought.

"Does that scare you?" he said. "My asking about a snuff movie?"

"Yes," she said.

"Me, too," he said, and smiled. "I've never seen one, either."

Explore it, she thought.

But she was afraid to.

"Think you might like that?" she asked.

Her heart was suddenly pounding again.

"Killing someone while you were laying her?"

He looked deep into her eyes as though searching for something there.

"Not if she knew it was going to happen," he said.

And suddenly she knew for certain that he was their man, and there was no postponing what would happen tonight.

He looked up at the clock.

"Time's up," he said. "Let's go outside."

12

The call to the squadroom came at twenty minutes to one. The call came from Monoghan, who was in a phone booth on the edge of the River Dix. He asked to talk to either Brown or Genero. Willis told him Brown and Genero were both out.

"So who's this?" Monoghan asked.

"Willis."

"What I got here," Monoghan said, "is a head and a pair of hands. These guys dragging the river turned up this aluminum case, like it's big enough to hold a man's head. And his hands. So that's what I got here. A head cut off at the neck, and a pair of hands cut off at the wrists."

"Uh-huh," Willis said.

"So earlier tonight I was with Brown and Genero back out behind this restaurant the Burgundy, and what we had there was the upper part of a torso in a garbage can, is what we had. And

214

now I got a head and a pair of hands, and it occurred to me this might be the same body here, this head and hands."

"Uh-huh," Willis said.

"So what I want to know, does Brown or Genero have a positive make on the stiff? 'Cause otherwise we now got a head to look at, and also some hands to print."

"Let me take a look at Brown's desk," Willis said. "I think he left some stuff here."

"Yeah, go take a look," Monoghan said.

"Hold on," Willis said.

"Yeah."

"Hold on, I'm putting you on hold."

"Yeah, fine," Monoghan said.

Willis pressed the hold button, and then went over to Brown's desk. He riffled through the papers there, and then stabbed at the lighted extension button, and picked up the receiver.

"Monoghan?"

"Yeah."

"From what I can gather, the body was identified as someone named Frank Sebastiani, male, white, thirty-four years old."

"That's what I got here, a white male around that age."

"I've got a picture here, too," Willis said.

"Whyn't you run on over with it?" Monoghan said. "We see we got the same stiff or not."

"Where are you?"

"Freezing my ass off on the drive here. Near the river."

"Which river?"

"The Dix."

"And where?"

"Hampton."

"Give me ten minutes," Willis said.

"Don't forget the picture," Monoghan said.

The apartment over the garage was perhaps twelve-feet wide by twenty-feet long. There was a neatly made double bed in the

215

room, and a dresser with a mirror over it, and an upholstered chair with a lamp behind it. The wall surrounding the mirror was covered with pictures of naked women snipped from men's magazines banned in 7-Eleven stores. All of the women were blondes. Like Marie Sebastiani. In the bottom drawer of the dresser, under a stack of Brayne's shirts, the detectives found a pair of crotchless black panties. The panties were a size five.

"Think they're Brayne's?" Hawes asked drily.

"What size you think the lady wears?" Brown asked.

"Could be a five," Hawes said, and shrugged.

"I thought you were an expert."

"On *bras* I'm an expert."

Men's socks, undershorts, sweaters, handkerchiefs in the other dresser drawers. Two sports jackets, several pairs of slacks, a suit, an overcoat, and three pairs of shoes in the single small closet. There was also a suitcase in the closet. Nothing in it. No indication anywhere in the apartment that Brayne had packed and taken off in a hurry. Even his razor and shaving cream were still on the sink in the tiny bathroom.

A tube of lipstick was in the cabinet over the sink.

Brown took off the top.

"Look like the lady's shade?" he asked Hawes. "Pretty careless if it's her, leavin' her o.c.p.'s in the dresser and her . . ."

"Her *what*?"

"Her open-crotch panties."

"Oh."

"You think she was dumb enough to be makin' it with him right here in this room?"

"Let's see what else we find," Hawes said.

What else they found was a sheaf of letters rubber-banded together. They found the letters in a cardboard shoe box on the top shelf of the closet. The letters were inside lavender-colored envelopes, but none of the envelopes had been stamped or mailed. The name "Jimmy" was scrawled on the front of each envelope.

"Hand-delivered," Hawes said.

"Mmm," Brown said, and they began reading the letters.
The letters were written in purple ink.
The first letter read:

> Jimmy,
> Just say when.
> *Marie*

It was dated July 18.
"When did he start working for them?" Brown asked.
"Fourth of July."
"Fast worker, this lady," Brown said.
The second letter was dated July 21. It described in excruciatingly passionate detail all the things Marie and Jimmy had done together the day before.
"This is dirty," Brown said, looking up.
"Yes," Hawes said. He was reading over Brown's shoulder.
There were twenty-seven letters in all. The letters chronicled a rather active sex life between the lady and the sorcerer's apprentice, Marie apparently having been compulsive about jotting down everything she had done to Jimmy in the recent past, and then outlining everything she hadn't yet done to him but which she planned to do to him in the foreseeable future, which—if the chronology was faithful—she did indeed get around to doing to him.
She did a lot of things to him.
The last letter was dated October 27, four days before the murder and dismemberment of the lady's husband. She suggested in this last letter that one of the things she wanted to do to Jimmy on Halloween night was tie him to the bed in his black silk undershorts and spread herself open over him in her black crotchless panties and then—
"You see any black silk undershorts in the dresser there?" Brown asked.
"No," Hawes said. "I'm reading."

217

"A celebration, do you think?" Brown asked. "All this stuff she planned to do to him on Halloween?"

"Maybe."

"Do hubby in, chop him up in little pieces, then come back here and have a witch's sabbath."

"Where does she call it that?"

"Call it what?"

"Witch's sabbath."

"*I'm* calling it that," Brown said. "Black silk undershorts, black o.c.p's . . ."

"So where's Brayne?" Hawes asked. "If they were planning a celebration . . ."

"Did you look under the bed?" Brown asked, and then turned suddenly toward the window.

Hawes turned at exactly the same moment.

An automobile had just pulled into the driveway.

At ten minutes to one—ten minutes after Bobby had suggested that they go outside—Eileen excused herself and went to the ladies' room. Annie, sitting at a table with an Italian sailor who was having difficulty making his needs understood, watched her as she crossed the room and made a left turn at the phone booths.

"Excuse me," Annie said.

By the time she got to the ladies' room, Eileen was already in one of the stalls. Annie did a quick check for feet. The other stalls were empty.

"Yes or no?" she asked.

"Yes," Eileen said.

Her voice from behind the closed door sounded odd.

"Are you sure?"

"I think so."

"You okay?"

"Fine. Checking out the hardware."

The door opened. Eileen looked pale. She went to the sink, touched up her lipstick, blotted it.

"You going out now?" Annie asked.

"Yes."

The same odd voice.

"Give me three minutes to get on the street," Annie said.

"Okay."

Annie went to the door.

"I'll be there," she said simply.

"Good," Eileen said.

Annie took one last look at her, and then went out.

"What I'm talking about is decency and honor," Peaches said.

It was very cold and they were walking along the street rapidly.

"I'm talking about a person's responsibility to another person," Peaches said, clinging to Parker's arm for warmth and nothing else.

Parker was beginning to feel married.

"You went to that party with *me*," Peaches said, "and not with Little Miss Muffet."

"If a person can't have a simple conversation with another person . . ."

"That wasn't a conversation," Peaches said. "That was a person-and-a-half exchanging deep sighs and meaningful glances."

"I don't think it's nice of you to make midget jokes," Parker said.

"Oh, was she a midget?" Peaches said. "I thought maybe she'd shrunk in the wash."

"That's just what I mean," Parker said.

"I thought maybe she was E.T. in drag."

"I'm sorry if you're upset," he said.

"I am upset."

"And I'm sorry."

He *was* sorry. He was thinking it was getting to be a very cold night after a lovely day in the tropics, and he would much prefer spending the winter in Peaches' probably warm and generous

219

bed here in town instead of in his own narrow, mean bed in his grubby little apartment away the hell out in Majesta. He was also thinking tomorrow was time enough to give Alice a call.

"What bothers me is I thought we were having such a good time together," Peaches said.

"We were. We still are. The night is young," he said.

"I thought you sort of liked me."

"I do like you. I like you a lot."

"I like you, too," Peaches said.

"So where's the problem? There's no problem. I don't see any problem. What we'll do," Parker said, "is we'll go back to your place, and we'll have a drink, and maybe watch some television . . ."

"That sounds nice," she said, and hugged his arm.

"It does, doesn't it?" he said. "It does sound nice."

"And we'll forget all about Eeansie-Beansie Spider."

"Who?" Parker said.

"Your little friend," Peaches said.

"I already forgot about her," Parker said.

They were just passing one of those subway-kiosk newsstands on the corner. The blind owner was kneeling over a stack of newspapers on the pavement, cutting the cord around them. Parker came up beside him. The blind man knew he was there, but he took his good sweet time cutting the cord. Parker waited; he prided himself on never having hassled a blind man in his life. The blind man finally hefted the papers up onto the newsstand and then walked around to the little door on the side of the stand and went in behind the counter.

"So?" he said.

Parker was looking down at the headline.

"You want a paper?" the blind man said.

The headline read:

2 COPS SHOT
4 MIDGETS SOUGHT

The car in the driveway of the Sebastiani house was a 1979 Cadillac Seville, silver-sided with a black hardtop, still in seemingly excellent condition. The woman who got out of the Caddy was in excellent condition herself, tall and leggy and wearing a black cloth coat the color of her hair. Hawes and Brown watched her from the upstairs window of the garage as she went directly to the front door of the house and rang the bell.

Hawes looked at his watch.

A few minutes before one in the morning.

"Who the hell is that?" he said.

They came out of Larry's Bar at exactly 1:00 A.M., twenty minutes after Bobby had first suggested they leave. A strong wind was blowing off the canal. He had insisted that she continue wearing his jacket, and she still had it draped over her shoulders. She hoped it wouldn't get in the way when she yanked the gun. Her hand hovered over the open top of her bag, seemingly resting there close to the shoulder strap. But close to the butt of the gun, too.

Bobby had his right hand in his pants pocket.

On the knife, she thought.

He had slashed his first victim in a doorway two blocks from the bar.

The second one in an alleyway on East Ninth.

The third on Canalside itself, heavily trafficked with hookers.

"Pretty cold out here," he said. "Not exactly what I had in mind."

Annie was the first of the three detectives to spot them coming out of the bar.

She had hit the street the moment she'd left Eileen in the ladies' room, and had taken up position in the darkened doorway of a closed Chinese noodle factory. It was very cold out here on the street, and she wasn't dressed for it. Skirt too damn short, blouse too flimsy. Eileen came out of the bar like a flare, red hair

221

blowing on the wind, the guy's jacket draped over her shoulders, made an immediate left turn, walking on the guy's right, her own right hand on the curb side and resting on her bag. The guy's right hand was in his pants pocket.

Two of the lamp posts on Fairview had been vandalized, and there were wide stretches of darkness between the light on the corner and the third one up. On the distant corner, a traffic light turned to red as flaming as Eileen's hair. The red hair was a plus. Easy to keep her in view. Annie gave them a twenty-yard lead, and then fell into step behind them, keeping close to the buildings on her left, the guy's blind side because he was turned to the right as he walked and talked. She cursed the hooker heels she was wearing because they made such a clatter on the sidewalk, but the guy seemed unaware of her presence behind them, just kept chatting up Eileen as they dissolved into the darkness between the lighted lamp posts.

Eileen's red hair was the beacon.

Kling, scanning the street from a vantage point diagonally across from the bar, was the second detective to spot them.

The street was dark where he waited in the shadow of an abandoned tool works, the lamp post globe shattered, but the woman was unmistakably Eileen. Never mind the red hair, he'd have known her if she was wearing a blonde wig. Knew every nuance of her walk, the long stride, the swing of her shoulders, the rhythmic jiggle of her buttocks. He was about to move out, cross the street and fall in behind them, when he saw Annie.

Good, he thought, she's in place.

He stayed on the opposite side of the street, ten feet behind Annie who was working hard to keep up without showing herself. Eileen and the guy were walking very fast, up toward the traffic light on the corner, which changed now, throwing a green wash onto the roadway. The formation could have been a classic tailing triangle—one cop behind the quarry, another cop ahead of them on the same side of the street, a third cop on the opposite side of the street—except that it was lacking the third cop.

Or so Kling thought.

Shanahan was the third cop.

He had been tailing Kling from the moment he'd spotted him peering through the plate-glass window of the bar. Pacing the street impatiently, always circling back to the bar, checking out the front door from across the street, then drifting off again, and back again, behaving very much like a person waiting for somebody to come out of there. When Eileen finally came out of the bar with a *second* blond guy, Shanahan's blond took off after them. Annie was up ahead, she had Eileen and *her* blond covered and in sight. But this other blond guy was still showing too much interest. Shanahan gave him a lead, and then fell in behind him again.

Up ahead, Eileen and her blond turned left at the traffic light, and disappeared around the corner.

Shanahan's blond hesitated only a moment.

Seemed undecided whether to make his move or not.

Then he pulled a gun and started across the street.

Annie recognized Kling at once.

He had a gun in his hand.

She didn't know whether she was more surprised by his presence here or by the gun in his hand. Too many thoughts clicked through her mind in the next three seconds. She thought He's going to blow it, the guy hasn't made his move yet. She thought Does Eileen know he's here? She thought—

But Eileen and her man were already around the corner and out of sight.

"Bert!" she shouted.

And in that instant Shanahan came thundering up yelling, "Stop! Police!"

*   *   *

Kling turned to see a man pointing an arm in a plaster cast at him.

He turned the other way and saw Annie running across the street.

"Mike!" Annie shouted.

Shanahan stopped dead in his tracks. Annie was waving her arms at him like a traffic cop.

"He's on the job!" she shouted.

Shanahan had earlier told Eileen that he and Lou Alvarez were just full of tricks. He hadn't realized, however, that Alvarez had sent another man to the Zone without telling him about it. That tricky, he didn't think Alvarez was. Shanahan's own little trick was a .32 revolver in his right hand, his finger inside the trigger guard, the gun and the hand encased in the plaster cast. He felt like an asshole now, the plaster cast still pointed at a guy Annie had just identified as a cop.

The realization came to all three of them in the same instant.

The traffic light on the corner turned red again as though signaling the coming of their mutual dawn.

Without a word, they looked up the street.

It was empty.

Eileen and her man were gone.

A minute ago, she'd had three backups.

Now she didn't have any.

Dolores Eisenberg was Frank Sebastiani's older sister.

Five-feet ten-inches tall, black hair and blue eyes, thirty-eight, thirty-nine years old. Hugging Marie to her when Brown and Hawes came over from the garage. Tears in the eyes of both women.

Marie introduced her to the cops.

Dolores seemed surprised to see them there.

"How do you do?" she said, and glanced at Marie.

"We're sorry for your trouble," Brown said.

224

An old Irish expression. Hawes wondered where he'd picked it up.

Dolores said, "Thank you," and then turned to Marie again. "I'm sorry it took me so long to get here," she said. "Max is in Cincinnati, and I had to find a sitter. God, wait'll he hears this. He's crazy about Frank."

"I know," Marie said.

"I'll have to call him again," Dolores said. "When Mom told me what happened, I tried to reach him at the hotel, but he was out. What time was that, when you called Mom?"

"It must've been around eleven-thirty," Marie said.

"Yeah, she called me right afterward. I felt like I'd been hit by a locomotive. I tried to get Max, I left a message for him to call me, but then I left the house around midnight, as soon as the sitter got there. I'll have to call him again."

She was still wearing her overcoat. She took it off now, revealing a trim black skirt and a crisp white blouse, and carried it familiarly to the coatrack. They were still standing in the entrance hall. The house seemed exceptionally still at this hour of the morning. The heater came on with a sudden whooosh.

"Would anyone like some coffee?" Dolores asked.

A take-charge lady, Hawes thought. Tragedy in the family, here she is at one in the morning, ready to make coffee.

"There's some on the stove," Marie said.

"Officers?" Dolores said.

"Thank you, no," Brown said.

"No, thanks," Hawes said.

"Marie? Honey, can I get a cup for you?"

"I'm all right, Dolores, thank you."

"Poor baby," Dolores said, and hugged her sister-in-law close again. Her arm still around her, she looked at Brown and said, "My mother told me you think Jimmy did it, is that right?"

"That's a strong possibility," Brown said, and looked at Marie.

"You haven't found him, though?"

"No, not yet."

225

"It's hard to believe," Dolores said, and shook her head. "My mother said you have to do an autopsy. I wish you wouldn't, really. That's really upsetting to her."

It occurred to Brown that she did not yet know her brother's body had been dismembered. Hadn't Marie told the family? He debated breaking the news, opted against it.

"Well, ma'am," he said, "an autopsy's mandatory in any trauma death."

"Still," Dolores said.

Brown was still looking at Marie. It had further occurred to him that on the phone with Dolores not an hour ago, she herself advised her sister-in-law about the autopsy. Yet now Dolores sounded as if the information had come from her mother. He tried to remember the exact content of the phone conversation. Marie's end of it, anyway.

Hello Dolores, no, not yet, I'm down in the kitchen.

Which meant her sister-in-law had asked her if she was in bed, or getting ready for bed, or whatever, and she'd told her No, I'm down here with two detectives. Which meant that Dolores *knew* there were two detectives here, so why had she looked so surprised to *find* them here?

They want to look at the garage room.

So you had to figure Dolores had asked her what two detectives were doing there. And she'd told her. And then the business about the autopsy. Which Dolores had just now talked about as if it had come from her mother. But if Dolores had called here just before leaving the house . . . well, wait a minute.

On the phone, Marie hadn't said anything about expecting her, nothing like "See you soon then," or "Hurry on over," or "Drive safely," just "I'll let you know," meaning about the autopsy, "Thanks for calling."

Brown decided to play it flat out.

He looked Dolores dead in the eye and said, "Did you call here about an hour ago?"

And the telephone rang.

Brown figured there had to be a god.

Because if the earlier ringing of the phone had visibly startled Marie, this time the ringing caused an immediate look of panic to flash in her eyes. She turned toward the kitchen as if it had suddenly burst into flames, made an abortive start out of the entrance hall, stopped, said, "I wonder ..." and then looked blankly at the detectives.

"Can't be Dolores again, can it?" Brown said.

"What?" Dolores said, puzzled.

"Better go answer it," Brown said.

"Yes," Marie said.

"I'll go with you," he said.

In the kitchen, the phone kept ringing.

Marie hesitated.

"Want me to get it?" Brown asked.

"No, I'll ... it may be my mother-in-law," she said, and headed immediately for the kitchen, Brown right behind her.

The phone kept ringing.

She was thinking You goddamn fool, I *told* you the cops were here!

She reached out for the receiver, her mind racing.

Brown was standing in the doorway to the kitchen now, his arms folded across his chest.

Marie lifted the receiver from the hook.

"Hello?" she said.

And listened.

Brown kept watching her.

"It's for you," she said, sounding relieved, and handed the receiver to him.

227

13

Parker felt like a real cop again.

A working detective.

The feeling was somewhat exhilarating.

The newspaper story accompanying the headline told him everything he needed to know about the liquor-store holdups tonight. The story extensively quoted Detective Meyer Meyer who had been interviewed in his room at Buenavista Hospital. Meyer had told the reporter that the heists and subsequent felony murders had been executed by four midgets being driven by a big blonde woman in a blue station wagon. One of the holdup victims had described the thieves as midgets. She had further told the police that one of the midgets was named Alice.

Parker did not have to be a detective to know that there couldn't be too many midgets named Alice in this city. But making the connection so quickly made him feel like a real cop again.

He put Peaches in a taxi—even though they were only four blocks from her apartment—told her he'd try to call her later, and then hailed a cruising patrol car. The two uniformed cops in the car advised Parker they were from the Three-One—which Parker knew anyway since the number of the precinct was on the side of the car—and they didn't know if they had authority to provide transportation for a detective from the Eight-Seven.

Parker said, "This is a homicide here, open the fucking door!"

The two uniformed cops looked at each other by way of consultation, and then the cop riding shotgun unlocked the back door for him. Parker sat in the back of the car like a common criminal, a metal grille separating him from the two cops up front.

"Four-oh-three Thompson Street," he told the driver.

"That's all the way down the Quarter," the driver complained.

"That's right, it should take you fifteen, twenty minutes."

"Half hour's more like it," the shotgun cop said, and then got on the walkie-talkie to tell his sergeant they were driving a bull from the Eight-Seven downtown.

The sergeant said, "Let me talk to him."

"He's in back," the shotgun cop said.

"Stop the car and let me talk to him," the sergeant said. He sounded very no-nonsense. Parker had met sergeants like him before. He loved trampling on sergeants like him.

They stopped the car and opened the back door. The shotgun cop handed the walkie-talkie in to Parker.

"What's the problem?" Parker said into it.

"Who's this?" the sergeant said.

"Detective Andrew Lloyd Parker," he said, "Eighty-Seventh Squad. Who's this?"

"Never mind who this is, what's the idea commandeering one of my cars?"

"The idea is homicide," Parker said. "The idea is two cops in the hospital. The idea is I gotta get downtown in a hurry, and I'd

229

hate like hell for the media to find out a sergeant from the Three-One maybe stood in the way of a timely arrest. That's the idea. You think you got it?"

There was a long silence.

"Who's your commanding officer?" the sergeant asked, trying to save face.

"Lieutenant Peter Byrnes," Parker said. "We finished here?"

"You can take the car downtown, but I'll be talking to your lieutenant," the sergeant said.

"Good, you talk to him," Parker said, and handed the walkie-talkie to the shotgun cop. "Let's get rolling," he said.

They closed the back door again. The driver set the car in motion.

"Hit the hammer," Parker said.

The blues looked sidelong at each other. This kind of thing didn't seem to warrant use of the siren.

"Hit the fucking hammer," Parker said.

The driver hit the siren switch.

They were sitting in the living room when Brown got off the phone. Marie and her sister-in-law side by side on the sofa, Hawes in an easy chair opposite them.

Brown walked in looking very solemn.

"Hal Willis," he said to Hawes.

"What's up?" Hawes said.

Brown tugged casually at his earlobe before he started talking again. Hawes picked up the signal at once. Little dog-and-pony act on the way.

"They found the rest of the body," Brown said.

Marie looked at him.

"Head and the hands," Brown said. "In the river. I'm sorry, ma'am," he said to Dolores, "but your brother's body was dismembered. I hate to break it to you this way."

"Oh my *God!*" Dolores said.

Marie was still looking at Brown.

"Guys dredging the river pulled up this aluminum case, head and the hands in it," he said.

Hawes was trying to catch the drift. He kept listening intently.

"Did you know this?" Dolores asked Marie.

Marie nodded.

"You knew he'd been . . . ?"

"Yes," she said. "I didn't tell Mom because I knew what it would do to her."

"Monoghan responded," Brown said to Hawes, "phoned the squad. Willis went on over with the stuff on my desk."

The stuff on his desk, Hawes thought. The reports, the positive ID, the poster he'd taken from the high school bulletin board.

"I hate to have to go over this another time, Mrs. Sebastiani," Brown said, "but I wonder if you can give me a description of your husband again. So we can close this out."

"I have it right here," Hawes said. He was beginning to catch on. Nobody closed out a case while the murderer was still running around loose. He took his notebook from the inside pocket of his jacket, flipped through the pages. "Male, white, thirty-four years old . . ." he said.

"That right?" Brown asked Marie.

"Yes," she said.

"Five-eleven," Hawes said, "one-seventy . . ."

"Mrs. Sebastiani?"

"Yes."

Eyes flashing with intelligence now. Hawes figured she was beginning to catch on, too. Didn't know exactly what was coming, but was bracing herself for it. Hawes didn't know exactly what was coming, either. But he had a hunch.

"Hair black," he said, "Eyes . . ."

"Why do we have to go over this again?" she said. "I identified the body, you have everything you . . ."

"My brother's hair was black, yes," Dolores said softly, and patted Marie's hand.

"Eyes blue," Hawes said.

231

"Blue eyes, yes," Dolores said. "Like mine."

"Will I have to come into the city again?" Marie asked. "To look at ... at what they ... they found in the ... ?"

"Mrs. Sebastiani," Brown said, "the head we found in the river doesn't match your husband's photograph."

Marie blinked at him.

Silence.

Then:

"Well ... does ... does that mean ... what does that mean?"

"It means the dead man isn't your husband," Brown said.

"Has someone made a mistake then?" Dolores asked at once. "Are you saying my brother isn't dead?"

"Mrs. Sebastiani," Brown said, "would you mind very much if I read you this description you gave me of Jimmy Brayne?"

"I really don't see why we have to go over this a hundred times," she said. "If you were doing your job right, you'd have *found* Jimmy by now."

Brown had already taken out his notebook.

"White male," he read, "thirty-two years old. Height, six feet. Weight, a hundred and eighty ..."

"Yes," she said impatiently.

Eyes alert now. Hawes had seen those eyes before. Desperate eyes, trapped eyes. Brown was closing in, and she knew it.

"Hair black, eyes brown."

"Yes," she said again.

"Mrs. Sebastiani, the eyes were brown."

"Yes, I just told you ..."

"On the head in the river. The eyes were brown." He turned to Dolores. "Does your brother have an appendectomy scar?" he asked.

"A what?"

"Did he ever have his appendix removed?"

"No. I don't understand what you ..."

"Was he ever in a skiing accident? Did he ever tear the cartilage on his ..."

"He never skied in his life," Dolores said.

She looked extremely puzzled now. She glanced at Marie.

"The techs printed the fingers and thumbs on both hands," Brown said. "We're running a comparison check right this minute. Was your brother ever in the service?"

"Yes. The Army."

"Would you know if Jimmy Brayne was ever in the service?"

"I don't know."

"Or in any security-sensitive job? How about you, Mrs. Sebastiani? You seem to know a lot about Jimmy Brayne, maybe you know whether he's ever been fingerprinted."

"All I know about him . . ."

"Right down to his beauty spot," Brown said, and snapped the notebook shut.

"Marie, what is he talking about?" Dolores asked.

"I think she knows what I'm talking about," Brown said.

Marie said nothing.

"If the prints come up blank," Brown said, "we've still got the head. Someone'll identify him. Sooner or later, we'll get a positive ID."

She still said nothing.

"He's Jimmy Brayne, isn't he?" Brown asked.

Silence.

"You and your husband killed Jimmy Brayne, didn't you?" he said.

She sat quite still, her hands folded on the lap of her robe.

"Mrs. Sebastiani," Brown said, "would you like to tell us where your husband is?"

Parker opened the door with a skeleton key.

On the sofa bed in the living room, a male midget and a female midget were asleep. They jumped up the minute the door opened.

"Hello," Parker said softly, and showed them the gun.

Wee Willie Winkie was one of the midgets. He was wearing

233

striped pajamas. He looked cute as a button, but his face went pale the moment he saw the gun. His wife, Corky, was wearing panties and a baby-doll nightgown. Pink. She grabbed a pillow and hugged it to her breasts as Parker approached the bed. Light from the hallway spilled illumination into the room. It glinted on the gun in Parker's hand. Corky's brown eyes were opened wide. She kept holding the pillow to her breasts. Parker thought she looked a little bit like Debbie Reynolds.

"Are the others asleep?" he whispered.

Willie nodded.

"Where?"

Willie pointed to a pair of closed doors.

"Up," Parker whispered.

They got out of bed. Corky looked embarrassed in only her nightgown and panties. She kept holding the pillow to her in front, but her back was exposed. Parker gestured with the gun.

"We're going to wake them up," he whispered. "Don't yell or I'll shoot you both."

In one of the bedrooms, Oliver Twist was asleep with a full-sized woman. The woman was very fat and very blonde. Parker remembered the old joke about the midget marrying the circus fat lady and running around the bed all night yelling, "Mine, all mine!"

He nudged the midget.

The midget popped up in bed.

Red hair all mussed, blue eyes wide.

"Shhhh," Parker said. "It's the police."

Oliver blinked. So did Willie. This was the first he was hearing of this. Up to now, he'd thought they were dealing with a burglar, which was bad enough. Now he knew it was a cop in here, his worst nightmare realized. He glanced at Corky, his eyes blaming his wife for her goddamn friendship with Little Annie Oakley and her trigger-happy finger.

"Wake up your lady," Parker said to Oliver.

Oliver nudged the fat blonde.

She rolled over.

He nudged her again.

"Go away," she said.

Parker pulled the blanket off her. She was wearing a long granny nightgown. She tried to pull the blanket back over her again, grasped futilely at only thin air, and then sat up, annoyed and still half-asleep.

"Police," Parker said, smiling.

"What?" she said, blinking.

"You the one did the driving?" he said.

"What driving?" she said.

"She don't know what driving," Parker said to Oliver, still smiling.

"Quentin did the driving," Oliver said. "This lady had nothing to do with any of it."

"Any of what?" the blonde said.

Quentin, Parker thought. The guy at the party.

"Where is he?" he asked.

"In the other room," Oliver said.

"Let's go tell him the party's over," Parker said. "Get out of bed. Both of you."

They got out of bed.

"Is this a joke?" the blonde whispered to Oliver.

"I don't think it's a joke," Oliver whispered back.

Parker herded the four of them into the other bedroom. The radiator was hissing, and the room was suffocatingly hot. Parker snapped on the lights. Quentin Forbes was in bed with Alice. Neither of them stirred. They had thrown back the covers in their sleep, and they were both naked. Alice looked as pretty as a little doll, her blonde hair fanned out over the pillow.

"Police!" Parker shouted, and they both jumped up at the same time. "Hello, Alice," he said, and smiled.

"Hello, Andy," she said, and smiled back.

"We have to get dressed now," he said, as if to a child.

"Okay," she said, and reached under the pillow.

Parker said it even before he saw the gun in her hand.

"Don't."

She hesitated.

"Please, Alice," he said. "Don't."

She must have discerned something in his eyes. She must have known she was looking into the eyes of a cop who had seen it all and heard it all.

"Okay," she said, and put down the gun.

Forbes said, "This is an outrage."

"It is, I know," Parker said.

"Let me see your badge," the blonde said.

Parker showed her his shield.

"What is this?" she asked.

"Let's get dressed now," he said, and went to the window and yelled down for the two uniformed cops from the Three-One.

There were only three pairs of handcuffs among them, and six people to cuff. This was a problem in the law of supply and demand. One of the blues went downstairs again and radioed for assistance, making it clear this wasn't a 10-13, they just needed some more handcuffs. The sergeant at the Twelfth wanted to know what two blues from the Three-One and a detective from the Eight-Seven were doing on his turf, but he sent a car around with the extra cuffs. By the time the cuffs arrived, Parker had personally searched the apartment. He'd found a valise full of money. He'd found a trunk with costumes and masks and wigs in it. He'd found four .22-caliber Zephyr revolvers and a Colt .45-caliber automatic.

He figured he had a case.

When they put the cuffs on her, Alice was wearing a pair of tailored gray slacks, a long-sleeved pink blouse, a double breasted navy-blue jacket with brass buttons, blue patent leather shoes with French heels, and a little navy-blue overcoat. She looked adorable.

As they went out of the apartment together, she said, "It didn't have to happen this way, you know."

"I know," Parker said.

Willis hoped there wasn't a gun in the room here. He hoped there wouldn't be shooting. With O'Brien along . . .

"Police," O'Brien said, and knocked on the door again.

Silence inside the room there.

Then the sound of a window scraping open.

"He's moving!" Willis said.

He was already backing away from the door and raising his right leg for a piston-kick. Arms wide for leverage, he looked like a football player going for the extra point. His leg lashed out, the sole and heel of his shoe hitting the door flat, just above the knob. The latch sprang, the door swung inward, O'Brien following it into the room, gun extended. Don't let there be another gun in here, Willis thought.

A man in his undershorts was halfway out the window.

"That's a long drop, mister," O'Brien said.

The man hesitated.

"Mr. Sebastiani?" Willis said.

The man still had one leg over the windowsill. There was no fire escape out there, Willis wondered where the hell he thought he was going.

"My name is Theo Hardeen," he said.

"So your wife mentioned," Willis said.

"My wife? I don't know what you're talking about."

They never knew what anyone was talking about.

"Mr. Sebastiani," Willis said, "at this very moment, your wife is driving in from Collinsworth with two detectives from the Eighty-Seventh Squad, upon whose instructions and advice we're . . ."

"I don't have any wife in . . ."

"They also have a chain saw in the car," O'Brien said.

"They found a chain saw in your garage," Willis said.

"There's a lot of blood on the saw," O'Brien said.

"Sir, we're arresting you for the crime of murder," Willis said, and then began reeling off Miranda-Escobedo by rote. Sebastiani listened to the recitation as though he were being lectured. He still had one leg over the windowsill.

"Mr. Sebastiani?" Willis said. "You want to come in off that window now?"

Sebastiani came in off the window.

"She blew it, huh?" he said.

"You both did," Willis said.

This time is for real, Carella thought.

No tricks this time.

This time I go west.

Swirling darkness, blinking lights, aurora borealis, murmuring voices, beeping sounds, everything so fake and far away, but everything so real and immediate, it was funny. Floating somewhere above himself, hovering above himself like the angel of death, "Wear this garlic around your neck," Grandma used to say, "it'll keep away the angel of death," but where's the garlic now, Grandma? Crisp white sheets and soft feather pillows, tomato sauce cooking on the old wood stove in the kitchen, your eyeglasses steaming up, the time Uncle Jerry ate the rat shit, thinking it was olives, everyone gone now, is Meyer dead, too?

Jesus, Meyer, don't be dead.

Please don't be dead.

Floating on the air above himself, looking down at himself, the big hero, some hero, open to the world, open to the hands and eyes of strangers, an open book, don't let Meyer be dead, let me hold you, Meyer, let me hold you, friend. Let's go in now, did someone say that years and years ago? Open him up now, open up the hero, big editorial conference out there, but no last-minute editorial decisions this time, no one here to say you can't kill the hero, big hero, some hero, cold-cocked by midgets, bang-bang, gotcha, close the book.

Exit.

But . . .

Please save that for later, okay? Save the final curtain for somewhere down the line, I'm a married man, give me a break. He almost laughed though nothing was funny, tried to laugh, wondered if he was smiling instead, heard someone say something through the fog rolling in off the water, heavy storm brewing out there, I never even learned to sail, he thought, I never had a yacht.

All the things I never did.

All the things I never had.

Well, listen, who's . . . ?

All the treasures.

Thirty-seven five a year doesn't buy treasures.

Ah, Jesus, Teddy, I never bought you treasures.

All the things I wanted to buy you.

Forgive me for the treasures, bless me father for I have sinned, A is for amethyst and B is for beryl, C is for coral and D is for diamonds, F is for furs and G is for gold and H is for heaven and I is for . . .

E is missing.

E is for exit.

But . . .

Please don't get ahead of me, please don't rush me, just give me a little time to finish the rest of the alphabet, I beg of you, please.

I is for me.

"Careful," someone said.

There's one hot-bed hotel the girls use, plus fifty or sixty rented rooms all over the Zone.

Shanahan talking.

239

Too many hours ago.

She had lost her backups, she knew that.

She didn't know what had happened on the street outside, but they were gone, that was for sure.

So here we are, she thought.

Alone at last.

You and me.

Face to face.

Not in that single hot-bed hotel, where there was a chance they might find her before the crack of dawn, but in one of those fifty or sixty rented rooms. Lady downstairs taking the money from him, looking at it on the palm of her hand as if she expected a tip besides, up the stairs to the third floor, the smells of cooking permeating the hallways, terrific spot for a honeymoon, key in the door, the door opening on a room with a bed and a dresser and a wooden chair and a lamp and a tattered window shade, and a small door at the far end leading into a bathroom with only a toilet bowl and a soiled sink.

"It's small, but it's cheerful," he'd said, grinning, and then he'd locked the door behind them and put the key into the same pocket with the knife.

That was almost an hour ago.

He'd been talking ever since.

She kept reminding him that time was money, wanting him to make his move, get it over with, but he kept laying twenty-dollar bills on her, "A dollar a minute, right?" he said, and the empty minutes of the night kept ticking away, and he made no move to approach her.

She wondered if she should bust him, anyway. Here we go, mister, it's the Law, run a lineup for the pair of hookers who'd described him, run the risk of them either chickening out or not remembering, run the further risk—even *with* a positive ID— that he'd talk his way out of it, walk away from it. Two hookers claiming they saw him chatting up the victims didn't add up to a conviction. No. If he was their man, he had to move on her before she could bust him. Come at her with the knife. No easy way out of this one, she thought. It's still him and me, alone together in this room. And all I can do is wait. And listen.

She was learning a lot about him.

He was lying on the bed with his hands behind his head, looking up at the ceiling, and she was sitting in the wooden chair across the room near the dresser, her bag on the floor near her dangling hand, and she felt like a psychiatrist listening to a patient. The room was warm enough, she had to say that for it. Sizzling hot radiator throwing heat, she was almost getting drowsy, that's all she needed. His jacket draped over the back of the wooden chair now, his voice droning into the room. She sat with both feet planted firmly on the floor, legs slightly apart, gun strapped to her ankle inside the right boot. She was ready for anything. But nothing came. Except talk.

". . . that maybe *she* was partly to blame for what happened, you know?" he said. "My mother. Listen, I love her to death, don't get me wrong, she's the one who made my freedom possible, may she rest in peace. But when you think of it another way, was it all my *father's* fault? Can I just hold him responsible? For laying Elga? I mean, isn't my *mother* partly to blame for what happened?"

Elga again.

Hardly a sentence out of his mouth without some mention of the housekeeper.

"She was a schoolteacher, you know, my mother, did I tell you that?"

Only a hundred times, Eileen thought.

"Put him through medical school, left me with Elga all the while I was growing up, well, listen, I don't blame her for that. She was teaching to support the family, you know, that was a lot of responsibility. Do you know the one about the kindergarten teacher who gets the obscene phone call? She picks up the phone, she says, 'Hello?' and the voice on the other end says, 'Doo-doo, pee-pee, ca-ca,' well, that's an old one, you probably

241

heard it. My mother didn't teach kindergarten, she was a high school teacher, worked in a tough school, long, hard hours, sometimes didn't get home till six or seven, had to correct papers all night long, I *hated* Elga. But what I'm saying, responsibility is a two-way street. If my father was laying Elga, maybe part of the fault was my mother's, do you see what I mean? She always said she hated teaching, but then why did she take it so seriously? Her sense of responsibility, sure. But shouldn't she have been responsible to her husband, too? To her son? Shouldn't she have taken care of *our* needs, too? I mean, shit, teaching didn't have to become an *obsession* with her, did it?"

I don't want to be your shrink, Eileen thought. I don't want to hear anything else about you, make your goddamn move!

But he wouldn't stop talking.

"Children sense things, don't you think?" he said. "I must have *known* something was wrong in that house. My father yelling at me all the time, my mother never there, there was tension in that house, you could cut it with a knife."

Silence.

She watched him on the bed.

Hands behind his head, staring up at the ceiling.

"I'll tell you the truth, I sometimes felt like killing her."

More silence.

Here it comes, Eileen thought.

"When I was a kid," he said.

And the silence lengthened.

"Fucking dedicated schoolteacher," he said.

She watched him.

"Ignoring the people who loved her."

Kept watching him. Ready. Waiting.

"I tried to make sense of it later, after she died. Left me all that money. This is for Robert's freedom to risk enjoying life. That was guilt talking, wasn't it? That was her guilt for having ignored us both."

Silence again.

"Do you know what she did once? Elga?"

"What did she do?"

"I was eight years old."

"What did she do?"

"She took off her bloomers."

Bloomers. A child's expression.

"Showed herself to me."

Silence.

"I ran away from her and locked myself in the bathroom."

Silence.

"My mother found me in there when she got home from school. Elga said I'd been a bad boy. Told my mother I'd locked myself in the bathroom and wouldn't come out. My mother asked me why I'd done that. Elga was standing right there. I said I was afraid of the lightning. It was raining that day. Elga smiled. The next time we were alone together, she ... she ... forced me to ..."

He sat up suddenly.

"Do you know the one about the guy who goes into a sex shop to buy a merkin? The clerk says, 'Did you want this sent, sir, or will you take it with you?' The guy says, 'No, I'll just eat it here.'" He laughed harshly and abruptly and then said, "How would you like me to eat *your* pussy?"

"Sure," she said.

"Then take off your bloomers."

He swung his legs over the side of the bed.

"Come over here and take off your bloomers."

"You come here," Eileen said.

He stood up.

He put his right hand in his pocket.

She thought Yes, take out the knife, you son of a bitch.

And then she thought No, don't, Bobby.

And was suddenly confused again.

"Bobby," she said wearily, "I'm a cop."

"Sure," he said, "a cop."

"I don't want to hurt you," she said.

"Then don't bullshit me!" he said angrily. "I've had enough bullshit in my life!"

"I'm a cop," she said, and took the gun out of her bag, and leveled it at him. "Let's go find some help for you, okay?"

He looked at her. A smile cracked over his face.

"Is this a trick?" he said.

"No trick. I'm a cop. Let's go, okay?"

"Go where? Where do you want to go, baby?" He was still smiling.

But his hand was still in his pocket.

"Find some people you can talk to," she said.

"About what? There's nothing I have to say to . . ."

"Put the knife on the floor, Bobby,"

She was standing now, almost in a policeman's crouch, the gun still leveled at him.

"What knife?" he said.

"The knife in your pocket, Bobby. Put it on the floor."

"I don't have a knife," he said.

"You have a knife, Bobby. Put it on the floor."

He took the knife out of his pocket.

"Good, now put it on the floor," she said.

"Suppose I don't?" he said.

"I know you will, Bobby."

"Suppose I lock myself in the bathroom instead?"

"No, you won't do that, Bobby. You're going to put the knife on the floor . . ."

"Like a good little boy, huh?"

"Bobby . . . I'm not your mother, I'm not Elga, I'm not going to hurt you. Just drop the knife on the floor . . ."

"Listen to the shrink," he said. "You're a fucking *hooker* is what you are, who the fuck do you think you're kidding?"

"Bobby, please drop the knife."

"Say pretty please," he said, and the blade snicked open.

The gun was in her hand, she had him cold.

"Don't move," she said.

The policeman's crouch more defined now, more deliberate.

He took a step toward her.

"I'm warning you, don't move!"

"Do you know the one about the guy who goes into a bank to hold it up? He sticks the gun in the teller's face and says, 'Don't muss a moovle, this is a fuck-up!' "

Another step toward her.

"This isn't fun anymore," he said, and sliced the knife across the air between them.

"Whoosh," he said.

And came at her.

Her first bullet took him in the chest, knocking him backward toward the bed. She fired again almost at once, hitting him in the shoulder this time, spinning him around, and then she fired a third time, shooting him in the back, knocking him over onto the bed, and then—she would never understand why—she kept shooting into his lifeless body, watching the eruptions of blood along his spine, saying over and over again, "I gave you a chance, I gave you a chance," until the gun was empty.

Then she threw the gun across the room and began screaming.

Some people never change.

Genero didn't even seem to know she couldn't hear him.

He was there at the hospital to tell Carella what a hero he'd been, shooting four teenagers who'd firebombed a building.

He sat in the hallway talking to Teddy, who was praying her husband wouldn't die, praying her husband wasn't already dead.

". . . and all at once they came running out," he said, "Steve would've been proud of me. They threw the firebomb at me, but that didn't scare me, I . . ."

A doctor in a green surgical gown was coming down the hallway.

There was blood on the gown.

She caught her breath.

"Mrs. Carella?" he said.

She read his lips.

At first she thought he said, "We shot him."

A puzzled look crossed her face.

He repeated it.

"We got it," he said.

She let out her breath.

"He'll be okay," the doctor said.

"He'll be okay," Genero repeated.

She nodded.

And then she cupped her hands to her face and began weeping.

Genero just sat there.

Annie talked to him in the hallway of the Seven-Two.

"The landlady called 911 because somebody was screaming upstairs," she said. "She caters to hookers, she wouldn't have called unless she thought it was very serious."

Kling nodded.

"She quieted down just a little while ago. She's down the hall in Interrogation. I'm not sure you ought to talk to her."

"Why not?" Kling said.

"I'm just not sure," Annie said.

He went down the hall.

He opened the door.

She was sitting at the long table in the Interrogation Room, the two-way mirror behind her. Just sitting there. Looking at her hands.

"I'm sorry if I screwed it up," he said.

"You didn't."

He sat opposite her.

"Are you okay?" he asked.

"No," she said.

He looked at her.

"I'm quitting," she said.

"What do you mean?"

"The force."

"No, you're not."

"I'm quitting, Bert. I don't like what it did to me, what it keeps doing to me."

"Eileen, you . . ."

"I'm quitting this city, too."

"Eileen . . ."

"This fucking city," she said, and shook her head.

He reached for her hand. She pulled it away.

"No," she said.

"What about me?" he said.

"What about me?" she said.

The phone rang at a little past two in the morning.

She picked up the receiver.

"Peaches?" the voice said. "This is Phil Hendricks at Camera Works, we talked earlier tonight."

Him again!

"What I want you to do," he said, "I want you to take off your blouse and go look at yourself in the mirror. Then I want you to . . ."

"Listen, you creep," she said, "if you call me one more time . . ."

"This is Andy Parker," he said. "I'm in a phone booth on the corner. Is it too late to come up?"

"You dope," she said.

It was the last trick of the night.

MT. PLEASANT BRANCH